# THE HUGO WINNERS

## Volumes One and Two

# THE
# HUGO WINNERS

*Volumes One and Two*

*Edited by*
Isaac Asimov

NELSON DOUBLEDAY, Inc.   Garden City, New York

Printed in the United States of America

# The Hugo Winners

## VOLUME I

THE DARFSTELLER by Walter M. Miller, Jr. Copyright © 1955 by Street & Smith Publications, Inc. Reprinted by courtesy of the author. Appeared originally in *Astounding Science Fiction*, January 1955. ALLAMAGOOSA by Eric Frank Russell. Copyright © 1955 by Street & Smith Publications, Inc. Reprinted by courtesy of Scott Meredith and the author. Appeared originally in *Astounding Science Fiction*, May 1955. EXPLORATION TEAM by Murray Leinster. Copyright © 1956 by Street & Smith Publications, Inc. Reprinted by courtesy of the author. Appeared originally in *Astounding Science Fiction*, March 1956. Included in COLONIAL SURVEY by Murray Leinster, Gnome Press 1957. THE STAR by Arthur C. Clarke. Copyright 1955 by Royal Publications, Inc. Reprinted by courtesy of Scott Meredith and the author. Appeared originally in *Infinity Science Fiction*, November 1955. Included in *The Other Side of the Sky* by Arthur C. Clarke, Harcourt, Brace, 1957 and A CENTURY OF SCIENCE FICTION edited by Damon Knight, Simon & Schuster, 1962. OR ALL THE SEAS WITH OYSTERS by Avram Davidson. Copyright © 1958 by Galaxy Publishing Corp. Reprinted by courtesy of Robert P. Mills and the author. Appeared originally in *Galaxy Science Fiction*, May 1958. Included in THE FOURTH GALAXY READER edited by H. L. Gold, Doubleday, 1959, and in SCIENCE FICTION-59 edited by Judith Merril, Gnome Press, 1959. THE BIG FRONT YARD by Clifford D. Simak. Copyright © 1958 by Street & Smith Publications, Inc. Reprinted by courtesy of Robert P. Mills and the author. Appeared originally in *Astounding Science Fiction*, October 1958. Included in THE WORLDS OF CLIFFORD SIMAK by Clifford D. Simak, Simon & Schuster, 1960. THE HELL-BOUND TRAIN by Robert Bloch. Copyright © 1958 by Mercury Press, Inc. Reprinted by courtesy of Harry Altshuler and the author. Appeared originally in *The Magazine of Fantasy and Science Fiction*, September 1958. FLOWERS FOR ALGERNON by Daniel Keyes. Copyright © 1959 by Daniel Keyes. Reprinted by courtesy of Robert P. Mills and the author. Appeared originally in *The Magazine of Fantasy and Science Fiction*, April 1959. Included in THE BEST FROM FANTASY AND SCIENCE FICTION—Ninth Series edited by Robert P. Mills, Doubleday, 1960. 5TH ANNUAL OF THE YEAR'S BEST SCIENCE FICTION edited by Judith Merril, Simon & Schuster, 1960; *Best Articles and Stories*, February 1961 and *Literary Cavalcade*, November 1961. THE LONGEST VOYAGE by Poul Anderson. Copyright © 1960 by Street & Smith Publications, Inc. Reprinted by courtesy of Scott Meredith and the author. Appeared originally in *Analog Science Fact and Fiction*, December 1960.

To all the True Conventioneers,
and, particularly,
to Pittsburgh

## ACKNOWLEDGMENTS

For help in the preparation of this book, the kindly services of Robert P. Mills and Sam Moskowitz are most gratefully acknowledged.

# CONTENTS

# INTRODUCTION

Let me introduce this book my own way, please; by which I mean I will begin by introducing myself.

I am Isaac Asimov and I am an old-timer.

Not, you understand, that I am (ha, ha) really old. Quite the contrary. I am rather young actually, being only mumblety-mumble years old and looking even younger!

I call myself an old-timer only because I started reading science fiction in 1929. Now this was only three years after Hugo Gernsback had inaugurated what is known to all True Believers as the Age of Science Fiction.

Gernsback was a Luxemburger who arrived in the United States in 1904. Fascinated by the new field of electronics, he ventured into publishing and put out a magazine devoted to the new science. Unable to keep himself down to the petty pace of actual events, he tried his hand at writing science fiction in order that he might forecast future developments in electronics and in science generally.

His own output, however, was insufficient for himself and, in 1926, he began publication of a magazine called *Amazing Stories*, the first periodical in the world to be devoted, exclusively, to tales of science fiction.

In the next few years a group of notable youngsters gathered about the magazine, and about a few more like it (*Wonder Stories, Astounding Stories*) that arose in *Amazing's* wake. That group made up the first science fiction fans.

The typical science fiction fan was an early teen-ager or even a pre-teener who worshipped science the way almost all his peers worshipped baseball. He dreamed of rocketships and new electronic marvels as others dreamed of homeruns and double-plays. And where his comrades shot cattle-rustlers with vigor, he himself blasted down the treacherous, be-tentacled monsters of Ganymede.

In short, among others, he was I!

At the start, we (myself and the others) had very little company in our specialized reveries. You can imagine the laughter to which we were subjected when sensible, hard-headed, practical, every-day people discovered we were reading crazy stories about atomic bombs, television, guided missiles, and rockets to the moon. All this was obvious crackpotism that could never come to pass, you see.

So we kept quiet about our lunacy and lived each month for those days when a new issue of one of our magazines was scheduled to reach the newsstands. We haunted the stands patiently on those days, and when the garish cover of the new issue finally came into sight, suffusing all the air about it with an electric glow, we passed over our quarter and reached out in trembling delight. (It is easy to duplicate the sensation in full adulthood. Everyone who has had a rich uncle die and leave him a million dollars after taxes knows exactly what the sensation is.)

Happiness reached a peak even more excessive when the astonishing discovery was made (as it eventually always was) that somewhere there existed another person who was interested in science fiction. Mind you, one always knew that somewhere, *in other cities,* they existed. After all, fans wrote endlessly to the various magazines, reporting on stories, criticizing the science content, demanding weekly publication, sneering at each other's views—and the magazine printed all the letters in microscopic print, with jovial asides from the editor.

But to find a fellow-fan in your own city, even in your own neighborhood!

It was a love affair on the spot. It was the tight union of a common interest unshared by the Philistines. The next step was a determined search for still other brethren, and the founding of a club. At weekly gatherings, the momentous issues of the day (Would *Astounding* adopt smooth edges? Was E. E. Smith's latest serial the equal of his immortal "Skylark of Space"?) were thrashed out.

The clubs grew larger and more active. Inter-city leagues of clubs were founded. Then, in 1939, the inevitable climax was reached. It was decided to hold a World Science Fiction Convention.

It was held in New York. Two hundred eager teen-agers attended, some coming from as far away as California. Editors attended and were astonished at the ardor and enthusiasm. The Guest of Honor was Frank R. Paul, the illustrator who had turned Gernsback's science fiction magazine covers into glowing dreams of fanciful machinery and horrid extra-terrestrial monsters.

I was there, too, already an "old-time fan" and now a writer, with three published stories to my credit. It made me a celebrity and I loved it. I signed autographs with a lofty dignity that was softened at the corners by just a touch of kindly condescension.

The success of that great gathering was enormous. We watched the old German science fiction movie, *Metropolis*. Fans shook hands with various editors and writers who, to their amazement, were not ten feet tall—but only seven or eight. We listened to talks on science fiction and, in fact, we could and did speak about science fiction and nothing but science fiction to anyone we met. For one short, golden day, we inhabited a tiny world in which science fiction was the exclusive interest.

I imagine Heaven must be a feeble imitation of that day.

There was nothing to do but repeat. In 1940, the 2nd Convention was held in Chicago; in 1941, the 3rd Convention was held in Denver.

Then came a pause called World War II. The lonely teen-agers of the '30s who had at last found each other, were now mostly in the Army, and those few who, for one reason or another, remained at home, initiated drives to send them science fiction magazines. (Pinup girls and letters from home are all very well in their way, but *our* boys in the foxholes needed those magazines to keep up their morale.)

In 1946, with peace restored and the atom bomb shedding a horrid glare of rationality over our crackpotism, the conventions were resumed and not a year has been missed since.

The 4th Convention was held at Los Angeles, and others have ranged as far north as Toronto (the 6th, in 1948), as far west as Seattle (the 19th, in 1961) and as far south as New Orleans (the 9th, in 1951). The 15th Convention crossed the ocean and was held in London. In 1952, no less than a thousand fans and professionals attended the 10th Convention held, like the 2nd, in Chicago.

Every Convention is notable and lovable, but the 1955 Convention is particularly memorable for two reasons.

It was held in Cleveland and it was the THIRTEENTH Convention. The organizing fans of the Cleveland area were therefore faced with the task of selecting a guest of honor who would not object to the evil connotations of the number, 13.

Someone was needed who was particularly sane and rational; some gentleman known to be fearless and intrepid. Naturally, he had also to be a witty and forceful speaker and, above all, he had to be devilishly handsome.

All this narrowed the field of possibilities in drastic fashion. In fact, only one candidate met all the requirements, and I accepted with my usual grace and charm.

With myself as Guest of Honor, the 13th Convention was obviously slated for immortality, but the organizing fans did not rest upon their laurels.

Until the 13th Convention, fans had occasionally voted on favorite novels, novelettes, short stories, artists, fan magazines, and so on. The results would be announced amid great jubilation. At the 11th Convention (Philadelphia, 1953) little space-ship models were handed out to winners. This, however, was a one-shot. At the 12th Convention (San Francisco, 1954) no awards of this type were made.

Well, then, the 13th Convention decided to make the space-ship award permanent. Mr. Ben Jason of Cleveland designed a new statuette, classic in its smooth simplicity, which at once—unofficially—was dubbed the Hugo after the immortal Gernsback. By 1958, the name was official.

Let the Philistines have their Oscars and their Emmys. *We* have the Hugos.

Hugos have been handed out at every convention since that epoch-making 13th. They have been reverently handed out on seven rafter-ringing occasions.

I watched the Hugos given out at the 13th Convention, smiling blandly from my post in the center of the head table. The next year, at the 14th Convention (New York, 1956), I watched more given out, again from a seat at the head table, a place that was mine by virtue of the fact that I was one of the featured speakers.

At both the 17th Convention (Detroit, 1959) and the 18th Convention (Pittsburgh, 1960) I was toastmaster and I handed out the Hugos with my very own hands.

But by the time the 19th Convention (Seattle, 1961) was over, a certain gnawing suspicion had found its way into the regions of my heart. I thought deeply and checked statistics and slowly the conviction grew and strengthened that a peculiar and unnatural situation prevailed in the science fiction world.

What it was, I can state simply. Although Hugos had been given out by car lots to all sorts of relatively insignificant personages, none —not one—had ever been awarded to *me*.

For months now I have brooded over the possibilities of revenge; as any red-blooded American boy would. I have discarded complicated schemes that involved poison-pen letters, mysterious and untraceable South American toxins, plastic bomb booby traps, and was almost at my wits' end, when the perfect opportunity presented itself.

The suggestion was made that someone collect the Hugo winners among the novelettes and short stories and place all of them within the pages of a single book. At least one story, sometimes two, had been given an award in this category on every occasion when Hugos were handed out except for the 11th Convention (Philadelphia, 1953) and the 15th Convention (London, 1957). Nine different stories were involved, winners at six different conventions. Thus the readers would find themselves with a lavish treat of the best-by-vote: over 100,000 words of superior fiction.

The person qualifying as editor for such an anthology would naturally have to be someone who had not himself received a Hugo, so that he could approach the job with the proper detachment. At the same time, he would have to be a person of note, sane and rational, fearless and intrepid, witty and forceful, and, above all, devilishly handsome.

All this was pointed out to Mr. Timothy Seldes at Doubleday and Company, and that fine gentleman agreed in every particular. Once again, the stringent requirements for the post seemed to cut down the possibilities to a single individual and I accepted with that lovable modesty that suits me so well.

And so here I have my revenge. If those wise guys, herein included among the authors, had not been so eager to grab at the Hugos, but had modestly held back the way I did, *they* might have edited this anthology.

I hope they have learned their lesson.

Anyway, here I am, and here are the Hugo winners.

*Isaac Asimov*
*West Newton, Massachusetts*

*1955*
*13th CONVENTION*
*CLEVELAND*

# Walter M. Miller, Jr.

I ought to have met Walter Miller at the 13th Convention (Cleveland, 1955) when his novelette "The Darfsteller" won its author a Hugo, but I didn't. When his name was called out by Anthony Boucher, (the toastmaster upon that occasion) a proxy came up to accept it. My disappointment was soothed a bit by the fact that the proxy was the charming Judith Merril, one of science fiction's best anthologists.

Things were different at the 14th Convention (New York, 1956). Walt wasn't taking a Hugo that time but he was there and he and I and Robert P. Mills had lunch together. Mills was editor of a new magazine *Venture Science Fiction* (an excellent venture indeed, which should have made out better than it did) and Walt and I were trying to write stories for it, so there was a great deal to discuss.

For this purpose, Mills took us both to a beautiful French restaurant for he spared no expense on such occasions, since he never picked up a check. I was at my most charming, witty, genial and learned, and interrupted my discourse only long enough to order the meal, which, naturally, I did in a French of the most elegant Parisian variety. This, after all, is only to be expected of one who, like myself, speaks, in ordinary life, that delightful patois that can only be described as High Brooklyn.

Now imagine that five years have passed, five years during which Walt and I have not met again. It is now time to write to Walt for permission to use "The Darfsteller." In doing so, I delicately recalled myself to him. Of course, I felt sure he could not have forgotten me. My only uncertainty was which of my many mind-stimulating comments he would lovingly cite as evidence that lunch with me was an occasion he would cherish in his memory forever.

In answering (and giving permission), he said, "Of course, I remember you. You ordered chitlin's in French."

But then, what can you expect of a Hugo-winner? Just to show you the greediness of this variety of writer, Walt did it again at the 19th Convention (Seattle, 1961) only worse. He carried off the biggest prize of all and won a Hugo for his novel, *A Canticle for Leibowitz*.

Fortunately, we can't include novels in this anthology. I wouldn't want to encourage Walt in this callous business of monopolizing Hugos.

# 1

# THE DARFSTELLER

"Judas, Judas" was playing at the Universal on Fifth Street, and the cast was entirely human. Ryan Thornier had been saving up for it for several weeks, and now he could afford the price of a matinée ticket. It had been a race for time between his piggy bank and the wallets of several "public-spirited" angels who kept the show alive, and the piggy bank had won. He could see the show before the wallets went flat and the show folded, as any such show was bound to do after a few limping weeks. A glow of anticipation suffused him. After watching the wretched mockery of dramaturgical art every day at the New Empire Theater where he worked as janitor, the chance to see real theater again would be like a breath of clean air.

He came to work an hour early on Wednesday morning and sped through his usual chores on overdrive. He finished his work before one o'clock, had a shower backstage, changed to street clothes, and went nervously upstairs to ask Imperio D'Uccia for the rest of the day off.

D'Uccia sat enthroned at a rickety desk before a wall plastered with photographs of lightly clad female stars of the old days. He heard the janitor's petition with a faint, almost oriental smile of apparent sympathy, then drew himself up to his full height of sixty-five inches, leaned on the desk with chubby hands to study Thornier with beady eyes.

"Off? So you wanna da day off? Mmmph—" He shook his head as if mystified by such an incomprehensible request.

The gangling janitor shifted his feet uneasily. "Yes, sir. I've finished up, and Jigger'll come over to stand by in case you need anything special." He paused. D'Uccia was studying his nails, frowning gravely. "I haven't asked for a day off in two years, Mr. D'Uccia," he added, "and I was sure you wouldn't mind after all the overtime I've—"

"Jigger," D'Uccia grunted. "Whoosa t'is Jigger?"

"Works at the Paramount. It's closed for repairs, and he doesn't mind—"

The theater manager grunted abruptly and waved his hands. "I don' pay no Jigger, I pay you. Whassa this all about? You swip the floor, you putsa things away, you all finish now, ah? You wanna day off. Thatsa whass wrong with the world, too mucha time loaf. Letsa machines work. More time to mek trouble." The theater manager came out from behind his desk and waddled to the door. He thrust his fat neck outside and looked up and down the corridor, then waddled back to confront Thornier with a short fat finger aimed at the employee's long and majestic nose.

"Whensa lass time you waxa the upstairs floor, hah?"

Thornier's jaw sagged forlornly. "Why, I—"

"Don'ta tell me no lie. Looka that hall. Sheeza feelth. *Look!* I want you to look." He caught Thornier's arm, tugged him to the doorway, pointed excitedly at the worn and ancient oak flooring. "Sheeza feelth ground in! See? When you wax, hah?"

A great shudder seemed to pass through the thin elderly man. He sighed resignedly and turned to look down at D'Uccia with weary gray eyes.

"Do I get the afternoon off, or don't I?" he asked hopelessly, knowing the answer in advance.

But D'Uccia was not content with a mere refusal. He began to pace. He was obviously deeply moved. He defended the system of free enterprise and the cherished traditions of the theater. He spoke eloquently of the golden virtues of industriousness and dedication to duty. He bounced about like a furious Pekingese yapping happily at a scarecrow. Thornier's neck reddened, his mouth went tight.

"Can I go now?"

"When you waxa da floor? Palisha da seats, fixa da lights? When you clean op the dressing room, hah?" He stared up at Thornier for a moment, then turned on his heel and charged to the window. He thrust his thumb into the black dirt of the window box, where several prize lilies were already beginning to bloom. "*Ha!*" he snorted. "Dry, like I thought! You think the bulbs a don't need a drink, hah?"

"But I watered them this morning. The sun—"

"Hah! You letsa little *fiori* wilt an die, hah? And you wanna the day off?"

It was hopeless. When D'Uccia drew his defensive mantle of calculated deafness or stupidity about himself, he became impenetrable to any request or honest explanation. Thornier sucked in a slow breath between his teeth, stared angrily at his employer for a moment, and seemed briefly ready to unleash an angry blast. Thinking better of it, he bit his lip, turned, and stalked wordlessly out of the office. D'Uccia followed him triumphantly to the door.

"Don' you go sneak off, now!" he called ominously, and stood smiling down the corridor until the janitor vanished at the head of the stairs. Then he sighed and went back to get his hat and coat. He was just preparing to leave when Thornier came back upstairs with a load of buckets, mops, and swabs.

The janitor stopped when he noticed the hat and coat, and his seamed face went curiously blank. "Going home, Mr. D'Uccia?" he asked icily.

"Yeh! I'ma worka too hard, the doctor say. I'ma need the sunshine. More frash air. I'ma go relax on the beach a while."

Thornier leaned on the mop handle and smiled nastily. "Sure," he said. "Letsa machines do da work."

The comment was lost on D'Uccia. He waved airily, strode off toward the stairway, and called an airy *"A rivederci!"* over his shoulder.

*"A rivederci, padrone,"* Thornier muttered softly, his pale eyes glittering from their crow's-feet wrappings. For a moment his face seemed to change—and once again he was Chaubrec's Adolfo, at the exit of the Commandant, Act II, scene *iv*, from "A Canticle for the Marsman."

Somewhere downstairs, a door slammed behind D'Uccia.

"Into death!" hissed Adolfo-Thornier, throwing back his head to laugh Adolfo's laugh. It rattled the walls. When its reverberations had died away, he felt a little better. He picked up his buckets and brooms and walked on down the corridor to the door of D'Uccia's office.

Unless "Judas, Judas" hung on through the week end, he wouldn't get to see it, since he could not afford a ticket to the evening performance, and there was no use asking D'Uccia for favors. While he waxed the hall, he burned. He waxed as far as D'Uccia's doorway, then stood staring into the office for several vacant minutes.

"I'm fed up," he said at last.

The office remained silent. The window-box lilies bowed to the breeze.

"You little creep!" he growled. "I'm through!"

The office was speechless. Thornier straightened and tapped his chest.

"I, Ryan Thornier, am walking out, you hear? The show is finished!"

When the office failed to respond, he turned on his heel and stalked downstairs. Minutes later, he came back with a small can of gold paint

and a pair of artists' brushes from the storeroom. Again he paused in
the doorway.

"Anything else I can do, Mr. D'Uccia?" he purred.

Traffic murmured in the street; the breeze rustled the lilies; the building creaked.

"Oh? You want me to wax in the wall-cracks, too? How could I have
forgotten!"

He clucked his tongue and went over to the window. Such lovely
lilies. He opened the paint can, set it on the window ledge, and then
very carefully he gilded each of the prize lilies, petals, leaves, and stalks,
until the flowers glistened like the work of Midas' hands in the sunlight. When he finished, he stepped back to smile at them in admiration for a moment, then went to finish waxing the hall.

He waxed it with particular care in front of D'Uccia's office. He
waxed under the throw rug that covered the worn spot on the floor
where D'Uccia had made a sharp left turn into his sanctum every
morning for fifteen years, and then he turned the rug over and dusted
dry wax powder into the pile. He replaced it carefully and pushed at
it a few times with his foot to make certain the lubrication was adequate. The rug slid about as if it rode on a bed of bird-shot.

Thornier smiled and went downstairs. The world was suddenly different somehow. Even the air smelled different. He paused on the landing to glance at himself in the decorative mirror.

Ah! the old trouper again. No more of the stooped and haggard menial. None of the wistfulness and weariness of self-perpetuated slavery.
Even with the gray at the temples and the lines in the face, here was
something of the old Thornier—or one of the *many* old Thorniers of
earlier days. Which one? Which one'll it be? Adolfo? Or Hamlet?
Justin, or J. J. Jones, from "The Electrocutioner"? Any of them, all of
them; for he was Ryan Thornier, star, in the old days.

"Where've you been, baby?" he asked his image with a tight smile of
approval, winked, and went on home for the evening. Tomorrow, he
promised himself, a new life would begin.

"But you've been making that promise for years, Thorny," said the
man in the control booth, his voice edged with impatience. "What do
you mean, 'you quit?' Did you tell D'Uccia you quit?"

Thornier smiled loftily while he dabbed with his broom at a bit of
dust in the corner. "Not exactly, Richard," he said. "But the *padrone*
will find it out soon enough."

The technician grunted disgust. "I don't understand you, Thorny.

Sure, if you *really* quit, that's swell—if you don't just turn around and get another job like this one."

"Never!" the old actor proclaimed resonantly, and glanced up at the clock. Five till ten. Nearly time for D'Uccia to arrive for work. He smiled to himself.

"If you really quit, what are you doing here today?" Rick Thomas demanded, glancing up briefly from the Maestro. His arms were thrust deep in the electronic entrails of the machine, and he wore a pencil-sized screwdriver tucked behind one ear. "Why don't you go home, if you quit?"

"Oh, don't worry, Richard. This time it's for real."

"Pssss!" An amused hiss from the technician. "Yeah, it was for real when you quit at the Bijou, too. Only then a week later you come to work here. So what now, Mercutio?"

"To the casting office, old friend. A bit part somewhere, perhaps." Thornier smiled on him benignly. "Don't concern yourself about me."

"Thorny, can't you get it through your head that theater's *dead*? There isn't any theater! No movies, no television either—except for dead men and the Maestro here." He slapped the metal housing of the machine.

"I *meant*," Thorny explained patiently, "'employment office,' and 'small job,' you . . . you machineage flintsmith. Figures of speech, solely."

"Yah."

"I thought you *wanted* me to resign my position, Richard."

"Yes! If you'll do something worthwhile with yourself. Ryan Thornier, star of 'Walkaway,' playing martyr with a scrub-bucket! Aaaak! You give me the gripes. And you'll do it again. You can't stay away from the stage, even if all you can do about it is mop up the oil drippings."

"You couldn't possibly understand," Thornier said stiffly.

Rick straightened to look at him, took his arms out of the Maestro and leaned on top of the cabinet. "I dunno, Thorny," he said in a softer voice. "Maybe I do. You're an actor, and you're always playing roles. Living them, even. You can't help it, I guess. But you *could* do a saner job of picking the parts you're going to play."

"The world has cast me in the role I play," Thornier announced with a funereal face.

Rick Thomas clapped a hand over his forehead and drew it slowly down across his face in exasperation. "I give up!" he groaned. "Look at you! Matinée idol, pushing a broom. Eight years ago, it made sense— *your* kind of sense, anyhow. Dramatic gesture. Leading actor defies

autodrama offer, takes janitor's job. Loyal to tradition, and the guild
—and all that. It made small headlines, maybe even helped the legit
stage limp along a little longer. But the audiences stopped bleeding for
you after a while, and then it stopped making even *your* kind of sense!"

Thornier stood wheezing slightly and glaring at him. "What would
*you* do," he hissed, "if they started making a little black box that could
be attached to the wall up there"—he waved to a bare spot above the
Maestro's bulky housing—"that could repair, maintain, operate, and
adjust—do all the things you do to that . . . that contraption. Suppose
nobody needed electronicians any more."

Rick Thomas thought about it a few moments, then grinned. "Well,
I guess I'd get a job making the little black boxes, then."

"You're not funny, Richard!"

"I didn't intend to be."

"You're . . . you're not an artist." Flushed with fury, Thornier
swept viciously at the floor of the booth.

A door slammed somewhere downstairs, far below the above-stage
booth. Thorny set his broom aside and moved to the window to watch.
The *clop, clop, clop* of bustling footsteps came up the central aisle.

"Hizzoner, da Imperio," muttered the technician, glancing up at the
clock. "Either that clock's two minutes fast, or else this was his morning to take a bath."

Thornier smiled sourly toward the main aisle, his eyes traveling after the waddling figure of the theater manager. When D'Uccia disappeared beneath the rear balcony, he resumed his sweeping.

"I don't see why you don't get a sales job, Thorny," Rick ventured,
returning to his work. "A good salesman is just an actor, minus the temperament. There's *lots* of demand for good actors, come to think of it.
Politicians, top executives, even generals—some of them seem to make
out on *nothing but* dramatic talent. History affirms it."

"Bah! I'm no schauspieler." He paused to watch Rick adjusting the
Maestro, and slowly shook his head. "Ease your conscience, Richard,"
he said finally.

Startled, the technician dropped his screwdriver, looked up quizzi-
cally. "*My* conscience? What the devil is uneasy about *my* conscience?"

"Oh, don't pretend. That's why you're always so concerned about
me. I know *you* can't help it that your . . . your trade has perverted a
great art."

Rick gaped at him in disbelief for a moment. "*You* think *I—*" He
choked. He colored angrily. He stared at the old ham and began to
curse softly under his breath.

Thornier suddenly lifted a finger to his mouth and went *shhhh!* His eyes roamed toward the back of the theater.

"That was only D'Uccia on the stairs," Rick began. "What—?"

"*Shhhh!*"

They listened. The janitor wore a rancid smile. Seconds later it came —first a faint yelp, then—

Bbbrroom*mmpb!*

It rattled the booth windows. Rick started up frowning.

"What the—?"

"*Shhhh!*"

The jolting jar was followed by a faint mutter of profanity.

"That's D'Uccia. What happened?"

The faint mutter suddenly became a roaring stream of curses from somewhere behind the balconies.

"Hey!" said Rick. "He must have hurt himself."

"Naah. He just found my resignation, that's all. See? I told you I'd quit."

The profane bellowing grew louder to the accompaniment of an elephantine thumping on carpeted stairs.

"He's not *that* sorry to see you go," Rick grunted, looking baffled.

D'Uccia burst into view at the head of the aisle. He stopped with his feet spread wide, clutching at the base of his spine with one hand and waving a golden lily aloft in the other.

"Lily gilder!" he screamed. "Pansy painter! You fancy-pantsy bom! Come out, you fonny fonny boy!"

Thornier thrust his head calmly through the control-booth window, stared at the furious manager with arched brows. "You calling me, Mr. D'Uccia?"

D'Uccia sucked in two or three gasping breaths before he found his bellow again.

"*Thornya!*"

"Yes, sir?"

"Itsa finish, you hear?"

"What's finished, boss?"

"Itsa finish. I'ma go see the servo man. I'ma go get me a swip-op machine. You gotta two wiks notice."

"Tell him you don't want any notice," Rick grunted softly from nearby. "Walk out on him."

"All right, Mr. D'Uccia," Thornier called evenly.

D'Uccia stood there sputtering, threatening to charge, waving the lily helplessly. Finally he threw it down in the aisle with a curse and whirled to limp painfully out.

"*Whew!*" Rick breathed. "What did you do?"

Thornier told him sourly. The technician shook his head.

"He won't fire you. He'll change his mind. It's too hard to hire any-body to do dirty-work these days."

"You heard him. He can buy an autojan installation. 'Swip-op' machine."

"Baloney! Dooch is too stingy to put out that much dough. Besides, he can't get the satisfaction of screaming at a machine."

Thornier glanced up wryly. "Why *can't* he?"

"Well—" Rick paused. "Ulp! . . . You're right. He can. He came up here and bawled out the Maestro once. Kicked it, yelled at it, shook it —like a guy trying to get his quarter back out of a telephone. Went away looking pleased with himself, too."

"Why not?" Thorny muttered gloomily. "People are machines to D'Uccia. And he's *fair* about it. He's willing to treat them all alike."

"But you're not going to stick around two weeks, are you?"

"Why not? It'll give me time to put out some feelers for a job."

Rick grunted doubtfully and turned his attention back to the ma-chine. He removed the upper front panel and set it aside. He opened a metal canister on the floor and lifted out a foot-wide foot-thick roll of plastic tape. He mounted it on a spindle inside the Maestro, and began feeding the end of the tape through several sets of rollers and guides. The tape appeared worm-eaten—covered with thousands of tiny punch-marks and wavy grooves. The janitor paused to watch the process with cold hostility.

"Is that the script-tape for the 'Anarch'?" he asked stiffly.

The technician nodded. "Brand new tape, too. Got to be careful how I feed her in. It's still got fuzz on it from the recording cuts." He stopped the feed mechanism briefly, plucked at a punch-mark with his awl, blew on it, then started the feed motor again.

"What happens if the tape gets nicked or scratched?" Thorny grunted curiously. "Actor collapse on stage?"

Rick shook his head. "Naa, it happens all the time. A scratch or a nick'll make a player muff a line or maybe stumble, then the Maestro catches the goof, and compensates. Maestro gets feedback from the stage, continuously directs the show. It can do a lot of compensating, too."

"I thought the whole show came from the tape."

The technician smiled. "It does, in a way. But it's more than a re-corded mechanical puppet show, Thorny. The Maestro watches the stage . . . no, more than that . . . the Maestro *is* the stage, an elec-

tronic analogue of it." He patted the metal housing. "All the actors' personality patterns are packed in here. It's more than a remote controller, the way most people think of it. It's a creative directing machine. It's even got pickups out in the audience to gauge reactions to—"

He stopped suddenly, staring at the old actor's face. He swallowed nervously. "Thorny *don't* look that way. I'm sorry. Here, have a cigarette."

Thorny accepted it with trembling fingers. He stared down into the gleaming maze of circuitry with narrowed eyes, watched the script-belt climb slowly over the rollers and down into the bowels of the Maestro.

"Art!" he hissed. "Theater! What'd they give you your degree in, Richard? Dramaturgical engineering?"

He shuddered and stalked out of the booth. Rick listened to the angry rattle of his heels on the iron stairs that led down to stage level. He shook his head sadly, shrugged, went back to inspecting the tape for rough cuts.

Thorny came back after a few minutes with a bucket and a mop. He looked reluctantly repentant. "Sorry, lad," he grunted. "I know you're just trying to make a living, and—"

"Skip it," Rick grunted curtly.

"It's just . . . well . . . this particular show. It gets me."

"This—? 'The Anarch,' you mean? What about it, Thorny? You play in it once?"

"Uh-uh. It hasn't been on the stage since the Nineties, except—well, it was almost revived ten years ago. We rehearsed for weeks. Show folded before opening night. No dough."

"You had a good part in it?"

"I was to play Andreyev," Thornier told him with a faint smile.

Rick whistled between his teeth. "The lead. That's too bad." He hoisted his feet to let Thorny mop under them. "Big disappointment, I guess."

"It's not that. It's just . . . well . . . 'The Anarch' rehearsals were the last time Mela and I were on stage together. That's all."

"Mela?" The technician paused, frowning. "Mela *Stone?*"

Thornier nodded.

Rick snatched up a copy of the uncoded script, waved it at him. "But she's in *this* version, Thorny! Know that! She's playing Marka."

Thornier's laugh was brief and brittle.

Rick reddened slightly. "Well, I mean her mannequin's playing it."

Thorny eyed the Maestro distastefully. "Your mechanical Svengali's playing its airfoam zombies in *all* roles, you mean."

"Oh, cut it out, Thorny. Be sore at the world if you want to, but don't blame me for what audiences want. And I didn't invent autodrama anyhow."

"I don't blame anybody. I merely detest that . . . that—" He punched at the base of the Maestro with his wet mop.

"You and D'Uccia," Rick grunted disgustedly. "Except—D'Uccia loves it when it's working O.K. It's just a machine, Thorny. Why hate it?"

"Don't need a reason to hate it," he said, snarly-petulant. "I hate air-cabs, too. It's a matter of taste, that's all."

"All right, but the public likes autodrama—whether it's by TV, stereo, or on stage. And they get what they want."

*"Why?"*

Rick snickered. "Well, it's their dough. Autodrama's portable, pre-dictable, duplicatable. And flexible. You can run 'Macbeth' tonight, the 'Anarch' tomorrow night, and 'King of the Moon' the next night—in the same house. No actor-temperament problems. No union prob-lems. Rent the packaged props, dolls, and tapes from Smithfield. Packaged theater. Systematized, mass-produced. In Coon Creek, Geor-gia, yet."

"Bah!"

Rick finished feeding in the script tape, closed the panel, and opened an adjacent one. He ripped the lid from a cardboard carton and dumped a heap of smaller tape-spools on the table.

"Are *those* the souls they sold to Smithfield?" Thornier asked, smil-ing at them rather weirdly.

The technician's stool scraped back and he exploded: "You know what they are!"

Thornier nodded, leaned closer to stare at them as if fascinated. He plucked one of them out of the pile, sighed down at it.

"If you say 'Alas, poor Yorick,' I'll heave you out of here!" Rick grated.

Thornier put it back with a sigh and wiped his hand on his coveralls. Packaged personalities. Actors' egos, analogized on tape. Real actors, once, whose dolls were now cast in the roles. The tapes contained com-plex psychophysiological data derived from months of psychic and so-matic testing, after the original actors had signed their Smithfield contracts. Data for the Maestro's personality matrices. Abstractions from the human psyche, incarnate in glass, copper, chromium. The souls they rented to Smithfield on a royalty basis, along with their flesh and blood likenesses in the dolls.

Rick loaded a casting spool onto its spindle, started it feeding through the pickups.

"What happens if you leave out a vital ingredient? Such as Mela Stone's tape, for instance," Thornier wanted to know.

"The doll'd run through its lines like a zombie, that's all," Rick explained. "No zip. No interpretation. Flat, deadpan, like a robot."

"They are robots."

"Not exactly. Remote marionettes for the Maestro, but interpreted. We did a run-through on 'Hamlet' once, without any actor tapes. Everybody talked in flat monotones, no expressions. It was a scream."

"Ha, ha," Thornier said grimly.

Rick slipped another tape on the spindle, clicked a dial to a new setting, started the feed again. "This one's Andreyev, Thornier—played by Peltier." He cursed suddenly, stopped the feed, inspected the tape anxiously, flipped open the pickup mechanism, and inspected it with a magnifier.

"What's wrong?" asked the janitor.

"Take-off's about worn out. Hard to keep its spacing right. I'm nervous about it getting hung up and chewing up the tape."

"No duplicate tapes?"

"Yeah. One set of extras. But the show opens tonight." He cast another suspicious look at the pickup glideway, then closed it and switched the feed again. He was replacing the panel when the feed mechanism stalled. A ripping sound came from inside. He muttered fluent profanity, shut off the drive, jerked away the panel. He held up a shredded ribbon of tape for Thorny to see, then flung it angrily across the booth. "Get out of here! You're a jinx!"

"Not till I finish mopping."

"Thorny, get D'Uccia for me, will you? We'll have to get a new pickup flown in from Smithfield before this afternoon. This is a helluva mess."

"Why not hire a human stand-in?" he asked nastily, then added: "Forgive me. That would be a perversion of your art, wouldn't it? Shall I get D'Uccia?"

Rick threw the Peltier spool at him. He ducked out with a chuckle and went to find the theater manager. Halfway down the iron stairs, he paused to look at the wide stage that spread away just beyond the folded curtains. The footlights were burning, and the gray-green floor looked clean and shimmering, with its checkerboard pattern of imbedded copper strips. The strips were electrified during the performance, and they fed the mannequins' energy-storage packs. The dolls had metallic disks in their soles, and rectifiers in their insteps. When batteries drained low, the Maestro moved the actor's foot an inch or so to contact the floor electrodes for periodic recharging during the play, since a doll would grow wobbly and its voice indistinct after a dozen minutes on internal power alone.

Thorny stared at the broad expanse of stage where no humans walked on performance night. D'Uccia's Siamese tomcat sat licking itself in the center of the stage. It glanced up at him haughtily, seemed to sniff, began licking itself again. He watched it for a moment, then called back upstairs to Rick.

"Energize the floor a minute, will you, Rick?"

"Huh? Why?"—a busy grunt.

"Want to check something."

"O.K., but then fetch D'Uccia."

He heard the technician snap a switch. The cat's calm hauteur exploded. The cat screamed, scrambled, barrel-rolled, amid a faint sputter of sparks. The cat did an Immelmann turn over the footlights, landed in the pit with a clawing crash, then scampered up the aisle with fur erect toward its haven beneath Imperio's desk.

"Whatthehell?" Rick growled, and thrust his head out of the booth.

"Shut it off now," said the janitor. "D'Uccia'll be here in a minute."

"With fangs showing!"

Thornier went to finish his routine clean-up. Gloom had begun to gather about him. He was leaving—leaving even this last humble role in connection with the stage. A fleeting realization of his own impotence came to him. Helpless. Helpless enough to seek petty revenges like vandalizing D'Uccia's window box and tormenting D'Uccia's cat, because there was not any real enemy at which he could strike out.

He put the realization down firmly, and stamped on it. *He* was Ryan Thornier, and never helpless, unless he willed it so. I'll make them know who I am just *once*, he thought, before I go. I'll make them remember, and they won't ever forget.

But that line of thought about playing one last great role, one last masterful interpretation, he knew was no good. "Thorny, if you ever played a one-last-great," Rick had said to him once, "there wouldn't be a thing left to live for, would there?" Rick had said it cynically, but it was true anyhow. And the pleasant fantasy was somehow alarming as well as pleasant.

The chic little woman in the white-plumed hat was explaining things carefully—with round vowels and precise enunciation—to the Playwright of the Moment, up-and-coming, with awed worshipfulness in his gaze as he listened to the pert little producer. "Stark realism, you see, is the milieu of autodrama," she said. "Always remember, Bernie, that consideration for the actors is a thing of the past. Study the drama of Rome—ancient Rome. If a play had a crucifixion scene, they got a slave for the part and crucified him. On stage, but *really!*"

The Playwright of the Moment laughed dutifully around his long cigarette holder. "So that's where they got the line: 'It's superb, but it's hell on the actors.' I must rewrite the murder scene in my 'George's Wake.' Do it with a hatchet, this time."

"Oh, now, *Bernie!* Mannequins don't bleed."

They both laughed heartily. "And they *are* expensive. Not hell on the actors, but hell on the budget."

"The Romans probably had the same problem. I'll bear it in mind."

Thornier saw them—the producer and the Playwright of the Moment—standing there in the orchestra when he came from backstage and across toward the center aisle. They lounged on the arms of their seats, and a crowd of production personnel and technicians milled about them. The time for the first run-through was approaching.

The small woman waved demurely to Thorny when she saw him making his way slowly through the throng, then turned to the playwright again. "Bernie, be a lamb and get me a drink, will you? I've got a butterfly."

"Surely. Hard, or soft?"

"Oh, hard. Scotch mist in a paper cup, please. There's a bar next door."

The playwright nodded a nod that was nearly a bow and shuffled away up the aisle. The woman caught at the janitor's sleeve as he passed.

"Going to snub me, Thorny?"

"Oh, hello, Miss Ferne," he said politely.

She leaned close and muttered: "Call me 'Miss Ferne' again and I'll claw you." The round vowels had vanished.

"O.K., Jade, but—" He glanced around nervously. Technicians milled about them. Ian Feria, the producer, watched them curiously from the wings.

"What's been doing with you, Thorny? Why haven't I seen you," she complained.

He gestured with the broom handle, shrugged. Jade Ferne studied his face a moment and frowned. "Why the agonized look, Thorny? Mad at me?"

He shook his head. "This play, Jade—'The Anarch,' well—" He glanced miserably toward the stage.

Memory struck her suddenly. She breathed a compassionate *ummm*. "The attempted revival, ten years ago—you were to be Andreyev. Oh, Thorny, I'd forgotten."

"It's all right." He wore a carefully tailored martyr's smile.

She gave his arm a quick pat. "I'll see you after the run-through, Thorny. We'll have a drink and talk old times."

He glanced around again and shook his head. "You've got new friends now, Jade. They wouldn't like it."

"The crew? Nonsense! They're not snobs."

"No, but they want your attention. Feria's trying to catch your eye right now. No use making them sore."

"All right, but after the run-through I'll see you in the mannequin room. I'll just slip away."

"If you want to."

"I do, Thorny. It's been so long."

The playwright returned with her Scotch mist and gave Thornier a hostilely curious glance.

"Bless your heart, Bernie," she said, the round vowels returning, then to Thornier: "Thorny, would you do me a favor? I've been trying to corner D'Uccia, but he's tied up with a servo salesman somewhere. Somebody's got to run and pick up a mannequin from the depot. The shipment was delivered, but the trucker missed a doll crate. We'll need it for the run-through. Could you—"

"Sure, Miss Ferne. Do I need a requisition order?"

"No, just sign the delivery ticket. And Thorny, see if the new part for the Maestro's been flown in yet. Oh, and one other thing—the Maestro chewed up the Peltier tape. We've got a duplicate, but we should have two, just to be safe."

"I'll see if they have one in stock," he murmured, and turned to go.

D'Uccia stood in the lobby with the salesman when he passed through. The theater manager saw him and smirked happily.

". . . Certain special features, of course," the salesman was saying. "It's an old building, and it wasn't designed with autojanitor systems in mind, like buildings are now. But we'll tailor the installation to fit your place, Mr. D'Uccia. We want to do the job *right*, and a packaged unit wouldn't do it."

"Yah, you gimme da price, hah?"

"We'll have an estimate for you by tomorrow. I'll have an engineer over this afternoon to make the survey, and he'll work up a layout tonight."

"Whatsa 'bout the demonstration, uh? Whatsa 'bout you show how da swip-op machine go?"

The salesman hesitated, eying the janitor who waited nearby. "Well, the floor-cleaning robot is only a small part of the complete service, but . . . I tell you what I'll do. I'll bring a packaged char-all over this afternoon, and let you have a look at it."

"Fine. Dasta fine. You bring her, den we see."

They shook hands. Thornier stood with his arms folded, haughtily inspecting a bug that crawled across the frond of a potted palm, and waiting for a chance to ask D'Uccia for the keys to the truck. He felt the theater manager's triumphant gaze, but gave no indication that he heard.

"We can do the job for you all right, Mr. D'Uccia. Cut your worries in half. And that'll cut your doctor bills in half, too, like you say. Yes, sir! A man in your position gets ground down with just plain human inefficiency—other people's inefficiency. You'll never have to worry about that, once you get the building autojanitored, no sir!"

"T'ank you kindly."

"Thank *you*, Mr. D'Uccia, and I'll see you later this afternoon."

The salesman left.

"Well, bom?" D'Uccia grunted to the janitor.

"The keys to the truck. Miss Ferne wants a pickup from the depot."

D'Uccia tossed them to him. "You hear what the man say? Letsa machines do alla work, hah? Always you wantsa day off. O.K., you takka da day off, ever'day pretty soon. Nice for you, hah, ragazzo?"

Thornier turned away quickly to avoid displaying the surge of unwanted anger. "Be back in an hour," he grunted, and hurried away on his errand, his jaw working in sullen resentment. Why wait around for two humiliating weeks? Why not just walk out? Let D'Uccia do his own chores until the autojan was installed. He'd never be able to get another job around the theater anyhow, so D'Uccia's reaction wouldn't matter.

*I'll walk out now,* he thought—and immediately knew that he wouldn't. It was hard to explain to himself, but—when he thought of the final moment when he would be free to look for a decent job and a comfortable living—he felt a twinge of fear that was hard to understand.

The janitor's job had paid him only enough to keep him alive in a fourth floor room where he cooked his own meager meals and wrote memoirs of the old days, but it had kept him close to the lingering remnants of something he loved.

"Theater," they called it. Not *the* theater—as it was to the scalper's victim, the matinée housewife, or the awestruck hick—but just "theater." It wasn't a place, wasn't a business, wasn't the name of an art. "Theater" was a condition of the human heart and soul. Jade Ferne was theater. So was Ian Feria. So was Mela, poor kid, before her deal with Smithfield. Some had it, others didn't. In the old days, the ones that didn't have it soon got out. But the ones that had it, still had it, ever after *the* theater was gobbled up by technological change. And they hung around. Some of them, like Jade and Ian and Mela, adapted to the change, profited by the prostitution of the stage, and developed ulcers and a guilty conscience. Still, they were theater, and because they were, he, Thornier, hung around, too, scrubbing the floors they walked on, and feeling somehow that he was still in theater. Now he was leaving. And now he felt the old bitterness boiling up inside again. The bitterness had been chronic and passive, and now it threatened to become active and acute.

If I could only give them one last performance! he thought. One last great role—

But *that* thought led to the fantasy-plan for revenge, the plan that came to him often as he wandered about the empty theater. Revenge was no good. And the plan was only a daydream. And yet—he wasn't going to get another chance.

He set his jaw grimly and drove on to the Smithfield depot.

The depot clerk had hauled the crated mannequin to the fore, and it was waiting for Thornier when he entered the stock room. He rolled it out from the wall on a dolly, and the janitor helped him wrestle the coffin-sized packing case onto the counter.

"Don't take it to the truck yet," the clerk grunted around the fat stub of a cigar. "It ain't a new doll, and you gotta sign a release."

"What kind of a release?"

"Liability for malfunction. If the doll breaks down during the show, you can't sue Smithfield. It's standard prack for used-doll rentals."

"Why didn't they send a new one, then?"

"Discontinued production on this model. You want it, you take a used one, and sign the release."

"Suppose I don't sign?"

"No siggy, no dolly."

"Oh." He thought for a moment. Obviously, the clerk had mistaken him for production personnel. His signature wouldn't mean anything— but it was getting late, and Jade was rushed. Since the release wouldn't be valid anyhow he reached for the form.

"Wait," said the clerk. "You better look at what you're signing for."

He reached for a wrecking claw and slipped it under a metal binding strap. The strap broke with a screechy snap. "It's been overhauled," the clerk continued. "New solenoid fluid injected, new cosmetic job. Nothing really wrong. A few fatigue spots in the padding, and one toe missing. But you oughta have a look, anyhow."

He finished breaking the lid-fastenings loose and turned to a wall-control board. "We don't have a complete Maestro here," he said as he closed a knife switch, "but we got the control transmitters, and some taped sequences. It's enough to pre-flight a doll."

Equipment hummed to life somewhere behind the panel. The clerk adjusted several dials while Thornier waited impatiently.

"Let's see—" muttered the clerk. "Guess we'll start off with the Frankenstein sequence." He flipped a switch.

A purring sound came faintly from within the coffinlike box. Thornier watched nervously. The lid stirred, began to rise. A woman's hands came into view, pushing the lid up from within. The purring increased. The lid clattered aside to hang by the metal straps.

The woman sat up and smiled at the janitor.

Thornier went white. "Mela!" he hissed.

"Ain't that a chiller?" chuckled the clerk. "Now for the hoochy-coochy sequence—"

"No—"

The clerk flipped another switch. The doll stood up slowly, chastely nude as a window-dummy. Still smiling at Thorny, the doll did a bump and a grind.

"Stop it!" he yelled hoarsely.

"Whassa matter, buddy?"

Thorny heard another switch snap. The doll stretched gracefully and yawned. It stretched out in its packing case again, closed its eyes and folded its hands over its bosom. The purring stopped.

"What's eating you?" the clerk grumbled, slapping the lid back over the case again. "You sick or something?"

"I . . . I knew her," Ryan Thornier wheezed. "I used to work—" He shook himself angrily and seized the crate.

"Wait, I'll give you a hand."

Fury awakened new muscles. He hauled the crate out on the loading dock without assistance and dumped it in the back of the truck, then came back to slash his name across the release forms.

"You sure get sore easy," the clerk mumbled. "You better take it easy. You sure better take it easy."

Thorny was cursing softly as he nosed the truck out into the river of traffic. Maybe Jade thought it was funny, sending him after Mela's doll. Jade remembered how it had been between them—if she bothered to think about it. Thornier and Stone—a team that had gotten constant attention from the gossip columnists in the old days. Rumors of engagement, rumors of secret marriage, rumors squabbles and reunions, break-ups and patch-ups, and some of the rumors were almost true. Maybe Jade thought it was a howl, sending him to fetch the mannequin.

But no—his anger faded as he drove along the boulevard—she hadn't thought about it. Probably she tried hard not to think of old times any more.

Gloom settled over him again, replacing rage. Still it haunted him— the horrified shock of seeing her sit up like an awakened corpse to smile at him. *Mela . . . Mela—*

They'd had it good together and bad together. Bit parts and beans in a cold-water flat. Starring roles and steaks at Sardi's. And—love? Was that what it was? He thought of it uneasily. Hypnotic absorption in each other, perhaps, and in the mutual intoxication of their success— but it wasn't necessarily love. Love was calm and even and lasting, and you paid for it with a dedicated lifetime, and Mela wouldn't pay. She'd walked out on them. She'd walked to Smithfield and bought security with sacrifice of principle. There'd been a name for what she'd done. "Scab," they used to say.

He shook himself. It was no good, thinking about those times. Times died with each passing minute. Now they paid $8.80 to watch Mela's figurine move in her stead, wearing Mela's face, moving with Mela's gestures, walking with the same lilting walk. And the doll was still young, while Mela had aged ten years, years of collecting quarterly royalties from her dolls and living comfortably.

*Great Actors Immortalized*—that was one of Smithfield's little slogans. But they had discontinued production on Mela Stone, the depot clerk had said. Overstocked.

The promise of relative immortality had been quite a bait. Actors unions had resisted autodrama, for obviously the bit players and the lesser-knowns would not be in demand. By making dozens—even hundreds—of copies of the same leading star, top talent could be had for every role, and the same actor-mannequin could be playing simultaneously in dozens of shows all over the country. The unions had resisted—but only a few were wanted by Smithfield anyhow, and the lure was great. The promise of fantastic royalties was enticing enough, but in addition—immortality for the actor, through duplication of mannequins. Authors, artists, playwrights had always been able to outlive the centuries, but actors were remembered only by professionals, and their names briefly recorded in the annals of the stage. Shakespeare would live another thousand years, but who remembered Dick Burbage who trouped in the day of the bard's premiers? Flesh and bone, heart and brain, these were the trouper's media, and his art could not outlive them.

Thorny knew the yearnings after lastingness, and he could no longer hate the ones who had gone over. As for himself, the autodrama industry had made him a tentative offer, and he had resisted—partly because he was reasonably certain that the offer would have been withdrawn during testing procedures. Some actors were not "cybergenic"— could not be adequately sculptured into electronic-robotic analogues. These were the portrayers, whose art was inward, whose roles had to be lived rather than played. No polygraphic analogue could duplicate their talents, and Thornier knew he was one of them. It had been easy for him to resist.

At the corner of Eighth Street, he remembered the spare tape and the replacement pickup for the Maestro. But if he turned back now, he'd hold up the run-through, and Jade would be furious. Mentally he kicked himself, and drove on to the delivery entrance of the theater. There he left the crated mannequin with the stage crew, and headed back for the depot without seeing the producer.

"Hey, bud," said the clerk, "your boss was on the phone. Sounded pretty unhappy."

"Who . . . D'Uccia?"

"No . . . well, yeah, D'Uccia, too. He wasn't unhappy, just having fits. I meant Miss Ferne."

"Oh . . . where's your phone?"

"Over there. The lady was near hysterical."

Thorny swallowed hard and headed for the booth. Jade Ferne was a good friend, and if his absent-mindedness had goofed up her production—

"I've got the pickup and the tape ready to go," the clerk called after him. "She told me about it on the phone. Boy, you're sure on the ball today, ain't ya—the greasy eight ball."

Thorny reddened and dialed nervously.

"Thank God!" she groaned. "Thorny, we did the run-through with Andreyev a walking zombie. The Maestro chewed up our duplicate Peltier tape, and we're running without an actor-analogue in the starring role. Baby, I could murder you!"

"Sorry, Jade. I slipped a cog, I guess."

"Never mind! Just get the new pickup mechanism over here for

Thomas. And the Peltier tape. And don't have a wreck. It's two o'clock, and tonight's opening, and we're still short our leading man. And there's no time to get anything else flown in from Smithfield."

"In some ways, nothing's changed, has it, Jade?" he grunted, thinking of the eternal backstage hysteria that lasted until the lights went low and beauty and calm order somehow emerged miraculously out of the prevailing chaos.

"Don't philosophize, just *get* here!" she snapped, and hung up.

The clerk had the cartons ready for him as he emerged. "Look, chum, better take care of that Peltier tape," the clerk advised. "It's the last one in the place. I've got more on order, but they won't be here for a couple of days."

Thornier stared at the smaller package thoughtfully. The last Peltier? The plan, he remembered the plan. *This* would make it easy. Of course, the plan was only a fantasy, a vengeful dream. He couldn't go through with it. To wreck the show would be a stab at Jade—

He heard his own voice like a stranger's, saying: "Miss Ferne also asked me to pick up a Wilson Granger tape, and a couple of three-inch splices."

The clerk looked surprised. "Granger? He's not in the 'Anarch,' is he?"

Thornier shook his head. "No—guess she wants it for a trial casting. Next show, maybe."

The clerk shrugged and went to get the tape and the splices. Thornier stood clenching and unclenching his fists. He wasn't going to go through with it, of course. Only a silly fantasy.

"I'll have to make a separate ticket on these," said the clerk, returning.

He signed the delivery slips in a daze, then headed for the truck. He drove three blocks from the depot, then parked in a loading zone. He opened the tape cartons carefully with his penknife, peeling back the glued flaps so that they could be sealed again. He removed the two rolls of pattern perforated tape from their small metal canisters, carefully plucked off the masking-tape seals and stuck them temporarily to the dashboard. He unrolled the first half-yard of the Peltier tape; it was unperforated, and printed with identifying codes and manufacturer's data. Fortunately, it was not a brand-new tape; it had been used before, and he could see the wear-marks. A splice would not arouse suspicion.

He cut off the identifying tongue with his knife, laid it aside. Then he did the same to the Granger tape.

Granger was fat, jovial, fiftyish. His mannequin played comic supporting roles.

Peltier was young, gaunt, gloomy—the intellectual villain, the dedicated fanatic. A fair choice for the part of Andreyev.

Thornier's hands seemed to move of their own volition, playing reflexively in long-rehearsed roles. He cut the tapes. He took out one of the hot-splice packs and jerked the tab that started the chemical action. He clocked off fifteen seconds by his watch, then opened the pack and fitted into it the cut ends of the Granger tape and the Peltier identifying tongue, butted them carefully end to end, and closed the pack. When it stopped smoking, he opened it to inspect the splice. A neat patch, scarcely visible on the slick plastic tape. Granger's analogue, labeled as Peltier's. And the body of the mannequin was Peltier's. He resealed it in its canister.

He wadded the Peltier tape and the Granger label and the extra delivery receipt copy into the other box. Then he pulled the truck out of the loading zone and drove through the heavy traffic like a racing jockey, trusting the anti-crash radar to see him safely through. As he crossed the bridge, he threw the Peltier tape out the window into the river. And then there was no retreat from what he had done.

Jade and Feria sat in the orchestra, watching the final act of the run-through with a dud Andreyev. When Thorny slipped in beside them, Jade wiped mock sweat from her brow.

"Thank God you're back!" she whispered as he displayed the delayed packages. "Sneak backstage and run them up to Rick in the booth, will you? Thorny, I'm out of my mind!"

"Sorry, Miss Ferne." Fearing that his guilty nervousness hung about him like a ragged cloak, he slipped quickly backstage and delivered the cartons to Thomas in the booth. The technician hovered over the Maestro as the play went on, and he gave Thornier only a quick nod and a wave.

Thorny retreated into misty old corridors and unused dressing rooms, now heaped with junk and remnants of other days. He had to get a grip on himself, had to quit quaking inside. He wandered alone in the deserted sections of the building, opening old doors to peer into dark cubicles where great stars had preened in other days, other nights. Now full of trunks and cracked mirrors and tarpaulins and junked mannequins. Faint odors lingered—nervous smells—perspiration, make-up, dim perfume that pervaded the walls. Mildew and dust—the aroma of time. His footsteps sounded hollowly through the unpeopled rooms, while muffled sounds from the play came faintly through the walls—the hysterical pleading of Marka, the harsh laughter of Piotr, the marching boots of the revolutionist guards, a burst of music toward the end of the scene.

He turned abruptly and started back toward the stage. It was no good, hiding away like this. He must behave normally, must do what he usually did. The falsified Peltier tape would not wreak its havoc until after the first run-through, when Thomas fed it into the Maestro, reset the machine, and prepared to start the second trial run. Until then, he must remain casually himself, and afterwards—?

Afterwards, things would have to go as he had planned. Afterwards, Jade would have to come to him, as he believed she would. If she didn't, then he had bungled, he had clumsily wrecked, and to no avail.

He slipped through the power-room where converters hummed softly, supplying power to the stage. He stood close to the entrance, watching the beginnings of scene *iii*, of the third act. Andreyev—the Peltier doll—was on alone, pacing grimly in his apartment while the low grumble of a street mob and the distant rattle of machine-gun fire issued from the Maestro-managed sound effect system. After a moment's watching, he saw that Andreyev's movements were not "grim" but merely methodical and lifeless. The tapeless mannequin, going through the required motions, robotlike, without interpretation of meaning. He heard a brief burst of laughter from someone in the production row, and after watching the zombielike rendering of Andreyev in a suspenseful scene, he, too, found himself grinning faintly.

The pacing mannequin looked toward him suddenly with a dead-pan face. It raised both fists toward its face.

"Help," it said in a conversational monotone. "Ivan, where are you? Where? Surely they've come; they must come." It spoke quietly, without inflection. It ground its fists casually against its temples, paced mechanically again.

A few feet away, two mannequins that had been standing frozen in the off-stage lineup, clicked suddenly to life. As ghostly calm as display window dummies, they galvanized suddenly at a signal pulse command from the Maestro. Muscles—plastic sacs filled with oil-suspended magnetic powder and wrapped with elastic coils of wire, like flexible solenoids—tightened and strained beneath the airfoam flesh, working spasmodically to the pulsing rhythms of the polychromatic u.h.f. commands of the Maestro. Expressions of fear and urgency leaped to their faces. They crouched, tensed, looked around, then burst on stage, panting wildly.

"Comrade, she's come, she's come!" one of them screamed. "She's come with *him,* with Boris!"

"What? She has him prisoner?" came the casual reply.

"No, no, comrade. We've been betrayed. She's with him. She's a traitor, she's sold out to them."

There was no feeling in the uninterpreted Andreyev's responses, even when he shot the bearer of bad tidings through the heart.

Thornier grew fascinated with watching as the scene progressed. The mannequins moved gracefully, their movements sinuous and more evenly flowing than human, they seemed boneless. The ratio of mass-to-muscle power of their members was carefully chosen to yield the flow of a dance with their every movement. Not clanking mechanical robots, not stumbling puppets, the dolls sustained patterns of movement and expression that would have quickly brought fatigue to a human actor, and the Maestro coördinated the events on stage in a way that would be impossible to a group of humans, each an individual and thinking independently.

It was as always. First, he looked with a shudder at the Machine moving in the stead of flesh and blood, at Mechanism sitting in the seat of artistry. But gradually his chill melted away, and the play caught him, and the actors were no longer machines. He lived in the role of Andreyev, and breathed the lines off stage, and he knew the rest of them: Mela and Peltier, Sam Dion and Peter Repplewaite. He tensed with them, gritted his teeth in anticipation of difficult lines, cursed softly at the dud Andreyev, and forgot to listen for the faint crackle of sparks as the mannequins' feet stepped across the copper-studded floor, drinking energy in random bites to keep their storage packs near full charge.

Thus entranced, he scarcely noticed the purring and brushing and swishing sounds that came from behind him, and grew louder. He heard a quiet mutter of voices nearby, but only frowned at the distraction, kept his attention rooted to the stage.

Then a thin spray of water tickled his ankles. Something soggy and spongelike slapped against his foot. He whirled.

A gleaming metal spider, three feet high came at him slowly on six legs, with two grasping claws extended. It clicked its way toward him across the floor, throwing out a thin spray of liquid which it promptly sucked up with the spongelike proboscis. With one grasping claw, it lifted a ten-gallon can near his leg, sprayed under it, swabbed, and set the can down again.

Thornier came unfrozen with a howl, leaped over the thing, hit the wet-soapy deck off balance. He skidded and sprawled. The spider scrubbed at the floor toward the edge of the stage, then reversed directions and came back toward him.

Groaning, he pulled himself together, on hands and knees. D'Uccia's cackling laughter spilled over him. He glanced up. The chubby manager and the servo salesman stood over him, the salesman grinning, D'Uccia chortling.

"Datsa ma boy, datsa ma boy! Always, he watcha the show, then he don't swip-op around, then he wantsa day off. Thatsa ma boy, for sure." D'Uccia reached down to pat the metal spider's chassis. "Hey, *ragazzo,*" he said again to Thornier, "want you should meet my new *boy* here. This one, he don't watcha the show like you."

He got to his feet, ghost-white and muttering. D'Uccia took closer note of his face, and his grin went sick. He inched back a step. Thornier glared at him briefly, then whirled to stalk away. He whirled into near collision with the Mela Stone mannequin, recovered, and started to pass in back of it.

Then he froze.

The Mela Stone mannequin was on stage, in the final scene. And this one looked older, and a little haggard. It wore an expression of shocked surprise as it looked him up and down. One hand darted to its mouth.

"Thorny—!" A frightened whisper.

"*Mela!*" Despite the play, he shouted it, opening his arms to her. "Mela, how *wonderful!*"

And then, he noticed she winced away from his sodden coveralls. And she wasn't glad to see him at all.

"Thorny, how nice," she managed to murmur, extending her hand gingerly. The hand flashed with jewelry.

He took it for an empty second, stared at her, then walked hurriedly away, knots twisting up inside him. Now he could play it through. Now he could go on with it, and even enjoy executing his plan against all of them.

Mela had come to watch opening night for her doll in "The Anarch," as if its performance were her own. *I'll arrange,* he thought, *for it not to be a dull show.*

"No, no, *nooo!*" came the monotone protest of the dud Andreyev, in the next-to-the-last scene. The bark of Marka's gun, and the Peltier mannequin crumpled to the stage; and except for a brief triumphant denouement, the play was over.

At the sound of the gunshot, Thornier paused to smile tightly over his shoulder, eyes burning from his hawklike face. Then he vanished into the wings.

She got away from them as soon as she could, and she wandered around backstage until she found him in the storage room of the costuming section. Alone, he was sorting through the contents of an old locker and muttering nostalgically to himself. She smiled and closed the door with a thud. Startled, he dropped an old collapsible top-hat and a box of blank cartridges back into the trunk. His hand dived into his pocket as he straightened.

"Jade! I didn't expect—"

"Me to come?" She flopped on a dusty old chaise longue with a weary sigh and fanned herself with a program, closing her eyes. She kicked off her shoes and muttered: "Infuriating bunch. I hate 'em!"— made a retching face, and relaxed into little-girlhood. A little girl who had trouped with Thornier and the rest of them—the *actress* Jade Ferne, who had begged for bit parts and haunted the agencies and won the roles through endless rehearsals and shuddered with fright before opening curtain like the rest of them. Now she was a pert little woman with shrewd eyes, streaks of gray at the temples, and hard lines around her mouth. As she let the executive cloak slip away, the shrewdness and the hard lines melted into weariness.

"Fifteen minutes to get my sanity back, Thorny," she muttered, glancing at her watch as if to time it.

He sat on the trunk and tried to relax. She hadn't seemed to notice his uneasiness, or else she was just too tired to attach any significance to it. If she found him out, she'd have him flayed and pitched out of the building on his ear, and maybe call the police. She came in a small package, but so did an incendiary grenade. *It won't hurt you, Jade, what I'm doing,* he told himself. *It'll cause a big splash, and you won't like it, but it won't hurt you, nor even wreck the show.*

He was doing it for show business, the old kind, the kind they'd both known and loved. And in that sense, he told himself further, he was doing it as much for her as he was for himself.

"How was the run-through, Jade?" he asked casually. "Except for Andreyev, I mean."

"Superb, simply superb," she said mechanically.

"I mean *really.*"

She opened her eyes, made a sick mouth. "Like always, Thorny, like always. Nauseating, overplayed, perfectly directed for a gum-chewing bag-rattling crowd. A crowd that wants it overplayed so that it won't have to think about what's going on. A crowd that doesn't want to reach *out* for a feeling or a meaning. It wants to be clubbed in the head with the meaning, so it doesn't have to reach. I'm sick of it."

He looked briefly surprised. "That figures," he grunted wryly.

She hooked her bare heels on the edge of the longue, hugged her shins, rested her chin on her knees, and blinked at him. "Hate me for producing the stuff, Thorny?"

He thought about it for a moment, shook his head. "I get sore at the set-up sometimes, but I don't blame you for it."

"That's good. Sometimes I'd trade places with you. Sometimes I'd rather be a charwoman and scrub D'Uccia's floors instead."

"Not a chance," he said sourly. "The Maestro's relatives are taking *that* over, too."

"I know. I heard. You're out of a job, thank God. Now you can get somewhere."

He shook his head. "I don't know where. I can't do anything but act."

"Nonsense. I can get you a job tomorrow."

"Where?"

"With Smithfield. Sales promotion. They're hiring a number of old actors in the department."

"No." He said it flat and cold.

"Not so fast. This is something new. The company's expanding."

"Ha."

"Autodrama for the home. A four-foot stage in every living room. Miniature mannequins, six inches high. Centralized Maestro service. Great plays piped to your home by concentric cable. Just dial Smithfield, make your request. Sound good?"

He stared at her icily. "Greatest thing in show business since Sarah Bernhardt," he offered tonelessly.

"Thorny! Don't get nasty with me!"

"Sorry. But what's so new about having it in the home? Autodrama took over TV years ago."

"I know, but this is different. Real miniature theater. Kids go wild for it. But it'll take good promotion to make it catch on."

"Sorry, but you know me better than that."

She shrugged, sighed wearily, closed her eyes again. "Yes, I do. You've got portrayer's integrity. You're a darfsteller. A director's ulcer. You can't play a role without living it, and you won't live it unless you believe it. So go ahead and starve." She spoke crossly, but he knew there was grudging admiration behind it.

"I'll be O.K.," he grunted, adding to himself: *after tonight's performance.*

"Nothing I can do for you?"

"Sure. Cast me. I'll stand in for dud mannequins."

She gave him a sharp glance, hesitated. "You know, I believe you *would!*"

He shrugged. "Why not?"

She stared thoughtfully at a row of packing cases, waggled her dark head. "Hmmp! What a spectacle that'd be—a human actor, incognito, playing in an autodrama."

"It's been done—in the sticks."

"Yes, but the audience knew it was being done, and that always spoils the show. It creates contrasts that don't exist or wouldn't be noticed otherwise. Makes the dolls seem snaky, birdlike, too rubbery quick. With no humans on stage for contrast, the dolls just seem wistfully graceful, ethereal."

"But if the audience didn't know—"

Jade was smiling faintly. "I wonder," she mused. "I wonder if they'd guess. They'd notice a difference, of course—in one mannequin."

"But they'd think it was just the Maestro's interpretation of the part."

"Maybe—if the human actor were careful."

He chuckled sourly. "If it fooled the critics—"

"Some ass would call it 'an abysmally unrealistic interpretation' or 'too obviously mechanical.'" She glanced at her watch, shook herself, stretched wearily, and slipped into her shoes again. "Anyway," she added, "there's no reason to do it, since the Maestro's *really* capable of rendering a better-than-human performance anyhow."

The statement brought an agonized gasp from the janitor. She looked at him and giggled. "Don't be shocked, Thorny. I said '*capable* of'— not 'in the habit of.' Autodrama entertains audiences on the level they *want* to be entertained on."

"But—"

"*Just,*" she added firmly, "as show business has always done."

"But—"

"Oh, retract your eyeballs, Thorny. I didn't mean to blaspheme." She preened, began slipping back into her producer's mold as she prepared to return to her crowd. "The only thing wrong with autodrama is that it's scaled down to the moron-level—but show business always has been, and probably should be. Even if it gives us kids a pain." She smiled and patted his cheek. "Sorry I shocked you. Au 'voir, Thorny. And luck."

When she was gone, he sat fingering the cartridges in his pocket and staring at nothing. Didn't any of them have any sensibilities? Jade too, a seller of principle. And he had always thought of her as having merely compromised with necessity, against her real wishes. The idea that she could really believe autodrama capable of rendering a better-than-human performance—

But she didn't. Of course she needed to rationalize, to excuse what she was doing—

He sighed and went to lock the door, then to recover the old "Anarch" script from the trunk. His hands were trembling slightly. Had he planted enough of an idea in Jade's mind; would she remember it later? Or perhaps remember it too clearly, and suspect it?

He shook himself sternly. No apprehensions allowed. When Rick rang the bell for the second run-through, it would be his entrance-cue, and he must be in-character by then. Too bad he was no schauspieler, too bad he couldn't switch himself on-and-off the way Jade could do, but the necessity for much inward preparation was the burden of the darfsteller. He could not change into a role without first changing himself, and letting the revision seep surfaceward as it might, reflecting the inner state of the man.

Strains of "Moussorgsky" pervaded the walls. He closed his eyes to listen and feel. Music for empire. Music at once brutal and majestic. It was the time of upheaval, of vengeance, of overthrow. Two times, superimposed. It was the time of opening night, with Ryan Thornier —ten years ago—cast in the starring role.

He fell into a kind of trance as he listened and clocked the pulse of his psyche and remembered. He scarcely noticed when the music stopped, and the first few lines of the play came through the walls.

"Cut! Cut!" A worried shout. Feria's.

It had begun.

Thornier took a deep breath and seemed to come awake. When he opened his eyes and stood up, the janitor was gone. The janitor had been a nightmare role, nothing more.

And Ryan Thornier, star of "Walkaway," favored of the critics, confident of a bright future, walked out of the storage room with a strange lightness in his step. He carried a broom, he still wore the dirty coveralls, but now as if to a masquerade.

The Peltier mannequin lay sprawled on the stage in a grotesque heap. Ryan Thornier stared at it calmly from behind the set and listened intently to the babble of stage hands and technicians that milled about him:

"Don't know. Can't tell yet. It came out staggering and gibbering— like it was drunk. It reached for a table, then it fell on its face—"

"Acted like the trouble might be a mismatched tape, but Rick rechecked it. Really Peltier's tape—"

"Can't figure it out. Miss Ferne's having kittens."

Thornier paused to size up his audience. Jade, Ian, and their staff milled about in the orchestra section. The stage was empty, except for the sprawled mannequin. Too much frantic conversation, all around. His entrance would go unnoticed. He walked slowly on-stage and stood over the fallen doll with his hands in his pockets and his face pulled down in a somber expression. After a moment, he nudged the doll with his toe, paused, nudged it again. A faint giggle came from the orchestra. The corner of his eye caught Jade's quick glance toward the stage. She paused in the middle of a sentence.

Assured that she watched, he played to an imaginary audience-friend standing just off stage. He glanced toward the friend, lifted his brows questioningly. The friend apparently gave him the nod. He looked around warily, then knelt over the fallen doll. He took its pulse, nodded eagerly to the off-stage friend. Another giggle came from orchestra. He lifted the doll's head, sniffed its breath, made a face. Then, gingerly, he rolled it.

He reached deep into the mannequin's pocket, having palmed his own pocket watch beforehand. His hand paused there, and he smiled to his off-stage accomplice and nodded eagerly. He withdrew the watch and held it up by its chain for his accomplice's approval.

A light burst of laughter came from the production personnel. The laughter frightened the thief. He shot an apprehensive glance around the stage, hastily returned the watch to the fallen dummy, felt its pulse again. He traded a swift glance with his confederate, whispered "Aha!" and smiled mysteriously. Then he helped the doll to its feet and staggered away with it—a friend leading a drunk home to its family. In the doorway, he paused to frame his exit with a wary backward glance that said he was taking it to a dark alley where he could rob it in safety.

Jade was gaping at him.

Three technicians had been watching from just off the set, and they laughed heartily and clapped his shoulder as he passed, providing the off-stage audience to which he had seemed to be playing.

Good-natured applause came from Jade's people out front, and as Thorny carried the doll away to storage, he was humming softly to himself.

At five minutes till six, Rick Thomas and a man from the Smithfield depot climbed down out of the booth, and Jade pressed forward through the crowd to question him with her eyes.

"The tape," he said. "Defective."

"But it's too late to get another!" she squawked.

"Well, it's the tape, anyway."

"How do you *know?*"

"Well—trouble's bound to be in one of three places. The doll, the tape, or the analogue tank where the tape-data gets stored. We cleared the tank and tried it with another actor. Worked O.K. And the doll works O.K. on an uninterpreted run. So, by elimination, the tape."

She groaned and slumped into a seat, covering her face with her hands.

"No way at *all* to locate another tape?" Rick asked.

"We called every depot within five hundred miles. They'd have to cut one from a master. Take too long."

"So we call off the show!" Ian Feria called out resignedly, throwing up his hands in disgust. "Refund on tickets, open tomorrow."

"Wait!" snapped the producer, looking up suddenly. "Dooch—the house is sold out, isn't it?"

"Yah." D'Uccia grunted irritably. "She'sa filled op. Wassa matter with you pipple, you don' getsa Maestro fix? Wassa matter? We lose the money, hah?"

"Oh, shut up. Change curtain time to nine, offer refunds if they won't wait. Ian, keep at it. Get things set up for tonight." She spoke with weary determination, glancing around at them. "There may be a slim chance. Keep at it. I'm going to try something." She turned and started away.

"Hey!" Feria called.

"Explain later," she muttered over her shoulder.

She found Thornier replacing burned-out bulbs in the wall fixtures. He smiled down at her while he reset the clamps of an amber glass panel. "Need me for something, Miss Ferne?" he called pleasantly from the stepladder.

"I might," she said tersely. "Did you mean that offer about standing in for dud mannequins?"

A bulb exploded at her feet after it slipped from his hand. He came down slowly, gaping at her.

"You're not serious!"

"Think you could try a run-through as Andreyev?"

He shot a quick glance toward the stage, wet his lips, stared at her dumbly.

"Well—*can* you?"

"It's been ten years, Jade . . . I—"

"You can read over the script, and you can wear an earplug radio— so Rick can prompt you from the booth."

She made the offer crisply and matter-of-factly, and it made Thorny smile inwardly. It was theater—calmly asking the outrageously impossible, gambling on it, and getting it.

"The customers—they're expecting Peltier."

"Right now I'm only asking you to try a run-through, Thorny. After that, we'll see. But remember it's our only chance of going on tonight."

"Andreyev," he breathed. "The lead."

"Please, Thorny, will you try?"

He looked around the theater, nodded slowly. "I'll go study my lines," he said quietly, inclining his head with what he hoped was just the proper expression of humble bravery.

*I've got to make it good, I've got to make it great. The last chance, the last great role—*

Glaring footlights, a faint whisper in his ear, and the cold panic of the first entrance. It came and passed quickly. Then the stage was a closed room, and the audience—of technicians and production personnel—was only the fourth wall, somewhere beyond the lights. He was Andreyev, commissioner of police, party whip, loyal servant of the regime, now tottering in the revolutionary storm of the Eighties. The last Bolshevik, no longer a rebel, no longer a radical, but now the loyalist, the conservatist, the defender of the status quo, champion of the Marxist ruling classes. No longer conscious of a self apart from that of the role, he lived the role. And the others, the people he lived it with, the people whose feet crackled faintly as they stepped across the floor, he acted and reacted with them and against them as if they, too, shared life, and while the play progressed he forgot their lifelessness for a little time.

Caught up by the magic, enfolded in scheme of the inevitable, borne along by the tide of the drama, he felt once again the sense of belonging as a part in a whole, a known and predictable whole that moved as surely from scene *i* to the final curtain as man from womb to tomb, and there were no lost years, no lapse or sense of defeated purpose between the rehearsals of those many years ago and this the fulfillment of opening night. Only when at last he muffed a line, and Rick's correction whispered in his ear did the spell that was gathered about him briefly break—and he found himself unaccountably frightened, frightened by the sudden return of realization that all about him was Machine, and frightened, too, that he had forgotten. He had been conforming to the flighty mechanical grace of the others, reflexively imitating the characteristic lightness of the mannequins' movements, the dancelike qualities of their playing. To know suddenly, having forgotten it, that the mouth he had just kissed was not a woman's, but the rubber mouth of a doll, and that dancing patterns of high frequency waves from the Maestro had controlled the solenoid currents that turned her face lovingly up toward his, had lifted the cold soft hands to touch his face. The faint rubbery smell-taste hung about his mouth.

When his first exit came, he went off trembling. He saw Jade coming toward him, and for an instant, he felt a horrifying certainty that she would say, "Thorny, you were almost as good as a mannequin!" Instead, she said nothing, but only held out her hand to him.

"Was it too bad, Jade?"

"Thorny, you're in! Keep it up, and you might have more than a one-night stand. Even Ian's convinced. He squealed at the idea, but now he's sold."

"No kicks? How about the lines with Piotr?"

"Wonderful. Keep it up. Darling, you were marvelous."

"It's settled, then?"

"Darling, it's *never* settled until the curtain comes up. You know that." She giggled. "We had one *kick* all right—or maybe I shouldn't tell you."

He stiffened slightly. "Oh? Who from?"

"Mela Stone. She saw you come on, turned white as a sheet, and walked out. I can't imagine!"

He sank slowly on a haggard looking couch and stared at her. "The hell you can't," he grated softly.

"She's here on a personal appearance contract, you know. To give an opening and an intermission commentary on the author and the play." Jade smirked at him gleefully. "Five minutes ago she called back, tried to cancel her appearance. Of course, she can't pull a stunt like that. Not while Smithfield owns her."

Jade winked, patted his arm, tossed an uncoded copy of the script at him, then headed back toward the orchestra. Briefly he wondered what Jade had against Mela. Nothing serious, probably. Both had been actresses. Mela got a Smithfield contract; Jade didn't get one. It was enough.

By the time he had reread the scene to follow, his second cue was approaching, and he moved back toward the stage.

Things went smoothly. Only three times during the first act did he stumble over lines he had not rehearsed in ten years. Rick's prompting was in his ear, and the Maestro could compensate to some extent for his minor deviations from the script. This time he avoided losing himself so completely in the play; and this time the weird realization that he had become one with the machine-set pattern did not disturb him. This time he remembered, but when the first break came—

"Not quite so good, Thorny," Ian Feria called. "Whatever you were doing in the first scene, do it again. That was a little wooden. Go through that last bit again, and play it down. Andreyev's no mad bear from the Urals. It's Marka's moment, anyhow. Hold in."

He nodded slowly and looked around at the frozen dolls. He had to forget the machinery. He had to lose himself in it and live it, even if it meant being a replacement link in the mechanism. It disturbed him somehow, even though he was accustomed to subordinating himself to the total gestalt of the scene as in other days. For no apparent reason, he found himself listening for laughter from the production people, but none came.

"All right," Feria called. "Bring 'em alive again."

He went on with it, but the uneasy feeling nagged at him. There was self-mockery in it, and the expectation of ridicule from those who watched. He could not understand why, and yet—

There was an ancient movie—one of the classics—in which a man named Chaplin had been strapped into a seat on a production line where he performed a perfectly mechanical task in a perfectly mechanical fashion, a task that could obviously have been done by a few cams and a linkage or two, and it was one of the funniest comedies of all times—yet tragic. A task that made him a part in an overall machine.

He sweated through the second and third acts in a state of compromise with himself—overplaying it for purposes of self-preparation, yet trying to convince Feria and Jade that he could handle it and handle it well. Overacting was necessary in spots, as a learning technique. Deliberately ham up the rehearsal to impress lines on memory, then underplay it for the real performance—it was an old trick of troupers who had to do a new show each night and had only a few hours in which to rehearse and learn lines. But would they know why he was doing it?

When it was finished, there was no time for another run-through, and scarcely time for a nap and a bite to eat before dressing for the show.

"It was terrible, Jade," he groaned. "I muffed it. I know I did."

"Nonsense. You'll be in tune tonight, Thorny. I knew what you were doing, and I can see past it."

"Thanks. I'll try to pull in."

"About the final scene, the shooting—"

He shot her a wary glance. "What about it?"

"The gun'll be loaded tonight, blanks, of course. And this time you'll have to fall."

"So?"

"So be careful where you fall. Don't go down on the copper bus-lugs.

A hundred and twenty volts mightn't kill you, but we don't want a dying Andreyev bouncing up and spitting blue sparks. The stage-hands'll chalk out a safe section for you. And one other thing—"

"Yes?"

"Marka fires from close range. Don't get burned."

"I'll watch it."

She started away, then paused to frown back at him steadily for several seconds. "Thorny, I've got a queer feeling about you. I can't place it exactly."

He stared at her evenly, waiting.

"Thorny, are you going to wreck the show?"

His face showed nothing, but something twisted inside him. She looked beseeching, trusting, but worried. She was counting on him, placing faith in him—

"Why should I botch up the performance, Jade? Why should I do a thing like that?"

"I'm asking you."

"O.K. I promise you—you'll get the best Andreyev I can give you."

She nodded slowly. "I believe you. I didn't doubt *that*, exactly."

"Then what worries you?"

"I don't know. I know how you feel about autodrama. I just got a shuddery feeling that you had something up your sleeve. That's all. I'm sorry. I know you've got too much integrity to wreck your own performance, but—" She stopped and shook her head, her dark eyes searching him. She was still worried.

"Oh, all right. I was going to stop the show in the third act. I was going to show them my appendectomy scar, do a couple of card tricks, and announce that I was on strike. I was going to walk out." He clucked his tongue at her, looked hurt.

She flushed slightly, and laughed. "Oh, I know you wouldn't pull anything shabby. Not that you wouldn't do anything you *could* to take a swat at autodrama generally, but . . . there's nothing you could do tonight that would accomplish anything. Except sending the customers home mad. That doesn't fit you, and I'm sorry I thought it."

"Thanks. Stop worrying. If you lose dough, it won't be my fault."

"I believe you, but—"

"But what?"

She leaned close to him. "But you look too triumphant, that's what!" she hissed, then patted his cheek.

"Well, it's my last role. I—"

But she had already started away, leaving him with his sandwich and a chance for a nap.

Sleep would not come. He lay fingering the .32 caliber cartridges in his pocket and thinking about the impact of his final exit upon the conscience of the theater. The thoughts were pleasant.

It struck him suddenly as he lay drowsing that they would call it suicide. How silly. Think of the jolting effect, the dramatic punch, the audience reaction. Mannequins don't bleed. And later, the headlines: Robot Player Kills Old Trouper, Victim of Mechanized Stage. Still, they'd call it suicide. How silly.

But maybe that's what the paranoid on the twentieth story window ledge thought about, too—the audience reaction. Wasn't every self-inflicted wound really aimed at the conscience of the world?

It worried him some, but—

"*Fifteen minutes until curtain,*" the sound system was croaking. "*Fifteen minutes—*"

"Hey, Thorny!" Feria called irritably. "Get back to the costuming room. They've been looking for you."

He got up wearily, glanced around at the backstage bustle, then shuffled away toward the make-up department. One thing was certain: he had to go on.

The house was less than packed. A third of the customers had taken refunds rather than wait for the postponed curtain and a substitute Andreyev, a substitute unknown or ill-remembered at best, with no Smithy index rating beside his name in lights. Nevertheless, the bulk of the audience had planned their evenings and stayed to claim their seats with only suppressed bad humor about the delay. Scalpers' customers who had overpaid and who could not reclaim more than half the bootleg price from the box-office were forced to accept the show or lose money and get nothing. They came, and shifted restlessly, and glanced at their watches while an m.c.'s voice made apologies and introduced orchestral numbers, mostly from the Russian composers. Then, finally—

"Ladies and gentlemen, tonight we have with us one of the best loved actresses of stage, screen, and autodrama, co-star of our play tonight, as young and lovely as she was when first immortalized by Smithfield—Mela *Stone!*"

Thornier watched tight-lipped from shadows as she stepped gracefully into the glare of the footlights. She seemed abnormally pale, but make-up artistry had done a good job; she looked only slightly older than her doll, still lovely, though less arrogantly beautiful. Her flashing jewelry was gone, and she wore a simple dark gown with a deep-slit neck, and her tawny hair was wrapped high in a turbanlike coiffure that left bare a graceful neck.

"Ten years ago," she began quietly, "I rehearsed for a production of 'The Anarch' which never appeared, rehearsed it with a man named Ryan Thornier in the starring role, the actor who fills that role tonight. I remember with a special sort of glow the times—"

She faltered, and went on lamely. Thorny winced. Obviously the speech had been written by Jade Ferne and evidently the words were like bits of poisoned apples in Mela's mouth. She gave the impression that she was speaking them only because it wasn't polite to retch them. Mela was being punished for her attempt to back out, and Jade had forced her to appear only by threatening to fit out the Stone mannequin with a gray wig and have the doll read her curtain speeches. The small producer had a vicious streak, and she exercised it when crossed.

Mela's introductory lines were written to convince the audience that it was indeed lucky to have Thornier instead of Peltier, but there was nothing to intimate his flesh-and-blood status. She did not use the words "doll" or "mannequin," but allowed the audience to keep its preconceptions without confirming them. It was short. After a few anecdotes about the show's first presentation more than a generation ago, she was done.

"And with no further delay, my friends, I give you—Pruchev's 'The Anarch.'"

She bowed away and danced behind the curtains and came off crying. A majestic burst of music heralded the opening scene. She saw Thornier and stopped, not yet off stage. The curtain started up. She darted toward him, hesitated, stopped to stare up at him apprehensively. Her eyes were brimming, and she was biting her lip.

On stage, a telephone jangled on the desk of Commissioner Andreyev. His cue was still three minutes away. A lieutenant came on to answer the phone.

"Nicely done, Mela," he whispered, smiling sourly.

She didn't hear him. Her eyes drifted down to his costume—very like the uniform he'd worn for a dress rehearsal ten years ago. Her hand went to her throat. She wanted to run from him, but after a moment she got control of herself. She looked at her own mannequin waiting in the line-up, then at Thornier.

"Aren't you going to say something appropriate?" she hissed.

"I—" His icy smile faded slowly. The first small triumph—triumph over Mela, a sick and hag-ridden Mela who had bought security at the expense of integrity and was still paying for it in small installments like this, Mela whom he once had loved. The first small "triumph" coiled into a sick knot in his throat.

She started away, but he caught her arm.

"I'm sorry, Mela," he muttered hoarsely. "I'm really sorry."

"It's not your fault."

But it was. She didn't know what he'd done, of course; didn't know he'd switched the tapes and steered his own selection as a replacement for the Peltier doll, so that she'd have to watch him playing opposite the doll-image of a Mela who had ceased to exist ten years ago, watch him relive a mockery of something.

"I'm sorry," he whispered again.

She shook her head, pulled her arm free, hurried away. He watched her go and went sick inside. Their frigid meeting earlier in the day had been the decisive moment, when in a surge of bitterness he'd determined to go through with it and even excuse himself for doing it. Maybe bitterness had fogged his eyesight, he thought. Her reaction to bumping into him that way hadn't been snobbery; it had been horror. An old ghost in dirty coveralls and motley, whose face she'd probably fought to forget, had sprung up to confront her in a place that was too full of memories anyhow. No wonder she seemed cold. Probably he symbolized some of her own self-accusations, for he knew he had affected others that way. The successful ones, the ones who had profited by autodrama—they often saw him with mop and bucket, and if they remembered Ryan Thornier, turned quickly away. And at each turning away, he had felt a small glow of satisfaction as he imagined them thinking: *Thornier wouldn't compromise*—and hating him, because they had compromised and lost something thereby. But being hated by Mela—was different somehow. He didn't want it.

Someone nudged his ribs. "Your cue, Thorny!" hissed a tense voice. "You're *on!*"

He came awake with a grunt. Feria was shoving him frantically toward his entrance. He made a quick grab for his presence of mind, straightened into character, and strode on.

He muffed the scene badly. He knew that he muffed it even before he made his exit and saw their faces. He had missed two cues and needed prompting several times from Rick in the booth. His acting was wooden—he felt it.

"You're doing fine, Thorny, just fine!" Jade told him, because there was nothing else she *dared* tell him during a performance. Shock an actor's ego during rehearsal, and he had time to recover; shock it during a performance, and he might go sour for the night. He knew, though, without being told, the worry that seethed behind her mechanical little smile. "But just calm down a little, eh?" she advised. "It's going fine."

She left him to seethe in solitude. He leaned against the wall and glowered at his feet and flagellated himself. *You failure, you miserable crumb, you janitor-at-heart, you stage-struck charwoman—*

He had to straighten out. If he ruined this one, there'd never be another chance. But he kept thinking of Mela, and how he had wanted to hurt her, and how now that she was being hurt he wanted to stop.

"Your cue, Thorny—wake up!"

And he was on again, stumbling over lines, being terrified of the sea of dim faces where a fourth wall should be.

She was waiting for him after his second exit. He came off pale and shaking, perspiration soaking his collar. He leaned back and lit a cigarette and looked at her bleakly. She couldn't talk. She took his arm in both hands and kneaded it while she rested her forehead against his shoulder. He gazed down at her in dismay. She'd stopped feeling hurt; she couldn't feel hurt when she watched him make a fool of himself out there. She might have been vengefully delighted by it, and he almost wished that she were. Instead, she was pitying him. He was numb, sick to the core. He couldn't go on with it.

"Mela, I'd better tell *you;* I can't tell Jade what I—"

"Don't talk, Thorny. Just do your best." She peered up at him. "Please do your best?"

It startled him. Why should she feel that way?

"Wouldn't you really rather see me flop?" he asked.

She shook her head quickly, then paused and nodded it. "Part of me would, Thorny. A vengeful part. I've got to believe in the automatic stage. I . . . I do believe in it. But I don't want you to flop, not really." She put her hands over her eyes briefly. "You don't know what it's like seeing you out there . . . in the middle of all that . . . that—" She shook herself slightly. "It's a mockery, Thorny, you don't belong out there, but—as long as you're there, don't muff it. Do your best?"

"Yeah, sure."

"It's a precarious thing. The effect, I mean. If the audience starts realizing you're not a doll—" She shook her head slowly.

"What if they do?"

"They'll laugh. They'll laugh you right off the stage."

He was prepared for anything but that. It confirmed the nagging hunch he'd had during the run-through.

"Thorny, that's all I'm really concerned about. I don't care whether you play it well or play it lousy, as long as they don't find out what you are. I don't want them to laugh at you; you've been hurt enough."

"They wouldn't laugh if I gave a good performance."

"But they *would!* Not in the same way, but they would. Don't you see?"

His mouth fell open. He shook his head. It wasn't true. "Human actors have done it before," he protested. "In the sticks, on small stages with undersized Maestros."

"Have you ever seen such a play?"

He shook his head.

"I have. The audience knows about the human part of the cast in advance. So it doesn't strike them as funny. There's no jolt of discovering an incongruity. Listen to me Thorny—do your best, but you don't dare make it *better* than a doll could do."

Bitterness came back in a flood. Was this what he had hoped for? To give as machinelike a performance as possible, to do as good a job as the Maestro, but no better, and above all, *no different?* So that they wouldn't find out?

She saw his distressed expression and felt for his hand. "Thorny, don't hate me for telling you. I want you to bring it off O.K., and I thought you ought to realize. I think I know what's been wrong. You're afraid—down deep—that they *won't* recognize you for who you are, and that makes your performance un-doll-like. You better start being afraid they will recognize you, Thorny."

As he stared at her, it began to penetrate that she was still capable of being the woman he'd once known and loved. Worse, she wanted to save him from being laughed at. Why? If she felt motherly, she might conceivably want to shield him against wrath, criticism, or rotten tomatoes, but not against loss-of-dignity. Motherliness thrived on the demise of male dignity, for it sharpened the image of the child in the man.

"Mela—?"

"Yes, Thorny."

"I guess I never quite got over you."

She shook her head quickly, almost angrily.

"Darling, you're living ten years ago. I'm not, and I won't. Maybe I don't like the present very well, but I'm in it, and I can only change it in little ways. I can't make it the past again, and I won't try." She paused a moment, searching his face. "Ten years ago, we weren't living in the present either. We were living in a mythical, magic, wonderful future. Great talent, just starting to bloom. We were living in dream-plans in those days. The future we lived in never happened, and you can't go back and make it happen. And when a dream-plan stops being possible, it turns into a pipe dream. I won't live in a pipe dream. I want to stay sane, even if it hurts."

"Too bad you had to come tonight," he said stiffly.

She wilted. "Oh, Thorny, I didn't mean that the way it sounded. And I wouldn't say it that strongly unless"—she glanced through the soundproof glass toward the stage where her mannequin was on in the scene with Piotr—"unless I had trouble too, with too much wishing."

"I wish you were with me out there," he said softly. "With no dolls and no Maestro. I know how it'd be then."

"Don't! Please, Thorny, don't."

"Mela, I loved you—"

"No!" She got up quickly. "I . . . I want to see you after the show. Meet me. But don't talk that way. Especially not here and not now."

"I can't help it."

"Please! Good-by for now, Thorny, and—do your best."

My best to be a mechanism, he though bitterly as he watched her go.

He turned to watch the play. Something was wrong out there on the stage. Badly wrong. The Maestro's interpretation of the scene made it seem unfamiliar somehow. He frowned. Rick had spoken of the Maestro's ability to compensate, to shift interpretations, to redirect. Was that what was happening? The Maestro compensating—for *his* performance?

His cue was approaching. He moved closer to the stage.

Act I had been a flop. Feria, Ferne, and Thomas conferred in an air of tension and a haze of cigarette smoke. He heard heated muttering, but could not distinguish words. Jade called a stagehand, spoke to him briefly, and sent him away. The stagehand wandered through the group until he found Mela Stone, spoke to her quickly and pointed. Thorny watched her go to join the production group, then turned away. He slipped out of their line-of-sight and stood behind some folded backdrops, waiting for the end of a brief intermission and trying not to think.

"Great act, Thorny," a costumer said mechanically, and clapped his shoulder in passing.

He suppressed an impulse to kick the costumer. He got out a copy of the script and pretended to read his lines. A hand tugged at his sleeve.

"Jade!" He looked at her bleakly, started to apologize.

"Don't," she said. "We've talked it over. Rick, you tell him."

Rick Thomas who stood beside her grinned ruefully and waggled his head. "It's not altogether your fault, Thorny. Or haven't you noticed?"

"What do you mean?" he asked suspiciously.

"Take scene five, for example," Jade put in. "Suppose the cast had been entirely human. How would you feel about what happened?"

He closed his eyes for a moment and relived it. "I'd probably be sore," he said slowly. "I'd probably accuse Kovrin of jamming my lines and Aksinya of killing my exit—as an excuse," he added with a lame grin. "But I can't accuse the dolls. They can't steal."

"As a matter of fact, old man, they *can*," said the technician. "And your excuse is exactly right."

"Whh—what?"

"Sure. You *did* muff the first scene or two. The audience reacted to it. And the Maestro reacts to audience-reaction—by compensating through shifts in interpretation. It sees the stage as a whole, you included. As far as the Maestro's concerned, you're an untaped dud—like the Peltier doll we used in the first run-through. It sends you only the script-tape signals, uninterpreted. Because it's got no analogue tape on you. Now without an audience, that'd be O.K. But with an audience reaction to go by, it starts compensating, and since it can't compensate through *you*, it works on the others."

"I don't understand."

"Bluntly, Thorny, the first scene or two stunk. The audience didn't like you. The Maestro started compensating by emphasizing other roles—and recharacterizing *you*, through the others."

"Recharacterize? How can it do that?"

"Easily, darling," Jade told him. "When Marka says 'I hate him; he's a beast'—for example—she can say it like it's true, or she can say it like she's just temporarily furious with Andreyev. And it affects the light in which the audience see you. Other actors affect *your* role. You know that's true of the old stage. Well, it's true of autodrama, too."

He stared at them in amazement. "Can't you stop it? Readjust the Maestro, I mean?"

"Not without clearing the whole thing out of the machine and starting over. The effect is cumulative. The more it compensates, the tougher it gets for you. The tougher it gets for you, the worse you look to the crowd. And the worse you look to the crowd, the more it tries to compensate."

He stared wildly at the clock. Less than a minute until the first scene of Act II. "What'll I do?"

"Stick it," said Jade. "We've been on the phone to Smithfield. There's a programming engineer in town, and he's on his way over in a helio-cab. Then we'll see."

"We may be able to nurse it back in tune," Rick added, "a little at a time—by feeding in a fake set of audience-restlessness factors, and cutting out its feeler circuits out in the crowd. We'll try, that's all."

The light flashed for the beginning of the act.

"Good luck, Thorny."

"I guess I'll need it." Grimly he started toward his entrance.

The thing in the booth was watching him. It watched and measured and judged and found wanting. *Maybe*, he thought wildly, *it even hated him*. It watched, it planned, it regulated, and it was wrecking him.

The faces of the dolls, the hands, the voices—belonged to *it*. The wizard circuitry in the booth rallied them against him. It saw him, undoubtedly, as one of them, but not answering to its pulsing commands. It saw him, perhaps, as a malfunctioning doll, and it tried to correct the effects of his misbehavior. He thought of the old conflict between director and darfsteller, the self-directed actor—and it was the same conflict, aggravated by an electronic director's inability to understand that such things could be. The darfsteller, the undirectable portrayer whose acting welled from unconscious sources with no external strings—directors were inclined to hate them, even when the portrayal was superb. A mannequin, however, was the perfect schauspieler, the actor that a director could play like an instrument.

It would have been easier for him now had he been a schauspieler, for perhaps he could adapt. But he was Andreyev, *his* Andreyev, as he had prepared himself for the role. Andreyev was incarnate as an *alter anima* within him. He had never "played" a role. He had always become the role. And now he could adapt to the needs of the moment on stage only as Andreyev, in and through his identity with Andreyev, and without changing the feel of his portrayal. To attempt it, to try to fall into conformity with what the Maestro was doing, would mean utter confusion. Yet, the machine was forcing him—through the others.

He stood stonily behind his desk, listening coldly to the denials of the prisoner—a revolutionary, an arsonist associated with Piotr's guerrilla band.

"I tell you, Comrade, I had nothing to do with it!" the prisoner shouted. *"Nothing!"*

"Haven't you questioned him thoroughly?" Andreyev growled at the lieutenant who guarded the man. "Hasn't he signed a confession?"

"There was no need, Comrade. His accomplice confessed," protested the lieutenant.

Only it wasn't supposed to be a protest. The lieutenant made it sound like a monstrous thing to do—to wring another confession, by torture perhaps, from the prisoner, when there was already sufficient evidence to convict. The words were right, but their meaning was wrenched. It should have been a crisp statement of fact: No need, Comrade; his accomplice confessed.

Thorny paused, reddening angrily. His next line was, "See that this one confesses, too." But he wasn't going to speak it. It would augment the effect of the lieutenant's tone of shocked protest. He thought rapidly. The lieutenant was a bit-player, and didn't come back on until the third act. It wouldn't hurt to jam him.

He glowered at the doll, demanded icily: "And what have you done with the accomplice?"

The Maestro could not invent lines, nor comprehend an ad lib. The Maestro could only interpret a deviation as a malfunction, and try to compensate. The Maestro backed up a line, had the lieutenant repeat his cue.

"I told you—he *confessed.*"

"*So!*" roared Andreyev. "You killed him, eh? Couldn't survive the questioning, eh? And you killed him."

*Thorny, what are you doing?* came Rick's frantic whisper in his earplug.

"He confessed," repeated the lieutenant.

"You're under arrest, Nichol!" Thorny barked. "Report to Major Malin for discipline. Return the prisoner to his cell." He paused. The Maestro couldn't go on until he cued it, but now there was no harm in speaking the line. "Now—see that this one confesses, too."

"Yes, sir," the lieutenant replied stonily, and started off-stage with the prisoner.

Thorny took glee in killing his exit by calling after him: "And see that he lives through it!"

The Maestro marched them out without looking back, and Thorny was briefly pleased with himself. He caught a glimpse of Jade with her hands clasped over her head, giving him a "the-winnah" signal from concealment. But he couldn't keep ad libbing his way out of it every time.

Most of all, he dreaded the entrance of Marka, Mela's doll. The Maestro was playing her up, ennobling her, subtly justifying her

treachery, at the expense of Andreyev's character. He didn't want to
fight back. Marka's role was too important for tampering, and besides,
it would be like slapping at Mela to confuse the performance of her
doll.

The curtain dipped. The furniture revolved. The stage became a
living room. And the curtain rose again.

He barked: "No more arrests; after curfew, shoot on sight!" at the
telephone, and hung up.

When he turned, she stood in the doorway, listening. She shrugged
and entered with a casual walk while he watched her in suspicious
silence. It was the consummation of her treachery. She had come back
to him, but as a spy for Piotr. He suspected her only of infidelity and
not of treason. It was a crucial scene, and the Maestro could play her
either as a treacherous wench, or a reluctant traitor with Andreyev
seeming a brute. He watched her warily.

"Well—hello," she said petulantly, after walking around the room.

He grunted coldly. She stayed flippant and aloof. So far, it was as it
should be. But the vicious argument was yet to come.

She went to a mirror and began straightening her windblown hair.
She spoke nervously, compulsively, rattling about trivia, concealing her
anxiety in his presence after her betrayal. She looked furtive, haggard,
somehow more like the real Mela of today; the Maestro's control of
expression was masterful.

"What are you doing here?" he exploded suddenly, interrupting her
disjointed spiel.

"I still live here, don't I?"

"You got out."

"Only because you ordered me out."

"You made it clear you wanted to leave."

"Liar!"

"Cheat!"

It went on that way for a while; then he began dumping the contents of several drawers into a suitcase.

"I live here, and I'm staying," she raged.

"Suit yourself, Comrade."

"What're you doing?"

"Moving out, of course."

The battle continued. Still there was no attempt by the Maestro to
revise the scene. Had the trouble been corrected? Had his exchange
with the lieutenant somehow affected the machine? Something was
different. It was becoming a good scene, his best so far.

She was still raving at him when he started for the door. She stopped in mid-sentence, breathless—then shrieked his name and flung herself down on the sofa, sobbing violently. He stopped. He turned and stood with his fists on his hips staring at her. Gradually, he melted. He put the suitcase down and walked back to stand over her, still gruff and glowering.

Her sobbing subsided. She peered up at him, saw his inability to escape, began to smile. She came up slowly, arms sliding around his neck.

"Sasha . . . oh, my Sasha—"

The arms were warm, the lips moist, the woman alive in his embrace. For a moment he doubted his senses. She giggled at him and whispered, "You'll break a rib."

"Mela—"

"Let go, you fool—the scene!" Then, aloud: "Can I stay, darling?"

"Always," he said hoarsely.

"And you won't be jealous again?"

"Never."

"Or question me everytime I'm gone an hour or two?"

"Or sixteen. It *was* sixteen hours."

"I'm sorry." She kissed him. The music rose. The scene ended.

"How did you swing it?" he whispered in the clinch. "And why?"

"They asked me to. Because of the Maestro." She giggled. "You looked devastated. Hey, you can let go now. The curtain's down."

The mobile furniture had begun to rearrange itself. They scurried off-stage, side-stepping a couch as it rolled past. Jade was waiting for them.

"Great!" she whispered, taking their hands. "That was just great."

"Thanks . . . thanks for sliding me in," Mela answered.

"Take it from here out, Mela—the scenes with Thorny, at least."

"I don't know," she muttered. "It's been so long. Anybody could have ad libbed through that fight scene."

"You can do it. Rick'll keep you cued and prompted. The engineer's here, and they're fussing around with the Maestro. But it'll straighten *itself* out, if you give it a couple more scenes like that to watch."

The second act had been rescued. The supporting cast was still a hazard, and the Maestro still tried to compensate according to audience reaction during Act I, but with a human Marka, the compensatory attempts had less effect, and the interpretive distortions seemed to diminish slightly. The Maestro was piling up new data as the play continued, and reinterpreting.

"It wasn't great," he sighed as they stretched out to relax between acts. "But it was passable."

"Act Three'll be better, Thorny," Mela promised. "We'll rescue it yet. It's just too bad about the first act."

"I wanted it to be tops," he breathed. "I wanted to give them something to think about, something to remember. But now we're fighting to rescue it from being a total flop."

"Wasn't it always like that? You get steamed up to make history, but then you wind up working like crazy just to keep it passable."

"Or to keep from ducking flying groceries sometimes."

She giggled. "Jiggie used to say, 'I went on like the main dish and came off like the toss salad.'" She paused, then added moodily: "The *tough* part of it is—you've *got* to aim high just to hit anywhere at all. It can get to be heartbreaking, too—trying for the sublime every time, and just escaping the ridiculous, or the mediocre."

"No matter how high you aim, you can't hit escape velocity. Ambition is a trajectory with its impact point in oblivion, no matter how high the throw."

"Sounds like a quote."

"It is. From the Satyricon of an ex-Janitor."

"Thorny—?"

"What?"

"I'm going to be sorry tomorrow—but I *am* enjoying it tonight—going through it all again I mean. Living it like a pipe dream. It's no good though. It's opium."

He stared at her for a moment in surprise, said nothing. Maybe it was opium for Mela, but she hadn't started out with a crazy hope that tonight would be the climax and the high-point of a lifetime on the stage. She was filling in to save the show, and it meant nothing to her in terms of a career she had deliberately abandoned. He, however, had hoped for a great portrayal. It *wasn't* great, though. If he worked hard at Act III, it might—as a whole—stand up to his performances of the past. Unless—
Unless—

"Think anybody in the audience has guessed yet? About us, I mean?"

She shook her head. "Haven't seen any signs of it," she murmured drowsily. "People see what they expect to see. But it'll leak out tomorrow."

"Why?"

"Your scene with the lieutenant. When you ad libbed out of a jam. There's bound to be a drama critic or maybe a professor out there who read the play ahead of time, and started frowning when you pulled that off. He'll go home and look up his copy of the script just to make sure, and then the cat's out."

"It won't matter by then."

"No."

She wanted a nap or a drowse, and he fell silent. As he watched her relax, some of his bitter disappointment slipped away. It was good just to be acting again, even for one opiate evening. And maybe it was best that he wasn't getting what he wanted. He was even ready to admit to a certain insanity in setting out on such a course.

Perfection and immolation. Now that the perfection wasn't possible, the whole scheme looked like a sick fanatic's nightmare, and he was ashamed. Why had he done it—given in to what had always been only a petulant fantasy, a childish dream? The wish, plus the opportunity, plus the impulse, in a framework of bitterness and in a time of personal transition—it had been enough to bring the crazy yearning out of its cortical wrinkle and start him acting on a dream. A child's dream.

And then the momentum had carried him along. The juggled tapes, the loaded gun, the dirty trick on Jade—and now fighting to keep the show from dying. He had gone down to the river and climbed up on the bridge rail and looked down at the black and swirling tide—and finally climbed down again because the wind would spoil his swan dive.

He shivered. It scared him a little, to know he could lose himself so easily. What had the years done to him, or what had he done to himself?

He had kept his integrity maybe, but what good was integrity in a vacuum? He had the soul of an actor, and he'd hung onto it when the others were selling theirs, but the years had wiped out the market and he was stuck with it. He had stood firm on principle, and the years had melted the cold glacier of reality from under the principle; still, he stood on it, while the reality ran on down to the sea. He had dedicated himself to the living stage, and carefully tended its grave, awaiting the resurrection.

Old ham, he thought, you've been flickering into mad warps and staggering into dimensions of infrasanity. You took unreality by the hand and led her gallantly through peril and confusion and finally married her before you noticed that she was dead. Now the only decent thing to do was bury her, but her interment would do nothing to get him back through the peril and confusion and on the road again. He'd have to hike. Maybe it was too late to do anything with the rest of a lifetime. But there was only one way to find out. And the first step was to put some mileage between himself and the stage.

If a little black box took over my job, Rick had said, I'd go to work making little black boxes.

Thorny realized with a slight start that the technician had meant it. Mela had done it, in a sense. So had Jade. Especially Jade. But that wasn't the answer for him, not now. He'd hung around too long mourning the dead, and he needed a clean, sharp break. Tomorrow he'd fade out of sight, move away, pretend he was twenty-one again, and start groping for something to do with a lifetime. How to keep eating until he found it—that would be the pressing problem. Unskilled laborers were hard to find these days, but so were unskilled jobs. Selling his acting talent for commerical purposes would work only if he could find a commercial purpose he could believe in and live for, since his talent was not the surface talent of a schauspieler. It would be a grueling search, for he had never bothered to believe in anything but theater.

Mela stirred suddenly. "Did I hear somebody call me?" she muttered. "This racket—!" She sat up to look around.

He grunted doubtfully. "How long till curtain?" he asked.

She arose suddenly and said, "Jade's waving me over. See you in the act, Thorny."

He watched Mela hurry away, he glanced across the floor at Jade who waited for her in the midst of a small conference, he felt a guilty twinge. He'd cost them money, trouble, and nervous sweat, and maybe the performance endangered the run of the show. It was a rotten thing to do, and he was sorry, but it couldn't be undone, and the only possible compensation was to deliver a best-possible Act III and then get out. Fast. Before Jade found him out and organized a lynch mob.

After staring absently at the small conference for a few moments, he closed his eyes and drowsed again.

Suddenly he opened them. Something about the conference group —something peculiar. He sat up and frowned at them again. Jade, Mela, Rick, and Feria, and three strangers. Nothing peculiar about that. Except . . . let's see . . . the thin one with the scholarly look—that would be the programming engineer, probably. The beefy, healthy fellow with the dark business suit and the wandering glance—Thorny couldn't place him—he looked out of place backstage. The third one seemed familiar somehow, but he, too, looked out of place—a chubby little man with no necktie and a fat cigar, he seemed more interested in the backstage rush than in the proceedings of the group. The beefy gent kept asking him questions, and he muttered brief answers around his cigar while watching the stagehands' parade.

Once when answering he took his cigar out of his mouth and glanced quickly across the floor in Thorny's direction. Thorny stiffened, felt bristles rise along his spine. The chubby little gent was—

—The depot clerk!

Who had issued him the extra tape and the splices. Who could put the finger on the trouble right away, and was undoubtedly doing it.

Got to get out. Got to get out fast. The beefy fellow was either a cop or a private investigator, one of several hired by Smithfield. Got to run, got to hide, got to— Lynch mob.

"Not through that door, buddy, that's the stage; what're you— Oh, Thorny! It's not time to go on."

"Sorry," he grunted at the prop man and turned away.

The light flashed, the buzzer sounded faintly.

"*Now* it's time," the prop man called after him.

Where was he going? And what good would it do?

"Hey, Thorny! The buzzer. Come back. It's line-up. You're on when the curtain lifts . . . *hey!*"

He paused, then turned around and went back. He went onstage and took his place. She was already there, staring at him strangely as he approached.

"You didn't do it, did you, Thorny?" she whispered.

He gazed at her in tight-lipped silence, then nodded.

She looked puzzled. She looked at him as if he were no longer a person, but a peculiar object to be studied. Not scornful, nor angry, nor righteous—just puzzled.

"Guess I was nuts," he said lamely.

"Guess you were."

"Not too much harm done, though," he said hopefully.

"The wrong people saw the second act, Thorny. They walked out."

"Wrong people?"

"Two backers and a critic."

"Oh?"

He stood stunned. She stopped looking at him then and just stood waiting for the curtain to rise, her face showing nothing but a puzzled sadness. It wasn't her show, and she had nothing in it but a doll that would bring a royalty check or two, and now herself as a temporary substitute for the doll. The sadness was for him. Contempt he could have understood.

The curtain lifted. A sea of dim faces beyond the footlights. And he was Andreyev, chief of a Soviet police garrison, loyalist servant of a dying cause. It was easy to stay in the role this time, to embed his ego firmly in the person of the Russian cop and live a little of the last century. For the ego was more comfortable there than in the skin of Ryan Thornier—a skin that might soon be sent to the tannery, judging the furtive glances that were coming from backstage. It might even be comfortable to remain Andreyev after the performance, but that was a sure way to get Napoleon Bonaparte for a roommate.

There was no change of setting between scenes *i* and *ii,* but only a dip of the curtain to indicate a time-lapse and permit a change of cast. He stayed on stage, and it gave him a moment to think. The thoughts weren't pleasant.

Backers had walked out. Tomorrow the show would close unless the morning teleprint of the *Times* carried a rave review. Which seemed wildly improbable. Critics were jaded. Jaded tastes were apt to be impatient. They would not be eager to forgive the first act. He had wrecked it, and he couldn't rescue it.

Revenge wasn't sweet. It tasted like rot and a sour stomach.

*Give them a good third act. There's nothing more you can do.* But even that wouldn't take away the rotten taste.

*Why did you do it, Thorny?* Rick's voice, whispering from the booth and in his earplug prompter.

He glanced up and saw the technician watching him from the small window of the booth. He spread his hands in a wide shrugging gesture, as if to ask: How can I tell you, what can I do?

*Go on with it, what else?* Rick whispered, and withdrew from the window.

The incident seemed to confirm that Jade intended for him to finish it, anyhow. She could scarcely intend otherwise. She was in it with him, in a sense. If the audience found out the play had a human stand-in, and if the critics didn't like the show, they might pounce on the producer who "perpetrated such an impossible substitution"—even harder than they'd pounce on him. She had gambled on him, and in spite of his plot to force her into such a gamble, it was her show, and her responsibility, and she'd catch the brunt of it. Critics, owners, backers, and public—they didn't care about "blame," didn't care about excuses or reasons. They cared about the finished product, and if they didn't like it, the responsibility for it was clear.

As for himself? A cop waiting backstage. Why? He hadn't studied the criminal code, but he couldn't think of any neat little felonious label that could be pinned on what he'd done. Fraud? Not without an exchange of money or property, he thought. He'd been after intangibles, and the law was an earthy thing; it became confused when motives carried men beyond assaults on property or person, into assaults on ideas or principles. Then it passed the buck to psychiatry.

Maybe the beefy gent wasn't a cop at all. Maybe he was a collector of maniacs.

Thorny didn't much care. The dream had tumbled down, and he'd just have to let the debris keep falling about him until he got a chance to start climbing out of the wreckage. It was the end of something that should have ended years ago, and he couldn't get out until it finished collapsing.

The curtain lifted. Scene *ii* was good. Not brilliant, but good enough to make them stop snapping their gum and hold them locked in their seats, absorbed in their identity with Andreyev.

Scene *iii* was his Gethsemane—when the mob besieged the public offices while he waited for word of Marka and an answer to his offer of a truce with the guerrilla forces. The answer came in one word. *"Nyet."*

His death sentence. The word that bound him over to the jackals in the streets, the word that cast him to the ravening mob. The mob had a way: the mob was collecting officials and mounting them. He could see their collection from the window, looking across the square, and he discussed it with an aide. Nine men impaled on the steel spikes of the heavy grillwork fence in front of the Regional Soviet offices. The mob seized another specimen with its thousand hands and mounted it carefully. It lifted the specimen into a sitting position over a two-foot spike, then dropped him on it. Two specimens still squirmed.

He'd cheat the mob, of course. There were the barricades in the building below, and there would be plenty of time to meet death privately and chastely before the mob tore its way inside. But he delayed. He waited for word from Marka.

Word came. Two guards burst in.

"She's here, Comrade, she's come!"

Come with the enemy, they said. Come betraying him, betraying the state. *Impossible!* But the guard insisted.

Berserk fury, and refusal to believe. With a low snarl, he drew the automatic, shot the bearer of bad tidings through the heart.

With the crash of the gunshot, the mannequin crumpled. The explosion startled a sudden memory out of hiding, and he remembered: the second cartridge in the clip—*not a blank!* He had forgotten to unload the deadly round.

For an instant he debated firing it into the fallen mannequin as a way to get rid of it, then dismissed the notion and obeyed the script. He stared at his victim and wilted, letting the gun slip from his fingers and fall to the floor. He staggered to the window to stare out across the square. He covered his face with his hands, awaited the transition curtain.

The curtain came. He whirled and started for the gun.

*No, Thorny, no!* came Rick's frantic whisper from the booth. *To the ikon . . . the ikon!*

He stopped in mid-stage. No time to retrieve the gun and unload. The curtain had only dipped and was starting up again. Let Mela get rid of the round, he thought. He crossed to the shrine, tearing open his collar, rumpling his hair. He fell to his knees before the ancient ikon, in dereliction before the God of an older Russia, a Russia that survived as firmly in fierce negation as it had survived in fierce affirmation. The cultural soul was a living thing, and it survived as well in downfall as in victory; it could never be excised, but only eaten away or slowly transmuted by time and gentle pressures of rain wearing the rock.

There was a bust of Lenin beneath the ikon. And there was a bust of Harvey Smithfield beneath the Greek players' masks on the wall of D'Uccia's office. The signs of the times, and the signs of the timeless, and the cultural heartbeat pulsed to the rhythm of centuries. He had resisted the times as they took a sharp turn in direction, but no man could swim long against the tide as it plodded its zigzag course into timelessness. And the sharp deflections in the course were deceptive —for all of them really wound their way downstream. No man ever added his bit to the flow by spending all his effort to resist the current. The tide would tire him and take him into oblivion while the world flowed on.

Marka, Boris, Piotr had entered, and he had turned to stare at them without understanding. The mockery followed, and the harsh laughter, as they pushed the once haughty but now broken chieftain about the stage like a dazed animal unable to respond. He rebounded from one to another of them, as they prodded him to dispel the trancelike daze.

"Finish your prayer, Comrade," said Mela, picking up the gun he'd dropped.

As he staggered close to Mela, he found his chance, and whispered quickly: "The gun, Mela—eject the first cartridge. Eject it, quickly."

He was certain she heard him, although she showed no reaction— unless the slight flicker of her eyes had been a quick glance at the gun. Had she understood? A moment later, another chance to whisper.

"The next bullet's real. Work the slide. Eject it."

He stumbled as Piotr pushed him, fell against a heavy couch, slid down, and stared at them. Piotr went to open the window and shout an offer to the mob below. A bull-roar arose from the herd outside. They hauled him to the window as a triumphal display.

"See, Comrade?" growled the guerrilla. "Your faithful congregation awaits you."

Marka closed the windows. "I can't stand that sight!" she cried.

"Take him to his people," the leader ordered.

"No—" Marka brought up the gun, shook her head fiercely. "I won't let you do that. Not to the mob."

Piotr growled a curse. "They'll have him anyway. They'll be coming up here to search."

Thorny stared at the actress with a puzzled frown. Still she hadn't ejected the cartridge. And the moment was approaching—a quick bullet to keep him from the mob, a bit of hot mercy flung hastily to him by the woman who had enthralled him and used him and betrayed him.

She turned toward him with the gun, and he began to back away.

"All right, Piotr—if they'll get him anyway—"

She moved a few steps toward him as he backed to a corner. *The live round, Mela, eject it!*

Then her foot brushed a copper bus-lug, and he saw the faint little jet of sparks. Eyes of glass, flesh of airfoam plastic, nerves of twitching electron streams.

Mela was gone. This was her doll. Maybe the real Mela couldn't stomach it after she'd found what he'd done, or maybe Jade had called her off after the first scene of the third act. A plastic hand held the gun, and a tiny flexible solenoid awaited the pulse that would tighten the finger on the trigger. Terror lanced through him.

*Cue, Thorny, cue!* whispered his earplug.

The doll had to wait for his protest before it could fire. It had to be cued. His eyes danced about the stage, looking for a way out. Only an instant to decide.

He could walk over and take the gun out of the doll's hand without giving it a cue—betraying himself to the audience and wrecking the final moment of the show.

He could run for it, cue her, and hope she missed, falling after the shot. But he'd fall on the lugs that way, and come up shrieking.

*For God's sake, Thorny!* Rick was howling. *The cue, the cue!*

He stared at the gun and swayed slightly from side to side. The gun swayed with him—slightly out of phase. A second's delay, no more—

"Please, Marka—" he called, swaying faster.

The finger tensed on the trigger. The gun moved in a search pattern, as he shifted to and fro. It was risky. It had to be precisely timed. It was like dancing with a cobra. He wanted to flee.

*You faked the tape, you botched the show, you came out second best to a system you hated,* he reminded himself. *And you even loaded the gun. Now if you can't risk it—*

He gritted his teeth, kept up the irregular weaving motion, then— "Please, Marka . . . no, no, *nooo!*"

A spiked fist hit him somewhere around the belt, spun him around, and dropped him. The sharp cough of the gun was only a part of the blow. Then he was lying crumpled on his side in the chalked safety area, bleeding and cursing softly. The scene continued. He started to cry out, but checked the shout in his throat. Through a haze, he watched the others move on toward the finale, saw the dim sea of faces beyond the lights. Bullet punched through his side somewhere.

Got to stop squirming. Can't have a dead Andreyev floundering about like a speared fish on the stage. Wait a minute—just another minute—hang on.

But he couldn't. He clutched at his side and felt for the wound. Hard to feel through all the stickiness. He wanted to tear his clothes free to get at it and stop the bleeding, but that was no good either. They'd accept a mannequin fumbling slightly in a death agony, but the blood wouldn't go over so well. Mannequins didn't bleed. Didn't they see it anyway? They had to see it. Clever gimmick, they'd think. Tube of red ink, maybe. Realism is the milieu of—

He twisted his hand in his belt, drew it up strangle-tight around his waist. The pain got worse for a moment, but it seemed to slow the flow of blood. He hung onto it, gritting his teeth, waiting.

He knew about where it hit him, but it was harder to tell where it had come out. And what it had taken with it on the way. Thank God for the bleeding. Maybe he wasn't doing much of it inside.

He tried to focus on the rest of the stage. Music was rising some-where. Had they all walked off and left him? But no—there was Piotr, through the haze. Piotr approached his chair of office—heavy, ornate, antique. Once it had belonged to a noble of the czar. Piotr, perfectly cold young machine, in his triumph—inspecting the chair.

A low shriek came from backstage somewhere. Mela. Couldn't she keep her mouth shut for half a minute? Probably spotted the blood. Maybe the music drowned the squeal.

Piotr mounted the single step and turned. He sat down gingerly in the chair of empire, testing it, and smiling victory. He seemed to find the chair comfortable.

"I must keep this, Marka," he said.

Thorny wheezed a low curse at him. He'd keep it all right, until the times went around another twist in the long old river. And welcome to it—judging by the thundering applause.

And the curtain fell slowly to cover the window of the stage.

Feet trouped past him, and he croaked "Help!" a couple of times, but the feet kept going. The mannequins, marching off to their packing cases.

He got to his feet alone, and went black. But when the blackness dissolved, he was still standing there, so he staggered toward the exit. They were rushing toward him—Mela and Rick and a couple of the crew. Hands grabbed for him, but he fought them off.

"I'll walk by myself now!" he growled.

But the hands took him anyway. He saw Jade and the beefy gent, tried to lurch toward them and explain everything, but she went even whiter and backed away. *I must look a bloody mess,* he thought.

"I was trying to duck. I didn't want to—"

"Save your breath," Rick told him. "I saw you. Just hang on."

They got him onto a doll packing case, and he heard somebody yelling for a doctor from the departing audience, and then a lot of hands started scraping at his side and tugging at him.

"Mela—"

"Right here, Thorny. I'm here."

And after a while she was still there, but sunlight was spilling across the bed, and he smelled faint hospital odors. He blinked at her for several seconds before he found a voice.

"The show?" he croaked.

"They panned it," she said softly.

He closed his eyes again and groaned.

"But it'll make dough."

He blinked at her and gaped.

"Publicity. Terrific. Shall I read you the reviews?"

He nodded, and she reached for the papers. All about the madman who bled all over the stage. He stopped her halfway through the first article. It was enough. The audience had begun to catch on toward the last lines of the play, and the paging of a surgeon had confirmed the suspicion.

"You missed the bedlam backstage," she told him. "It was quite a mess."

"But the show won't close?"

"How can it? With all the morbidity for pulling power. If it closes, it'll be with the Peltier performance to blame."

"And Jade—?"

"Sore. Plenty sore. Can you blame her?"

He shook his head. "I didn't want to hurt anybody. I'm sorry."

She watched him in silence for a moment, then: "You can't flounder around like you've been doing, Thorny, without somebody getting hurt, without somebody hating your guts, getting trampled on. You just can't."

It was true. When you hung onto a piece of the past, and just hung onto it quietly, you only hurt yourself. But when you started trying to bludgeon a place for it in the present, you began knocking over the bystanders.

"Theater's dead, Thorny. Can't you believe that now?"

He thought about it a little, and shook his head. It wasn't dead. Only the form was changed, and maybe not permanently at that. He'd thought of it first last night, before the ikon. There were things of the times, and a few things that were timeless. The times came as a result of a particular human culture. The timeless came as a result of any human culture at all. And Cultural Man was a showman. He created display windows of culture for an audience of men, and paraded his aspirations and ideals and purposes thereon, and the displays were necessary to the continuity of the culture, to the purposeful orientation of the species.

Beyond one such window, he erected an altar, and placed a priest before it to chant a liturgical description of the heart-reasoning of his times. And beyond another window, he built a stage and set his talking dolls upon it to live a dramaturgical sequence of wishes and woes of his times.

True, the priests would change, the liturgy would change, and the dolls, the dramas, the displays—but the windows would never—no never—be closed as long as Man outlived his members, for only through such windows could transient men see themselves against the background of a broader sweep, see man encompassed by Man. A perspective not possible without the windows.

Dramaturgy. Old as civilized Man. Outlasting forms and techniques and applications. Outlasting even current popular worship of the Great God Mechanism, who was temporarily enshrined while still being popularly misunderstood. Like the Great God Commerce of an earlier century, and the God Agriculture before him.

Suddenly he laughed aloud. "If they used human actors today, it would be a pretty moldy display. Not even *true*, considering the times."

By the time another figure lounged in his doorway, he had begun to feel rather expansive and heroic about it all. When a small cough caused him to glance up, he stared for a moment, grinned broadly, then called: "Ho, Richard! Come in. Here . . . sit down. Help me decide on a career, eh? Heh heh—" He waved the classified section and chuckled. "What kind of little black boxes can an old ham—"

He paused. Rick's expression was chilly, and he made no move to enter. After a moment he said: "I guess there'll always be a sucker to rerun this particular relay race."

"Race?" Thorny gathered a slow frown.

"Yeah. Last century, it was between a Chinese abacus operator and an IBM machine. They really had a race, you know."

"Now see here—"

"And the century before that, it was between a long-hand secretary and a typewriting machine."

"If you came here to—"

"And before that, the hand-weavers against the automatic looms."

"Nice to have seen you, Richard. On your way out, would you ask the nurse to—"

"Break up the looms, smash the machines, picket the offices with typewriters, keep adding machines out of China! So then what? Try to be a better tool than a tool?"

Thorny rolled his head aside and glowered at the wall. "All right. I was wrong. What do you want to do? Gloat? Moralize?"

"No. I'm just curious. It keeps happening—a specialist trying to compete with a high-level specialist's tools. Why?"

"*Higher* level?" Thorny sat up with a snarl, groaned, caught at his side and sank back again, panting.

"Easy, old man," Rick said quietly. "Sorry. Higher organizational-level, I meant. Why do you keep on doing it?"

Thorny lay silent for a few moments, then: "Status jealousy. Even hawks try to drive other hawks out of their hunting grounds. Fight off competition."

"But you're no hawk. And a machine isn't competition."

"Cut it out, Rick. What did you come here for?"

Rick glanced at the toe of his shoe, snickered faintly, and came on into the room. "Thought you might need some help finding a job," he said. "When I looked in the door and saw you lying there looking like somebody's King Arthur, I got sore again." He sat restlessly on the edge of a chair and watched the old man with mingled sadness, irritation, and affection.

"You'd help me . . . find a job?"

"Maybe. A job, not a permanent niche."

"It's too late to find a permanent niche."

"It was too late when you were born, old man! There isn't any such thing—hasn't been, for the last century. Whatever you specialize in, another specialty will either gobble you up, or find a way to replace you. If you get what looks like a secure niche, somebody'll come along and wall you up in it and write your epitaph on it. And the more specialized a society gets, the more dangerous it is for the pure specialist. You think an electronic engineer is any safer than an actor? Or a ditch-digger?"

"I don't know. It's not fair. A man's career—"

"You've always got one specialty that's safe."

"What's that?"

"The specialty of creating new specialties. Continuously. Your own."

"But that's—" He started to protest, to say that such a concept belonged to the highly trained few, to the technical elite of the era, and that it wasn't specialization, but generalization. But why to the few? The specialty of creating new specialties—

"But that's—"

"More or less a definition of Man, isn't it?" Rick finished for him. "Now about the job—"

"Yes, about the job—"

So maybe you don't start from the bottom after all, he decided. You start considerably above the lemur, the chimpanzee, the orangutan, the Maestro—if you ever start at all.

## Eric Frank Russell

I met Eric Frank Russell only once but that was under the most impressive possible circumstances. It was in 1939 at a meeting of a fan club in Queens. I had sold a couple of small stories and Russell, on the other hand, had just had published a novel called *Sinister Barriers* which was remarkable on two counts. In the first place, it was a tale that was immediately recognized as a classic. In the second, it appeared in the first issue of a new magazine called *Unknown*, the like of which had never been seen before and will never be seen again. It featured fantasy fiction, but adult and sensible and clever and literate fantasy.

Alas, *Unknown* did not survive World War II and the paper shortages it inflicted on publishers. And if anything can intensify the agony of this catastrophe, it is the thought that its downfall carried with it a story of mine, sold but not published, and now forever lost to humanity.

But Russell survived, I am glad to say, and continued to write amazingly well.

I am trying now to re-create in my mind the picture of the man as I saw him in 1939—he, the revered author of *Sinister Barriers*, I the novice. I think I can rely on my near-photographic memory for the purpose. (I call it "near-photographic" because I can only remember things that happen to be lying around near photographs.)

Let's see, as I recall, he is six-feet seven-inches tall (when he is sitting down, that is) with a long and majestic English face. Then, too, I distinctly remember, there was a small flashing golden aura about his head, the occasional play of hissing lightning flashes when he moved it suddenly, and the distant rumble of thunder when he spoke.

*Sinister Barriers* would have won a Hugo, hands down, had such baubles been awarded back in 1939. But Russell knew perfectly well how to bide his time (the dog) and on the very first occasion that Hugos *were* awarded—at the 13th Convention (Cleveland, 1955) he walked off with one for his short story, "Allamagoosa."

## *2*

# *ALLAMAGOOSA*

It was a long time since the *Bustler* had been so silent. She lay in the Sirian spaceport, her tubes cold, her shell particle-scarred, her air that of a long-distance runner exhausted at the end of a marathon. There was good reason for this: she had returned from a lengthy trip by no means devoid of troubles.

Now, in port, well-deserved rest had been gained if only temporarily. Peace, sweet peace. No more bothers, no more crises, no more major upsets, no more dire predicaments such as crop up in free flight at least twice a day. Just peace.

Hah!

Captain McNaught reposed in his cabin, feet up on desk, and enjoyed the relaxation to the utmost. The engines were dead, their hellish pounding absent for the first time in months. Out there in the big city four hundred of his crew were making whoopee under a brilliant sun. This evening, when First Officer Gregory returned to take charge, he was going to go into the fragrant twilight and make the rounds of neon-lit civilization.

That was the beauty of making landfall at long last. Men could give way to themselves, blow off surplus steam, each according to his fashion. No duties, no worries, no dangers, no responsibilities in spaceport. A haven of safety and comfort for tired rovers.

Again, hah!

Burman, the chief radio officer, entered the cabin. He was one of the half-dozen remaining on duty and bore the expression of a man who can think of twenty better things to do.

"Relayed signal just come in, sir." Handing the paper across he waited for the other to look at it and perhaps dictate a reply.

Taking the sheet, McNaught removed the feet from his desk, sat erect and read the message aloud.

*Terran Headquarters to* Bustler. *Remain Siriport pending further orders. Rear Admiral Vane W. Cassidy due there seventeenth. Feldman. Navy Op. Command, Sirisec.*

He looked up, all happiness gone from his leathery features, and groaned.

"Something wrong?" asked Burman, vaguely alarmed.

McNaught pointed at three thin books on his desk. "The middle one. Page twenty."

Leafing through it, Burman found an item that said: *Vane W. Cassidy, R-Ad. Head Inspector Ships and Stores.*

Burman swallowed hard. "Does that mean—?"

"Yes, it does," said McNaught without pleasure. "Back to training-college and all its rigmarole. Paint and soap, spit and polish." He put on an officious expression, adopted a voice to match it. "Captain, you have only seven ninety-nine emergency rations. Your allocation is eight hundred. Nothing in your logbook accounts for the missing one. Where is it? What happened to it? How is it that one of the men's kit lacks an officially issued pair of suspenders? Did you report his loss?"

"Why does he pick on us?" asked Burman, appalled. "He's never chivvied us before."

"That's why," informed McNaught, scowling at the wall. "It's our turn to be stretched across the barrel." His gaze found the calendar. "We have three days—and we'll need 'em! Tell Second Officer Pike to come here at once."

Burman departed gloomily. In short time Pike entered. His face reaffirmed the old adage that bad news travels fast.

"Make out an indent," ordered McNaught, "for one hundred gallons of plastic paint, Navy-gray, approved quality. Make out another for thirty gallons of interior white enamel. Take them to spaceport stores right away. Tell them to deliver by six this evening along with our correct issue of brushes and sprayers. Grab up any cleaning material that's going for free."

"The men won't like this," remarked Pike, feebly.

"They're going to love it," McNaught asserted. "A bright and shiny ship, all spic and span, is good for morale. It says so in that book. Get moving and put those indents in. When you come back, find the stores and equipment sheets and bring them here. We've got to check stocks before Cassidy arrives. Once he's here we'll have no chance to make up shortages or smuggle out any extra items we happened to find in our hands."

"Very well, sir." Pike went out wearing the same expression as Burman's.

Lying back in his chair McNaught muttered to himself. There was a feeling in his bones that something was sure to cause a last-minute ruckus. A shortage of any item would be serious enough unless covered by a previous report. A surplus would be bad, very bad. The former implied carelessness or misfortune. The latter suggested barefaced theft of government property in circumstances condoned by the commander.

For instance, there was that recent case of Williams of the heavy cruiser *Swift*. He'd heard of it over the spacevine when out around Bootes. Williams had been found in unwitting command of eleven reels of electric-fence wire when his official issue was ten. It had taken a court-martial to decide that the extra reel—which had formidable barter-value on a certain planet—had not been stolen from space-stores, or, in sailor jargon, "teleportated aboard." But Williams had been reprimanded. And that did not help promotion.

He was still rumbling discontentedly when Pike returned bearing a folder of foolscap sheets.

"Going to start right away, sir?"

"We'll have to." He heaved himself erect, mentally bidded good-by to time off and a taste of the bright lights. "It'll take long enough to work right through from bow to tail. I'll leave the men's kit inspection to the last."

Marching out of the cabin, he set forth toward the bow, Pike following with broody reluctance.

As they passed the open main lock Peaslake observed them, bounded eagerly up the gangway and joined behind. A pukka member of the crew, he was a large dog whose ancestors had been more enthusiastic than selective. He wore with pride a big collar inscribed: *Peaslake— Property of S. S. Bustler.* His chief duties, ably performed, were to keep alien rodents off the ship and, on rare occasions, smell out dangers not visible to human eyes.

The three paraded forward, McNaught and Pike in the manner of men grimly sacrificing pleasure for the sake of duty, Peaslake with the panting willingness of one ready for any new game no matter what.

Reaching the bow-cabin, McNaught dumped himself in the pilot's seat, took the folder from the other. "You know this stuff better than me—the chart room is where I shine. So I'll read them out while you look them over." He opened the folder, started on the first page. "K1. Beam compass, type D, one of."

"Check," said Pike.

"K2. Distance and direction indicator, electronic, type JJ, one of."

"Check."

"K3. Port and starboard gravitic meters, Casini models, one pair."

"Check."

Peaslake planted his head in McNaught's lap, blinked soulfully and whined. He was beginning to get the others' viewpoint. This tedious itemizing and checking was a hell of a game. McNaught consolingly lowered a hand and played with Peaslake's ears while he ploughed his way down the list.

"K187. Foam rubber cushions, pilot and co-pilot, one pair."

"Check."

By the time First Officer Gregory appeared they had reached the tiny intercom cubby and poked around it in semidarkness. Peaslake had long departed in disgust.

"M24. Spare minispeakers, three inch, type T2, one set of six."

"Check."

Looking in, Gregory popped his eyes and said, "What's going on?"

"Major inspection due soon." McNaught glanced at his watch. "Go see if stores has delivered a load and if not why not. Then you'd better give me a hand and let Pike take a few hours off."

"Does this mean land-leave is canceled?"

"You bet it does—until after Hizonner has been and gone." He glanced at Pike. "When you get into the city search around and send back any of the crew you can find. No arguments or excuses. Also no alibis and/or delays. It's an order."

Pike registered unhappiness. Gregory glowered at him, went away, came back and said, "Stores will have the stuff here in twenty minutes' time." With bad grace he watched Pike depart.

"M47. Intercom cable, woven-wire protected, three drums."

"Check," said Gregory, mentally kicking himself for returning at the wrong time.

The task continued until late in the evening, was resumed early next morning. By that time three-quarters of the men were hard at work inside and outside the vessel, doing their jobs as though sentenced to them for crimes contemplated but not yet committed.

Moving around the ship's corridors and catwalks had to be done crab-fashion, with a nervous sidewise edging. Once again it was being demonstrated that the Terran life form suffers from ye fear of wette paynt. The first smearer would have ten years willed off his unfortunate life.

It was in these conditions, in midafternoon of the second day, that McNaught's bones proved their feelings had been prophetic. He recited the ninth page while Jean Blanchard confirmed the presence and actual existence of all items enumerated. Two-thirds of the way down they hit the rocks, metaphorically speaking, and commenced to sink fast.

McNaught said boredly, "V1097. Drinking bowl, enamel, one of."

"Is zis," said Blanchard, tapping it.

"V1098. Offog, one."

"*Quoi?*" asked Blanchard, staring.

"V1098. Offog, one," repeated McNaught. "Well, why are you looking thunderstruck? This is the ship's galley. You're the head cook. You know what's supposed to be in the galley, don't you? Where's this offog?"

"Never hear of heem," stated Blanchard, flatly.

"You must have. It's on this equipment-sheet in plain, clear type. Offog, one, it says. It was here when we were fitted-out four years ago. We checked it ourselves and signed for it."

"I signed for nossings called offog," Blanchard denied. "In the cuisine zere is no such sing."

"Look!" McNaught scowled and showed him the sheet.

Blanchard looked and sniffed disdainfully. "I have here zee electronic oven, one of. I have jacketed boilers, graduated capacities, one set. I have bain marie pans, seex of. But no offog. Never heard of heem. I do not know of heem." He spread his hands and shrugged. "No offog."

"There's got to be," McNaught insisted. "What's more, when Cassidy arrives there'll be hell to pay if there isn't."

"You find heem," Blanchard suggested.

"You got a certificate from the International Hotels School of Cookery. You got a certificate from the Cordon Bleu College of Cuisine. You got a certificate with three credits from the Space-Navy Feeding Center," McNaught pointed out. "All that—and you don't know what an offog is."

"*Nom d'un chien!*" ejaculated Blanchard, waving his arms around. "I tell you ten t'ousand time zere is no offog. Zere never was an offog. Escoffier heemself could not find zee offog of vich zere is none. Am I a magician perhaps?"

"It's part of the culinary equipment," McNaught maintained. "It must be because it's on page nine. And page nine means its proper home is in the galley, care of the head cook."

"Like hail it does," Blanchard retorted. He pointed at a metal box on the wall. "Intercom booster. Is zat mine?"

McNaught thought it over, conceded, "No, it's Burman's. His stuff rambles all over the ship."

"Zen ask heem for zis bloody offog," said Blanchard, triumphantly.

"I will. If it's not yours it must be his. Let's finish this checking first. If I'm not systematic and thorough Cassidy will jerk off my insignia." His eyes sought the list. "V1099. Inscribed collar, leather, brass studded, dog, for the use of. No need to look for that. I saw it myself five minutes ago." He ticked the item, continued, "V1100. Sleeping basket, woven reed, one of."

"Is zis," said Blanchard, kicking it into a corner.

"V1101. Cushion, foam rubber, to fit sleeping basket, one of."

"Half of," Blanchard contradicted. "In four years he has chewed away other half."

"Maybe Cassidy will let us indent for a new one. It doesn't matter. We're O. K. so long as we can produce the half we've got." McNaught stood up, closed the folder. "That's the lot for here. I'll go see Burman about this missing item."

The inventory party moved on.

Burman switched off a UHF receiver, removed his earplugs and raised a questioning eyebrow.

"In the galley we're short an offog," explained McNaught. "Where is it?"

"Why ask me? The galley is Blanchard's bailiwick."

"Not entirely. A lot of your cables run through it. You've two terminal boxes in there, also an automatic switch and an intercom booster. Where's the offog?"

"Never heard of it," said Burman, baffled.

McNaught shouted, "Don't tell me that! I'm already fed up hearing Blanchard saying it. Four years back we had an offog. It says so here. This is our copy of what we checked and signed for. It says we signed for an offog. Therefore we must have one. It's got to be found before Cassidy gets here."

"Sorry, sir," sympathized Burman. "I can't help you."

"You can think again," advised McNaught. "Up in the bow there's a direction and distance indicator. What do *you* call it?"

"A didin," said Burman, mystified.

"And," McNaught went on, pointing at the pulse transmitter, "what do you call *that?*"

"The opper-popper."

"Baby names, see? Didin and opper-popper. Now rack your brains and remember what you called an offog four years ago."

"Nothing," asserted Burman, "has ever been called an offog to my knowledge."

"Then," demanded McNaught ,"why did we sign for one?"

"I didn't sign for anything. You did all the signing."

"While you and others did the checking. Four years ago, presumably in the galley, I said, 'Offog, one,' and either you or Blanchard pointed to it and said, 'Check.' I took somebody's word for it. I have to take other specialists' words for it. I am an expert navigator, familiar with all the latest navigational gadgets but not with other stuff. So I'm compelled to rely on people who know what an offog is—or ought to."

Burman had a bright thought. "All kinds of oddments were dumped in the main lock, the corridors and the galley when we were fitted-out. We had to sort through a deal of stuff and stash it where it properly belonged, remember? This offog-thing might be any place today. It isn't necessarily my responsibility or Blanchard's."

"I'll see what the other officers say," agreed McNaught, conceding the point. "Gregory, Worth, Sanderson or one of the others may be coddling the item. Wherever it is, it's got to be found. Or accounted for in full if it's been expended."

He went out. Burman pulled a face, inserted his earplugs, resumed fiddling with his apparatus. An hour later McNaught came back wearing a scowl.

"Positively," he announced with ire, "there is no such thing on the ship. Nobody knows of it. Nobody can so much as guess at it."

"Cross it off and report it lost," Burman suggested.

"What, when we're hard aground? You know as well as I do that loss and damage must be signaled at time of occurrence. If I tell Cassidy the offog went west in space, he'll want to know when, where, how and why it wasn't signaled. There'll be a real ruckus if the contraption happens to be valued at half a million credits. I can't dismiss it with an airy wave of the hand."

"What's the answer then?" inquired Burman, innocently ambling straight into the trap.

"There's one and only one," McNaught announced. "*You* will manufacture an offog."

"Who? Me?" said Burman, twitching his scalp.

"You and no other. I'm fairly sure the thing is your pigeon, anyway."

"Why?"

"Because it's typical of the baby names used for your kind of stuff. I'll bet a month's pay that an offog is some sort of scientific allamagoosa. Something to do with fog, perhaps. Maybe a blind-approach gadget."

"The blind-approach transceiver is called 'the fumbly,'" Burman informed.

"There you are!" said McNaught as if that clinched it. "So you will make an offog. It will be completed by six tomorrow evening and ready for my inspection then. It had better be convincing, in fact pleasing. In fact its function will be convincing."

Burman stood up, let his hands dangle, and said in hoarse tones, "How can I make an offog when I don't even know what it is?"

"Neither does Cassidy know," McNaught pointed out, leering at him. "He's more of a quantity surveyor than anything else. As such he counts things, looks at things, certifies that they exist, accepts advice on whether they are functionally satisfactory or worn out. All we need do is concoct an imposing allamagoosa and tell him it's the offog."

"Holy Moses!" said Burman, fervently.

"Let us not rely on the dubious assistance of Biblical characters," McNaught reproved. "Let us use the brains that God has given us. Get a grip on your soldering-iron and make a topnotch offog by six tomorrow evening. That's an order!"

He departed, satisfied with this solution. Behind him, Burman gloomed at the wall and licked his lips once, twice.

Rear Admiral Vane W. Cassidy arrived right on time. He was a short, paunchy character with a florid complexion and eyes like those of a long-dead fish. His gait was an important strut.

"Ah, captain, I trust that you have everything shipshape."

"Everything usually is," assured McNaught, glibly. "I see to that." He spoke with conviction.

"Good!" approved Cassidy. "I like a commander who takes his responsibilities seriously. Much as I regret saying so, there are a few who do not." He marched through the main lock, his cod-eyes taking note of the fresh white enamel. "Where do you prefer to start, bow or tail?"

"My equipment-sheets run from bow backward. We may as well deal with them the way they're set."

"Very well." He trotted officiously toward the nose, paused on the way to pat Peaslake and examine his collar. "Well cared-for, I see. Has the animal proved useful?"

"He saved five lives on Mardia by barking a warning."

"The details have been entered in your log, I suppose?"

"Yes, sir. The log is in the chart room awaiting your inspection."

"We'll get to it in due time." Reaching the bow-cabin, Cassidy took a seat, accepted the folder from McNaught, started off at businesslike pace. "K1. Beam compass, type D, one of."

"This is it, sir," said McNaught, showing him.

"Still working properly?"

"Yes, sir."

They carried on, reached the intercom-cubby, the computer room, a succession of other places back to the galley. Here, Blanchard posed in freshly laundered white clothes and eyed the newcomer warily.

"V147. Electronic oven, one of."

"Is zis," said Blanchard, pointing with disdain.

"Satisfactory?" inquired Cassidy, giving him the fishy-eye.

"Not beeg enough," declared Blanchard. He encompassed the entire galley with an expressive gesture. "Nossings beeg enough. Place too small. Eversings too small. I am chef de cuisine an' she is a cuisine like an attic."

"This is a warship, not a luxury liner," Cassidy snapped. He frowned at the equipment-sheet. "V148. Timing device, electronic oven, attachment thereto, one of."

"Is zis," spat Blanchard, ready to sling it through the nearest port if Cassidy would first donate the two pins.

Working his way down the sheet, Cassidy got nearer and nearer while nervous tension built up. Then he reached the critical point and said, "V1098. Offog, one."

"*Morbleu!*" said Blanchard, shooting sparks from his eyes, "I have say before an' I say again, zere never was—"

"The offog is in the radio room, sir," McNaught chipped in hurriedly.

"Indeed?" Cassidy took another look at the sheet. "Then why is it recorded along with galley equipment?"

"It was placed in the galley at time of fitting-out, sir. It's one of those portable instruments left to us to fix up where most suitable."

"Hm-m-m! Then it should have been transferred to the radio room list. Why didn't you transfer it?"

"I thought it better to wait for your authority to do so, sir."

The fish-eyes registered gratification. "Yes, that is quite proper of you, captain. I will transfer it now." He crossed the item from sheet nine, initialed it, entered it on sheet sixteen, initialed that. "V1099. Inscribed collar, leather . . . oh, yes, I've seen that. The dog was wearing it."

He ticked it. An hour later he strutted into the radio room. Burman stood up, squared his shoulders but could not keep his feet or hands from fidgeting. His eyes protruded slightly and kept straying toward McNaught in silent appeal. He was like a man wearing a porcupine in his britches.

"V1098. Offog, one," said Cassidy in his usual tone of brooking no nonsense.

Moving with the jerkiness of a slightly uncoördinated robot, Burman pawed a small box fronted with dials, switches and colored lights. It looked like a radio ham's idea of a fruit machine. He knocked down a couple of switches. The lights came on, played around in intriguing combinations.

"This is it, sir," he informed with difficulty.

"Ah!" Cassidy left his chair and moved across for a closer look. "I don't recall having seen this item before. But there are so many different models of the same things. Is it still operating efficiently?"

"Yes, sir."

"It's one of the most useful things in the ship," contributed McNaught, for good measure.

"What does it *do?*" inquired Cassidy, inviting Burman to cast a pearl of wisdom before him.

Burman paled.

Hastily, McNaught said, "A full explanation would be rather involved and technical but, to put it as simply as possible, it enables us to strike a balance between opposing gravitational fields. Variations in lights indicate the extent and degree of unbalance at any given time."

"It's a clever idea," added Burman, made suddenly reckless by this news, "based upon Finagle's Constant."

"I see," said Cassidy, not seeing at all. He resumed his seat, ticked the offog and carried on. "Z44. Switchboard, automatic, forty-line intercom, one of."

"Here it is, sir."

Cassidy glanced at it, returned his gaze to the sheet. The others used his momentary distraction to mop perspiration from their foreheads.

Victory had been gained.

All was well.

For the third time, hah!

Rear Admiral Vane W. Cassidy departed pleased and complimentary. Within one hour the crew bolted to town. McNaught took turns with Gregory at enjoying the gay lights. For the next five days all was peace and pleasure.

On the sixth day Burman brought in a signal, dumped it upon McNaught's desk and waited for the reaction. He had an air of gratification, the pleasure of one whose virtue is about to be rewarded.

*Terran Headquarters to* Bustler. *Return here immediately for overhaul and refitting. Improved power plant to be installed. Feldman. Navy Op. Command. Sirisec.*

"Back to Terra," commented McNaught, happily. "And an overhaul will mean at least one month's leave." He eyed Burman. "Tell all officers on duty to go to town at once and order the crew aboard. The men will come running when they know why."

"Yes, sir," said Burman, grinning.

Everyone was still grinning two weeks later when the Siriport had receded far behind and Sol had grown to a vague speck in the sparkling mist of the bow starfield. Eleven weeks still to go, but it was worth it. Back to Terra. Hurrah!

In the captain's cabin the grins abruptly vanished one evening when Burman suddenly developed the willies. He marched in, chewed his bottom lip while waiting for McNaught to finish writing in the log.

Finally, McNaught pushed the book away, glanced up, frowned. "What's the matter with you? Got a bellyache or something?"

"No, sir. I've been thinking."

"Does it hurt that much?"

"I've been thinking," persisted Burman in funereal tones. "We're going back for overhaul. You know what that means? We'll walk off the ship and a horde of experts will walk onto it." He stared tragically at the other. "Experts, I said."

"Naturally they'll be experts," McNaught agreed. "Equipment cannot be tested and brought up to scratch by a bunch of dopes."

"It will require more than a mere expert to bring the offog up to scratch," Burman pointed out. "It'll need a genius."

McNaught rocked back, swapped expressions like changing masks. "Jumping Judas! I'd forgotten all about that thing. When we get to Terra we won't blind *those* boys with science."

"No, sir, we won't," endorsed Burman. He did not add "any more" but his face shouted aloud, "You got me into this. You get me out of it." He waited a time while McNaught did some intense thinking, then prompted, "What do you suggest, sir?"

Slowly the satisfied smile returned to McNaught's features as he answered, "Break up the contraption and feed it into the disintegrator."

"That doesn't solve the problem," said Burman. "We'll still be short an offog."

"No we won't. Because I'm going to signal its loss owing to the hazards of space-service." He closed one eye in an emphatic wink. "We're in free flight right now." He reached for a message-pad and scribbled on it while Burman stood by vastly relieved.

*Bustler to Terran Headquarters. Item V1098, Offog one, came apart under gravitational stress while passing through twin-sun field Hector Major-Minor. Material used as fuel. McNaught, Commander. Bustler.*

Burman took it to the radio room and beamed it Earthward. All was peace and progress for another two days. The next time he went to the captain's cabin he went running and worried.

"General call, sir," he announced breathlessly and thrust the message into the other's hands.

*Terran Headquarters for relay all sectors. Urgent and Important. All ships grounded forthwith. Vessels in flight under official orders will make for nearest spaceport pending further instructions. Welling. Alarm and Rescue Command. Terra.*

"Something's gone bust," commented McNaught, undisturbed. He traipsed to the chart room, Burman following. Consulting the charts, he dialed the intercom phone, got Pike in the bow and ordered, "There's a panic. All ships grounded. We've got to make for Zaxtedport, about three days' run away. Change course at once. Starboard seventeen degrees, declination ten." Then he cut off, griped, "Bang goes that sweet month on Terra. I never did like Zaxted, either. It stinks. The crew will feel murderous about this and I don't blame them."

"What d'you think has happened, sir?" asked Burman. He looked both uneasy and annoyed.

"Heaven alone knows. The last general call was seven years ago when the *Starider* exploded halfway along the Mars run. They grounded every ship in existence while they investigated the cause." He rubbed his chin, pondered, went on, "And the call before that one was when the entire crew of the *Blowgun* went nuts. Whatever it is this time, you can bet it's serious."

"It wouldn't be the start of a space war?"

"Against whom?" McNaught made a gesture of contempt. "Nobody has the ships with which to oppose us. No, it's something technical. We'll learn of it eventually. They'll tell us before we reach Zaxted or soon afterward."

They did tell him. Within six hours. Burman rushed in with face full of horror.

"What's eating you now?" demanded McNaught, staring at him.

"The offog," stuttered Burman. He made motions as though brushing off invisible spiders.

"What of it?"

"It's a typographical error. In your copy it should read off. dog."

The commander stared owlishly.

"Off. dog?" echoed McNaught, making it sound like foul language.

"See for yourself." Dumping the signal on the desk, Burman bolted out, left the door swinging. McNaught scowled after him, picked up the message.

*Terran Headquarters to Bustler. Your report V1098, ship's official dog Peaslake. Detail fully circumstances and manner in which animal came apart under gravitational stress. Cross-examine crew and signal all coincidental symptoms experienced by them. Urgent and Important. Welling. Alarm and Rescue Command. Terra.*

In the privacy of his cabin McNaught commenced to eat his nails. Every now and again he went a little cross-eyed as he examined them for nearness to the flesh.

*1956*
*14th CONVENTION*
*NEW YORK*

## Murray Leinster

Murray Leinster is the acknowledged dean of science fiction. He is a *real* old-timer. I look up to him with the respect and reverence due one of such ancient and patriarchal grandeur. After all, in the 1930s, when all the world was green and new, Murray Leinster wrote some of the stories that set my young and eager heart to pounding wildly. Little did I imagine then that the day would come I would meet, and even touch, so god-like a man.

I must admit, though, that it is deucedly irritating to be part of a field with so uncharacteristic a dean, however god-like.

After all, you know what a dean is *supposed* to be like. He should be a benign greybeard who makes an impressive appearance and who knows how to smile benevolently at awed looks and humble greetings. Above all, he does not sully the sanctity of his position by competing with younger men.

Certainly, Leinster should be just such a dean. He had a story, "The Runaway Skyscraper," in the June 1926 issue of *Amazing Stories,* which was only the third issue of the oldest science fiction magazine. Surely he should be entitled to take his ease now.

Isn't it hard then, that Leinster, quick and spry as any young squirt, has continued to write copiously to this very day, and manages to do it so well that at the 14th Convention (New York, 1956) he carried off a Hugo for "Exploration Team."

I pointed out the inappropriateness of his behavior, and, more in sorrow than in anger, explained that as dean he had his dignity to think of. I urged him to return the Hugo and offered to keep it for him.

It pains me to report that he merely laughed at this and skipped gaily off, holding his Hugo so that anyone might see it—completely lost to shame.

# 3

# EXPLORATION TEAM

I

The nearer moon went by overhead. It was jagged and irregular in shape, and was probably a captured asteroid. Huyghens had seen it often enough, so he did not go out of his quarters to watch it hurtle across the sky with seemingly the speed of an atmosphere-flier, occulting the stars as it went. Instead, he sweated over paper work, which should have been odd because he was technically a felon and all his labors on Loren Two felonious. It was odd, too, for a man to do paper work in a room with steel shutters and a huge bald eagle—untethered —dozing on a three-inch perch set in the wall. But paper work was not Huyghens' real task. His only assistant had tangled with a nightwalker and the furtive Kodius Company ships had taken him away to where Kodius Company ships came from. Huyghens had to do two men's work in loneliness. To his knowledge, he was the only man in this solar system.

Below him, there were snufflings. Sitka Pete got up heavily and padded to his water pan. He lapped the refrigerated water and sneezed violently. Sourdough Charley waked and complained in a rumbling growl. There were divers other rumblings and mutterings below. Huyghens called reassuringly, "Easy there!" and went on with his work. He finished a climate report, and fed figures to a computer, and while it hummed over them he entered the inventory totals in the station log, showing what supplies remained. Then he began to write up the log proper.

"Sitka Pete," he wrote, "has apparently solved the problem of killing individual sphexes. He has learned that it doesn't do to hug them and that his claws can't penetrate their hide—not the top hide, anyhow. To-day Semper notified us that a pack of sphexes had found the scent-trail *to the station. Sitka hid downwind until they arrived. Then he charged from the rear and brought his paws together on both sides of a sphex's head in a terrific pair of slaps. It must have been like two twelve-inch shells arriving from opposite directions at the same time. It must have scrambled the sphex's brains as if they were eggs. It dropped dead. He killed two more with such mighty pairs of wallops. Sourdough Charley watched, grunting, and when the sphexes turned on Sitka, he charged in his turn. I, of course, couldn't shoot too close to him, so he might have fared badly but that Faro Nell came pouring out of the bear quarters to help. The diversion enabled Sitka Pete to resume the use of his new technic, towering on his hind legs and swinging his paws in the new and grisly fashion. The fight ended promptly. Semper flew and screamed above the scrap, but as usual did not join in. Note: Nugget, the cub, tried to mix in but his mother cuffed him out of the way. Sourdough and Sitka ignored him as usual. Kodius Champion's genes are sound!"*

The noises of the night went on outside. There were notes like organ tones—song lizards. There were the tittering giggling cries of night-walkers—not to be tittered back at. There were sounds like tack hammers, and doors closing, and from every direction came noises like hiccups in various keys. These were made by the improbable small creatures which on Loren Two took the place of insects.

Huyghens wrote out:

*"Sitka seemed ruffled when the fight was over. He painstakingly used his trick on every dead or wounded sphex, except those he'd killed with it, lifting up their heads for his pile-driver-like blows from two directions at once, as if to show Sourdough how it was done. There was much grunting as they hauled the carcasses to the incinerator. It almost seemed—"*

The arrival bell clanged, and Huyghens jerked up his head to stare at it. Semper, the eagle, opened icy eyes. He blinked.

Noises. There was a long, deep, contented snore from below. Something shrieked, out in the jungle. Hiccups. Clatterings, and organ notes—

The bell clanged again. It was a notice that a ship aloft somewhere had picked up the beacon beam—which only Kodius Company ships should know about—and was communicating for a landing. But there shouldn't be any ships in this solar system just now! This was the only habitable planet of the sun, and it had been officially declared uninhabitable by reason of inimical animal life. Which meant sphexes. Therefore no colony was permitted, and the Kodius Company broke the law. And there were few graver crimes than unauthorized occupation of a new planet.

The bell clanged a third time. Huyghens swore. His hand went out to cut off the beacon—but that would be useless. Radar would have fixed it and tied it in with physical features like the nearby sea and the Sere Plateau. The ship could find the place, anyhow, and descend by daylight.

"The devil!" said Huyghens. But he waited yet again for the bell to ring. A Kodius Company ship would double-ring to reassure him. But there shouldn't be a Kodius Company ship for months.

The bell clanged singly. The space phone dial flickered and a voice came out of it, tinny from stratospheric distortion:

*"Calling ground! Calling ground! Crete Line ship Odysseus calling ground on Loren Two. Landing one passenger by boat. Put on your field lights."*

Huyghens' mouth dropped open. A Kodius Company ship would be welcome. A Colonial Survey ship would be extremely unwelcome, because it would destroy the colony and Sitka and Sourdough and Faro Nell and Nugget—and Semper—and carry Huyghens off to be tried for unauthorized colonization and all that it implied.

But a commercial ship, landing one passenger by boat— There was simply no circumstances under which that would happen. Not to an unknown, illegal colony. Not to a furtive station!

Huyghens flicked on the landing-field lights. He saw the glare in the field outside. Then he stood up and prepared to take the measures required by discovery. He packed the paper work he'd been doing into the disposal safe. He gathered up all personal documents and tossed them in. Every record, every bit of evidence that the Kodius Company maintained this station went into the safe. He slammed the door. He touched his finger to the disposal button, which would destroy the contents and melt down even the ashes past their possible use for evidence in court.

Then he hesitated. If it were a Survey ship, the button had to be pressed and he must resign himself to a long term in prison. But a Crete Line ship—if the space phone told the truth—was not threatening. It was simply unbelievable.

He shook his head. He got into travel garb and armed himself. He went down into the bear quarters, turning on lights as he went. There were startled snufflings and Sitka Pete reared himself very absurdly to a sitting position to blink at him. Sourdough Charley lay on his back with his legs in the air. He'd found it cooler, sleeping that way. He rolled over with a thump. He made snorting sounds which somehow

sounded cordial. Faro Nell padded to the door of her separate apartment—assigned her so that Nugget would not be underfoot to irritate
the big males.

Huyghens, as the human population of Loren Two, faced the work
force, fighting force, and—with Nugget—four-fifths of the terrestrial
nonhuman population of the planet. They were mutated Kodiak bears,
descendants of the Kodius Champion for whom the Kodius Company
was named. Sitka Pete was a good twenty-two hundred pounds of lumbering, intelligent carnivore. Sourdough Charley would weigh within
a hundred pounds of that figure. Faro Nell was eighteen hundred
pounds of female charm—and ferocity. Then Nugget poked his muz-
zle around his mother's furry rump to see what was toward, and he was
six hundred pounds of ursine infancy. The animals looked at Huyghens expectantly. If he'd had Semper riding on his shoulder, they'd
have known what was expected of them.

"Let's go," said Huyghens. "It's dark outside, but somebody's coming.
And it may be bad!"

He unfastened the outer door of the bear quarters. Sitka Pete went
charging clumsily through it. A forthright charge was the best way to
develop any situation—if one was an oversized male Kodiak bear. Sourdough went lumbering after him. There was nothing hostile immediately outside. Sitka stood up on his hind legs—he reared up a solid
twelve feet—and sniffed the air. Sourdough methodically lumbered to
one side and then the other, sniffing in his turn. Nell came out, nine-
tenths of a ton of daintiness, and rumbled admonitorily at Nugget, who
trailed her closely. Huyghens stood in the doorway, his night-sighted
gun ready. He felt uncomfortable at sending the bears ahead into a
Loren Two jungle at night. But they were qualified to scent danger,
and he was not.

The illumination of the jungle in a wide path toward the landing
field made for weirdness in the look of things. There were arching
giant ferns and columnar trees which grew above them, and the extraordinary lanceolate underbrush of the jungle. The flood lamps, set
level with the ground, lighted everything from below. The foliage,
then, was brightly lit against the black night-sky—brightly lit enough to
dim-out the stars. There were astonishing contrasts of light and shadow
everywhere.

"On ahead!" commanded Huyghens, waving. "Hup!"

He swung the bear-quarters door shut. He moved toward the landing field through the lane of lighted forest. The two giant male Kodiaks
lumbered ahead. Sitka Pete dropped to all fours and prowled. Sour-

dough Charley followed closely, swinging from side to side. Huyghens came alertly behind the two of them, and Faro Nell brought up the rear with Nugget following her closely.

It was an excellent military formation for progress through dangerous jungle. Sourdough and Sitka were advance-guard and point, respectively, while Faro Nell guarded the rear. With Nugget to look after, she was especially alert against attack from behind. Huyghens was, of course, the striking force. His gun fired explosive bullets which would discourage even sphexes, and his night-sight—a cone of light which went on when he took up the trigger-slack—told exactly where they would strike. It was not a sportsmanlike weapon, but the creatures of Loren Two were not sportsmanlike antagonists. The night-walkers, for example— But night-walkers feared light. They attacked only in a species of hysteria if it were too bright.

Huyghens moved toward the glare at the landing field. His mental state was savage. The Kodius Company station on Loren Two was completely illegal. It happened to be necessary, from one point of view, but it was still illegal. The tinny voice on the space phone was not convincing, in ignoring that illegality. But if a ship landed, Huyghens could get back to the station before men could follow, and he'd have the disposal safe turned on in time to protect those who'd sent him here.

But he heard the faraway and high harsh roar of a landing-boat rocket—not a ship's bellowing tubes—as he made his way through the unreal-seeming brush. The roar grew louder as he pushed on, the three big Kodiaks padding here and there, sniffing thoughtfully, making a perfect defensive-offensive formation for the particular conditions of this planet.

He reached the edge of the landing field, and it was blindingly bright, with the customary divergent beams slanting skyward so a ship could check its instrument landing by sight. Landing fields like this had been standard, once upon a time. Nowadays all developed planets had landing grids—monstrous structures which drew upon ionospheres for power and lifted and drew down star ships with remarkable gentleness and unlimited force. This sort of landing field would be found where a survey-team was at work, or where some strictly temporary investigation of ecology or bacteriology was under way, or where a newly authorized colony had not yet been able to build its landing grid. Of course it was unthinkable that anybody would attempt a settlement in defiance of the law!

Already, as Huyghens reached the edge of the scorched open space, the night-creatures had rushed to the light like moths on Earth. The air was misty with crazily gyrating, tiny flying things. They were innumerable and of every possible form and size, from the white midges of the night and multi-winged flying worms to those revoltingly naked-looking larger creatures which might have passed for plucked flying monkeys if they had not been carnivorous and worse. The flying things soared and whirred and danced and spun insanely in the glare. They made peculiarly plaintive humming noises. They almost formed a lamp-lit ceiling over the cleared space. They did hide the stars. Staring upward, Huyghens could just barely make out the blue-white flame of the space-boat's rocket through the fog of wings and bodies.

The rocket-flame grew steadily in size. Once, apparently, it tilted to adjust the boat's descending course. It went back to normal. A speck of incandescence at first, it grew until it was like a great star, and then a more-than-brilliant moon, and then it was a pitiless glaring eye. Huyghens averted his gaze from it. Sitka Pete sat lumpily—more than a ton of him—and blinked wisely at the dark jungle away from the light. Sourdough ignored the deepening, increasing rocket roar. He sniffed the air delicately. Faro Nell held Nugget firmly under one huge paw and licked his head as if tidying him up to be seen by company. Nugget wriggled.

The roar became that of ten thousand thunders. A warm breeze below outward from the landing-field. The rocket boat hurled downward, and its flame touched the mist of flying things, and they shriveled and burned and were hot. Then there were churning clouds of dust everywhere, and the center of the field blazed terribly—and something slid down a shaft of fire, and squeezed it flat, and sat on it—and the flame went out. The rocket boat sat there, resting on its tail fins, pointing toward the stars from which it came.

There was a terrible silence after the tumult. Then, very faintly, the noises of the night came again. There were sounds like those of organ pipes, and very faint and apologetic noises like hiccups. All these sounds increased, and suddenly Huyghens could hear quite normally. Then a side-port opened with a quaint sort of clattering, and something unfolded from where it had been inset into the hull of the space boat, and there was a metal passageway across the flame-heated space on which the boat stood.

A man came out of the port. He reached back in and shook hands very formally. He climbed down the ladder rungs to the walkway. He marched above the steaming baked area, carrying a traveling bag. He reached the end of the walk and stepped gingerly to the ground. He moved hastily to the edge of the clearing. He waved to the space boat. There were ports. Perhaps someone returned the gesture. The walkway folded briskly back up to the hull and vanished in it. A flame exploded into being under the tail fins. There were fresh clouds of monstrous, choking dust and a brightness like that of a sun. There was noise past the possibility of endurance. Then the light rose swiftly through the dust cloud, and sprang higher and climbed more swiftly still. When Huyghens' ears again permitted him to hear anything, there was only a diminishing mutter in the heavens and a small bright speck of light ascending to the sky and swinging eastward as it rose to intercept the ship which had let it descend.

The night noises of the jungle went on. Life on Loren Two did not need to heed the doings of men. But there was a spot of incandescence in the day-bright clearing, and a short, brisk man looked puzzledly about him with a traveling bag in his hand.

Huyghens advanced toward him as the incandescence dimmed. Sourdough and Sitka preceded him. Faro Nell trailed faithfully, keeping a maternal eye on her offspring. The man in the clearing stared at the parade they made. It would be upsetting, even after preparation, to land at night on a strange planet, and to have the ship's boat and all links with the rest of the cosmos depart, and then to find one's self approached—it might seem stalked—by two colossal male Kodiak bears, with a third bear and a cub behind them. A single human figure in such company might seem irrelevant.

The new arrival gazed blankly. He moved, startled. Then Huyghens called:

"Hello, there! Don't worry about the bears! They're friends!"

Sitka reached the newcomer. He went warily downwind from him and sniffed. The smell was satisfactory. Man-smell. Sitka sat down with the solid impact of more than a ton of bear-meat landing on packed dirt. He regarded the man amiably. Sourdough said *"Whoosh!"* and went on to sample the air beyond the clearing. Huyghens approached. The newcomer wore the uniform of the Colonial Survey. That was bad. It bore the insignia of a senior officer. Worse.

"Hah!" said the just-landed man. "Where are the robots? What in all the nineteen hells are these creatures? Why did you shift your station? I'm Roane, here to make a progress report on your colony."

Huyghens said:

"What colony?"

"Loren Two Robot Installation—" Then Roane said indignantly, "Don't tell me that that idiot skipper dropped me at the wrong place! This is Loren Two, isn't it? And this is the landing field. But where are your robots? You should have the beginning of a grid up! What the devil's happened here and what are these beasts?"

Huyghens grimaced.

"This," he said politely, "is an illegal, unlicensed settlement. I'm a criminal. These beasts are my confederates. If you don't want to associate with criminals you needn't, of course, but I doubt if you'll live till morning unless you accept my hospitality while I think over what to do about your landing. In reason, I ought to shoot you."

Faro Nell came to a halt behind Huyghens, which was her proper post in all out-door movement. Nugget, however, saw a new human. Nugget was a cub, and, therefore, friendly. He ambled forward ingratiatingly. He was four feet high at the shoulders, on all fours. He wriggled bashfully as he approached Roane. He sneezed, because he was embarrassed.

His mother overtook him swiftly and cuffed him to one side. He wailed. The wail of a six-hundred-pound Kodiak bear-cub is a remarkable sound. Roane gave ground a pace.

"I think," he said carefully, "that we'd better talk things over. But if this is an illegal colony, of course you're under arrest and anything you say will be used against you."

Huyghens grimaced again.

"Right," he said. "But now if you'll walk close to me, we'll head back to the station. I'd have Sourdough carry your bag—he likes to carry things—but he may need his teeth. We've half a mile to travel." He turned to the animals. "Let's go!" he said commandingly. "Back to the station! Hup!"

Grunting, Sitka Pete arose and took up his duties as advanced point of a combat team. Sourdough trailed, swinging widely to one side and another. Huyghens and Roane moved together. Faro Nell and Nugget brought up the rear. Which, of course, was the only relatively safe way for anybody to travel on Loren Two, in the jungle, a good half mile from one's fortresslike residence.

But there was only one incident on the way back. It was a night-walker, made hysterical by the lane of light. It poured through the underbrush, uttering cries like maniacal laughter.

Sourdough brought it down, a good ten yards from Huyghens. When it was all over, Nugget bristled up to the dead creature, uttering cub-growls. He feigned to attack it.

His mother whacked him soundly.

## II

There were comfortable, settling-down noises below. The bears grunted and rumbled, but ultimately were still. The glare from the landing field was gone. The lighted lane through the jungle was dark again. Huyghens ushered the man from the space boat up into his living quarters. There was a rustling stir, and Semper took his head from under his wing. He stared coldly at the two humans. He spread monstrous, seven-foot wings and fluttered them. He opened his beak and closed it with a snap.

"That's Semper," said Huyghens. "Semper Tyrannis. He's the rest of the terrestrial population here. Not being a fly-by-night sort of creature, he didn't come out to welcome you."

Roane blinked at the huge bird, perched on a three-inch-thick perch set in the wall.

"An eagle?" he demanded. "Kodiak bears—mutated ones you say, but still bears—and now an eagle? You've a very nice fighting unit in the bears."

"They're pack animals, too," said Huyghens. "They can carry some hundreds of pounds without losing too much combat efficiency. And there's no problem of supply. They live off the jungle. Not sphexes, though. Nothing will eat a sphex, even if it can kill one."

He brought out glasses and a bottle. He indicated a chair. Roane put down his traveling bag. He took a glass.

"I'm curious," he observed. "Why Semper Tyrannis? I can understand Sitka Pete and Sourdough Charley as names. The home of their ancestors makes them fitting. But why Semper?"

"He was bred for hawking," said Huyghens. "You sic a dog on something. You sic Semper Tyrannis. He's too big to ride on a hawking glove, so the shoulders of my coats are padded to let him ride there. He's a flying scout. I've trained him to notify us of sphexes, and in flight he carries a tiny television camera. He's useful, but he hasn't the brains of the bears."

Roane sat down and sipped at his glass.

"Interesting . . . very interesting! But this is an illegal settlement. I'm a Colonial Survey officer. My job is reporting on progress according to plan, but nevertheless I have to arrest you. Didn't you say something about shooting me?"

Huyghens said doggedly:

"I'm trying to think of a way out. Add up all the penalties for ille-

gal colonization and I'd be in a very bad fix if you got away and reported this set-up. Shooting you would be logical."

"I see that," said Roane reasonably. "But since the point has come
up—I have a blaster trained on you from my pocket."

Huyghens shrugged.

"It's rather likely that my human confederates will be back here before your friends. You'd be in a very tight fix if my friends came back
and found you more or less sitting on my corpse."

Roane nodded.

"That's true, too. Also it's probable that your fellow terrestrials
wouldn't co-operate with me as they have with you. You seem to have
the whip hand, even with my blaster trained on you. On the other
hand, you could have killed me quite easily after the boat left, when
I'd first landed. I'd have been quite unsuspicious. So you may not really
intend to murder me."

Huyghens shrugged again.

"So," said Roane, "since the secret of getting along with people is
that of postponing quarrels—suppose we postpone the question of who
kills whom? Frankly, I'm going to send you to prison if I can. Unlawful
colonization is very bad business. But I suppose you feel that you have
to do something permanent about me. In your place I probably should,
too. Shall we declare a truce?"

Huyghens indicated indifference. Roane said vexedly:

"Then I do! I have to! So—"

He pulled his hand out of his pocket and put a pocket blaster on the
table. He leaned back, defiantly.

"Keep it," said Huyghens. "Loren Two isn't a place where you live
long unarmed." He turned to a cupboard. "Hungry?"

"I could eat," admitted Roane.

Huyghens pulled out two mealpacks from the cupboard and inserted
them in the readier below. He set out plates.

"Now—what happened to the official, licensed, authorized colony
here?" asked Roane briskly. "License issued eighteen months ago.
There was a landing of colonists with a drone fleet of equipment and
supplies. There've been four ship-contacts since. There should be
several thousand robots being industrious under adequate human
supervision. There should be a hundred-mile-square clearing, planted
with food plants for later human arrivals. There should be a landing
grid at least half-finished. Obviously there should be a space beacon
to guide ships to a landing. There isn't. There's no clearing visible from
space. That Crete Line ship has been in orbit for three days, trying

to find a place to drop me. Her skipper was fuming. Your beacon is
the only one on the planet, and we found it by accident. What
happened?"

Huyghens served the food. He said dryly:

"There could be a hundred colonies on this planet without any one
knowing of any other. I can only guess about your robots, but I suspect
they ran into sphexes."

Roane paused, with his fork in his hand.

"I read up on this planet, since I was to report on its colony. A sphex
is part of the inimical animal life here. Cold-blooded belligerent carnivore, not a lizard but a genus all its own. Hunts in packs. Seven to
eight hundred pounds, when adult. Lethally dangerous and simply too
numerous to fight. They're why no license was ever granted to human
colonists. Only robots could work here, because they're machines.
What animal attacks machines?"

Huyghens said:

"What machine attacks animals? The sphexes wouldn't bother robots, of course, but would robots bother the sphexes?"

Roane chewed and swallowed.

"Hold it! I'll agree that you can't make a hunting-robot. A machine
can discriminate, but it can't decide. That's why there's no danger of
a robot revolt. They can't decide to do something for which they have
no instructions. But this colony was planned with full knowledge of
what robots can and can't do. As ground was cleared, it was enclosed
in an electric fence which no sphex could touch without frying."

Huyghens thoughtfully cut his food. After a moment:

"The landing was in the wintertime," he observed. "It must have
been, because the colony survived a while. And at a guess, the last
ship-landing was before thaw. The years are eighteen months long
here, you know."

Roane admitted:

"It was in winter that the landing was made. And the last ship-
landing was before spring. The idea was to get mines in operation for
material, and to have ground cleared and enclosed in sphex-proof
fence before the sphexes came back from the tropics. They winter there,
I understand."

"Did you ever see a sphex?" Huyghens asked. Then added, "No, of
course not. But if you took a spitting cobra and crossed it with a wildcat, painted it tan-and-blue and then gave it hydrophobia and homicidal mania at once—why you might have one sphex. But not the race
of sphexes. They can climb trees, by the way. A fence wouldn't stop
them."

"An electrified fence," said Roane. "Nothing could climb that!"

"No one animal," Huyghens told him. "But sphexes are a race. The smell of one dead sphex brings others running with blood in their eyes. Leave a dead sphex alone for six hours and you've got them around by the dozen. Two days and there are hundreds. Longer, and you've got thousands of them! They gather to caterwaul over their dead pal and hunt for whoever or whatever killed him."

He returned to his meal. A moment later he said:

"No need to wonder what happened to your colony. During the winter the robots burned out a clearing and put up an electrified fence according to the book. Come spring, the sphexes came back. They're curious, among their other madnesses. A sphex would try to climb the fence just to see what was behind it. He'd be electrocuted. His carcass would bring others, raging because a sphex was dead. Some of them would try to climb the fence—and die. And their corpses would bring others. Presently the fence would break down from the bodies hanging on it, or a bridge of dead beasts' carcasses would be built across it—and from as far downwind as the scent carried there'd be loping, raging, scent-crazed sphexes racing to the spot. They'd pour into the clearing through or over the fence, squalling and screeching for something to kill. I think they'd find it."

Roane ceased to eat. He looked sick.

"There were . . . pictures of sphexes in the data I read. I suppose that would account for . . . everything."

He tried to lift his fork. He put it down again.

"I can't eat," he said abruptly.

Huyghens made no comment. He finished his own meal, scowling. He rose and put the plates into the top of the cleaner. There was a whirring. He took them out of the bottom and put them away.

"Let me see those reports, eh?" he asked dourly. "I'd like to see what sort of a set-up they had—those robots."

Roane hesitated and then opened his traveling bag. There was a microviewer and reels of films. One entire reel was labeled "Specifications for Construction, Colonial Survey," which would contain detailed plans and all requirements of material and workmanship for everything from desks, office, administrative personnel, for use of, to landing grids, heavy-gravity planets, lift-capacity one hundred thousand Earth-tons. But Huyghens found another. He inserted it and spun the control swiftly here and there, pausing only briefly at index frames until he came to the section he wanted. He began to study the information with growing impatience.

"Robots, robots, robots!" he snapped. "Why don't they leave them where they belong—in cities to do the dirty work, and on airless planets where nothing unexpected ever happens! Robots don't belong in new colonies! Your colonists depended on them for defense! Dammit, let a man work with robots long enough and he thinks all nature is as limited as they are! This is a plan to set up a controlled environment! On Loren Two! Controlled environment—" He swore, luridly. "Complacent, idiotic, desk-bound half-wits!"

"Robots are all right," said Roane. "We couldn't run civilization without them."

"But you can't tame a wilderness with 'em!" snapped Huyghens. "You had a dozen men landed, with fifty assembled robots to start with. There were parts for fifteen hundred more—and I'll bet anything I've got that the ship-contacts landed more still."

"They did," admitted Roane.

"I despise 'em," growled Huyghens. "I feel about 'em the way the old Greeks and Romans felt about slaves. They're for menial work—the sort of work a man will perform for himself, but that he won't do for another man for pay. Degrading work!"

"Quite aristocratic!" said Roane with a touch of irony. "I take it that robots clean out the bear quarters downstairs."

"No!" snapped Huyghens. "I do! They're my friends! They fight for me! They can't understand the necessity and no robot would do the job right!"

He growled, again. The noises of the night went on outside. Organ tones and hiccupings and the sound of tack hammers and slamming doors. Somewhere there was a singularly exact replica of the discordant squeaking of a rusty pump.

"I'm looking," said Huyghens at the micro-viewer, "for the record of their mining operations. An open-pit operation wouldn't mean a thing. But if they had driven a tunnel, and somebody was there supervising the robots when the colony was wiped out, there's an off-chance he survived a while."

Roane regarded him with suddenly intent eyes.

"And—"

"Dammit," snapped Huyghens, "if so I'll go see! He'd . . . they'd have no chance at all, otherwise. Not that the chance is good in any case!"

Roane raised his eyebrows.

"I'm a Colonial Survey officer," he said. "I've told you I'll send you to prison if I can. You've risked the lives of millions of people, maintaining non-quarantine communication with an unlicensed planet. If you did rescue somebody from the ruins of the robot colony, does it occur to you that they'd be witnesses to your unauthorized presence here?"

Huyghens spun the viewer again. He stopped. He switched back and forth and found what he wanted. He muttered in satisfaction: "They did run a tunnel!" Aloud he said, "I'll worry about witnesses when I have to."

He pushed aside another cupboard door. Inside it were the odds and ends a man makes use of to repair the things about his house that he never notices until they go wrong. There was an assortment of wires, transistors, bolts, and similar stray items that a man living alone will need. When to his knowledge he's the only inhabitant of a solar system, he especially needs such things.

"What now?" asked Roane mildly.

"I'm going to try to find out if there's anybody left alive over there. I'd have checked before if I'd known the colony existed. I can't prove they're all dead, but I may prove that somebody's still alive. It's barely two weeks' journey away from here! Odd that two colonies picked spots so near!"

He absorbedly picked over the oddments he'd selected. Roane said vexedly:

"Confound it! How can you check whether somebody's alive some hundreds of miles away—when you didn't know he existed half an hour ago?"

Huyghens threw a switch and took down a wall panel, exposing electronic apparatus and circuits behind. He busied himself with it.

"Ever think about hunting for a castaway?" he asked over his shoulder. "There's a planet with some tens of millions of square miles on it. You know there's a ship down. You've no idea where. You assume the survivors have power—no civilized man will be without power very long, so long as he can smelt metals!—but making a space beacon calls for high-precision measurements and workmanship. It's not to be improvised. So what will your ship-wrecked civilized man do, to guide a rescue ship to the one or two square miles he occupies among some tens of millions on the planet?"

Roane fretted visibly.

"What?"

"He's had to go primitive, to begin with," Roane explained. "He cooks his meat over a fire, and so on. He has to make a strictly primitive signal. It's all he can do without gauges and micrometers and very special tools. But he can fill all the planet's atmosphere with a signal that searchers for him can't miss. You see?"

Roane thought irritably. He shook his head.

"He'll make," said Huyghens, "a spark transmitter. He'll fix its output at the shortest frequency he can contrive—it'll be somewhere in the five-to-fifty-meter wave-band, but it will tune very broad—and it will be a plainly human signal. He'll start it broadcasting. Some of those frequencies will go all around the planet under the ionosphere. Any ship that comes in under the radio roof will pick up his signal, get a fix on it, move and get another fix, and then go straight to where the castaway is waiting placidly in a hand-braided hammock, sipping whatever sort of drink he's improvised out of the local vegetation."

Roane said grudgingly:

"Now that you mention it, of course—"

"My space phone picks up microwaves," said Huyghens, "I'm shifting a few elements to make it listen for longer stuff. It won't be efficient, but it will pick up a distress signal if one's in the air. I don't expect it, though."

He worked. Roane sat still a long time, watching him. Down below, a rhythmic sort of sound arose. It was Sourdough Charley, snoring. He lay on his back with his legs in the air. He'd discovered that he slept cooler that way. Sitka Pete grunted in his sleep. He was dreaming. In the general room of the station Semper, the eagle, blinked his eyes rapidly and then tucked his head under a gigantic wing and went to sleep. The noises of the Loren Two jungle came through the steel-shuttered windows. The nearer moon—which had passed overhead not long before the ringing of the arrival bell—again came soaring over the eastern horizon. It sped across the sky at the apparent speed of an atmosphere-flier. Overhead, it could be seen to be a jagged irregular mass of rock or metal, plunging blindly about the great planet forever.

Inside the station, Roane said angrily:

"See here, Huyghens! You've reason to kill me. Apparently you don't intend to. You've excellent reason to leave that robot colony strictly alone. But you're preparing to help, if there's anybody alive to need it. And yet you're a criminal—and I mean a criminal! There've been some ghastly bacteria exported from planets like Loren Two! There've been plenty of lives lost in consequence, and you're risking more! Why do you do it? Why do you do something that could produce monstrous results to other beings?"

Huyghens grunted.

"You're only assuming there are no sanitary and quarantine precautions taken in my communications. As a matter of fact, there are. They're taken, all right! As for the rest, you wouldn't understand."

"I don't understand," snapped Roane, "but that's no proof I can't! Why are you a criminal?"

Huyghens painstakingly used a screwdriver inside the wall panel. He delicately lifted out a small electronic assembly. He carefully began to fit in a spaghettied new assembly with larger units.

"I'm cutting my amplification here to hell-and-gone," he observed, "but I think it'll do. I'm doing what I'm doing," he added calmly, "I'm being a criminal because it seems to me befitting what I think I am. Everybody acts according to his own real notion of himself. You're a conscientious citizen, and a loyal official, and a well-adjusted personality. You consider yourself an intelligent rational animal. But you don't act that way! You're reminding me of my need to shoot you or something similar, which a merely rational animal would try to make me forget. You happen, Roane, to be a man. So am I. But I'm aware of it. Therefore, I deliberately do things a merely rational animal wouldn't, because they're my notion of what a man who's more than a rational animal should do."

He very carefully tightened one small screw after another. Roane said annoyedly:

"Oh. Religion."

"Self-respect," corrected Huyghens. "I don't like robots. They're too much like rational animals. A robot will do whatever it can that its supervisor requires it to do. A merely rational animal will do whatever it can that circumstances require it to do. I wouldn't like a robot unless it had some idea of what was befitting it and would spit in my eye if I tried to make it do something else. The bears downstairs, now— They're no robots! They are loyal and honorable beasts, but they'd turn and tear me to bits if I tried to make them do something against their nature. Faro Nell would fight me and all creation together, if I tried to harm Nugget. It would be unintelligent and unreasonable and irrational. She'd lose out and get killed. But I like her that way! And I'll fight you and all creation when you make me try to do something against my nature. I'll be stupid and unreasonable and irrational about it." Then he grinned over his shoulder. "So will you. Only you don't realize it."

He turned back to his task. After a moment he fitted a manual-control knob over a shaft in his haywire assembly.

"What did somebody try to make you do?" asked Roane shrewdly. "What was demanded of you that turned you into a criminal? What are you in revolt against?"

Huyghens threw a switch. He began to turn the knob which controlled the knob of his makeshift-modified receiver.

"Why," he said amusedly, "when I was young the people around me tried to make me into a conscientious citizen and a loyal employee and a well-adjusted personality. They tried to make me into a highly intelligent rational animal and nothing more. The difference between us, Roane, is that I found it out. Naturally, I rev—"

He stopped short. Faint, crackling, crisp frying sounds came from the speaker of the space phone now modified to receive what once were called short waves.

Huyghens listened. He cocked his head intently. He turned the knob very, very slowly. Then Roane made an arrested gesture, to call attention to something in the sibilant sound. Huyghens nodded. He turned the knob again, with infinitesimal increments.

Out of the background noise came a patterned mutter. As Huyghens shifted the tuning, it grew louder. It reached a volume where it was unmistakable. It was a sequence of sounds like discordant buzzing. There were three half-second buzzings with half-second pauses between. A two-second pause. Three full-second buzzings with half-second pauses between. Another two-second pause and three half-second buzzings, again. Then silence for five seconds. Then the pattern repeated.

"The devil!" said Huyghens. "That's a human signal! Mechanically made, too! In fact, it used to be a standard distress-call. It was termed an S O S, though I've no idea what that meant. Anyhow, somebody must have read old-fashioned novels, some time, to know about it. And so someone is still alive over at your licensed, but now smashed-up, robot colony. And they're asking for help. I'd say they're likely to need it."

He looked at Roane.

"The intelligent thing to do is sit back and wait for a ship—either of my friends or yours. A ship can help survivors or castaways much better than we can. A ship can even find them more easily. But maybe time is important to the poor devils! So I'm going to take the bears and see if I can reach them. You can wait here, if you like. What say? Travel on Loren Two isn't a picnic! I'll be fighting nearly every foot of the way. There's plenty of 'inimical animal life' here!"

Roane snapped angrily:

"Don't be a fool! Of course I'm coming! What do you take me for? And two of us should have four times the chance of one!"

Huyghens grinned.

"Not quite. You forget Sitka Pete and Sourdough Charley and Faro

Nell. There'll be five of us if you come, instead of four. And, of course, Nugget has to come—and he'll be no help—but Semper may make up for him. You won't quadruple our chances, Roane, but I'll be glad to have you if you want to be stupid and unreasonable and not at all rational—and come along."

### III

There was a jagged spur of stone looming precipitously over a river-valley. A thousand feet below, a broad stream ran westward to the sea. Twenty miles to the east, a wall of mountains rose sheer against the sky. Its peaks seemed to blend to a remarkable evenness of height. There was rolling, tumbled ground between for as far as the eye could see.

A speck in the sky came swiftly downward. Great pinions spread, and flapped, and icy eyes surveyed the rocky space. With more great flappings, Semper the eagle came to ground. He folded his huge wings and turned his head jerkily, his eyes unblinking. A tiny harness held a miniature camera against his chest. He strutted over the bare stone to the highest point. He stood there, a lonely and arrogant figure in the vastness.

There came crashings and rustlings, and then snuffling sounds. Sitka Pete came lumbering out into the clear space. He wore a harness too, and a pack. The harness was complex, because it had not only to hold a pack in normal travel, but, when he stood on his hind legs, it must not hamper the use of his forepaws in combat.

He went cagily all over the open area. He peered over the edge of the spur's farthest tip. He prowled to the other side and looked down. He scouted carefully. Once he moved close to Semper and the eagle opened his great curved beak and uttered an indignant noise. Sitka paid no attention.

He relaxed, satisfied. He sat down untidily, his hind legs sprawling. He wore an air approaching benevolence as he surveyed the landscape about and below him.

More snufflings and crashings. Sourdough Charley came into view with Huyghens and Roane behind him. Sourdough carried a pack, too. Then there was a squealing and Nugget scurried up from the rear, impelled by a whack from his mother. Faro Nell appeared, with the carcass of a staglike animal lashed to her harness.

"I picked this place from a space photo," said Huyghens, "to make a directional fix from. I'll get set up."

He swung his pack from his shoulders to the ground. He extracted an obviously self-constructed device which he set on the ground. It had a whip aerial, which he extended. Then he plugged in a considerable length of flexible wire and unfolded a tiny, improvised directional aerial with an even tinier booster at its base. Roane slipped his pack from his shoulders and watched. Huyghens slipped headphones over his ears. He looked up and said sharply:

"Watch the bears, Roane. The wind's blowing up the way we came. Anything that trails us—sphexes, for example—will send its scent on before. The bears will tell us."

He busied himself with the instruments he'd brought. He heard the hissing, frying, background noise which could be anything at all except a human signal. He reached out and swung the small aerial around. Rasping, buzzing tones came in, faintly and then loudly. This receiver, though, had been made for this particular wave band. It was much more efficient than the modified space phone had been. It picked up three short buzzes, three long ones, and three short ones again. Three dots, three dashes, and three dots. Over and over again. S O S. S O S. S O S.

Huyghens took a reading and moved the directional aerial a carefully measured distance. He took another reading. He shifted it yet again and again, carefully marking and measuring each spot and taking notes of the instrument readings. When he finished, he had checked the direction of the signal not only by loudness but by phase— he had as accurate a fix as could possibly be had with portable apparatus.

Sourdough growled softly. Sitka Pete whiffed the air and arose from his sitting position. Faro Nell whacked Nugget, sending him whimpering to the farthest corner of the flea place. She stood bristling, facing down-hill the way they'd come.

"Damn!" said Huyghens.

He got up and waved his arm at Semper, who had turned his head at the stirrings. Semper squawked in a most un-eaglelike fashion and dived off the spur and was immediately fighting the down-draught beyond it. As Huyghens reached his weapon, the eagle came back overhead. He went magnificently past, a hundred feet high, careening and flapping in the tricky currents. He screamed, abruptly, and circled and screamed again. Huyghens swung a tiny vision plate from its strap to where he could look into it. He saw, of course, what the little camera on Semper's chest could see—reeling, swaying terrain as Semper saw it, though without his breadth of field. There were moving objects to be seen through the shifting trees. Their coloring was unmistakable.

"Sphexes," said Huyghens dourly. "Eight of them. Don't look for them to follow our track, Roane. They run parallel to a trail on either side. That way they attack in breadth and all at once when they catch up. And listen! The bears can handle anything they tangle with! It's our job to pick off the loose ones! And aim for the body! The bullets explode."

He threw off the safety of his weapon. Faro Nell, uttering thunderous growls, went padding to a place between Sitka Pete and Sourdough. Sitka glanced at her and made a whuffing noise, as if derisive of her blood-curdling sounds. Sourdough grunted in a somehow solid fashion. He and Sitka moved farther away from Nell to either side. They would cover a wider front.

There was no other sign of life than the shrillings of the incredibly tiny creatures which on this planet were birds, and Faro Nell's deep-bass, raging growls, and then the click of Roane's safety going off as he got ready to use the weapon Huyghens had given him.

Semper screamed again, flapping low above the treetops, following parti-colored, monstrous shapes beneath.

Eight blue-and-tan fiends came racing out of the underbrush. They had spiny fringes, and horns, and glaring eyes, and they looked as if they had come straight out of hell. On the instant of their appearance they leaped, emitting squalling, spitting squeals that were like the cries of fighting tomcats ten thousand times magnified. Huyghens' rifle cracked, and its sound was wiped out in the louder detonation of its bullet in sphexian flesh. A tan-and-blue monster tumbled over, shrieking. Faro Nell charged, the very impersonation of white-hot fury. Roane fired, and his bullet exploded against a tree. Sitka Pete brought his massive forepaws in a clapping, monstrous ear-boxing motion. A sphex died.

Then Roane fired again. Sourdough Charley whuffed. He fell forward upon a spitting bi-colored fiend, rolled him over, and raked with his hind claws. The belly-hide of the sphex was tenderer than the rest. The creature rolled away, snapping at its own wounds. Another sphex found itself shaken loose from the tumult about Sitka Pete. It whirled to leap on him from behind—and Huyghens fired very coldly—and two plunged upon Faro Nell and Roane blasted one and Faro Nell disposed of the other in truly awesome fury. Then Sitka Pete heaved himself erect—seeming to drip sphexes—and Sourdough waddled over and pulled one off and killed it and went back for another. And both rifles cracked together and there was suddenly nothing left to fight.

The bears prowled from one to another of the corpses. Sitka Pete rumbled and lifted up a limp head. Crash! Then another. He went over the lot, whether or not they showed signs of life. When he had finished, they were wholly still.

Semper came flapping down out of the sky. He had screamed and fluttered overhead as the fight went on. Now he landed with a rush. Huyghens went soothingly from one bear to another, calming them with his voice. It took longest to calm Faro Nell, licking Nugget with impassioned solicitude and growling horribly as she licked.

"Come along, now," said Huyghens, when Sitka showed signs of intending to sit down again. "Heave these carcasses over a cliff. Come along! Sitka! Sourdough! Hup!"

He guided them as the two big males somewhat fastidiously lifted up the nightmarish creatures they and the guns together had killed, and carried them to the edge of the spur of stone. They let the dead beasts go bouncing and sliding down into the valley.

"That," said Huyghens, "is so their little pals will gather round them and caterwaul their woe where there's no trail of ours to give them ideas. If we'd been near a river, I'd have dumped them in to float down-river and gather mourners wherever they stranded. Around the station I incinerate them. If I had to leave them, I'd make tracks away. About fifty miles upwind would be a good idea."

He opened the pack Sourdough carried and extracted giant sized swabs and some gallons of antiseptic. He tended the three Kodiaks in turn, swabbing not only the cuts and scratches they'd received, but deeply soaking their fur where there could be suspicion of spilled sphex blood.

"This antiseptic deodorizes, too," he told Roane. "Or we'd be trailed by any sphex who passed to leeward of us. When we start off, I'll swab the bears' paws for the same reason."

Roane was very quiet. He'd missed his first shot with a bullet-firing weapon—a beam hasn't the stopping-power of an explosive bullet—but he'd seemed to grow savagely angry with himself. The last few seconds of the fight, he'd fired very deliberately and every bullet hit. Now he said bitterly:

"If you're instructing me so I can carry on should you be killed, I doubt that it's worth while!"

Huyghens felt in his pack and unfolded the enlargements he'd made of the space photos of this part of the planet. He carefully oriented the map with distant landmarks. He drew a painstakingly accurate line across the photo.

"The S O S signal comes from somewhere close to the robot colony," he reported. "I think a little to the south of it. Probably from a mine they'd opened up, on the far side—of course—of the Sere Plateau. See how I've marked this map? Two fixes, one from the station and one from here. I came away off-course to get a fix here so we'd have two position-lines to the transmitter. The signal could have come from the other side of the planet. But it doesn't."

"The odds would be astronomical against other castaways," protested Roane.

"No-o-o-o," said Huyghens. "Ships have been coming here. To the robot-colony. One could have crashed. And I have friends, too."

He repacked his apparatus and gestured to the bears. He led them beyond the scene of combat and very carefully swabbed off their paws, so they could not possibly leave a trail of sphex-blood scent behind them. He waved Semper, the eagle, aloft.

"Let's go," he told the Kodiaks. "Yonder! Hup!"

The party headed downhill and into the jungle again. Now it was Sourdough's turn to take the lead, and Sitka Pete prowled more widely behind him. Faro Nell trailed the men, with Nugget. She kept an extremely sharp eye upon the cub. He was a baby, still. He only weighed six hundred pounds. And of course she watched against danger from the rear.

Overhead, Semper fluttered and flew in giant circles and spirals, never going very far away. Huyghens referred constantly to the screen which showed what the air-borne camera saw. The image tilted and circled and banked and swayed. It was by no means the best air-reconnaissance that could be imagined. But it was the best that would work. Presently Huyghens said:

"We swing to the right, here. The going's bad straight ahead, and it looks like a pack of sphexes has killed and is feeding."

Roane was upset. He was dissatisfied with himself. So he said:

"It's against reason for carnivores to be as thick as you say! There has to be a certain amount of other animal life for every meat-eating beast! Too many of them would eat all the game and starve!"

"They're gone all winter," explained Huyghens, "which around here isn't as severe as you might think. And a good many animals seem to breed just after the sphexes go south. Also, the sphexes aren't around all the warm weather. There's a sort of peak, and then for a matter of weeks you won't see a one of them, and suddenly the jungle swarms with them again. Then, presently, they head south. Apparently they're migratory in some fashion, but nobody knows." He said dryly: "There haven't been many naturalists around on this planet. The animal life is inimical."

Roane fretted. He was a senior officer in the Colonial Survey, and he was accustomed to arrival at a partly or completely-finished colonial set-up, and to pass upon the completion or non-completion of the planned installation as designed. Now he was in an intolerably hostile environment, depending upon an illegal colonist for his life, engaged upon a demoralizingly indefinite enterprise—because the mechanical spark-signal could be working long after its constructors were dead— and his ideas about a number of matters were shaken. He was alive, for example, because of three giant Kodiak bears and a bald eagle. He and Huyghens could have been surrounded by ten thousand robots, and they'd have been killed. Sphexes and robots would have ignored each other, and sphexes would have made straight for the men, who'd have had less than four seconds in which to discover for themselves that they were attacked, prepare to defend themselves, and kill eight sphexes.

Roane's convictions as a civilized man were shaken. Robots were marvelous contrivances for doing the expected: accomplishing the planned; coping with the predicted. But they also had defects. Robots could only follow instructions—if this thing happens, do this, if that thing happens do that. But before something else, neither this nor that, robots were helpless. So a robot civilization worked only in an environment where nothing unanticipated ever turned up, and human supervisors never demanded anything unexpected. Roane was appalled. He'd never encountered the truly unpredictable before in all his life and career.

He found Nugget, the cub, ambling uneasily in his wake. The cub flattened his ears miserably when Roane glanced at him. It occurred to the man that Nugget was receiving a lot of disciplinary thumpings from Faro Nell. He was knocked about physically, pretty much as Roane was being knocked about psychologically. His lack of information and unfitness for independent survival in this environment was being hammered into him.

"Hi, Nugget," said Roane ruefully. "I feel just about the way you do!"

Nugget brightened visibly. He frisked. He tended to gambol. He looked very hopefully up into Roane's face—and he stood four feet high at the shoulder and would overtop Roane if he stood erect.

Roane reached out and patted Nugget's head. It was the first time in all his life that he'd ever petted an animal.

He heard a snuffling sound behind him. Skin crawled at the back of his neck. He whirled.

Faro Nell regarded him—eighteen hundred pounds of she-bear only ten feet away and looking into his eyes. For one panicky instant Roane went cold all over. Then he realized that Faro Nell's eyes were not burning. She was not snarling. She did not emit those blood-curdling sounds which the bare prospect of danger to Nugget had produced up on the rocky spur. She looked at him blandly. In fact, after a moment she swung off on some independent investigation of a matter that had aroused her curiosity.

The traveling party went on, Nugget frisking beside Roane and tending to bump into him out of pure cub-clumsiness. Now and again he looked adoringly at Roane, in the instant and overwhelming affection of the very young.

Roane trudged on. Presently he glanced behind again. Faro Nell was now ranging more widely. She was well satisfied to have Nugget in the immediate care of a man. From time to time he got on her nerves.

A little while later, Roane called ahead.

"Huyghens! Look here! I've been appointed nursemaid to Nugget!"

Huyghens looked back.

"Oh, slap him a few times and he'll go back to his mother."

"The devil I will!" said Roane querulously. "I like it!"

The traveling party went on.

When night fell, they camped. There could be no fire, of course, because all the minute night-things about would come eagerly to dance in the glow. But there could not be darkness, equally, because night-walkers hunted in the dark. So Huyghens set out the barrier lamps which made a wall of twilight about their halting place, and the stag-like creature Faro Nell had carried became their evening meal. Then they slept—at least the men did—and the bears dozed and snorted and waked and dozed again. But Semper sat immobile with his head under his wing on a tree limb. And presently there was a glorious cool hush and all the world glowed in morning light diffused through the jungle by a newly risen sun. And they arose, and traveled again.

This day they stopped stock-still for two hours while sphexes puzzled over the trail the bears had left. Huyghens discoursed calmly on the need for an anti-scent, to be used on the boots of men and the paws of bears, which would make the following of their trails unpopular with sphexes. And Roane seized upon the idea and absorbedly suggested that a sphex-repellent odor might be worked out, which would make a human revolting to a sphex. If that were done—why—humans could go freely about unmolested.

"Like stink-bugs," said Huyghens, sardonically. "A very intelligent idea! Very rational! You can feel proud!"

And suddenly Roane, very obscurely, was not proud of the idea at all.

They camped again. On the third night they were at the base of that remarkable formation, the Sere Plateau, which from a distance looked like a mountain-range but was actually a desert tableland. And it was not reasonable for a desert to be raised high, while lowlands had rain, but on the fourth morning they found out why. They saw, far, far away, a truly monstrous mountain-mass at the end of the long-way expanse of the plateau. It was like the prow of a ship. It lay, so Huyghens observed, directly in line with the prevailing winds, and divided them as a ship's prow divides the waters. The moisture-bearing air-currents flowed beside the plateau, not over it, and its interior was pure sere desert in the unscreened sunshine of high altitudes.

It took them a full day to get halfway up the slope. And here, twice as they climbed, Semper flew screaming over aggregations of sphexes to one side of them or the other. These were much larger groups than Huyghens had ever seen before—fifty to a hundred monstrosities together, where a dozen was a large hunting-pack elsewhere. He looked in the screen which showed him what Semper saw, four to five miles away. The sphexes padded uphill toward the Sere Plateau in a long line. Fifty—sixty—seventy tan-and-azure beasts out of hell.

"I'd hate to have that bunch jump us," he said candidly to Roane. "I don't think we'd stand a chance."

"Here's where a robot tank would be useful," Roane observed.

"Anything armored," conceded Huyghens. "One man in an armored station like mine would be safe. But if he killed a sphex he'd be besieged. He'd have to stay holed up, breathing the smell of dead sphex, until the odor had gone away. And he mustn't kill any others or he'd be besieged until winter came."

Roane did not suggest the advantages of robots in other directions. At that moment, for example, they were working their way up a slope which averaged fifty degrees. The bears climbed without effort despite their burdens. For the men it was infinite toil. Semper, the eagle, manifested impatience with bears and men alike, who crawled so slowly up an incline over which he soared.

He went ahead up the mountainside and teetered in the air-currents at the plateau's edge. Huyghens looked in the visionplate by which he reported.

"How the devil," panted Roane—they had stopped for a breather, and the bears waited patiently for them—"do you train bears like these? I can understand Semper."

"I don't train them," said Huyghens, staring into the plate. "They're mutations. In heredity the sex-linkage of physical characteristics is standard stuff. But there's been some sound work done on the gene-linkage of psychological factors. There was need, on my home planet, for an animal who could fight like a fiend, live off the land, carry a pack and get along with men at least as well as dogs do. In the old days they'd have tried to breed the desired physical properties into an animal who already had the personality they wanted. Something like a giant dog, say. But back home they went at it the other way about. They picked the wanted physical characteristics and bred for the personality —the psychology. The job got done over a century ago—a Kodiak bear named Kodius Champion was the first real success. He had everything that was wanted. These bears are his descendants."

"They look normal," commented Roane.

"They are!" said Huyghens warmly. "Just as normal as an honest dog! They're not trained, like Semper. They train themselves!" He looked back into the plate in his hands, which showed the ground five and six and seven thousand feet higher. "Semper, now, is a trained bird without too much brains. He's educated—a glorified hawk. But the bears want to get along with men. They're emotionally dependent on us! Like dogs. Semper's a servant, but they're companions and friends. He's trained, but they're loyal. He's conditioned. They love us. He'd abandon me if he ever realized he could—he thinks he can only eat what men feed him. But the bears wouldn't want to. They like us. I admit that I like them. Maybe because they like me."

Roane said deliberately:

"Aren't you a trifle loose-tongued, Huyghens? I'm a Colonial Survey officer. I have to arrest you sooner or later. You've told me something that will locate and convict the people who set you up here. It shouldn't be hard to find where bears were bred for psychological mutations, and where a bear named Kodius Champion left descendants! I can find out where you came from now, Huyghens!"

Huyghens looked up from the plate with its tiny swaying television image, relayed from where Semper floated impatiently in mid-air.

"No harm done," he said amiably. "I'm a criminal there, too. It's officially on record that I kidnaped these bears and escaped with them. Which, on my home planet, is about as heinous a crime as a man can commit. It's worse than horse-theft back on Earth in the old days. The kin and cousins of my bears are highly thought of. I'm quite a criminal, back home."

Roane stared.

"Did you steal them?" he demanded.

"Confidentially," said Huyghens, "no. But prove it!" Then he said: "Take a look in this plate. See what Semper can see up at the plateau's edge."

Roane squinted aloft, where the eagle flew in great sweeps and dashes. Somehow, by the experience of the past few days, Roane knew that Semper was screaming fiercely as he flew. He made a dart toward the plateau's border.

Roane looked at the transmitter picture. It was only four inches by six, but it was perfectly without grain and in accurate color. It moved and turned as the camera-bearing eagle swooped and circled. For an instant the screen showed the steeply sloping mountainside, and off at one edge the party of men and bears could be seen as dots. Then it swept away and showed the top of the plateau.

There were sphexes. A pack of two hundred trotted toward the desert interior. They moved at leisure, in the open. The viewing camera reeled, and there were more. As Roane watched and as the bird flew higher, he could see still other sphexes moving up over the edge of the plateau from a small erosion-defile here and another one there. The Sere Plateau was alive with the hellish creatures. It was inconceivable that there should be game enough for them to live on. They were visible as herds of cattle would be visible on grazing planets.

It was simply impossible.

"Migrating," observed Huyghens. "I said they did. They're headed somewhere. Do you know, I doubt that it would be healthy for us to try to cross the plateau through such a swarm of sphexes?"

Roane swore, in abrupt change of mood.

"But the signal's still coming through! Somebody's alive over at the robot colony! Must we wait till the migration's over?"

"We don't know," Huyghens pointed out, "that they'll stay alive. They may need help badly. We have to get to them. But at the same time—"

He glanced at Sourdough Charley and Sitka Pete, clinging patiently to the mountainside while the men rested and talked. Sitka had managed to find a place to sit down, though one massive paw anchored him in his place.

Huyghens waved his arm, pointing in a new direction.

"Let's go!" he called briskly. "Let's go! Yonder! Hup!"

## IV

They followed the slopes of the Sere Plateau, neither ascending to its level top—where sphexes congregated—nor descending into the foot-hills where sphexes assembled. They moved along hillsides and moun-tain-flanks which sloped anywhere from thirty to sixty degrees, and they did not cover much distance. They practically forgot what it was to walk on level ground. Semper, the eagle, hovered overhead during the daytime, not far away. He descended at nightfall for his food from the pack of one of the bears.

"The bears aren't doing too well for food," said Huyghens dryly. "A ton of bear needs a lot to eat. But they're loyal to us. Semper hasn't any loyalty. He's too stupid. But he's been conditioned to think that he can only eat what men feed him. The bears know better, but they stick to us regardless. I rather like these bears."

It was the most self-evident of understatements. This was at an en-campment on the top of a massive boulder which projected from a mountainous stony wall. This was six days from the start of their jour-ney. There was barely room on the boulder for all the party. And Faro Nell fussily insisted that Nugget should be in the safest part, which meant near the mountain-flank. She would have crowded the men outward, but Nugget whimpered for Roane. Wherefore, when Roane moved to comfort him, Faro Nell contentedly drew back and snorted at Sitka and Sourdough and they made room for her near the edge.

It was a hungry camp. They had come upon tiny rills upon occa-sion, flowing down the mountain side. Here the bears had drunk deeply and the men had filled canteens. But this was the third night, and there had been no game at all. Huyghens made no move to bring out food for Roane or himself. Roane made no comment. He was be-ginning to participate in the relationship between bears and men, which was not the slavery of the bears but something more. It was two-way. He felt it.

"It would seem," he said fretfully, "that since the sphexes don't seem to hunt on their way uphill, that there should be some game. They ignore everything as they file uphill."

This was true enough. The normal fighting formation of sphexes was line abreast, which automatically surrounded anything which offered to flee and outflanked anything which offered fight. But here they ascended the mountain in long lines, one after the other, following apparently long-established trails. The wind blew along the slopes and carried scent only sidewise. But the sphexes were not diverted from their chosen paths. The long processions of hideous blue-and-tawny creatures—it was hard to think of them as natural beasts, male and female and laying eggs like reptiles on other planets—simply climbed.

"There've been other thousands of beasts before them," said Huyghens. "They must have been crowding this way for days or even weeks. We've seen tens of thousands in Semper's camera. They must be uncountable, altogether. The first-comers ate all the game there was, and the last-comers have something else on whatever they use for minds."

Roane protested: "But so many carnivores in one place is impossible! I know they are here, but they can't be!"

"They're cold-blooded," Huyghens pointed out. "They don't burn food to sustain body-temperature. After all, lots of creatures go for long periods without eating. Even bears hibernate. But this isn't hibernation—or estivation, either."

He was setting up the radiation-wave receiver in the darkness. There was no point in attempting a fix here. The transmitter was on the other side of the Sere Plateau, which inexplicably swarmed with the most ferocious and deadly of all the creatures of Loren Two. The men and bears would commit suicide by crossing here.

But Huyghens turned on the receiver. There came the whispering, scratchy sound of background-noise. Then the signal. Three dots, three dashes, three dots. Three dots, three dashes, three dots. It went on and on and on. Huyghens turned it off. Roane said:

"Shouldn't we have answered that signal before we left the station? To encourage them?"

"I doubt they have a receiver," said Huyghens. "They won't expect an answer for months, anyhow. They'd hardly listen all the time, and if they're living in a mine-tunnel and trying to sneak out for food to stretch their supplies—why, they'll be too busy to try to make complicated recorders or relays."

Roane was silent for a moment or two.

"We've got to get food for the bears," he said presently. "Nugget's weaned, and he's hungry."

"We will," Huyghens promised. "I may be wrong, but it seems to me that the number of sphexes climbing the mountain is less than yesterday and the day before. We may have just about crossed the path of their migration. They're thinning out. When we're past their trail, we'll have to look out for night-walkers and the like again. But I think they wiped out all animal life on their migration-route."

He was not quite right. He was waked in darkness by the sound of slappings and the grunting of bears. Feather-light puffs of breeze beat upon his face. He struck his belt-lamp sharply and the world was hidden by a whitish film which snatched itself away. Something flapped. Then he saw the stars and the emptiness on the edge of which they camped. Then big white things flapped toward him.

Sitka Pete whuffed mightily and swatted. Faro Nell grunted and swung. She caught something in her claws. She crunched. The light went off as Huyghens realized. Then he said:

"Don't shoot, Roane!" He listened, and heard the sounds of feeding in the dark. It ended. "Watch this!" said Huyghens.

The belt-light came on again. Something strangely-shaped and pallid like human skin reeled and flapped crazily toward him. Something else. Four. Five—ten—twenty—more . . .

A huge hairy paw reached up into the light-beam and snatched a flying thing out of it. Another great paw. Huyghens shifted the light and the three great Kodiaks were on their hind legs, swatting at creatures which flittered insanely, unable to resist the fascination of the glaring lamp. Because of their wild gyrations it was impossible to see them in detail, but they were those unpleasant night-creatures which looked like plucked flying monkeys but were actually something quite different.

The bears did not snarl or snap. They swatted, with a remarkable air of businesslike competence and purpose. Small mounds of broken things built up about their feet.

Suddenly there were no more. Huyghens snapped off the light. The bears crunched and fed busily in the darkness.

"Those things are carnivores *and* blood-suckers, Roane," said Huyghens calmly. "They drain their victims of blood like vampire bats —they've some trick of not waking them—and when they're dead the whole tribe eats. But bears have thick furs, and they wake when they're touched. And they're omnivorous—they'll eat anything but sphexes, and like it. You might say that those night-creatures came to lunch. But they stayed. They are it—for the bears, who are living off the country as usual."

Roane uttered a sudden exclamation. He made a tiny light, and blood flowed down his hand. Huyghens passed over his pocket kit of antiseptic and bandages. Roane stanched the bleeding and bound up his hand. Then he realized that Nugget chewed on something. When he turned the light, Nugget swallowed convulsively. It appeared that he had caught and devoured the creature which had drawn blood from Roane. But Roane had lost none to speak of, at that.

In the morning they started along the sloping scarp of the plateau once more. During the morning, Roane said painfully:

"Robots wouldn't have handled those vampire-things, Huyghens."

"Oh, they could be built to watch for them," said Huyghens, tolerantly. "But you'd have to swat for yourself. I prefer the bears."

He led the way on. Here their jungle-formation could not apply. On a steep slope the bears ambled comfortably, the tough pads of their feet holding fast on the slanting rock, but the men struggled painfully. Twice Huyghens halted to examine the ground about the mountains' bases through binoculars. He looked encouraged as they went on. The monstrous peak which was like the bow of a ship at the end of the Sere Plateau was visibly nearer. Toward midday, indeed, it looked high above the horizon, no more than fifteen miles away. And at midday Huyghens called a final halt.

"No more congregations of sphexes down below," he said cheerfully, "and we haven't seen a climbing line of them in miles." The crossing of a sphex-trail meant simply waiting until one party had passed, and then crossing before another came in view. "I've a hunch we've crossed their migration-route. Let's see what Semper tells us!"

He waved the eagle aloft. And Semper, like all creatures other than men, normally functioned only for the satisfaction of his appetite, and then tended to loaf or sleep. He had ridden the last few miles perched on Sitka Pete's pack. Now he soared upward and Huyghens watched in the small vision-plate.

Semper went soaring—and the image on the plate swayed and turned and turned—and in minutes was above the plateau's edge. And here there was some vegatation and the ground rolled somewhat, and there were even patches of brush. But as Semper towered higher still, the inner desert appeared. But nearby it was clear of beasts. Only once, when the eagle banked sharply and the camera looked along the long dimension of the plateau, did Huyghens see any sign of the blue-and-tan beasts. There he saw what looked like masses amounting to herds. But, of course, carnivores do not gather in herds.

"We go straight up," said Huyghens in satisfaction. "We cross the plateau here—and we can edge downwind a bit, even. I think we'll find something interesting on our way to your robot colony."

He waved to the bears to go ahead uphill.

They reached the top hours later—barely before sunset. And they saw game. Not much, but game at the grassy, brushy border of the desert. Huyghens brought down a shaggy ruminant which surely would not live on a desert. When night fell there was an abrupt chill in the air. It was much colder than night-temperatures on the slopes. The air was thin. Roane thought confusedly and presently guessed at the cause. In the lee of the prow-mountain the air was calm. There were no clouds. The ground radiated its heat to empty space. It could be bitterly cold in the nighttime, here.

"And hot by day," Huyghens agreed when he mentioned it. "The sunshine's terrifically hot where the air is thin, but on most mountains there's wind. By day, here, the ground will tend to heat up like the surface of a planet without atmosphere. It may be a hundred and forty or fifty degrees on the sand at midday. But it should be cold at night."

It was. Before midnight Huyghens built a fire. There could be no danger of night-walkers where the temperature dropped to freezing.

In the morning the men were stiff with cold, but the bears snorted and moved about briskly. They seemed to revel in the morning chill. Sitka and Sourdough Charley, in fact, became festive and engaged in a mock fight, whacking each other with blows that were only feigned, but would have crushed in the skull of any man. Nugget sneezed with excitement as he watched them. Faro Nell regarded them with female disapproval.

They went on. Semper seemed sluggish. After a single brief flight he descended and rode on Sitka's pack, as on the previous day. He perched there, surveying the landscape as it changed from semi-arid to pure desert in their progress. His air was arrogant. But he would not fly. Soaring birds do not like to fly when there are no winds to make currents of which to take advantage. On the way, Huyghens painstakingly pointed out to Roane exactly where they were on the enlarged photograph taken from space, and the exact spot from which the distress-signal seemed to come.

"You're doing it in case something happens to you," said Roane. "I admit it's sense, but—what could I do to help those survivors even if I got to them, without you?"

"What you've learned about sphexes would help," said Huyghens. "The bears would help. And we left a note back at my station. Whoever grounds at the landing field back there—and the beacon's working again—will find instructions to come to the place we're trying to reach."

Roane plodded alongside him. The narrow non-desert border of the Sere Plateau was behind them, now. They marched across powdery desert sand.

"See here," said Roane. "I want to know something! You tell me you're listed as a bear-thief on your home planet. You tell me it's a lie— to protect your friends from prosecution by the Colonial Survey. You're on your own, risking your life every minute of every day. You took a

risk in not shooting me. Now you're risking more in going to help men
who'd have to be witnesses that you were a criminal. What are you
doing it for?"

Huyghens grinned.

"Because I don't like robots. I don't like the fact that they're sub-
duing men—making men subordinate to them."

"Go on," insisted Roane. "I don't see why disliking robots should
make you a criminal. Nor men subordinating themselves to robots,
either!"

"But they are," said Huyghens mildly. "I'm a crank, of course. But—
I live like a man on this planet. I go where I please and do what I please.
My helpers, the bears, are my friends. If the robot colony had been a
success, would the humans in it have lived like men? Hardly! They'd
have to live the way the robots let them! They'd have to stay inside a
fence the robots built. They'd have to eat foods that robots could raise,
and no others. Why—a man couldn't move his bed near a window,
because if he did the house-tending robots couldn't work! Robots would
serve them—the way the robots determined—but all they'd get out of it
would be jobs servicing the robots!"

Roane shook his head.

"As long as men want robot service, they have to take the service
that robots can give. If you don't want those services—"

"I want to decide what I want," said Huyghens, again mildly, "instead of being limited to choose among what I'm offered. On my home
planet we halfway tamed it with dogs and guns. Then we developed
the bears, and we finished the job with them. Now there's population-
pressure and the room for bears and dogs—and men—is dwindling.
More and more people are being deprived of the power of decision,
and being allowed only the power of choice among the things robots
allow. The more we depend on robots, the more limited those choices
become. We don't want our children to limit themselves to wanting
what robots can provide! We don't want them shriveling to where they
abandon everything robots can't give—or won't! We want them to be
men—and women. Not damned automatons who live *by* pushing
robot-controls so they can live *to* push robot-controls. If that's not sub-
ordination to robots—"

"It's an emotional argument," protested Roane. "Not everybody feels
that way."

"But I feel that way," said Huyghens. "And so do a lot of others.
This is a big galaxy and it's apt to contain some surprises. The one sure
thing about a robot and a man who depends on them is that they can't
handle the unexpected. There's going to come a time when we

need men who can. So on my home planet, some of us asked for Loren Two, to colonize. It was refused—too dangerous. But men can colonize anywhere if they're men. So I came here to study the planet. Especially the sphexes. Eventually, we expected to ask for a license again, with proof that we could handle even those beasts. I'm already doing it in a mild way. But the Survey licensed a robot colony—and where is it?"

Roane made a sour face.

"You picked the wrong way to go about it, Huyghens. It was illegal. It is. It was the pioneer spirit, which is admirable enough, but wrongly directed. After all, it was pioneers who left Earth for the stars. But—"

Sourdough raised up on his hind legs and sniffed the air. Huyghens swung his rifle around to be handy. Roane slipped off the safety-catch of his own. Nothing happened.

"In a way," said Roane vexedly, "you're talking about liberty and freedom, which most people think is politics. You say it can be more. In principle, I'll concede it. But the way you put it, it sounds like a freak religion."

"It's self-respect," corrected Huyghens.

"You may be—"

Faro Nell growled. She bumped Nugget with her nose, to drive him closer to Roane. She snorted at him. She trotted swiftly to where Sitka and Sourdough faced toward the broader, sphex-filled expanse of the Sere Plateau. She took up her position between them.

Huyghens gazed sharply beyond them and then all about.

"This could be bad!" he said softly. "But luckily there's no wind. Here's a sort of hill. Come along, Roane!"

He ran ahead, Roane following and Nugget plumping heavily with him. They reached the raised place—actually a mere hillock no more than five or six feet above the surrounding sand, with a distorted cactus-like growth protruding from the ground. Huyghens stared again. He used his binoculars.

"One sphex," he said curtly. "Just one! And it's out of all reason for a sphex to be alone! But it's not rational for them to gather in hundreds of thousands, either!" He wetted his finger and held it up. "No wind at all."

He used the binoculars again.

"It doesn't know we're here," he added. "It's moving away. Not another one in sight—" He hesitated, biting his lips. "Look here, Roane! I'd like to kill that one lone sphex and find out something. There's a fifty per cent chance I could find out something really important. But— I might have to run. If I'm right—" Then he said grimly, "It'll have to be done quickly. I'm going to ride Faro Nell—for speed. I doubt Sitka or Sourdough would stay behind. But Nugget can't run fast enough. Will you stay here with him?"

Roane drew in his breath. Then he said calmly:

"You know what you're doing. Of course."

"Keep your eyes open. If you see anything, even at a distance, shoot and we'll be back—fast! Don't wait until something's close enough to hit. Shoot the instant you see anything—if you do!"

Roane nodded. He found it peculiarly difficult to speak again. Huyghens went over to the embattled bears. He climbed up on Faro Nell's back, holding fast by her shaggy fur.

"Let's go!" he snapped. "That way! Hup!"

The three Kodiaks plunged away at a dead run, Huyghens lurching and swaying on Faro Nell's back. The sudden rush dislodged Semper from his perch. He flapped wildly and got aloft. Then he followed effortfully, flying low.

It happened very quickly. A Kodiak bear can travel as fast as a race horse on occasion. These three plunged arrow-straight for a spot perhaps half a mile distant, where a blue-and-tawny shape whirled to face them. There was the crash of Huyghens' weapon from where he rode on Faro Nell's back—the explosion of the weapon and the bullet was one sound. The somehow unnatural spiky monster leaped and died.

Huyghens jumped down from Faro Nell. He became feverishly busy at something on the ground—where the parti-colored sphex had fallen. Semper banked and whirled and came down to the ground. He watched, with his head on one side.

Roane stared, from a distance. Huyghens was doing something to the dead sphex. The two male bears prowled about. Faro Nell regarded Huyghens with intense curiosity. Back at the hillock, Nugget whimpered a little. Roane patted him roughly. Nugget whimpered more loudly. In the distance, Huyghens straightened up and took three steps toward Faro Nell. He mounted. Sitka turned his head back toward Roane. He seemed to see or sniff something dubious. He reared upward. He made a noise, apparently, because Sourdough ambled to his side. The two great beasts began to trot back. Semper flapped wildly and—lacking wind—lurched crazily in the air. He landed on Huyghens' shoulder and his talons clung there.

Then Nugget howled hysterically and tried to swarm up Roane, as a cub tries to swarm up the nearest tree in time of danger. Roane collapsed, and the cub upon him—and there was a flash of stinking scaly hide, while the air was filled with the snarling, spitting squeals of a sphex in full leap. The beast had overjumped, aiming at Roane and the cub while both were upright and arriving when they had fallen. It went tumbling.

Roane heard nothing but the fiendish squalling, but in the distance Sitka and Sourdough were coming at rocketship speed. Faro Nell let out a roar and fairly split the air. And then there was a furry cub streaking toward her, bawling, while Roane rolled to his feet and snatched up his gun. He raged through pure instinct. The sphex crouched to pursue the cub and Roane swung his weapon as a club. He was literally too close to shoot—and perhaps the sphex had only seen the fleeing bear-cub. But he swung furiously.

And the sphex whirled. Roane was toppled from his feet. An eight-hundred-pound monstrosity straight out of hell—half wildcat and half spitting cobra with hydrophobia and homicidal mania added—such a monstrosity is not to be withstood when in whirling its body strikes one in the chest.

That was when Sitka arrived, bellowing. He stood on his hind legs, emitting roars like thunder, challenging the sphex to battle. He waddled forward. Huyghens arrived, but he could not shoot with Roane in the sphere of an explosive bullet's destructiveness. Faro Nell raged and snarled, torn between the urge to be sure that Nugget was unharmed, and the frenzied fury of a mother whose offspring has been endangered.

Mounted on Faro Nell, with Semper clinging idiotically to his shoulder, Huyghens watched helplessly as the sphex spat and squalled at Sitka, having only to reach out one claw to let out Roane's life.

## v

They got away from there, though Sitka seemed to want to lift the limp carcass of his victim in his teeth and dash it repeatedly to the ground. He seemed doubly raging because a man—with whom all Kodius Champion's descendants had an emotional relationship—had been mishandled. But Roane was not grievously hurt. He bounced and swore as the bears raced for the horizon. Huyghens had flung him up on Sourdough's pack and snapped for him to hold on. He bumped and chattered furiously:

"Dammit, Huyghens! This isn't right! Sitka got some deep scratches! That horror's claws may be poisonous!"

But Huyghens snapped, "Hup! Hup!" to the bears, and they continued their race against time. They went on for a good two miles, when Nugget wailed despairingly of his exhaustion and Faro Nell halted firmly to nuzzle him.

"This may be good enough," said Huyghens. "Considering that there's no wind and the big mass of beasts is down the plateau and there were only those two around here. Maybe they're too busy to hold a wake, even! Anyhow—"

He slid to the ground and extracted the antiseptic and swabs.

"Sitka first," snapped Roane. "I'm all right!"

Huyghens swabbed the big bear's wounds. They were trivial, because Sitka Pete was an experienced sphex-fighter. Then Roane grudgingly let the curiously-smelling stuff—it reeked of ozone—be applied to the slashes on his chest. He held his breath as it stung. Then he said dourly:

"It was my fault, Huyghens. I watched you instead of the landscape. I couldn't imagine what you were doing."

"I was doing a quick dissection," Huyghens told him. "By luck, that first sphex was a female, as I hoped. And she was just about to lay her eggs. Ugh! And now I know why the sphexes migrate, and where, and how it is that they don't need game up here."

He slapped a quick bandage on Roane. He led the way eastward, still putting distance between the dead sphexes and his party. It was a crisp walk, only, but Semper flapped indignantly overhead, angry that he was not permitted to ride again.

"I'd dissected them before," said Huyghens. "Not enough's been known about them. Some things needed to be found out if men were ever to be able to live here."

"With bears?" asked Roane ironically.

"Oh, yes," said Huyghens. "But the point is that sphexes come to the desert here to breed—to mate and lay their eggs for the sun to hatch. It's a particular place. Seals return to a special place to mate—and the males at least don't eat for weeks on end. Salmon return to their native streams to spawn. They don't eat, and they die afterward. And eels—I'm using Earth examples, Roane—travel some thousands of miles to the Sargasso to mate and die. Unfortunately, sphexes don't appear to die, but it's clear that they have an ancestral breeding place and that they come here to the Sere Plateau to deposit their eggs!"

Roane plodded onward. He was angry: angry with himself because he hadn't taken elementary precautions; because he'd felt too safe, as a man in a robot-served civilization forms the habit of doing; because he hadn't used his brain when Nugget whimpered, in even a bear-cub's awareness that danger was near.

"And now," Huyghens added, "I need some equipment that the robot colony had. With it, I think we can make a start toward making this a planet that men can live like men on!"

Roane blinked.

"What's that?"

"Equipment," said Huyghens impatiently. "It'll be at the robot colony. Robots were useless because they wouldn't pay attention to sphexes. They'd still be. But take out the robot controls and the machines will do! They shouldn't be ruined by a few months' exposure to weather!"

Roane marched on and on. Presently he said:

"I never thought you'd want anything that came from that colony, Huyghens!"

"Why not?" demanded Huyghens impatiently. "When men make machines do what they want, that's all right. Even robots—when they're where they belong. But men will have to handle flame-casters in the job I want them for. There have to be some, because there was a hundred-mile clearing to be burned off. And Earth-sterilizers—intended to kill the seeds of any plants that robots couldn't handle. We'll come back up here, Roane, and at the least we'll destroy the spawn of these infernal beasts! If we can't do more than that—just doing that every year will wipe out the race in time. There are probably other hordes than this, with other breeding places. But we'll find them, too. We'll make this planet into a place where men from my world can come— and still be men!"

Roane said sardonically:

"It was sphexes that beat the robots. Are you sure you aren't planning to make this world safe for robots?"

Huyghens laughed shortly.

"You've only seen one night-walker," he said. "And how about those things on the mountain-slope—which would have drained you of blood and then feasted? Would you care to wander about this planet with only a robot bodyguard, Roane? Hardly! Men can't live on this planet with only robots to help them—and stop them from being fully men! You'll see!"

They found the colony after only ten days more of travel and after many sphexes and more than a few staglike creatures and shaggy ruminants had fallen to their weapons and the bears. But first they found the survivors of the colony.

There were three of them, hard-bitten and bearded and deeply embittered. When the electrified fence went down, two of them were away at a mine-tunnel, installing a new control-panel for the robots who worked in it. The third was in charge of the mining operation. They were alarmed by the stopping of communication with the colony and went back in a tank-truck to find out what had happened, and only the fact that they were unarmed saved them. They found sphexes prowling and caterwauling about the fallen colony, in numbers they still did not wholly believe. And the sphexes smelled men inside the armored vehicle, but couldn't break in. In turn, the men couldn't kill them, or they'd have been trailed to the mine and besieged there for as long as they could kill an occasional monster.

The survivors stopped all mining—of course—and tried to use remote-controlled robots for revenge and to get supplies for them. Their mining-robots were not designed for either task. And they had no weapons. They improvised miniature throwers of burning rocket-fuel, and they sent occasional prowling sphexes away screaming with scorched hides. But this was useful only because it did not kill the beasts. And it cost fuel. In the end they barricaded themselves and used the fuel only to keep a spark-signal going against the day when another ship came to seek the colony. They stayed in the mine as in a prison, on short rations, waiting without real hope. For diversion they could only contemplate the mining-robots they could not spare fuel to run and which could not do anything but mine.

When Huyghens and Roane reached them, they wept. They hated robots and all things robotic only a little less than they hated sphexes. But Huyghens explained, and armed them with weapons from the packs of the bears, and they marched to the dead colony with the male Kodiaks as point and advance-guard, and with Faro Nell bringing up the rear. They killed sixteen sphexes on the way. In the now over-grown clearing there were four more. In the shelters of the colony they found only foulness and the fragments of what had been men. But there was some food—not much, because the sphexes clawed at anything that smelled of men, and had ruined the plastic packets of radiation-sterilized food. But there were some supplies in metal containers which were not destroyed.

And there was fuel, which men could dispense when they got to the control-panels of the equipment. There were robots everywhere, bright and shining and ready for operation, but immobile, with plants growing up around and over them.

They ignored those robots. But lustfully they fueled tracked flame-casters—adapting them to human rather than robot operation—and the giant soil-sterilizer which had been built to destroy vegetation that robots could not be made to weed out or cultivate. And they headed back for the Sere Plateau, burning-eyed and filled with hate.

But Nugget became a badly spoiled bear-cub, because the freed men approved passionately of anything that would even grow up to kill sphexes. They petted him to excess, when they camped.

And they reached the plateau by a sphex-trail to the top. And Semper scouted for sphexes, and the giant Kodiaks disturbed them and the sphexes came squalling and spitting to destroy them—and while Roane and Huyghens fired steadily, the great machines swept up with their special weapons. The Earth-sterilizer, it was found, was deadly against animal life as well as seeds, when its diathermic beam was raised and aimed. But it had to be handled by a man. No robot could decide just when it was to be used, and against what target.

Presently the bears were not needed, because the scorched corpses of sphexes drew live ones from all parts of the plateau even in the absence of noticeable breezes. The official business of the sphexes was presumably finished, but they came to caterwaul and seek vengeance—which they did not find. Presently the survivors of the robot colony drove machines—as men needed to do, here—in great circles around the hugest heap of slaughtered fiends, destroying new arrivals as they came. It was such a killing as men had never before made on any planet, but there would not be many left of the sphex-horde which had bred in this particular patch of desert. There might be other hordes elsewhere, and other breeding places, but the normal territory of this mass of monsters would see few of them this year.

Or next year, either. Because the soil-sterilizer would go over the dug-up sand where the sphex-spawn lay hidden for the sun to hatch. And the sun would never hatch them.

But Huyghens and Roane, by that time, were camped on the edge of the plateau with the Kodiaks. They were technically upwind from the scene of slaughter—and somehow it seemed more befitting for the men of the robot colony to conduct it. After all, it was those men whose companions had been killed.

There came an evening when Huyghens amiably cuffed Nugget away from where he sniffed too urgently at a stag-steak cooking on the campfire. Nugget ambled dolefully behind the protecting form of Roane and sniveled.

"Huyghens," said Roane painfully, "we've got to come to a settlement of our affairs. I'm a Colonial Survey officer. You're an illegal colonist. It's my duty to arrest you."

Huyghens regarded him with interest.

"Will you offer me lenience if I tell on my confederates," he asked mildly, "or may I plead that I can't be forced to testify against myself?"

Roane said vexedly:

"It's irritating! I've been an honest man all my life, but—I don't believe in robots as I did, except in their place. And their place isn't here. Not as the robot colony was planned, anyhow. The sphexes are nearly wiped out, but they won't be extinct and robots can't handle them. Bears and men will have to live here or—the people who do will have to spend their lives behind sphex-proof fences, accepting only what robots can give them. And there's much too much on this planet for people to miss it! To live in a robot-managed controlled environment on a planet like Loren Two wouldn't . . . it wouldn't be self-respecting!"

"You wouldn't be getting religious, would you?" asked Huyghens dryly. "That was your term for self-respect before."

Semper, the eagle, squawked indignantly as Sitka Pete almost stepped on him, approaching the fire. Sitka Pete sniffed, and Huyghens spoke to him sharply, and he sat down with a thump. He remained sitting in an untidy lump, looking at the steak and drooling.

"You don't let me finish!" protested Roane querulously. "I'm a Colonial Survey officer, and it's my job to pass on the work that's done on a planet before any but the first-landed colonists may come there to live. And of course to see that specifications are followed. Now—the robot colony I was sent to survey was practically destroyed. As designed, it wouldn't work. It couldn't survive."

Huyghens grunted. Night was falling. He turned the meat over the fire.

"Now, in emergencies," said Roane carefully, "colonists have the right to call on any passing ship for aid. Naturally! So— I've always been an honest man before, Huyghens—my report will be that the colony as designed was impractical, and that it was overwhelmed and destroyed except for three survivors who holed up and signaled for help. They did, you know!"

"Go on," grunted Huyghens.

"So," said Roane querulously, "it just happened—just happened, mind you—that a ship with you and Sitka and Sourdough and Faro Nell on board—and Nugget and Semper, too, of course—picked up the distress-call. So you landed to help the colonists. And you did. That's the story. Therefore it isn't illegal for you to be here. It was only illegal for you to be here when you were needed. But we'll pretend you weren't."

Huyghens glanced over his shoulder in the deepening night. He said calmly:

"I wouldn't believe that if I told it myself. Do you think the Survey will?"

"They're not fools," said Roane tartly. "Of course they won't! But when my report says that because of this unlikely series of events it is practical to colonize the planet, whereas before it wasn't—and when my report proves that a robot colony alone is stark nonsense, but that with bears and men from your world added, so many thousand colonists can be received per year— And when that much is true, anyhow—"

Huyghens seemed to shake a little as a dark silhouette against the flames. A little way off, Sourdough sniffed the air hopefully. With a bright light like the fire, presently naked-looking flying things might appear to be slapped down out of the air. They were succulent—to a bear.

"My reports carry weight," insisted Roane. "The deal will be offered, anyhow! The robot colony organizers will have to agree or they'll have to fold up. It's true! And your people can hold them up for nearly what terms they choose."

Huyghens' shaking became understandable. It was laughter.

"You're a lousy liar, Roane," he said, chuckling. "Isn't it unintelligent and unreasonable and irrational to throw away a lifetime of honesty just to get me out of a jam? You're not acting like a rational animal, Roane. But I thought you wouldn't, when it came to the point."

Roane squirmed.

"That's the only solution I can think of. But it'll work."

"I accept it," said Huyghens, grinning. "With thanks. If only because it means another few generations of men living like men on a planet that is going to take a lot of taming. And—if you want to know —because it keeps Sourdough and Sitka and Nell and Nugget from being killed because I brought them here illegally."

Something pressed hard against Roane. Nugget, the cub, pushed urgently against him in his desire to get closer to the fragrantly cooking meat. He edged forward. Roane toppled from where he squatted on the ground. He sprawled. Nugget sniffed luxuriously.

"Slap him," said Huyghens. "He'll move back."

"I won't!" said Roane indignantly from where he lay. "I won't do it! He's my friend!"

# Arthur C. Clarke

If Arthur C. Clarke had more hair and were considerably more handsome, he could easily be mistaken for me.

He is just about my age and has been writing just about as long. He has written science fiction novels and has published collections of his science fiction short stories, as I have. He has been professionally trained in science as I have (he in astronomy, I in chemistry) and has published books on "straight science" as I have.

On top of that, where I was Guest of Honor at the 13th Convention (Cleveland, 1955), he was Guest of Honor at the 14th Convention (New York, 1956). It was at the 14th Convention that I grew to know Arthur well and learned to love him, for, indeed, he is a lovable fellow and a witty conversationalist.

From one standpoint, however, he leaves much to be desired as a friend. Ordinarily, I am in an impregnable position when it comes to conserving my tender ego. When I find myself in the company of someone whose fiction I suspect to be more successful than mine, I cleverly change the subject to non-fiction. When it is non-fiction at which I am about to take a back seat, I discourse learnedly on fiction.

Only with Arthur are both approaches rudely blocked. His science fiction, alas, is among the most imaginative and carefully thought out you can find anywhere; while his non-fiction is both authoritative, clear, and written with fascinating skill. Worst of all, I cannot even fall back on the last resort of sheer quantity, since Arthur is almost as prolific in both fact and fiction as I am.

The final straw was the fact that Arthur did with ease and aplomb what I could not. At the Convention at which *he* was the Guest of Honor, he rose from his seat to accept a Hugo for his short story "The Star," and so excellent a story was it and so well-preserved was the award, that I found my traitorous hands applauding with wild joy.

Nevertheless, I must admit that some mornings, as I comb my luxuriant shock of brown, wavy hair, I find myself rather pleased that Arthur is a bit on the bald side. Serves him right, say I.

# THE STAR

It is three thousand light-years to the Vatican. Once I believed that space could have no power over Faith. Just as I believed that the heavens declared the glory of God's handiwork. Now I have seen that handiwork, and my faith is sorely troubled.

I stare at the crucifix that hangs on the cabin wall above the Mark VI computer, and for the first time in my life I wonder if it is no more than an empty symbol.

I have told no one yet, but the truth cannot be concealed. The data are there for anyone to read, recorded on the countless miles of magnetic tape and the thousands of photographs we are carrying back to Earth. Other scientists can interpret them as easily as I can—more easily, in all probability. I am not one who would condone that tampering with the Truth which often gave my Order a bad name in the olden days.

The crew is already sufficiently depressed, I wonder how they will take this ultimate irony. Few of them have any religious faith, yet they will not relish using this final weapon in their campaign against me —that private, good-natured but fundamentally serious war which lasted all the way from Earth. It amused them to have a Jesuit as chief astrophysicist: Dr. Chandler, for instance, could never get over it (why are medical men such notorious atheists?). Sometimes he would meet me on the observation deck, where the lights are always low so that the stars shine with undiminished glory. He would come up to me in the gloom and stand staring out of the great oval port, while the heavens crawled slowly round us as the ship turned end over end with the residual spin we had never bothered to correct.

"Well, Father," he would say at last. "It goes on forever and forever, and perhaps *Something* made it. But how you can believe that Something has a special interest in us and our miserable little world—that just beats me." Then the argument would start, while the stars and nebulae would swing around us in silent, endless arcs beyond the flawlessly clear plastic of the observation port.

It was, I think, the apparent incongruity of my position which . . . yes, *amused* . . . the crew. In vain I would point to my three papers in the *Astrophysical Journal,* my five in the *Monthly Notices of the Royal Astronomical Society.* I would remind them that our Order has long been famous for its scientific works. We may be few now, but ever since the eighteenth century we have made contributions to astronomy and geophysics out of all proportions to our numbers.

Will my report on the Phoenix Nebula end our thousand years of history? It will end, I fear, much more than that.

I do not know who gave the Nebula its name, which seems to me a very bad one. If it contains a prophecy, it is one which cannot be verified for several thousand million years. Even the word nebula is misleading: this is a far smaller object than those stupendous clouds of mist—the stuff of unborn stars—which are scattered throughout the length of the Milky Way. On the cosmic scale, indeed, the Phoenix Nebula is a tiny thing—a tenuous shell of gas surrounding a single star.

Or what is left of a star . . .

The Rubens engraving of Loyola seems to mock me as it hangs there above the spectrophotometer tracings. What would *you,* Father, have made of this knowledge that has come into my keeping, so far from the little world that was all the universe you knew? Would your faith have risen to the challenge, as mine has failed to do?

You gaze into the distance, Father, but I have traveled a distance beyond any that you could have imagined when you founded our Order a thousand years ago. No other survey ship has been so far from Earth: we are at the very frontiers of the explored universe. We set out to reach the Phoenix Nebula, we succeeded, and we are homeward bound with our burden of knowledge. I wish I could lift that burden from my shoulders, but I call to you in vain across the centuries and the light-years that lie between us.

On the book you are holding the words are plain to read. AD MAIOREM DEI GLORIAM the message runs, but it is a message I can no longer believe. Would you still believe it, if you could see what we have found?

We knew, of course, what the Phoenix Nebula was. Every year, in *our* galaxy alone, more than a hundred stars explode, blazing for a few hours or days with thousands of times their normal brilliance before they sink back into death and obscurity. Such are the ordinary novae —the commonplace disasters of the universe. I have recorded the spectrograms and light-curves of dozens, since I started working at the lunar observatory.

But three or four times in every thousand years occurs something beside which even a nova pales into total insignificance.

When a star becomes a *supernova*, it may for a little while outshine all the massed suns of the galaxy. The Chinese astronomers watched this happen in 1054 A.D., not knowing what it was they saw. Five centuries later, in 1572, a supernova blazed in Cassiopeia so brilliantly that it was visible in the daylight sky. There have been three more in the thousand years that have passed since then.

Our mission was to visit the remnants of such a catastrophe, to reconstruct the events that led up to it, and, if possible, to learn its cause. We came slowly in through the concentric shells of gas that had been blasted out six thousand years before, yet were expanding still. They were immensely hot, radiating still with a fierce violet light, but far too tenuous to do us any damage. When the star had exploded, its outer layers had been driven upwards with such speed that they had escaped completely from its gravitational field. Now they formed a hollow shell large enough to engulf a thousand solar systems, and at its center burned the tiny, fantastic object which the star had now become—a white dwarf, smaller than the Earth yet weighing a million times as much.

The glowing gas shells were all around us, banishing the normal night of interstellar space. We were flying into the center of a cosmic bomb that had detonated millennia ago and whose incandescent fragments were still hurtling apart. The immense scale of the explosion, and the fact that the debris already covered a volume of space many billions of miles across, robbed the scene of any visible movement. It would take decades before the unaided eye could detect any motion in these tortured wisps and eddies of gas, yet the sense of turbulent expansion was overwhelming.

We had checked our primary drive hours before, and were drifting slowly towards the fierce little star ahead. Once it had been a sun like our own, but it had squandered in a few hours the energy that should have kept it shining for a million years. Now it was a shrunken miser, hoarding its resources as if trying to make amends for its prodigal youth.

No one seriously expected to find planets. If there had been any before the explosion, they would have been boiled into puffs of vapor, and their substance lost in the greater wreckage of the star itself. But we made the automatic search, as always when approaching an unknown sun, and presently we found a single small world circling the star at an immense distance. It must have been the Pluto of this vanished solar system, orbiting on the frontiers of the night. Too far from the central sun ever to have known life, its remoteness had saved it from the fate of all its lost companions.

The passing fires had seared its rocks and burnt away the mantle of frozen gas that must have covered it in the days before the disaster. We landed, and we found the Vault.

Its builders had made sure that we should. The monolithic marker that stood above the entrance was now a fused stump, but even the first long-range photographs told us that here was the work of intelligence. A little later we detected the continent-wide pattern of radioactivity that had been buried in the rock. Even if the pylon above the Vault had been destroyed, this would have remained, an immovable and all but eternal beacon calling to the stars. Our ship fell towards this gigantic bull's-eye like an arrow into its target.

The pylon must have been a mile high when it was built, but now it looked like a candle that had melted down into a puddle of wax. It took us a week to drill through the fused rock, since we did not have the proper tools for a task like this. We were astronomers, not archaeologists, but we could improvise. Our original program was forgotten: this lonely monument, reared at such labor at the greatest possible distance from the doomed sun, could have only one meaning. A civilization which knew it was about to die had made its last bid for immortality.

It will take us generations to examine all the treasures that were placed in the Vault. *They* had plenty of time to prepare, for their sun must have given its first warnings many years before the final detonation. Everything that they wished to preserve, all the fruits of their genius, they brought here to this distant world in the days before the end, hoping that some other race would find them and that they would not be utterly forgotten.

If only they had had a little more time! They could travel freely enough between the planets of their own sun, but they had not yet learned to cross the interstellar gulfs, and the nearest solar system was a hundred light-years away.

Even if they had not been so disturbingly human as their sculpture shows, we could not have helped admiring them and grieving for their fate. They left thousands of visual records and the machines for projecting them, together with elaborate pictorial instructions from which it will not be difficult to learn their written language. We have examined many of these records, and brought to life for the first time in six thousand years the warmth and beauty of a civilization which in many ways must have been superior to our own. Perhaps they only showed us the best, and one can hardly blame them. But their worlds were very lovely, and their cities were built with a grace that matches anything of ours. We have watched them at work and play, and listened to their musical speech sounding across the centuries. One scene is still before my eyes—a group of children on a beach of strange blue sand, playing in the waves as children play on Earth.

And sinking into the sea, still warm and friendly and life-giving, is the sun that will soon turn traitor and obliterate all this innocent happiness.

Perhaps if we had not been so far from home and so vulnerable to loneliness, we should not have been so deeply moved. Many of us had seen the ruins of ancient civilizations on other worlds, but they had never affected us so profoundly.

This tragedy was unique. It was one thing for a race to fail and die, as nations and cultures have done on Earth. But to be destroyed so completely in the full flower of its achievement, leaving no survivors—how could that be reconciled with the mercy of God?

My colleagues have asked me that, and I have given what answers I can. Perhaps you could have done better, Father Loyola, but I have found nothing in the *Exercitia Spiritualia* that helps me here. They were not an evil people: I do not know what gods they worshipped, if indeed they worshipped any. But I have looked back at them across the centuries, and have watched while the loveliness they used their last strength to preserve was brought forth again into the light of their shrunken sun.

I know the answers that my colleagues will give when they get back to Earth. They will say that the universe has no purpose and no plan, that since a hundred suns explode every year in our galaxy, at this very moment some race is dying in the depths of space. Whether that race has done good or evil during its lifetime will make no difference in the end: there is no divine justice, *for there is no God*.

Yet, of course, what we have seen proves nothing of the sort. Anyone who argues thus is being swayed by emotion, not logic. God has no need to justify His actions to man. He who built the universe can destroy it when He chooses. It is arrogance—it is perilously near blasphemy—for us to say what He may or may not do.

This I could have accepted, hard though it is to look upon whole worlds and peoples thrown into the furnace. But there comes a point when even the deepest faith must falter, and now, as I look at my calculations, I know I have reached that point at last.

We could not tell, before we reached the nebula, how long ago the explosion took place. Now, from the astronomical evidence and the record in the rocks of that one surviving planet, I have been able to date it very exactly. I know in what year the light of this colossal conflagration reached Earth. I know how brilliantly the supernova whose corpse now dwindles behind our speeding ship once shone in terrestrial skies. I know how it must have blazed low in the East before sunrise, like a beacon in that Oriental dawn.

There can be no reasonable doubt: the ancient mystery is solved at last. Yet—O God, there were so many stars you *could* have used.

What was the need to give these people to the fire, that the symbol of their passing might shine above Bethlehem?

*1958*
*16th CONVENTION*
*LOS ANGELES*

Avram Davidson won his way into my heart with a short story in *The Magazine of Fantasy and Science Fiction* in which a character refers to *me*.

It was with no little dismay then, that I met the gentleman himself at the 17th Convention (Detroit, 1959) for it was then I found out exactly what it was that had gained entrance to my heart. It explained the tickling sensation in my chest and the periodic sieges of heartburn that had been overcoming me; for be it known, oh, gentle readers, that Avram is mostly Beard.

Now there are beards and beards. There are prissy Vandykes that bespeak the scholarly man of culture; there are the little token bits of hair that spell beatnik; there are the oddly shaped beavers that mark the Civil War general.

Here, however, we have a full black beard, rippling its mighty length down Avram's majestically rotund figure. Avram need wear no tie, collar nor shirt stud. In fact, Avram need wear no belt buckle. It is only necessary for a man with a red lantern to precede Avram wherever he goes, lest the sight of the Beard coming upon people unexpectedly produce fainting spells and, in crowds, destructive panic.

But the Beard has its uses. Avram is a dangerous man in any battle of wits, and a sharp retort delivered in his deceptively sweet voice could wreak real damage, were it not softened and gentled by passage through the numerous filter-like crannies and byways of the Beard. His deftest repartee is in that way turned into mellifluously caressing remarks that make him beloved by all.

Furthermore, at those times when he chooses to knot his Beard around his waist and out of the way, so that his hands can reach the typewriter unencumbered, he can write darned good stories. One of them, "Or All the Seas with Oysters," won for him the Hugo at the 16th Convention (Los Angeles, 1958) at which point, I have been told (I wasn't there in person) his Beard turned momentarily red with joy.

# 5

# OR ALL THE SEAS WITH OYSTERS

When the man came in to the F & O Bike Shop, Oscar greeted him with a hearty "Hi, there!" Then, as he looked closer at the middle-aged visitor with the eyeglasses and business suit, his forehead creased and he began to snap his thick fingers.

"Oh, say, I know you," he muttered. "Mr.—um—name's on the tip of my tongue, doggone it . . ." Oscar was a barrel-chested fellow. He had orange hair.

"Why, sure you do," the man said. There was a Lion's emblem in his lapel. "Remember, you sold me a girl's bicycle with gears, for my daughter? We got to talking about that red French racing bike your partner was working on—"

Oscar slapped his big hand down on the cash register. He raised his head and rolled his eyes up. "Mr. Whatney!" Mr. Whatney beamed. "Oh, *sure*. Gee, how could I forget? And we went across the street afterward and had a couple a beers. Well, how you *been*, Mr. Whatney? I guess the bike—it was an English model, wasn't it? Yeah. It must of given satisfaction or you would of been back, huh?"

Mr. Whatney said the bicycle was fine, just fine. Then he said, "I understand there's been a change, though. You're all by yourself now. Your partner . . ."

Oscar looked down, pushed his lower lip out, nodded. "You heard, huh? Ee-up. I'm all by myself now. Over three months now."

The partnership had come to an end three months ago, but it had been faltering long before then. Ferd liked books, long-playing records and high-level conversation. Oscar liked beer, bowling and women. Any women. Any time.

The shop was located near the park; it did a big trade in renting bicycles to picnickers. If a woman was barely old enough to be *called* a woman, and not quite old enough to be called an *old* woman, or if she was anywhere in between, and if she was alone, Oscar would ask, "How does that machine feel to you? All right?"

"Why . . . I guess so."

Taking another bicycle, Oscar would say, "Well, I'll just ride along a little bit with you, to make sure. Be right back, Ferd." Ferd always nodded gloomily. He knew that Oscar would not be right back. Later, Oscar would say, "Hope you made out in the shop as good as I did in the park."

"Leaving me all alone here all that time," Ferd grumbled.

And Oscar usually flared up. "Okay, then, next time *you* go and leave *me* stay here. See if I begrudge you a little fun." But he knew, of course, that Ferd—tall, thin, pop-eyed Ferd—would never go. "Do you good," Oscar said, slapping his sternum. "Put hair on your chest."

Ferd muttered that he had all the hair on his chest that he needed. He would glance down covertly at his lower arms; they were thick with long black hair, though his upper arms were slick and white. It was already like that when he was in high school, and some of the others would laugh at him—call him "Ferdie the Birdie." They knew it bothered him, but they did it anyway. How was it possible—he wondered then; he still did now—for people deliberately to hurt someone else who hadn't hurt them? How was it possible?

He worried over other things. All the time.

"The Communists—" He shook his head over the newspaper. Oscar offered an advice about the Communists in two short words. Or it might be capital punishment. "Oh, what a terrible thing if an innocent man was to be executed," Ferd moaned. Oscar said that was the guy's tough luck.

"Hand me that tire-iron," Oscar said.

And Ferd worried even about other people's minor concerns. Like the time the couple came in with the tandem and the baby-basket on it. Free air was all they took; then the woman decided to change the diaper and one of the safety pins broke.

"Why are there never any safety pins?" the woman fretted, rummaging here and rummaging there. "There are *never* any safety pins."

Ferd made sympathetic noises, went to see if he had any; but, though he was sure there'd been some in the office, he couldn't find them. So they drove off with one side of the diaper tied in a clumsy knot.

At lunch, Ferd said it was too bad about the safety pins. Oscar dug his teeth into a sandwich, tugged, tore, chewed, swallowed. Ferd liked to experiment with sandwich spreads—the one he liked most was cream-cheese, olives, anchovy and avocado, mashed up with a little mayonnaise—but Oscar always had the same pink luncheon-meat.

"It must be difficult with a baby." Ferd nibbled. "Not just traveling, but raising it."

Oscar said, "Jeez, there's drugstores in every block, and if you can't read, you can at least reckernize them."

"Drugstores? Oh, to buy safety pins, you mean."

"Yeah. Safety pins."

"But . . . you know . . . it's true . . . there's never any safety pins when you look."

Oscar uncapped his beer, rinsed the first mouthful around. "Aha! Always plenny of clothes hangers, though. Throw 'em out every month, next month same closet's full of 'm again. Now whatcha wanna do in your spare time, you invent a device which it'll make safety pins outa clothes hangers."

Ferd nodded abstractedly. "But in my spare time I'm working on the French racer . . ." It was a beautiful machine, light, low-slung, swift, red and shining. You felt like a bird when you rode it. But, good as it was, Ferd knew he could make it better. He showed it to everybody who came in the place until his interest slackened.

Nature was his latest hobby, or, rather, reading about Nature. Some kids had wandered by from the park one day with tin cans in which they had put salamanders and toads, and they proudly showed them to Ferd. After that, the work on the red racer slowed down and he spent his spare time on natural history books.

"Mimicry!" he cried to Oscar. "A wonderful thing!"

Oscar looked up interestedly from the bowling scores in the paper. "I seen Edie Adams on TV the other night, doing her imitation of Marilyn Monroe. Boy, oh, boy."

Ferd was irritated, shook his head. "Not that kind of mimicry. I mean how insects and arachnids will mimic the shapes of leaves and twigs and so on, to escape being eaten by birds or other insects and arachnids."

A scowl of disbelief passed over Oscar's heavy face. "You mean they change their *shapes?* What you giving me?"

"Oh, it's true. Sometimes the mimicry is for aggressive purposes, though—like a South African turtle that looks like a rock and so the fish swim up to it and then it catches them. Or that spider in Sumatra.

When it lies on its back, it looks like a bird dropping. Catches butterflies that way."

Oscar laughed, a disgusted and incredulous noise. It died away as he turned back to the bowling scores. One hand groped at his pocket, came away, scratched absently at the orange thicket under the shirt, then went patting his hip pocket.

"Where's that pencil?" he muttered, got up, stomped into the office, pulled open drawers. His loud cry of "Hey!" brought Ferd into the tiny room.

"What's the matter?" Ferd asked.

Oscar pointed to a drawer. "Remember that time you claimed there were no safety pins here? Look—whole gahdamn drawer is full of 'em."

Ferd stared, scratched his head, said feebly that he was certain he'd looked there before . . .

A contralto voice from outside asked, "Anybody here?"

Oscar at once forgot the desk and its contents, called, "Be right with you," and was gone. Ferd followed him slowly.

There was a young woman in the shop, a rather massively built young woman, with muscular calves and a deep chest. She was pointing out the seat of her bicycle to Oscar, who was saying "Uh-huh" and looking more at her than at anything else. "It's just a little too far forward ("Uh-huh"), as you can see. A wrench is all I need ("Uh-huh"). It was silly of me to forget my tools."

Oscar repeated, "Uh-huh" automatically, then snapped to. "Fix it in a jiffy," he said, and—despite her insistence that she could do it herself —he did fix it. Though not quite in a jiffy. He refused money. He prolonged the conversation as long as he could.

"Well, thank *you*," the young woman said. "And now I've got to go."

"That machine feel all right to you now?"

"Perfectly. Thanks—"

"Tell you what, I'll just ride along with you a little bit, just—"

Pear-shaped notes of laughter lifted the young woman's bosom. "Oh, you couldn't keep up with me! My machine is a *racer!*"

The moment he saw Oscar's eye flit to the corner, Ferd knew what he had in mind. He stepped forward. His cry of "No" was drowned out by his partner's loud, "Well, I guess this racer here can keep up with yours!"

The young woman giggled richly, said, well, they would see about that, and was off. Oscar, ignoring Ferd's outstretched hand, jumped on the French bike and was gone. Ferd stood in the doorway, watching the two figures, hunched over their handlebars, vanish down the road into the park. He went slowly back inside.

It was almost evening before Oscar returned, sweaty but smiling. Smiling broadly. "Hey, what a babe!" he cried. He wagged his head, he whistled, he made gestures, noises like escaping steam. "Boy, oh, boy, what an afternoon!"

"Give me the bike," Ferd demanded.

Oscar said, yeah, sure; turned it over to him and went to wash. Ferd looked at the machine. The red enamel was covered with dust; there was mud spattered and dirt and bits of dried grass. It seemed soiled—degraded. He had felt like a swift bird when he rode it . . .

Oscar came out wet and beaming. He gave a cry of dismay, ran over.

"Stand away," said Ferd, gesturing with the knife. He slashed the tires, the seat and seat cover, again and again.

"You crazy?" Oscar yelled. "You outa your mind? Ferd, no, don't, Ferd—"

Ferd cut the spokes, bent them, twisted them. He took the heaviest hammer and pounded the frame into shapelessness, and then he kept on pounding till his breath was gasping.

"You're not only crazy," Oscar said bitterly, "you're rotten jealous. You can go to hell." He stomped away.

Ferd, feeling sick and stiff, locked up, went slowly home. He had no taste for reading, turned out the light and fell into bed, where he lay awake for hours, listening to the rustling noises of the night and thinking hot, twisted thoughts.

They didn't speak to each other for days after that, except for the necessities of the work. The wreckage of the French racer lay behind the shop. For about two weeks, neither wanted to go out back where he'd have to see it.

One morning Ferd arrived to be greeted by his partner, who began to shake his head in astonishment even before he started speaking. "How did you *do* it, how did you *do* it, Ferd? Jeez, what a beautiful job—I gotta hand it to you—no more hard feelings, huh, Ferd?"

Ferd took his hand. "Sure, sure. But what are you talking about?"

Oscar led him out back. There was the red racer, all in one piece, not a mark or scratch on it, its enamel bright as ever. Ferd gaped. He squatted down and examined it. It *was* his machine. Every change, every improvement he had made, was there.

He straightened up slowly. "Regeneration . . ."

"Huh? What say?" Oscar asked. Then, "Hey, kiddo, you're all white.

Whad you do, stay up all night and didn't get no sleep? Come on in and siddown. But I still don't see how you done it."

Inside, Ferd sat down. He wet his lips. He said, "Oscar—listen—"

"Yeah?"

"Oscar. You know what regeneration is? No? Listen. Some kinds of lizards, you grab them by the tail, the tail breaks off and they grow a new one. If a lobster loses a claw, it regenerates another one. Some kinds of worms—and hydras and starfish—you cut them into pieces, each piece will grow back the missing parts. Salamanders can regenerate lost hands, and frogs can grow legs back."

"No kidding, Ferd. But, uh, I mean: Nature. Very interesting. But to get back to the bike now—how'd you manage to fix it so good?"

"I never touched it. It regenerated. Like a newt. Or a lobster."

Oscar considered this. He lowered his head, looked up at Ferd from under his eyebrows. "Well, now, Ferd . . . Look . . . How come all broke bikes don't do that?"

"This isn't an ordinary bike. I mean it isn't a real bike." Catching Oscar's look, he shouted, "Well, it's *true!*"

The shout changed Oscar's attitude from bafflement to incredulity. He got up. "So for the sake of argument, let's say all that stuff about the bugs and the eels or whatever the hell you were talking about is true. But they're alive. A bike ain't." He looked down triumphantly.

Ferd shook his leg from side to side, looked at it. "A crystal isn't, either, but a broken crystal can regenerate itself if the conditions are right. Oscar, go see if the safety pins are still in the desk. Please, Oscar?"

He listened as Oscar, muttering, pulled the desk drawers out, rummaged in them, slammed them shut, tramped back.

"Naa," he said. "All gone. Like that lady said that time, and you said, there never are any safety pins when you want 'em. They disap—Ferd? What're—"

Ferd jerked open the closet door, jumped back as a shoal of clothes hangers clattered out.

"And like *you* say," Ferd said with a twist of his mouth, "on the other hand, there are always plenty of clothes hangers. There weren't any here before."

Oscar shrugged. "I don't see what you're getting at. But anybody could of got in here and took the pins and left the hangers. *I* could of— but I didn't. Or *you* could of. Maybe—" He narrowed his eyes. "Maybe you walked in your sleep and done it. You better see a doctor. Jeez, you look rotten."

Ferd went back and sat down, put his head in his hands. "I *feel* rotten. I'm scared, Oscar. Scared of what?" He breathed noisily. "I'll tell you. Like I explained before, about how things that live in the wild places, they mimic other things there. Twigs, leaves . . . toads that look like rocks. Well, suppose there are . . . things . . . that live in people places. Cities. Houses. These things could imitate—well, other kinds of things you find in people places—"

"*People* places, for crise sake!"

"Maybe they're a different kind of life-form. Maybe they get their nourishment out of the elements in the air. You know what safety pins *are*—these other kinds of them? Oscar, the safety pins are the pupa-forms and then they, like, *hatch*. Into the larval-forms. Which look just like coat hangers. They feel like them, even, but they're not. Oscar, they're not, not really, not really, not . . ."

He began to cry into his hands. Oscar looked at him. He shook his head.

After a minute, Ferd controlled himself somewhat. He snuffled. "All these bicycles the cops find, and they hold them waiting for owners to show up, and then we buy them at the sale because no owners show up because there aren't any, and the same with the ones the kids are always trying to sell us, and they say they just found them, and they really did because they were never made in a factory. They grew. They grow. You smash them and throw them away, they regenerate."

Oscar turned to someone who wasn't there and waggled his head. "Hoo, boy," he said. Then, to Ferd: "You mean one day there's a safety pin and the next day instead there's a coat hanger?"

Ferd said, "One day there's a cocoon; the next day there's a moth. One day there's an egg; the next day there's a chicken. But with . . . these it doesn't happen in the open daytime where you can see it. But at night, Oscar—at night you can *hear* it happening. All the little noises in the nighttime, Oscar—"

Oscar said, "Then how come we ain't up to our belly-button in bikes? If I had a bike for every coat hanger—"

But Ferd had considered that, too. If every codfish egg, he explained, or every oyster spawn grew to maturity, a man could walk across the ocean on the backs of all the codfish or oysters there'd be. So many died, so many were eaten by predatory creatures, that Nature had to produce a maximum in order to allow a minimum to arrive at maturity. And Oscar's question was: then who, uh, eats the, uh, coat hangers?

Ferd's eyes focused through wall, buildings, park, more buildings, to the horizon. "You got to get the picture. I'm not talking about real pins or hangers. I got a name for the others—'false friends,' I call them. In high school French, we had to watch out for French words that looked like English words, but really were different. 'Faux amis,' they call them. False friends. Pseudo-pins. Pseudo-hangers . . . Who eats them? I don't know for sure. Pseudo-vacuum cleaners, maybe?"

His partner, with a loud groan, slapped his hands against his thighs. He said, "Ferd, Ferd, for crise sake. You know what's the trouble with you? You talk about oysters, but you forgot what they're good for. You forgot there's two kinds of people in the world. Close up them books, them bug books and French books. Get out, mingle, meet people. Soak up some brew. You know what? The next time Norma—that's this broad's name with the racing bike—the next time she comes here, *you* take the red racer and *you* go out in the woods with her. I won't mind. And I don't think she will, either. Not *too* much."

But Ferd said no. "I never want to touch the red racer again. I'm afraid of it."

At this, Oscar pulled him to his feet, dragged him protestingly out to the back and forced him to get on the French machine. "Only way to conquer your fear of it!"

Ferd started off, white-faced, wobbling. And in a moment was on the ground, rolling and thrashing, screaming.

Oscar pulled him away from the machine.

"It threw me!" Ferd yelled. "It tried to kill me! Look—blood!"

His partner said it was a bump that threw him—it was his own fear. The blood? A broken spoke. Grazed his cheek. And he insisted Ferd get on the bicycle again, to conquer his fear.

But Ferd had grown hysterical. He shouted that no man was safe— that mankind had to be warned. It took Oscar a long time to pacify him and to get him to go home and into bed.

He didn't tell all this to Mr. Whatney, of course. He merely said that his partner had gotten fed up with the bicycle business.

"It don't pay to worry and try to change the world," he pointed out. "I always say take things the way they are. If you can't lick 'em, join 'em."

Mr. Whatney said that was his philosophy, exactly. He asked how things were, since.

"Well . . . not *too* bad. I'm engaged, you know. Name's Norma. Crazy about bicycles. Everything considered, things aren't bad at all. More work, yes, but I can do things all my own way, so . . ."

Mr. Whatney nodded. He glanced around the shop. "I see they're still making drop-frame bikes," he said, "though, with so many women wearing slacks, I wonder they bother."

Oscar said, "Well, I dunno. I kinda like it that way. Ever stop to think that bicycles are like people? I mean, of all the machines in the world, only bikes come male and female."

Mr. Whatney gave a little giggle, said that was *right*, he had never thought of it like that before. Then Oscar asked if Mr. Whatney had anything in particular in mind—not that he wasn't always welcome.

"Well, I wanted to look over what you've got. My boy's birthday is coming up—"

Oscar nodded sagely. "Now here's a job," he said, "which you can't get it in any other place but here. Specialty of the house. Combines the best features of the French racer and the American standard, but it's made right here, and it comes in three models—Junior, Intermediate and Regular. Beautiful, ain't it?"

Mr. Whatney observed that, say, that might be just the ticket. "By the way," he asked, "what's become of the French racer, the red one, used to be here?"

Oscar's face twitched. Then it grew bland and innocent and he leaned over and nudged his customer. "Oh, *that* one. Old Frenchy? Why, I put *him* out to stud!"

And they laughed and they laughed, and after they told a few more stories they concluded the sale, and they had a few beers and they laughed some more. And then they said what a shame it was about poor Ferd, poor old Ferd, who had been found in his own closet with an unraveled coat hanger coiled tightly around his neck.

*1959*
*17th* *CONVENTION*
*DETROIT*

# Clifford D. Simak

Clifford D. Simak is one of the oldest and most nearly invisible of my friends. It came to pass after this fashion.

In 1938, before I had published any stories of my own, I, like all science fiction fans, considered myself a redoubtable critic of the medium, and I never hesitated to write letters to the editor denouncing those stories I disliked, and doing so, moreover, in the most uncompromising tones imaginable. I did so in connection with a story entitled "Rule 18" by Clifford D. Simak.

Cliff promptly wrote me a letter asking me for more details of what he had done wrong so that he could improve himself. (No, he was not being sarcastic; he really meant it. That's the kind of guy he is.) This forced me to reread the story and to realize that what really bothered me was Cliff's habit of jumping suddenly from one scene to the next, changing time, place and personnel in complete abandon.

At first reading, this was unsettling, but the second time round, I saw the point. It introduced a sense of swift action and, properly handled, it lent a mood of heightened drama. I wrote a letter of apology and, without even a twinge of conscience, adopted the device myself in the stories I was then trying to write.

Our friendship was established and we corresponded thereafter for over twenty years without once meeting each other. As the fates would have it, those conventions I attended, he could not, and those which he attended, I could not. Even at the 17th Convention (Detroit, 1959) when I handed out the Hugo awarded his story "The Big Front Yard," it was accepted by proxy.

And then, finally, on October 20, 1961, we both found ourselves in New York simultaneously. I had forgiven him, by then, his lack of consideration in winning a Hugo, and we had lunch together. After 23 years, I met Cliff in the flesh.

Now I know very well what the proper denouement should be: Old time pen-pals meet after many years and long-held illusions are shattered.

Sorry. Truth is duller than fiction. It was as though we had always known each other in person. We had a delightful lunch together; a pair of old friends communicating for once in a slightly modified fashion, by sound-waves rather than through marks on paper.

And we still correspond.

# 6

# THE BIG FRONT YARD

Hiram Taine came awake and sat up in his bed.

Towser was barking and scratching at the floor.

"Shut up," Taine told the dog.

Towser cocked quizzical ears at him and then resumed the barking and scratching at the floor.

Taine rubbed his eyes. He ran a hand through his rat's-nest head of hair. He considered lying down again and pulling up the covers.

But not with Towser barking.

"What's the matter with you, anyhow?" he asked Towser, with not a a little wrath.

"*Whuff*," said Towser, industriously proceeding with his scratching at the floor.

"If you want out," said Taine, "all you got to do is open the screen door. You know how it is done. You do it all the time."

Towser quit his barking and sat down heavily, watching his master getting out of bed.

Taine put on his shirt and pulled on his trousers, but didn't bother with his shoes.

Towser ambled over to a corner, put his nose down to the baseboard and snuffled moistly.

"You got a mouse?" asked Taine.

"*Whuff*," said Towser, most emphatically.

"I can't ever remember you making such a row about a mouse," Taine said, slightly puzzled. "You must be off your rocker."

It was a beautiful summer morning. Sunlight was pouring through the open window.

Good day for fishing, Taine told himself, then remembered that there'd be no fishing, for he had to go out and look up that old four-poster maple bed that he had heard about up Woodman way. More than likely, he thought, they'd want twice as much as it was worth. It was getting so, he told himself, that a man couldn't make an honest dollar. Everyone was getting smart about antiques.

He got up off the bed and headed for the living room.

"Come on," he said to Towser.

Towser came along, pausing now and then to snuffle into corners and to whuffle at the floor.

"You got it bad," said Taine.

Maybe it's a rat, he thought. The house was getting old.

He opened the screen door and Towser went outside.

"Leave that woodchuck be today," Taine advised him. "It's a losing battle. You'll never dig him out."

Towser went around the corner of the house.

Taine noticed that something had happened to the sign that hung on the post beside the driveway. One of the chains had become unhooked and the sign was dangling.

He padded out across the driveway slab and the grass, still wet with dew, to fix the sign. There was nothing wrong with it—just the unhooked chain. Might have been the wind, he thought, or some passing urchin. Although probably not an urchin. He got along with kids. They never bothered him, like they did some others in the village. Banker Stevens, for example. They were always pestering Stevens.

He stood back a way to be sure the sign was straight.

It read, in big letters:

### HANDY MAN

And under that, in smaller lettering:

### *I fix anything*

And under that:

#### ANTIQUES FOR SALE

### *What have you got to trade?*

Maybe, he told himself, he'd ought to have two signs, one for his fix-it shop and one for antiques and trading. Some day, when he had the time, he thought, he'd paint a couple of new ones. One for each side of the driveway. It would look neat that way.

He turned around and looked across the road at Turner's Woods. It was a pretty sight, he thought. A sizable piece of woods like that right at the edge of town. It was a place for birds and rabbits and woodchucks and squirrels and it was full of forts built through generations by the boys of Willow Bend.

Some day, of course, some smart operator would buy it up and start a housing development or something equally objectionable and when that happened a big slice of his own boyhood would be cut out of his life.

Towser came around the corner of the house. He was sidling along, sniffing at the lowest row of siding and his ears were cocked with interest.

"That dog is nuts," said Taine and went inside.

He went into the kitchen, his bare feet slapping on the floor.

He filled the teakettle, set it on the stove and turned the burner on underneath the kettle.

He turned on the radio, forgetting that it was out of kilter.

When it didn't make a sound, he remembered and, disgusted, snapped it off. That was the way it went, he thought. He fixed other people's stuff, but never got around to fixing any of his own.

He went into the bedroom and put on his shoes. He threw the bed together.

Back in the kitchen the stove had failed to work again. The burner beneath the kettle was still cold.

Taine hauled off and kicked the stove. He lifted the kettle and held his palm above the burner. In a few seconds he could detect some heat.

"Worked again," he told himself.

Some day, he knew, kicking the stove would fail to work. When that happened, he'd have to get to work on it. Probably wasn't more than a loose connection.

He put the kettle back onto the stove.

There was a clatter out in front and Taine went out to see what was going on.

Beasly, the Horton's yardboy-chauffeur-gardener-et cetera was backing a rickety old truck up the driveway. Beside him sat Abbie Horton, the wife of H. Henry Horton, the village's most important citizen. In the back of the truck, lashed on with ropes and half-protected by a garish red and purple quilt, stood a mammoth television set. Taine recognized it from of old. It was a good ten years out of date and still, by any standard, it was the most expensive set ever to grace any home in Willow Bend.

Abbie hopped out of the truck. She was an energetic, bustling, bossy woman.

"Good morning, Hiram," she said. "Can you fix this set again?"

"Never saw anything that I couldn't fix," said Taine, but nevertheless he eyed the set with something like dismay. It was not the first time he had tangled with it and he knew what was ahead.

"It might cost you more than it's worth," he warned her. "What you really need is a new one. This set is getting old and—"

"That's just what Henry said," Abbie told him, tartly. "Henry wants to get one of the color sets. But I won't part with this one. It's not just TV, you know. It's a combination with radio and a record player and the wood and style are just right for the other furniture, and besides—"

"Yes, I know," said Taine, who'd heard it all before.

Poor old Henry, he thought. What a life the man must lead. Up at that computer plant all day long, shooting off his face and bossing everyone, then coming home to a life of petty tyranny.

"Beasly," said Abbie, in her best drill-sergeant voice, "you get right up there and get that thing untied."

"Yes'm," Beasly said. He was a gangling, loose-jointed man who didn't look too bright.

"And see you be careful with it. I don't want it all scratched up."

"Yes'm," said Beasly.

"I'll help," Taine offered.

The two climbed into the truck and began unlashing the old monstrosity.

"It's heavy," Abbie warned. "You two be careful of it."

"Yes'm," said Beasly.

It was heavy and it was an awkward thing to boot, but Beasly and Taine horsed it around to the back of the house and up the stoop and through the back door and down the basement stairs, with Abbie following eagle-eyed behind them, alert to the slightest scratch.

The basement was Taine's combination workshop and display room for antiques. One end of it was filled with benches and with tools and machinery and boxes full of odds and ends and piles of just plain junk were scattered everywhere. The other end housed a collection of rickety chairs, sagging bedposts, ancient highboys, equally ancient lowboys, old coal scuttles painted gold, heavy iron fireplace screens and a lot of other stuff that he had collected from far and wide for as little as he could possibly pay for it.

He and Beasly set the TV down carefully on the floor. Abbie watched them narrowly from the stairs.

"Why, Hiram," she said, excited, "you put a ceiling in the basement. It looks a whole lot better."

"Huh?" asked Taine.

"The ceiling. I said you put in a ceiling."

Taine jerked his head up and what she said was true. There was a ceiling there, but he'd never put it in.

He gulped a little and lowered his head, then jerked it quickly up and had another look. The ceiling was still there.

"It's not that block stuff," said Abbie with open admiration. "You can't see any joints at all. How did you manage it?"

Taine gulped again and got back his voice. "Something I thought up," he told her weakly.

"You'll have to come over and do it to our basement. Our basement is a sight. Beasly put the ceiling in the amusement room, but Beasly is all thumbs."

"Yes'm," Beasly said contritely.

"When I get the time," Taine promised, ready to promise anything to get them out of there.

"You'd have a lot more time," Abbie told him acidly, "if you weren't gadding around all over the country buying up that broken-down old furniture that you call antiques. Maybe you can fool the city folks when they come driving out here, but you can't fool me."

"I make a lot of money out of some of it," Taine told her calmly.

"And lose your shirt on the rest of it," she said.

"I got some old china that is just the kind of stuff you are looking for," said Taine. "Picked it up just a day or two ago. Made a good buy on it. I can let you have it cheap."

"I'm not interested," she said and clamped her mouth tight shut. She turned around and went back up the stairs.

"She's on the prod today," Beasly said to Taine. "It will be a bad day. It always is when she starts early in the morning."

"Don't pay attention to her," Taine advised.

"I try not to, but it ain't possible. You sure you don't need a man? I'd work for you cheap."

"Sorry, Beasly. Tell you what—come over some night soon and we'll play some checkers."

"I'll do that, Hiram. You're the only one who ever asks me over. All the others ever do is laugh at me or shout."

Abbie's voice came bellowing down the stairs. "Beasly, are you coming? Don't go standing there all day. I have rugs to beat."

"Yes'm," said Beasly, starting up the stairs.

At the truck, Abbie turned on Taine with determination: "You'll get that set fixed right away? I'm lost without it."

"Immediately," said Taine.

He stood and watched them off, then looked around for Towser, but the dog had disappeared. More than likely he was at the woodchuck hole again, in the woods across the road. Gone off, thought Taine, without his breakfast, too.

The teakettle was boiling furiously when Taine got back to the kitchen. He put coffee in the maker and poured in the water. Then he went downstairs.

The ceiling was still there.

He turned on all the lights and walked around the basement, staring up at it.

It was a dazzling white material and it appeared to be translucent—up to a point, that is. One could see into it, but he could not see through it. And there were no signs of seams. It was fitted neatly and tightly around the water pipes and the ceiling lights.

Taine stood on a chair and rapped his knuckles against it sharply. It gave out a bell-like sound, almost exactly as if he'd rapped a fingernail against a thinly-blown goblet.

He got down off the chair and stood there, shaking his head. The whole thing was beyond him. He had spent part of the evening repairing Banker Stevens' lawn mower and there'd been no ceiling then.

He rummaged in a box and found a drill. He dug out one of the smaller bits and fitted it in the drill. He plugged in the cord and climbed on the chair again and tried the bit against the ceiling. The whirling steel slid wildly back and forth. It didn't make a scratch. He switched off the drill and looked closely at the ceiling. There was not a mark upon it. He tried again, pressing against the drill with all his strength. The bit went *ping* and the broken end flew across the basement and hit the wall.

Taine stepped down off the chair. He found another bit and fitted it in the drill and went slowly up the stairs, trying to think. But he was too confused to think. That ceiling should not be up there, but there it was. And unless he went stark, staring crazy and forgetful as well, he had not put it there.

In the living room, he folded back one corner of the worn and faded carpeting and plugged in the drill. He knelt and started drilling in the floor. The bit went smoothly through the old oak flooring, then stopped. He put on more pressure and the drill spun without getting any bite.

And there wasn't supposed to be anything underneath that wood! Nothing to stop a drill. Once through the flooring, it should have dropped into the space between the joists.

Taine disengaged the drill and laid it to one side.

He went into the kitchen and the coffee now was ready. But before he poured it, he pawed through a cabinet drawer and found a pencil flashlight. Back in the living room he shone the light into the hole that the drill had made.

There was something shiny at the bottom of the hole.

He went back to the kitchen and found some day-old doughnuts and poured a cup of coffee. He sat at the kitchen table, eating doughnuts and wondering what to do.

There didn't appear, for the moment at least, much that he could do. He could putter around all day trying to figure out what had happened to his basement and probably not be any wiser than he was right now.

His money-making Yankee soul rebelled against such a horrid waste of time.

There was, he told himself, that maple four-poster that he should be getting to before some unprincipled city antique dealer should run afoul of it. A piece like that, he figured, if a man had any luck at all, should sell at a right good price. He might turn a handsome profit on it if he only worked it right.

Maybe, he thought, he could turn a trade on it. There was the table model TV set that he had traded a pair of ice skates for last winter. Those folks out Woodman way might conceivably be happy to trade the bed for a reconditioned TV set, almost like brand new. After all, they probably weren't using the bed and, he hoped fervently, had no idea of the value of it.

He ate the doughnuts hurriedly and gulped down an extra cup of coffee. He fixed a plate of scraps for Towser and set it outside the door. Then he went down into the basement and got the table TV set and put it in the pickup truck. As an afterthought, he added a reconditioned shotgun which would be perfectly all right if a man were careful not to use these far-reaching, powerful shells, and a few other odds and ends that might come in handy on a trade.

He got back late, for it had been a busy and quite satisfactory day. Not only did he have the four-poster loaded on the truck, but he had as well a rocking chair, a fire screen, a bundle of ancient magazines, an old-fashioned barrel churn, a .walnut highboy and a Governor Winthrop on which some half-baked, slap-happy decorator had applied a coat of apple-green paint. The television set, the shotgun and five dollars had gone into the trade. And what was better yet, he'd managed it so well that the Woodman family probably was dying of laughter at this very moment about how they'd taken him.

He felt a little ashamed of it—they'd been such friendly people. They had treated him so kindly and had him stay for dinner and had sat and talked with him and shown him about the farm and even asked him to stop by if he went through that way again.

He'd wasted the entire day, he thought, and he rather hated that, but maybe it had been worth it to build up his reputation out that way as the sort of character who had softening of the head and didn't know the value of a dollar. That way, maybe some other day, he could do some more business in the neighborhood.

He heard the television set as he opened the back door, sounding loud and clear, and he went clattering down the basement stairs in something close to a panic. For now that he'd traded off the table model, Abbie's set was the only one downstairs and Abbie's set was broken.

It was Abbie's set, all right. It stood just where he and Beasly had put it down that morning and there was nothing wrong with it—nothing wrong at all. It was even televising color.

*Televising color!*

He stopped at the bottom of the stairs and leaned against the railing for support.

The set kept right on televising color.

Taine stalked the set and walked around behind it.

The back of the cabinet was off, leaning against a bench that stood behind the set, and he could see the innards of it glowing cheerily.

He squatted on the basement floor and squinted at the lighted innards and they seemed a good deal different from the way that they should be. He'd repaired the set many times before and he thought he had a good idea of what the working parts would look like. And now they all seemed different, although just how he couldn't tell.

A heavy step sounded on the stairs and a hearty voice came booming down to him.

"Well, Hiram, I see you got it fixed."

Taine jackknifed upright and stood there slightly frozen and completely speechless.

Henry Horton stood foursquarely and happily on the stairs, looking very pleased.

"I told Abbie that you wouldn't have it done, but she said for me to come over anyway— Hey, Hiram, it's in color! How did you do it, man?"

Taine grinned sickly. "I just got fiddling around," he said.

Henry came down the rest of the stairs with a stately step and stood before the set, with his hands behind his back, staring at it fixedly in his best executive manner.

He slowly shook his head. "I never would have thought," he said, "that it was possible."

"Abbie mentioned that you wanted color."

"Well, sure. Of course I did. But not on this old set. I never would have expected to get color on this set. How did you do it, Hiram?"

Taine told the solemn truth. "I can't rightly say," he said.

Henry found a nail keg standing in front of one of the benches and rolled it out in front of the old-fashioned set. He sat down warily and relaxed into solid comfort.

"That's the way it goes," he said. "There are men like you, but not very many of them. Just Yankee tinkerers. You keep messing around with things, trying one thing here and another there and before you know it you come up with something."

He sat on the nail keg, staring at the set.

"It's sure a pretty thing," he said. "It's better than the color they have in Minneapolis. I dropped in at a couple of the places the last time I was there and looked at the color sets. And I tell you honest, Hiram, there wasn't one of them that was as good as this."

Taine wiped his brow with his shirt sleeve. Somehow or other, the basement seemed to be getting warm. He was fine sweat all over.

Henry found a big cigar in one of his pockets and held it out to Taine.

"No, thanks. I never smoke."

"Perhaps you're wise," said Henry. "It's a nasty habit."

He stuck the cigar into his mouth and rolled it east to west.

"Each man to his own," he proclaimed expansively. "When it comes to a thing like this, you're the man to do it. You seem to think in mechanical contraptions and electronic circuits. Me, I don't know a thing about it. Even in the computer game, I still don't know a thing about it; I hire men who do. I can't even saw a board or drive a nail. But I can organize. You remember, Hiram, how everybody snickered when I started up the plant?"

"Well, I guess some of them did, at that."

"You're darn tooting they did. They went around for weeks with their hands up to their faces to hide smart-aleck grins. They said, what does Henry think he's doing, starting up a computer factory out here in the sticks; he doesn't think he can compete with those big companies in the east, does he? And they didn't stop their grinning until I sold a couple of dozen units and had orders for a year or two ahead."

He fished a lighter from his pocket and lit the cigar carefully, never taking his eyes off the television set.

"You got something there," he said, judiciously, "that may be worth a mint of money. Some simple adaptation that will fit on any set. If you can get color on this old wreck, you can get color on any set that's made."

He chuckled moistly around the mouthful of cigar. "If RCA knew what was happening here this minute, they'd go out and cut their throats."

"But I don't know what I did," protested Taine.

"Well, that's all right," said Henry, happily. "I'll take this set up to the plant tomorrow and turn loose some of the boys on it. They'll find out what you have here before they're through with it."

He took the cigar out of his mouth and studied it intently, then popped it back in again.

"As I was saying, Hiram, that's the difference in us. You can do the stuff, but you miss the possibilities. I can't do a thing, but I can organize it once the thing is done. Before we get through with this, you'll be wading in twenty dollar bills clear up to your knees."

"But I don't have—"

"Don't worry. Just leave it all to me. I've got the plant and whatever money we may need. We'll figure out a split."

"That's fine of you," said Taine mechanically.

"Not at all," Henry insisted, grandly. "It's just my aggressive, grasping sense of profit. I should be ashamed of myself, cutting in on this."

He sat on the keg, smoking and watching the TV perform in exquisite color.

"You know, Hiram," he said, "I've often thought of this, but never got around to doing anything about it. I've got an old computer up at the plant that we will have to junk because it's taking up room that we really need. It's one of our early models, a sort of experimental job that went completely sour. It sure is a screwy thing. No one's ever been able to make much out of it. We tried some approaches that probably were wrong—or maybe they were right, but we didn't know enough to make them quite come off. It's been standing in a corner all these years and I should have junked it long ago. But I sort of hate to do it. I wonder if you might not like it—just to tinker with."

"Well, I don't know," said Taine.

Henry assumed an expansive air. "No obligation, mind you. You may not be able to do a thing with it—I'd frankly be surprised if you could, but there's no harm in trying. Maybe you'll decide to tear it down for the salvage you can get. There are several thousand dollars worth of equipment in it. Probably you could use most of it one way or another."

"It might be interesting," conceded Taine, but not too enthusiastically.

"Good," said Henry, with an enthusiasm that made up for Taine's lack of it. "I'll have the boys cart it over tomorrow. It's a heavy thing. I'll send along plenty of help to get it unloaded and down into the basement and set up."

Henry stood up carefully and brushed cigar ashes off his lap.

"I'll have the boys pick up the TV set at the same time," he said. "I'll have to tell Abbie you haven't got it fixed yet. If I ever let it get into the house, the way it's working now, she'd hold onto it."

Henry climbed the stairs heavily and Taine saw him out the door into the summer night.

Taine stood in the shadow, watching Henry's shadowed figure go across the Widow Taylor's yard to the next street behind his house. He took a deep breath of the fresh night air and shook his head to try to clear his buzzing brain, but the buzzing went right on.

Too much had happened, he told himself. Too much for any single day—first the ceiling and now the TV set. Once he had a good night's sleep he might be in some sort of shape to try to wrestle with it.

Towser came around the corner of the house and limped slowly up the steps to stand beside his master. He was mud up to his ears.

"You had a day of it, I see," said Taine. "And, just like I told you, you didn't get the woodchuck."

"*Woof,*" said Towser, sadly.

"You're just like a lot of the rest of us," Taine told him, severely. "Like me and Henry Horton and all the rest of us. You're chasing something and you think you know what you're chasing, but you really don't. And what's even worse, you have no faint idea of why you're chasing it."

Towser thumped a tired tail upon the stoop.

Taine opened the door and stood to one side to let Towser in, then went in himself.

He went through the refrigerator and found part of a roast, a slice or two of luncheon meat, a dried-out slab of cheese and half a bowl of cooked spaghetti. He made a pot of coffee and shared the food with Towser.

Then Taine went back downstairs and shut off the television set. He found a trouble lamp and plugged it in and poked the light into the innards of the set.

He squatted on the floor, holding the lamp, trying to puzzle out what had been done to the set. It was different, of course, but it was a little hard to figure out in just what ways it was different. Someone had tinkered with the tubes and had them twisted out of shape and there were little white cubes of metal tucked here and there in what seemed to be an entirely haphazard and illogical manner—although, Taine admitted to himself, there probably was no haphazardness. And the circuit, he saw, had been rewired and a good deal of wiring had been added.

But the most puzzling thing about it was that the whole thing seemed to be just jury-rigged—as if someone had done no more than a hurried, patch-up job to get the set back in working order on an emergency and temporary basis.

Someone, he thought!

And who had that someone been?

He hunched around and peered into the dark corners of the basement and he felt innumerable and many-legged imaginary insects running on his body.

Someone had taken the back off the cabinet and leaned it against the bench and had left the screws which held the back laid neatly in a row upon the floor. Then they had jury-rigged the set and jury-rigged it far better than it had ever been before.

If this was a jury-job, he wondered, just what kind of job would it have been if they had had the time to do it up in style?

They hadn't had the time, of course. Maybe they had been scared off when he had come home—scared off even before they could get the back on the set again.

He stood up and moved stiffly away.

First the ceiling in the morning—and now, in the evening, Abbie's television set.

And the ceiling, come to think of it, was not a ceiling only. Another liner, if that was the proper term for it, of the same material as the ceiling, had been laid beneath the floor, forming a sort of boxed-in area between the joists. He had struck that liner when he had tried to drill into the floor.

And what, he asked himself, if all the house were like that, too?

There was just one answer to it all: *There was something in the house with him!*

Towser had heard that *something* or smelled it or in some other manner sensed it and had dug frantically at the floor in an attempt to dig it out, as if it were a woodchuck.

Except that this, whatever it might be, certainly was no woodchuck.

He put away the trouble light and went upstairs.

Towser was curled up on a rug in the living room beside the easy chair and beat his tail in polite decorum in greeting to his master.

Taine stood and stared down at the dog. Towser looked back at him with satisfied and sleepy eyes, then heaved a doggish sigh and settled down to sleep.

Whatever Towser might have heard or smelled or sensed this morning, it was quite evident that as of this moment he was aware of it no longer.

Then Taine remembered something else.

He had filled the kettle to make water for the coffee and had set it on the stove. He had turned on the burner and it had worked the first time.

He hadn't had to kick the stove to get the burner going.

He woke in the morning and someone was holding down his feet and he sat up quickly to see what was going on.

But there was nothing to be alarmed about; it was only Towser who had crawled into bed with him and now lay sprawled across his feet.

Towser whined softly and his back legs twitched as he chased dream rabbits.

Taine eased his feet from beneath the dog and sat up, reaching for his clothes. It was early, but he remembered suddenly that he had left all of the furniture he had picked up the day before out there in the truck and should be getting downstairs where he could start reconditioning it.

Towser went on sleeping.

Taine stumbled to the kitchen and looked out of the window and there, squatted on the back stoop, was Beasly, the Horton man-of-all-work.

Taine went to the back door to see what was going on.

"I quit them, Hiram," Beasly told him. "She kept on pecking at me every minute of the day and I couldn't do a thing to please her, so I up and quit."

"Well, come on in," said Taine. "I suppose you'd like a bite to eat and a cup of coffee."

"I was kind of wondering if I could stay here, Hiram. Just for my keep until I can find something else."

"Let's have breakfast first," said Taine, "then we can talk about it."

He didn't like it, he told himself. He didn't like it at all. In another hour or so Abbie would show up and start stirring up a ruckus about how he'd lured Beasly off. Because, no matter how dumb Beasly might be, he did a lot of work and took a lot of nagging and there wasn't anyone else in town who would work for Abbie Horton.

"Your ma used to give me cookies all the time," said Beasly. "Your ma was a real good woman, Hiram."

"Yes, she was," said Taine.

"My ma used to say that you folks were quality, not like the rest in town, no matter what kind of airs they were always putting on. She said your family was among the first settlers. Is that really true, Hiram?"

"Well, not exactly first settlers, I guess, but this house has stood here for almost a hundred years. My father used to say there never was a night during all those years that there wasn't at least one Taine beneath its roof. Things like that, it seems, meant a lot to father."

"It must be nice," said Beasly, wistfully, "to have a feeling like that. You must be proud of this house, Hiram."

"Not really proud; more like belonging. I can't imagine living in any other house."

Taine turned on the burner and filled the kettle. Carrying the kettle back, he kicked the stove. But there wasn't any need to kick it; the burner was already beginning to take on a rosy glow.

Twice in a row, Taine thought. This thing is getting better!

"Gee, Hiram," said Beasly, "this is a dandy radio."

"It's no good," said Taine. "It's broke. Haven't had the time to fix it."

"I don't think so, Hiram. I just turned it on. It's beginning to warm up."

"It's beginning to— Hey, let me see!" yelled Taine.

Beasly told the truth. A faint hum was coming from the tubes.

A voice came in, gaining in volume as the set warmed up. It was speaking gibberish.

"What kind of talk is that?" asked Beasly.

"I don't know," said Taine, close to panic now.

First the television set, then the stove and now the radio!

He spun the tuning knob and the pointer crawled slowly across the dial face instead of spinning across as he remembered it, and station after station sputtered and went past.

He tuned in the next station that came up and it was strange lingo, too—and he knew by then exactly what he had.

Instead of a $39.50 job, he had here on the kitchen table an all-band receiver like they advertised in the fancy magazines.

He straightened up and said to Beasly: "See if you can get someone speaking English. I'll get on with the eggs."

He turned on the second burner and got out the frying pan. He put it on the stove and found eggs and bacon in the refrigerator.

Beasly got a station that had band music playing.

"How's that?" he asked.

"That's fine," said Taine.

Towser came out from the bedroom, stretching and yawning. He went to the door and showed he wanted out.

Taine let him out.

"If I were you," he told the dog, "I'd lay off that woodchuck. You'll have all the woods dug up."

"He ain't digging after any woodchuck, Hiram."

"Well, a rabbit, then."

"Not a rabbit, either. I snuck off yesterday when I was supposed to be beating rugs. That's what Abbie got so sore about."

Taine grunted, breaking eggs into the skillet.

"I snuck away and went over to where Towser was. I talked with him and he told me it wasn't a woodchuck or a rabbit. He said it was something else. I pitched in and helped him dig. Looks to me like he found an old tank of some sort buried out there in the woods."

"Towser wouldn't dig up any tank," protested Taine. "He wouldn't care about anything except a rabbit or a woodchuck."

"He was working hard," insisted Beasly. "He seemed to be excited."

"Maybe the woodchuck just dug his hole under this old tank or whatever it might be."

"Maybe so," Beasly agreed. He fiddled with the radio some more. He got a disk jockey who was pretty terrible.

Taine shoveled eggs and bacon onto plates and brought them to the table. He poured big cups of coffee and began buttering the toast.

"Dive in," he said to Beasly.

"This is good of you, Hiram, to take me in like this. I won't stay no longer than it takes to find a job."

"Well, I didn't exactly say—"

"There are times," said Beasly, "when I get to thinking I haven't got a friend and then I remember your ma, how nice she was to me and all—"

"Oh, all right," said Taine.

He knew when he was licked.

He brought the toast and a jar of jam to the table and sat down, beginning to eat.

"Maybe you got something I could help you with," suggested Beasly, using the back of his hand to wipe egg off his chin.

"I have a load of furniture out in the driveway. I could use a man to help me get it down into the basement."

"I'll be glad to do that," said Beasly. "I am good and strong. I don't mind work at all. I just don't like people jawing at me."

They finished breakfast and then carried the furniture down into the basement. They had some trouble with the Governor Winthrop, for it was an unwieldy thing to handle.

When they finally horsed it down, Taine stood off and looked at it. The man, he told himself, who slapped paint onto that beautiful cherry-wood had a lot to answer for.

He said to Beasly: "We have to get the paint off that thing there. And we must do it carefully. Use paint remover and a rag wrapped around a spatula and just sort of roll it off. Would you like to try it?"

"Sure, I would. Say, Hiram, what will we have for lunch?"

"I don't know," said Taine. "We'll throw something together. Don't tell me you're hungry."

"Well, it was sort of hard work, getting all that stuff down here."

"There are cookies in the jar on the kitchen shelf," said Taine. "Go and help yourself."

When Beasly went upstairs, Taine walked slowly around the basement. The ceiling, he saw, was still intact. Nothing else seemed to be disturbed.

Maybe that television set and the stove and radio, he thought, was just their way of paying rent to me. And if that were the case, he told himself, whoever they might be, he'd be more than willing to let them stay right on.

He looked around some more and could find nothing wrong.

He went upstairs and called to Beasly in the kitchen.

"Come on out to the garage, where I keep the paint. We'll hunt up some remover and show you how to use it."

Beasly, a supply of cookies clutched in his hand, trotted willingly behind him.

As they rounded the corner of the house they could hear Towser's muffled barking. Listening to him, it seemed to Taine that he was get-ting hoarse.

Three days, he thought—or was it four?

"If we don't do something about it," he said, "that fool dog is going to get himself wore out."

He went into the garage and came back with two shovels and a pick.

"Come on," he said to Beasly. "We have to put a stop to this before we have any peace."

Towser had done himself a noble job of excavation. He was almost completely out of sight. Only the end of his considerably bedraggled tail showed out of the hole he had clawed in the forest floor.

Beasly had been right about the tanklike thing. One edge of it showed out of one side of the hole.

Towser backed out of the hole and sat down heavily, his whiskers dripping clay, his tongue hanging out of the side of his mouth.

"He says that it's about time that we showed up," said Beasly.

Taine walked around the hole and knelt down. He reached down a hand to brush the dirt off the projecting edge of Beasly's tank. The clay was stubborn and hard to wipe away, but from the feel of it the tank was heavy metal.

Taine picked up a shovel and rapped it against the tank. The tank gave out a clang.

They got to work, shoveling away a foot or so of topsoil that lay above the object. It was hard work and the thing was bigger than they had thought and it took some time to get it uncovered, even roughly.

"I'm hungry," Beasly complained.

Taine glanced at his watch. It was almost one o'clock.

"Run on back to the house," he said to Beasly. "You'll find something in the refrigerator and there's milk to drink."

"How about you, Hiram? Ain't you ever hungry?"

"You could bring me back a sandwich and see if you can find a trowel."

"What you want a trowel for?"

"I want to scrape the dirt off this thing and see what it is."

He squatted down beside the thing they had unearthed and watched Beasly disappear into the woods.

"Towser," he said, "this is the strangest animal you ever put to ground."

A man, he told himself, might better joke about it—if to do no more than keep his fear away.

Beasly wasn't scared, of course. Beasly didn't have the sense to be scared of a thing like this.

Twelve feet wide by twenty long and oval shaped. About the size, he thought, of a good-size living room. And there never had been a tank of that shape or size in all of Willow Bend.

He fished his jackknife out of his pocket and started to scratch away the dirt at one point on the surface of the thing. He got a square inch of free dirt and it was no metal such as he had ever seen. It looked for all the world like glass.

He kept on scraping at the dirt until he had a clean place as big as an outstretched hand.

It wasn't any metal. He'd almost swear to that. It looked like cloudy glass—like the milk-glass goblets and bowls he was always on the lookout for. There were a lot of people who were plain nuts about it and they'd pay fancy prices for it.

He closed the knife and put it back into his pocket and squatted, looking at the oval shape that Towser had discovered.

And the conviction grew: Whatever it was that had come to live with him undoubtedly had arrived in the same contraption. From space or time, he thought, and was astonished that he thought it, for he'd never thought such a thing before.

He picked up his shovel and began to dig again, digging down this time, following the curving side of this alien thing that lay within the earth.

And as he dug, he wondered. What should he say about this—or should he say anything? Maybe the smartest course would be to cover it again and never breathe a word about it to a living soul.

Beasly would talk about it, naturally. But no one in the village would pay attention to anything that Beasly said. Everyone in Willow Bend knew Beasly was cracked.

Beasly finally came back. He carried three inexpertly-made sandwiches wrapped in an old newspaper and a quart bottle almost full of milk.

"You certainly took your time," said Taine, slightly irritated.

"I got interested," Beasly explained.

"Interested in what?"

"Well, there were three big trucks and they were lugging a lot of heavy stuff down into the basement. Two or three big cabinets and a lot of other junk. And you know Abbie's television set? Well, they took the set away. I told them that they shouldn't, but they took it anyway."

"I forgot," said Taine. "Henry said he'd send the computer over and I plumb forgot."

Taine ate the sandwiches, sharing them with Towser, who was very grateful in a muddy way.

Finished, Taine rose and picked up his shovel.

"Let's get to work," he said.

"But you got all that stuff down in the basement."

"That can wait," said Taine. "This job we have to finish."

It was getting dusk by the time they finished.

Taine leaned wearily on his shovel.

Twelve feet by twenty across the top and ten feet deep—and all of it, every bit of it, made of the milk-glass stuff that sounded like a bell when you whacked it with a shovel.

They'd have to be small, he thought, if there were many of them, to live in a space that size, especially if they had to stay there very long.

And that fitted in, of course, for if they weren't small they couldn't now be living in the space between the basement joists.

If they were really living there, thought Taine. If it wasn't all just a lot of supposition.

Maybe, he thought, even if they had been living in the house, they might be there no longer—for Towser had smelled or heard or somehow sensed them in the morning, but by that very night he'd paid them no attention.

Taine slung his shovel across his shoulder and hoisted the pick.

"Come on," he said, "let's go. We've put in a long, hard day."

They tramped out through the brush and reached the road. Fireflies were flickering off and on in the woody darkness and the street lamps were swaying in the summer breeze. The stars were hard and bright.

Maybe they still were in the house, thought Taine. Maybe when they found out that Towser had objected to them, they had fixed it so he'd be aware of them no longer.

They probably were highly adaptive. It stood to good reason they would have to be. It hadn't taken them too long, he told himself grimly, to adapt to a human house.

He and Beasly went up the gravel driveway in the dark to put the tools away in the garage and there was something funny going on, for there was no garage.

There was no garage and there was no front on the house and the driveway was cut off abruptly and there was nothing but the curving wall of what apparently had been the end of the garage.

They came up to the curving wall and stopped, squinting unbelieving in the summer dark.

There was no garage, no porch, no front of the house at all. It was as if someone had taken the opposite corners of the front of the house and bent them together until they touched, folding the entire front of the building inside the curvature of the bent-together corners.

Taine now had a curved-front house. Although it was, actually, not as simple as all that, for the curvature was not in proportion to what actually would have happened in case of such a feat. The curve was long and graceful and somehow not quite apparent. It was as if the front of the house had been eliminated and an illusion of the rest of the house had been summoned to mask the disappearance.

Taine dropped the shovel and the pick and they clattered on the driveway gravel. He put his hand up to his face and wiped it across his eyes, as if to clear his eyes of something that could not possibly be there.

And when he took the hand away it had not changed a bit.

There was no front to the house.

Then he was running around the house, hardly knowing he was running, and there was a fear inside of him at what had happened to the house.

But the back of the house was all right. It was exactly as it had always been.

He clattered up the stoop with Beasly and Towser running close behind him. He pushed open the door and burst into the entry and scrambled up the stairs into the kitchen and went across the kitchen in three strides to see what had happened to the front of the house.

At the door between the kitchen and the living room he stopped and his hands went out to grasp the door jamb as he stared in disbelief at the windows of the living room.

It was night outside. There could be no doubt of that. He had seen the fireflies flickering in the brush and weeds and the street lamps had been lit and the stars were out.

But a flood of sunlight was pouring through the windows of the living room and out beyond the windows lay a land that was not Willow Bend.

"Beasly," he gasped, "look out there in front!"

Beasly looked.

"What place is that?" he asked.

"That's what I'd like to know."

Towser had found his dish and was pushing it around the kitchen floor with his nose, by way of telling Taine that it was time to eat.

Taine went across the living room and opened the front door. The garage, he saw, was there. The pickup stood with its nose against the open garage door and the car was safe inside.

There was nothing wrong with the front of the house at all.

But if the front of the house was all right, that was all that was.

For the driveway was chopped off just a few feet beyond the tail end of the pickup and there was no yard or woods or road. There was just a desert—a flat, far-reaching desert, level as a floor, with occasional boulder piles and haphazard clumps of vegetation and all of the ground covered with sand and pebbles. A big blinding sun hung just above a horizon that seemed much too far away and a funny thing about it was that the sun was in the north, where no proper sun should be. It had a peculiar whiteness, too.

Beasly stepped out on the porch and Taine saw that he was shivering like a frightened dog.

"Maybe," Taine told him, kindly, "you'd better go back in and start making us some supper."

"But, Hiram—"

"It's all right," said Taine. "It's bound to be all right."

"If you say so, Hiram."

He went in and the screen door banged behind him and in a minute Taine heard him in the kitchen.

He didn't blame Beasly for shivering, he admitted to himself. It was a sort of shock to step out of your front door into an unknown land. A man might eventually get used to it, of course, but it would take some doing.

He stepped down off the porch and walked around the truck and around the garage corner and when he rounded the corner he was half prepared to walk back into familiar Willow Bend—for when he had gone in the back door the village had been there.

There was no Willow Bend. There was more of the desert, a great deal more of it.

He walked around the house and there was no back to the house. The back of the house now was just the same as the front had been before—the same smooth curve pulling the sides of the house together.

He walked on around the house to the front again and there was desert all the way. And the front was still all right. It hadn't changed at all. The truck was there on the chopped-off driveway and the garage was open and the car inside.

Taine walked out a way into the desert and hunkered down and scooped up a handful of the pebbles and the pebbles were just pebbles.

He squatted there and let the pebbles trickle through his fingers.

In Willow Bend there was a back door and there wasn't any front. Here, wherever here might be, there was a front door, but there wasn't any back.

He stood up and tossed the rest of the pebbles away and wiped his dusty hands upon his breeches.

Out of the corner of his eye he caught a sense of movement on the porch and there they were.

A line of tiny animals, if animals they were, came marching down the steps, one behind another. They were four inches high or so and they went on all four feet, although it was plain to see that their front feet were really hands, not feet. They had ratlike faces that were vaguely human, with noses long and pointed. They looked as if they might have scales instead of hide, for their bodies glistened with a rippling motion as they walked. And all of them had tails that looked very much like the coiled-wire tails one finds on certain toys and the tails stuck straight up above them, quivering as they walked.

They came down the steps in single file, in perfect military order, with half a foot or so of spacing between each one of them.

They came down the steps and walked out into the desert in a straight, undeviating line as if they knew exactly where they might be bound. There was something deadly purposeful about them and yet they didn't hurry.

Taine counted sixteen of them and he watched them go out into the desert until they were almost lost to sight.

There go the ones, he thought, who came to live with me. They are the ones who fixed up the ceiling and who repaired Abbie's television set and jiggered up the stove and radio. And more than likely, too, they were the ones who had come to Earth in the strange milk-glass contraption out there in the woods.

And if they had come to Earth in that deal out in the woods, then what sort of place was this?

He climbed the porch and opened the screen door and saw the neat, six-inch circle his departing guests had achieved in the screen to get out of the house. He made a mental note that some day, when he had the time, he would have to fix it.

He went in and slammed the door behind him.

"Beasly," he shouted.

There was no answer.

Towser crawled from beneath the love seat and apologized.

"It's all right, pal," said Taine. "That outfit scared me, too."

He went into the kitchen. The dim ceiling light shone on the overturned coffee pot, the broken cup in the center of the floor, the upset bowl of eggs. One broken egg was a white and yellow gob on the linoleum.

He stepped down on the landing and saw that the screen door in the back was wrecked beyond repair. Its rusty mesh was broken—exploded might have been a better word—and a part of the frame was smashed.

Taine looked at it in wondering admiration.

"The poor fool," he said. "He went straight through it without opening it at all."

He snapped on the light and went down the basement stairs. Halfway down he stopped in utter wonderment.

To his left was a wall—a wall of the same sort of material as had been used to put in the ceiling.

He stooped and saw that the wall ran clear across the basement, floor to ceiling, shutting off the workshop area.

And inside the workshop, what?

For one thing, he remembered, the computer that Henry had sent over just this morning. Three trucks, Beasly had said—three truckloads of equipment delivered straight into their paws!

Taine sat down weakly on the steps.

They must have thought, he told himself, that he was co-operating! Maybe they had figured that he knew what they were about and so went along with them. Or perhaps they thought he was paying them for fixing up the TV set and the stove and radio.

But to tackle first things first, why had they repaired the TV set and the stove and radio? As a sort of rental payment? As a friendly gesture? Or as a sort of practice run to find out what they could about this world's technology? To find, perhaps, how their technology could be adapted to the materials and conditions on this planet they had found?

Taine raised a hand and rapped with his knuckles on the wall beside the stairs and the smooth white surface gave out a pinging sound.

He laid his ear against the wall and listened closely and it seemed to him he could hear a low-key humming, but if so it was so faint he could not be absolutely sure.

Banker Stevens' lawn mower was in there, behind the wall, and a lot of other stuff waiting for repair. They'd take the hide right off him, he thought, especially Banker Stevens. Stevens was a tight man.

Beasly must have been half-crazed with fear, he thought. When he had seen those things coming up out of the basement, he'd gone clean off his rocker. He'd gone straight through the door without even bothering to try to open it and now he was down in the village yapping to anyone who'd stop to listen to him.

No one ordinarily would pay Beasly much attention, but if he yapped long enough and wild enough, they'd probably do some checking. They'd come storming up here and they'd give the place a going over and they'd stand goggle-eyed at what they found in front and pretty soon some of them would have worked their way around to sort of running things.

And it was none of their business, Taine stubbornly told himself, his ever-present business sense rising to the fore. There was a lot of real estate lying around out there in his front yard and the only way anyone could get to it was by going through the house. That being the case, it stood to reason that all that land out there was his. Maybe it wasn't any good at all. There might be nothing there. But before he had other people overrunning it, he'd better check and see.

He went up the stairs and out into the garage.

The sun was still just above the northern horizon and there was nothing moving.

He found a hammer and some nails and a few short lengths of plank in the garage and took them in the house.

Towser, he saw, had taken advantage of the situation and was sleeping in the gold-upholstered chair. Taine didn't bother him.

Taine locked the back door and nailed some planks across it. He locked the kitchen and the bedroom windows and nailed planks across them, too.

That would hold the villagers for a while, he told himself, when they came tearing up here to see what was going on.

He got his deer rifle, a box of cartridges, a pair of binoculars and an old canteen out of a closet. He filled the canteen at the kitchen tap and stuffed a sack with food for him and Towser to eat along the way, for there was no time to wait and eat.

Then he went into the living room and dumped Towser out of the gold-upholstered chair.

"Come on, Tows," he said. "We'll go and look things over."

He checked the gasoline in the pickup and the tank was almost full.

He and the dog got in and he put the rifle within easy reach. Then he backed the truck and swung it around and headed out, north, across the desert.

It was easy traveling. The desert was as level as a floor. At times it got a little rough, but no worse than a lot of the back roads he traveled hunting down antiques.

The scenery didn't change. Here and there were low hills, but the desert itself kept on mostly level, unraveling itself into that far-off horizon. Taine kept on driving north, straight into the sun. He hit some sandy stretches, but the sand was firm and hard and he had no trouble.

Half an hour out he caught up with the band of things—all sixteen of them—that had left the house. They were still traveling in line at their steady pace.

Slowing down the truck, Taine traveled parallel with them for a time, but there was no profit in it; they kept on traveling their course, looking neither right nor left.

Speeding up, Taine left them behind.

The sun stayed in the north, unmoving, and that certainly was queer. Perhaps, Taine told himself, this world spun on its axis far more slowly than the Earth and the day was longer. From the way the sun appeared to be standing still, perhaps a good deal longer.

Hunched above the wheel, staring out into the endless stretch of desert, the strangeness of it struck him for the first time with its full impact.

This was another world—there could be no doubt of that—another planet circling another star, and where it was in actual space no one on Earth could have the least idea. And yet, through some machination of those sixteen things walking straight in line, it also was lying just outside the front door of his house.

Ahead of him a somewhat larger hill loomed out of the flatness of the desert. As he drew nearer to it, he made out a row of shining objects lined upon its crest. After a time he stopped the truck and got out with the binoculars.

Through the glasses, he saw that the shining things were the same sort of milk-glass contraptions as had been in the woods. He counted eight of them, shining in the sun, perched upon some sort of rock-gray cradles. And there were other cradles empty.

He took the binoculars from his eyes and stood there for a moment, considering the advisibility of climbing the hill and investigating closely. But he shook his head. There'd be time for that later on. He'd better keep on moving. This was not a real exploring foray, but a quick reconnaissance.

He climbed into the truck and drove on, keeping watch upon the gas gauge. When it came close to half full he'd have to turn around and go back home again.

Ahead of him he saw a faint whiteness above the dim horizon line and he watched it narrowly. At times it faded away and then came in again, but whatever it might be was so far off he could make nothing of it.

He glanced down at the gas gauge and it was close to the halfway mark. He stopped the pickup and got out with the binoculars.

As he moved around to the front of the machine he was puzzled at how slow and tired his legs were and then remembered—he should have been in bed many hours ago. He looked at his watch and it was two o'clock and that meant, back on Earth, two o'clock in the morning. He had been awake for more than twenty hours and much of that time he had been engaged in the backbreaking work of digging out the strange thing in the woods.

He put up the binoculars and the elusive white line that he had been seeing turned out to be a range of mountains. The great, blue, craggy mass towered up above the desert with the gleam of snow on its peaks and ridges. They were a long way off, for even the powerful glasses brought them in as little more than a misty blueness.

He swept the glasses slowly back and forth and the mountains extended for a long distance above the horizon line.

He brought the glasses down off the mountains and examined the desert that stretched ahead of him. There was more of the same that he had been seeing—the same floorlike levelness, the same occasional mounds, the self-same scraggy vegetation.

And a house!

His hands trembled and he lowered the glasses, then put them up to his face again and had another look. It was a house, all right. A funny-looking house standing at the foot of one of the hillocks, still shadowed by the hillock so that one could not pick it out with the naked eye.

It seemed to be a small house. Its roof was like a blunted cone and it lay tight against the ground, as if it hugged or crouched against the ground. There was an oval opening that probably was a door, but there was no sign of windows.

He took the binoculars down again and stared at the hillock. Four or five miles away, he thought. The gas would stretch that far and even if it didn't he could walk the last few miles into Willow Bend.

It was queer, he thought, that a house should be all alone out here. In all the miles he'd traveled in the desert he'd seen no sign of life beyond the sixteen little ratlike things that marched in single file, no sign of artificial structure other than the eight milk-glass contraptions resting in their cradles.

He climbed into the pickup and put it into gear. Ten minutes later he drew up in front of the house, which still lay within the shadow of the hillock.

He got out of the pickup and hauled his rifle after him. Towser leaped to the ground and stood with his hackles up, a deep growl in his throat.

"What's the matter, boy?" asked Taine.

Towser growled again.

The house stood silent. It seemed to be deserted.

The walls were built, Taine saw, of rude, rough masonry crudely set together, with a crumbling, mudlike substance used in lieu of mortar. The roof originally had been of sod and that was queer, indeed, for there was nothing that came close to sod upon this expanse of desert. But now, although one could see the lines where the sod strips had been fitted together, it was nothing more than earth baked hard by the desert sun.

The house itself was featureless, entirely devoid of any ornament, with no attempt at all to soften the harsh utility of it as a simple shelter. It was the sort of thing that a shepherd people might have put together. It had the look of age about it; the stone had flaked and crumbled in the weather.

Rifle slung beneath his arm, Taine paced toward it. He reached the door and glanced inside and there was darkness and no movement.

He glanced back for Towser and saw that the dog had crawled beneath the truck and was peering out and growling.

"You stick around," said Taine. "Don't go running off."

With the rifle thrust before him, Taine stepped through the door into the darkness. He stood for a long moment to allow his eyes to become accustomed to the gloom.

Finally he could make out the room in which he stood. It was plain and rough, with a rude stone bench along one wall and queer unfunctional niches hollowed in another. One rickety piece of wooden furniture stood in a corner, but Taine could not make out what its use might be.

An old and deserted place, he thought, abandoned long ago. Perhaps a shepherd people might have lived here in some long-gone age, when the desert had been a rich and grassy plain.

There was a door into another room and as he stepped through it he heard the faint, far-off booming sound and something else as well—the sound of pouring rain! From the open door that led out through the back he caught a whiff of salty breeze and he stood there frozen in the center of that second room.

Another one!

Another house that led to another world!

He walked slowly forward, drawn toward the outer door, and he stepped out into a cloudy, darkling day with the rain streaming down from wildly racing clouds. Half a mile away, across a field of jumbled broken, iron-gray boulders, lay a pounding sea that raged upon the coast, throwing great spumes of angry spray high into the air.

He walked out from the door and looked up at the sky, and the rain drops pounded at his face with a stinging fury. There was a chill and a dampness in the air and the place was eldritch—a world jerked straight from some ancient Gothic tale of goblin and of sprite.

He glanced around and there was nothing he could see, for the rain blotted out the world beyond this stretch of coast, but behind the rain he could sense or seemed to sense a presence that sent shivers down his spine. Gulping in fright, Taine turned around and stumbled back again through the door into the house.

One world away, he thought, was far enough; two worlds away was more than one could take. He trembled at the sense of utter loneliness that tumbled in his skull and suddenly this long-forsaken house became unbearable and he dashed out of it.

Outside the sun was bright and there was welcome warmth. His clothes were damp from rain and little beads of moisture lay on the rifle barrel.

He looked around for Towser and there was no sign of the dog. He was not underneath the pickup; he was nowhere in sight.

Taine called and there was no answer. His voice sounded lone and hollow in the emptiness and silence.

He walked around the house, looking for the dog, and there was no back door to the house. The rough rock walls of the sides of the house pulled in with that funny curvature and there was no back to the house at all.

But Taine was not interested; he had known how it would be. Right now he was looking for his dog and he felt the panic rising in him. Somehow it felt a long way from home.

He spent three hours at it. He went back into the house and Towser was not there. He went into the other world again and searched among the tumbled rocks and Towser was not there. He went back to the desert and walked around the hillock and then he climbed to the crest of it and used the binoculars and saw nothing but the lifeless desert, stretching far in all directions.

Dead-beat with weariness, stumbling, half asleep even as he walked, he went back to the pickup.

He leaned against it and tried to pull his wits together.

Continuing as he was would be a useless effort. He had to get some sleep. He had to go back to Willow Bend and fill the tank and get some extra gasoline so that he could range farther afield in his search for Towser.

He couldn't leave the dog out here—that was unthinkable. But he had to plan, he had to act intelligently. He would be doing Towser no good by stumbling around in his present shape.

He pulled himself into the truck and headed back for Willow Bend, following the occasional faint impressions that his tires had made in the sandy places, fighting a half-dead drowsiness that tried to seal his eyes shut.

Passing the higher hill on which the milk-glass things had stood, he stopped to walk around a bit so he wouldn't fall asleep behind the wheel. And now, he saw, there were only seven of the things resting in their cradles.

But that meant nothing to him now. All that meant anything was to hold off the fatigue that was closing down upon him, to cling to the wheel and wear off the miles, to get back to Willow Bend and get some sleep and then come back again to look for Towser.

Slightly more than halfway home he saw the other car and watched it in numb befuddlement, for this truck that he was driving and the car at home in his garage were the only two vehicles this side of his house.

He pulled the pickup to a halt and tumbled out of it.

The car drew up and Henry Horton and Beasly and a man who wore a star leaped quickly out of it.

"Thank God we found you, man!" cried Henry, striding over to him.

"I wasn't lost," protested Taine. "I was coming back."

"He's all beat out," said the man who wore the star.

"This is Sheriff Hanson," Henry said. "We were following your tracks."

"I lost Towser," Taine mumbled. "I had to go and leave him. Just leave me be and go and hunt for Towser. I can make it home."

He reached out and grabbed the edge of the pickup's door to hold himself erect.

"You broke down the door," he said to Henry. "You broke into my house and you took my car—"

"We had to do it, Hiram. We were afraid that something might have happened to you. The way that Beasly told it, it stood your hair on end."

"You better get him in the car," the sheriff said. "I'll drive the pickup back."

"But I have to hunt for Towser!"

"You can't do anything until you've had some rest."

Henry grabbed him by the arm and led him to the car and Beasly held the rear door open.

"You got any idea what this place is?" Henry whispered conspiratorially.

"I don't positively know," Taine mumbled. "Might be some other—"

Henry chuckled. "Well, I guess it doesn't really matter. Whatever it may be, it's put us on the map. We're in all the newscasts and the papers are plastering us in headlines and the town is swarming with reporters and cameramen and there are big officials coming. Yes, sir, I tell you, Hiram, this will be the making of us—"

Taine heard no more. He was fast asleep before he hit the seat.

He came awake and lay quietly in the bed and he saw the shades were drawn and the room was cool and peaceful.

It was good, he thought, to wake in a room you knew—in a room that one had known for his entire life, in a house that had been the Taine house for almost a hundred years.

Then memory clouted him and he sat bolt upright.

And now he heard it—the insistent murmur from outside the window.

He vaulted from the bed and pulled one shade aside. Peering out, he saw the cordon of troops that held back the crowd that overflowed his back yard and the back yards back of that.

He let the shade drop back and started hunting for his shoes, for he was fully dressed. Probably Henry and Beasly, he told himself, had dumped him into bed and pulled off his shoes and let it go at that. But he couldn't remember a single thing of it. He must have gone dead to the world the minute Henry had bundled him into the back seat of the car.

He found the shoes on the floor at the end of the bed and sat down upon the bed to pull them on.

And his mind was racing on what he had to do.

He'd have to get some gasoline somehow and fill up the truck and stash an extra can or two into the back and he'd have to take some food and water and perhaps his sleeping bag. For he wasn't coming back until he found his dog.

He got on his shoes and tied them, then went out into the living room. There was no one there, but there were voices in the kitchen.

He looked out the window and the desert lay outside, unchanged. The sun, he noticed, had climbed higher in the sky, but out in his front yard it was still forenoon.

He looked at his watch and it was six o'clock and from the way the shadows had been falling when he'd peered out of the bedroom window, he knew that it was 6:00 P.M. He realized with a guilty start that he must have slept almost around the clock. He had not meant to sleep that long. He hadn't meant to leave Towser out there that long.

He headed for the kitchen and there were three persons there—Abbie and Henry Horton and a man in military garb.

"There you are," cried Abbie merrily. "We were wondering when you would wake up."

"You have some coffee cooking, Abbie?"

"Yes, a whole pot full of it. And I'll cook up something else for you."

"Just some toast," said Taine. "I haven't got much time. I have to hunt for Towser."

"Hiram," said Henry, "this is Colonel Ryan, National Guard. He has his boys outside."

"Yes, I saw them through the window."

"Necessary," said Henry. "Absolutely necessary. The sheriff couldn't handle it. The people came rushing in and they'd have torn the place apart. So I called the governor."

"Taine," the colonel said, "sit down. I want to talk with you."

"Certainly," said Taine, taking a chair. "Sorry to be in such a rush, but I lost my dog out there."

"This business," said the colonel, smugly, "is vastly more important than any dog could be."

"Well, colonel, that just goes to show that you don't know Towser. He's the best dog I ever had and I've had a lot of them. Raised him from a pup and he's been a good friend all these years—"

"All right," the colonel said, "so he is a friend. But still I have to talk with you."

"You just sit and talk," Abbie said to Taine. "I'll fix up some cakes and Henry brought over some of that sausage that we get out on the farm."

The back door opened and Beasly staggered in to the accompaniment of a terrific metallic banging. He was carrying three empty five-gallon gas cans in one hand and two in the other hand and they were bumping and banging together as he moved.

"Say," yelled Taine, "what's going on here?"

"Now, just take it easy," Henry said. "You have no idea the problems that we have. We wanted to get a big gas tank moved through here, but we couldn't do it. We tried to rip out the back of the kitchen to get it through, but we couldn't—"

"You did what!"

"We tried to rip out the back of the kitchen," Henry told him calmly. "You can't get one of those big storage tanks through an ordinary door. But when we tried, we found that the entire house is boarded up inside with the same kind of material that you used down in the basement. You hit it with an axe and it blunts the steel—"

"But, Henry, this is my house and there isn't anyone who has the right to start tearing it apart."

"Fat chance," the colonel said. "What I would like to know, Taine, what is that stuff that we couldn't break through?"

"Now you take it easy, Hiram," cautioned Henry. "We have a big new world waiting for us out there—"

"It isn't waiting for you or anyone," yelled Taine.

"And we have to explore it and to explore it we need a stockpile of gasoline. So since we can't have a storage tank, we're getting together as many gas cans as possible and then we'll run a hose through here—"

"But, Henry—"

"I wish," said Henry sternly, "that you'd quit interrupting me and let me have my say. You can't even imagine the logistics that we face. We're bottlenecked by the size of a regulation door. We have to get supplies out there and we have to get transport. Cars and trucks won't be so bad. We can disassemble them and lug them through piecemeal, but a plane will be a problem."

"You listen to me, Henry. There isn't anyone going to haul a plane through here. This house has been in my family for almost a hundred years and I own it and I have a right to it and you can't come in high-handed and start hauling stuff through it."

"But," said Henry plaintively, "we need a plane real bad. You can cover so much more ground when you have a plane."

Beasly went banging through the kitchen with his cans and out into the living room.

The colonel sighed. "I had hoped, Mr. Taine, that you would understand how the matter stood. To me it seems very plain that it's your patriotic duty to co-operate with us in this. The government, of course, could exercise the right of eminent domain and start condemnation action, but it would rather not do that. I'm speaking unofficially, of course, but I think it's safe to say the government would much prefer to arrive at an amicable agreement."

"I doubt," Taine said, bluffing, not knowing anything about it, "that the right to eminent domain would be applicable. As I understand it, it applies to buildings and to roads—"

"This is a road," the colonel told him flatly. "A road right through your house to another world."

"First," Taine declared, "the government would have to show it was in the public interest and that refusal of the owner to relinquish title amounted to an interference in government procedure and—"

"I think," the colonel said, "that the government can prove it is in the public interest."

"I think," Taine said angrily, "I better get a lawyer."

"If you really mean that," Henry offered, ever helpful, "and you want to get a good one—and I presume you do—I would be pleased to recommend a firm that I am sure would represent your interests most ably and be, at the same time, fairly reasonable in cost."

The colonel stood up, seething. "You'll have a lot to answer, Taine. There'll be a lot of things the government will want to know. First of all, they'll want to know just how you engineered this. Are you ready to tell that?"

"No," said Taine, "I don't believe I am."

And he thought with some alarm: They think that I'm the one who did it and they'll be down on me like a pack of wolves to find out just how I did it. He had visions of the FBI and the state department and the Pentagon and, even sitting down, he felt shaky in the knees.

The colonel turned around and marched stiffly from the kitchen. He went out the back and slammed the door behind him.

Henry looked at Taine speculatively.

"Do you really mean it?" he demanded. "Do you intend to stand up to them?"

"I'm getting sore," said Taine. "They can't come in here and take over without even asking me. I don't care what anyone may think, this is my house. I was born here and I've lived here all my life and I like the place and—"

"Sure," said Henry. "I know just how you feel."

"I suppose it's childish of me, but I wouldn't mind so much if they showed a willingness to sit down and talk about what they meant to do once they'd taken over. But there seems no disposition to even ask me what I think about it. And I tell you, Henry, this is different than it seems. This isn't a place where we can walk in and take over, no matter what Washington may think. There's something out there and we better watch our step—"

"I was thinking," Henry interrupted, "as I was sitting here, that your attitude is most commendable and deserving of support. It has occurred to me that it would be most unneighborly of me to go on sitting here and leave you in the fight alone. We could hire ourselves a fine array of legal talent and we could fight the case and in the meantime we could form a land and development company and that way we could make sure that this new world of yours is used the way it should be used.

"It stands to reason, Hiram, that I am the one to stand beside you, shoulder to shoulder, in this business since we're already partners in this TV deal."

"What's this about TV?" shrilled Abbie, slapping a plate of cakes down in front of Taine.

"Now, Abbie," Henry said patiently, "I have explained to you already that your TV set is back of that partition down in the basement and there isn't any telling when we can get it out."

"Yes, I know," said Abbie, bringing a platter of sausages and pouring a cup of coffee.

Beasly came in from the living room and went bumbling out the back.

"After all," said Henry, pressing his advantage, "I would suppose I had some hand in it. I doubt you could have done much without the computer I sent over."

And there it was again, thought Taine. Even Henry thought he'd been the one who did it.

"But didn't Beasly tell you?"

"Beasly said a lot, but you know how Beasly is."

And that was it, of course. To the villagers it would be no more than another Beasly story—another whopper that Beasly had dreamed up. There was no one who believed a word that Beasly said.

Taine picked up the cup and drank his coffee, gaining time to shape an answer and there wasn't any answer. If he told the truth, it would sound far less believable than any lie he'd tell.

"You can tell me, Hiram. After all, we're partners."

He's playing me for a fool, thought Taine. Henry thinks he can play anyone he wants for a fool and sucker.

"You wouldn't believe me if I told you, Henry."

"Well," Henry said, resignedly, getting to his feet, "I guess that part of it can wait."

Beasly came tramping and banging through the kitchen with another load of cans.

"I'll have to have some gasoline," said Taine, "if I'm going out for Towser."

"I'll take care of that right away," Henry promised smoothly. "I'll send Ernie over with his tank wagon and we can run a hose through here and fill up those cans. And I'll see if I can find someone who'll go along with you."

"That's not necessary. I can go alone."

"If we had a radio transmitter. Then you could keep in touch."

"But we haven't any. And, Henry, I can't wait. Towser's out there somewhere—"

"Sure, I know how much you thought of him. You go out and look for him if you think you have to and I'll get started on this other business. I'll get some lawyers lined up and we'll draw up some sort of corporate papers for our land development—"

"And, Hiram," Abbie said, "will you do something for me, please?"

"Why, certainly," said Taine.

"Would you speak to Beasly. It's senseless the way he's acting. There wasn't any call for him to up and leave us. I might have been a little sharp with him, but he's so simple-minded he's infuriating. He ran off and spent half a day helping Towser at digging out that woodchuck and—"

"I'll speak to him," said Taine.

"Thanks, Hiram. He'll listen to you. You're the only one he'll listen to. And I wish you could have fixed my TV set before all this came about. I'm just lost without it. It leaves a hole in the living room. It matched my other furniture, you know."

"Yes I know," said Taine.

"Coming, Abbie?" Henry asked, standing at the door.

He lifted a hand in a confidential farewell to Taine. "I'll see you later, Hiram. I'll get it all fixed up."

I just bet you will, thought Taine.

He went back to the table, after they were gone, and sat down heavily in a chair.

The front door slammed and Beasly came panting in, excited.

"Towser's back!" he yelled. "He's coming back and he's driving in the biggest woodchuck you ever clapped your eyes on."

Taine leaped to his feet.

"Woodchuck! That's an alien planet. It hasn't any woodchucks."

"You come and see," yelled Beasly.

He turned and raced back out again, with Taine following close behind.

It certainly looked considerably like a woodchuck—a sort of man-size woodchuck. More like a woodchuck out of a children's book, perhaps, for it was walking on its hind legs and trying to look dignified even while it kept a weather eye on Towser.

Towser was back a hundred feet or so, keeping a wary distance from the massive chuck. He had the pose of a good sheepherding dog, walking in a crouch, alert to head off any break that the chuck might make.

The chuck came up close to the house and stopped. Then it did an about-face so that it looked back across the desert and it hunkered down.

It swung its massive head to gaze at Beasly and Taine and in the limpid brown eyes Taine saw more than the eyes of an animal.

Taine walked swiftly out and picked up the dog in his arms and hugged him tight against him. Towser twisted his head around and slapped a sloppy tongue across his master's face.

Taine stood with the dog in his arms and looked at the man-size chuck and felt a great relief and an utter thankfulness.

Everything was all right now, he thought. Towser had come back.

He headed for the house and out into the kitchen.

He put Towser down and got a dish and filled it at the tap. He placed it on the floor and Towser lapped at it thirstily, slopping water all over the linoleum.

"Take it easy, there," warned Taine. "You don't want to overdo it."

He hunted in the refrigerator and found some scraps and put them in Towser's dish.

Towser wagged his tail with doggish happiness.

"By rights," said Taine, "I ought to take a rope to you, running off like that."

Beasly came ambling in.

"That chuck is a friendly cuss," he announced. "He's waiting for someone."

"That's nice," said Taine, paying no attention.

He glanced at the clock.

"It's seven-thirty," he said. "We can catch the news. You want to get it Beasly?"

"Sure. I know right where to get it. That fellow from New York."

"That's the one," said Taine.

He walked into the living room and looked out the window. The man-size chuck had not moved. He was sitting with his back to the house, looking back the way he'd come.

Waiting for someone, Beasly had said, and it looked as if he might be, but probably it was all just in Beasly's head.

And if he were waiting for someone, Taine wondered, who might that someone be? *What* might that someone be? Certainly by now the word had spread out that there was a door into another world. And how many doors, he wondered, had been opened through the ages?

Henry had said that there was a big new world out there waiting for Earthmen to move in. And that wasn't it at all. It was the other way around.

The voice of the news commentator came blasting from the radio in the middle of a sentence:

" . . . finally got into the act. Radio Moscow said this evening that the Soviet delegate will make representations in the U.N. tomorrow for the internationalization of this other world and the gateway to it.

"From that gateway itself, the home of a man named Hiram Taine, there is no news. Complete security had been clamped down and a cordon of troops form a solid wall around the house, holding back the crowds. Attempts to telephone the residence are blocked by a curt voice which says that no calls are being accepted for that number. And Taine himself has not stepped from the house."

Taine walked back into the kitchen and sat down.

"He's talking about you," Beasly said importantly.

"Rumor circulated this morning that Taine, a quiet village repair man and dealer in antiques, and until yesterday a relative unknown, had finally returned from a trip which he made out into this new and unknown land. But what he found, if anything, no one yet can say. Nor is there any further information about this other place beyond the fact that it is a desert and, to the moment, lifeless.

"A small flurry of excitement was occasioned late yesterday by the finding of some strange object in the woods across the road from the residence, but this area likewise was swiftly cordoned off and to the moment Colonel Ryan, who commands the troops, will say nothing of what actually was found.

"Mystery man of the entire situation is one Henry Horton, who seems to be the only unofficial person to have entry to the Taine house. Horton, questioned earlier today, had little to say, but managed to suggest an air of great conspiracy. He hinted he and Taine were partners in some mysterious venture and left hanging in midair the half impression that he and Taine had collaborated in opening the new world.

"Horton, it is interesting to note, operates a small computer plant and it is understood on good authority that only recently he delivered a computer to Taine, or at least some sort of machine to which considerable mystery is attached. One story is that this particular machine had been in the process of development for six or seven years.

"Some of the answers to the matter of how all this did happen and what actually did happen must wait upon the findings of a team of scientists who left Washington this evening after an all-day conference at the White House, which was attended by representatives from the military, the state department, the security division and the special weapons section.

"Throughout the world the impact of what happened yesterday at Willow Bend can only be compared to the sensation of the news, almost twenty years ago, of the dropping of the first atomic bomb. There is some tendency among many observers to believe that the implications of Willow Bend, in fact, may be even more earth-shaking than were those at Hiroshima.

"Washington insists, as is only natural, that this matter is of internal concern only and that it intends to handle the situation as it best affects the national welfare.

"But abroad there is a rising storm of insistence that this is not a matter of national policy concerning one nation, but that it necessarily must be a matter of worldwide concern.

"There is an unconfirmed report that a U.N. observer will arrive in Willow Bend almost momentarily. France, Britain, Bolivia, Mexico and India have already requested permission of Washington to send observers to the scene and other nations undoubtedly plan to file similar requests.

"The world sits on edge tonight, waiting for the word from Willow Bend and—"

Taine reached out and clicked the radio to silence.

"From the sound of it," said Beasly, "we're going to be overrun by a batch of foreigners."

Yes, thought Taine, there might be a batch of foreigners, but not exactly in the sense that Beasly meant. The use of the word, he told himself, so far as any human was concerned, must be outdated now. No man of Earth ever again could be called a foreigner with alien life next door—literally next door. What were the people of the stone house?

And perhaps not the alien life of one planet only, but the alien life of many. For he himself had found another door into yet another planet and there might be many more such doors and what would these other worlds be like, and what was the purpose of the doors?

Someone, *something*, had found a way of going to another planet short of spanning light-years of lonely space—a simpler and a shorter way than flying through the gulfs of space. And once the way was open, then the way stayed open and it was as easy as walking from one room to another.

But one thing—one ridiculous thing—kept puzzling him and that was the spinning and the movement of the connected planets, of all the planets that must be linked together. You could not, he argued, establish solid, factual links between two objects that move independently of one another.

And yet, a couple of days ago, he would have contended just as stolidly that the whole idea on the face of it was fantastic and impossible. Still it had been done. And once one impossibility was accomplished, what logical man could say with sincerity that the second could not be?

The doorbell rang and he got up to answer it.

It was Ernie, the oil man.

"Henry said you wanted some gas and I came to tell you I can't get it until morning."

"That's all right," said Taine. "I don't need it now."

And swiftly slammed the door.

He leaned against it, thinking: I'll have to face them sometime. I can't keep the door locked against the world. Sometime, soon or late, the Earth and I will have to have this out.

And it was foolish, he thought, for him to think like this, but that was the way it was.

He had something here that the Earth demanded; something that Earth wanted or thought it wanted. And yet, in the last analysis, it was his responsibility. It had happened on his land, it had happened in his house; unwittingly, perhaps, he'd even aided and abetted it.

And the land and house are mine, he fiercely told himself, and that world out there was an extension of his yard. No matter how far or where it went, an extension of his yard.

Beasly had left the kitchen and Taine walked into the living room. Towser was curled up and snoring gently in the gold-upholstered chair.

Taine decided he would let him stay there. After all, he thought, Towser had won the right to sleep anywhere he wished.

He walked past the chair to the window and the desert stretched to its far horizon and there before the window sat the man-size woodchuck and Beasly side by side, with their backs turned to the window and staring out across the desert.

Somehow it seemed natural that the chuck and Beasly should be sitting there together—the two of them, it appeared to Taine, might have a lot in common.

And it was a good beginning—that a man and an alien creature from this other world should sit down companionably together.

He tried to envision the setup of these linked worlds, of which Earth was now a part, and the possibilities that lay inherent in the fact of linkage rolled thunder through his brain.

There would be contact between the Earth and these other worlds and what would come of it?

And come to think of it, the contact had been made already, but so naturally, so undramatically, that it failed to register as a great, important meeting. For Beasly and the chuck out there were contact and if it all should go like that, there was absolutely nothing for one to worry over.

This was no haphazard business, he reminded himself. It had been planned and executed with the smoothness of long practice. This was not the first world to be opened and it would not be the last.

The little ratlike things had spanned space—how many light-years of space one could not even guess—in the vehicle which he had unearthed out in the woods. They then had buried it, perhaps as a child might hide a dish by shoving it into a pile of sand. Then they had come to this very house and had set up the apparatus that had made this house a tunnel between one world and another. And once that had been done, the need of crossing space had been canceled out forever. There need be but one crossing and that one crossing would serve to link the planets.

And once the job was done the little ratlike things had left, but not before they had made certain that this gateway to their planet would stand against no matter what assault. They had sheathed the house inside the studdings with a wonder-material that would resist an ax and that, undoubtedly, would resist much more than a simple ax.

And they had marched in drill-order single file out to the hill where eight more of the space machines had rested in their cradles. And now there were only seven there, in their cradles on the hill, and the rat-like things were gone and, perhaps, in time to come, they'd land on another planet and another doorway would be opened, a link to yet another world.

But more, Taine thought, than the linking of mere worlds. It would be, as well, the linking of the peoples of those worlds.

The little ratlike creatures were the explorers and the pioneers who sought out other Earthlike planets and the creature waiting with Beasly just outside the window must also serve its purpose and perhaps in time to come there would be a purpose which man would also serve.

He turned away from the window and looked around the room and the room was exactly as it had been ever since he could remember it. With all the change outside, with all that was happening outside, the room remained unchanged.

This is the reality, thought Taine, this is all the reality there is. Whatever else may happen, this is where I stand—this room with its fireplace blackened by many winter fires, the bookshelves with the old thumbed volumes, the easy-chair, the ancient worn carpet—worn by beloved and unforgotten feet through the many years.

And this also, he knew, was the lull before the storm.

In just a little while the brass would start arriving—the team of scientists, the governmental functionaries, the military, the observers from the other countries, the officials from the U.N.

And against all these, he realized, he stood weaponless and shorn of his strength. No matter what a man might say or think, he could not stand off the world.

This was the last day that this would be the Taine house. After almost a hundred years, it would have another destiny.

And for the first time in all those years there'd be no Taine asleep beneath its roof.

He stood looking at the fireplace and the shelves of books and he sensed the old, pale ghosts walking in the room and he lifted a hesitant hand as if to wave farewell, not only to the ghosts but to the room as well. But before he got it up, he dropped it to his side.

What was the use, he thought.

He went out to the porch and sat down on the steps.

Beasly heard him and turned around.

"He's nice," he said to Taine, patting the chuck upon the back. "He's exactly like a great big teddy bear."

"Yes, I see," said Taine.

"And best of all, I can talk with him."

"Yes, I know," said Taine, remembering that Beasly could talk with Towser, too.

He wondered what it would be like to live in the simple world of Beasly. At times, he decided, it would be comfortable.

The ratlike things had come in the spaceship, but why had they come to Willow Bend, why had they picked this house, the only house in all the village where they would have found the equipment that they needed to build their apparatus so easily and so quickly? For there was no doubt that they had cannibalized the computer to get the equipment they needed. In that, at least, Henry had been right. Thinking back on it, Henry, after all, had played quite a part in it.

Could they have foreseen that on this particular week in this particular house the probability of quickly and easily doing what they had come to do had stood very high?

Did they, with all their other talents and technology, have clairvoyance as well?

"There's someone coming," Beasly said.

"I don't see a thing."

"Neither do I," said Beasly, "but Chuck told me that he saw them."

"Told you!"

"I told you we been talking. There, I can see them too."

They were far off, but they were coming fast—three dots rode rapidly out of the desert.

He sat and watched them come and he thought of going in to get the rifle, but he didn't stir from his seat upon the steps. The rifle would do no good, he told himself. It would be a senseless thing to get it; more than that, a senseless attitude. The least that man could do, he thought, was to meet these creatures of another world with clean and empty hands.

They were closer now and it seemed to him that they were sitting in invisible chairs that traveled very fast.

He saw that they were humanoid, to a degree at least, and there were only three of them.

They came in with a rush and stopped very suddenly a hundred feet or so from where he sat upon the steps.

He didn't move or say a word—there was nothing he could say. It was too ridiculous.

They were, perhaps, a little smaller than himself, and black as the ace of spades, and they wore skin tight shorts and vests that were somewhat oversize and both the shorts and vests were the blue of April skies.

But that was not the worst of it.

They sat on saddles, with horns in front and stirrups and a sort of bedroll tied on the back, but they had no horses.

The saddles floated in the air, with the stirrups about three feet above the ground and the aliens sat easily in the saddles and stared at him and he stared back at them.

Finally he got up and moved forward a step or two and when he did that the three swung from the saddles and moved forward, too, while the saddles hung there in the air, exactly as they'd left them.

Taine walked forward and the three walked forward until they were no more than six feet apart.

"They say hello to you," said Beasly. "They say welcome to you."

"Well, all right, then, tell them— Say, how do you know all this!"

"Chuck tells me what they say and I tell you. You tell me and I tell him and he tells them. That's the way it works. That is what he's here for."

"Well, I'll be—," said Taine. "So you can really talk to him."

"I told you that I could," stormed Beasly. "I told you that I could talk to Towser, too, but you thought that I was crazy."

"Telepathy!" said Taine. And it was worse than ever now. Not only had the ratlike things known all the rest of it, but they'd known of Beasly, too.

"What was that you said, Hiram?"

"Never mind," said Taine. "Tell that friend of yours to tell them I'm glad to meet them and what can I do for them?"

He stood uncomfortably and stared at the three and he saw that their vests had many pockets and that the pockets were crammed, probably with their equivalent of tobacco and handkerchiefs and pocket knives and such.

"They say," said Beasly, "that they want to dicker."

"Dicker?"

"Sure, Hiram. You know, trade."

Beasly chuckled thinly. "Imagine them laying themselves open to a Yankee trader. That's what Henry says you are. He says you can skin a man on the slickest—"

"Leave Henry out of this," snapped Taine. "Let's leave Henry out of something."

He sat down on the ground and the three sat down to face him.

"Ask them what they have in mind to trade."

"Ideas," Beasly said.

"Ideas! That's a crazy thing—"

And then he saw it wasn't.

Of all the commodities that might be exchanged by an alien people, ideas would be the most valuable and the easiest to handle. They'd take no cargo room and they'd upset no economies—not immediately, that is—and they'd make a bigger contribution to the welfare of the cultures than trade in actual goods.

"Ask them," said Taine, "what they'll take for the idea back of those saddles they are riding."

"They say, what have you to offer?"

And that was the stumper. That was the one that would be hard to answer.

Automobiles and trucks, the internal gas engine—well, probably not. Because they already had the saddles. Earth was out of date in transportation from the viewpoint of these people.

Housing architecture—no, that was hardly an idea and, anyhow, there was that other house, so they knew of houses.

Cloth? No, they had cloth.

Paint, he thought. Maybe paint was it.

"See if they are interested in paint," Taine told Beasly.

"They say, what is it? Please explain yourself."

"O.K., then. Let's see. It's a protective device to be spread over almost any surface. Easily packaged and easily applied. Protects against weather and corrosion. It's decorative, too. Comes in all sorts of colors. And its cheap to make."

"They shrug in their mind," said Beasly. "They're just slightly interested. But they'll listen more. Go ahead and tell them."

And that was more like it, thought Taine.

That was the kind of language that he could understand.

He settled himself more firmly on the ground and bent forward slightly, flicking his eyes across the three deadpan, ebony faces, trying to make out what they might be thinking.

There was no making out. Those were three of the deadest pans he had ever seen.

It was all familiar. It made him feel at home. He was in his element.

And in the three across from him, he felt somehow subconsciously, he had the best dickering opposition he had ever met. And that made him feel good too.

"Tell them," he said, "that I'm not quite sure. I may have spoken up too hastily. Paint, after all, is a mighty valuable idea."

"They say, just as a favor to them, not that they're really interested, would you tell them a little more."

Got them hooked, Taine told himself. If he could only play it right—

He settled down to dickering in earnest.

Hours later Henry Horton showed up. He was accompanied by a very urbane gentleman, who was faultlessly turned out and who carried beneath his arm an impressive attaché case.

Henry and the man stopped on the steps in sheer astonishment.

Taine was squatted on the ground with a length of board and he was daubing paint on it while the aliens watched. From the daubs here and there upon their anatomies, it was plain to see the aliens had been doing some daubing of their own. Spread all over the ground were other lengths of half-painted boards and a couple of dozen old cans of paint.

Taine looked up and saw Henry and the man.

"I was hoping," he said, "that someone would show up."

"Hiram," said Henry, with more importance than usual, "may I present Mr. Lancaster. He is a special representative of the United Nations."

"I'm glad to meet you, sir," said Taine. "I wonder if you would—"

"Mr. Lancaster," Henry explained grandly, "was having some slight difficulty getting through the lines outside, so I volunteered my services. I've already explained to him our joint interest in this matter."

"It was very kind of Mr. Horton," Lancaster said. "There was this stupid sergeant—"

"It's all in knowing," Henry said, "how to handle people."

The remark, Taine noticed, was not appreciated by the man from the U.N.

"May I inquire, Mr. Taine," asked Lancaster, "exactly what you're doing?"

"I'm dickering," said Taine.

"Dickering. What a quaint way of expressing—"

"An old Yankee word," said Henry quickly, "with certain connotations of its own. When you trade with someone you are exchanging goods, but if you're dickering with him you're out to get his hide."

"Interesting," said Lancaster. "And I suppose you're out to skin these gentlemen in the sky-blue vests—"

"Hiram," said Henry, proudly, "is the sharpest dickerer in these parts. He runs an antique business and he has to dicker hard—"

"And may I ask," said Lancaster, ignoring Henry finally, "what you might be doing with these cans of paint? Are these gentlemen potential customers for paint or—"

Taine threw down the board and rose angrily to his feet.

"If you'd both shut up!" he shouted. "I've been trying to say something ever since you got here and I can't get in a word. And I tell you, it's important—"

"Hiram!" Henry exclaimed in horror.

"It's quite all right," said the U.N. man. "We *have* been jabbering. And now, Mr. Taine?"

"I'm backed into a corner," Taine told him, "and I need some help. I've sold these fellows on the idea of paint, but I don't know a thing about it—the principle back of it or how it's made or what goes into it or—"

"But, Mr. Taine, if you're selling them the paint, what difference does it make—"

"I'm not selling them the paint," yelled Taine. "Can't you understand that? They don't want the paint. They want the *idea* of paint, the principle of paint. It's something that they never thought of and they're interested. I offered them the paint idea for the idea of their saddles and I've almost got it—"

"Saddles? You mean those things over there, hanging in the air?"

"That is right. Beasly, would you ask one of our friends to demonstrate a saddle?"

"You bet I will," said Beasly.

"What," demanded Henry, "has Beasly got to do with this?"

"Beasly is an interpreter. I guess you'd call him a telepath. You remember how he always claimed he could talk with Towser?"

"Beasly was always claiming things."

"But this time he was right. He tells Chuck, that funny-looking monster, what I want to say and Chuck tells these aliens. And these aliens tell Chuck and Chuck tells Beasly and Beasly tells me."

"Ridiculous!" snorted Henry. "Beasly hasn't got the sense to be . . . what did you say he was?"

"A telepath," said Taine.

One of the aliens had gotten up and climbed into a saddle. He rode it forth and back. Then he swung out of it and sat down again.

"Remarkable," said the U.N. man. "Some sort of antigravity unit, with complete control. We could make use of that, indeed."

He scraped his hand across his chin.

"And you're going to exchange the idea of paint for the idea of that saddle?"

"That's exactly it," said Taine, "but I need some help. I need a chemist or a paint manufacturer or someone to explain how paint is made. And I need some professor or other who'll understand what they're talking about when they tell me the idea of the saddle."

"I see," said Lancaster. "Yes, indeed, you have a problem. Mr. Taine, you seem to me a man of some discernment—"

"Oh, he's all of that," interrupted Henry. "Hiram's quite astute."

"So I suppose you'll understand," said the U.N. man, "that this whole procedure is quite irregular—"

"But it's not," exploded Taine. "That's the way they operate. They open up a planet and then they exchange ideas. They've been doing that with other planets for a long, long, time. And ideas are all they want, just the new ideas, because that is the way to keep on building a technology and culture. And they have a lot of ideas, sir, that the human race can use."

"That is just the point," said Lancaster. "This is perhaps the most important thing that has ever happened to us humans. In just a short year's time we can obtain data and ideas that will put us ahead—theoretically, at least—by a thousand years. And in a thing that is so important, we should have experts on the job—"

"But," protested Henry, "you can't find a man who'll do a better dickering job than Hiram. When you dicker with him your back teeth aren't safe. Why don't you leave him be? He'll do a job for you. You can get your experts and your planning groups together and let Hiram front for you. These folks have accepted him and have proved they'll do business with him and what more do you want? All he needs is a little help."

Beasly came over and faced the U.N. man.

"I won't work with no one else," he said. "If you kick Hiram out of here, then I go with him. Hiram's the only person who ever treated me like a human—"

"There, you see!" Henry said, triumphantly.

"Now, wait a second, Beasly," said the U.N. man. "We could make it worth your while. I should imagine that an interpreter in a situation such as this could command a handsome salary."

"Money don't mean a thing to me," said Beasly. "It won't buy me friends. People still will laugh at me."

"He means it, mister," Henry warned. "There isn't anyone who can be as stubborn as Beasly. I know; he used to work for us."

The U.N. man looked flabbergasted and not a little desperate.

"It will take you quite some time," Henry pointed out, "to find another telepath—leastwise one who can talk to these people here."

The U.N. man looked as if he were strangling. "I doubt," he said, "there's another one on Earth."

"Well, all right," said Beasly, brutally, "let's make up our minds. I ain't standing here all day."

"All right," cried the U.N. man. "You two go ahead. Please, will you go ahead? This is a chance we can't let slip through our fingers. Is there anything you want? Anything I can do for you?"

"Yes, there is," said Taine. "There'll be the boys from Washington and bigwigs from other countries. Just keep them off my back."

"I'll explain most carefully to everyone. There'll be no interference."

"And I need that chemist and someone who'll know about the saddles. And I need them quick. I can stall these boys a little longer, but not for too much longer."

"Anyone you need," said the U.N. man. "Anyone at all. I'll have them here in hours. And in a day or two there'll be a pool of experts waiting for whenever you may need them—on a moment's notice."

"Sir," said Henry, unctuously, "that's most co-operative. Both Hiram and I appreciate it greatly. And now, since this is settled, I understand that there are reporters waiting. They'll be interested in your statement."

The U.N. man, it seemed, didn't have it in him to protest. He and Henry went tramping up the stairs.

Taine turned around and looked out across the desert.

"It's a big front yard," he said.

## Robert Bloch

Robert Bloch likes to say that he has the heart of a little boy—pickled in alcohol on his desk.

And I think he has, for this mild, gentle soul, who gazes benignly at the world from his lanky, sharp-featured height, writes the most grisly tales imaginable. Notably, he wrote the story entitled "Alfred Hitchcock's Psycho" which, when it was first written, was known simply as *Psycho*.

I met Bob rather slightly at the 11th Convention (Philadelphia, 1953) but our real friendship dates from the 13th Convention (Cleveland, 1955). Thereafter we carried on a correspondence that saw weekly letters exchanged for four years—until Bob was carried by the tidal wave of "Alfred Hitchcock's Psycho" into the engulfing arms of Hollywood where he disappeared (I hope, not forever) from the ken of mortal man.

Bob is one of the three science fiction personalities who, for his wit, humor, presence of mind and general amiability, serves as perennial toastmaster at the conventions. (Anthony Boucher, mystery reviewer for the New York *Times,* and beloved one-time editor of *The Magazine of Fantasy and Science Fiction* is the second.)

On the occasion of the 17th Convention (Detroit, 1959), Bob and I shared the role of toastmaster. Influenced by the usual course of events at the Academy Award dinner in Hollywood we got up after the banquet in our glisten and glitter and announced the Hugo winners in alternation.

It was Bob's turn when we came to the short-story award and he opened the envelope and remained standing and staring, his eyes slightly protruding and his Adam's apple bobbing slowly up and down. I looked over his shoulder and the card he held announced his own story, "The Hell-Bound Train" to be the winner.

With a gay laugh, I plucked the card from his nerveless fingers, and announced the result. I placed the Hugo in his trembling hands and guided him to a seat where he might for just a moment be alone with his glory.

# 7

# THE HELL-BOUND TRAIN

When Martin was a little boy, his Daddy was a Railroad Man. Daddy never rode the high iron, but he walked the tracks for the CB&Q, and he was proud of his job. And every night when he got drunk, he sang this old song about *That Hell-Bound Train*.

Martin didn't quite remember any of the words, but he couldn't forget the way his Daddy sang them out. And when Daddy made the mistake of getting drunk in the afternoon and got squeezed between a Pennsy tank-car and an *AT&SF* gondola, Martin sort of wondered why the Brotherhood didn't sing the song at his funeral.

After that, things didn't go so good for Martin, but somehow he always recalled Daddy's song. When Mom up and ran off with a traveling salesman from Keokuk (Daddy must have turned over in his grave, knowing she'd done such a thing, and with a *passenger,* too!) Martin hummed the tune to himself every night in the Orphan Home. And after Martin himself ran away, he used to whistle the song softly at night in the jungles, after the other bindlestiffs were asleep.

Martin was on the road for four-five years before he realized he wasn't getting anyplace. Of course he'd tried his hand at a lot of things —picking fruit in Oregon, washing dishes in a Montana hash-house, stealing hub-caps in Denver and tires in Oklahoma City—but by the time he'd put in six months on the chain-gang down in Alabama he knew he had no future drifting around this way on his own.

So he tried to get on the railroad like his Daddy had and they told him that times were bad.

But Martin couldn't keep away from the railroads. Wherever he traveled, he rode the rods; he'd rather hop a freight heading north in sub-zero weather than lift his thumb to hitch a ride with a Cadillac headed for Florida. Whenever he managed to get hold of a can of Sterno, he'd sit there under a nice warm culvert, think about the old days, and often as not he'd hum the song about *That Hell-Bound Train.* That was the train the drunks and the sinners rode—the gambling men and the grifters, the big-time spenders, the skirt-chasers, and all the jolly crew. It would be really fine to take a trip in such good company, but Martin didn't like to think of what happened when that train finally pulled into the Depot Way Down Yonder. He didn't figure on spending eternity stoking boilers in Hell, without even a Company Union to protect him. Still, it would be a lovely ride. If there was *such* a thing as a Hell-Bound Train. Which, of course, there wasn't.

At least Martin didn't *think* there was, until that evening when he found himself walking the tracks heading south, just outside of Appleton Junction. The night was cold and dark, the way November nights are in the Fox River Valley, and he knew he'd have to work his way down to New Orleans for the winter, or maybe even Texas. Somehow he didn't much feel like going, even though he'd heard tell that a lot of those Texas automobiles had solid gold hub-caps.

No sir, he just wasn't cut out for petty larceny. It was worse than a sin—it was unprofitable, too. Bad enough to do the Devil's work, but then to get such miserable pay on top of it! Maybe he'd better let the Salvation Army convert him.

Martin trudged along humming Daddy's song, waiting for a rattler to pull out of the Junction behind him. He'd have to catch it—there was nothing else for him to do.

But the first train to come along came from the other direction, roaring towards him along the track from the south.

Martin peered ahead, but his eyes couldn't match his ears, and so far all he could recognize was the sound. It *was* a train, though; he felt the steel shudder and sing beneath his feet.

And yet, how could it be? The next station south was Neenah-Menasha, and there was nothing due out of there for hours.

The clouds were thick overhead, and the field-mists rolled like a cold fog in a November midnight. Even so, Martin should have been able to see the headlight as the train rushed on. But there was only the whistle, screaming out of the black throat of the night. Martin could recognize the equipment of just about any locomotive ever built, but he'd never heard a whistle that sounded like this one. It wasn't signalling; it was screaming like a lost soul.

He stepped to one side, for the train was almost on top of him now. And suddenly there it was, looming along the tracks and grinding to a stop in less time than he'd believed possible. The wheels hadn't been oiled, because they screamed too, screamed like the damned. But the train slid to a halt and the screams died away into a series of low, groaning sounds, and Martin looked up and saw that this was a passenger train. It was big and black, without a single light shining in the engine cab or any of the long string of cars; Martin couldn't read any lettering on the sides, but he was pretty sure this train didn't belong on the Northwestern Road.

He was even more sure when he saw the man clamber down out of the forward car. There was something wrong about the way he walked, as though one of his feet dragged, and about the lantern he carried. The lantern was dark, and the man held it up to his mouth and blew, and instantly it glowed redly. You don't have to be a member of the Railway Brotherhood to know that this is a mighty peculiar way of lighting a lantern.

As the figure approached, Martin recognized the conductor's cap perched on his head, and this made him feel a little better for a moment —until he noticed that it was worn a bit too high, as though there might be something sticking up on the forehead underneath it.

Still, Martin knew his manners, and when the man smiled at him, he said, "Good evening, Mr. Conductor."

"Good evening, Martin."

"How did you know my name?"

The man shrugged. "How did you know I was the Conductor?"

"You *are*, aren't you?"

"To you, yes. Although other people, in other walks of life, may recognize me in different roles. For instance, you ought to see what I look like to the folks out in Hollywood." The man grinned. "I travel a great deal," he explained.

"What brings you here?" Martin asked.

"Why, you ought to know the answer to that, Martin. I came because you needed me. Tonight, I suddenly realized you were backsliding. Thinking of joining the Salvation Army, weren't you?"

"Well—" Martin hesitated.

"Don't be ashamed. To err is human, as somebody-or-other once said. *Reader's Digest*, wasn't it? Never mind. The point is, I felt you needed me. So I switched over and came your way."

"What for?"

"Why, to offer you a ride, of course. Isn't it better to travel comfortably by train than to march along the cold streets behind a Salvation Army band? Hard on the feet, they tell me, and even harder on the eardrums."

"I'm not sure I'd care to ride your train, sir," Martin said. "Considering where I'm likely to end up."

"Ah, yes. The old argument." The Conductor sighed. "I suppose you'd prefer some sort of bargain, is that it?"

"Exactly," Martin answered.

"Well, I'm afraid I'm all through with that sort of thing. There's no shortage of prospective passengers any more. Why should I offer you any special inducements?"

"You must want me, or else you wouldn't have bothered to go out of your way to find me."

The Conductor sighed again. "There you have a point. Pride was always my besetting weakness, I admit. And somehow I'd hate to lose you to the competition, after thinking of you as my own all these years." He hesitated. "Yes, I'm prepared to deal with you on your own terms, if you insist."

"The terms?" Martin asked.

"Standard proposition. Anything you want."

"Ah," said Martin.

"But I warn you in advance, there'll be no tricks. I'll grant you any wish you can name—but in return, you must promise to ride the train when the time comes."

"Suppose it never comes?"

"It will."

"Suppose I've got the kind of a wish that will keep me off forever?"

"There is no such wish."

"Don't be too sure."

"Let me worry about that," the Conductor told him. "No matter what you have in mind, I warn you that I'll collect in the end. And there'll be none of this last-minute hocus-pocus, either. No last-hour repentances, no blonde *frauleins* or fancy lawyers showing up to get you off. I offer a clean deal. That is to say, you'll get what you want, and I'll get what I want."

"I've heard you trick people. They say you're worse than a used-car salesman."

"Now, wait a minute—"

"I apologize," Martin said, hastily. "But it *is* supposed to be a fact that you can't be trusted."

"I admit it. On the other hand, you seem to think you have found a way out."

"A sure-fire proposition."

"Sure-fire? Very funny!" The man began to chuckle, then halted. "But we waste valuable time, Martin. Let's get down to cases. What do you want from me?"

Martin took a deep breath. "I want to be able to stop Time."

"Right now?"

"No. Not yet. And not for everybody. I realize that would be impossible, of course. But I want to be able to stop Time for myself. Just once, in the future. Whenever I get to a point where I know I'm happy and contented, that's where I'd like to stop. So I can just keep on being happy forever."

"That's quite a proposition," the Conductor mused. "I've got to admit I've never heard anything just like it before—and believe me, I've listened to some lulus in my day." He grinned at Martin. "You've really been thinking about this, haven't you?"

"For years," Martin admitted. Then he coughed. "Well, what do you say?"

"It's not impossible, in terms of your own *subjective* time-sense," the Conductor murmured. "Yes, I think it could be arranged."

"But I mean *really* to stop. Nor for me just to *imagine* it."

"I understand. And it can be done."

"Then you'll agree?"

"Why not? I promised you, didn't I? Give me your hand."

Martin hesitated. "Will it hurt very much? I mean, I don't like the sight of blood, and—"

"Nonsense! You've been listening to a lot of poppycock. We already have made our bargain, my boy. I merely intend to put something into your hand. The ways and means of fulfilling your wish. After all, there's no telling at just what moment you may decide to exercise the agreement, and I can't drop everything and come running. So it's better if you can regulate matters for yourself."

"You're going to give me a Time-stopper?"

"That's the general idea. As soon as I can decide what would be practical." The Conductor hesitated. "Ah, the very thing! Here, take my watch."

He pulled it out of his vest-pocket; a railroad watch in a silver case. He opened the back and made a delicate adjustment; Martin tried to see just exactly what he was doing, but the fingers moved in a blinding blur.

"There we are," the Conductor smiled. "It's all set, now. When you finally decide where you'd like to call a halt, merely turn the stem in reverse and unwind the watch until it stops. When it stops, Time stops, for you. Simple enough?" And the Conductor dropped the watch into Martin's hand.

The young man closed his fingers tightly around the case. "That's all there is to it, eh?"

"Absolutely. But remember—you can stop the watch only once. So you'd better make sure that you're satisfied with the moment you choose to prolong. I caution you in all fairness; make very certain of your choice."

"I will." Martin grinned. "And since you've been so fair about it, I'll be fair, too. There's one thing you seem to have forgotten. It doesn't really matter *what* moment I choose. Because once I stop Time for myself, that means I stay where I am forever. I'll never have to get any older. And if I don't get any older, I'll never die. And if I never die, then I'll never have to take a ride on your train."

The Conductor turned away. His shoulders shook convulsively, and he may have been crying. "And you said *I* was worse than a used-car salesman," he gasped, in a strangled voice.

Then he wandered off into the fog, and the train-whistle gave an impatient shriek, and all at once it was moving swiftly down the track, rumbling out of sight in the darkness.

Martin stood there, blinking down at the silver watch in his hand. If it wasn't that he could actually see it and feel it there, and if he couldn't smell that peculiar odor, he might have thought he'd imagined the whole thing from start to finish—train, Conductor, bargain, and all.

But he had the watch, and he could recognize the scent left by the train as it departed, even though there aren't many locomotives around that use sulphur and brimstone as fuel.

And he had no doubts about his bargain. That's what came of thinking things through to a logical conclusion. Some fools would have settled for wealth, or power, or Kim Novak. Daddy might have sold out for a fifth of whiskey.

Martin knew that he'd made a better deal. Better? It was foolproof. All he needed to do now was choose his moment.

He put the watch in his pocket and started back down the railroad track. He hadn't really had a destination in mind before, but he did now. He was going to find a moment of happiness. . . .

Now young Martin wasn't altogether a ninny. He realized perfectly well that happiness is a relative thing; there are conditions and degrees of contentment, and they vary with one's lot in life. As a hobo, he was often satisfied with a warm handout, a double-length bench in the park, or a can of Sterno made in 1957 (a vintage year). Many a time he had reached a state of momentary bliss through such simple agencies, but he was aware that there were better things. Martin determined to seek them out.

Within two days he was in the great city of Chicago. Quite naturally, he drifted over to West Madison Street, and there he took steps to elevate his role in life. He became a city bum, a panhandler, a moocher. Within a week he had risen to the point where happiness was a meal in a regular one-arm luncheon joint, a two-bit flop on a real army cot in a real flophouse, and a full fifth of muscatel.

There was a night, after enjoying all three of these luxuries to the full, when Martin thought of unwinding his watch at the pinnacle of intoxication. But he also thought of the faces of the honest johns he'd braced for a handout today. Sure, they were squares, but they were prosperous. They wore good clothes, held good jobs, drove nice cars. And for them, happiness was even more ecstatic—they ate dinner in fine hotels, they slept on innerspring mattresses, they drank blended whiskey.

Squares or no, they had something there. Martin fingered his watch, put aside the temptation to hock it for another bottle of muscatel, and went to sleep determined to get himself a job and improve his happiness-quotient.

When he awoke he had a hangover, but the determination was still with him. Before the month was out Martin was working for a general contractor over on the South Side, at one of the big rehabilitation projects. He hated the grind, but the pay was good, and pretty soon he got himself a one-room apartment out on Blue Island Avenue. He was accustomed to eating in decent restaurants now, and he bought himself a comfortable bed, and every Saturday night he went down to the corner tavern. It was all very pleasant, but—

The foreman liked his work and promised him a raise in a month. If he waited around, the raise would mean that he could afford a second-hand car. With a car, he could even start picking up a girl for a date now and then. Other fellows on the job did, and they seemed pretty happy.

So Martin kept on working, and the raise came through and the car came through and pretty soon a couple of girls came through.

The first time it happened, he wanted to unwind his watch immediately. Until he got to thinking about what some of the older men always said. There was a guy named Charlie, for example, who worked alongside him on the hoist. "When you're young and don't know the score, maybe you get a kick out of running around with those pigs. But after a while, you want something better. A nice girl of your own. That's the ticket."

Martin felt he owed it to himself to find out. If he didn't like it better, he could always go back to what he had.

Almost six months went by before Martin met Lillian Gillis. By that time he'd had another promotion and was working inside, in the office. They made him go to night school to learn how to do simple book-keeping, but it meant another fifteen bucks extra a week, and it was nicer working indoors.

And Lillian *was* a lot of fun. When she told him she'd marry him, Martin was almost sure that the time was now. Except that she was sort of—well, she was a *nice* girl, and she said they'd have to wait until they were married. Of course, Martin couldn't expect to marry her until he had a little more money saved up, and another raise would help, too.

That took a year. Martin was patient, because he knew it was going to be worth it. Every time he had any doubts, he took out his watch and looked at it. But he never showed it to Lillian, or anybody else. Most of the other men wore expensive wristwatches and the old silver railroad watch looked just a little cheap.

Martin smiled as he gazed at the stem. Just a few twists and he'd have something none of these other poor working slobs would ever have. Permanent satisfaction, with his blushing bride—

Only getting married turned out to be just the beginning. Sure, it was wonderful, but Lillian told him how much better things would be if they could move into a new place and fix it up. Martin wanted decent furniture, a TV set, a nice car.

So he started taking night courses and got a promotion to the front office. With the baby coming, he wanted to stick around and see his son arrive. And when it came, he realized he'd have to wait until it got a little older, started to walk and talk and develop a personality of its own.

About this time the company sent him out on the road as a trouble-shooter on some of those other jobs, and now he *was* eating at those good hotels, living high on the hog and the expense-account. More than once he was tempted to unwind his watch. This was the good life. . . . Of course, it would be even better if he just didn't have to *work*. Sooner or later, if he could cut in on one of the company deals, he could make a pile and retire. Then everything would be ideal.

It happened, but it took time. Martin's son was going to high school before he really got up there into the chips. Martin got a strong hunch that it was now or never, because he wasn't exactly a kid any more.

But right about then he met Sherry Westcott, and she didn't seem to think he was middle-aged at all, in spite of the way he was losing hair and adding stomach. She taught him that a *toupee* would cover the bald spot and a cummerbund could cover the potgut. In fact, she taught him quite a lot and he so enjoyed learning that he actually took out his watch and prepared to unwind it.

Unfortunately, he chose the very moment that the private detectives broke down the door of the hotel room, and then there was a long stretch of time when Martin was so busy fighting the divorce action that he couldn't honestly say he was enjoying any given moment.

When he made the final settlement with Lil he was broke again, and Sherry didn't seem to think he was so young, after all. So he squared his shoulders and went back to work.

He made his pile, eventually, but it took longer this time, and there wasn't much chance to have fun along the way. The fancy dames in the fancy cocktail lounges didn't seem to interest him any more, and neither did the liquor. Besides, the Doc had warned him off that.

But there were other pleasures for a rich man to investigate. Travel, for instance—and not riding the rods from one hick burg to another, either. Martin went around the world by plane and luxury liner. For a while it seemed as though he would find his moment after all, visiting the Taj Mahal by moonlight. Martin pulled out the battered old watchcase, and got ready to unwind it. Nobody else was there to watch him—

And that's why he hesitated. Sure, this was an enjoyable moment, but he was alone. Lil and the kid were gone, Sherry was gone, and somehow he'd never had time to make any friends. Maybe if he found new congenial people, he'd have the ultimate happiness. That must be the answer—it wasn't just money or power or sex or seeing beautiful things. The real satisfaction lay in friendship.

So on the boat trip home, Martin tried to strike up a few acquaintances at the ship's bar. But all these people were much younger, and Martin had nothing in common with them. Also they wanted to dance and drink, and Martin wasn't in condition to appreciate such pastimes. Nevertheless, he tried.

Perhaps that's why he had the little accident the day before they docked in San Francisco. "Little accident" was the ship's doctor's way of describing it, but Martin noticed he looked very grave when he told him to stay in bed, and he'd called an ambulance to meet the liner at the dock and take the patient right to the hospital.

At the hospital, all the expensive treatment and the expensive smiles and the expensive words didn't fool Martin any. He was an old man with a bad heart, and they thought he was going to die.

But he could fool them. He still had the watch. He found it in his coat when he put on his clothes and sneaked out of the hospital.

He didn't have to die. He could cheat death with a single gesture—and he intended to do it as a free man, out there under a free sky.

That was the real secret of happiness. He understood it now. Not even friendship meant as much as freedom. This was the best thing of all—to be free of friends or family or the furies of the flesh.

Martin walked slowly beside the embankment under the night sky. Come to think of it, he was just about back where he'd started, so many years ago. But the moment was good, good enough to prolong forever. Once a bum, always a bum.

He smiled as he thought about it, and then the smile twisted sharply and suddenly, like the pain twisting sharply and suddenly in his chest. The world began to spin and he fell down on the side of the embankment.

He couldn't see very well, but he was still conscious, and he knew what had happened. Another stroke, and a bad one. Maybe this was it. Except that he wouldn't be a fool any longer. He wouldn't wait to see what was still around the corner.

Right now was his chance to use his power and save his life. And he was going to do it. He could still move, nothing could stop him.

He groped in his pocket and pulled out the old silver watch, fumbling with the stem. A few twists and he'd cheat death, he'd never have to ride that Hell-Bound Train. He could go on forever.

*Forever.*

Martin had never really considered the word before. To go on forever—but *how?* Did he *want* to go on forever, like this; a sick old man, lying helplessly here in the grass?

No. He couldn't do it. He wouldn't do it. And suddenly he wanted very much to cry, because he knew that somewhere along the line he'd outsmarted himself. And now it was too late. His eyes dimmed, there was a roaring in his ears . . .

He recognized the roaring, of course, and he wasn't at all surprised to see the train come rushing out of the fog up there on the embankment. He wasn't surprised when it stopped, either, or when the Conductor climbed off and walked slowly towards him.

The Conductor hadn't changed a bit. Even his grin was still the same.

"Hello, Martin," he said. "All aboard."

"I know," Martin whispered. "But you'll have to carry me. I can't walk. I'm not even really talking any more, am I?"

"Yes you are," the Conductor said. "I can hear you fine. And you can walk, too." He leaned down and placed his hand on Martin's chest. There was a moment of icy numbness, and then, sure enough, Martin could walk after all.

He got up and followed the Conductor along the slope, moving to the side of the train.

"In here?" he asked.

"No, the next car," the Conductor murmured. "I guess you're entitled to ride Pullman. After all, you're quite a successful man. You've tasted the joys of wealth and position and prestige. You've known the pleasures of marriage and fatherhood. You've sampled the delights of dining and drinking and debauchery, too, and you traveled high, wide and handsome. So let's not have any last-minute recriminations."

"All right," Martin sighed. "I can't blame you for my mistakes. On the other hand, you can't take credit for what happened, either. I worked for everything I got. I did it all on my own. I didn't even need your watch."

"So you didn't," the Conductor said, smiling. "But would you mind giving it back to me now?"

"Need it for the next sucker, eh?" Martin muttered.

"Perhaps."

Something about the way he said it made Martin look up. He tried to see the Conductor's eyes, but the brim of his cap cast a shadow. So Martin looked down at the watch instead.

"Tell me something," he said, softly. "If I give you the watch, what will you do with it?"

"Why, throw it into the ditch," the Conductor told him. "That's all I'll do with it." And he held out his hand.

"What if somebody comes along and finds it? And twists the stem backwards, and stops Time?"

"Nobody would do that," the Conductor murmured. "Even if they knew."

"You mean, it was all a trick? This is only an ordinary, cheap watch?"

"I didn't say that," whispered the Conductor. "I only said that no one has ever twisted the stem backwards. They've all been like you, Martin —looking ahead to find that perfect happiness. Waiting for the moment that never comes."

The Conductor held out his hand again.

Martin sighed and shook his head. "You cheated me after all."

"You cheated yourself, Martin. And now you're going to ride that Hell-Bound Train."

He pushed Martin up the steps and into the car ahead. As he entered, the train began to move and the whistle screamed. And Martin stood there in the swaying Pullman, gazing down the aisle at the other passengers. He could see them sitting there, and somehow it didn't seem strange at all.

Here they were; the drunks and the sinners, the gambling men and the grifters, the big-time spenders, the skirt-chasers, and all the jolly crew. They knew where they were going, of course, but they didn't seem to give a damn. The blinds were drawn on the windows, yet it was light inside, and they were all living it up—singing and passing the bottle and roaring with laughter, throwing the dice and telling their jokes and bragging their big brags, just the way Daddy used to sing about them in the old song.

"Mighty nice traveling companions," Martin said. "Why, I've never seen such a pleasant bunch of people. I mean, they seem to be really enjoying themselves!"

The Conductor shrugged. "I'm afraid things won't be quite so jazzy when we pull into that Depot Way Down Yonder."

For the third time, he held out his hand. "Now, before you sit down, if you'll just give me that watch. A bargain's a bargain—"

Martin smiled. "A bargain's a bargain," he echoed. "I agreed to ride your train if I could stop Time when I found the right moment of happiness. And I think I'm about as happy right here as I've ever been."

Very slowly, Martin took hold of the silver watch-stem.

"No!" gasped the Conductor. "No!"

But the watch-stem turned.

"Do you realize what you've done?" the Conductor yelled. "Now we'll never reach the Depot! We'll just go on riding, all of us—forever!"

Martin grinned. "I know," he said. "But the fun is in the trip, not the destination. You taught me that. And I'm looking forward to a wonderful trip. Look, maybe I can even help. If you were to find me another one of those caps, now, and let me keep this watch—"

And that's the way it finally worked out. Wearing his cap and carrying his battered old silver watch, there's no happier person in or out of this world—now and forever—than Martin. Martin, the new Brakeman on That Hell-Bound Train.

*1960*
*18th CONVENTION*
*PITTSBURGH*

*Daniel Keyes*

It is difficult, as you all by now realize, for me to hand out Hugos, convinced as I am that in any one year, any of half a dozen stories of my own, rightly deserved the victory. Naturally, I mask this feeling with consummate skill and I believe I gave myself away only once.

That was at the 18th Convention (Pittsburgh, 1960)—a convention which, I might say as a purely personal opinion, was the best and most wonderful convention of all—when I found myself handing out the Hugo to Daniel Keyes for the story "Flowers for Algernon."

Now here was a story which struck me so forcefully that I was actually lost in admiration as I read it. So lost in admiration was I for the delicacy of his feeling, for the sure way in which he plucked at my heartstrings, for the skill with which he handled the remarkable *tour de force* involved in his method of telling the story, that I completely forgot to hate him.

When I announced the Hugo for that story in Pittsburgh, therefore, a sudden access of warmth entered my tones which must have shown, by comparison, that the cheer with which I handed out the other Hugos was synthetic.

My winged words cleft the air impassionedly as I delivered an impromptu encomium on the manifold excellences of Daniel Keyes. "How did he do it?" I demanded of the Muses. "How did he do it?"

I then looked up at a level about nine or ten feet from the floor in order to encounter the face of this giant whom I had never, until that moment, met.

A hand plucked at my elbow and I brought my eyes down to ordinary man-height. And, from the round and gentle face of Daniel Keyes, issued the immortal words: "Listen, when you find out how I did it, let me know, will you? I want to do it again."

# 8

# FLOWERS FOR ALGERNON

*progris riport 1—martch 5, 1965*

Dr. Strauss says I shud rite down what I think and evrey thing that happins to me from now on. I dont know why but he says its importint so they will see if they will use me. I hope they use me. Miss Kinnian says maybe they can make me smart. I want to be smart. My name is Charlie Gordon. I am 37 years old. I have nuthing more to rite now so I will close for today.

*progris riport 2—martch 6*

I had a test today. I think I faled it. And I think maybe now they wont use me. What happind is a nice young man was in the room and he had some white cards and ink spillled all over them. He sed Charlie what do yo see on this card. I was very skared even tho I had my rabits foot in my pockit because when I was a kid I always faled tests in school and I spillled ink to.

I told him I saw a inkblot. He said yes and it made me feel good. I thot that was all but when I got up to go he said Charlie we are not thru yet. Then I dont remember so good but he wantid me to say what was in the ink. I dint see nuthing in the ink but he said there was picturs there other pepul saw some picturs. I couldnt see any picturs. I reely tryed. I held the card close up and then far away. Then I said if I had my glases I coud see better I usally only ware my glases in the movies or TV but I said they are in the closit in the hall. I got them. Then I said let me see that card agen I bet Ill find it now.

I tryed hard but I only saw the ink. I told him maybe I need new glases. He rote something down on a paper and I got skared of faling the test. I told him it was a very nice inkblot with littel points all around the edges. He looked very sad so that wasnt it. I said please let me try agen. Ill get it in a few minits becaus Im not so fast somtimes. Im a slow reeder too in Miss Kinnians class for slow adults but I'm trying very hard.

He gave me a chance with another card that had 2 kinds of ink spilled on it red and blue.

He was very nice and talked slow like Miss Kinnian does and he explaned it to me that it was a *raw shok*. He said pepul see things in the ink. I said show me where. He said think. I told him I think a ink-blot but that wasn't rite eather. He said what does it remind you—pretend something. I closed my eyes for a long time to pretend. I told him I pretend a fowntan pen with ink leeking all over a table cloth.

I dont think I passed the *raw shok* test

### *progris riport 3—martch 7*

Dr Strauss and Dr Nemur say it dont matter about the inkblots. They said that maybe they will still use me. I said Miss Kinnian never gave me tests like that one only spelling and reading. They said Miss Kinnian told that I was her bestist pupil in the adult nite school becaus I tryed the hardist and I reely wantid to lern. They said how come you went to the adult nite scool all by yourself Charlie. How did you find it. I said I asked pepul and sumbody told me where I shud go to lern to read and spell good. They said why did you want to. I told them becaus all my life I wantid to be smart and not dumb. But its very hard to be smart. They said you know it will probly be tempirery. I said yes. Miss Kinnian told me. I dont care if it herts.

Later I had more crazy tests today. The nice lady who gave it to me told me the name and I asked her how do you spellit so I can rite it my progris riport. THEMATIC APPERCEPTION TEST. I dont know the frist 2 words but I know what *test* means. You got to pass it or you get bad marks. This test lookd easy becaus I coud see the picturs. Only this time she dint want me to tell her the picturs. That mixd me up. She said make up storys about the pepul in the picturs.

I told her how can you tell storys about pepul you never met. I said why shud I make up lies. I never tell lies any more becaus I always get caut.

She told me this test and the other one the raw-shok was for getting personality. I laffed so hard. I said how can you get that thing from inkblots and fotos. She got sore and put her picturs away. I don't care. It was sily. I gess I faled that test too.

Later some men in white coats took me to a difernt part of the hospitil and gave me a game to play. It was like a race with a white mouse. They called the mouse Algernon. Algernon was in a box with a lot of twists and turns like all kinds of walls and they gave me a pencil and a paper with lines and lots of boxes. On one side it said START and on the other end it said FINISH. They said it was *amazed* and that Algernon and me had the same *amazed* to do. I dint see how we could have the same *amazed* if Algernon had a box and I had a paper but I dint say nothing. Anyway there wasnt time because the race started.

One of the men had a watch he was trying to hide so I wouldnt see it so I tryed not to look and that made me nervus.

Anyway that test made me feel worser than all the others because they did it over 10 times with different *amazeds* and Algernon won every time. I dint know that mice were so smart. Maybe thats because Algernon is a white mouse. Maybe white mice are smarter than other mice.

### *progris riport 4—Mar 8*

Their going to use me! Im so excited I can hardly write. Dr Nemur and Dr Strauss had a argament about it first. Dr Nemur was in the office when Dr Strauss brot me in. Dr Nemur was worryed about using me but Dr Strauss told him Miss Kinnian rekemmended me the best from all the people who she was teaching. I like Miss Kinnian becaus shes a very smart teacher. And she said Charlie your going to have a second chance. If you volenteer for this experament you mite get smart. They dont know if it will be perminint but theirs a chance. Thats why I said ok even when I was scared because she said it was an operashun. She said dont be scared Charlie you done so much with so little I think you deserv it most of all.

So I got scaird when Dr. Nemur and Dr. Strauss argud about it. Dr. Strauss said I had something that was very good. He said I had a good *motorvation*. I never even knew I had that. I felt proud when he said that not every body with an eye-q of 68 had that thing. I dant know what it is or where I got it but he said Algernon had it too. Algernons *motor-vation* is the cheese they put in his box. But it cant be that because I didn't eat any cheese this week.

Then he told Dr Nemur something I dint understand so while they were talking I wrote down some of the words.

He said Dr. Nemur I know Charlie is not what you had in mind as the first of your new brede of intelek** (coudnt get the word) superman. But most people of his low ment** are host** and uncoop** they are usually dull apath** and hard to reach. He has a good natcher hes intristed and eager to please.

Dr Nemur said remember he will be the first human beeng ever to have his intelijence tripled by surgicle meens.

Dr. Strauss said exakly. Look at how well hes lerned to read and write for his low mentel age its as grate an acheve** as you and I lerning einstines therey of **vity without help. That shows the inteness motor-vation. Its comparat** a tremen** achev** I say we use Charlie.

I dint get all the words but it sounded like Dr Strauss was on my side and like the other one wasnt.

Then Dr Nemur nodded he said all right maybe your right. We will use Charlie. When he said that I got so exited I jumped up and shook his hand for being so good to me. I told him thank you doc you wont be sorry for giving me a second chance. And I mean it like I told him. After the operashun Im gonna try to be smart. Im gonna try awful hard.

### progris riport 5—Mar 10

Im skared. Lots of the nurses and the people who gave me the tests came to bring me candy and wish me luck. I hope I have luck. I got my rabits foot and my lucky penny. Only a black cat crossed me when I was comming to the hospitil. Dr Strauss says dont be supersitis Charlie this is science. Anyway Im keeping my rabits foot with me.

I asked Dr Strauss if Ill beat Algernon in the race after the operashun and he said maybe. If the operashun works Ill show that mouse I can be as smart as he is. Maybe smarter. Then Ill be abel to read better and spell the words good and know lots of things and be like other people. I want to be smart like other people. If it works perminint they will make everybody smart all over the wurld.

They dint give me anything to eat this morning. I dont know what that eating has to do with getting smart. Im very hungry and Dr. Nemur took away my box of candy. That Dr Nemur is a grouch. Dr Strauss says I can have it back after the operashun. You cant eat befor a operashun . . .

### progress report 6—Mar 15

The operashun dint hurt. He did it while I was sleeping. They took off the bandijis from my head today so I can make a PROGRESS REPORT. Dr. Nemur who looked at some of my other ones says I spell PROGRESS wrong and told me how to spell it and REPORT too. I got to try and remember that.

I have a very bad memary for spelling. Dr Strauss says its ok to tell about all the things that happin to me but he says I should tell more about what I feel and what I think. When I told him I dont know how to think he said try. All the time when the bandijis were on my eyes I tryed to think. Nothing happened. I dont know what to think about. Maybe if I ask him he will tell me how I can think now that Im suppose to get smart. What do smart people think about. Fancy things I suppose. I wish I knew some fancy things alredy.

### progress report 7—mar 19

Nothing is happining. I had lots of tests and different kinds of races with Algernon. I hate that mouse. He always beats me. Dr. Strauss said I got to play those games. And he said some time I got to take those tests over again. Those inkblots are stupid. And those pictures are stupid too. I like to draw a picture of a man and a woman but I wont make up lies about people.

I got a headache from trying to think so much. I thot Dr Strauss was my frend but he dont help me. He dont tell me what to think or when Ill get smart. Miss Kinnian dint come to see me. I think writing these progress reports are stupid too.

### progress report 8—Mar 23

Im going back to work at the factory. They said it was better I shud go back to work but I cant tell anyone what the operashun was for and I have to come to the hospitil for an hour evry night after work. They are gonna pay me mony every month for learning to be smart.

Im glad Im going back to work because I miss my job and all my frends and all the fun we have there.

Dr Strauss says I shud keep writing things down but I dont have to do it every day just when I think of something or something speshul happins. He says dont get discoridged because it takes time and it happins slow. He says it took a long time with Algernon before he got 3 times smarter than he was before. Thats why Algernon beats me all the time because he had that operashun too. That makes me feel better. I coud probly do that *amazed* faster than a reglar mouse. Maybe some day Ill beat him. That would be something. So far Algernon looks smart perminent.

*Mar 25* (I dont have to write PROGRESS REPORT on top any

more just when I hand it in once a week for Dr Nemur. I just have to put the date on. That saves time)

We had a lot of fun at the factery today. Joe Carp said hey look where Charlie had his operashun what did they do Charlie put some brains in. I was going to tell him but I remembered Dr Strauss said no. Then Frank Reilly said what did you do Charlie forget your key and open your door the hard way. That made me laff. Their really my friends and they like me.

Sometimes somebody will say hey look at Joe or Frank or George he really pulled a Charlie Gordon. I dont know why they say that but they always laff. This morning Amos Borg who is the 4 man at Donnegans used my name when he shouted at Ernie the office boy. Ernie lost a packige. He said Ernie for godsake what are you trying to be a Charlie Gordon. I dont understand why he said that.

*Mar* 28 Dr Strauss came to my room tonight to see why I dint come in like I was suppose to. I told him I dont like to race with Algernon any more. He said I dont have to for a while but I shud come in. He had a present for me. I thot it was a little television but it wasnt. He said I got to turn it on when I go to sleep. I said your kidding why shud I turn it on when Im going to sleep. Who ever herd of a thing like that. But he said if I want to get smart I got to do what he says. I told him I dint think I was going to get smart and he puts his hand on my sholder and said Charlie you dont know it yet but your getting smarter all the time. You wont notice for a while. I think he was just being nice to make me feel good because I dont look any smarter.

Oh yes I almost forgot. I asked him when I can go back to the class at Miss Kinnians school. He said I wont go their. He said that soon Miss Kinnian will come to the hospitil to start and teach me speshul.

*Mar* 29 That crazy TV kept up all night. How can I sleep with something yelling crazy things all night in my ears. And the nutty pictures. Wow. I don't know what it says when Im up so how am I going to know when Im sleeping.

Dr Strauss says its ok. He says my brains are lerning when I sleep and that will help me when Miss Kinnian starts my lessons in the hospitl (only I found out it isn't a hospitil its a labatory.) I think its all crazy. If you can get smart when your sleeping why do people go to school. That thing I don't think will work. I use to watch the late show and the late late show on TV all the time and it never made me smart. Maybe you have to sleep while you watch it.

*progress report 9—April 3*

Dr Strauss showed me how to keep the TV turned low so now I can sleep. I don't hear a thing. And I still dont understand what it says. A few times I play it over in the morning to find out what I lerned when I was sleeping and I don't think so. Miss Kinnian says Maybe its another langwidge. But most times it sounds american. It talks faster then even Miss Gold who was my teacher in 6 grade.

I told Dr. Strauss what good is it to get smart in my sleep. I want to be smart when Im awake. He says its the same thing and I have two minds. Theres the *subconscious* and the *conscious* (thats how you spell it). And one dont tell the other one what its doing. They dont even talk to each other. Thats why I dream. And boy have I been having crazy dreams. Wow. Ever since that night TV. The late late late show.

I forgot to ask him if it was only me or if everybody had those two minds.

(I just looked up the word in the dictionary Dr Strauss gave me. The word is *subconscious. adj. Of the nature of mental operations yet not present in consciousness; as, subconscious conflict of desires.*) There's more but I still dont know what it means. This isnt a very good dictionary for dumb people like me.

Anyway the headache is from the party. My friends from the factery Joe Carp and Frank Reilly invited me to go to Muggsys Saloon for some drinks. I don't like to drink but they said we will have lots of fun. I had a good time.

Joe Carp said I shoud show the girls how I mop out the toilet in the factory and he got me a mop. I showed them and everyone laffed when I told that Mr. Donnegan said I was the best janiter he ever had because I like my job and do it good and never miss a day except for my operashun.

I said Miss Kinnian always said Charlie be proud of your job because you do it good.

Everybody laffed and we had a good time and they gave me lots of drinks and Joe said Charlie is a card when hes potted. I dont know what that means but everybody likes me and we have fun. I cant wait to be smart like my best friends Joe Carp and Frank Reilly.

I dont remember how the party was over but I think I went out to buy a newspaper and coffe for Joe and Frank and when I came back there was no one their. I looked for them all over till late. Then I dont remember so good but I think I got sleepy or sick. A nice cop brot me back home Thats what my landlady Mrs Flynn says.

But I got a headache and a big lump on my head. I think maybe I fell but Joe Carp says it was the cop they beat up drunks some times. I don't think so. Miss Kinnian says cops are to help people. Anyway I got a bad headache and Im sick and hurt all over. I dont think Ill drink anymore.

*April* 6 I beat Algernon! I dint even know I beat him until Burt the tester told me. Then the second time I lost because I got so exited I fell off the chair before I finished. But after that I beat him 8 more times. I must be getting smart to beat a smart mouse like Algernon. But I dont *feel* smarter.

I wanted to race Algernon some more but Burt said thats enough for one day. They let me hold him for a minit. Hes not so bad. Hes soft like a ball of cotton. He blinks and when he opens his eyes their black and pink on the eges.

I said can I feed him because I felt bad to beat him and I wanted to be nice and make friends. Burt said no Algernon is a very specshul mouse with an operashun like mine, and he was the first of all the animals to stay smart so long. He told me Algernon is so smart that every day he has to solve a test to get his food. Its a thing like a lock on a door that changes every time Algernon goes in to eat so he has to lern something new to get his food. That made me sad because if he coudnt lern he woud be hungry.

I don't think its right to make you pass a test to eat. How woud Dr Nemur like it to have to pass a test every time he wants to eat. I think Ill be friends with Algernon.

*April* 9 Tonight after work Miss Kinnian was at the laboratory. She looked like she was glad to see me but scared. I told her dont worry Miss Kinnian Im not smart yet and she laffed. She said I have confidence in you Charlie the way you struggled so hard to read and right better than all the others. At werst you will have it for a littel wile and your doing somthing for science.

We are reading a very hard book. Its called *Robinson Crusoe* about a man who gets merooned on a dessert Iland. Hes smart and figers out all kinds of things so he can have a house and food and hes a good swimmer. Only I feel sorry because hes all alone and has no frends. But I think their must be somebody else on the iland because theres a picture with his funny umbrella looking at footprints. I hope he gets a frend and not be lonly.

*April* 10 Miss Kinnian teaches me to spell better. She says look at a word and close your eyes and say it over and over until you remember. I have lots of truble with *through* that you say *threw* and *enough* and *tough* that you dont say *enew and tew*. You got to say *enuff* and *tuff*. Thats how I use to write it before I started to get smart. Im confused but Miss Kinnian says theres no reason in spelling.

*Apr* 14 Finished *Robinson Crusoe*. I want to find out more about what happens to him but Miss Kinnian says thats all there is. *Why.*

*Apr* 15 Miss Kinnian says Im lerning fast. She read some of the Progress Reports and she looked at me kind of funny. She says Im a fine person and Ill show them all. I asked her why. She said never mind but I shouldnt feel bad if I find out everybody isnt nice like I think. She said for a person who god gave so little to you done more then a lot of people with brains they never even used. I said all my friends are smart people but there good. They like me and they never did anything that wasnt nice. Then she got something in her eye and she had to run out to the ladys room.

*Apr* 16 Today, I lerned, the *comma,* this is a comma (,) a period, with a tail, Miss Kinnian, says its importent, because, it makes writing, better, she said, somebody, coud lose, a lot of money, if a comma, isnt, in the, right place, I dont have, any money, and I dont see, how a comma, keeps you, from losing it,

*Apr* 17 I used the comma wrong. Its punctuation. Miss Kinnian told me to look up long words in the dictionary to lern to spell them. I said whats the difference if you can read it anyway. She said its part of your education so now on Ill look up all the words Im not sure how to spell. It takes a long time to write that way but I only have to look up once and after that I get it right.

You got to mix them up, she showed? me" how. to mix! them (and now; I can! mix up all kinds" of punctuation, in! my writing? There, are lots! of rules? to lern; but Im gettin'g them in my head.

One thing I like about, Dear Miss Kinnian: (thats the way it goes in a business letter if I ever go into business) is she, always gives me' a reason" when—I ask. She's a gen'ius! I wish I cou'd be smart" like, her;

(Puncuation, is; fun!)

*April* 18 What a dope I am! I didn't even understand what she was talking about. I read the grammar book last night and it explanes the whole thing. Then I saw it was the same way as Miss Kinnian was trying to tell me, but I didn't get it.

Miss Kinnian said that the TV working in my sleep helped out. She and I reached a plateau. Thats a flat hill.

After I figured out how puncuation worked, I read over all my old Progress Reports from the beginning. Boy, did I have crazy spelling and punctuation! I told Miss Kinnian I ought to go over the pages and fix all the mistakes but she said, "No, Charlie, Dr. Nemur wants them just as they are. That's why he let you keep them after they were photostated, to see your own progress. You're coming along fast, Charlie."

That made me feel good. After the lesson I went down and played with Algernon. We don't race any more.

*April* 20 I feel sick inside. Not sick like for a doctor, but inside my chest it feels empty like getting punched and a heartburn at the same time. I wasn't going to write about it, but I guess I got to, because its important. Today was the first time I ever stayed home from work.

Last night Joe Carp and Frank Reilly invited me to a party. There were lots of girls and some men from the factory. I remembered how sick I got last time I drank too much, so I told Joe I didn't want anything to drink. He gave me a plain coke instead.

We had a lot of fun for a while. Joe said I should dance with Ellen and she would teach me the steps. I fell a few times and I couldn't understand why because no one else was dancing besides Ellen and me. And all the time I was tripping because somebody's foot was always sticking out.

Then when I got up I saw the look on Joe's face and it gave me a funny feeling in my stomack. "He's a scream," one of the girls said. Everybody was laughing.

"Look at him. He's blushing. Charlie is blushing."

"Hey, Ellen, what'd you do to Charlie? I never saw him act like that before."

I didn't know what to do or where to turn. Everyone was looking at me and laughing and I felt naked. I wanted to hide. I ran outside and I threw up. Then I walked home. It's a funny thing I never knew that Joe and Frank and the others liked to have me around all the time to make fun of me.

Now I know what it means when they say "to pull a Charlie Gordon."

I'm ashamed.

## progress report 11

*April* 21 Still didn't go into the factory. I told Mrs. Flynn my land-lady to call and tell Mr. Donnegan I was sick. Mrs. Flynn looks at me very funny lately like she's scared.

I think it's a good thing about finding out how everybody laughs at me. I thought about it a lot. It's because I'm so dumb and I don't even know when I'm doing something dumb. People think it's funny when a dumb person can't do things the same way they can.

Anyway, now I know I'm getting smarter every day. I know punc-tuation and I can spell good. I like to look up all the hard words in the dictionary and I remember them. I'm reading a lot now, and Miss Kin-nian says I read very fast. Sometimes I even understand what I'm read-ing about, and it stays in my mind. There are times when I can close my eyes and think of a page and it all comes back like a picture.

Besides history, geography and arithmetic, Miss Kinnian said I should start to learn foreign languages. Dr. Strauss gave me some more tapes to play while I sleep. I still don't understand how that conscious and unconscious mind works, but Dr. Strauss says not to worry yet. He asked me to promise that when I start learning college subjects next week I wouldn't read any books on psychology—that is, until he gives me permission.

I feel a lot better today, but I guess I'm still a little angry that all the time people were laughing and making fun of me because I wasn't so smart. When I become intelligent like Dr. Strauss says, with three times my I.Q. of 68, then maybe I'll be like everyone else and people will like me.

I'm not sure what an I.Q. is. Dr. Nemur said it was something that measured how intelligent you were—like a scale in the drugstore weighs pounds. But Dr. Strauss had a big argument with him and said an I.Q. didn't weigh intelligence at all. He said an I.Q. showed how much intelligence you could get, like the numbers on the outside of a measuring cup. You still had to fill the cup up with stuff.

Then when I asked Burt, who gives me my intelligence tests and works with Algernon, he said that both of them were wrong (only I had to promise not to tell them he said so). Burt says that the I.Q. meas-ures a lot of different things including some of the things you learned already, and it really isn't any good at all.

So I still don't know what I.Q. is except that mine is going to be over 200 soon. I didn't want to say anything, but I don't see how if they don't know *what* it is, or *where* it is—I don't see how they know *how much* of it you've got.

Dr. Nemur says I have to take a *Rorshach Test* tomorrow. I wonder what *that* is.

*April 22* I found out what a Rorshach is. It's the test I took before the operation—the one with the inkblots on the pieces of cardboard.

I was scared to death of those inkblots. I knew the man was going to ask me to find the pictures and I knew I couldn't. I was thinking to myself, if only there was some way of knowing what kind of pictures were hidden there. Maybe there weren't any pictures at all. Maybe it was just a trick to see if I was dumb enough to look for something that wasn't there. Just thinking about that made me sore at him.

"All right, Charlie," he said, "you've seen these cards before, remember?"

"Of course I remember."

The way I said it, he knew I was angry, and he looked surprised. "Yes, of course. Now I want you to look at this. What might this be? What do you see on this card? People see all sorts of things in these ink-blots. Tell me what it might be for you—what it makes you think of."

I was shocked. That wasn't what I had expected him to say. "You mean there are no pictures hidden in those inkblots?"

He frowned and took off his glasses. "What?"

"Pictures. Hidden in the inkblots. Last time you told me everyone could see them and you wanted me to find them too."

He explained to me that the last time he had used almost the exact same words he was using now. I didn't believe it, and I still have the suspicion that he misled me at the time just for the fun of it. Unless— I don't know any more—could I have been *that* feeble-minded?

We went through the cards slowly. One looked like a pair of bats tugging at something. Another one looked like two men fencing with swords. I imagined all sorts of things. I guess I got carried away. But I didn't trust him any more, and I kept turning them around, even looking on the back to see if there was anything there I was supposed to catch. While he was making his notes, I peeked out of the corner of my eye to read it. But it was all in code that looked like this:

$$WF + A \qquad DdF - Ad\ orig. \qquad WF - A$$
$$SF + obj$$

The test still doesn't make sense to me. It seems to me that anyone could make up lies about things that they didn't really imagine? Maybe I'll understand it when Dr. Strauss lets me read up on psychology.

*April* 25 I figured out a new way to line up the machines in the factory, and Mr. Donnegan says it will save him ten thousand dollars a year in labor and increased production. He gave me a $25 bonus.

I wanted to take Joe Carp and Frank Reilly out to lunch to celebrate, but Joe said he had to buy some things for his wife, and Frank said he was meeting his cousin for lunch. I guess it'll take a little time for them to get used to the changes in me. Everybody seems to be frightened of me. When I went over to Amos Borg and tapped him, he jumped up in the air.

People don't talk to me much any more or kid around the way they used to. It makes the job kind of lonely.

*April* 27 I got up the nerve today to ask Miss Kinnian to have dinner with me tomorrow night to celebrate my bonus.

At first she wasn't sure it was right, but I asked Dr. Strauss and he said it was okay. Dr. Strauss and Dr. Nemur don't seem to be getting along so well. They're arguing all the time. This evening I heard them shouting. Dr. Nemur was saying that it was *his* experiment and *his* research, and Dr. Strauss shouted back that he contributed just as much, because he found me through Miss Kinnian and he performed the operation. Dr. Strauss said that someday thousands of neurosurgeons might be using his technique all over the world.

Dr. Nemur wanted to publish the results of the experiment at the end of this month. Dr. Strauss wanted to wait a while to be sure. Dr. Strauss said Dr. Nemur was more interested in the Chair of Psychology at Princeton than he was in the experiment. Dr. Nemur said Dr. Strauss was nothing but an opportunist trying to ride to glory on *his* coattails.

When I left afterwards, I found myself trembling. I don't know why for sure, but it was as if I'd seen both men clearly for the first time. I remember hearing Burt say Dr. Nemur had a shrew of a wife who was pushing him all the time to get things published so he could become famous. Burt said that the dream of her life was to have a big shot husband.

*April* 28 I don't understand why I never noticed how beautiful Miss Kinnian really is. She has brown eyes and feathery brown hair that comes to the top of her neck. She's only thirty-four! I think from the beginning I had the feeling that she was an unreachable genius—and very, very old. Now, every time I see her she grows younger and more lovely.

We had dinner and a long talk. When she said I was coming along so fast I'd be leaving her behind, I laughed.

"It's true, Charlie. You're already a better reader than I am. You can read a whole page at a glance while I can take in only a few lines at a time. And you remember every single thing you read. I'm lucky if I can recall the main thoughts and the general meaning."

"I don't feel intelligent. There are so many things I don't understand."

She took out a cigarette and I lit for her. "You've got to be a *little* patient. You're accomplishing in days and weeks what it takes normal people to do in a lifetime. That's what makes it so amazing. You're like a giant sponge now, soaking things in. Facts, figures, general knowledge. And soon you'll begin to connect them, too. You'll see how different branches of learning are related. There are many levels, Charlie, like steps on a giant ladder that take you up higher and higher to see more and more of the world around you.

"I can see only a little bit of that, Charlie, and I won't go much higher than I am now, but you'll keep climbing up and up, and see more and more, and each step will open new worlds that you never even knew existed." She frowned. "I hope . . . I just hope to God—"

"What?"

"Never mind, Charles. I just hope I wasn't wrong to advise you to go into this in the first place."

I laughed. "How could that be? It worked, didn't it? Even Algernon is still smart."

We sat there silently for a while and I knew what she was thinking about as she watched me toying with the chain of my rabbit's foot and my keys. I didn't want to think of that possibility any more than elderly people want to think of death. I *knew* that this was only the beginning. I knew what she meant about levels because I'd seen some of them already. The thought of leaving her behind made me sad.

I'm in love with Miss Kinnian.

### progress report 12

*April* 30 I've quit my job with Donnegan's Plastic Box Company. Mr. Donnegan insisted it would be better for all concerned if I left. What did I do to make them hate me so?

The first I knew of it was when Mr. Donnegan showed me the petition. Eight hundred names, everyone in the factory, except Fanny Girden. Scanning the list quickly, I saw at once that hers was the only missing name. All the rest demanded that I be fired.

Joe Carp and Frank Reilly wouldn't talk to me about it. No one else would either, except Fanny. She was one of the few people I'd known who set her mind to something and believed it no matter what the rest of the world proved, said or did—and Fanny did not believe that I should have been fired. She had been against the petition on principle and despite the pressure and threats she'd held out.

"Which don't mean to say," she remarked, "that I don't think there's something mighty strange about you, Charlie. Them changes. I don't know. You used to be a good, dependable, ordinary man—not too bright maybe, but honest. Who knows what you done to yourself to get so smart all of a sudden. Like everybody around here's been saying, Charlie, it's not right."

"But how can you say that, Fanny? What's wrong with a man becoming intelligent and wanting to acquire knowledge and understanding of the world around him?"

She stared down at her work and I turned to leave. Without looking at me, she said: "It was evil when Eve listened to the snake and ate from the tree of knowledge. It was evil when she saw that she was naked. If not for that none of us would ever have to grow old and sick, and die."

Once again, now, I have the feeling of shame burning inside me. This intelligence has driven a wedge between me and all the people I once knew and loved. Before, they laughed at me and despised me for my ignorance and dullness; now, they hate me for my knowledge and understanding. What in God's name do they want of me?

They've driven me out of the factory. Now I'm more alone than ever before. . . .

*May* 15 Dr. Strauss is very angry at me for not having written any progress reports in two weeks. He's justified because the lab is now paying me a regular salary. I told him I was too busy thinking and reading. When I pointed out that writing was such a slow process that it made me impatient with my poor handwriting, he suggested I learn to type. It's much easier to write now because I can type seventy-five words a minute. Dr. Strauss continually reminds me of the need to speak and write simply so people will be able to understand me.

I'll try to review all the things that happened to me during the last two weeks. Algernon and I were presented to the *American Psychological Association* sitting in convention with the *World Psychological Association*. We created quite a sensation. Dr. Nemur and Dr. Strauss were proud of us.

I suspect that Dr. Nemur, who is sixty—ten years older than Dr. Strauss—finds it necessary to see tangible results of his work. Undoubtedly the result of pressure by Mrs. Nemur.

Contrary to my earlier impressions of him, I realize that Dr. Nemur is not at all a genius. He has a very good mind, but it struggles under the spectre of self-doubt. He wants people to take him for a genius. Therefore it is important for him to feel that his work is accepted by the world. I believe that Dr. Nemur was afraid of further delay because he worried that someone else might make a discovery along these lines and take the credit from him.

Dr. Strauss on the other hand might be called a genius, although I feel his areas of knowledge are too limited. He was educated in the tradition of narrow specialization; the broader aspects of background were neglected far more than necessary—even for a neuro-surgeon.

I was shocked to learn the only ancient languages he could read were Latin, Greek and Hebrew, and that he knows almost nothing of mathematics beyond the elementary levels of the calculus of variations. When he admitted this to me, I found myself almost annoyed. It was as if he'd hidden this part of himself in order to deceive me, pretending —as do many people I've discovered—to be what he is not. No one I've ever known is what he appears to be on the surface.

Dr. Nemur appears to be uncomfortable around me. Sometimes when I try to talk to him, he just looks at me strangely and turns away. I was angry at first when Dr. Strauss told me I was giving Dr. Nemur an inferiority complex. I thought he was mocking me and I'm oversensitive at being made fun of.

How was I to know that a highly respected psycho-experimentalist like Nemur was unacquainted with Hindustani and Chinese? It's absurd when you consider the work that is being done in India and China today in the very field of his study.

I asked Dr. Strauss how Nemur could refute Rahajamati's attack on his method if Nemur couldn't even read them in the first place. That strange look on Strauss' face can mean only one of two things. Either he doesn't want to tell Nemur what they're saying in India, or else— and this worries me—Dr. Strauss doesn't know either. I must be careful to speak and write clearly and simply so people won't laugh.

*May* 18 I am very disturbed. I saw Miss Kinnian last night for the first time in over a week. I tried to avoid all discussions of intellectual concepts and to keep the conversation on a simple, everyday level, but she just stared at me blankly and asked me what I meant about the mathematical variance equivalent in Dorbermann's *Fifth Concerto*.

When I tried to explain she stopped me and laughed. I guess I got angry, but I suspect I'm approaching her on the wrong level. No matter what I try to discuss with her, I am unable to communicate. I must review Vrostadt's equations on *Levels of Semantic Progression*. I find I don't communicate with people much any more. Thank God for books and music and things I can think about. I am alone at Mrs. Flynn's boarding house most of the time and seldom speak to anyone.

*May* 20 I would not have noticed the new dishwasher, a boy of about sixteen, at the corner diner where I take my evening meals if not for the incident of the broken dishes.

They crashed to the floor, sending bits of white china under the tables. The boy stood there, dazed and frightened, holding the empty tray in his hand. The catcalls from the customers (the cries of "hey, there go the profits!" . . . "*Mazeltov!*" . . . and "well, *he* didn't work here very long . . ." which invariably seems to follow the breaking of glass or dishware in a public restaurant) all seemed to confuse him.

When the owner came to see what the excitement was about, the boy cowered as if he expected to be struck. "All right! All right, you dope," shouted the owner, "don't just stand there! Get the broom and sweep that mess up. A broom . . . a broom, you idiot! It's in the kitchen!"

The boy saw he was not going to be punished. His frightened expression disappeared and he smiled as he came back with the broom to sweep the floor. A few of the rowdier customers kept up the remarks, amusing themselves at his expense.

"Here, sonny, over here there's a nice piece behind you . . ."

"He's not so dumb. It's easier to break 'em than wash 'em!"

As his vacant eyes moved across the crowd of onlookers, he slowly mirrored their smiles and finally broke into an uncertain grin at the joke he obviously did not understand.

I felt sick inside as I looked at his dull, vacuous smile, the wide, bright eyes of a child, uncertain but eager to please. They were laughing at him because he was mentally retarded.

And I had been laughing at him too.

Suddenly I was furious at myself and all those who were smirking at him. I jumped up and shouted, "Shut up! Leave him alone! It's not his fault he can't understand! He can't help what he is! But he's still a human being!"

The room grew silent. I cursed myself for losing control. I tried not to look at the boy as I walked out without touching my food. I felt ashamed for both of us.

How strange that people of honest feelings and sensibility, who would not take advantage of a man born without arms or eyes—how such people think nothing of abusing a man born with low intelligence. It infuriated me to think that not too long ago I had foolishly played the clown.

And I had almost forgotten.

I'd hidden the picture of the old Charlie Gordon from myself because now that I was intelligent it was something that had to be pushed out of my mind. But today in looking at that boy, for the first time I saw what I had been. *I was just like him!*

Only a short time ago, I learned that people laughed at me. Now I can see that unknowingly I joined with them in laughing at myself. That hurts most of all.

I have often reread my progress reports and seen the illiteracy, the childish naïveté, the mind of low intelligence peering from a dark room, through the keyhole at the dazzling light outside. I see that even in my dullness I knew I was inferior, and that other people had something I lacked—something denied me. In my mental blindness, I thought it was somehow connected with the ability to read and write, and I was sure that if I could get those skills I would automatically have intelligence too.

Even a feeble-minded man wants to be like other men.

A child may not know how to feed itself, or what to eat, yet it knows of hunger.

This then is what I was like. I never knew. Even with my gift of intellectual awareness, I never really knew.

This day was good for me. Seeing the past more clearly, I've decided to use my knowledge and skills to work in the field of increasing human intelligence levels. Who is better equipped for this work? Who else has lived in both worlds? These are my people. Let me use my gift to do something for them.

Tomorrow, I will discuss with Dr. Strauss how I can work in this area. I may be able to help him work out the problems of widespread use of the technique which was used on me. I have several good ideas of my own.

There is so much that might be done with this technique. If I could be made into a genius, what about thousands of others like myself? What fantastic levels might be achieved by using this technique on normal people? On *geniuses*?

There are so many doors to open. I am impatient to begin.

*progress report 13*

*May* 23 It happened today. Algernon bit me. I visited the lab to see him as I do occasionally, and when I took him out of his cage, he snapped at my hand. I put him back and watched him for a while. He was unusually disturbed and vicious.

*May* 24 Burt, who is in charge of the experimental animals, tells me that Algernon is changing. He is less co-operative; he refuses to run the maze any more; general motivation has decreased. And he hasn't been eating. Everyone is upset about what this may mean.

*May* 25 They've been feeding Algernon, who now refuses to work the shifting-lock problem. Everyone identifies me with Algernon. In a way we're both the first of our kind. They're all pretending that Algernon's behavior is not necessarily significant for me. But it's hard to hide the fact that some of the other animals who were used in this experiment are showing strange behavior.

Dr. Strauss and Dr. Nemur have asked me not to come to the lab any more. I know what they're thinking but I can't accept it. I am going ahead with my plans to carry their research forward. With all due respect to both these fine scientists, I am well aware of their limitations. If there is an answer, I'll have to find it out for myself. Suddenly, time has become very important to me.

*May* 29 I have been given a lab of my own and permission to go ahead with the research. I'm onto something. Working day and night. I've had a cot moved into the lab. Most of my writing time is spent on the notes which I keep in a separate folder, but from time to time I feel it necessary to put down my moods and thoughts from sheer habit.

I find the *calculus of intelligence* to be a fascinating study. Here is the place for the application of all the knowledge I have acquired.

*May* 31 Dr. Strauss thinks I'm working too hard. Dr. Nemur says I'm trying to cram a lifetime of research and thought into a few weeks. I know I should rest, but I'm driven on by something inside that won't let me stop. I've got to find the reason for the sharp regression in Algernon. I've got to know *if* and *when* it will happen to me.

*June* 4

## LETTER TO DR. STRAUSS (*copy*)

Dear Dr. Strauss:

Under separate cover I am sending you a copy of my report entitled, "The Algernon-Gordon Effect: A Study of Structure and Function of Increased Intelligence," which I would like to have published.

As you see, my experiments are completed. I have included in my report all of my formulae, as well as mathematical analysis in the appendix. Of course, these should be verified.

Because of its importance to both you and Dr. Nemur (and need I say to myself, too?) I have checked and rechecked my results a dozen times in the hope of finding an error. I am sorry to say the results must stand. Yet for the sake of science, I am grateful for the little bit that I here add to the knowledge of the function of the human mind and of the laws governing the artificial increase of human intelligence.

I recall your once saying to me that an experimental *failure* or the *disproving* of a theory was as important to the advancement of learning as a success would be. I know now that this is true. I am sorry, however, that my own contribution to the field must rest upon the ashes of the work of two men I regard so highly.

Yours truly,
Charles Gordon

*June* 5 I must not become emotional. The facts and the results of my experiments are clear, and the more sensational aspects of my own rapid climb cannot obscure the fact that the tripling of intelligence by the surgical technique developed by Drs. Strauss and Nemur must be viewed as having little or no practical applicability (at the present time) to be the increase of human intelligence.

As I review the records and data on Algernon, I see that although he is still in his physical infancy, he has regressed mentally. Motor activity is impaired; there is a general reduction of glandular activity; there is an accelerated loss of coordination.

There are also strong indications of progressive amnesia.

As will be seen by my report, these and other physical and mental deterioration syndromes can be predicted with significant results by the application of my formula.

The surgical stimulus to which we were both subjected has resulted in an intensification and acceleration of all mental processes. The unforeseen development, which I have taken the liberty of calling the *Algernon-Gordon Effect*, is the logical extension of the entire intelligence speed-up. The hypothesis here proven may be described simply in the following terms: Artificially increased intelligence deteriorates at a rate of time directly proportional to the quantity of the increase.

I feel that this, in itself, is an important discovery.

As long as I am able to write, I will continue to record my thoughts in these progress reports. It is one of my few pleasures. However, by all indications, my own mental deterioration will be very rapid.

I have already begun to notice signs of emotional instability and forgetfulness, the first symptoms of the burnout.

*June* 10 Deterioration progressing. I have become absent-minded. Algernon died two days ago. Dissection shows my predictions were right. His brain had decreased in weight and there was a general smoothing out of cerebral convolutions, as well as a deepening and broadening of brain fissures.

I guess the same thing is or will soon be happening to me. Now that it's definite, I don't want it to happen.

I put Algernon's body in a cheese box and buried him in the back yard. I cried.

*June* 15 Dr. Strauss came to see me again. I wouldn't open the door and I told him to go away. I want to be left to myself. I am touchy and irritable. I feel the darkness closing in. It's hard to throw off thoughts of suicide. I keep telling myself how important this journal will be.

It's a strange sensation to pick up a book you enjoyed just a few months ago and discover you don't remember it. I remembered how great I thought John Milton was, but when I picked up *Paradise Lost* I couldn't understand it at all. I got so angry I threw the book across the room.

I've got to try to hold on to some of it. Some of the things I've learned. Oh, God, please don't take it all away.

*June* 19 Sometimes, at night, I go out for a walk. Last night, I couldn't remember where I lived. A policeman took me home. I have the strange feeling that this has all happened to me before—a long time ago. I keep telling myself I'm the only person in the world who can describe what's happening to me.

*June* 21 Why can't I remember? I've got to fight. I lie in bed for days and I don't know who or where I am. Then it all comes back to me in a flash. Fugues of amnesia. Symptoms of senility—second childhood. I can watch them coming on. It's so cruelly logical. I learned so much and so fast. Now my mind is deteriorating rapidly. I won't let it happen. I'll fight it. I can't help thinking of the boy in the restaurant, the blank expression, the silly smile, the people laughing at him. No—please—not that again. . . .

*June 22* I'm forgetting things that I learned recently. It seems to be following the classic pattern—the last things learned are the first things forgotten. Or is that the pattern? I'd better look it up again. . . .

I re-read my paper on the *Algernon-Gordon Effect* and I get the strange feeling that it was written by someone else. There are parts I don't even understand.

Motor activity impaired. I keep tripping over things, and it becomes increasingly difficult to type.

*June 23* I've given up using the typewriter. My coordination is bad. I feel I'm moving slower and slower. Had a terrible shock today. I picked up a copy of an article I used in my research, Krueger's *Uber psychische Ganzheit,* to see if it would help me understand what I had done. First I thought there was something wrong with my eyes. Then I realized I could no longer read German. I tested myself in other languages. All gone.

*June 30* A week since I dared to write again. It's slipping away like sand through my fingers. Most of the books I have are too hard for me now. I get angry with them because I know that I read and understood them just a few weeks ago.

I keep telling myself I must keep writing these reports so that somebody will know what is happening to me. But it gets harder to form the words and remember spellings. I have to look up even simple words in the dictionary now and it makes me impatient with myself.

Dr. Strauss comes around almost every day, but I told him I wouldn't see or speak to anybody. He feels guilty. They all do. But I don't blame anyone. I knew what might happen. But how it hurts.

*July 7* I don't know where the week went. Todays Sunday I know because I can see through my window people going to church. I think I stayed in bed all week but I remember Mrs. Flynn bringing food to me a few times. I keep saying over and over I've got to do something but then I forget or maybe its just easier not to do what I say I'm going to do.

I think of my mother and father a lot these days. I found a picture of them with me taken at a beach. My father has a big ball under his arm and my mother is holding me by the hand. I dont remember them the way they are in the picture. All I remember is my father drunk most of the time and arguing with mom about money.

He never shaved much and he used to scratch my face when he hugged me. My Mother said he died but Cousin Miltie said he heard his dad say that my father ran away with another woman. When I asked my mother she slapped me and said my father was dead. I dont think I ever found out the truth but I dont care much. (He said he was going to take me to see cows on a farm once but he never did. He never kept his promises. . . .)

*July* 10 My landlady Mrs. Flynn is very worried about me. She says the way I lay around all day and dont do anything I remind her of her son before she threw him out of the house. She said she doesn't like loafers. If Im sick its one thing, but if Im a loafer thats another thing and she won't have it. I told her I think Im sick.

I try to read a little bit every day, mostly stories, but sometimes I have to read the same thing over and over again because I don't know what it means. And its hard to write. I know I should look up all the words in the dictionary but its so hard and Im so tired all the time.

Then I got the idea that I would only use the easy words instead of the long hard ones. That saves time. I put flowers on Algernons grave about once a week. Mrs Flynn thinks Im crazy to put flowers on a mouses grave but I told her that Algernon was special.

*July* 14 Its sunday again. I dont have anything to do to keep me busy now because my television set is broke and I dont have any money to get it fixed. (I think I lost this months check from the lab. I dont remember)

I get awful headaches and asperin doesnt help me much. Mrs. Flynn knows Im really sick and she feels very sorry for me. Shes a wonderful woman whenever someone is sick.

*July* 22 Mrs. Flynn called a strange doctor to see me. She was afraid I was going to die. I told the doctor I wasnt too sick and I only forget sometimes. He asked me did I have any friends or relatives and I said no I dont have any. I told him I had a friend called Algernon once but he was a mouse and we used to run races together. He looked at me kind of funny like he thought I was crazy. He smiled when I told him I used to be a genius. He talked to me like I was a baby and he winked at Mrs. Flynn. I got mad and chased him out because he was making fun of me the way they all used to.

*July* 24 I have no more money and Mrs Flynn says I got to go to work somewhere and pay the rent because I havent paid for two months. I dont know any work but the job I used to have at Donnegans Box Company. I dont want to go back because they all knew me when I was smart and maybe they'll laugh at me. But I dont know what else to do to get money.

*July* 25 I was looking at some of my old progress reports and its very funny but I cant read what I wrote. I can make out some of the words but they dont make sense.

Miss Kinnian came to the door but I said go away I dont want to see you. She cried and I cried too but I wouldnt let her in because I didn't want her to laugh at me. I told her I didnt like her any more. I told her I didnt want to be smart any more. Thats not true. I still love her and I still want to be smart but I had to say that so shed go away. She gave Mrs. Flynn money to pay the rent. I dont want that. I got to get a job.

Please . . . please let me not forget how to read and write. . . .

*July* 27 Mr. Donnegan was very nice when I came back and asked him for my old job of janitor. First he was very suspicious but I told him what happened to me then he looked very sad and put his hand on my shoulder and said Charlie Gordon you got guts.

Everybody looked at me when I came downstairs and started working in the toilet sweeping it out like I used to. I told myself Charlie if they make fun of you dont get sore because you remember their not so smart as you once thot they were. And besides they were once your friends and if they laughted at you that doesnt mean anything because they liked you too.

One of the new men who came to work there after I went away made a nasty crack he said hey Charlie I hear your a very smart fella a real quiz kid. Say something intelligent. I felt bad but Joe Carp came over and grabbed him by the shirt and said leave him alone you lousy cracker or I'll break your neck. I didnt expect Joe to take my part so I guess hes really my friend.

Later Frank Reilly came over and said Charlie if anybody bothers you or trys to take advantage you call me or Joe and we will set em straight. I said thanks Frank and I got choked up so I had to turn around and go into the supply room so he wouldnt see me cry. Its good to have friends.

*July* 28 I did a dumb thing today I forgot I wasnt in Miss Kinnians class at the adult center any more like I use to be. I went in and sat down in my old seat in the back of the room and she looked at me funny and she said Charles. I dint remember she ever called me that before only Charlie so I said hello Miss Kinnian Im redy for my lesin today only I lost my reader that we was using. She startid to cry and run out of the room and everybody looked at me and I saw they wasnt the same pepul who use to be in my class.

Then all of a suddin I remembered some things about the operashun and me getting smart and I said holy smoke I reely pulled a Charlie Gordon that time. I went away before she come back to the room.

Thats why Im going away from New York for good. I dont want to do nothing like that agen. I dont want Miss Kinnian to feel sorry for me. Evry body feels sorry at the factery and I dont want that eather so Im going someplace where nobody knows that Charlie Gordon was once a genus and now he cant even reed a book or rite good.

Im taking a cuple of books along and even if I cant reed them Ill practise hard and maybe I wont forget every thing I lerned. If I try reel hard maybe Ill be a littel bit smarter than I was before the operashun. I got my rabits foot and my luky penny and maybe they will help me.

If you ever reed this Miss Kinnian dont be sorry for me Im glad I got a second chanse to be smart becaus I lerned a lot of things that I never even new were in this world and Im grateful that I saw it all for a littel bit. I dont know why Im dumb agen or what I did wrong maybe its because I dint try hard enuff. But if I try and practis very hard maybe Ill get a littl smarter and know what all the words are. I remember a littel bit how nice I had a feeling with the blue book that has the torn cover when I red it. Thats why Im gonna keep trying to get smart so I can have that feeling agen. Its a good feeling to know things and be smart. I wish I had it rite now if I did I would sit down and reed all the time. Anyway I bet Im the first dumb person in the world who ever found out somthing importent for science. I remember I did somthing but I dont remember what. So I gess its like I did it for all the dumb pepul like me.

Goodbye Miss Kinnian and Dr. Strauss and evreybody. And P.S. please tell Dr Nemur not to be such a grouch when pepul laff at him and he would have more frends. Its easy to make frends if you let pepul laff at you. Im going to have lots of frends where I go.

P.P.S. Please if you get a chanse put some flowrs on Algernons grave in the bak yard. . . .

*1961*
*19th CONVENTION*
*SEATTLE*

There is a secret to the pronunciation of Poul Anderson's first name that only Scandinavians know.

In the summer of 1959, Poul Anderson and his wife were crossing the country by car and decided to stop off for a visit at the Asimovs. (It was either that or run into the Atlantic Ocean.)

This gave me a chance to see him; a chance that doesn't happen often, for he lives on "the Coast," while I live in a Boston suburb.

In any case, we had a pleasant time of it and a sizable portion of the evening was spent in alternately reciting his first name. First he would say it, then I would say it, then he would say it, then I would say it, and so on. I distinctly heard the pronunciation *he* gave it (a delicate perversion of the vowel which must be heard to be believed) but all I could come up with was "Pole."

Poor Poul gave up at last with a smile of forbearance on his face and admitted that everyone said "Pole."

It was about this time that I was coming to admire all things Scandinavian with great intensity (you ought to hear me tell of my experiences at a smorgasbord-type restaurant at which I committed such heroic carnage that there were moments afterward when it seemed that an operation would be necessary) and Poul may have had much to do with it. He is tall, has blond wavy hair and an incredibly youthful appearance. There is much of the Viking in him and it breathes through all his stories. Yet he is, withal, a gentle soul whose conversation is a particular delight for he is equally at home in the sciences and in the humanities.

That fall we met again at the 17th Convention (Detroit, 1959) and, as Toastmaster, it was my delight and pleasure to introduce Poul as Guest of Honor.

His great moment, however, came at the 19th Convention (Seattle, 1961) when his novelette, "The Longest Voyage," won the Hugo. I could not attend that convention, so I did not witness the award, and my love and affection for Poul has therefore remained without alloy.

9

# THE LONGEST VOYAGE

When first we heard of the Sky Ship, we were on an island whose name, as nearly as Montalirian tongues can wrap themselves about so barbarous a noise, was Yarzik. That was almost a year after the *Golden Leaper* sailed from Lavre Town, and we judged we had come halfway round the world. So befouled was our poor caravel with weeds and shells that all sail could scarce drag her across the sea. What drinking water remained in the butts was turned green and evil, the biscuit was full of worms, and the first signs of scurvy had appeared on certain crewmen.

"Hazard or no," decreed Captain Rovic, "we must land somewhere." A gleam I remembered appeared in his eyes. He stroked his red beard and murmured, "Besides, it's long since we asked for the Aureate Cities. Perhaps this time they'll have intelligence of such a place."

Steering by that ogre planet which climbed daily higher as we bore westward, we crossed such an emptiness that mutinous talk broke out afresh. In my heart I could not blame the crew. Imagine, my lords. Day upon day upon day where we saw naught but blue waters, white foam, high clouds in a tropic sky; heard only the wind, *whoosh* of waves, creak of timbers, sometimes at night the huge sucking and rushing as a sea monster breached. These were terrible enough to common sailors, unlettered men who still thought the world must be flat. But then to have Tambur hang forever above the bowsprit, and climb, so that all could see we must eventually pass directly beneath that brooding thing . . . and what upbore it? the crew mumbled in the forecastle. Would an angered God not let fall down on us?

So a deputation waited on Captain Rovic. Very timid and respectful they were, those rough burly men, as they asked him to turn about. But their comrades massed below, muscled sun-blackened bodies taut in the ragged kilts, with daggers and belaying pins ready to hand. We officers on the quarterdeck had swords and pistols, true. But we numbered a mere six, including that frightened boy who was myself, and aged Froad the astrologue, whose robe and white beard were reverend to see but of small use in a fight.

Rovic stood mute for a long while after the spokesman had voiced this demand. The stillness grew, until the empty shriek of wind in our shrouds, the empty glitter of ocean out to the world's rim, became all there was. Most splendid our master looked, for he had donned scarlet hose and bell-tipped shoon when he knew the deputation was coming: as well as helmet and corselet polished to mirror brightness. The plumes blew around that blinding steel head and the diamonds on his fingers flashed against the rubies in his sword hilt. Yet when at last he spoke, it was not as a knight of the Queen's court, but in the broad Anday of his fisher boyhood.

"So 'tis back ye'd wend, lads? Wi' a fair wind an' a warm sun, liefer ye'd come about an' beat half round the globe? How ye're changed from yere fathers! Ken ye nay the legend, that once all things did as man commanded, an' 'twas an Andayman's lazy fault that now men must work? For see ye, 'twas nay too much that he told his ax to cut down a tree for him, an' told the faggots to walk home, but when he told 'em to carry him, then God was wroth an' took the power away. Though to be sure, as recompense God gave all Andaymen sea-luck, dice-luck, an' love-luck. What more d'ye ask for, lads?"

Bewildered at this response, the spokesman wrung his hands, flushed, looked at the deck, and stammered that we'd all perish miserably . . . starve, or thirst, or drown, or be crushed under that horrible moon, or sail off the world's edge . . . the *Golden Leaper* had come farther than ship had sailed since the Fall of Man, and if we returned at once, our fame would live forever—

"But can ye eat fame, Etien?" asked Rovic, still mild and smiling. "We've had fights an' storms, aye, an' merry carouses too; but devil an Aureate City we've seen, though well ye ken they lie out here someplace, stuffed wi' treasure for the first bold man who'll come plunder 'em. What ails yere gutworks, lad? Is't nay an easy cruise? What would the foreigners say? How will yon arrogant cavaliers o' Sathayn, yon grubby chapmen o' Woodland, laugh—nay alone at us, but at all Montalir—did we turn back!"

Thus he jollied them. Only once did he touch his sword, half drawing it, as if absent-mindedly, when he recalled how we had weathered the hurricane off Xingu. But they remembered the mutiny that followed then, and how that same sword had pierced three armed sailors who attacked him together. His dialect told them he would let bygones

lie forgotten: if they would. His bawdy promises of sport among lascivi-
ous heathen tribes yet to be discovered, his recital of treasure legends,
his appeal to their pride as seamen and Montalirians, soothed fear. And
then in the end, when he saw them malleable, he dropped the provincial speech. He stood forth on the quarterdeck with burning casque and
tossing plumes, and the flag of Montalir blew its sea-faded colors above
him, and he said as the knights of the Queen say:

"Now you know I do not propose to turn back until the great globe
has been rounded and we bring to Her Majesty that gift which is
most peculiarly ours to give. The which is not gold or slaves, nor even
that lore of far places that she and her most excellent Company
of Merchant Adventurers desire. No, what we shall lift in our hands to
give her, on that day when again we lie by the long docks of Lavre,
shall be our achievement: that we did this thing which no men have
dared in all the world erenow, and did it to her glory."

A while longer he stood, through a silence full of the sea's noise.
Then he said quietly, "Dismissed," turned on his heel and went back
into his cabin.

So we continued for some days more, the men subdued but not un-
cheerful, the officers taking care to hide their doubts. I found myself
busied, not so much with the clerical duties for which I was paid or
the study of captaincy for which I was apprenticed—both these amounting to little by now—as with assisting Froad the astrologue. In these
balmy airs he could carry on his work even on shipboard. To him it
scarce mattered whether we sank or swam; he had lived more than a
common span of years already. But the knowledge of the heavens to
be gained here, that was something else. At night, standing on the fore-
deck with quadrant, astrolabe, and telescope, drenched in the radiance
from above, he resembled some frosty-bearded saint in the windows
of Provien Minster.

"See there, Zhean." His thin hand pointed above seas that glowed
and rippled with light, past the purple sky and the few stars still daring
to show themselves, toward Tambur. Huge it was in full phase at midnight, sprawling over seven degrees of sky, a shield or barry of soft
vert and azure, splotched with angry sable that could be seen to move
across its face. The firefly moon we had named Siett twinkled near
the hazy edge of the giant. Balant, espied rarely and low on the horizon
in our part of the world, here stood high: a crescent, but with the dark
part of the disk tinged by luminous Tambur.

"Observe," declared Froad, "there's no doubt left, one can *see* how it
rotates on an axis, and how storms boil up in its air. Tambur is no

longer the dimmest of frightened legends, nor a dreadful apparition seen to rise as we entered unknown waters; Tambur is real. A world like our own. Immensely bigger, certes, but still a spheroid in space: around which our own world moves, always turning the same hemisphere to her monarch. The conjectures of the ancients are triumphantly confirmed. Not merely that our world is round, *pouf,* that's obvious to anyone . . . but that we move about a greater center, which in turn has an annual path about the sun. But, then, how big is the sun?"

"Siett and Balant are inner satellites of Tambur," I rehearsed, struggling for comprehension. "Vieng, Darou, and the other moons commonly seen at home, have paths outside our own world's. Aye. But what holds it all up?"

"That I don't know. Mayhap the crystal sphere containing the stars exerts an inward pressure. The same pressure, maybe, that hurled mankind down onto the earth, at the time of the Fall From Heaven."

That night was warm, but I shivered, as if those had been winter stars. "Then," I breathed, "there may also be men on . . . Siett, Balant, Vieng . . . even on Tambur?"

"Who knows? We'll need many lifetimes to find out. And what lifetimes they'll be! Thank the good God, Zhean, that you were born in this dawn of the coming age."

Froad returned to making measurements. A dull business, the other officers thought; but by now I had learned enough of the mathematic arts to understand that from these endless tabulations might come the true size of the earth, of Tambur, sun and moons and stars, the path they took through space and the direction of Paradise. So the common sailors, who muttered and made signs against evil as they passed our instruments, were closer to fact than Rovic's gentlemen: for indeed Froad practiced a most potent gramarye.

At length we saw weeds floating on the sea, birds, towering cloud masses, all the signs of land. Three days later we raised an island. It was an intense green under those calm skies. Surf, still more violent than in our hemisphere, flung against high cliffs, burst in a smother of foam and roared back down again. We coasted carefully, the palomers aloft to seek an approach, the gunners standing by our cannon with lighted matches. For not only were there unknown currents and shoals—familiar hazards—but we had had brushes with canoe-sailing cannibals in the past. Especially did we fear the eclipses. My lords can visualize how in that hemisphere the sun each day must go behind Tambur. In that longitude the occurrence was about midafternoon

and lasted nearly ten minutes. An awesome sight: the primary planet
—for so Froad now called it, a planet akin to Diell or Coint, with our
own world humbled to a mere satellite thereof!—become a black disk
encircled with red, up in a sky suddenly full of stars. A cold wind blew
across the sea, and even the breakers seemed hushed. Yet so impudent
is the soul of man that we continued about our duties, stopping only
for the briefest prayer as the sun disappeared, thinking more about the
chance of shipwreck in the gloom than of God's Majesty.

So bright is Tambur that we continued to work our way around the
island at night. From sunup to sunup, twelve mortal hours, we kept
the *Golden Leaper* slowly moving. Toward the second noon, Captain
Rovic's persistence was rewarded. An opening in the cliffs revealed a
long fjord. Swampy shores overgrown with saltwater trees told us that
while the tides rose high in that bay, it was not one of those roosts so
dreaded by mariners. The wind being against us, we furled sail and
lowered the boats, towing in our caravel by the power of oars. This was
a vulnerable moment, especially since we had perceived a village within the fjord. "Should we not stand out, master, and let them come first
to us?" I ventured.

Rovic spat over the rail. "I've found it best never to show doubt,"
said he. "If a canoe fleet should assail us, we'll give 'em a whiff of grape-
shot and trust to break their nerve. But I think, thus showing ourselves fearless of them from the very first, we're less likely to meet
treacherous ambuscade later."

He proved right.

In the course of time, we learned we had come upon the eastern
end of a large archipelago. The inhabitants were mighty seafarers,
considering that they had only outrigger dugouts to travel in. These,
however, were often a hundred feet long. With forty paddles, or with
three bast-sailed masts, such a vessel could almost match our best
speed, and was more maneuverable. However, the small cargo space
limited their range of travel.

Though they lived in houses of wood and thatch, possessing only
stone tools, the natives were cultivated folk. They farmed as well as
fished; their priests had an alphabet. Tall and vigorous, somewhat
darker and less hairy than we, they were impressive to behold: whether
nude as was common, or in full panoply of cloth and feathers and shell
ornaments. They had formed a loose empire throughout the archipelago, raided islands lying farther north and carried on a brisk trade
within their own borders. Their whole nation they called the Hisagazi,
and the island on which we had chanced was Yarzik.

This we learned slowly, as we mastered somewhat their tongue. For we were several weeks at that town. The duke of the island, Guzan, made us welcome, supplying us with food, shelter, and helpers as we required. For our part, we pleased them with glassware, bolts of Wondish cloth, and suchlike trade goods. Nonetheless we encountered many difficulties. The shore above high-water mark being too swampy for beaching a vessel as heavy as ours, we must build a drydock before we could careen. Numerous of us took a flux from some disease, though all recovered in time, and this slowed us further.

"Yet I think our troubles will prove a blessing," Rovic told me one night. As had become his habit, once he learned I was a discreet amanuensis, he confided certain thoughts in me. The captain is ever a lonely man; and Rovic, fisher lad, freebooter, self-taught navigator, victor over the Grand fleet of Sathayn and ennobled by the Queen herself, must have found the keeping of that necessary aloofness harder than would a gentleman born.

I waited silent, there in the grass hut they had given him. A soapstone lamp threw wavering light and enormous shadows over us; something rustled the thatch. Outside, the damp ground sloped past houses on stilts and murmurous fronded trees, to the fjord where it shimmered under Tambur. Faintly I heard drums throb, a chant and stamping of feet around some sacrificial fire. Indeed the cool hills of Montalir seemed far.

Rovic leaned back his muscular form, y-clad a mere seaman's kilt in this heat. He had had them fetch him a civilized chair from the ship. "For see you, young fellow," he continued, "at other times we'd have established just enough communication to ask about gold. Well, we might also try to get a few sailing directions. But all in all, we'd hear little except the old story—'aye, foreign lord, indeed there's a kingdom where the very streets are paved with gold . . . a hundred miles west'— anything to get rid of us, eh? But in this prolonged stay, I've asked out the duke and the idolater priests more subtly. I've been so coy about whence we came and what we already know, that they've let slip a gobbet of knowledge they'd not otherwise have disgorged on the rack itself."

"The Aureate Cities?" I cried.

"Hush! I'd not have the crew get excited and out of hand. Not yet."

His leathery, hooknosed face turned strange with thought. "I've always believed those cities an old wives' tale," he said. My shock must have been mirrored to his gaze, for he grinned and went on, "A useful one. Like a lodestone on a stick, it's dragging us around the world." His mirth faded. Again he got that look, which was not unlike the look of Froad considering the heavens. "Aye, of course I want gold, too.

But if we find none on this voyage, I'll not care. I'll just capture a few
ships of Eralia or Sathayn when we're back in home waters, and pay
for the voyage thus. I spoke God's truth that day on the quarterdeck,
Zhean, that this journey was its own goal; until I can give it to Queen
Odela, who once gave me the kiss of ennoblement."

He shook himself out of his reverie and said in a brisk tone: "Having
led him to believe I already knew the most of it, I teased from Duke
Guzan the admission that on the main island of this Hisagazi empire
is something I scarce dare think about. A ship of the gods, he says, and
an actual live god who came from the stars therein. Any of the natives
will tell you this much. The secret reserved to the noble folk is that this
is no legend or mummery, but sober fact. Or so Guzan claims. I know
not what to think. But . . . he took me to a holy cave and showed me an
object from that ship. It was some kind of clockwork mechanism, I
believe. What, I know not. But of a shining silvery metal such as I've
never seen before. The priest challenged me to break it. The metal was
not heavy; must have been thin. But it blunted my sword, splintered
a rock I pounded with, and my diamond ring would not scratch it."

I made signs against evil. A chill went along me, spine and skin and
scalp, until I prickled all over. For the drums were muttering in a jungle
dark, and the waters lay like quicksilver beneath gibbous Tambur,
and each afternoon that planet ate the sun. Oh, for the bells of Provien,
across windswept Anday downs!

When the *Golden Leaper* was seaworthy again, Rovic had no trouble
gaining permission to visit the Hisagazian emperor on the main island.
He would, indeed, have found difficulty in not doing so. By now the
canoes had borne word of us from one end of the realm to another,
and the great lords were all agog to see these blue-eyed strangers. Sleek
and content once more, we disentangled ourselves from the arms of
tawny wenches and embarked. Up anchor, up sail, with chanties
whose echoes sent sea birds whirling above the steeps, and we stood
out to sea. This time we were escorted. Guzan himself was our pilot,
a big middle-aged man whose handsomeness was not much injured by
the livid green tattoos his folk affected on face and body. Several of
his sons spread their pallets on our decks, while a swarm of warriors
paddled alongside.

Rovic summoned Etien the boatswain to him in his cabin. "You're
a man of some wit," he said. "I give you charge of keeping our crew
alert, weapons ready, however peaceful this may look."

"Why, master!" The scarred brown face sagged with near dismay.
"Think you the natives plot a treachery?"

"Who can tell?" said Rovic. "Now, say naught to the crew. They've no skill in dissembling. Did greed or fear rise among 'em, the natives would sense as much, and grow uneasy—which would worsen the attitude of our own men, until none but God's Daughter could tell what'd happen. Only see to it, as casually as you're able, that our arms are ever close by and that our folk stay together."

Etien collected himself, bowed, and left the cabin. I made bold to ask what Rovic had in mind.

"Nothing, yet," said he. "However, I did hold in these fists a piece of clockwork such as the Grand Ban of Giair never imagined; and yarns were spun me of a Ship which flew down from heaven, bearing a god or a prophet. Guzan thinks I know more than I do, and hopes we'll be a new, disturbing element in the balance of things, by which he may further his own ambitions. He did not take all those fighting men along by accident. As for me . . . I intend to learn more about this."

He sat a while at his table, staring at a sunbeam which sickled up and down the wainscot as the ship rocked. Finally: "Scripture tells us man dwelt beyond the stars before the Fall. The astrologues of the past generation or two have told us the planets are corporeal bodies like this earth. A traveler from Paradise—"

I left with my head in a roar.

We made an easy passage among scores of islands. After several days we raised the main one, Ulas-Erkila. It is about a hundred miles long, forty miles across at the widest, rising steep and green toward central mountains dominated by a volcanic cone. The Hisagazi worship two sorts of gods, watery and fiery, and believe this Mount Ulas houses the latter. When I saw that snowpeak afloat in the sky above emerald ridges, staining the blue with smoke, I could feel what the pagans did. The holiest act a man can perform among them is to cast himself into the burning crater of Ulas, and many an aged warrior is carried up the mountain that he may do so. Women are not allowed on the slopes.

Nikum, the royal seat, is situated at the head of a fjord like the village where we had been staying. But Nikum is rich and extensive, being about the size of Roann. Many houses are made from timber rather than thatch; there is also a massive basalt temple atop a cliff, overlooking the city, with orchards, jungle, and mountains at its back. So great are the tree trunks available to them for pilings, the Hisagazi have built here a regular set of docks like those at Lavre—instead of moorings and floats that can rise or fall with the tides, such as most harbors throughout the world are content with. We were offered a berth of honor at the central wharf, but Rovic made the excuse that our ship was awkward to handle and got us tied at the far end.

"In the middle, we'd have the watchtower straight above us," he muttered to me. "And they may not have discovered the bow here, but their javelin throwers are good. Also, we'd have an easy approach to our ship, plus a clutter of moored canoes between us and the bay mouth. Here, though, a few of us could hold the pier whilst the others ready for quick departure."

"But have we anything to fear, master?" I asked.

He gnawed his mustache. "I know not. Much depends on what they really believe about this god-ship of theirs . . . as well as what the truth is. But come all death and hell against us, we'll not return without that truth for Queen Odela."

Drums rolled and feathered spearmen leaped as our officers disembarked. A royal catwalk had been erected above high-water level. (Common townsfolk in this realm swim from house to house when the tide laps their thresholds, or take a coracle if they have burdens to carry.) Across the graceful span of vines and canes lay the palace, which was a long building made from logs, the roof pillars carved into fantastic god-shapes.

Iskilip, Priest-Emperor of the Hisagazi, was an old and corpulent man. A soaring headdress of plumes, a feather robe, a wooden scepter topped with a human skull, his own facial tattoos, his motionlessness, all made him seem unhuman. He sat on a dais, under sweet-smelling torches. His sons sat crosslegged at his feet, his courtiers on either side. Down the long walls were ranged his guardsmen. They had not our custom of standing to attention; but they were big supple young men, with shields and corselets of scaly seamonster leather, with flint axes and obsidian spears that could kill as easily as iron. Their heads were shaven, which made them look the fiercer.

Iskilip greeted us well, called for refreshment, bade us be seated on a bench not much lower than his dais. He asked many perceptive questions. Wide-ranging, the Hisagazi knew of islands far beyond their own chain. They could even point the direction and tell us roughly the distance of a many-castled country they named Yurakadak, though one of them had traveled that far himself. Judging by their third-hand description, what could this be but Giair, which the Wondish adventurer Hanas Tolasson had reached overland? It blazed in me that we were indeed rounding the world. Only after that glory had faded a little did I again heed the talk.

"As I told Guzan," Rovic was saying, "another thing which drew us hither was the tale that you were blessed with a Ship from heaven. And he showed me this was true."

A hissing went down the hall. The princes grew stiff, the courtiers blanked their countenances, even the guardsmen stirred and muttered. Remotely through the walls I heard the rumbling, nearing tide. When Iskilip spoke, through the mask of himself, his voice had gone whetted: "Have you forgotten that these things are not for the uninitiate to see, Guzan?"

"No, Holy One," said the duke. Sweat sprang forth among the devils on his face, but it was not the sweat of fear. "However, this captain knew. His people also . . . as nearly as I could learn . . . he still has trouble speaking so I can understand . . . his people are initiate too. The claim seems reasonable, Holy One. Look at the marvels they brought. The hard, shining stone-which-is-not-stone, as in this long knife I was given, is that not like the stuff of which the Ship is built? The tubes which make distant things look close at hand, such as he has given you, Holy One, is this not akin to the far-seer the Messenger possesses?"

Iskilip leaned forward, toward Rovic. His scepter hand trembled so much that the pegged jaws of the skull clattered together. "Did the Star People themselves teach you to make all this?" he cried. "I never imagined . . . The Messenger never spoke of any others—"

Rovic held up both palms. "Not so fast, Holy One, I pray you," said he. "We are poorly versed in your tongue. I couldn't recognize a word just now."

This was his deceit. All his officers had been ordered to feign a knowledge of Hisagazi less than they really possessed. (We had improved our command of it by secret practicing with each other.) Thus he had an unimpeachable device for equivocation.

"Best we talk of this in private, Holy One," suggested Guzan, with a glance at the courtiers. They returned him a jealous glare.

Iskilip slouched in his gorgeous regalia. His words fell blunt enough, but in the weak tone of an old, uncertain man. "I know not. If these strangers are already initiate, certes we can show them what we have. But otherwise—if profane ears heard the Messenger's own tale—"

Guzan raised a dominator's hand. Bold and ambitious, long thwarted in his petty province, he had taken fire this day. "Holy One," he said, "why has the full story been withheld all these years? In part to keep the commoners obedient, aye. But also, did you and your councillors not fear that all the world might swarm hither, greedy for knowledge, if it knew, and we should then be overwhelmed? Well, if we let the blue-eyed men go home with curiosity unsatisfied, I think they are sure to return in strength. So we have naught to lose by revealing the truth to them. If they have never had a Messenger of their own, if they can be of no real use to us, time enough to kill them. But if they have indeed been visited like us, what might we and they not do together!"

This was spoken fast and softly, so that we Montalirians should not understand. And indeed our gentlemen failed to do so. I, having young ears, got the gist; and Rovic preserved such a fatuous smile of incomprehension that I knew he was seizing every word.

So in the end they decided to take our leader—and my insignificant self, for no Hisagazian magnate goes anywhere quite unattended—up to the temple. Iskilip led the way in person, with Guzan and two brawny princes behind. A dozen spearmen brought up the rear. I thought Rovic's blade would be scant use if trouble came, but set my lips firmly together and made myself walk behind him. He looked as eager as a child on Thanksday Morning, teeth agleam in the pointed beard, a plumed bonnet slanted rakish over his brow. None would have thought him aware of any peril.

We left about sundown; in Tambur's hemisphere, folk make less distinction between day and night than our people must. Having observed Siett and Balant in high tide position, I was not surprised that Nikum lay nearly drowned. And yet, as we wound up the cliff trail toward the temple, methought I had never seen a view more alien.

Below us lay a sheet of water, on which the long grass roofs of the city appeared to float; the crowded docks, where our own ship's masts and spars raked above heathen figureheads; the fjord, winding between precipices toward its mouth, where the surf broke white and terrible on the skerries. The heights above us seemed altogether black, against a fire-colored sunset that filled nigh half the sky and bloodied the waters. Wan through those clouds I glimpsed the thick crescent of Tambur, banded in a heraldry no man could read. A basalt column chipped into the shape of a head loomed in outline athwart the planet. Right and left of the path grew sawtoothed grasses, summer-dry. The sky was pale at the zenith, dark purple in the east, where the first few stars had appeared. Tonight I found no comfort in the stars. We all walked silent. The bare native feet made no noise. My own shoes went *pad-pad* and the bells on Rovic's toes raised a tiny jingle.

The temple was a bold piece of work. Within a quadrangle of basalt walls guarded by tall stone heads lay several buildings of the same material. Only the fresh-cut fronds that roofed them were alive. With Iskilip to lead us, we brushed past acolytes and priests to a wooden cabin behind the sanctum. Two guardsmen stood watch at its door, but they knelt for Iskilip. The emperor rapped with his curious scepter.

My mouth was dry and my heart thunderous. I expected almost any being hideous or radiant to stand in the doorway as it was opened. Astonishing, then, to see just a man, and of no great stature. By lamplight within I discerned his room, clean, austere, but not uncomfortable; this could have been any Hisagazian dwelling. He himself wore a simple bast skirt. The legs beneath were bent and thin, old man's shanks. His body was also thin, but still erect, the white head proudly carried. In complexion he was darker than a Montalirian, lighter than a Hisagazian, with brown eyes and thin beard. His visage differed subtly, in nose and lips and slope of jaw, from any other race I had ever encountered. But he was human.

Naught else.

We entered the cabin, shutting out the spearmen. Iskilip doddered through a half-religious ceremony of introduction. I saw Guzan and the princes shift their stance, restless and unawed. Their class had long been party to this. Rovic's face was unreadable. He bowed with full courtliness to Val Nira, Messenger of Heaven, and explained our presence in a few words. But as he spoke, their eyes met and I saw him take the star man's measure.

"Aye, this is my home," said Val Nira. Habit spoke for him; he had given this account to so many young nobles that the edges were worn off it. As yet he had not observed our metallic instruments, or else had not grasped their significance to him. "For . . . forty-three years, is that right, Iskilip? I have been treated as well as might be. If at times I was near screaming from loneliness, that is what an oracle must expect."

The emperor stirred, uneasy in his robe. "His demon left him," he explained. "Now he is simple human flesh. That's the real secret we keep. It was not ever thus. I remember when he first came. He prophesied immense things, and all the people wailed and went on their faces. But sithence his demon has gone back to the stars, and the once potent weapon he bore has equally been emptied of its force. The people would not believe this, however, so we still pretend otherwise, or there would be unrest among them."

"Affecting your own privileges," said Val Nira. His tone was tired and sardonic. "Iskilip was young then," he added to Rovic, "and the imperial succession was in doubt. I gave him my influence. He promised in return to do certain things for me."

"I tried, Messenger," said the monarch. "Ask all the sunken canoes and drowned men if I did not try. But the will of the gods was otherwise."

"Evidently." Val Nira shrugged. "These islands have few ores, Captain Rovic, and no person capable of recognizing those I required. It's too far to the mainland for Hisagazian canoes. But I don't deny you tried, Iskilip . . . then." He cocked an eyebrow back at us. "This is the first time foreigners have been taken so deeply into the imperial confidence, my friends. Are you certain you can get back out again, alive?"

"Why, why, why, they're our guests!" blustered Iskilip and Guzan, almost in each other's mouths.

"Besides," smiled Rovic, "I had most of the secret already. My own country has secrets of its own, to set against this. Yes, I think we might well do business, Holy One."

The emperor trembled. His voice cracked across. "Have you indeed a Messenger too?"

"*What?*" For a numbed moment Val Nira stared at us. Red and white pursued each other across his countenance. Then he sat down on the bench and began to weep.

"Well, not precisely." Rovic laid a hand on the shaking shoulder, "I confess no heavenly vessel had docked at Montalir. But we've certain other secrets, belike equally valuable." Only I, who knew his moods somewhat, could sense the tauntness in him. He locked eyes with Guzan and stared the duke down as a wild animal tamer does. And all the while, motherly gentle, he spoke with Val Nira. "I take it, friend, your Ship was wrecked on these shores, but could be repaired if you had certain materials?"

"Yes . . . yes . . . listen—" Stammering and gulping at the thought he might see his home again ere he died, Val Nira tried to explain.

The doctrinal implications of what he said are so astounding, even dangerous, that I feel sure my lords would not wish me to repeat much. However, I do not believe they are false. If the stars are indeed suns like our own, each attended by planets like our own, this demolishes the crystal-sphere theory. But Froad, when he was told later, did not think that mattered to the true religion. Scripture has never said in so many words that Paradise lies directly above the birthplace of God's Daughter; this was merely assumed, during those centuries when the earth was believed to be flat. Why should Paradise not be those planets of other suns, where men dwell in magnificence, men who possess all the ancient arts and flit from star to star as casually as we might go from Lavre to West Alayn?

Val Nira believed our ancestors had been cast away on this world, several thousand years ago. They must have been fleeing the consequences of some crime or heresy, to come so far from any human domain. Somehow their ship was wrecked, the survivors went back to savagery, only by degrees have their descendants regained a little knowledge. I cannot see where this explanation contradicts the dogma of the Fall. Rather, it amplifies it. The Fall was not the portion of all mankind, but only of a few—our own tainted blood—while the others continued to dwell prosperous and content in the heavens.

Even today, our world lies far off the trade lanes of the Paradise folk. Very few of them nowadays have any interest in seeking new worlds. Val Nira, though, was such a one. He traveled at hazard for months until he chanced upon our earth. Then the curse seized him, too. Something went wrong. He descended upon Ulas-Erkila, and the Ship would fly no more.

"I know what the damage is," he said ardently. "I've not forgotten. How could I? No day has passed in all these years that I didn't recite to myself what must be done. A certain subtle engine in the Ship requires quicksilver." (He and Rovic must spend some time talking ere they deduced this must be what he meant by the word he used.) "When the engine failed, I landed so hard that its tanks burst. All the quicksilver, what I had in reserve as well as what I was employing, poured forth. So much, in that hot enclosed space, would have poisoned me. I fled outside, forgetting to close the doorway. The deck being canted, the quicksilver ran after me. By the time I had recovered from blind panic, a tropical rainstorm had carried off all the fluid metal. A series of unlikely accidents, yes, that's what's condemned me to a life's exile. It really would have made more sense to perish outright!"

He clutched Rovic's hand, staring up from his seat at the captain who stood over him. "Can you actually get quicksilver?" he begged. "I need no more than the volume of a man's head. Only that, and a few repairs easily made with tools in the Ship. When this cult grew up around me, I must needs release certain things I possessed, that each provincial temple might have a relic. But I took care never to give away anything important. Whatever I need is all there. A gallon of quicksilver, and— Oh, God, my wife may even be alive, on Terra!"

Guzan, at least, had begun to understand the situation. He gestured to the princes, who hefted their axes and stepped a little closer. The door was shut on the guard escort, but a shout would bring their spears into this cabin. Rovic looked from Val Nira to Guzan, whose face was grown ugly with tension. My captain laid hand on hilt. In no other way did he seem to feel any nearness of trouble.

"I take it, milord," he said lightly, "you're willing that the Heaven Ship be made to fly again."

Guzan was jarred. He had never expected this. "Why, of course," he exclaimed. "Why not?"

"Your tame god would depart you. What then becomes of your power in Hisagazia?"

"I . . . I'd not thought of that," Iskilip stuttered.

Val Nira's eyes shuttled among us, as if watching a game of paddle-ball. His thin body shook. "No," he whimpered. "You can't. You can't keep me!"

Guzan nodded. "In a few more years," he said, not unkindly, "you would depart in death's canoe anyhow. If meanwhile we held you against your will, you might not speak the right oracles for us. Nay, be at ease; we'll get your flowing stone." With a slitted glance at Rovic: "Who shall fetch it?"

"My own folk," said the knight. "Our ship can readily reach Giair, where there are civilized nations who surely have the quicksilver. We could return within a year, I think."

"Accompanied by a fleet of adventurers, to help you seize the sacred vessel?" asked Guzan bluntly. "Or . . . once out of our islands . . . you might not proceed to Yurakadak at all. You might continue the whole way home, and tell your Queen, and return with all the power she commands."

Rovic lounged against a roof post, like a big pouncecat at its ease in ruffles and hose and scarlet cape. His right hand continued to rest on his sword pommel. "Only Val Nira could make that Ship go, I suppose," he drawled. "Does it matter who aids him in making repairs? Surely you don't think either of our nations could conquer Paradise!"

"The Ship is very easy to operate," chattered Val Nira. "Anyone can fly it in air. I showed many nobles what levers to use. It's navigating among the stars which is more difficult. No nation on this world could even reach my people unaided—let alone fight them—but why should you think of fighting? I've told you a thousand times, Iskilip, the dwellers in the Milky Way are dangerous to none, helpful to all. They have so much wealth they're hard put to find a use for most of it. Gladly would they spend large amounts to help all the peoples on this world become civilized again." With an anxious, half hysterical look at Rovic: "Fully civilized, I mean. We'll teach you our arts. We'll give you engines, automata, homunculi, that do all the toilsome work; and boats that fly through the air; and regular passenger service on those ships that ply between the stars—"

"These things you have promised for forty years," said Iskilip. "We've only your word."

"And, finally, a chance to confirm his word," I blurted.

Guzan said with calculated grimness: "Matters are not that simple, Holy One. I've watched these men from across the ocean for weeks, while they lived on Yarzik. Even on their best behavior, they're a fierce and greedy lot. I trust them no further than my eyes reach. This very night I see how they've befooled us. They know our language better than they ever admitted. And they misled us to believe they might have some inkling of a Messenger. If the Ship were indeed made to fly again, with them in possession, who knows what they might choose to do?"

Rovic's tone softened still further, "What do you propose, Guzan?"

"We can discuss that another time."

I saw knuckles tighten around stone axes. For a moment, only Val Nira's unsteady breathing was heard. Guzan stood heavy in the lamplight, rubbing his chin, the small black eyes turned downward in thoughtfulness. At last he shook himself. "Perhaps," he said crisply, "a crew mainly Hisagazian could sail your ship, Rovic, and fetch the flowing stone. A few of your men could go along to instruct ours. The rest could remain here as hostages."

My captain made no reply. Val Nira groaned, "You don't understand! You're squabbling over nothing! When my people come here, there'll be no more war, no more oppression, they'll cure you of all such diseases. They'll show friendship to all and favor to none. I beg you—"

"Enough," said Iskilip. His own words fell ragged. "We shall sleep on all this. If anyone can sleep after so much strangeness."

Rovic looked past the emperor's plumes, into the face of Guzan. "Before we decide anything—" His fingers tightened on the sword hilt till the nails turned white. Some thought had sprung up within him. But he kept his tone even. "First I want to see that Ship. Can we go there tomorrow?"

Iskilip was the Holy One, but he stood huddled in his feather robe. Guzan nodded agreement.

We bade our goodnights and went forth under Tambur. The planet was waxing toward full, flooding the courtyard with cold luminance, but the hut was shadowed by the temple. It remained a black outline, with a narrow lamplight rectangle of doorway in the middle. There was etched the frail body of Val Nira, who had come from the stars. He watched us till we had gone out of sight.

On the way down the path, Guzan and Rovic bargained in curt words. The Ship lay two days' march inland, on the slopes of Mount Ulas. We would go in a joint party to inspect it, but a mere dozen

Montalirians were to be allowed. Afterward we would debate our course of action.

Lanthorns glowed yellow at our caravel's poop. Refusing Iskilip's hospitality, Rovic and I returned thither for the night. A pikeman on guard at the gangway inquired what I had learned. "Ask me tomorrow," I said feebly. "My head's in too much of a whirl."

"Come into my cabin, lad, for a stoup ere we retire," the captain invited me.

God knows I needed wine. We entered the low little room, crowded with nautical instruments, with books, and with printed charts that looked quaint to me now I had seen a little of those spaces where the cartographer drew mermaids and windsprites. Rovic sat down behind his table, gestured me to a chair opposite, and poured from a carafe into two goblets of Quaynish crystal. Then I knew he had momentous thoughts in his head—far more than the problem of saving our lives.

We sipped a while, unspeaking. I heard the *lap-lap* of wavelets on our hull, the tramp of men on watch, the rustle of distant surf: otherwise nothing. At last Rovic leaned back, staring at the ruby wine on the table. I could not read his expression.

"Well, lad," said he, "what do you think?"

"I know not what to think, master."

"You and Froad are a little prepared for this idea that the stars are other suns. You're educated. As for me, I've seen so much eldritch in my day that this seems quite believable. The rest of our people, though—"

"An irony that barbarians like Guzan should long have been familiar with the concept—having had the old man from the sky to preach it privily to their class for more than forty years— Is he indeed a prophet, master?"

"He denies it. He plays prophet because he must, but it's evident all the dukes and earls of this realm know it's a trick. Iskilip is senile, more than half converted to his own artificial creed. He was mumbling about prophecies Val Nira made long ago, true prophecies. Bah! Tricks of memory and wishfulness. Val Nira is as human and fallible as I am. We Montalirians are the same flesh as these Hisagazi, even if we have learned the use of metal before they did. Val Nira's people know more in turn than us; but they're still mortals, by Heaven. I *must* remember that they are."

"Guzan remembers."

"Bravo, lad!" Rovic's mouth bent upward, one-sidedly. "He's a clever one, and bold. When he came, he saw his chance to stop stagnating as the petty lord of an outlying island. He'll not let that chance slip without a fight. Like many a double-dealer before him, he accuses us of plotting the very things he hopes to do."

"But what does he hope for?"

"My guess would be, he wants the Ship for himself. Val Nira said it was easy to fly. Navigation between the stars would be too difficult for anyone save him; nor could any man in his right mind hope to play pirate along the Milky Way. However . . . if the Ship stayed right here, on this earth, rising no higher than a mile above ground . . . the warlord who used it might conquer more widely than Lame Darveth himself."

I was aghast. "Do you mean Guzan would not even try to seek out Paradise?"

Rovic scowled so blackly at his wine that I saw he wanted aloneness. I stole off to my bunk in the poop.

The captain was up before dawn, readying our folk. Plainly he had reached some decision, and it was not pleasant. But once he set a course, he seldom left it. He was long in conference with Etien, who came out of the cabin looking frightened. As if to reassure himself, the boatswain ordered the men about all the more harshly.

Our allowed dozen were to be Rovic, Froad, myself, Etien, and eight crewmen. All were supplied with helmets and corselets, muskets and edged weapons. Since Guzan had told us there was a beaten path to the Ship, we assembled a supply cart on the dock. Etien supervised its lading. I was astonished to see that nearly all it carried, till the axles groaned, was barrels of gunpowder. "But we're not taking cannon!" I protested.

"Skipper's orders," rapped Etien. He turned his back on me. After a glance at Rovic's face, no one ventured to ask him the reason. I remembered we would be going up a mountainside. A wagonful of powder, with lit fuse, set rolling down toward a hostile army, might win a battle. But did Rovic anticipate open conflict so soon?

Certes his orders to the men and officers remaining behind suggested as much. They were to stay aboard the *Golden Leaper*, holding her ready for instant fight or flight.

As the sun rose, we said our morning prayers to God's Daughter and marched down the docks. The wood banged hollow under our boots. A few thin mists drifted on the bay; Tambur's crescent hung wan above. Nikum Town was hushed as we passed through.

Guzan met us at the temple. A son of Iskilip was supposedly in charge, but the duke ignored that youth as much as we did. They had a hundred guardsmen with them, scaly-coated, shaven-headed, tattooed with storms and dragons. The early sunlight gleamed off obsidian spearheads. Our approach was watched in silence. But when we drew up before those disorderly ranks, Guzan trod forth. He was also y-clad in leather, and carried the sword Rovic had given him on Yarzik. The dew shimmered on his feather cloak. "What have you in that wagon?" he demanded.

"Supplies," Rovic answered.

"For four days?"

"Send home all but ten of your men," said Rovic coolly, "and I'll send back this cart."

Their eyes clashed, until Guzan turned and gave his orders. We started off, a few Montalirians surrounded by pagan warriors. The jungle lay ahead of us, a deep and burning green, rising halfway up the slope of Ulas. Then the mountain became naked black, up to the snow that edged its smoking crater.

Val Nira walked between Rovic and Guzan. Strange, I thought, that the instrument of God's will for us was so shriveled. He ought to have walked tall and haughty, with a star on his brow.

During the day, at night when we made camp, and again the next day, Rovic and Froad questioned him eagerly about his home. Of course, all their talk was in fragments. Nor did I hear everything, since I must take my turn at pulling our wagon along that narrow, upward, damnable trail. The Hisagazi have no draft animals, therefore they make very little use of the wheel and have no proper roads. But what I did hear kept me long awake.

Ah, greater marvels than the poets have imagined for Elf Land! Entire cities built in a single tower half a mile high. The sky made to glow so that there is no true darkness after sunset. Food not grown in the earth, but manufactured in alchemical laboratories. The lowest peasant owning a score of machines which serve him more subtly and humbly than might a thousand slaves—owning an aerial carriage which can fly him around his world in less than a day—owning a crystal window on which theatrical images appear, to beguile his abundant leisure. Argosies between suns, stuffed with the wealth of a thousand planets; yet every ship unarmed and unescorted, for there are no pirates and this realm has long ago come to such good terms with the other starfaring nations that war has also ceased. (These other countries, it seems, are more akin to the supernatural than Val Nira's, in that the races composing them are not human, though able to speak and reason.) In this happy land there is little crime. When it does occur, the criminal is soon captured by the arts of the provost corps; yet he is not hanged, nor even transported overseas. Instead, his mind is cured of the wish to violate any law. He returns home to live as an especially honored citizen, since all know he is now completely trustworthy. As for the government—but here I lost the thread of discourse. I believe it is in form a republic, but in practice a devoted fellowship of men, chosen by examination, who see to the welfare of everyone else.

Surely, I thought, this was Paradise!

Our sailors listened with mouths agape. Rovic's mien was reserved, but he gnawed his mustaches incessantly. Guzan, to whom this was an old tale, grew rough of manner. Plain to see, he disliked our intimacy with Val Nira, and the ease wherewith we grasped ideas that were spoken.

But then, we came of a nation which has long encouraged natural philosophy and improvement of all mechanic arts. I myself, in my short lifetime, had witnessed the replacement of the waterwheel in regions where there are few streams, by the modern form of windmill. The pendulum clock was invented the year before I was born. I had read many romances about the flying machines which no few men have tried to devise. Living at such a dizzy pace of progress, we Montalirians were well prepared to entertain still vaster concepts.

At night, sitting up with Froad and Etien around a campfire, I spoke somewhat of this to the savant. "Ah," he crooned, "today Truth stood unveiled before me. Did you hear what the starman said? The three laws of planetary motion about a sun, and the one great law of attraction which explains them? Dear saints, that law can be put in a single short sentence, and yet the development will keep mathematicians busy for three hundred years!"

He stared past the flames, and the other fires around which the heathen men slept, and the jungle gloom, and the angry volcanic glow in heaven. I started to query him. "Leave be, lad," grunted Etien. "Can ye nay tell when a man's in love?"

I shifted my position, a little closer to the boatswain's stolid, comforting bulk. "What do you think of all this?" I asked, softly, for the jungle whispered and croaked on every side.

"Me, I stopped thinking a while back," he said. "After yon day on the quarterdeck, when the skipper jested us into sailing wi' him though we went off the world's edge an' tumbled down in foam amongst the nether stars . . . well, I'm but a poor sailor man, an' my one chance o' regaining home is to follow the skipper."

"Even beyond the sky?"

"Less hazard to that, maybe, than sailing on around the world. The little man swore his vessel was safe, an' that there're no storms between the suns."

"Can you trust his word?"

"Oh, aye. Even a knocked-about old palomer like me has seen enough o' men to ken when a one's too timid an' eagersome to stand by a lie. I fear not the folk in Paradise, nor does the skipper. Except in some way—" Etien rubbed his bearded jaw, scowling. "In some way I can nay wholly grasp, they affright Rovic. He fears nay they'll come hither wi' torch an' sword; but there's somewhat else about 'em that frets him."

I felt the ground shudder, ever so faintly. Ulas had cleared his throat. "It does seem we'd be daring God's anger—"

"That's nay what gnaws on the skipper's mind. He was never an over-pious man." Etien scratched himself, yawned, and climbed to his feet. "Glad I am to be nay the skipper. Let him think over what's best to do. Time ye an' me was asleep."

But I slept little that night.

Rovic, I think, rested well. Yet as the next day wore on, I could see haggardness on him. I wondered why. Did he think the Hisagazi would turn on us? If so, why had he come at all? As the slope steepened, the wagon drew so toilsome to push and drag that my fears died for lack of breath.

Yet when we came upon the Ship, toward evening, I forgot my weariness. And after one amazed volley of oaths, our mariners rested silent on their pikes. The Hisagazi, never talkative, crouched low in token of awe. Only Guzan remained erect among them. I glimpsed his expression as he stared at the marvel. It was a look of lust.

Wild was that place. We had gone above timberline, so the land was a green sea below us, edged with silvery ocean. Here we stood among tumbled black boulders, with cinders and spongy tufa underfoot. The mountain rose in steeps and scarps and ravines, up to the snows and the smoke, which rose another mile into a pale chilly sky. And here stood the Ship.

And the Ship was beauty.

I remember. In length—height, rather, since it stood on its tail—it was about equal to our own caravel, in form not unlike a lance head, in color a shining white untarnished after forty years. That was all. But words are paltry, my lord. What can they show of clean soaring curves, of iridescence on burnished metal, of a thing which was proud and lovely and in its very shape aquiver to be off? How can I conjure back the glamor which hazed that Ship whose keel had cloven starlight?

We stood there a long time. My vision blurred. I wiped my eyes, angry to be seen so affected, until I noticed one tear glisten in Rovic's red beard. But the captain's visage was quite blank. When he spoke, he said merely, in a flat voice, "Come, let's make camp."

The Hisagazian guardsmen dared approach no closer than these several hundred yards, to so potent an idol as the Ship had become. Our own mariners were glad enough to maintain the same distance. But after dark, when all else was in order, Val Nira led Rovic, Froad, Guzan, and myself to the vessel.

As we approached, a double door in the side swung noiselessly open and a metal gangplank descended therefrom. Glowing in Tambur's light, and in the dull clotted red reflected off the smoke clouds, the Ship was already as strange as I could endure. When it thus opened itself to me, as if a ghost stood guard, I whimpered and fled. The cinders crunched beneath my boots; I caught a whiff of sulfurous air.

But at the edge of camp I rallied myself enough to look again. The dark ground blotted all light, so that the Ship appeared alone with its grandeur. Presently I went back.

The interior was lit by luminous panels, cool to the touch. Val Nira explained that the great engine which drove it—as if the troll of folk-lore were put on a treadmill—was intact, and would furnish power at the flick of a lever. As nearly as I could understand what he said, this was done by changing the metallic part of ordinary salt into light . . . so I do not understand after all. The quicksilver was required for a part of the controls, which channeled power from the engine into another mechanism that hurtled the Ship skyward. We inspected the broken container. Enormous indeed had been the impact of landing, to twist and bend that thick alloy so. And yet Val Nira had been shielded by invisible forces, and the rest of the Ship had not suffered important damage. He fetched some tools, which flamed and hummed and whirled, and demonstrated a few repair operations on the broken part. Obviously he would have no trouble completing the work—and then he need only pour in a gallon of quicksilver, to bring his vessel alive again.

Much else did he show us that night. I shall say naught of this, for I cannot even remember such strangeness very clearly, let alone find words. Suffice it that Rovic, Froad, and Zhean spent a few hours in Elf Hill.

So, too, did Guzan. Though he had been taken here once before, as part of his initiation, he had never been shown this much erenow. Watching him, however, I saw less marveling in him than greed.

No doubt Rovic observed the same. There was little which Rovic did not observe. When we departed the Ship, his silence was not stunned like Froad's or my own. At the time, I thought in a vague fashion that he fretted over the trouble Guzan was certain to make. Now, looking back, I believe his mood was sadness.

Sure it is that long after we others were in our bedrolls, he stood alone, looking at the planetlit Ship.

Early in a cold dawn, Etien shook me awake. "Up, lad, we've work to do. Load yere pistols an' belt on yere dirk."

"What? What's to happen?" I fumbled with a hoarfrosted blanket. Last night seemed a dream.

"The skipper's nay said, but plainly he awaits a fight. Report to the wagon an' help us move into yon flying tower." Etien's thick form heel-squatted a moment longer beside me. Then, slowly: "Methinks Guzan has some idea o' murdering us all, here on the mountain. One officer an' a few crewmen can be made to sail the *Golden Leaper* for him, to Giair an' back. The rest o' us would be less trouble to him wi' our weasands slit."

I crawled forth, teeth clattering in my head. After arming myself, I snatched some food from the common store. The Hisagazi on the march carry dried fish and a sort of bread made from a powdered weed. Only the saints knew when I'd next get a chance to eat. I was the last to join Rovic at the cart. The natives were drifting sullenly toward us, unsure what we intended.

"Let's go, lads," said Rovic. He gave his orders. Four men started manhandling the wagon across the rocky trail toward the Ship, where this gleamed among mists. We others stood by, weapons ready. Almost at once Guzan hastened toward us, with Val Nira toiling in his wake.

Anger darkened his countenance. "What are you doing?" he barked.

Rovic gave him a calm stare. "Why, milord, as we may be here for some time, inspecting the wonders aboard the Ship—"

"What?" interrupted Guzan. "What do you mean? Have you not seen enough for one visit? We must get home again, and prepare to sail after the flowing stone."

"Go if you wish," said Rovic. "I choose to linger. And since you don't trust me, I reciprocate the feeling. My folk will stay in the Ship, which can be defended if necessary."

Guzan stormed and raged, but Rovic ignored him. Our men continued hauling the cart over the uneven ground. Guzan signaled his spearmen, who approached in a disordered but alert mass. Etien spoke a command. We fell into line. Pikes slanted forward, muskets took aim.

Guzan stepped back. We had demonstrated firearms for him at his own home island. Doubtless he could overwhelm us with sheer numbers, were he determined enough, but the cost would be heavy. "No reason to fight, is there?" purred Rovic. "I am only taking a sensible precaution. The Ship is a most valuable prize. It could bring Paradise for all . . . or dominion over this earth for one. There are those who'd prefer the latter. I've not accused you of being among them. However, in prudence I'd liefer keep the Ship for my hostage and my fortress, as long as it pleases me to remain here."

I think then I was convinced of Guzan's real intentions, not as a surmise of ours but as plain fact. Had he truly wished to attain the stars, his one concern would have been to keep the Ship safe. He would not have reached out, snatched little Val Nira in his powerful hands, and dragged the starman backward like a shield against our fire. Not that his intent matters, save to my own conscience. Wrath distorted his patterned visage. He screamed at us, "Then I'll keep a hostage too! And much good may your shelter do you!"

The Hisagazi milled about, muttering, hefting their spears and axes, but not prepared to follow us. We grunted our way across the black mountainside. The sun strengthened. Froad twisted his beard. "Dear me, master captain," he said, "think you they'll lay siege to us?"

"I'd not advise anyone to venture forth alone," said Rovic dryly.

"But without Val Nira to explain things, what use for us to stay at the Ship? Best we go back. I've mathematic texts to consult—my head's aspin with the law that binds the turning planets—I must ask the man from Paradise what he knows of—"

Rovic interrupted with a gruff order to three men, that they help lift a wheel wedged between two stones. He was in a savage temper. I confess his action seemed mad to me. If Guzan intended treachery, we had gained little by immobilizing ourselves in the Ship, where he could starve us. Better to let him attack in the open, where we would have a chance of fighting our way through. On the other hand, if Guzan did not plan to fall on us in the jungle—or any other time—then this was senseless provocation on our part. But I dared not question.

When we had brought our wagon up to the Ship, its gangplank again descended for us. The sailors started and cursed. Rovic forced himself out of his own bitterness, to speak soothing words. "Easy, lads. I've been aboard already, ye ken. Naught harmful within. Now we must tote our powder thither, an' stow it as I've planned."

Being slight of frame, I was not set to carrying the heavy casks, but put at the foot of the gangplank to watch the Hisagazi. We were too far away to distinguish words, but I saw how Guzan stood up on a boulder and harangued them. They shook their weapons at us and whooped. But they did not venture to attack. I wondered wretchedly what this was all about. If Rovic had foreseen us besieged, that would explain why he brought so much powder along . . . no, it would not, for there was more than a dozen men could shoot off in weeks of musketry, even had we had enough lead along . . . and we had almost no food! I looked past the poisonous volcano clouds, to Tambur where storms raged that could engulf all our earth, and wondered what demons lurked here to possess men.

I sprang to alertness at an indignant shout from within. Froad! Almost, I ran up the gangway, then remembered my duty. I heard Rovic roar him down and order the crewfolk to carry on. Froad and Rovic must have gone alone into the pilot's compartment and talked for an hour or more. When the old man emerged, he protested no longer. But as he walked down the gangway, he wept.

Rovic followed, grimmer of countenance than I had ever seen a man erenow. The sailors filed after, some looking appalled, some relieved, but chiefly watching the Hisagazian camp. They were simple mariners; the Ship was little to them save an alien and disquieting thing. Last came Etien, walking backward down the metal plank as he uncoiled a long string.

"Form square!" barked Rovic. The men snapped into position. "Best get within, Zhean and Froad," said the captain. "You can better carry extra ammunition than fight." He placed himself in the van.

I tugged Froad's sleeve. "Please, I beg you, master, what's happening?" But he sobbed too much to answer.

Etien crouched with flint and steel in his hands. He heard me—for otherwise we were all deathly silent—and said in a hard voice: "We placed casks o' powder throughout this hull, lad, wi' powder trains to join 'em. Here's the fuse to the whole."

I could not speak, could not even think, so monstrous was this. As if from immensely far away, I heard the click of stone on steel in Etien's fingers, heard him blow on the spark and add: "A good idea, methinks. I said t'other eventide, I'd follow the skipper wi'out fear o' God's curse —but better 'tis not to tempt Him overmuch."

"Forward march!" Rovic's sword blazed clear of the scabbard.

Our feet scrunched loud and horrible on the mountain as we quickstepped away. I did not look back. I could not. I was still fumbling in a nightmare. Since Guzan would have moved to intercept us anyhow, we proceeded straight toward his band. He stepped forward as we halted at the camp's edge. Val Nira slunk shivering after him. I heard the words dimly:

"Well, Rovic, what now? Are you ready to go home?"

"Yes," said the captain. His voice was dull. "All the way home."

Guzan squinted in rising suspiciousness. "Why did you abandon your wagon? What did you leave behind?"

"Supplies. Come, let's march."

Val Nira stared at the cruel shapes of our pikes. He must wet his lips a few times ere he could quaver, "What are you talking about? There's no reason to leave food there. It would spoil in all the time until . . . until—" He faltered as he looked into Rovic's eyes. The blood drained from him.

"What have you done?" he whispered.

Suddenly Rovic's free hand went up, to cover his face. "What I must," he said thickly. "Daughter of God, forgive me."

The starman regarded us an instant more. Then he turned and ran. Past the astonished warriors he burst, out onto the cindery slope, toward his Ship.

"Come back!" bellowed Rovic. "You fool you'll never—"

He swallowed hard. As he looked after that small, stumbling, lonely shape, hurrying across a fire mountain toward the Beautiful One, the sword sank in his grasp. "Perhaps it's best," he said, like a benediction.

Guzan raised his own sword. In scaly coat and blowing feathers, he was a figure as impressive as steel-clad Rovic. "Tell me what you've done," he snarled, "or I'll kill you this moment!"

He paid our muskets no heed. He, too, had had dreams.

He, too, saw them end, when the Ship exploded.

Even that adamantine hull could not withstand a wagonload of carefully placed gunpowder, set off at one time. There came a crash that knocked me to my knees, and the hull cracked open. White-hot chunks of metal screamed across the slopes. I saw one of them strike a boulder and split it in twain. Val Nira vanished, destroyed too quickly to have seen what happened; so in the ultimate, God was merciful to him. Through the flames and smokes and the doomsday noise which followed, I saw the Ship fall. It rolled down the slope, strewing its own mangled guts behind. Then the mountainside grumbled and slid in pursuit, and buried it, and dust hid the sky.

More than this, I have no heart to remember.

The Hisagazi shrieked and fled. They must have thought all hell come to earth. Guzan stood his ground. As the dust enveloped us, hiding the grave of the Ship and the white volcano crater, turning the sun red, he sprang at Rovic. A musketeer raised his weapon. Etien slapped it down. We stood and watched those two men fight, up and over the shaken cinder land, and knew in our private darkness that this was their right. Sparks flew where the blades clamored together. At last Rovic's skill prevailed. He took Guzan in the throat.

We gave Guzan decent burial and went down through the jungle.

That night the guardsmen rallied their courage enough to attack us. We were aided by our muskets, but must chiefly use sword and pike. We hewed our way through them because we had no other place to go than the sea.

They gave up, but carried word ahead of us. When we reached Nikum, all the forces Iskilip could raise were besieging the *Golden Leaper* and waiting to oppose Rovic's entry. We formed a square again, and no matter how many thousands they had, only a score or so could reach us at any time. Nonetheless, we left six good men in the crimsoned mud of those streets. When our people on the caravel realized Rovic was coming back, they bombarded the town. This ignited the thatch roofs and distracted the enemy enough that a sortie from the ship was able to effect a juncture with us. We chopped our way to the pier, got aboard, and manned the capstan.

Outraged and very brave, the Hisagazi paddled their canoes up to our hull, where our cannon could not be brought to bear. They stood on each other's shoulders to reach our rail. One band forced itself aboard, and the fight was fierce which cleared them from the decks. That was when I got the shattered collarbone which plagues me to this day.

But in the end, we came out of the fjord. A fresh east wind was blowing. With all sail aloft, we outran the foe. We counted our dead, bound our wounds, and slept.

Next dawning, awakened by the pain of my shoulder and the worse pain within, I mounted the quarterdeck. The sky was overcast. The wind had stiffened; the sea ran cold and green, whitecaps out to a cloud-gray horizon. Timbers groaned and rigging skirled. I stood an hour facing aft, into the chill wind that numbs pain.

When I heard boots behind me, I did not turn around. I knew they were Rovic's. He stood beside me a long while, bareheaded. I noticed that he was starting to turn gray.

Finally, not yet regarding me, still squinting into the air that lashed tears from our eyes, he said: "I had a chance to talk Froad over, that day. He was grieved, but owned I was right. Has he spoken to you about it?"

"No," I said.

"None of us are ever likely to speak of it much," said Rovic.

After another time: "I was not afraid Guzan or anyone else would seize the Ship and try to turn conqueror. We men of Montalir should well be able to deal with any such rogues. Nor was I afraid of the Paradise dwellers. That poor little man could only have been telling truth. They would never have harmed us . . . willingly. They would have brought precious gifts, and taught us their own esoteric arts, and let us visit all their stars."

"Then why?" I got out.

"Someday Froad's successors will solve the riddles of the universe," he said. "Someday our descendants will build their own Ship, and go forth to whatever destiny they wish."

Spume blew up and around us, until our hair was wet. I tasted the salt on my lips.

"Meanwhile," said Rovic, "we'll sail the seas of this earth, and walk its mountains, and chart and subdue and come to understand it. Do you see, Zhean? That is what the Ship would have taken from us."

Then I was also made able to weep. He laid his hand on my uninjured shoulder and stood with me while the *Golden Leaper,* all sail set, proceeded westward.

I can't resist having the final word . . .

Every good story reflects credit upon its author and all the authors I know, without exception, cheerfully accept such credit, and do not willingly allow any of it to escape.

In particular, any suggestion that the editor of a magazine deserves any specific credit for the good writing of the stories appearing in it, is met with unfavorable reactions ranging from gently derisive to violently negative.

However, I will let you into a professional secret if you will promise not to reveal the source of your information. An editor, whether he wants to or not, places his mark upon the magazine and every story in it. He selects the stories that are to appear and thus sets the tone for the magazine. He talks endlessly to authors who come to visit him and writes letters to those who do not. He encourages, inspires, offers suggestions, donates ideas. He asks for revision and points out room for improvement even at the cost of securing for himself a vaster and more articulate unpopularity than human flesh and blood ought to be required to endure.

Let me list, then, the editors responsible for seeing the Hugo winners in print, before they became Hugo winners.

For "The Darfsteller," "Allamagoosa," "Exploration Team," "The Big Front Yard," and "The Longest Voyage," we have John W. Campbell, Jr., to thank. John is large, indecently intelligent, fearfully articulate and dreadfully opinionated on every conceivable subject. He is a dangerous man to argue with for he will convince you that white is plaid and when you are ready to die for your new belief, will turn about and as painstakingly convince you that plaid is black. No one has so influenced the field as has he.

The editorial responsibility for "The Star" belongs to Larry T. Shaw.

Larry is short and very soft-spoken, so that it is necessary to lean your ear against his mouth to realize that he has lost his temper and is shouting. He wears glasses thicker than he is and smokes a pipe somewhat longer than he is; and on a very small budget ran a darned good magazine for as long as money held out at all.

"Or All the Seas with Oysters" appeared in Horace L. Gold's magazine. Horace's personality, quite different from that of John Campbell, is nevertheless just as overpowering. His tongue-lashings of authors who have failed to live up to their own standards are notorious but when the author, smarting and bleeding, condescended to patch his story as suggested, he was generally rewarded with the knowledge that somehow his story had been greatly improved. (I can testify to this of personal knowledge for no author smarts as sharply or bleeds as copiously under such conditions as do I—or finds his stories as drastically changed for the better.)

For "The Hell-Bound Train," we have Anthony Boucher; witty, genial, understanding, and the composer of the gentlest and most soothing letters of rejection that can possibly exist. He, more than anyone else, learned how to give science fiction the delicate aura of literature. Tony earned love under the most unfavorable possible conditions for he was loved even by the authors whose stories he rejected.

Finally, Robert P. Mills can move up as the editor responsible for "Flowers for Algernon." He stepped into Anthony Boucher's shoes when Tony retired as editor. They weren't easy shoes to wear properly but Bob managed to do it well. Tall and gangling, a keeper of his temper under the most trying of circumstances, Bob doesn't really look the part of science fiction editor. He is widely felt to be "too normal" for this role, and that gives rise to a sense of uneasiness among science fiction authors who have never in their lives suffered from being "too normal." But the uneasiness is unjustified. Under that normal and good-looking exterior, there beats a warm and screwball heart.

I know all these gentlemen personally. They have all, on one occasion or another, told me what a lousy writer I was; and I invariably answered by telling them what lousy editors they were (prudently waiting till they were out of earshot, of course). But every one of them (plus some others who are not represented in this anthology) helped me often and, I am sure, helped every author they could reach.

This help should be acknowledged far more often and far more publicly than it is, and I am glad to have an opportunity here to strike a blow for justice and right-thinking.

*Isaac Asimov*

# APPENDIX

## THE HUGO AWARDS

The notion of a science fiction award arose in early 1953 in Philadelphia. A gentleman by the name of Hal Lynch, having watched the Academy Awards on television, was struck by the idea, which he passed on at once to those fans who were organizing the 11th Convention (Philadelphia, 1953).

After numerous misadventures, the awards were designed and hand-machined by Jack McKnight of Lansdale, Pennsylvania. He produced them deftly, racing against time, in a remarkable demonstration of skillful labor-of-love. The awards were small stainless-steel rocketships, finned at base and center and set on a cylindrical wooden base on which an appropriately inscribed plaque was set.

There was no feeling at the time that such an award ought to be repeated and, in fact, at the 12th Convention (San Francisco, 1954) there were no awards. The 13th Convention (Cleveland, 1955), however, decided to present what was officially termed "The Second Annual Science Fiction Achievement Award," and that was the true beginning of the Hugo as an annual feature.

The manufacture of the Hugos for the 13th Convention was once again an Odyssey of complication and near-despair, for the Conventions are one and all conducted by impecunious fans who must raise money by squeezing blood out of turnips. And while money won't buy happiness, lack of money won't buy Hugos.

A new Hugo was designed by Ben Jason of Cleveland. It differed from the McKnight version in appearance chiefly in that it was larger, lacked the central fins and was set on a cubical base. The crucial difference, however, was that the Jason design could be mass-produced, while the McKnight design could not be.

The annual production of standardized Hugos was now possible. Ben Jason plugged hard for this and, in the main, won his point. Most Conventions since 1955 have used his design, which is now considered standard. Mr. Jason possesses the original mold and has personally supervised the construction for a number of the post-Cleveland Conventions. He has been commissioned to do the work for the 20th Convention (Chicago, 1962) and the 21st Convention (Washington, 1963).

The Jason-designed Hugo is that which decorates the cover-jacket of this book.

A full list of the Hugo winners through 1961 has been prepared by Ed Wood, of Idaho Falls, Idaho, a prominent science fiction fan with an encyclopedic knowledge of the field. This list has been made available to me by Earl Kemp, chairman of the committee that is organizing the 20th Convention, which will be held in the month in which this book is published.

Here is the list:

## 11TH CONVENTION—PHILADELPHIA, 1953

#1 Fan Personality—Forrest J. Ackerman
Interior Illustrator—Virgil Finlay
Cover Artist—Ed Emshwiller; Hannes Bok (tie)
Excellence in Fact Articles—Willy Ley
New Science Fiction Author or Artist—Philip José Farmer
Professional Magazine—*Galaxy* and *Astounding Science Fiction* (tie)
Novel—THE DEMOLISHED MAN by Alfred Bester

## 13TH CONVENTION—CLEVELAND, 1955

Novel—THEY'D RATHER BE RIGHT by Mark Clifton and Frank Riley
*Novelette—"The Darfsteller" by Walter M. Miller, Jr.
*Short Story—"Allamagoosa" by Eric Frank Russell
Professional Magazine—*Astounding Science Fiction*
Illustrator—Frank Kelly Freas
Amateur Publication—*Fantasy Times*

## 14TH CONVENTION—NEW YORK, 1956

Novel—DOUBLE STAR by Robert A. Heinlein
*Novelette—"Exploration Team" by Murray Leinster
*Short Story—"The Star" by Arthur C. Clarke
Feature Writer—Willy Ley
Professional Magazine—*Astounding Science Fiction*
Illustrator—Frank Kelly Freas
Most Promising New Author—Robert Silverberg
Amateur Publication—*Inside & Science Fiction Advertiser*
Critic—Damon Knight

## 15TH CONVENTION—LONDON, 1957

Professional Magazine, American—*Astounding Science Fiction*
Professional Magazine, British—*New Worlds Science Fiction*
Amateur Publication—*Science Fiction Times*

## 16TH CONVENTION—LOS ANGELES, 1958

Novel—THE BIG TIME by Fritz Leiber
*Short Story—"Or All the Seas with Oysters," by Avram Davidson

Professional Magazine—*Magazine of Fantasy and Science Fiction*
Illustrator—Frank Kelly Freas
Motion Picture—*The Incredible Shrinking Man* by Richard Matheson
Most Outstanding Actifan—Walter A. Willis

## 17TH CONVENTION—DETROIT, 1959

Novel—A CASE OF CONSCIENCE by James Blish
*Novelette—"The Big Front Yard" by Clifford D. Simak
*Short Story—"The Hell-Bound Train" by Robert Bloch
Illustrator—Frank Kelly Freas
Professional Magazine—*Magazine of Fantasy and Science Fiction*
Amateur Publication—*FANAC*
Most Promising New Author—Brian W. Aldiss

## 18TH CONVENTION—PITTSBURGH, 1960

Novel—*Starship Trooper,* by Robert A. Heinlein
*Short Fiction—"Flowers for Algernon," by Daniel Keyes
Professional Magazine—*Magazine of Fantasy and Science Fiction*
Amateur Publication—*Cry of the Nameless*
Illustrator—Ed Emshwiller
Dramatic Presentation—*The Twilight Zone,* by Rod Serling
Special Award—Hugo Gernsback as "The Father of Magazine Science
   Fiction"

## 19TH CONVENTION—SEATTLE, 1961

Novel—*A Canticle for Leibowitz* by Walter M. Miller, Jr.
*Short Story—"The Longest Voyage," by Poul Anderson
Professional Magazine—*Analog Science Fact and Fiction*
Amateur Publication—*Who Killed Science Fiction?* by Earl Kemp
Illustrator—Ed Emshwiller
Dramatic Presentation—*The Twilight Zone* by Rod Serling

* Winners presented in this anthology

# *The Hugo Winners*

## VOLUME II

# CONTENTS

To the memory of Hugo Gernsback,
grandfather of us all

# HERE I AM AGAIN

## by Isaac Asimov

Some nine years ago, it had seemed necessary to prepare an anthology of those science fiction novelettes and short stories that had won Hugos —the awards handed out for the best-of-the-year at the World Science Fiction Conventions held each Labor Day weekend in various cities.

Needed as editor of such an anthology was someone who was a person of note, sane and rational, fearless and intrepid, witty and forceful and, above all, devilishly handsome. In addition, he had to be someone who (through some grotesque miscarriage of justice) had never won a Hugo.

Since I (Isaac Asimov) had at that time never won a Hugo and since all the required adjectives were quite notoriously applicable to myself, I was at once chosen as editor by that estimable publishing house, Doubleday & Co., Inc.

The anthology was published in 1962 under the title of *The Hugo Winners* and was an enormous success, partly by the nature of the excellent prize-winning stories it contained and partly by that indefinable cachet I lent it as editor. (Do not bother to volunteer definitions, please!)

Once it was published, though, I faced a dilemma:

(a) The stories in *The Hugo Winners* included only those prize-winning items up to and including the 19th Convention in 1961—but Hugo awards would continue to be made. This meant that sooner or later a second anthology would have to be prepared. Naturally, I wanted to be editor of the second anthology, too, but in order to do that I had to maintain my qualification as the very best science fiction writer in the world never to have won a Hugo. (Or to have won a Hugo, either, but I'm too modest to say that.)

(b) On the other hand, I wanted to win a Hugo.

These two, you see, are mutually exclusive. As a logician would say:

if *a*, then *not-b*; and if *b*, then *not-a*. Either way I would be unhappy.

Since I am sane and rational, I sat down and figured out the chances. On the one hand, everybody was going to read *The Hugo Winners* and, in particular, read the introduction in which I movingly described the injustice inflicted on me in the matter of the Hugos. Clearly, one and all would dissolve in tears. Obviously, every fan club in the United States would decide that as soon as they were in a position to run a World Convention they would see to it that one of my sterling science fiction stories would be awarded the Hugo it so richly and automatically deserved.

On the other hand, since 1958, I had written hardly any science fiction aside from an occasional slight short-short, so there was nothing to give me a Hugo *for*.

A weighing of these two propositions proved clearly that I would have to get a Hugo for nothing. It seemed an odd thing to arrange, but I am far too fine a person to disappoint a fan club. If they wanted to give me a Hugo for nothing, I would take it—or even grab it, if they hesitated.

The year 1962 passed with a convention in Chicago which was erratic in the way of Hugos and did not hand an individual award in the short story division but granted one to Brian Aldiss's "Hothouse" series as a whole—five stories which, taken together, are virtually a novel and therefore cannot be included within the purview of an anthology of shorter pieces. (Besides I don't travel very long distances and everyone knew I wouldn't be in Chicago.)

But then came 1963 and Washington, D.C., was going to run the convention that year, and I can go as far as Washington. In plenty of time, George Scithers, who was handling the details, called me to ask if I would come down and be part of a panel-discussion.

With pretended casualness, I asked, "Don't you want me as master of ceremonies?"

You see, usually when I attend a convention, I am master of ceremonies because of my graceful wit and charming presence, and that means I hand out the Hugos—to other people. Here was George Scithers, going to considerable lengths to make sure I would be there at the convention and yet he was not asking me to be master of ceremonies.

"No," he said, just as casually, "Ted Sturgeon is going to be master of ceremonies."

Ordinarily, I would have kicked and screamed and then gone into a prolonged pout. This time, though, I merely chuckled. "Sure, George," I said, "I'll be there."

You see, my keen analytical mind told me that Sturgeon was going to be master of ceremonies so he could give me a Hugo. I couldn't very well be master of ceremonies myself and give myself a Hugo, could I? I'm far too modest, as anyone can tell.

But then, just about a week before the convention, with my hotel room reserved, my car tuned up, and everything, George called again. "Isaac," he said, "Ted can't make it after all because of family complications. I know this is short notice, but can you be master of ceremonies after all?"

I had to say, yes, but my heart sank. No Hugo after all!

I went to Washington in pensive mood. I greeted George curtly and occupied my seat at the head table during the banquet sullenly, occasionally eying the audience in a markedly morose manner.

Eventually, I had to give up and begin reading off the list of nominees in the various categories and then read the winner in each and then hand out the Hugo.

There was only one thing to do and I did it. I handed out those Hugos savagely, snarling at each winner as he came up to get the object. When Fred Pohl, a friend of my childhood, approached to pick up one on behalf of a winner, I cried out as he came bounding up, "Break a leg, friend of my childhood!" (But he didn't. Nobody would do the least little thing to oblige me.)

I grew more and more eloquent as Hugo after Hugo was awarded and when only one was left, I hit the peak of invective. With the closed envelope still in my hand, I asked the audience to take note of the fact that no Hugo was ever awarded me, and I told them why. I raised a fist high to heaven and said, "It's anti-Semitic prejudice, that's what it is. You're all a bunch of Nazis."

And with that cold, unimpassioned statement, I opened the envelope and it said, "For putting the science in science fiction—Isaac Asimov."

I had really gotten my Hugo for nothing after all. The original plan had indeed been to have Ted Sturgeon hand me a Hugo, as I had thought. He had really had to stay away against his will and George Scithers had said, "Oh, well, let Isaac give it to himself. It'll make it all the funnier and he's the only writer in science fiction who can give himself a Hugo and not be embarrassed."

A lot he cared that I stood there for ten minutes, trying to accept my Hugo with an air of modest surprise, while the audience laughed itself silly. And he still hasn't explained what he meant by saying that I was the only writer in science fiction who could give himself a Hugo and not be embarrassed. I don't get that at all.

Clearly, though, this was a Hugo for nothing, and would not disqualify me from editing further volumes of Hugo winners. At least, I intended to argue the point in this fashion.

But then came 1966 and the 24th Convention in Cleveland. Again I was invited and again I was to be master of ceremonies. This time though, a new and unprecedented category was offered for the Hugos. It was to be that of a "novel series"; that is, an interconnected group of three or more novels.

Naturally, such an award would be the most impressive one ever offered, since a Hugo is coveted more for a long item than for a short one, and this was the longest item possible. Besides it was the only category which asked for a vote on best-of-all-time, rather than merely best-of-the-year.

I won't stretch this out. When the best novel-series award came up, I was shoved to one side and little Harlan Ellison ran up to make the announcement, and the winner (however did you guess?) was Isaac Asimov for "The Foundation Series."

This time I had a Hugo for something, and the biggest single Hugo ever handed out. Recognition at last, but this time—good-bye anthology.

Came 1970.

Lawrence P. Ashmead, Doubleday's most genial and lovable editor, said, "Isaac, it's time we did *The Hugo Winners, Volume Two.*"

I said sadly, "So it is. Whom ought we to get as the editor?"

"Why, you, of course," said Larry.

"Impossible," I said, "I've won two Hugos."

"That may well be so," said Larry, "but we still need a person of note, sane and rational, fearless and intrepid, witty and forceful, and, above all, devilishly handsome, and is there any science fiction writer but yourself who can possibly fill these qualifications?"

You know, that had never occurred to me!

Larry was obviously right, so, with that modest smile that is the hallmark of my personality, I said, "Larry, you're perfectly correct, and I should have seen that for myself."

Here I am again then, and here is *The Hugo Winners, Volume Two.*

*1963*
*21st* CONVENTION
*WASHINGTON*

# Jack Vance

I have a certain system for introducing prize-winning stories, and the core of it is that I never talk about the stories.

Why should I, after all? They are prize-winners and therefore may be accepted as good stories. It may be that you, as a particular reader, will disagree with the consensus—but only you can tell that, and I wouldn't argue you out of your opinion just by telling you loudly that the story is great. Besides, the story is right here and surely you would rather read it than listen to me talk about it.

So what do I do? Easy! I talk about the authors.

The world of the science fiction writer is a tight one and a friendly one. We're in a minority. All writers are, anyway, because we are misunderstood by normal people. Our charming eccentricities are dismissed as evidence of serious neurotic disorders. Our habit of sitting in a chair and carefully working out intricate and thoughtful story lines with our eyes closed is dismissed as a disgusting sign of feckless sloth, just because we snore a little in the process.

Even among writers generally, the science fiction writer stands out as peculiar. Writers may get ideas, but science fiction writers get *crazy* ideas.

But we like one another, and we meet at conventions and sometimes in between conventions; and we talk, and laugh, and eat and drink, and sometimes just huddle together for security against a world that considers us queer because we have that rare and frightening characteristic—sanity.

All right, then. You don't know these queer people and I do—so I'll tell you about them.

At least, I'll tell you about all of them except those few, those very few, whom I've never met and with whom I've never corresponded. The chances of one of those just happening to come up is laughably small, so let's all laugh because here comes that chance.

I have never met Jack Vance, nor have I ever corresponded with him. But don't worry! I'll get another crack at him later in the anthology and I will think of something!

# THE DRAGON MASTERS

The apartments of Joaz Banbeck, carved deep from the heart of a lime-stone crag, consisted of five principal chambers, on five different levels. At the top were the reliquarium and a formal council chamber: the first a room of somber magnificence housing the various archives, tro-phies and mementos of the Banbecks; the second a long narrow hall, with dark wainscoting chest-high and a white plaster vault above, ex-tending the entire width of the crag, so that balconies overlooked Ban-beck Vale at one end and Kergan's Way at the other.

Below were Joaz Banbeck's private quarters: a parlor and bed-chamber, then next his study and finally, at the bottom, a work-room where Joaz permitted none but himself.

Entry to the apartments was through the study, a large L-shaped room with an elaborate groined ceiling, from which depended four garnet-encrusted chandeliers. These were now dark. Into the room came only a watery gray light from four honed-glass plates on which, in the manner of a *camera obscura*, were focused views across Banbeck Vale. The walls were paneled with lignified reed. A rug patterned in angles, squares and circles of maroon, brown and black covered the floor.

In the middle of the study stood a naked man.

His only covering was the long, fine, brown hair which flowed down his back, the golden torc which clasped his neck. His features were sharp and angular, his body thin. He appeared to be listening, or perhaps meditating. Occasionally he glanced at a yellow marble globe on a nearby shelf, whereupon his lips would move, as if he were committing to memory some phrase or sequence of ideas.

At the far end of the study a heavy door eased open.

A flower-faced young woman peered through, her expression mischievous, arch. At the sight of the naked man, she clapped her hands to her mouth, stifling a gasp. The naked man turned—but the heavy door had already swung shut.

For a moment he stood deep in frowning reflection, then slowly went to the wall on the inside leg of the L. He swung out a section of the bookcase and passed through the opening. Behind him the bookcase thudded shut. Descending a spiral staircase he came out into a chamber rough-hewn from the rock: Joaz Banbeck's private work-room. A bench supported tools, metal shapes and fragments, a bank of electro-motive cells, oddments of circuitry: the current objects of Joaz Banbeck's curiosity.

The naked man glanced at the bench. He picked up one of the devices and inspected it with something like condescension, though his gaze was as clear and wondering as that of a child.

Muffled voices from the study penetrated to the work room. The naked man raised his head to listen, then stooped under the bench. He lifted a block of stone, slipped through the gap into a dark void. Replacing the stone, he took up a luminous wand, and set off down a narrow tunnel, which presently dipped to join a natural cavern. At irregular intervals luminous tubes exuded a wan light, barely enough to pierce the murk.

The naked man jogged forward swiftly, the silken hair flowing like a nimbus behind him.

Back in the study the minstrel-maiden Phade and an elderly seneschal were at odds. "Indeed I saw him!" Phade insisted. "With these two eyes of mine, one of the sacerdotes, standing thus and so, as I have described." She tugged angrily at his elbow. "Do you think me bereft of my wits, or hysterical?"

Rife the seneschal shrugged, committing himself neither one way nor the other. "I do not see him now." He climbed the staircase, peered into the sleeping parlor. "Empty. The doors above are bolted." He peered owlishly at Phade. "And I sat at my post in the entry."

"You sat sleeping. Even when I came past you snored!"

"You are mistaken; I did but cough."

"With your eyes closed, your head lolling back?"

Rife shrugged once more. "Asleep or awake, it is all the same. Admitting that the creature gained access, how did he leave? I was wakeful after you summoned me, as you must agree."

"Then remain on guard, while I find Joaz Banbeck." Phade ran down the passage which presently joined Bird Walk, so called for the series of fabulous birds of lapis, gold, cinnabar, malachite and marcasite inlaid into the marble. Through an arcade of green and gray jade in spiral columns she passed out into Kergan's Way, a natural defile which formed the main thoroughfare of Banbeck Village. Reaching the portal, she summoned a pair of lads from the fields. "Run to the brooder, find Joaz Banbeck! Hasten, bring him here; I must speak with him."

The boys ran off toward a low cylinder of black brick a mile to the north.

Phade waited. With the sun Skene at its nooning, the air was warm. The fields of vetch, bellegarde and spharganum gave off a pleasant odor. Phade went to lean against a fence. Now she began to wonder about the urgency of her news, even its basic reality. "No!" she told herself fiercely. "I saw! I saw!"

At either side tall white cliffs rose to Banbeck Verge, with mountains and crags beyond, and, spanning all, the dark sky flecked with feathers of cirrus. Skene glittered dazzling bright, a minuscule flake of brilliance.

Phade sighed, half-convinced of her own mistake. Once more, less vehemently, she reassured herself. Never before had she seen a sacerdote; why should she imagine one now?

The boys, reaching the brooder, had disappeared into the dust of the exercise pens. Scales gleamed and winked; grooms, dragon-masters, armorers in black leather moved about their work.

After a moment Joaz Banbeck came into view.

He mounted a tall thin-legged Spider, urged it to the full extent of its head-jerking lope, pounded down the track toward Banbeck Village. Phade's uncertainty grew. Might Joaz become exasperated, would he dismiss her news with an unbelieving stare? Uneasily she watched his approach. Coming to Banbeck Vale only a month before, she still felt unsure of her status. Her preceptors had trained her diligently in the barren little valley to the south where she had been born, but the disparity between teaching and practical reality at times bewildered her. She had learned that all men obeyed a small and identical group of behaviors. Joaz Banbeck, however, observed no such limits, and Phade found him completely unpredictable. She knew him to be a relatively young man, though his appearance provided no guide to his age. He had a pale austere face in which gray eyes shone like crystals, a long thin mouth which suggested flexibility, yet never curved far from a straight line. He moved languidly; his voice carried no vehemence; he made no pretense of skill with either saber or pistol; he seemed deliberately to shun any gesture which might win the admiration or affection of his subjects. Yet he had both.

Phade originally had thought him cold, but presently changed her mind. He was, so she decided, a man bored and lonely, with a quiet humor which at times seemed rather grim. But he treated her without discourtesy, and Phade, testing him with all her hundred and one coquetries, not infrequently thought to detect a spark of response.

Joaz Banbeck dismounted from the Spider, ordered it back to its quarters. Phade came diffidently forward, and Joaz turned her a quizzical look. "What requires so urgent a summons? Have you remembered the nineteenth location?"

Phade flushed in confusion. Artlessly she had described the painstaking rigors of her training; Joaz now referred to an item in one of the classifications which had slipped her mind.

Phade spoke rapidly, excited once more. "I opened the door into your study, softly, gently. And what did I see? A sacerdote, naked in his hair! He did not hear me. I shut the door, I ran to fetch Rife. When we returned—the chamber was empty!"

Joaz's eyebrows contracted a trifle; he looked up the valley. "Odd." After a moment he asked, "You are sure that he saw nothing of you?"

"No. I think not. Yet, when I returned with stupid old Rife he had disappeared! Is it true that they know magic?"

"As to that, I cannot say," replied Joaz.

They returned up Kergan's Way, traversed tunnels and rock-walled corridors, finally came to the entry chamber.

Rife once more dozed at his desk. Joaz signaled Phade back and, going quietly forward, thrust aside the door to his study. He glanced here and there, nostrils twitching.

The room was empty.

He climbed the stairs, investigated the sleeping-parlor, returned to the study. Unless magic were indeed involved, the sacerdote had provided himself a secret entrance. With this thought in mind, he swung back the bookcase door, descended to the workshop and again tested the air for the sour-sweet odor of the sacerdotes. A trace? Possibly.

Joaz examined the room inch by inch, peering from every angle. At last, along the wall below the bench, he discovered a barely perceptible crack, marking out an oblong.

Joaz nodded with dour satisfaction. He rose to his feet and returned to his study. He considered his shelves: what was here to interest a sacerdote? Books, folios, pamphlets? Had they even mastered the art of reading? When next I meet a sacerdote I must inquire, thought Joaz vaguely; at least he will tell me the truth. On second thought, he knew the question to be ludicrous; the sacerdotes, for all their nakedness, were by no means barbarians, and in fact had provided him his four vision-panes—a technical engineering feat of no small skill.

He inspected the yellowed marble globe which he considered his most valued possession: a representation of mythical Eden. Apparently it had not been disturbed. Another shelf displayed models of the Banbeck dragons: the rust-red Termagant; the Long-horned Murderer and its cousin the Striding Murderer; the Blue Horror; the Fiend, low to the ground, immensely strong, tail tipped with a steel barbell; the ponderous Jugger, skullcap polished and white as an egg. A little apart stood the progenitor of the entire group: a pearl-pallid creature upright on two legs, with two versatile central members, a pair of multi-articulated brachs at the neck.

Beautifully detailed though these models might be, why should they pique the curiosity of a sacerdote? No reason whatever, when most of the originals could be studied daily without hindrance.

What of the workshop, then? Joaz rubbed his long pale chin. He had no illusions about the value of his work. It was idle tinkering and no more. Joaz put aside conjecture. Most likely the sacerdote had come upon no specific mission, the visit perhaps being part of a continued inspection. But why?

A pounding at the door: old Rife's irreverent fist. Joaz opened to him.

"Joaz Banbeck, a notice from Ervis Carcolo of Happy Valley. He wishes to confer with you, and at this moment awaits your response on Banbeck Verge."

"Very well," said Joaz. "I will confer with Ervis Carcolo."

"Here? Or on Banbeck Verge?"

"On the Verge, in half an hour."

## II

Ten miles from Banbeck Vale, across a wind-scoured wilderness of ridges, crags, spines of stone, amazing crevasses, barren fells and fields of tumbled boulders, lay Happy Valley. As wide as Banbeck Vale but only half as long and half as deep, its bed of wind-deposited soil was only half as thick and correspondingly less productive.

The Chief Councillor of Happy Valley was Ervis Carcolo, a thick-bodied short legged man with a vehement face, a heavy mouth, a disposition by turns jocose and wrathful. Unlike Joaz Banbeck, Carcolo enjoyed nothing more than his visits to the dragon barracks, where he treated dragon-masters, grooms and dragons alike to a spate of bawled invective.

Ervis Carcolo was an energetic man, intent upon restoring Happy Valley to the ascendancy it had enjoyed some twelve generations before. During those harsh times, before the advent of the dragons, men fought their own battles. The men of Happy Valley had been notably daring, deft and ruthless. Banbeck Vale, the Great Northern Rift, Clewhaven, Sadro Valley, Phosphor Gulch: all acknowledged the authority of the Carcolos.

Then down from space came a ship of the Basics, or grephs, as they were known at that time. The ship killed or took prisoner the entire population of Clewhaven. It attempted as much in the Great Northern Rift, but only partially succeeded; then bombarded the remaining settlements with explosive pellets.

When the survivors crept back to their devastated valleys, the dominance of Happy Valley was a fiction. A generation later, during the Age of Wet Iron, even the fiction collapsed. In a climactic battle Goss Carcolo was captured by Kergan Banbeck and forced to emasculate himself with his own knife.

Five years of peace elapsed, and then the Basics returned. After depopulating Sadro Valley, the great black ship landed in Banbeck Vale, but the inhabitants had taken warning and had fled into the mountains. Toward nightfall twenty-three of the Basics sallied forth behind their precisely trained warriors: several platoons of Heavy Troops, a squad of Weaponeers—these hardly distinguishable from the men of Aerlith—and a squad of Trackers: these emphatically different. The sunset storm broke over the Vale, rendering the flyers from the ship useless, which allowed Kergan Banbeck to perform the amazing feat which made his name a legend on Aerlith. Rather than joining the terrified flight of his people to the High Jambles, he assembled sixty warriors and shamed them to courage with jeers and taunts.

It was a suicidal venture—fitting the circumstances.

Leaping from ambush they hacked to pieces one platoon of the Heavy Troops, routed the others, and captured the twenty-three Basics almost before they realized that anything was amiss. The Weaponeers stood back, frantic with frustration, unable to use their weapons for fear of destroying their masters. The Heavy Troopers blundered forward to attack, halting only when Kergan Banbeck performed an unmistakable pantomime to make it clear that the Basics would be the first to die.

Confused, the Heavy Troopers drew back. Kergan Banbeck, his men and the twenty-three captives escaped into the darkness.

The long Aerlith night passed. The dawn storm swept out of the east, thundered overhead, retreated majestically into the west; Skene rose like a blazing atom.

Three men emerged from a Basic ship: a Weaponeer and a pair of Trackers. They climbed the cliffs to Banbeck Verge, while above flitted a small Basic flyer, no more than a buoyant platform, diving and veering in the wind like a poorly balanced kite. The three men trudged south toward the High Jambles, a region of chaotic shadows and lights, splintered rock and fallen crags, boulders heaped on boulders. It was the traditional refuge of hunted men.

Halting in front of the Jambles, the Weaponeer called out for Kergan Banbeck, asking him to parley.

Kergan Banbeck came forth. There ensued the strangest colloquy in the history of Aerlith. The Weaponeer spoke the language of men with difficulty, his lips, tongue and glottal passages more adapted to the language of the Basics.

"You are restraining twenty-three of our Revered. It is necessary that you usher them forth, in all humility." He spoke soberly, with an air of gentle melancholy, neither asserting, commanding nor urging. As his linguistic habits had been shaped to Basic patterns, so had his mental processes.

Kergan Banbeck, a tall spare man with varnished black eyebrows, black hair shaped and varnished into a crest of five tall spikes, gave a bark of humorless laughter. "What of the Aerlith folk killed, what of the folk seized aboard your ship?"

The Weaponeer bent forward earnestly, himself an impressive man with a noble aquiline head. He was hairless except for small rolls of wispy yellow fleece. His skin shone as if burnished. His ears, where he differed most noticeably from the unadapted men of Aerlith, were small, fragile flaps. He wore a simple garment of dark blue and white, carried no weapons save a small multi-purpose ejector. With complete poise and quiet reasonableness he responded to Kergan Banbeck's question: "The Aerlith folk who have been killed are dead. Those aboard the ship will be merged into the under-stratum, where the infusion of fresh blood is of value."

Kergan Banbeck inspected the Weaponeer with contemptuous deliberation. In some respects, thought Kergan Banbeck, this modified and carefully inbred man resembled the sacerdotes of his own planet, notably in the clear fair skin, the strongly modeled features, the long legs and arms.

Perhaps telepathy was at work, or perhaps a trace of the characteristic sour-sweet odor had been carried to him: turning his head he noticed a sacerdote standing among the rocks not fifty feet away—a man naked except for his golden torc and long brown hair blowing behind him like a pennant. By the ancient etiquette, Kergan Banbeck looked through him, pretended that he had no existence. The Weaponeer after a swift glance did likewise.

"I demand that you release the folk of Aerlith from your ship," said Kergan Banbeck in a flat voice.

The Weaponeer smilingly shook his head, bent his best efforts to the task of making himself intelligible. "These persons are not under discussion. Their"—he paused, seeking words—"their destiny is . . . parceled, quantum-type, ordained. Established. Nothing can be said more."

Kergan Banbeck's smile became a cynical grimace. He stood aloof and silent while the Weaponeer croaked on. The sacerdote came slowly forward, a few steps at a time. "You will understand," said the Weaponeer, "that a pattern for events exists. It is the function of such as myself to shape events so that they will fit the pattern." He bent, with a graceful sweep of arm, and seized a small jagged pebble. "Just as I can grind this bit of rock to fit a round aperture."

Kergan Banbeck reached forward, took the pebble, tossed it high over the tumbled boulders. "That bit of rock you shall never shape to fit a round hole."

The Weaponeer shook his head in mild deprecation. "There is always more rock."

"And there are always more holes," declared Kergan Banbeck.

"To business then," said the Weaponeer. "I propose to shape this situation to its correct arrangement."

"What do you offer in exchange for the twenty-three grephs?"

The Weaponeer gave his shoulder an uneasy shake. The ideas of this man were as wild, barbaric and arbitrary as the varnished spikes of his hair-dress. "If you desire I will give you instruction and advice, so that—"

Kergan Banbeck made a sudden sharp gesture. "I make three conditions." The sacerdote now stood only ten feet away, face blind, gaze vague. "First," said Kergan Banbeck, "a guarantee against future attacks upon the men of Aerlith. Five grephs must always remain in our custody as hostages. Second—further to secure the perpetual validity of the guarantee—you must deliver me a space-ship, equipped, energized and armed. And you must instruct me in its use."

The Weaponeer threw back his head and made a series of bleating sounds through his nose.

"Third," continued Kergan Banbeck, "you must release all the men and women presently aboard your ship."

The Weaponeer blinked, spoke rapid hoarse words of amazement to the Trackers. They stirred, uneasy and impatient, watching Kergan Banbeck sidelong as if he were not only savage, but mad. Overhead hovered the flyer; the Weaponeer looked up and seemed to derive encouragement from the sight. Turning back to Kergan Banbeck with a firm fresh attitude, he spoke as if the previous interchange had never occurred. "I have come to instruct you that the twenty-three Revered must be instantly released."

Kergan Banbeck repeated his own demands. "You must furnish me a space-ship, you must raid no more, you must release the captives. Do you agree, yes or no?"

The Weaponeer seemed confused. "This is a peculiar situation—indefinite, unquantizable."

"Can you not understand me?" barked Kergan Banbeck in exasperation. He glanced at the sacerdote, an act of questionable decorum, then performed in manner completely unconventional: "Sacerdote, how can I deal with this blockhead? He does not seem to hear me."

The sacerdote moved a step nearer, his face as bland and blank as before. Living by a doctrine which proscribed active or intentional interference in the affairs of other men, he could make to any question only a specific and limited answer. "He hears you, but there is no meeting of ideas between you. His thought structure is derived from that of his masters. It is incommensurable with yours. As to how you must deal with him, I cannot say."

Kergan Banbeck looked back to the Weaponeer. "Have you heard what I asked of you? Did you understand my conditions for the release of the grephs?"

"I heard you distinctly," replied the Weaponeer. "Your words have no meaning, they are absurdities, paradoxes. Listen to me carefully. It is ordained, complete, a quantum of destiny, that you deliver to us the Revered. It is irregular, it is not ordainment that you should have a ship, or that your other demands be met."

Kergan Banbeck's face became red. He half-turned toward his men but, restraining his anger, spoke slowly and with careful clarity. "I have something you want. You have something I want. Let us trade."

For twenty seconds the two men stared eye to eye. Then the Weaponeer drew a deep breath. "I will explain in your words, so that you will comprehend. Certainties—no, not certainties: definites . . . Definites exist. These are units of certainty, quanta of necessity and order. Existence is the steady succession of these units, one after the other. The activity of the universe can be expressed by reference to these units. Irregularity, absurdity—these are like—half of a man, with half of a brain, half of a heart, half of all his vital organs. Neither are allowed to exist. That you hold twenty-three Revered as captives is such an absurdity: an outrage to the rational flow of the universe."

Kergan Banbeck threw up his hands, turned once more to the sacerdote. "How can I halt his nonsense? How can I make him see reason?"

The sacerdote reflected. "He speaks not nonsense, but rather a language you fail to understand. You can make him understand your language by erasing all knowledge and training from his mind, and replacing it with patterns of your own."

Kergan Banbeck fought back an unsettling sense of frustration and unreality. In order to elicit exact answers from a sacerdote, an exact question was required; indeed it was remarkable that this sacerdote stayed to be questioned. Thinking carefully, he asked, "How do you suggest that I deal with this man?"

"Release the twenty-three grephs." The sacerdote touched the twin knobs at the front of his golden torc: a ritual gesture indicating that, no matter how reluctantly, he had performed an act which conceivably might alter the course of the future. Again he tapped his torc and intoned, "Release the grephs; he will then depart."

Kergan Banbeck cried out in unrestrained anger. "Who then do you serve? Man or greph? Let us have the truth! Speak!"

"By my faith, by my creed, by the truth of my *tand,* I serve no one but myself." The sacerdote turned his face toward the great crag of Mount Gethron and moved slowly off. The wind blew his long fine hair to the side.

Kergan Banbeck watched him go, then with cold decisiveness turned back to the Weaponeer. "Your discussion of certainties and absurdities is interesting. I feel that you have confused the two. Here is certainty from my viewpoint: I will not release the twenty-three grephs unless you meet my terms. If you attack us further, I will cut them in half, to illustrate and realize your figure of speech, and perhaps convince you that absurdities are possible. I say no more."

The Weaponeer shook his head slowly, pityingly. "Listen, I will explain. Certain conditions are unthinkable. They are unquantized, un-destined—"

"Go," thundered Kergan Banbeck. "Otherwise you will join your twenty-three revered grephs, and I will teach you how real the unthinkable can become!"

The Weaponeer and the two Trackers, croaking and muttering, turned, retreated from the Jambles to Banbeck Verge, descended into the valley. Over them the flyer fluttered like a falling leaf.

Watching from their retreat among the crags, the men of Banbeck Vale presently witnessed a remarkable scene. Half an hour after the Weaponeer had returned to the ship, he came leaping forth once again: dancing, cavorting. Others followed him—Weaponeers, Trackers, Heavy Troopers and eight more grephs—all jerking, jumping, running back and forth in distracted steps. The ports of the ship flashed lights of various colors, and there came a slow rising sound of tortured machinery.

"They have gone mad!" muttered Kergan Banbeck. He hesitated an instant, then gave an order. "Assemble every man! We attack while they are helpless!"

Down from the High Jambles rushed the men of Banbeck Vale. As they descended the cliffs, a few of the captured men and women from Sadro Valley came timidly forth from the ship, and meeting no restraint fled to freedom across Banbeck Vale. Others followed—and now the Banbeck warriors reached the valley floor.

Besides the ship the insanity had quieted. The out-worlders huddled quietly beside the hull. There came a sudden mind-shattering explosion: a blankness of yellow and white fire. The ship disintegrated. A great crater marred the valley floor; fragments of metal began to fall among the attacking Banbeck Warriors.

Kergan Banbeck stared at the scene of destruction.

Slowly, his shoulders sagging, he summoned his people and led them back to their ruined valley. At the rear, marching single-file, tied together with ropes, came the twenty-three grephs, dull eyed, pliant, already remote from their previous existence.

The texture of Destiny was inevitable. The present circumstances could not apply to twenty-three of the Revered. The mechanism must therefore adjust to insure the halcyon progression of events. The twenty-three, hence, were something other than the Revered: a different order of creature entirely.

If this were true, what were they? Asking each other the question in sad, croaking undertones, they marched down the cliff into Banbeck Vale.

III

Across the long Aerlith years the fortunes of Happy Valley and Banbeck Vale fluctuated with the capabilities of the opposing Carcolos and

Banbecks. Golden Banbeck, Joaz's grandfather, was forced to release Happy Valley from clientship when Uttern Carcolo, an accomplished dragon-breeder, produced the first Fiends. Golden Banbeck, in his turn, developed the Juggers, but allowed an uneasy truce to continue.

Further years passed. Ilden Banbeck, the son of Golden, a frail ineffectual man, was killed in a fall from a mutinous Spider. With Joaz yet an ailing child, Grode Carcolo decided to try his chances against Banbeck Vale. He failed to reckon with old Handel Banbeck, granduncle to Joaz and Chief Dragon-master.

The Happy Valley forces were routed on Starbreak Fell. Grode Carcolo was killed and young Ervis gored by a Murderer. For various reasons, including Handel's age and Joaz's youth, the Banbeck army failed to press to a decisive advantage. Ervis Carcolo, though exhausted by loss of blood and pain, withdrew in some degree of order, and for further years a suspicious truce held between the neighboring valleys.

Joaz matured into a saturnine young man who, if he excited no enthusiastic affection from his people, at least aroused no violent dislike. He and Ervis Carcolo were united in a mutual contempt. At the mention of Joaz's study, with its books, scrolls, models and plans, its complicated viewing-system across Banbeck Vale (the optics furnished, it was rumored, by the sacerdotes), Carcolo would throw up his hands in disgust. "Learning? Pah! What avails all this rolling in bygone vomit? Where does it lead? He should have been born a sacerdote. He is the same sort of sour-mouthed cloud-minded weakling!"

An itinerant named Dae Alvonso, who combined the trades of minstrel, child-buyer, psychiatrist and chiropractor, reported Carcolo's obloquies to Joaz, who shrugged. "Ervis Carcolo should breed himself to one of his own Juggers," said Joaz. "He would thereby produce an impregnable creature with the Jugger's armor and his own unflinching stupidity."

The remark in due course returned to Ervis Carcolo, and by coincidence touched him in a particularly sore spot. Secretly he had been attempting an innovation at his brooders: a dragon almost as massive as the Jugger, with the savage intelligence and agility of the Blue Horror. But Ervis Carcolo worked with an intuitive and over-optimistic approach, ignoring the advice of Bast Givven, his Chief Dragon-master.

The eggs hatched; a dozen spratlings survived. Ervis Carcolo nurtured them with alternate doses of tenderness and objurgation. Eventually the dragons matured.

Carcolo's hoped-for combination of fury and impregnability was realized in four sluggish, irritable creatures, with bloated torsos, spindly legs, insatiable appetites. ("As if one can breed a dragon by commanding it: 'Exist!'" sneered Bast Givven to his helpers, and advised them: "Be wary of the beasts; they are competent only at luring you within reach of their brachs.")

The time, effort, facilities and provender wasted upon the useless hybrid had weakened Carcolo's army. Of the fecund Termagants he had no lack. There was a sufficiency of Long-horned Murderers and Striding Murderers; but the heavier and more specialized types, especially Juggers, were far from adequate to his plans.

The memory of Happy Valley's ancient glory haunted his dreams. First he would subdue Banbeck Vale; and often he planned the ceremony whereby he would reduce Joaz Banbeck to the office of apprentice barracks-boy.

Ervis Carcolo's ambitions were complicated by a set of basic difficulties. Happy Valley's population had doubled but, rather than extending the city by breaching new pinnacles or driving tunnels, Carcolo constructed three new dragon brooders, a dozen barracks and an enormous training compound. The folk of the valley could choose either to cram the fetid existing tunnels or build ramshackle dwellings along the base of the cliff. Brooders, barracks, training compound and huts encroached on Happy Valley's already inadequate fields. Water was diverted from the pond to maintain the brooders. Enormous quantities of produce went to feed dragons. The folk of Happy Valley, under-nourished, sickly, miserable, shared none of Carcolo's aspirations, and their lack of enthusiasm infuriated him.

In any event, when the itinerant Dae Alvonso repeated Joaz Banbeck's recommendation that Ervis Carcolo breed himself to a Jugger, Carcolo seethed with choler. "Bah! What does Joaz Banbeck know about dragon-breeding? I doubt if he understands his own dragon-talk." He referred to the means by which orders and instructions were transmitted to the dragons: a secret jargon distinctive to every army. To learn an opponent's dragon-talk was the prime goal of every Dragon-master, for he thereby gained a degree of control over his enemies' forces. "I am a practical man, worth two of him," Carcolo went on. "Can he design, nurture, rear and teach dragons? Can he impose discipline, teach ferocity? No. He leaves all this to his Dragon-masters, while he lolls on a couch eating sweetmeats, campaigning only against the patience of his minstrel-maidens. They say that by astrological divination he predicts the return of the Basics, that he walks with his neck cocked, watching the sky. Is such a man deserving of power and a prosperous life? I say no! Is Ervis Carcolo of Happy Valley such a man? I say yes, and this I will demonstrate!"

Dae Alvonso judiciously held up his hand. "Not so fast. He is more alert than you think. His dragons are in prime condition; he visits them often. And as for the Basics—"

"Do not speak to me of Basics," stormed Carcolo. "I am no child to be frightened by bugbears!"

Again Dae Alvonso held up his hand. "Listen. I am serious, and you can profit by my news. Joaz Banbeck took me into his private study—"

"The famous study, indeed!"

"From a cabinet he brought out a ball of crystal mounted on a black box."

"Aha!" jeered Carcolo. "A crystal ball!"

Dae Alvonso went on placidly, ignoring the interruption. "I examined this globe, and indeed it seemed to hold all of space. Within it floated stars and planets, all the bodies of the cluster. 'Look well,' said Joaz Banbeck, 'you will never see the like of this anywhere. It was built by the olden men and brought to Aerlith when our people first arrived.'

" 'Indeed,' I said. 'And what is this object?'

" 'It is a celestial armamentarium,' said Joaz. 'It depicts all the nearby stars, and their positions at any time I choose to specify. Now'—here he pointed—'see this white dot? This is our sun. See this red star? In the old almanacs it is named Coralyne. It swings near us at irregular intervals, for such is the flow of stars in this cluster. These intervals have always coincided with the attacks of the Basics.' Here I expressed astonishment; Joaz assured me regarding the matter. 'The history of men on Aerlith records six attacks by the Basics, or grephs as they were originally known. Apparently as Coralyne swings through space the Basics scour nearby worlds for hidden dens of humanity. The last of these was long ago during the time of Kergan Banbeck, with the results you know about. At that time Coralyne passed close in the heavens. For the first time since then, Coralyne is once more close at hand.' This," Alvonso told Carcolo, "is what Joaz Banbeck told me, and this is what I saw."

Carcolo was impressed in spite of himself. "Do you mean to tell me," demanded Carcolo, "that within this globe swim all the stars of space?"

"As to that, I cannot vouch," replied Dae Alvonso. "The globe is set in a black box, and I suspect that an inner mechanism projects images or perhaps luminous spots which simulate the stars. Either way it is a marvelous device, one which I would be proud to own. I offered Joaz several precious objects in exchange. But he would have none of them."

Carcolo curled his lip in disgust. "You and your stolen children. Have you no shame?"

"No more than my customers," said Dae Alvonso stoutly. "As I recall, I have dealt profitably with you on several occasions."

Ervis Carcolo turned away, pretended to watch a pair of Termagants exercising with wooden scimitars. The two men stood by a stone fence, behind which scores of dragons practiced evolutions, dueled with spears and swords, strengthened their muscles. Scales flashed. Dust rose up under splayed stamping feet. The acrid odor of dragon-sweat permeated the air.

Carcolo muttered. "He is crafty, that Joaz. He knew you would report to me in detail."

Dae Alvonso nodded. "Precisely. His words were—but perhaps I should be discreet." He glanced slyly toward Carcolo from under shaggy white eyebrows.

"Speak," said Ervis Carcolo gruffly.

"Very well. Mind you, I quote Joaz Banbeck. 'Tell blundering old Carcolo that he is in great danger. If the Basics return to Aerlith, as well they may, Happy Valley is absolutely vulnerable and will be ruined. Where can his people hide? They will be herded into the black ship and transported to a cold new planet. If Carcolo is not completely heartless he will drive new tunnels, prepare hidden avenues. Otherwise—'"

"Otherwise what?" demanded Carcolo.

"'Otherwise there will be no more Happy Valley, and no more Ervis Carcolo.'"

"Bah," said Carcolo in a subdued voice. "The young jackanapes barks in shrill tones."

"Perhaps he extends an honest warning. His further words—but I fear to offend Your Dignity."

"Continue! Speak!"

"These are his words—but no. I dare not repeat them. Essentially he considers your efforts to create an army ludicrous. He contrasts your intelligence unfavorably to his own. He predicts—"

"Enough!" roared Ervis Carcolo, waving his fists. "He is a subtle adversary, but why do you lend yourself to his tricks?"

Dae Alvonso shook his frosty old head. "I merely repeat, with reluctance, that which you demand to hear. Now then, since you have wrung me dry, do me some profit. Will you buy drugs, elixirs, wambles or potions? I have here a salve of eternal youth which I stole from the Demie Sacerdote's personal coffer. In my train are both boy and girl children, obsequious and handsome, at a fair price. I will listen to your woes, cure your lisp, guarantee a placidity of disposition. Or perhaps you would buy dragon eggs?"

"I need none of those," grunted Carcolo. "Especially dragon's eggs which hatch to lizards. As for children, Happy Valley seethes with them. Bring me a dozen sound Juggers and you may depart with a hundred children of your choice."

Dae Alvonso shook his head sadly and lurched away. Carcolo slumped against the fence, staring across the dragon pens.

The sun hung low over the crags of Mount Despoire. Evening was close at hand.

This was the most pleasant time of the Aerlith day, when the winds ceased, leaving a vast velvet quiet. Skene's blaze softened to a smoky yellow, with a bronze aureole. The clouds of the approaching evening storm gathered, rose, fell, shifted, swirled; glowing and changing in every tone of gold, orange-brown, gold-brown and dusty violet.

Skene sank; the golds and oranges became oak-brown and purple. Lightning threaded the clouds, and the rain fell in a black curtain. In the barracks men moved with vigilance, for now the dragons became unpredictable, by turns watchful, torpid, quarrelsome. With the passing of the rain, evening became night, and a cool quiet breeze drifted through the valleys. The dark sky began to burn and dazzle with the stars of the cluster. One of the most effulgent twinkled red, green, white, red, green.

Ervis Carcolo studied this star thoughtfully. One idea led to another, and presently to a course of action which seemed to dissolve the entire tangle of uncertainties and dissatisfactions which marred his life.

Carcolo twisted his mouth into a sour grimace. He must make overtures to that popinjay Joaz Banbeck. But, if this were unavoidable so be it!

Hence, the following morning, shortly after Phade the minstrel-maiden discovered the sacerdote in Joaz's study, a messenger appeared in the Vale, inviting Joaz Banbeck up to Banbeck Verge for a conference with Ervis Carcolo.

IV

Ervis Carcolo waited on Banbeck Verge with Chief Dragon-master Bast Givven and a pair of young fuglemen. Behind, in a row, stood their mounts: four glistening Spiders, brachs folded, legs splayed at exactly identical angles.

These were Carcolo's newest breed. He was immoderately proud of them. The barbs surrounding the horny visages were clasped with cinnabar cabochons; a round target enameled black and studded with a central spike covered each chest. The men wore the traditional black leather breeches, with short maroon cloaks and black leather helmets, with long flaps slanting back across the ears and down to the shoulders.

The four men waited, patient or restless as their natures dictated, surveying the well-tended length of Banbeck Vale. To the south stretched fields of various food-stuffs: vetch, bellegarde, moss-cake, a loquat grove. Directly opposite, near the mouth of Clybourne Crevasse, the shape of the crater created by the explosion of the Basic ship could still be seen. North lay more fields, then the dragon compounds, consisting of black-brick barracks, a brooder, an exercise field. Beyond lay Banbeck Jambles—an area of wasteland, where ages previously a section of the cliff had fallen, creating a wilderness of tumbled rock, similar to the High Jambles under Mount Gethron, but smaller in compass.

One of the young fuglemen rather tactlessly commented upon the evident prosperity of Banbeck Vale. Ervis Carcolo listened glumly a moment or two, then turned a haughty stare toward the offender.

"Notice the dam," said the fugleman. "We waste half our water in seepage."

"True," said the other. "The rock facing is a good idea. I wonder why we don't do something similar."

Carcolo started to speak, but thought better of it. With a growling sound in his throat, he turned away. Bast Givven made a sign; the fuglemen hastily fell silent.

A few moments later Givven announced: "Joaz Banbeck has set forth."

Carcolo peered down toward Kergan's Way. "Where is his company? Does he choose to ride alone?"

"So it seems."

A few minutes later Joaz Banbeck appeared on Banbeck Verge riding a Spider caparisoned in gray and red velvet. Joaz wore a loose lounge cloak of soft brown cloth over a gray shirt and gray trousers, with a long-billed hat of blue velvet. He held up his hand in casual greeting.

Brusquely Ervis Carcolo returned the salute, and with a jerk of his head sent Givven and the fuglemen off out of ear-shot.

Carcolo said gruffly, "You sent me a message by old Alvonso."

Joaz nodded. "I trust he rendered my remarks accurately?"

Carcolo grinned wolfishly. "At times he felt obliged to paraphrase."

"Tactful old Dae Alvonso."

"I am given to understand," said Carcolo, "that you consider me rash, ineffectual, callous to the best interests of Happy Valley. Alvonso admitted that you used the word 'blunderer' in reference to me."

Joaz smiled politely. "Sentiments of this sort are best transmitted through intermediaries."

Carcolo made a great show of dignified forbearance. "Apparently you feel that another Basic attack is imminent."

"Just so," agreed Joaz, "if my theory, which puts their home by the star Coralyne, is correct. In which case, as I pointed out to Alvonso, Happy Valley is seriously vulnerable."

"And why not Banbeck Vale as well?" barked Carcolo.

Joaz stared at him in surprise. "Is it not obvious? I have taken precautions. My people are housed in tunnels, rather than huts. We have several escape routes, should this prove necessary, both to the High Jambles and to Banbeck Jambles."

"Very interesting." Carcolo made an effort to soften his voice. "If your theory is accurate—and I pass no immediate judgment—then perhaps I would be wise to take similar measures. But I think in different terms. I prefer attack to passive defense."

"Admirable," said Joaz Banbeck. "Important deeds are done by men such as you."

Carcolo became a trifle pink in the face. "This is neither here nor there," he said. "I have come to propose a joint project. It is entirely novel, but carefully thought out. I have considered various aspects of this matter for several years."

"I attend you with great interest," said Joaz.

Carcolo blew out his cheeks. "You know the legends as well as I, perhaps better. Our people came to Aerlith as exiles during the War of the Ten Stars. The Nightmare Coalition apparently had defeated the Old Rule, but how the war ended"—he threw up his hands—"who can say?"

"There is a significant indication," said Joaz. "The Basics revisit Aerlith and ravage us at their pleasure. We have seen no men visiting except those who serve the Basics."

"Men?" Carcolo demanded scornfully. "I call them something else. Nevertheless, this is no more than a deduction, and we are ignorant as to the course of history. Perhaps Basics rule the cluster; perhaps they plague us only because we are weak and weaponless. Perhaps we are the last men. Perhaps the Old Rule is resurgent. And never forget that many years have elapsed since the Basics last appeared on Aerlith."

"Many years have elapsed since Aerlith and Coralyne were in such convenient apposition."

Carcolo made an impatient gesture. "A supposition, which may or may not be relevant. Let me explain the basic axiom of my proposal. It is simple enough. I feel that Banbeck Vale and Happy Valley are too small a compass for men such as ourselves. We deserve larger scope."

Joaz agreed. "I wish it were possible to ignore the practical difficulties involved."

"I am able to suggest a method to counter these difficulties," asserted Carcolo.

"In that case," said Joaz, "power, glory and wealth are as good as ours."

Carcolo glanced at him sharply, slapped his breeches with the gold-beaded tassel to his scabbard. "Reflect," he said. "The sacerdotes inhabited Aerlith before us. How long no one can say. It is a mystery. In fact, what do we know of the sacerdotes? Next to nothing. They trade their metal and glass for our food. They live in deep caverns. Their creed is disassociation, reverie, detachment, whatever one may wish to call it—totally incomprehensible to one such as myself." He challenged Joaz with a look; Joaz merely fingered his long chin. "They put themselves forward as simple metaphysical cultists. Actually they are a very mysterious people. Has anyone yet seen a sacerdote woman? What of the blue lights? What of the lightning towers, what of the sacerdote magic? What of weird comings and going by night, what of strange shapes moving across the sky, perhaps to other planets?"

"The tales exist, certainly," said Joaz. "As to the degree of credence to be placed in them—"

"Now we reach the meat of my proposal!" declared Ervis Carcolo. "The creed of the sacerdotes apparently forbids shame or regard for consequence. Hence, they are forced to answer any question put to them. Nevertheless, creed or no creed, they completely befog any information an assiduous man is able to wheedle from them."

Joaz inspected him curiously. "Evidently you have made the attempt."

Ervis Carcolo nodded. "Why should I deny it? I have questioned three sacerdotes with determination and persistence. They answered all my questions with gravity and calm reflection, but told me nothing." He shook his head in vexation. "Therefore, I suggest that we apply coercion."

"You are a brave man."

Carcolo shook his head modestly. "I would dare no direct measures. But they must eat. If Banbeck Vale and Happy Valley cooperate, we can apply the very cogent persuasion of hunger. Presently their words may be more to the point."

Joaz considered a moment or two. Ervis Carcolo twitched his scabbard tassel. "Your plan," said Joaz at last, "is not a frivolous one, and is ingenious—at least at first glance. What sort of information do you hope to secure? In short, what are your ultimate aims?"

Carcolo sidled close, prodded Joaz with his forefinger. "We know nothing of the outer worlds. We are marooned on this miserable planet of stone and wind while life passes us by. You assume that Basics rule the cluster. But suppose you are wrong? Suppose the Old Rule has returned? Think of the rich cities, the gay resorts, the palaces, the pleasure-islands! Look up into the night sky. Ponder the bounties which might be ours! You ask how can we implement these desires? I respond, the process may be so simple that the sacerdotes will reveal it without reluctance."

"You mean—"

"Communication with the worlds of men! Deliverance from this lonely little world at the edge of the universe!"

Joaz Banbeck nodded dubiously. "A fine vision. But the evidence suggests a situation far different, namely the destruction of man and the Human Empire."

Carcolo held out his hands in a gesture of open-minded tolerance. "Perhaps you are right. But why should we not make inquiries of the sacerdotes? Concretely I propose as follows: that you and I agree to the mutual cause I have outlined. Next, we request an audience with the Demie Sacerdote. We put our questions. If he responds freely, well and good. If he evades, then we act together. No more food to the sacerdotes until they tell us plainly what we want to hear."

"Other valleys exist," said Joaz thoughtfully.

Carcolo made a brisk gesture. "We can deter any such trade by persuasion or by the power of our dragons."

"The essence of your idea appeals to me," said Joaz. "But I fear that all is not so simple."

Carcolo rapped his thigh smartly with the tassel. "And why not?"

"In the first place, Coralyne shines bright in the sky. This is our first concern. Should Coralyne pass and the Basics not attack—then is the time to pursue this matter. Again—and perhaps more to the point—I doubt that we can starve the sacerdotes into submission. In fact, I consider it impossible."

Carcolo blinked. "In what wise?"

"They walk naked through sleet and storm; do you think they fear hunger? And there is wild lichen to be gathered. How could we forbid this? You might dare some sort of coercion, but not I. The tales told of the sacerdotes may be superstition—or they may be understatement."

Ervis Carcolo heaved a deep disgusted sigh. "Joaz Banbeck, I took you for a man of decision. But you merely pick flaws."

"These are not flaws. They are major errors which would lead to disaster."

"Well then. Do you have any suggestions of your own?"

Joaz fingered his chin. "If Coralyne recedes and we are still on Aerlith—rather than in the hold of the Basic ship—then let us plan to plunder the secrets of the sacerdotes. In the meantime I strongly recommend that you prepare Happy Valley against a new raid. You are overextended, with your new brooders and barracks. Let them rest, while you dig yourself secure tunnels!"

Ervis Carcolo stared straight across Banbeck Vale. "I am not a man to defend. I attack!"

"You will attack heat-beams and ion-rays with your dragons?"

Ervis Carcolo turned his gaze back to Joaz Banbeck. "Can I consider us allies in the plan I have proposed?"

"In its broadest principles, certainly. However I don't care to cooperate in starving or otherwise coercing the sacerdotes. It might be dangerous, as well as futile."

For an instant Carcolo could not control his detestation of Joaz Banbeck. His lip curled, his hands clenched. "Danger? Pah! What danger from a handful of naked pacifists?"

"We do not know that they are pacifists. We do know that they are men."

Carcolo once more became brightly cordial. "Perhaps you are right. But essentially at least we are allies."

"To a degree."

"Good. I suggest that in the case of the attack you fear, we act together, with a common strategy."

Joaz nodded distantly. "This might be effective."

"Let us coordinate our plans. Let us assume that the Basics drop down into Banbeck Vale. I suggest that your folk take refuge in Happy Valley, while the Happy Valley army joins with yours to cover their retreat. And likewise, should they attack Happy Valley, my people will take temporary refuge with you in Banbeck Vale."

Joaz laughed in sheer amusement. "Ervis Carcolo, what sort of lunatic do you take me for? Return to your valley, put aside your foolish grandiosities, dig yourself protection. And fast! Coralyne is bright!"

Carcolo stood stiffly. "Do I understand that you reject my offer of alliance?"

"Not at all. But I cannot undertake to protect you and your people if you will not help yourselves. Meet my requirements, satisfy me that you are a fit ally—then we shall speak further of alliance."

Ervis Carcolo whirled on his heel, signaled to Bast Givven and the two young fuglemen. With no further word or glance he mounted his splendid Spider, goaded him into a sudden leaping run across the Verge and up the slope toward Starbreak Fell. His men followed, somewhat less precipitously.

Joaz watched them go, shaking his head in sad wonder. Then, mounting his own Spider, he returned down the trail to the floor of Banbeck Vale.

v

The long Aerlith day, equivalent to six of the old Diurnal Units, passed.

In Happy Valley there was grim activity, a sense of purpose and impending decision. The dragons exercised in tighter formation. The fuglemen and cornets called orders with harsher voices. In the armory bullets were cast, powder was mixed, swords were ground and honed.

Ervis Carcolo drove himself with dramatic bravado, wearing out Spider after Spider as he sent his dragons through various evolutions. In the case of the Happy Valley forces, these were for the most part Termagants—small active dragons with rust-red scales, narrow darting heads, chisel-sharp fangs. Their brachs were strong and well-developed. They used lance, cutlass or mace with equal skill. A man pitted against a Termagant stood no chance, for the scales warded off bullets as well as any blow the man might have strength enough to deal. On the other hand a single slash of fang, the rip of a scythe-like claw, meant death to the man.

The Termagants were fecund and hardy and throve even under the conditions which existed in the Happy Valley brooders; hence their predominance in Carcolo's army. This was a situation not to the liking of Bast Givven, Chief Dragon-master, a spare wiry man with a flat crooked-nosed face, eyes black and blank as drops of ink on a plate. Habitually terse and tight-lipped, he waxed almost eloquent in opposition to the attack upon Banbeck Vale. "Look you, Ervis Carcolo. We are able to deploy a horde of Termagants, with sufficient Striding Murderers and Long-horned Murderers. But Blue Horrors, Fiends and Juggers—no! We are lost if they trap us on the fells!"

"I do not plan to fight on the fells," said Carcolo. "I will force battle upon Joaz Banbeck. His Juggers and Fiends are useless on the cliffs. And in the matter of Blue Horrors we are almost his equal."

"You overlook a single difficulty," said Bast Givven.

"And what is this?"

"The improbability that Joaz Banbeck plans to permit all this. I allow him greater intelligence than that."

"Show me evidence!" charged Carcolo. "What I know of him suggests vacillation and stupidity! So we will strike—hard!" Carcolo smacked fist into palm. "Thus we will finish the haughty Banbecks!"

Bast Givven turned to go. Carcolo wrathfully called him back. "You show no enthusiasm for this campaign!"

"I know what our army can do and what it cannot do," said Givven bluntly. "If Joaz Banbeck is the man you think he is, we might succeed. If he has even the sagacity of a pair of grooms I listened to ten minutes ago, we face disaster."

In a voice thick with rage, Carcolo said, "Return to your Fiends and Juggers. I want them quick as Termagants."

Bast Givven went his way. Carcolo jumped on a nearby Spider, kicked it with his heels. The creature sprang forward, halted sharply, twisted its long neck about to look Carcolo in the face. Carcolo cried, "Hust, hust! Forward at speed, smartly now! Show these louts what snap and spirit mean!" The Spider jumped ahead with such vehemence that Carcolo tumbled over backward, landing on his neck, where he lay groaning.

Grooms came running and assisted him to a bench where he sat cursing in a steady low voice. A surgeon examined, pressed, prodded, recommended that Carcolo take to his couch and administered a sedative potion.

Carcolo was carried to his apartments beneath the west wall of Happy Valley and placed under the care of his wives. He slept for twenty hours. When he awoke the day was half gone.

He wished to arise, but found himself too stiff to move and, groaning, lay back. Presently he called for Bast Givven, who appeared and listened without comment to Carcolo's adjurations.

Evening arrived. The dragons returned to the barracks. There was nothing to do now but wait for daybreak.

During the long night Carcolo underwent a variety of treatments: massage, hot baths, infusions and poultices. He exercised with diligence, and as the night reached its end he declared himself fit. Overhead the star Coralyne vibrated poisonous colors—red, green, white— by far the brightest star of the cluster. Carcolo refused to look up at the star, but its radiance struck through the corners of his eyes whenever he walked on the valley floor.

Dawn approached. Carcolo planned to march at the earliest moment the dragons were manageable. A flickering to the east told of the oncoming dawn storm, still invisible across the horizon. With great caution the dragons were mustered from their barracks and ordered into a marching column. There were almost three hundred Termagants; eighty-five Striding Murderers, as many Long-horned Murderers; a hundred Blue Horrors; fifty-two squat, immensely powerful Fiends, their tails tipped with spiked steel balls; eighteen Juggers. They growled and muttered evilly among themselves, watching an opportunity to kick each other or to snip a leg from an unwary groom. Darkness stimulated their latent hatred for humanity—though they had been taught nothing of their past, nor the circumstances by which they had become enslaved.

The dawn lightning blazed, outlining the vertical steeples and astonishing peaks of the Malheur Mountains. Overhead passed the storm, with wailing gusts of wind and thrashing banks of rain, moving on toward Banbeck Vale. The east glowed with a gray-green pallor, and Carcolo gave the signal to march.

Still stiff and sore he hobbled to his Spider, mounted, ordered the creature into a special and dramatic curvet. Carcolo had miscalculated. Malice of the night still gripped the mind of the dragon. It ended its curvet with a lash of the neck which once again dashed Carcolo to the ground, where he lay half-mad with pain and frustration.

He tried to rise; collapsed; tried again; fainted.

Five minutes he lay unconscious, then seemed to rouse himself by sheer force of will. "Lift me," he whispered huskily. "Tie me into the saddle. We must march." This being manifestly impossible, no one made a move. Carcolo raged, finally called hoarsely for Bast Givven. "Proceed; we cannot stop now. You must lead the troops."

Givven nodded glumly. This was an honor for which he had no stomach.

"You know the battle-plan," wheezed Carcolo. "Circle north of the Fang, cross the Skanse with all speed, swing north around Blue Crevasse, then south along Banbeck Verge. There Joaz Banbeck may be expected to discover you. You must deploy so that when he brings up his Juggers you can topple them back with Fiends. Avoid committing our Juggers. Harry him with Termagants; reserve the Murderers to strike wherever he reaches the edge. Do you understand me?"

"As you explain it, victory is certain," muttered Bast Givven.

"And so it is, unless you blunder grievously. Ah, my back! I can't move. While the great battle rages I must sit by the brooder and watch eggs hatch! Now go! Strike hard for Happy Valley!"

Givven gave an order. The troops set forth.

Termagants darted into the lead, followed by silken Striding Murderers and the heavier Long-horned Murderers, their fantastic chest-spike tipped with steel. Behind came the ponderous Juggers, grunting, gurgling, teeth clashing together with the vibration of their steps. Flanking the Juggers marched the Fiends, carrying heavy cutlasses, flourishing their terminal steel balls as a scorpion carries his sting. Then at the rear came the Blue Horrors, who were both massive and quick, good climbers, no less intelligent than the Termagants. To the flanks rode a hundred men: dragon-masters, knights, fuglemen and cornets. They were armed with swords, pistols and large-bore blunderbusses.

Carcolo watched from a stretcher till the last of his forces had passed from view, then commanded himself carried back to the portal which led into the Happy Valley caves.

Never before had the caves seemed so dingy and shallow. Sourly he eyed the straggle of huts along the cliff, built of rock, slabs of resin-impregnated lichen, canes bound with tar. With the Banbeck campaign at an end, he would set about cutting new chambers and halls into the cliff. The splendid decorations of Banbeck Village were well-known. Happy Valley would be even more magnificent. The halls would glow with opal and nacre, silver and gold . . . And yet, to what end? If events went as planned, there was his great dream in prospect. And then, what consequence a few paltry decorations in the tunnels of Happy Valley?

Groaning, he allowed himself to be laid on his couch and entertained himself picturing the progress of his troops. By now they should be working down from Dangle Ridge, circling the mile-high Fang.

He tentatively stretched his arms, worked his legs. His muscles protested. Pain shot back and forth along his body—but it seemed as if the injuries were less than before . . . By now the army would be mounting the ramparts which rimmed that wide area of upland fell known as the Skanse . . . The surgeon brought Carcolo a potion. He drank and slept, to awake with a start. What was the time? His troops might well have joined battle!

He ordered himself carried to the outer portal; then, still dissatisfied, commanded his servants to transport him across the valley to the new dragon brooder, the walkway of which commanded a view up and down the valley. Despite the protests of his wives, here he was conveyed, and made as comfortable as bruises and sprains permitted.

He settled himself for an indeterminate wait. But news was not long in coming.

Down the North Trail came a cornet on a foam-bearded Spider. Carcolo sent a groom to intercept him and, heedless of aches and pains, raised himself from his couch. The cornet threw himself off his mount, staggered up the ramp, sagged exhausted against the rail.

"Ambush!" he panted. "Bloody disaster!"

"Ambush?" groaned Carcolo in a hollow voice. "Where?"

"As we mounted the Skanse Ramparts. They waited till our Termagants and Murderers were over, then charged with Horrors, Fiends and Juggers. They cut us apart, drove us back, then rolled boulders on our Juggers! Our army is broken!"

Carcolo sank back on the couch, lay staring at the sky. "How many are lost?"

"I do not know. Givven called the retreat. We withdrew in the best style possible."

Carcolo lay as if comatose. The cornet flung himself down on a bench.

A column of dust appeared to the north, which presently dissolved and separated to reveal a number of Happy Valley dragons. All were wounded. They marched, hopped, limped, dragged themselves at random, croaking, glaring, bugling. First came a group of Termagants, darting ugly heads from side to side; then a pair of Blue Horrors, brachs twisting and clasping almost like human arms; then a Jugger, massive, toad-like, legs splayed out in weariness. Even as it neared the barracks it toppled, fell with a thud and lay still, legs and talons jutting into the air.

Down from the North Trail rode Bast Givven, dust-stained and haggard. He dismounted from his drooping Spider, mounted the ramp. With a wrenching effort, Carcolo once more raised himself on the couch.

Givven reported in a voice so even and light as to seem careless, but even the insensitive Carcolo was not deceived. He asked in puzzlement: "Exactly where did the ambush occur?"

"We mounted the Ramparts by way of Chloris Ravine. Where the Skanse falls off into the ravine a porphyry outcrop juts up and over. Here they awaited us."

Carcolo hissed through his teeth. "Amazing."

Bast Givven gave the faintest of nods.

Carcolo said, "Assume that Joaz Banbeck set forth during the dawnstorm, an hour earlier than I would think possible. Assume that he forced his troops at a run. How could he reach the Skanse Ramparts before us even so?"

"By my reckoning," said Givven, "ambush was no threat until we had crossed the Skanse. I had planned to patrol Barchback, all the way down Blue Fell and across Blue Crevasse."

Carcolo gave somber agreement. "How then did Joaz Banbeck bring his troops to the Ramparts so soon?"

Givven turned, looked up the valley, where wounded dragons and men still straggled down the North Trail. "I have no idea."

"A drug?" puzzled Carcolo. "A potion to pacify the dragons? Could he have made bivouac on the Skanse the whole night long?"

"The last is possible," admitted Givven grudgingly. "Under Barch Spike are empty caves. If he quartered his troops here during the night, then he had only to march across the Skanse to waylay us."

Carcolo grunted. "Perhaps we have underestimated Joaz Banbeck." He sank back on his couch with a groan. "Well, then, what are our losses?"

The reckoning made dreary news. Of the already inadequate squad of Juggers, only six remained. From a force of fifty-two Fiends, forty survived and of these five were sorely wounded. Termagants, Blue Horrors and Murderers had suffered greatly. A large number had been torn apart in the first onslaught. Many others had been toppled down the Ramparts to strew their armored husks through the detritus. Of the hundred men, twelve had been killed by bullets, another fourteen by dragon attack. A score more were wounded in various degree.

Carcolo lay back, his eyes closed and his mouth working feebly.

"The terrain alone saved us," said Givven. "Joaz Banbeck refused to commit his troops to the ravine. If there were any tactical error on either side, it was his. He brought an insufficiency of Termagants and Blue Horrors."

"Small comfort," growled Carcolo. "Where is the balance of the army?"

"We have good position on Dangle Ridge. We have seen none of Banbeck's scouts, either man or Termagant. He may conceivably believe we have retreated to the valley. In any event his main forces were still collected on the Skanse."

Carcolo, by an enormous effort, raised himself to his feet.

He tottered across the walkway to look down into the dispensary. Five Fiends crouched in vats of balsam, muttering and sighing. A Blue Horror hung in a sling, whining as surgeons cut broken fragments of armor from its gray flesh. As Carcolo watched, one of the Fiends raised itself high on its anterior legs, foam gushing from its gills. It cried out in a peculiar, poignant tone and fell back dead into the vat of balsam.

Carcolo turned back to Givven. "This is what you must do. Joaz Banbeck surely has sent forth patrols. Retire along Dangle Ridge. Then, taking all concealment from the patrols, swing up into one of the Despoire Cols. Tourmaline Col will serve. This is my reasoning. Banbeck will assume that you are retiring to Happy Valley, so he will hurry south behind the Fang, to attack as you come down off Dangle Ridge. As he passes below Tourmaline Col, you have the advantage. You may well destroy Joaz Banbeck there with all his troops."

Bast Givven shook his head decisively. "What if his patrols locate us in spite of our precautions? He need only follow our tracks to bottle us into Tourmaline Col, with no escape except over Mount Despoire or out on Starbreak Fell. And if we venture out on Starbreak Fell his Juggers will destroy us in minutes."

Ervis Carcolo sagged back down upon the couch. "Bring the troops back to Happy Valley. We will regroup and await another occasion."

## VI

Cut into the cliff south of the crag which housed Joaz's apartments was a large chamber known as Kergan's Hall. The proportions of the room, the simplicity and lack of ornament, the massive antique furniture contributed to the sense of lingering personality, as well as an odor unique to the room. This odor exhaled from naked stone walls, the petrified moss parquetry, old wood—a rough ripe redolence which Joaz had always disliked, together with every other aspect of the room. The dimensions seemed arrogant in their extent. The lack of ornament impressed him as rude, if not brutal. One day it occurred to Joaz that he disliked not the room but Kergan Banbeck himself, together with the entire system of overblown legends which surrounded him.

The room nevertheless in many respects was pleasant. Three tall groined windows overlooked the vale. The casements were set with small square panes of green-blue glass in muntins of black ironwood. The ceiling likewise was paneled in wood, and here a certain amount of the typical Banbeck intricacy had been permitted. There were mock pilaster capitals with gargoyle heads, a frieze carved with conventionalized fern-fronds. The furniture consisted of three pieces: two tall carved chairs and a massive table, all polished dark wood, all of enormous antiquity.

Joaz had found a use for the room. The table supported a carefully detailed relief map of the district, on a scale of three inches to the mile. At the center was Banbeck Vale, on the right hand Happy Valley, separated by a turmoil of crags and chasms, cliffs, spikes, walls and five titanic peaks: Mount Gethron to the south, Mount Despoire in the center, Barch Spike, the Fang and Mount Halcyon to the north.

At the front of Mount Gethron lay the High Jambles, then Starbreak Fell extended to Mount Despoire and Barch Spike. Beyond Mount Despoire, between the Skanse Ramparts and Barchback, the Skanse reached all the way to the tormented basalt ravines and bluffs at the foot of Mount Halcyon.

As Joaz stood studying the map, into the room came Phade. She was mischievously quiet. But Joaz sensed her nearness by the scent of incense, in the smoke of which she had steeped herself before seeking out Joaz. She wore a traditional holiday costume of Banbeck maidens: a tight-fitting sheath of dragon intestine, with muffs of brown fur at neck, elbows and knees. A tall cylindrical hat, notched around the upper edge, perched on her rich brown curls, and from the top of this hat soared a red plume.

Joaz feigned unconsciousness of her presence. She came up behind him to tickle his neck with the fur of her neck-piece. Joaz pretended stolid indifference. Phade, not at all deceived, put on a face of woeful concern. "Must we all be slain? How goes the war?"

"For Banbeck Vale the war goes well. For poor Ervis Carcolo and Happy Valley the war goes ill indeed."

"You plan his destruction," Phade intoned a voice of hushed accusation. "You will kill him! Poor Ervis Carcolo!"

"He deserves no better."

"But what will befall Happy Valley?"

Joaz Banbeck shrugged idly. "Changes for the better."

"Will you seek to rule?"

"Not I."

"Think!" whispered Phade. "Joaz Banbeck, Tyrant of Banbeck Vale, Happy Valley, Phosphor Gulch, Glore, the Tarn, Clewhaven and the Great Northern Rift."

"Not I," said Joaz. "Perhaps you would rule in my stead?"

"Oh! Indeed! What changes there would be! I'd dress the sacerdotes in red and yellow ribbons. I'd order them to sing and dance and drink May wine. The dragons I'd send south to Arcady, except for a few gentle Termagants to nursemaid the children. And no more of these furious battles. I'd burn the armor and break the swords; I'd—"

"My dear little flutterbug," said Joaz with a laugh. "What a swift reign you'd have indeed!"

"Why swift? Why not forever? If men had no means to fight—"

"And when the Basics came down—you'd throw garlands around their necks?"

"Pah. They shall never be seen again. What do they gain by molesting a few remote valleys?"

"Who knows what they gain? We are free men. Perhaps the last free men in the universe. Who knows? And will they be back? Coralyne is bright in the sky!"

Phade became suddenly interested in the relief map. "And your current war—dreadful. Will you attack, will you defend?"

"This depends on Ervis Carcolo," said Joaz. "I need only wait till he exposes himself." Looking down at the map he added thoughtfully, "He is clever enough to do me damage, unless I move with care."

"And what if the Basics come while you bicker with Carcolo?"

Joaz smiled. "Perhaps we shall all flee to the Jambles. Perhaps we shall all fight."

"I will fight beside you," declared Phade, striking a brave attitude. "We will attack the great Basic space-ship, braving the heat-rays, fending off the power-bolts. We will storm to the very portal. We will pull the nose of the first marauder who shows himself!"

"At one point your otherwise sage strategy falls short," said Joaz. "How does one find the nose of a Basic?"

"In that case," said Phade, "we shall seize their—" She turned her head at a sound in the hall. Joaz strode across the room, flung back the door. Old Rife the porter sidled forward. "You told me to call when the bottle either overturned or broke. Well, it's done both."

Joaz pushed past Rife, ran down the corridor. "What means this?" demanded Phade. "Rife, what have you said to disturb him?"

Rife shook his head fretfully. "I am as perplexed as you. A bottle is pointed out to me. 'Watch this bottle day and night'—so I am commanded. And also, 'When the bottle breaks or tips, call me at once.' I tell myself that here in all truth is a sinecure. And I wonder, does Joaz consider me so senile that I will rest content with a make-work task such as watching a bottle? I am old, my jaws tremble, but I am not witless. To my surprise the bottle breaks! The explanation admittedly is simple. It fell to the floor. Nevertheless, without knowledge of what it all means, I obey orders and notify Joaz Banbeck."

Phade had been squirming impatiently. "Where then is this bottle?"

"In the studio of Joaz Banbeck."

Phade ran off as swiftly as the tight sheath about her thighs permitted: through a transverse tunnel, across Kergan's Way by a covered bridge, then up at a slant toward Joaz's apartments.

Down the long hall ran Phade, through the anteroom where a bottle lay shattered on the floor, into the studio, where she halted in astonishment. No one was to be seen. She noticed a section of shelving which stood at an angle. Quietly, timorously, she stole across the room, peered down into the workshop.

The scene was an odd one. Joaz stood negligently, smiling a cool smile, as across the room a naked sacerdote gravely sought to shift a barrier which had sprung down across an area of the wall. But the gate was cunningly locked in place, and the sacerdote's efforts were to no avail.

He turned, glanced briefly at Joaz, then started for the exit into the studio.

Phade sucked in her breath and backed away.

The sacerdote came out into the studio, started for the door.

"Just a moment," said Joaz. "I wish to speak to you."

The sacerdote paused, turned his head in mild inquiry. He was a young man, his face bland, blank, almost beautiful. Fine transparent skin stretched over his pale bones. His eyes—wide, blue, innocent—seemed to stare without focus. He was delicate of frame and sparsely fleshed. His hands were thin, with fingers trembling in some kind of nervous imbalance. Down his back, almost to his waist, hung the mane of long light-brown hair.

Joaz seated himself with ostentatious deliberation, never taking his eyes from the sacerdote. Presently he spoke in a voice pitched at an ominous level. "I find your conduct far from ingratiating." This was a declaration requiring no response, and the sacerdote made none.

"Please sit," said Joaz. He indicated a bench. "You have a great deal of explaining to do."

Was it Phade's imagination? Or did a spark of something like wild amusement flicker and die almost instantaneously in the sacerdote's eyes? But again he made no response. Joaz, adapting to the peculiar rules by which communication with the sacerdotes must be conducted, asked, "Do you care to sit?"

"It is immaterial," said the sacerdote. "Since I am standing now, I will stand."

Joaz rose to his feet and performed an act without precedent. He pushed the bench behind the sacerdote, rapped the back of the knobby knees, thrust the sacerdote firmly down upon the bench. "Since you are sitting now," said Joaz, "you might as well sit."

With gentle dignity the sacerdote regained his feet. "I shall stand."

Joaz shrugged. "As you wish. I intend to ask you some questions. I hope that you will cooperate and answer with precision."

The sacerdote blinked owlishly.

"Will you do so?"

"Certainly. I prefer, however, to return the way I came."

Joaz ignored the remark. "First," he asked, "why do you come to my study?"

The sacerdote spoke carefully, in the voice of one talking to a child. "Your language is vague. I am confused and must not respond, since I am vowed to give only truth to anyone who requires it."

Joaz settled himself in his chair. "There is no hurry. I am ready for a long discussion. Let me ask you then: did you have impulses which you can explain to me, which persuaded or impelled you to come to my studio?"

"Yes."

"How many of these impulses did you recognize?"

"I don't know."

"More than one?"

"Perhaps."

"Less than ten?"

"I don't know."

"Hmm . . . Why are you uncertain?"

"I am not uncertain."

"Then why can't you specify the number as I requested?"

"There is no such number."

"I see . . . You mean, possibly, that there are several elements of a single motive which directed your brain to signal your muscles in order that they might carry you here?"

"Possibly."

Joaz's thin lips twisted in a faint smile of triumph. "Can you describe an element of the eventual motive?"

"Yes."

"Do so, then."

There was an imperative, against which the sacerdote was proof. Any form of coercion known to Joaz—fire, sword, thirst, mutilation— these to a sacerdote were no more than inconveniences; he ignored them as if they did not exist. His personal inner world was the single world of reality. Either acting upon or reacting against the affairs of the Utter Men demeaned him. Absolute passivity and absolute candor were his necessary courses of action. Understanding something of this,

Joaz rephrased his command: "Can you think of an element of the motive which impelled you to come here?"

"Yes."

"What is it?"

"A desire to wander about."

"Can you think of another?"

"Yes."

"What is it?"

"A desire to exercise myself by walking."

"I see . . . Incidentally, are you trying to evade answering my question?"

"I answer such questions as you put to me. So long as I do so, so long as I open my mind to all who seek knowledge—for this is our creed— there can be no question of evasion."

"So you say. However, you have not provided me an answer that I find satisfactory."

The sacerdote's reply to the comment was an almost imperceptible widening of the pupils.

"Very well then," said Joaz Banbeck. "Can you think of another element to this complex motive we have been discussing?"

"Yes."

"What is it?"

"I am interested in antiques. I came to your study to admire your relics of the old worlds."

"Indeed?" Joaz raised his eyebrows. "I am lucky to possess such fascinating treasures. Which of my antiques interests you particularly?"

"Your books. Your maps. Your great globe of the Arch-world."

"The Arch-world? Eden?"

"This is one of its names."

Joaz pursed his lips. "So you come here to study my antiques. Well then, what other elements to this motive exist?"

The sacerdote hesitated an instant. "It was suggested to me that I come here."

"By whom?"

"By the Demie."

"Why did he so suggest?"

"I am uncertain."

"Can you conjecture?"

"Yes."

"What are these conjectures?"

The sacerdote made a small bland gesture with the fingers of one hand. "The Demie might wish to become an Utter Man, and so seeks to learn the principles of your existence. Or the Demie might wish to change the trade articles. The Demie might be fascinated by my descriptions of your antiques. Or the Demie might be curious regarding the focus of your vision-panels. Or—"

"Enough. Which of these conjectures, and of other conjectures you have not yet divulged, do you consider most probable?"

"None."

Joaz raised his eyebrows once more. "How do you justify this?"

"Since any desired number of conjectures can be formed, the denominator of any probability-ratio is variable and the entire concept becomes arithmetically meaningless."

Joaz grinned wearily. "Of the conjectures which to this moment have occurred to you, which do you regard as the most likely?"

"I suspect that the Demie might think it desirable that I come here to stand."

"What do you achieve by standing?"

"Nothing."

"Then the Demie does not send you here to stand."

To Joaz's assertion, the sacerdote made no comment.

Joaz framed a question with great care. "What do you believe that the Demie hopes you will achieve by coming here to stand?"

"I believe that he wishes me to learn how Utter Men think."

"And you learn how I think by coming here?"

"I am learning a great deal."

"How does it help you?"

"I don't know."

"How many times have you visited my study?"

"Seven times."

"Why were you chosen specially to come?"

"The synod has approved my *tand*. I may well be the next Demie."

Joaz spoke over his shoulder to Phade. "Brew tea." He turned back to the sacerdote. "What is a *tand*?"

The sacerdote took a deep breath. "My *tand* is the representation of my soul."

"Hmm. What does it look like?"

The sacerdote's expression was unfathomable. "It cannot be described."

"Do I have one?"

"No."

Joaz shrugged. "Then you can read my thoughts."

Silence.

"Can you read my thoughts?"

"Not well."

"Why should you wish to read my thoughts?"

"We are alive in the universe together. Since we are not permitted to act, we are obliged to know."

Joaz smiled skeptically. "How does knowledge help you, if you will not act upon it?"

"Events follow the Rationale, as water drains into a hollow and forms a pool."

"Bah!" said Joaz, in sudden irritation. "Your doctrine commits you to non-interference in our affairs, nevertheless you allow your 'Rationale' to create conditions by which events are influenced. Is this correct?"

"I am not sure. We are a passive people."

"Still, your Demie must have had a plan in mind when he sent you here. Is this not correct?"

"I cannot say."

Joaz veered to a new line of questioning. "Where does the tunnel behind my workshop lead?"

"Into a cavern."

Phade set a silver pot before Joaz. He poured and sipped reflectively. Of contests there were numberless varieties. He and the sacerdote were engaged in a hide-and-seek game of words and ideas. The sacerdote was schooled in patience and supple evasions, to counter which Joaz could bring pride and determination. The sacerdote was handicapped by an innate necessity to speak truth. Joaz, on the other hand, must grope like a man blindfolded, unacquainted with the goal he sought, ignorant of the prize to be won. Very well, thought Joaz, let us continue. We shall see whose nerves fray first. He offered tea to the sacerdote, who refused with a shake of the head so quick and of such small compass as to seem a shudder.

Joaz made a gesture signifying it was all the same to him. "Should you desire sustenance or drink," he said, "please let it be known. I enjoy our conversation so inordinately that I fear I may prolong it to the limits of your patience. Surely you would prefer to sit?"

"No."

"As you wish. Well, then, back to our discussion. This cavern you mentioned: is it inhabited by sacerdotes?"

"I fail to understand your question."

"Do sacerdotes use the cavern?"

"Yes."

Eventually, fragment by fragment, Joaz extracted the information that the cavern connected with a series of chambers, in which the sacerdotes smelted metal, boiled glass, ate, slept, performed their rituals. At one time there had been an opening into Banbeck Vale, but long ago this had been blocked. Why? There were wars throughout the cluster; bands of defeated men were taking refuge upon Aerlith, settling in rifts and valleys. The sacerdotes preferred a detached existence and had shut their caverns away from sight. Where was this opening? The sacerdote seemed vague. To the north end of the valley. Behind Banbeck Jambles? Possibly. But trading between men and sacerdotes was conducted at a cave entrance below Mount Gethron. Why? A matter of usage, declared the sacerdote. In addition this location was more readily accessible to Happy Valley and Phosphor Gulch. How many sacerdotes lived in these caves? Uncertainty. Some might have died, others might have been born. Approximately how many this morning? Perhaps five hundred.

At this juncture the sacerdote was swaying and Joaz was hoarse. "Back to your motive—or the elements of your motives—for coming to my studio. Are they connected in any manner with the star Coralyne, and a possible new coming of the Basics, or the grephs, as they were formerly called?"

Again the sacerdote seemed to hesitate. Then: "Yes."

"Will the sacerdotes help us against the Basics, should they come?"

"No." This answer was terse and definite.

"But I assume that the sacerdotes wish the Basics driven off?"

No answer.

Joaz rephrased his words. "Do the sacerdotes wish the Basics repelled from Aerlith?"

"The Rationale bids us stand aloof from affairs of men and non-men alike."

Joaz curled his lip. "Suppose the Basics invaded your cave and dragged you off to the Coralyne planet. Then what?"

The sacerdote almost seemed to laugh. "The question cannot be answered."

"Would you resist the Basics if they made the attempt?"

"I cannot answer your question."

Joaz laughed. "But the answer is not no?"

The sacerdote assented.

"Do you have weapons, then?"

The sacerdote's mild blue eyes seemed to droop. Secrecy? Fatigue? Joaz repeated the question.

"Yes," said the sacerdote. His knees sagged, but he snapped them tight.

"What kind of weapons?"

"Numberless varieties. Projectiles, such as rocks. Piercing weapons, such as broken sticks. Cutting and slashing weapons, such as cooking utensils." His voice began to fade as if he were moving away. "Poisons: arsenic, sulfur, triventidum, acid, black-spore. Burning weapons, such as torches and lenses to focus the sunlight. Weapons to suffocate: ropes, nooses, slings and cords. Cisterns, to drown the enemy . . ."

"Sit down. Rest," Joaz urged him. "Your inventory interests me, but its total effect seems inadequate. Have you other weapons which might decisively repel the Basics should they attack you?"

The question, by design or chance, was never answered. The sacerdote sank to his knees, slowly, as if praying. He fell forward on his face, then sprawled to the side. Joaz sprang forward, yanked up the drooping head by its hair. The eyes, half-open, revealed a hideous white expanse. "Speak!" croaked Joaz. "Answer my last question! Do you have weapons—or a weapon—to repel a Basic attack?"

The pallid lips moved. "I don't know."

Joaz frowned, peered into the waxen face, drew back in bewilderment. "The man is dead," he whispered.

## VII

Phade looked up from drowsing on a couch, face pink, hair tossed. "You have killed him!" she cried in a voice of hushed horror.

"No. He has died—or caused himself to die."

Phade staggered blinking across the room, sidled close to Joaz, who pushed her absently away. Phade scowled, shrugged and then, as Joaz paid her no heed, marched from the room.

Joaz sat back, staring at the limp body. "He did not tire," muttered Joaz, "until I verged upon secrets."

Presently he jumped to his feet, went to the entry hall, sent Rife to fetch a barber. An hour later the corpse, stripped of hair, lay on a wooden pallet covered by a sheet, and Joaz held in his hands a rude wig fashioned from the long hair.

The barber departed. Servants carried away the corpse. Joaz stood alone in his studio, tense and light-headed. He removed his garments, to stand naked as the sacerdote. Gingerly he drew the wig across his scalp and examined himself in a mirror. To a casual eye, where the difference? Something was lacking: the torc. Joaz fitted it about his neck. Once more he examined his reflection, with dubious satisfaction.

He entered the workshop, hesitated, disengaged the trap, cautiously pulled away the stone slab. On hands and knees he peered into the tunnel and, since it was dark, held forward a glass vial of luminescent algae. In the faint light the tunnel seemed empty.

Irrevocably putting down his fears, Joaz clambered through the opening. The tunnel was narrow and low. Joaz moved forward tentatively, nerves thrilling with wariness. He stopped often to listen, but heard nothing but the whisper of his own pulse.

After perhaps a hundred yards the tunnel broke out into a natural cavern. Joaz stopped and stood indecisively straining his ears through the gloom. Luminescent vials fixed to the walls at irregular intervals provided a measure of light, enough to delineate the direction of the cavern. It seemed to be north, parallel to the length of the valley. Joaz set forth once again, halting to listen every few yards.

To the best of his knowledge the sacerdotes were a mild unaggressive folk, but they were also intensely secretive. How would they respond to the presence of an interloper? Joaz could not be sure, and proceeded with great caution.

The cavern rose, fell, widened, narrowed. Joaz presently came upon evidences of use: small cubicles, hollowed into the walls, lit by candelabra holding tall vials of luminous stuff. In two of the cubicles Joaz came upon sacerdotes, the first asleep on a reed rug, the second sitting crosslegged, gazing fixedly at a contrivance of twisted metal rods. They gave Joaz no attention; he continued with a more confident step.

The cave sloped downward, widened like a cornucopia and suddenly broke into a cavern so enormous that Joaz thought for a startled instant that he had stepped out into the starless night.

The ceiling reached beyond the flicker of the myriad lamps, fires and glowing vials. Ahead and to the left smelters and forges were in operation; then a twist in the cavern wall obscured something of the view. Joaz glimpsed a tiered, tubular construction which seemed to be some sort of workshop, for a large number of sacerdotes were occupied at complicated tasks. To the right was a stack of bales, a row of bins containing goods of unknown nature.

Joaz for the first time saw sacerdote women: neither the nymphs nor the half-human witches of popular legend. Like the men they seemed pallid and frail, with sharply defined features; like the men they moved with care and deliberation; like the men they wore only their waist-long hair. There was little conversation and no laughter. Rather there was an atmosphere of not unhappy placidity and concentration. The cavern exuded a sense of time, use and custom. The stone floor was polished by endless padding of bare feet. The exhalations of many generations had stained the walls.

No one heeded Joaz.

He moved slowly forward, keeping to the shadows, and paused under the stack of bales. To the right the cavern dwindled by irregular proportions into a vast horizontal funnel, receding, twisting, telescoping, losing all reality in the dim light.

Joaz searched the entire sweep of vast cavern. Where would be the armory, with the weapons whose existence the sacerdote, by the very act of dying, had promised him? Joaz turned his attention once more to the left, straining to see detail in the odd tiered workshop which rose fifty feet from the stone floor. A strange edifice, thought Joaz, craning his neck; one whose nature he could not entirely comprehend. But every aspect of the great cavern—so close beside Banbeck Vale, and so remote—was strange and marvelous. Weapons? They might be anywhere. Certainly he dared seek no further for them.

There was nothing more he could learn without risk of discovery. He turned back the way he had come: up the dim passage, past the occasional side cubicles, where the two sacerdotes remained as he had found them before: the one asleep, the other intent on the contrivance of twisted metal. He plodded on and on.

Had he come so far? Where was the fissure which led to his own apartments? Had he passed it by, must he search? Panic rose in his throat, but he continued, watching carefully. There, he had not gone wrong. There it opened to his right, a fissure almost dear and familiar. He plunged into it, walked with long loping strides, like a man under water, holding his luminous tube ahead.

An apparition rose before him, a tall white shape.

Joaz stood rigid. The gaunt figure bore down upon him. Joaz pressed against the wall. The figure stalked forward, and suddenly shrank to human scale. It was the young sacerdote whom Joaz had shorn and left for dead. He confronted Joaz, mild blue eyes bright with reproach and contempt. "Give me my torc."

With numb fingers Joaz removed the golden collar. The sacerdote took it, but made no move to clasp it upon himself. He looked at the hair which weighed heavy upon Joaz's scalp. With a foolish grimace Joaz doffed the disheveled wig, proffered it. The sacerdote sprang back as if Joaz had become a cave-goblin. Sidling past, as far from Joaz as the wall of the passage allowed, he paced swiftly off down the tunnel. Joaz dropped the wig to the floor, stared down at the unkempt pile of hair. He turned and looked after the sacerdote, a pallid figure which soon became one with the murk. Slowly Joaz continued up the tunnel.

There. An oblong blank of light, the opening to his workshop. He crawled through, back to the real world. Savagely, with all his strength, he thrust the slab back in the hole and slammed down the gate which originally had trapped the sacerdote.

Joaz's garments lay where he had tossed them. Wrapping himself in a cloak, he went to the outer door and looked forth into the anteroom, where Rife sat dozing. Joaz snapped his fingers. "Fetch masons, with mortar, steel and stone."

Joaz bathed with diligence, rubbing himself time after time with emulsion, rinsing and rerinsing himself. Emerging from the bath he took the waiting masons into his workshop and ordered the sealing of the hole.

Then he took himself to his couch. Sipping a cup of wine, he let his mind rove and wander . . .

Recollection became reverie. Reverie became dream. Joaz once again traversed the tunnel, on feet light as thistledown, down the long cavern, and the sacerdotes in their cubicles now raised their heads to look after him. At last he stood in the entrance to the great underground void, and once more looked right and left in awe. Now he drifted across the floor, past sacerdotes laboring earnestly over fires and anvils. Sparks rose from retorts, blue gas flickered above melting metal.

Joaz moved beyond to a small chamber cut into the stone. Here sat an old man, thin as a pole, his waist-long mane of hair snow-white. The man examined Joaz with fathomless blue eyes, and spoke, but his voice was muffled, inaudible. He spoke again; the words rang loud in Joaz's mind.

"I bring you here to caution you, lest you do us harm, and with no profit to yourself. The weapon you seek is both non-existent and beyond your imagination. Put it outside your ambition."

By great effort Joaz managed to stammer, "The young sacerdote made no denial. This weapon must exist!"

"Only with the narrow limits of special interpretation. The lad can speak no more than the literal truth, nor can he act with other than grace. How can you wonder why we hold ourselves apart? You Utter folk find purity incomprehensible; you thought to advantage yourself, but achieved nothing but an exercise in rat-like stealth. Lest you try again with greater boldness I must abase myself to set matters correct. I assure you, this so-called weapon is absolutely beyond your control."

First shame, then indignation came over Joaz. He cried out, "You do not understand my urgencies! Why should I act differently? Coralyne is close; the Basics are at hand. Are you not men? Why will you not help us defend the planet?"

The Demie shook his head, and the white hair rippled with hypnotic slowness. "I quote you the Rationale: passivity, complete and absolute. This implies solitude, sanctity, quiescence, peace. Can you imagine the anguish I risk in speaking to you? I intervene, I interfere, at vast pain of the spirit. Let there be an end to it. We have made free with your studio, doing you no harm, offering you no indignity. You have paid a visit to our hall, demeaning a noble young man in the process. Let us be quits! Let there be no further spying on either side. Do you agree?"

Joaz heard his voice respond, quite without his conscious prompting. It sounded more nasal and shrill than he liked. "You offer this agreement now when you have learned your fill of my secrets, but I know none of yours."

The Demie's face seemed ro recede and quiver. Joaz read contempt, and in his sleep he tossed and twitched. He made an effort to speak in a voice of calm reason: "Come, we are men together. Why should we be at odds? Let us share our secrets, let each help the other. Examine my archives at your leisure, and then allow me to study this existent but non-existent weapon. I swear it shall be used only against the Basics, for the protection of both of us."

The Demie's eyes sparkled. "No."

"Why not?" argued Joaz. "Surely you wish us no harm?"

"We are detached and passionless. We await your extinction. You are the Utter men, the last of humanity. And when you are gone, your dark thoughts and grim plots will be gone. Murder and pain and malice will be gone."

"I cannot believe this," said Joaz. "There may be no men in the cluster, but what of the universe? The Old Rule reached far! Sooner or later men will return to Aerlith."

The Demie's voice became plangent. "Do you think we speak only from faith? Do you doubt our knowledge?"

"The universe is large. The Old Rule reached far."

"The last men dwell on Aerlith," said the Demie. "The Utter men and the Sacerdotes. You shall pass; we will carry forth the Rationale like a banner of glory, through all the worlds of the sky."

"And how will you transport yourselves on this mission?" Joaz asked cunningly. "Can you fly to the stars as naked as you walk the fells?"

"There will be a means. Time is long."

"For your purposes, Time needs to be long. Even on the Coralyne planets there are men. Enslaved, reshaped in body and mind, but men. What of them? It seems that you are wrong, that you are guided by faith indeed."

The Demie fell silent. His face seemed to stiffen.

"Are these not facts?" asked Joaz. "How do you reconcile them with your faith?"

The Demie said mildly, "Facts can never be reconciled with faith. By our faith, these men, if they exist, will also pass. Time is long. O the worlds of brightness: they await us!"

"It is clear," said Joaz, "that you ally yourselves with the Basics and hope for our destruction. This can only change our attitudes toward you. I fear that Ervis Carcolo was right and I wrong."

"We remain passive," said the Demie. His face wavered, seemed to swim with mottled colors. "Without emotion, we will stand witness to the passing of the Utter men, neither helping nor hindering."

Joaz spoke in fury. "Your faith, your Rationale—whatever you call it—misleads you. I make you this threat: if you fail to help us, you will suffer as we suffer."

"We are passive. We are indifferent."

"What of your children? The Basics make no difference between us. They will herd you to their pens as readily as they do us. Why should we fight to protect you?"

The Demie's face faded, became splotched with transparent mist. His eyes glowed like rotten meat. "We need no protection," he howled. "We are secure."

"You will suffer our fate," cried Joaz, "I promise you this!"

The Demie collapsed suddenly into a small dry husk, like a dead mosquito. With incredible speed, Joaz fled back through the caves, the tunnels, up through his work-room, his studio, into his bed chamber where now he jerked upright, eyes starting, throat distended, mouth dry.

The door opened; Rife's head appeared. "Did you call, sir?"

Joaz raised himself on his elbows and looked around the room. "No. I did not call."

Rife withdrew. Joaz settled back on the couch, lay staring at the ceiling.

He had dreamed a most peculiar dream. Dream? A synthesis of his own imaginings? Or, in all verity, a confrontation and exchange between two minds? Impossible to decide, and perhaps irrelevant. The event carried its own conviction.

Joaz swung his legs over the side of the couch and blinked at the floor. Dream or colloquy, it was all the same. He rose to his feet, donned sandals and a robe of yellow fur, limped morosely up to the Council Room and stepped out on a sunny balcony.

The day was two-thirds over. Shadows hung dense along the western cliffs. Right and left stretched Banbeck Vale. Never had it seemed more prosperous or more fruitful, and never before unreal: as if he were a stranger to the planet. He looked north along the great bulwark of stone which rose sheer to Banbeck Verge. This too was unreal, a façade behind which lived the sacerdotes. He gauged the rock face, superimposing a mental projection of the great cavern. The cliff toward the north end of the vale must be scarcely more than a shell!

Joaz turned his attention to the exercise field, where Juggers were thudding briskly through defensive evolutions. How strange was the quality of life, which had produced Basic and Jugger, sacerdote and himself. He thought of Ervis Carcolo, and wrestled with sudden exasperation. Carcolo was a distraction most unwelcome at the present time. There would be no tolerance when Carcolo was finally brought to account.

A light step behind him, the pressure of fur, the touch of gay hands, the scent of incense. Joaz's tensions melted.

If there were no such creatures as minstrel-maidens, it would be necessary to invent them.

Deep under Banbeck Scarp, in a cubicle lit by a twelve-vial candelabra, a naked white-haired man sat quietly. On a pedestal at the level of his eyes rested his *tand,* an intricate construction of gold rods and silver wire, woven and bent seemingly at random. The fortuitousness of the design, however, was only apparent. Each curve symbolized an aspect of Final Sentience. The shadow cast upon the wall represented the Rationale, evershifting, always the same. The object was sacred to the sacerdotes, and served as a source of revelation.

There was never an end to the study of the *tand.* New intuitions were continually derived from some heretofore-overlooked relationship of angle and curve. The nomenclature was elaborate: each part, juncture, sweep and twist had its name; each aspect of the relationships between the various parts was likewise categorized. Such was the cult of the *tand:* abstruse, exacting, without compromise. At his puberty rites the young sacerdote might study the original *tand* for as long as he chose. Then each must construct a duplicate *tand,* relying upon memory alone. Then occurred the most significant event of his lifetime: the viewing of his *tand* by a synod of elders.

In awesome stillness, for hours at a time they would ponder his creation, weigh the infinitesimal variations of proportion, radius, sweep and angle. So they would infer the initiate's quality, judge his personal attributes, determine his understanding of Final Sentience, the Rationale and the Basis.

Occasionally the testimony of the *tand* revealed a character so tainted as to be reckoned intolerable. The vile *tand* would be cast into a furnace, the molten metal consigned to a latrine, the unlucky initiate expelled to the face of the planet, to live on his own terms.

The naked white-haired Demie, contemplating his own beautiful *tand*, sighed, moved restlessly. He had been visited by an influence so ardent, so passionate, so simultaneously cruel and tender, that his mind was oppressed. Unbidden, into his mind, came a dark seep of doubt.

Can it be, he asked himself, that we have insensibly wandered from the true Rationale? Do we study our *tands* with blinded eyes? . . . How to know, oh how to know! All is relative ease and facility in orthodoxy, yet how can it be denied that good is in itself undeniable? Absolutes are the most uncertain of all formulations, while the uncertainties are the most real . . .

Twenty miles over the mountains, in the long pale light of the Aerlith afternoon, Ervis Carcolo planned his own plans. "By daring, by striking hard, by cutting deep can I defeat him! In resolve, courage and endurance, I am more than his equal. Not again will he trick me, to slaughter my dragons and kill my men! Oh, Joaz Banbeck, how I will pay you for your deceit!" He raised his arms in wrath. "Oh Joaz Banbeck, you whey-faced sheep!" Carcolo smote the air with his fist. "I will crush you like a clod of dry moss!"

He frowned and rubbed his round red chin. But how? Where? He had every advantage! Carcolo pondered his possible stratagems. "He will expect me to strike. So much is certain. Doubtless he will again wait in ambush. So I will patrol every inch, but this too he will expect and so be wary lest I thunder upon him from above. Will he hide behind Despoire, or along Northguard, to catch me as I cross the Skanse? If so, I must approach by another route—through Maudlin Pass and under Mount Gethron? Then, if he is tardy in his march I will meet him on Banbeck Verge. And if he is early, I stalk him through the peaks and chasms . . ."

## VIII

With the cold rain of dawn pelting down upon them, with the trail illuminated only by lightning-glare, Ervis Carcolo, his dragons and his men set forth. When the first sparkle of sunlight struck Mount Despoire, they had already traversed Maudlin Pass.

So far, so good, exulted Ervis Carcolo. He stood high in his stirrups to scan Starbreak Fell. No sign of the Banbeck forces. He waited, scanning the far edge of Northguard Ridge, black against the sky. A minute passed. Two minutes. The men beat their hands together, the dragons rumbled and muttered fretfully.

Impatience began to prickle along Carcolo's ribs. He fidgeted and cursed. Could not the simplest of plans be carried through without mistake? But now the flicker of a heliograph from Barch Spike, and another to the southeast from the slopes of Mount Gethron. Carcolo waved forward his army; the way lay clear across Starbreak Fell. Down from Maudlin Pass surged the Happy Valley army: first the Long-horned Murderers, steel-spiked and crested with steel prongs; then the rolling red seethe of the Termagants, darting their heads as they ran; and, behind, the balance of the forces.

Starbreak Fell spread wide before them, a rolling slope strewn with flinty meteoric fragments which glinted like flowers on the gray-green moss. To all sides rose majestic peaks, snow blazing white in the clear morning light: Mount Gethron, Mount Despoire, Barch Spike and, far to the south, Clew Taw.

The scouts converged from left and right. They brought identical reports: no sign of Joaz Banbeck or his troops. Carcolo began to toy with a new possibility. Perhaps Joaz Banbeck had not deigned to take the field. The idea enraged him and filled him with a great joy: if so, Joaz would pay dearly for his neglect.

Halfway across Starbreak Fell they came upon a pen occupied by two hundred of Joaz Banbeck's spratling Fiends. Two old men and a boy tended the pen, and watched the Happy Valley horde advance with manifest terror.

But Carcolo rode past leaving the pen unmolested. If he won the day, it would become part of his spoils. If he lost, the spratling Fiends could do him no harm.

The old men and the boy stood on the roof of their turf hut, watching Carcolo and his troops pass: the men in black uniforms and black peaked caps with back-slanting ear-flaps; the dragons bounding, crawling, loping, plodding, according to their kind, scales glinting: the dull red and maroon of Termagants; the poisonous shine of the Blue Horrors; the black-green Fiends; the gray and brown Juggers and Murderers. Ervis Carcolo rode on the right flank, Bast Givven rode to the rear. And now Carcolo hastened the pace, haunted by the anxiety that Joaz Banbeck might bring his Fiends and Juggers up Banbeck Scarp before he arrived to thrust him back—assuming that Joaz Banbeck had been caught napping.

But Carcolo reached Banbeck Verge without challenge.

He shouted out in triumph, waved his cap high. "Joaz Banbeck the sluggard! Let him try now the ascent of Banbeck Scarp!" And Ervis Carcolo surveyed Banbeck Vale with the eye of a conqueror.

Bast Givven seemed to share none of Carcolo's triumph, and kept an uneasy watch to north and south and to the rear.

Carcolo observed him peevishly from the corner of his eye and presently called out, "Ho, ho, then! What's amiss?"

"Perhaps much. Perhaps nothing," said Bast Givven, searching the landscape.

Carcolo blew out his mustaches. Givven went on, in the cool voice which so completely irritated Carcolo. "Joaz Banbeck seems to be tricking us as before."

"Why do you say this?"

"Judge for yourself. Would he allow us advantage without claiming a miser's price?"

"Nonsense!" muttered Carcolo. "The sluggard is fat with his last victory." But he rubbed his chin and peered uneasily down into Banbeck Vale. From here it seemed curiously quiet. There was a strange inactivity in the fields and barracks. A chill began to grip Carcolo's heart —then he cried out. "Look at the brooder: there are the Banbeck dragons!"

Givven squinted down into the vale, glanced sidewise at Carcolo. "Three Termagants, in egg." He straightened, abandoned all interest in the vale and scrutinized the peaks and ridges to the north and east. "Assume that Joaz Banbeck set out before dawn, came up to the Verge, by the Slickenslides, crossed Blue Fell in strength—"

"What of Blue Crevasse?"

"He avoids Blue Crevasse to the north, comes over Barchback, steals across the Skanse and around Barch Spike . . ."

Carcolo studied Northguard Ridge with new and startled awareness. A quiver of movement, the glint of scales?

"Retreat!" roared Carcolo. "Make for Barch Spike! They're behind us!"

Startled, his army broke ranks, fled across Banbeck Verge, up into the harsh spurs of Barch Spike. Joaz, his strategy discovered, launched squads of Murderers to intercept the Happy Valley army, to engage and delay and, if possible, deny them the broken slopes of Barch Spike.

Carcolo calculated swiftly. His own Murderers he considered his finest troops, and held them in great pride. Purposely now he delayed, hoping to engage the Banbeck skirmishers, quickly destroy them and still gain the protection of the Barch declivities.

The Banbeck Murderers, however, refused to close, and scrambled for height up Barch Spike. Carcolo sent forward his Termagants and Blue Horrors.

With a horrid snarling the two lines met. The Banbeck Termagants rushed up, to be met by Carcolo's Striding Murderers and forced into humping pounding flight.

The main body of Carcolo's troops, excited at the sight of retreating foes, could not be restrained. They veered off from Barch Spike, plunged down upon Starbreak Fell. The striding Murderers overtook the Banbeck Termagants, climbed up their backs, toppled them over squealing and kicking, then knifed open the exposed pink bellies.

Banbeck's Long-horned Murderers came circling, struck from the flank into Carcolo's Striding Murderers, goring with steel-tipped horns, impaling on lances.

Somehow they overlooked Carcolo's Blue Horrors who sprang down upon them. With axes and maces they laid the Murderers low, performing the rather grisly entertainment of clambering on a subdued Murderer, seizing the horn, stripping back horn, skin and scales, from head to tail. So Joaz Banbeck lost thirty Termagants and perhaps two dozen Murderers. Nevertheless, the attack served its purpose, allowing him to bring his knights, Fiends and Juggers down from Northguard before Carcolo could gain the heights of Barch Spike.

Carcolo retreated in a slantwise line up the pocked slopes, and meanwhile sent six men across the fell to the pen where the spratling Fiends milled in fear at the battle. The men broke the gates, struck down the two old men, herded the young fiends across the fell toward the Banbeck troops. The hysterical spratlings obeyed their instincts. They clasped themselves to the neck of whatever dragon they first encountered, which thereupon became sorely hampered, for its own instincts prevented it from detaching the spratling by force.

This ruse, a brilliant improvisation, created enormous disorder among the Banbeck troops. Ervis Carcolo now charged with all his power directly into the Banbeck center. Two squads of Termagants fanned out to harass the men. His Murderers—the only category in which he outnumbered Joaz Banbeck—were sent to engage Fiends, while Carcolo's own Fiends, pampered, strong, glistening with oily strength, snaked in toward the Juggers. Under the great brown hulks they darted, lashing the fifty-pound steel ball at the tip of their tails against the inner side of the Jugger's legs.

A roaring melee ensued. Battle-lines were uncertain. Both men and dragons were crushed, torn apart, hacked to bits. The air sang with bullets, whistled with steel, reverberated to trumpeting, whistles, shouts, screams and bellows.

The reckless abandon of Carcolo's tactics achieved results out of proportion to his numbers. His Fiends burrowed ever deeper into the crazed and almost helpless Banbeck Juggers, while the Carcolo Murderers and Blue Horrors held back the Banbeck Fiends. Joaz Banbeck himself, assailed by Termagants, escaped with his life only by fleeing around behind the battle, where he picked up the support of a squad of Blue Horrors. In a fury he blew a withdrawal signal, and his army backed off down the slopes, leaving the ground littered with struggling and kicking bodies.

Carcolo, throwing aside all restraint, rose in his saddle and signaled to commit his own Juggers, which so far he had treasured like his own children.

Shrilling, hiccuping, they lumbered down into the seethe, tearing away great mouthfuls of flesh to right and left, ripping apart lesser dragons with their brachs, treading on Termagants, seizing Blue Horrors and Murderers, flinging them wailing and clawing through the air. Six Banbeck knights sought to stem the charge, firing their muskets point-blank into the demoniac faces; they went down and were seen no more.

Down on Starbreak Fell tumbled the battle. The nucleus of the fighting became less concentrated, the Happy Valley advantage dissipated. Carcolo hesitated, a long heady instant.

He and his troops alike were afire; the intoxication of unexpected success tingled in their brains—but here on Starbreak Fell, could they counter the odds posed by the greater Banbeck forces? Caution dictated that Carcolo withdraw up Barch Spike, to make the most of his limited victory. Already a strong platoon of Fiends had grouped and were maneuvering to charge his meager force of Juggers. Bast Givven approached, clearly expecting the word to retreat. But Carcolo still waited, reveling in the havoc being wrought by his paltry six Juggers.

Bast Givven's saturnine face was stern. "Withdraw, withdraw! It's annihilation when their flanks bear in on us!"

Carcolo seized his elbow. "Look! See where those Fiends gather, see where Joaz Banbeck rides! As soon as they charge, send six Striding Murderers from either side; close in on him, kill him!"

Givven opened his mouth to protest, looked where Carcolo pointed, rode to obey the orders.

Here came the Banbeck Fiends, moving with stealthy certainty toward the Happy Valley Juggers. Joaz, raising in his saddle, watched their progress. Suddenly from either side the Striding Murderers were on him. Four of his knights and six young cornets, screaming alarm, dashed back to protect him; there was clanging of steel on steel and steel on scale. The Murderers fought with sword and mace. The knights, their muskets useless, countered with cutlasses, one by one going under.

Rearing on hind legs the Murderer corporal hacked down at Joaz, who desperately fended off the blow. The Murderer raised sword and mace together—and from fifty yards a musket pellet smashed into its ear. Crazy with pain, it dropped its weapons, fell forward upon Joaz, writhing and kicking. Banbeck Blue Horrors came to attack; the Murderers darted back and forth over the thrashing corporal, stabbing down at Joaz, kicking at him, finally fleeing the Blue Horrors.

Ervis Carcolo groaned in disappointment. By a half-second only had he fallen short of victory. Joaz Banbeck, bruised, mauled, perhaps wounded, had escaped with his life.

Over the crest of the hill came a rider: an unarmed youth whipping a staggering Spider. Bast Givven pointed him out to Carcolo. "A messenger from the Valley, in urgency."

The lad careened down the fell toward Carcolo, shouting ahead, but his message was lost in the din of battle. At last he drew close. "The Basics, the Basics!"

Carcolo slumped like a half-empty bladder. "Where?"

"A great black ship, half the valley wide. I was up on the heath, I managed to escape." He pointed, whimpered.

"Speak, boy!" husked Carcolo. "What do they do?"

"I did not see; I ran to you."

Carcolo gazed across the battle-field; the Banbeck Fiends had almost reached his Juggers, who were backing slowly, with heads lowered, fangs fully extended.

Carcolo threw up his hands in despair. He ordered Givven, "Blow a retreat, break clear!"

Waving a white kerchief he rode around the battle to where Joaz Banbeck still lay on the ground, the quivering Murderer only just now being lifted from his legs. Joaz stared up, his face white as Carcolo's kerchief. At the sight of Carcolo his eyes grew wide and dark, his mouth became still.

Carcolo blurted, "The Basics have come once more; they have dropped into Happy Valley, they are destroying my people."

Joaz Banbeck, assisted by his knights, gained his feet. He stood swaying, arms limp, looking silently into Carcolo's face.

Carcolo spoke once more. "We must call truce. This battle is waste! With all our forces let us march to Happy Valley and attack the monsters before they destroy all of us! Ah, think what we could have achieved with the weapons of the sacerdotes!"

Joaz stood silent. Another ten seconds passed. Carcolo cried angrily, "Come now, what do you say?"

In a hoarse voice Joaz spoke, "I say no truce. You rejected my warning. You thought to loot Banbeck Vale. I will show you no mercy."

Carcolo gaped, his mouth a red hole under the sweep of his mustaches. "But the Basics—"

"Return to your troops. You as well as the Basics are my enemy. Why should I choose between you? Prepare to fight for your life; I give you no truce."

Carcolo drew back a face as pale as Joaz's own. "Never shall you rest! Even though you win this battle here on Starbreak Fell, yet you shall never know victory. I will persecute you until you cry for relief."

Banbeck motioned to his knights. "Whip this dog back to his own."

Carcolo backed his Spider from the threatening flails, turned, loped away.

The tide of battle had turned. The Banbeck Fiends now had broken past his Blue Horrors. One of his Juggers was gone; another, facing three sidling Fiends, snapped its great jaws, waved its monstrous sword. The Fiends flicked and feinted with their steel balls, scuttled forward. The Jugger chopped, shattered its sword on the rock-hard armor of the Fiends; they were underneath, slamming their steel balls into the monstrous legs. It tried to hop clear, toppled majestically. The Fiends slit its belly, and now Carcolo had only five Juggers left.

"Back!" he cried. "Disengage!"

Up Barch Spike toiled his troops, the battle-front a roaring seethe of scales, armor, flickering metal. Luckily for Carcolo his rear was to the high ground, and after ten terrible minutes he was able to establish an orderly retreat.

Two more Juggers had fallen. The three remaining scrambled free. Seizing boulders, they hurled them down into the attackers, who, after a series of sallies and lunges, were well content to break clear. In any event Joaz, after hearing Carcolo's news, was of no disposition to spend further troops.

Carcolo, waving his sword in desperate defiance, led his troops back around Barch Spike, presently down across the dreary Skanse. Joaz turned back to Banbeck Vale. The news of the Basic raid had spread to all ears. The men rode sober and quiet, looking behind and overhead. Even the dragons seemed infected, and muttered restlessly among themselves.

As they crossed Blue Fell the almost omnipresent wind died. The stillness added to the oppression.

Termagants, like the men, began to watch the sky. Joaz wondered, how could they know, how could they sense the Basics? He himself searched the sky, and as his army passed down over the scarp he thought to see high over Mount Gethron, a fitting little black rectangle, which presently disappeared behind a crag.

## IX

Ervis Carcolo and the remnants of his army raced pell-mell down from the Skanse, through the wilderness of ravines and gulches at the base of Mount Despoire, out on the barrens to the west of Happy Valley. All pretense of military precision had been abandoned.

Carcolo led the way, his Spider sobbing with fatigue. Behind in disarray pounded first Murderers and Blue Horrors, with Termagants hurrying along behind. Then the Fiends, racing low to the ground, steel balls grinding on rocks, sending up sparks. Far in the rear lumbered the Juggers and their attendants.

Down to the verge of Happy Valley plunged the army and pulled up short, stamping and squealing. Carcolo jumped from his Spider, ran to the brink, stood looking down into the valley.

He had expected to see the ship, yet the actuality of the thing was so immediate and intense as to shock him. It was a tapered cylinder, glossy and black, resting in a field of legumes not far from ramshackle Happy Town. Polished metal disks at either end shimmered and glistened with fleeting films of color. There were three entrance ports—forward, central and aft—and from the central port a ramp had been extended to the ground.

The Basics had worked with ferocious efficiency. From the town straggled a line of people, herded by Heavy Troopers. Approaching the ship they passed through an inspection apparatus controlled by a pair of Basics. A series of instruments and the eyes of the Basics appraised each man, woman and child, classified them by some system not instantly obvious, whereupon the captives were either hustled up the ramp into the ship or prodded into a nearby booth.

Peculiarly, no matter how many persons entered, the booth never seemed to fill.

Carcolo rubbed his forehead with trembling fingers, turned his eyes to the ground. When once more he looked up, Bast Givven stood beside him, and together they stared down into the valley.

From behind came a cry of alarm. Starting around, Carcolo saw a black rectangular flyer sliding silently down from above Mount Gethron.

Waving his arms Carcolo ran for the rocks, bellowing orders to take cover. Dragons and men scuttled up the gulch. Overhead slid the flyer. A hatch opened, releasing a load of explosive pellets. They struck with a great rattling volley, and up into the air flew pebbles, rock splinters, fragments of bone, scales, skin and flesh. All who failed to reach cover were shredded.

The Termagants fared relatively well. The Fiends, though battered and scraped, had all survived. Two of the Juggers had been blinded, and could fight no more till they had grown new eyes.

The flyer slid back once more. Several of the men fired their muskets —an act of apparently futile defiance, but the flyer was struck and damaged. It twisted, veered, soared up in a roaring curve, swooped over its back, plunged toward the mountainside, crashed in a brilliant orange gush of fire. Carcolo shouted in maniac glee, jumped up and down, ran to the verge of the cliff, shook his fist at the ship below. He quickly quieted, to stand glum and shivering.

Then, turning to the ragged cluster of men and dragons who once more had crept down from the gulch, Carcolo cried hoarsely, "What do you say? Shall we fight? Shall we charge down upon them?"

There was silence.

Bast Givven replied in a colorless voice, "We are helpless. We can accomplish nothing. Why commit suicide?"

Carcolo turned away, heart too full for words. Givven spoke the obvious truth. They would either be killed or dragged aboard the ship; and then, on a world too strange for imagining, be put to uses too dismal to be borne.

Carcolo clenched his fists and looked westward with bitter hatred. "Joaz Banbeck, you brought me to this! When I might yet have fought for my people you detained me!"

"The Basics were here already," said Givven with unwelcome rationality. "We could have done nothing since we had nothing to do with."

"We could have fought!" bellowed Carcolo. "We might have swept down the Crotch and come upon them with all force! A hundred warriors and four hundred dragons—are these to be despised?"

Bast Givven judged further argument to be pointless. He pointed. "They now examine our brooders."

Carcolo turned to look, gave a wild laugh. "They are astonished! They are awed! And well have they a right to be."

Givven agreed. "I imagine the sight of a Fiend or a Blue Horror—not to mention a Jugger—gives them pause for reflection."

Down in the valley the grim business had ended. The Heavy Troopers marched back into the ship. A pair of enormous men twelve feet high came forth, lifted the booth, carried it up the ramp into the ship. Carcolo and his men watched with protruding eyes. "Giants!"

Bast Givven chuckled dryly. "The Basics stare at our Juggers, we ponder their Giants."

The Basics presently returned to the ship. The ramp was drawn up, the ports closed. From a turret in the bow came a shaft of energy, touching each of the three brooders in succession, and each exploded with great eruption of black bricks.

Carcolo moaned softly under his breath, but said nothing.

The ship trembled, floated. Carcolo bellowed an order; men and dragons rushed for cover. Flattened behind boulders they watched the black cylinder rise from the valley, drift to the west. "They make for Banbeck Vale," said Bast Givven.

Carcolo laughed, a cackle of mirthless glee. Bast Givven looked at him sidelong. Had Ervis Carcolo become addled? He turned away. A matter of no great moment.

Carcolo came to a sudden resolve. He stalked to one of the Spiders, mounted, swung around to face his men. "I ride to Banbeck Vale. Joaz Banbeck has done his best to despoil me; I shall do my best against him. I give no orders: come or stay as you wish. Only remember! Joaz Banbeck would not allow us to fight the Basics!"

He rode off. The men stared into the plundered valley, turned to look after Carcolo. The black ship was just now slipping over Mount Despoire. There was nothing for them in the valley. Grumbling and muttering, they summoned the bone-tired dragons and set off up the dreary mountainside.

Ervis Carcolo rode his Spider at a plunging run across the Skanse. Tremendous crags soared to either side, the blazing sun hung halfway up the black sky. Behind, the Skanse Ramparts; ahead, Barchback, Barch Spike and Northguard Ridge.

Oblivious to the fatigue of his Spider, Carcolo whipped it on. Gray-green moss pounded back from its wild feet, the narrow head hung low, foam trailed from its gill-vents. Carcolo cared nothing. His mind was empty of all but hate—for the Basics, for Joaz Banbeck, for Aerlith, for man, for human history.

Approaching Northguard the Spider staggered and fell. It lay moaning, neck outstretched, legs trailing back. Carcolo dismounted in disgust. He looked back down the long rolling slope of the Skanse to see how many of his troops had followed him. A man riding a Spider at a modest lope turned out to be Bast Givven, who presently came up beside him and inspected the fallen Spider. "Loosen the surcingle. He will recover the sooner." Carcolo glared, thinking to hear a new note in Givven's voice. Nevertheless he bent over the foundered dragon and slipped loose the broad bronze buckle. Givven dismounted, stretched his arms, massaged his thin legs. He pointed. "The Basic ship descends into Banbeck Vale."

Carcolo nodded grimly. "I would be an audience to the landing." He kicked the Spider. "Come, get up, have you not rested enough? Do you wish me to walk?"

The Spider whimpered its fatigue, but nevertheless struggled to its feet. Carcolo started to mount, but Bast Givven laid a restraining hand on his shoulder. Carcolo looked back in outrage: here was impertinence! Givven said calmly, "Tighten the surcingle, otherwise you will fall on the rocks and once more break your bones."

Uttering a spiteful phrase under his breath, Carcolo clasped the buckle back into position. The Spider cried out in despair. Paying no heed, Carcolo mounted, and the Spider moved off with trembling steps.

Barch Spike rose ahead like the prow of a white ship, dividing Northguard Ridge from Barchback. Carcolo paused to consider the landscape, tugging his mustaches.

Givven was tactfully silent. Carcolo looked back down the Skanse to the listless straggle of his army, then set off to the left.

Passing close under Mount Gethron, skirting the High Jambles, they descended an ancient water-course to Banbeck Verge. Though perforce they had come without great speed, the Basic ship had moved no faster. It had only started to settle into the vale, the disks at bow and stern swirling with furious colors.

Carcolo grunted bitterly. "Trust Joaz Banbeck to scratch his own

itch. Not a soul in sight! He's taken to his tunnels, dragons and all."
Pursing his mouth he rendered a mincing parody of Joaz's voice:
"'Ervis Carcolo, my dear friend, there is but one answer to attack: dig
tunnels!' And I replied to him, 'Am I a sacerdote to live underground?
Burrow and delve, Joaz Banbeck, do as you will. I am but an old-time
man; I go under the cliffs only when I must.'"

Givven gave the faintest of shrugs.

Carcolo went on, "Tunnels or not, they'll winkle him out. If need
be they'll blast open the entire valley. They've no lack of tricks."

Givven grinned sardonically. "Joaz Banbeck knows a trick or two
—as we know to our sorrow."

"Let him capture two dozen Basics today," snapped Carcolo. "Then
I'll concede him a clever man." He stalked away to the very brink of the
cliff, standing in full view of the Basic ship. Givven watched without
expression.

Carcolo pointed. "Aha! Look there!"

"Not I," said Givven. "I respect the Basic weapons too greatly."

"Pah!" spat Carcolo. Nevertheless he moved a trifle back from the
brink. "There are dragons in Kergan's Way. For all Joaz Banbeck's talk
of tunnels." He gazed north along the valley a moment or two, then
threw up his hands in frustration. "Joaz Banbeck will not come up
here to me. There is nothing I can do. Unless I walk down into the
village, seek him out and strike him down, he will escape me."

"Unless the Basics captured the two of you and confined you in the
same pen," said Givven.

"Bah!" muttered Carcolo, and moved off to one side.

x

The vision-plates which allowed Joaz Banbeck to observe the length
and breadth of Banbeck Vale for the first time were being put to practical use.

He had evolved the scheme while playing with a set of old lenses,
and dismissed it as quickly. Then one day, while trading with the sacerdotes in the cavern under Mount Gethron, he had proposed that they
design and supply the optics for such a system.

The blind old sacerdote who conducted the trading gave an ambiguous reply. The possibility of such a project, under certain circumstances, might well deserve consideration. Three months passed. The
scheme receded to the back of Joaz Banbeck's mind. Then the sacerdote in the trading-cave inquired if Joaz still planned to install the
viewing system. If so he might take immediate delivery of the optics.

Joaz agreed to the barter price, returned to Banbeck Vale with four heavy crates. He ordered the necessary tunnels driven, installed the lenses, and found that with the study darkened he could command all quarters of Banbeck Vale.

Now, with the Basic ship darkening the sky, Joaz Banbeck stood in his study, watching the descent of the great black hulk.

At the back of the chamber maroon portieres parted. Clutching the cloth with taut fingers stood the minstrel-maiden Phade. Her face was pale, her eyes bright as opals. In a husky voice she called, "The ship of death. It has come to gather souls!"

Joaz turned her a stony glance and turned back to the honed-glass screen. "The ship is clearly visible."

Phade ran forward, clasped Joaz's arm, swung around to look into his face. "Let us try to escape into the High Jambles. Don't let them take us so soon!"

"No one deters you," said Joaz indifferently. "Escape in any direction you choose."

Phade stared at him blankly, then turned her head and watched the screen. The great black ship sank with sinister deliberation, the disks at bow and stern now shimmering mother-of-pearl. Phade looked back to Joaz, licked her lips. "Are you not afraid?"

Joaz smiled thinly. "What good to run? Their Trackers are swifter than Murderers, more vicious than Termagants. They can smell you a mile away, take you from the very center of the Jambles."

Phade shivered with superstitious horror. She whispered, "Let them take me dead, then. I can't go with them alive."

Joaz suddenly cursed. "Look where they land! In our best field of bellegarde!"

"What is the difference?"

" 'Difference?' Must we stop eating because they pay their visit?"

Phade looked at him in a daze, beyond comprehension. She sank slowly to her knees and began to perform the ritual gestures of the Theurgic cult. Hands palm down to either side, slowly up till the back of the hand touched the ears, and the simultaneous protrusion of the tongue; over and over again, eyes staring with hypnotic intensity into emptiness.

Joaz ignored the gesticulations, until Phade, her face screwed up into a fantastic mask, began to sigh and whimper. Then he swung the flaps of his jacket into her face. "Give over your folly!"

Phade collapsed moaning to the floor. Joaz's lips twitched in annoyance. Impatiently he hoisted her erect. "Look you, these Basics are

neither ghouls nor angels of death. They are no more than pallid Termagants, the basic stock of our dragons. So now, give over your idiocy,
or I'll have Rife take you away."

"Why do you not make ready? You watch and do nothing."

"There is nothing more that I can do."

Phade drew a deep shuddering sigh, stared dully at the screen. "Will
you fight them?"

"Naturally."

"How can you hope to counter such miraculous power?"

"We will do what we can. They have not yet met our dragons."

The ship came to rest in a purple and green vine-field across the valley, near the mouth of Clybourne Crevasse. The port slid back and a
ramp rolled forth. "Look," said Joaz, "there you see them."

Phade stared at the queer pale shapes who had come tentatively out
on the ramp. "They seem strange and twisted, like silver puzzles for
children."

"They are the Basics. From their eggs came our dragons. They have
done as well with men: look, here are their Heavy Troops."

Down the ramp, four abreast, in exact cadence, marched the Heavy
Troops, to half fifty yards in front of the ship. There were three squads
of twenty: short squat men with massive shoulders, thick necks and
stern, down-drawn faces. They wore armor fashioned from overlap-
ping scales of black and blue metal, a wide belt slung with pistol and
sword. Black epaulettes, extending past their shoulders, supported a
short ceremonial flap of black cloth ranging down their backs. Their
helmets bore a crest of sharp spikes. Their knee-high boots were armed
with kick-knives.

A number of Basics now rode forth. Their mounts were creatures
only remotely resembling men. They ran on hands and feet, backs high
off the ground. Their heads were long and hairless, with quivering
loose lips. The Basics controlled them with negligent touches of a quirt,
and once on the ground set them cantering smartly through the bellegarde. Meanwhile a team of Heavy Troopers rolled a three-wheeled
mechanism down the ramp, directed its complex snout toward the
village.

"Never before have they prepared so carefully," muttered Joaz. "Here
come the Trackers." He counted. "Only two dozen? Perhaps they are
hard to breed. Generations pass slowly with men; dragons lay a clutch
of eggs every year . . ."

The Trackers moved to the side and stood in a loose restless group:
gaunt creatures seven feet tall, with bulging black eyes, beaked noses,

small undershot mouths pursed as if for kissing. From narrow shoulders long arms dangled and swung like ropes. As they waited they flexed their knees, staring sharply up and down the valley, in constant restless motion. After them came a group of Weaponeers—unmodified men wearing loose cloth smocks and cloth hats of green and yellow. They brought with them two more three-wheeled contrivances which they at once began to adjust and test.

The entire group became still and tense.

The Heavy Troopers stepped forward with a stumping, heavy-legged gait, hands ready at pistols and swords. "Here they come," said Joaz. Phade made a quiet desperate sound, knelt and once more began to perform Theurgic gesticulations. Joaz in disgust ordered her from the study. He went to a panel equipped with a bank of six direct-wire communications, the construction of which he had personally supervised. He spoke into three of the telephones, assuring himself that his defenses were alert, then returned to the honed-glass screens.

Across the field of bellegarde came the Heavy Troopers, faces heavy, hard, marked with down-veering creases. Upon either flank the Weaponeers trundled their three-wheeled mechanisms, but the Trackers waited beside the ship. About a dozen Basics rode behind the Heavy Troopers, carrying bulbous weapons on their backs.

A hundred yards from the portal into Kergan's Way, beyond the range of the Banbeck muskets, the invaders halted. A Heavy Trooper ran to one of the Weaponeers' carts, thrust his shoulders under a harness and stood erect. He now carried a gray machine, from which extended a pair of black globes. The Trooper scuttled toward the village like an enormous rat, while from the black globes streamed a flux, intended to interfere with the neural currents of the Banbeck defenders, and so immobilize them.

Explosions sounded. Puffs of smoke appeared from nooks and vantages through the crags. Bullets spat into the ground beside the Trooper. Several caromed off his armor.

At once heat-beams from the ship stabbed against the cliff walls. In his study Joaz Banbeck smiled. The smoke puffs were decoys. The actual shots came from other areas. The Trooper, dodging and jerking, avoided a rain of bullets and ran under the portal, above which two men waited. Affected by the flux, they tottered, stiffened, but nevertheless dropped a great stone which struck the Trooper where the neck joined his shoulders and hurled him to the ground.

He thrashed his arms and legs up and down, rolled over and over. Then, bouncing to his feet, he raced back into the valley, soaring and bounding, finally to stumble, plunge headlong to the ground and lay kicking and quivering.

The Basic army watched with no apparent concern or interest.

There was a moment of inactivity. Then from the ship came an invisible field of vibration, traveling across the face of the cliff.

Where the focus struck, puffs of dust arose and loose rock became dislodged. A man, lying on a ledge, sprang to his feet, dancing and twisting, plunged two hundred feet to his death. Passing across one of Joaz Banbeck's spy-holes, the vibration was carried into the study where it set up a nerve-grinding howl. The vibration passed along the cliff. Joaz rubbed his aching head.

Meanwhile the Weaponeers discharged one of their instruments. First there came a muffled explosion, then through the air curved a wobbling gray sphere. Inaccurately aimed, it struck the cliff and burst in a great gush of yellow-white gas. The mechanism exploded once more, and this time lobbed the bomb accurately into Kergan's Way—which was now deserted. The bomb produced no effect.

In his study Joaz waited grimly. To now the Basics had taken only tentative, almost playful, steps. More serious efforts would surely follow.

Wind dispersed the gas; the situation remained as before. The casualties so far had been one Heavy Trooper and one Banbeck rifleman.

From the ship now came a stab of red flame, harsh, decisive. The rock at the portal shattered. Slivers sang and spun; the Heavy Troopers jogged forward.

Joaz spoke into his telephone, bidding his captains caution, lest in counter-attacking against a feint they expose themselves to a new gas bomb.

But the Heavy Troopers stormed into Kergan's Way—in Joaz's mind an act of contemptuous recklessness. He gave a curt order.

Out from passages and areas swarmed his dragons: Blue Horrors, Fiends, Termagants.

The squat Troopers stared with sagging jaws. Here were unexpected antagonists! Kergan's Way resounded with their calls and orders. First they fell back, then, with the courage of desperation, fought furiously. Up and down Kergan's Way raged the battle.

Certain relationships quickly became evident. In the narrow defile neither the Trooper pistols nor the steel-weighted tails of the Fiends could be used effectively. Cutlasses were useless against dragon-scale, but the pincers of the Blue Horrors, the Termagant daggers, the axes, swords, fangs and claws of the Fiends, did bloody work against the

Heavy Troopers. A single Trooper and a single Termagant were approximately a match; though the Trooper, gripping the dragon with massive arms, tearing away its brachs, breaking back its neck, won more often than the Termagant. But if two or three Termagants confronted a single Trooper, he was doomed. As soon as he committed himself to one, another would crush his legs, blind him or hack open his throat.

So the Troopers fell back to the valley floor, leaving twenty of their fellows dead in Kergan's Way. The Banbeck men once more opened fire, but once more with minor effect.

Joaz watched from his study, wondering as to the next Basic tactic. Enlightenment was not long in coming. The Heavy Troopers regrouped and stood panting, while the Basics rode back and forth receiving information, admonishing, advising, chiding.

From the black ship came a gush of energy, to strike the cliff above Kergan's Way. The study rocked with the concussion.

Joaz backed away from the vision-plates. What if a ray struck one of his collecting lenses? Might not the energy be guided and reflected directly toward him?

He departed his study as it shook to a new explosion.

He ran through a passage, descended a staircase, emerged into one of the central galleries, to find apparent confusion. White-faced women and children, retiring deeper into the mountain, pushed past dragons and men in battle-gear entering one of the new tunnels. Joaz watched for a moment or two to satisfy himself that the confusion held no panic, then joined his warriors in the tunnel leading north.

In some past era an entire section of the cliff at the head of the valley had sloughed off, creating a jungle of piled rock and boulders: the Banbeck Jambles. Here, through a fissure, the new tunnel opened; and here Joaz went with his warriors. Behind them, down the valley, sounded the rumble of explosions as the black ship began to demolish Banbeck Village.

Joaz, peering around a boulder, watched in a fury, as great slabs of rock began to scale away from the cliff.

Then he stared in astonishment, for to the Basic troops had come an extraordinary reinforcement: eight Giants twice an ordinary man's stature—barrel-chested monsters, gnarled of arm and legs, with pale eyes, shocks of tawny hair. They wore brown and red armor with black epaulettes, and carried swords, maces and blast-cannon slung over their backs.

Joaz considered. The presence of the Giants gave him no reason to alter his central strategy, which in any event was vague and intuitive. He must be prepared to suffer losses, and could only hope to inflict greater losses on the Basics. But what did they care for the lives of their troops? Less than he cared for his dragons. And if they destroyed Banbeck Village, ruined the Vale, how could he do corresponding damage to them?

He looked over his shoulder at the tall white cliffs, wondering how closely he had estimated the position of the sacerdote's hall. And now he must act; the time had come.

He signaled to a small boy, one of his own sons, who took a deep breath, hurled himself blindly away from the shelter of the rocks, ran helter-skelter out to the valley floor. A moment later his mother ran forth to snatch him up and dash back into the Jambles.

"Done well," Joaz commended them. "Done well indeed." Cautiously he again looked forth through the rocks. The Basics were gazing intently in his direction.

For a long moment, while Joaz tingled with suspense, it seemed that they had ignored his ploy. They conferred, came to a decision, flicked the leathery buttocks of their mounts with their quirts. The creatures pranced sidewise, then loped north up the valley. The Trackers fell in behind, then came the Heavy Troopers moving at a humping quickstep. The Weaponeers followed with their three-wheeled mechanisms, and ponderously at the rear came the eight Giants.

Across the fields of bellegarde and vetch, over vines, hedges, beds of berries and stands of oil-pod tramped the raiders, destroying with a certain morose satisfaction.

The Basics prudently halted before the Banbeck Jambles, while the Trackers ran ahead like dogs, clambering over the first boulders, rearing high to test the air for odor, peering, listening, pointing, twittering doubtfully to each other. The Heavy Troopers moved in carefully, and their near presence spurred on the Trackers.

Abandoning caution, they bounded into the heart of the Jambles, emitting squeals of horrified consternation when a dozen Blue Horrors dropped among them. They clawed out heat-guns, in their excitement burning friend and foe alike. With silken ferocity the Blue Horrors ripped them apart. Screaming for aid, kicking, flailing, thrashing, those who were able fled as precipitously as they had come.

Only twelve from the original twenty-four regained the valley floor; and even as they did so, even as they cried out in relief at winning free from death, a squad of Long-horned Murderers burst out upon them, and these surviving Trackers were knocked down, gored, hacked.

The Heavy Troopers charged forward with hoarse calls of rage, aiming pistols, swinging swords; but the Murderers retreated to the shelter of the boulders.

Within the Jambles the Banbeck men had appropriated the heat-guns dropped by the Trackers. Warily coming forward, they tried to burn the Basics. But, unfamiliar with the weapons, the men neglected either to focus or condense the flame. The Basics were no more than mildly singed. Hastily they whipped their mounts back out of range. The Heavy Troopers, halting not a hundred feet in front of the Jambles, sent in a volley of explosive pellets, which killed two of the Banbeck knights and forced the others back.

## XI

At a discreet distance the Basics appraised the situation. The Weaponeers came up and, while awaiting instructions, conferred in low tones with the mounts.

One of these Weaponeers was now summoned and given orders. He divested himself of all his weapons and holding his empty hands in the air marched forward to the edge of the Jambles. Choosing a gap between a pair of ten-foot boulders, he resolutely entered the rock-maze.

A Banbeck knight escorted him to Joaz. Here, by chance, were also half a dozen Termagants. The Weaponeer paused uncertainly, made a mental readjustment, approached the Termagants. Bowing respectfully he started to speak. The Termagants listened without interest, and presently one of the knights directed him to Joaz.

"Dragons do not rule men on Aerlith," said Joaz dryly. "What is your message?"

The Weaponeer looked dubiously toward the Termagants, then somberly back to Joaz. "You are authorized to act for the entire warren?" He spoke slowly in a dry bland voice, selecting his words with conscientious care.

Joaz repeated shortly, "What is your message?"

"I bring an integration from my masters."

" 'Integration?' I do not understand you."

"An integration of the instantaneous vectors of destiny. An interpretation of the future. They wish the sense conveyed to you in the following terms: 'Do not waste lives, both ours and your own. You are valuable to us and will be given treatment in accordance with this value. Surrender to the Rule. Cease the wasteful destruction of enterprise.' "

Joaz frowned. "Destruction of 'enterprise?' "

"The reference is to the content of your genes. The message is at its end. I advise you to accede. Why waste your blood, why destroy yourselves? Come forth now with me. All will be for the best."

Joaz gave a brittle laugh. "You are a slave. How can you judge what is best for us?"

The Weaponeer blinked. "What choice is there for you? All residual pockets of disorganized life are to be expunged. The way of facility is best." He inclined his head respectfully toward the Termagants. "If you doubt me, consult your own Revered Ones. They will advise you."

"There are no Revered Ones here," said Joaz. "The dragons fight with us and for us; they are our fellow-warriors. But I have an alternate proposal. Why do not you and your fellows join us? Throw off your slavery, become free men! We will take the ship and go searching for the old worlds of men."

The Weaponeer exhibited only polite interest. "'Worlds of men?' There are none of them. A few residuals such as yourself remain in the desolate regions. All are to be expunged. Would you not prefer to serve the Rule?"

"Would you not prefer to be a free man?"

The Weaponeer's face showed mild bewilderment. "You do not understand me. If you choose—"

"Listen carefully," said Joaz. "You and your fellows can be your own masters, live among other men."

The Weaponeer frowned. "Who would wish to be a wild savage? To whom would we look for law, control, direction, order?"

Joaz threw up his hands in disgust, but made one last attempt. "I will provide all these; I will undertake such a responsibility. Go back, kill all the Basics—the Revered Ones, as you call them. These are my first orders."

"Kill them?" The Weaponeer's voice was soft with horror.

"Kill them." Joaz spoke as if to a child. "Then we men will possess the ship. We will go to find the worlds where men are powerful—"

"There are no such worlds."

"Ah, but there must be! At one time men roamed every star in the sky."

"No longer."

"What of Eden?"

"I know nothing of it."

Joaz threw up his hands. "Will you join us?"

"What would be the meaning of such an act?" said the Weaponeer gently. "Come then. Lay down your arms, submit to the Rule." He glanced doubtfully toward the Termagants. "Your own Revered Ones will receive fitting treatment. Have no fear on this account."

"You fool! These 'Revered Ones' are slaves, just as you are a slave to the Basics! We breed them to serve us, just as you are bred! Have at least the grace to recognize your own degradation!"

The Weaponeer blinked. "You speak in terms I do not completely understand. You will not surrender then?"

"No. We will kill all of you, if our strength holds out."

The Weaponeer bowed, turned, departed through the rocks. Joaz followed, peered out over the valley floor.

The Weaponeer made his report to the Basics, who listened with characteristic detachment. They gave an order, and the Heavy Troopers, spreading out in a skirmish line, moved slowly in toward the rocks.

Behind lumbered the Giants, blasters slung forward at the ready, and about twenty Trackers, survivors of the first foray. The Heavy Troopers reached the rocks, peered in. The Trackers clambered above, searching for ambushes, and finding none, signaled back. With great caution the Heavy Troopers entered the Jambles, necessarily breaking formation. Twenty feet they advanced, fifty feet, a hundred feet. Emboldened, the vengeful Trackers sprang forward over the rocks . . . and up surged the Termagants.

Screaming and cursing the Trackers scrambled back, pursued by the dragons. The Heavy Troopers recoiled, then swung up their weapons, fired. Two Termagants were struck under the lower armpits, their most vulnerable spot. Floundering, they tumbled down among the rocks. Others, maddened, jumped squarely down upon the Troopers. There was roaring, squealing, cries of shock and pain. The Giants lumbered up, and grinning vastly plucked away the Termagants, wrenched off their heads, flung them high over the rocks. Those Termagants who were able scuttled back, leaving half a dozen Heavy Troopers wounded, two with their throats torn open.

Again the Heavy Troopers moved forward, with the Trackers reconnoitering above, but more warily. The Trackers froze, yelled a warning. The Heavy Troopers stopped short, calling to each other, swinging their guns nervously. Overhead the Trackers scrambled back, and through the rocks, over the rocks, came dozens of Fiends and Blue Horrors.

The Heavy Troopers, grimacing dourly, fired their pistols; and the air reeked with the stench of burning scale, exploded viscera. The dragons surged in upon the men, and now began a terrible battle among the rocks, with the pistols, the maces, even the swords useless for lack of room.

The Giants lumbered forward and in turn were attacked by Fiends. Astonished, the idiotic grins faded from their faces; they hopped awkwardly back from the steel-weighted tails, but among the rocks the Fiends were also at a disadvantage, their steel balls clattering and jarring away from rock more often than flesh.

The Giants, recovering, discharged their chest-projectors into the melée. Fiends were torn apart as well as Blue Horrors and Heavy Troopers, the Giants making no distinction.

Over the rocks came another wave of dragons: Blue Horrors. They slid down on the heads of the Giants, clawing, stabbing, tearing. In a frenzy the Giants tore at the creatures, flung them to the ground, stamped on them, and the Heavy Troopers burnt them with their pistols.

From nowhere, for no reason, there came a lull.

Ten seconds, fifteen seconds passed, with no sound but whimpering and moaning from wounded dragons and men. A sense of imminence weighted the air, and here came the Juggers, looming through the passages.

For a brief period Giants and Juggers looked each other face to face. Then Giants groped for their blast-projectors, while Blue Horrors sprang down once more, grappling the Giant arms. The Juggers stumped quickly forward. Dragon-brachs grappled Giant arms; bludgeons and maces swung, dragon armor and man armor crushed and ground apart. Man and dragon tumbled over and over, ignoring pain, shock, mutilation.

The struggle became quiet. Sobbing and wheezing replaced the roars, and presently eight Juggers, superior in mass and natural armament, staggered away from eight destroyed Giants.

The Troopers meanwhile had drawn together, standing back to back in clots. Step by step, burning with heat-beams the screaming Horrors, Termagants and Fiends who lunged after them, they retreated toward the valley floor, and finally won free of the rocks. The pursuing Fiends, anxious to fight in the open, sprang into their midst, while from the flanks came Long-horned Murderers and Striding Murderers. In a spirit of reckless jubilation, a dozen men riding Spiders, carrying blast-cannon taken from the fallen Giants, charged the Basics and Weaponeers, who waited beside the rather casual emplacement of three-wheeled weapons. The Basics, without shame, jerked their man-mounts around and fled toward the black ship.

The Weaponeers swiveled their mechanisms, aimed, discharged

bursts of energy. One man fell, two men, three men—then the others were among the Weaponeers, who were soon hacked to pieces . . . including the persuasive individual who had served as envoy.

Several of the men, whooping and hooting, set out in chase of the Basics. But the human mounts, springing along like monstrous rabbits, carried the Basics as fast as the Spiders carried the men.

From the Jambles came a horn signal. The mounted men halted, wheeled back; the entire Banbeck force turned and retreated full speed into the Jambles.

The Troopers stumbled a few defiant steps in pursuit, then halted in sheer fatigue.

Of the original three squads, not enough men to make up a single squad survived. The eight Giants had perished, all Weaponeers and almost the entire group of Trackers.

The Banbeck forces gained the Jambles with seconds only to spare. From the black ship came a volley of explosive pellets, to shatter the rocks at the spot where they had disappeared.

On a wind-polished cape of rock above Banbeck Vale Ervis Carcolo and Bast Givven had watched the battle.

The rocks hid the greater part of the fighting. The cries and clangor rose faint and tinny, like insect noise. There would be the glint of dragon scale, glimpses of running men, the shadow and flicker of movement, but not until the mangled forces of the Basics staggered forth did the outcome of the battle reveal itself. Carcolo shook his head in sour bewilderment. "The crafty devil, Joaz Banbeck! He's turned them back. He's slaughtered their best!"

"It would appear," said Bast Givven, "that dragons armed with fangs, swords and steel balls are more effective than men with guns and heatbeams—at least in close quarters."

Carcolo grunted. "I might have done as well myself, under like circumstances." He turned Bast Givven a waspish glance.

"Do you not agree?"

"Certainly. Beyond question."

"Of course," Carcolo went on, "I had not the advantage of preparation. The Basics surprised me, but Joaz Banbeck labored under no such handicap." He looked back down into Banbeck Vale, where the Basic ship was bombarding the Jambles, shattering rocks into splinters. "Do they plan to blast the Jambles out of the valley? In which case, of course, Joaz Banbeck would have no further refuge. Their strategy is clear. And as I suspected: reserve forces!"

Another thirty Troopers had marched down the ramp to stand immobile in the trampled field before the ship.

Carcolo pounded his fist into his palm. "Bast Givven, listen now, listen carefully! For it is in our power to do a great deed, to reserve our fortunes! Notice Clybourne Crevasse, how it opens into the Vale, directly behind the Basic ship."

"Your ambition will yet cost us our lives."

Carcolo laughed. "Come, Givven, how many times does a man die? What better way to lose a life than in the pursuit of glory?"

Bast Givven turned, surveyed the meager remnants of the Happy Valley army. "We could win glory by trouncing a dozen sacerdotes. Flinging ourselves upon a Basic ship is hardly needful."

"Nevertheless," said Ervis Carcolo, "that is how it must be. I ride ahead, you marshal the forces and follow. We meet at the head of Clybourne Crevasse, on the west edge of the Vale!"

XII

Stamping his feet, muttering nervous curses, Ervis Carcolo waited at the head of Clybourne Crevasse.

Unlucky chance after chance paraded before his imagination. The Basics might surrender to the difficulties of Banbeck Vale and depart. Joaz Banbeck might attack across the open fields to save Banbeck Village from destruction and so destroy himself. Bast Givven might be unable to control the disheartened men and mutinous dragons of Happy Valley. Any of these situations might occur; any would expunge Carcolo's dreams of glory and leave him a broken man.

Back and forth he paced the scarred granite. Every few seconds he peered down into Banbeck Vale. Every few seconds he turned to scan the bleak skylines for the dark shapes of his dragons, the taller silhouettes of his men.

Beside the Basic ship waited a scanty two squads of Heavy Troopers: those who had survived the original attack and the reserves. They squatted in silent groups, watching the leisurely destruction of Banbeck Village. Fragment by fragment, the spires, towers and cliffs which had housed the Banbeck folk cracked off, slumped down into an ever-growing mound of rubble. An even heavier barrage poured against the Jambles. Boulders broke like eggs. Rock splinters drifted down the valley.

A half hour passed. Ervis Carcolo seated himself glumly on a rock.

A jingle, the pad of feet: Carcolo bounded to his feet. Winding across the skyline came the sorry remnants of his forces, the men dispirited, the Termagants surly and petulant, a mere handful each of Fiends, Blue Horrors and Murderers.

Carcolo's shoulders sagged. What could be accomplished with a force so futile as this? He took a deep breath. Show a brave front! Never say die! He assumed his bluffest mien. Stepping forward, he cried out, "Men, dragons! Today we have known defeat, but the day is not over. The time of redemption is at hand; we shall revenge ourselves on both the Basics and Joaz Banbeck!"

He searched the faces of his men, hoping for enthusiasm. They looked back at him without interest. The dragons, their understanding less complete, snorted softly, hissed and whispered. "Men and dragons!" bawled Carcolo. "You ask me, how shall we achieve these glories? I answer, follow where I lead! Fight where I fight! What is death to us, with our valley despoiled?"

Again he inspected his troops, once more finding only listlessness and apathy. Carcolo stifled the roar of frustration which rose into his throat, and turned away. "Advance!" he called gruffly over his shoulder. Mounting his drooping Spider, he set off down Clybourne Crevasse.

The Basic ship pounded the Jambles and Banbeck Village with equal vehemence. From a vantage on the west rim of the valley Joaz Banbeck watched the blasting of corridor after familiar corridor. Apartments and halls hewn earnestly from the rock, carved, tooled, polished across the generations—all opened, destroyed, pulverized. Now the target became that spire which contained Joaz Banbeck's private apartments, with his study, his workroom, the Banbeck reliquarium.

Joaz clenched and unclenched his fists, furious at his own helplessness. The goal of the Basics was clear. They intended to destroy Banbeck Vale, to exterminate as completely as possible the men of Aerlith —and what could prevent them?

Joaz studied the Jambles. The old talus had been splintered away almost to the sheer face of the cliff. Where was the opening into the Great Hall of the sacerdotes? His far-fetched hypotheses were diminishing to futility. Another hour would see the utter devastation of Banbeck Village.

Joaz tried to control a sickening sense of frustration. How to stop the destruction? He forced himself to calculate. Clearly, an attack across the valley floor was equivalent to suicide. But behind the black ship opened a ravine similar to that in which Joaz stood concealed: Clybourne Crevasse. The ship's entry gaped wide, Heavy Troopers squatted listlessly to the side. Joaz shook his head with a sour grimace. Inconceivable that the Basics could neglect so obvious a threat.

Still—in their arrogance might they not overlook the possibility of so insolent an act?

Indecision tugged Joaz forward and backward. And now a barrage of explosive pellets split open the spire which housed his apartments. The reliquarium, the ancient trove of the Banbeck's, was about to be destroyed . . . Joaz made a blind gesture, jumped to his feet, called the closest of his dragon-masters.

"Assemble the Murderers, three squads of Termagants, two dozen Blue Horrors, ten Fiends, all the riders. We climb to Banbeck Verge. We descend Clybourne Crevasse. We attack the ship!"

The dragon-master departed. Joaz gave himself to gloomy contemplation. If the Basics intended to draw him into a trap, they were about to succeed.

The dragon-master returned. "The force is assembled."

"We ride."

Up the ravine surged men and dragons, emerging upon Banbeck Verge. Swinging south, they came to the head of Clybourne Crevasse.

A knight at the head of the column suddenly signaled a halt. When Joaz approached he pointed out marks on the floor of the crevasse. "Dragons and men have passed here recently."

Joaz studied the tracks. "Heading down the crevasse."

"Yes."

Joaz dispatched a party of scouts who presently came galloping wildly back. "Ervis Carcolo, with men and dragons, is attacking the ship!"

Joaz wheeled his Spider and plunged headlong down the dim passage, followed by his army.

Outcries and screams of battle reached their ears as they approached the mouth of the crevasse. Bursting out on the valley floor Joaz came upon a scene of desperate carnage, with dragon and Heavy Trooper hacking, stabbing, burning, blasting. Where was Ervis Carcolo?? Joaz recklessly rode to look into the entry port. It hung wide! Ervis Carcolo then had forced his way into the ship!

A trap? Or had he effectuated Joaz's own plan of seizing the ship? What of the Heavy Troopers? Would the Basics sacrifice forty warriors to capture a handful of men? Unreasonable—but now the Heavy Troopers were holding their own. They had formed a phalanx, they now concentrated the energy of their weapons on those dragons who yet opposed them. A trap? If so, it was sprung—unless Ervis Carcolo already had captured the ship. Joaz rose in his saddle, signaled his company. "Attack!"

The Heavy Troopers were doomed. Striding Murderers hewed from above, Long-horned Murderers thrust from below, Blue Horrors pinched, clipped, dismembered. The battle was done, but Joaz, with men and Termagants, had already charged up the ramp. From within came the hum and throb of power, and also human sounds—cries and shouts of fury.

The sheer ponderous bulk struck at Joaz. He stopped short, peered uncertainly into the ship. Behind him his men waited, muttering under their breath.

Joaz asked himself, "Am I as brave as Ervis Carcolo? What is bravery, in any case? I am completely afraid: I dare not enter, I dare not stay outside." He put aside all caution and rushed forward, followed by his men and a horde of scuttling Termagants.

Even as Joaz entered the ship he knew Ervis Carcolo had not succeeded. Above him the guns still sang and hissed. Joaz's apartments splintered apart. Another tremendous volley struck into the Jambles, laying bare the naked stone of cliff, and what was hitherto hidden: the edge of a tall opening.

Joaz, inside the ship, found himself in an ante-chamber. The inner port was closed. He sidled forward, peered through a rectangular pane into what seemed a lobby or staging chamber. Ervis Carcolo and his knights crouched against the far wall, casually guarded by about twenty Weaponeers. A group of Basics rested in an alcove to the side, relaxed, quiet, their attitude one of contemplation.

Carcolo and his men were not completely subdued. As Joaz watched Carcolo lunged furiously forward. A purple crackle of energy punished him, hurled him back against the wall.

From the alcove one of the Basics, staring across the inner chamber, took note of Joaz Banbeck. He flicked out with his brach, touched a rod. An alarm whistle sounded, the outer port slid shut. A trap? An emergency process? The result was the same. Joaz motioned to four men, heavily burdened. They came forward, kneeled, placed on the deck four of the blast cannon which the Giants had carried into the Jambles.

Joaz swung his arm. Cannon belched; metal creaked, melted; acrid odors permeated the room. The hole was still too small. "Again!" The cannon flamed; the inner port vanished.

Into the gap sprang Weaponeers, firing their energy guns. Purple fire cut into the Banbeck ranks. Men curled, twisted, wilted, fell with clenched fingers and contorted faces. Before the cannon could respond, red-scaled shapes scuttled forward: Termagants. Hissing and wailing, they swarmed over the Weaponeers, on into the staging chamber. In front of the alcove occupied by the Basics they stopped short, as if in astonishment. The men crowding after fell silent. Even Carcolo watched in fascination.

Basic stock confronted its derivative, each seeing in the other its caricature. The Termagants crept forward with sinister deliberation. The Basics waved their brachs, whistled, fluted. The Termagants scuttled forward, sprang into the alcove.

There was a horrid tumbling and croaking. Joaz, sickened at some elementary level, was forced to look away. The struggle was soon over.

There was silence in the alcove. Joaz turned to examine Ervis Carcolo, who stared back, rendered inarticulate by anger, humiliation, pain and fright.

Finally finding his voice Carcolo made an awkward gesture of menace and fury. "Be off with you," he croaked. "I claim this ship. Unless you would lie in your own blood, leave me to my conquest!"

Joaz snorted contemptuously, turned his back on Carcolo, who sucked in his breath, and with a whispered curse, lurched forward. Bast Givven seized him, drew him back. Carcolo struggled. Givven talked earnestly into his ear, and Carcolo at last relaxed, half-weeping.

Joaz meanwhile examined the chamber. The walls were blank, gray; the deck was covered with resilient black foam. There was no obvious illumination, but light was everywhere, exuding from the walls. The air chilled the skin, and smelled unpleasantly acrid: an odor which Joaz had not previously noticed. He coughed. His ear-drums rang.

A frightening suspicion became certainty. On heavy legs he lunged for the port, beckoning to his troops. "Outside, they poison us!" He stumbled out on the ramp, gulped fresh air. His men and Termagants followed, and then in a stumbling rush came Ervis Carcolo and his men. Under the hulk of the great ship the group stood gasping, tottering on limp legs, eyes dim and swimming.

Above them, oblivious or careless of their presence, the ship's guns sent forth another barrage. The spire housing Joaz's apartments tottered, collapsed. The Jambles were no more than a heap of rock splinters drifting into a high arched opening. Inside the opening Joaz glimpsed a dark shape, a glint, a shine, a structure—then he was distracted by an ominous sound at his back. From a port at the other end of the ship, a new force of Heavy Troopers had alighted. Three new squads of twenty men each, accompanied by a dozen Weaponeers with four of the rolling projectors.

Joaz sagged back in dismay.

He glanced along his troops. They were in no condition either to attack or defend. A single alternative remained: flight. "Make for Cly-bourne Crevasse," he called thickly.

Stumbling, lurching, the remnants of the two armies fled under the brow of the great black ship. Behind them Heavy Troopers swung smartly forward, but without haste.

Rounding the ship, Joaz stopped short. In the mouth of Clybourne Crevasse waited a fourth squad of Heavy Troopers, with another Weaponeer and his weapon.

Joaz looked to right and left, up and down the valley. Which way to run, where to turn? The Jambles? They were non-existent. Motion, slow and ponderous in the opening previously concealed by tumbled rock caught his attention. A dark object moved forth. A shutter drew back, a bright disk glittered. Almost instantly a pencil of milky blue radiance lanced at, into, through the end-disk of the Basic ship.

Within, tortured machinery whined, simultaneously up and down the scale, to inaudibility at either end. The luster of the end-disks vanished. They became gray, dull; the whisper of power and life previously pervading the ship gave way to dead quiet. The ship itself was dead, and its mass, suddenly unsupported, crushed groaning into the ground.

The Heavy Troopers gazed up in consternation at the hulk which had brought them to Aerlith. Joaz, taking advantage of their indecision, called, "Retreat! North—up the valley!"

The Heavy Troopers doggedly followed. The Weaponeers however cried out an order to halt. They emplaced their weapons, brought them to bear on the cavern behind the Jambles. Within the opening naked shapes moved with frantic haste. There was slow shifting of massive machinery, a change of lights and shadows, and the milky blue shaft of radiance struck forth once more. It flicked down.

Weaponeers, weapons, two-thirds of the Heavy Troopers vanished like moths in a furnace. The surviving Heavy Troopers halted, retreated uncertainly toward the ship.

In the mouth of Clybourne Crevasse waited the remaining squad of Heavy Troopers. The single Weaponeer crouched over his three-wheeled mechanism.

With fateful care he made his adjustments. Within the dark opening the naked sacerdotes worked furiously, thrusting, wedging, the strain of their sinews and hearts and minds communicating itself to every man in the valley. The shaft of milky-blue light sprang forth, but too soon: it melted the rock a hundred yards south of Clybourne Crevasse, and now from the Weaponeer's gun came a splash of orange and green flame. Seconds later the mouth of the sacerdote's cavern erupted. Rocks, bodies, fragments of metal, glass, rubber arched through the air.

The sound of the explosion reverberated through the valley. And the dark object in the cavern was destroyed, was no more than tatters and shreds of metal.

Joaz took three deep breaths, throwing off the effects of the narcotic gas by sheer power of will. He signaled to his Murderers. "Charge! Kill!"

The Murderers loped forward.

The Heavy Troopers threw themselves flat, aimed their weapons, but soon died. In the mouth of Clybourne Crevasse the final squad of Troopers charged wildly forth, to be instantly attacked by Termagants and Blue Horrors who had sidled along the face of the cliff. The Weaponeer was gored by a Murderer. There was no further resistance in the valley, and the ship lay open to attack.

Joaz led the way back up the ramp, through the entry into the now dim staging-chamber. The blast-cannon captured from the Giants lay where his men had dropped them.

Three portals led from the chamber, and these were swiftly burned down. The first revealed a spiral ramp. The second, a long empty hall lined with tiers of bunks. The third, a similar hall in which the bunks were occupied. Pale faces peered from the tiers, pallid hands flickered. Up and down the central corridor marched squat matrons in gray gowns. Ervis Carcolo rushed forward, buffeting the matrons to the deck, peering into the bunks. "Outside," he bellowed. "You are rescued, you are saved. Outside quickly, while there is opportunity."

But there was only meager resistance to overcome from a half-dozen Weaponeers and Trackers, none whatever from twenty Mechanics—these, short thin men with sharp features and dark hair—and none from the sixteen remaining Basics.

All were marched off the ship as prisoners.

XIII

Quiet filled the valley floor, the silence of exhaustion.

Men and dragons sprawled in the trampled fields. The captives stood in a dejected huddle beside the ship. Occasionally an isolated sound came to emphasize the silence: the creak of cooling metal within the ship, the fall of a loose rock from the shattered cliffs; an occasional murmur from the liberated Happy Valley folk, who sat in a group apart from the surviving warriors.

Ervis Carcolo alone seemed restless. For a space he stood with his back to Joaz, slapping his thigh with his scabbard tassel. He contemplated the sky where Skene, a dazzling atom, hung close over the western cliffs, then turned, studied the shadowed gap at the north of the valley, filled with the twisted remains of the sacerdotes' construction. He gave his thigh a final slap, looked toward Joaz Banbeck, turned to stalk through the huddle of Happy Valley folk, making brusque motions of no particular significance, pausing here and there to harangue or cajole, apparently attempting to instill spirit and purpose into his defeated people.

In this purpose he was unsuccessful. Presently he swung sharply about and marched across the field to where Joaz Banbeck lay outstretched.

Carcolo stared down. "Well, then," he said bluffly. "The battle is over, the ship is won."

Joaz raised himself upon one elbow. "True."

"Let us have no misunderstanding on one point," said Carcolo. "Ship and contents are mine. An ancient rule defines the rights of him who is first to attack. On this rule I base my claim."

Joaz looked up in surprise, and seemed almost amused. "By a rule even more ancient, I have already assumed possession."

"I dispute this assertion," said Carcolo hotly. "Who—"

Joaz held up his hand wearily. "Silence, Carcolo! You are alive now only because I am sick of blood and violence. Do not test my patience!"

Carcolo turned away, twitching his scabbard tassel with restrained fury. He looked up the valley, turned back to Joaz. "Here come the sacerdotes, who in fact demolished the ship. I remind you of my proposal, by which we might have prevented this destruction and slaughter."

Joaz smiled. "You made your proposal only two days ago. Further, the sacerdotes possess no weapons."

Carcolo stared as if Joaz had taken leave of his wits. "Then how did they destroy the ship?"

Joaz shrugged. "I can only make conjectures."

Carcolo asked sarcastically, "And what direction do these conjectures lead?"

"I wonder if they had constructed the frame of a space-ship. I wonder if they turned the propulsion beam against the Basic ship."

Carcolo pursed his mouth dubiously. "Why should the sacerdotes build themselves a space-ship?"

"The Demie approaches. Why do you not put your question to him?"

"I will do so," said Carcolo with dignity.

But the Demie, followed by four younger sacerdotes and walking with the air of a man in a dream, passed without speaking.

Joaz rose to his knees and watched after him. The Demie apparently planned to mount the ramp and enter the ship. Joaz jumped to his feet, followed, barred the way to the ramp.

Politely he asked, "What do you seek, Demie?"

"I seek to board the ship."

"To what end? I ask, of course, from sheer curiosity."

The Demie inspected him a moment without reply. His face was haggard and tight. His eyes gleamed like frost-stars. Finally he replied, in a voice hoarse with emotion. "I wish to determine if the ship can be repaired."

Joaz considered a moment, then spoke in a gentle rational voice. "The information can be of little interest to you. Would the sacerdotes place themselves so completely under my command?"

"We obey no one."

"In that case, I can hardly take you with me when I leave."

The Demie swung around, and for a moment seemed as if he would walk away. His eyes fell on the shattered opening at the end of the vale, and he turned back.

He spoke, not in the measured voice of a sacerdote, but in a burst of grief and fury. "This is your doing! You preen yourself, you count yourself resourceful and clever. You forced us to act, and thereby violate ourselves and our dedication!"

Joaz nodded, with a faint grim smile. "I knew the opening must lie behind the Jambles. I wondered if you might be building a space-ship; I hoped that you might protect yourselves against the Basics, and so serve my purposes. I admit your charges. I used you and your construction as a weapon, to save myself and my people. Did I do wrong?"

"Right or wrong—who can weigh? You wasted our effort across more than eight hundred Aerlith years! You destroyed more than you can ever replace."

"I destroyed nothing, Demie. The Basics destroyed your ship. If you had cooperated with us in the defense of Banbeck Vale this disaster would have never occurred. You choose neutrality. You thought yourselves immune from our grief and pain. As you see, such is not the case."

"And meanwhile our labor of eight hundred and twelve years goes to naught," the Demie said.

Joaz asked with feigned innocence, "Why did you need a space-ship? Where do you plan to travel?"

The Demie's eyes burst with flames as intense as those of Skene. "When the race of men is gone, then we go abroad. We move across the galaxy. We re-populate the terrible old worlds, and the new universal history starts from that day, with the past wiped clean as if it never existed. If the grephs destroy you, what is it to us? We await only the death of the last man in the universe."

"Do you not consider yourselves men?"

"We are as you know us—above-men."

At Joaz's shoulder someone laughed coarsely. Joaz turned his head to see Ervis Carcolo. "'Overmen?'" mocked Carcolo. "Poor naked waifs of the caves! What can you display to prove your superiority?"

The Demie's mouth drooped, the lines of his face deepened. "We have our *tands*. We have our knowledge. We have our strength."

Carcolo turned away with another coarse laugh. Joaz said in a subdued voice, "I feel more pity for you than you ever felt for us."

Carcolo returned. "And where did you learn to build a space-ship? From your own efforts? Or from the work of men before you, men of the old times?"

"We are the ultimate men," said the Demie. "We know all that men have ever thought, spoken or devised. We are the last and the first. And when the under-folk are gone, we shall renew the cosmos as innocent and fresh as rain."

"But men have never gone and will never go," said Joaz. "A setback, yes. But is not the universe wide? Somewhere are the worlds of men. With the help of the Basics and their Mechanics, I will repair the ship and go forth to find these worlds."

"You will seek in vain," said the Demie.

"These worlds do not exist?"

"The Human Empire is dissolved. Men exist only in feeble groups."

"What of Eden, old Eden?"

"A myth, no more."

"My marble globe, what of that?"

"A toy. An imaginative fabrication."

"How can you be sure?" asked Joaz, troubled in spite of himself.

"Have I not said that we know all of history? We can look into our *tands* and see deep into the past, until the recollections are dim and misty, and never do we remember planet Eden."

Joaz shook his head stubbornly. "There must be an original world from which men came. Call it Earth or Tempe or Eden; somewhere it exists."

The Demie started to speak, then in a rare show of irresolution held his tongue. Joaz said, "Perhaps you are right. Perhaps we are the last men. But I shall go forth to look."

"I shall come with you," said Ervis Carcolo.

"You will be fortunate to find yourself alive tomorrow," said Joaz.

Carcolo drew himself up. "Do not dismiss my claim to the ship so carelessly!"

Joaz struggled for words, but could find none. What to do with the unruly Carcolo? He could not find in himself enough harshness to do what he knew should be done. He temporized, turned his back on Carcolo.

"Now you know my plans," he told the Demie. "If you do not interfere with me, I shall not interfere with you."

The Demie moved slowly back. "Go then. We are a passive race. We despise ourselves for our activity of today. Perhaps it was our greatest mistake . . . But go, seek your forgotten world. You will only perish somewhere among the stars. We will wait, as already we have waited." He turned and walked away, followed by the four younger sacerdotes, who had all the time stood gravely to the side.

Joaz called after him. "And if the Basics come again? Will you fight with us? Or against us?"

The Demie made no response, but walked to the north, the long white hair swinging down his thin shoulder-blades.

Joaz watched him a moment, gazed up and down the ruined valley, shook his head in wonder and puzzlement, turned back to study the great black ship.

Skene touched the western cliffs. There was an instant dimming of light, a sudden chill.

Carcolo approached him. "Tonight I shall hold my folk here in Banbeck Vale, and send them home on the morrow. Meanwhile, I suggest that you board the ship with me and make a preliminary survey."

Joaz took a deep breath. Why could it not come easier for him? Carcolo had twice sought his life, and, had positions been reversed, would have shown him no mercy. He forced himself to act. His duty to himself, to his people, to his ultimate goal, was clear.

He called to those of his knights who carried the captured heat-guns. They approached.

Joaz said, "Take Carcolo into Clybourne Crevasse. Execute him at once."

Protesting, bellowing, Carcolo was dragged off. Joaz turned away with a heavy heart, and sought Bast Givven. "I take you for a sensible man."

"I regard myself so."

"I set you in charge of Happy Valley. Take your folk home, before darkness falls."

Bast Givven silently went to his people. They stirred, and presently departed Banbeck Vale.

Joaz crossed the valley floor to the tumble of rubble which choked Kergan's Way. He choked with fury as he looked upon the destruction, and for a moment almost wavered in his resolve. Might it not be fit to fly the black ship to Coralyne and take revenge on the Basics? He walked around to stand under the spire which had housed his apartments, and by some strange freak of chance came upon a rounded fragment of yellow marble.

Weighing this in his palm he looked up into the sky where Coralyne already twinkled red, and tried to bring order to his mind.

The Banbeck folk had emerged from the deep tunnels. Phade the minstrel-maiden came to find him. "What a terrible day," she murmured. "What awful events. What a great victory."

Joaz tossed the bit of yellow marble back into the rubble. "I feel much the same way. And where it all ends, no one knows less than I!"

*1964*
*22nd* CONVENTION
SAN FRANCISCO (OAKLAND)

## Poul Anderson

Poul Anderson is of Danish extraction and as that old song from *South Pacific* says, "There is nothing like a Dane." Poul knows the Nordic and Teutonic mythology the way I know the Greek (although, oddly enough, I am not a Greek).

But that is not what I want to talk about.

We science fiction writers are concerned with the present world as well as with the future one, and we have our disagreements in outlook on all the great problems that agitate the public generally. Consider the war in Vietnam, for instance:

The Vietnam issue has divided the microcosm of the science fiction writer, as it has the United States as a whole. I, myself, for instance, am a liberal and, in connection with Vietnam, I am a dove. I always have been. Practically everyone thinks *now* that getting into an Asian land-war was a mistake, but I thought so even when we were in the process of getting into it and said so loudly.

Naturally, then, when a statement was handed around at a science fiction convention urging immediate withdrawal from Vietnam, a couple of years ago, I signed it at once. That statement with a number of names of science fiction personalities attached, was published in a science fiction magazine.

But there are conservatives among us, too, and prominent in that list is Poul Anderson. When he heard of the dove statement, he helped prepare a hawk statement in which signers urged the government to remain in Vietnam until its aims were achieved. The competing statement was also published.

Fears were expressed at the time that this would create storms and divisions among science fiction writers and would break up our camaraderie in a tempest of controversy. Well, if the statements have done so, I haven't noticed it. Our mutual identification as fellow science fiction writers persists above and beyond lesser divisions.

To be specific, Poul knows that I am a "fuzzy-minded pinko" and I know that he is a "narrow-minded hardhat" (not that either of us would ever use such terms), but we love each other anyway, and our relations with each other in these last couple of years have not suffered at all.

May I point out that to disagree without rancor and to engage in rational argument without emotional disintegration is a faculty that need not be confined to the science fiction world. It would be great if that large world outside could boast of it as well.

# 2

# NO TRUCE WITH KINGS

"Song, Charlie! Give's a song!"

"Yay, Charlie!"

The whole mess was drunk, and the junior officers at the far end of the table were only somewhat noisier than their seniors near the colonel. Rugs and hangings could not much muffle the racket, shouts, stamping boots, thump of fists on oak and clash of cups raised aloft, that rang from wall to stony wall. High up among shadows that hid the rafters they hung from, the regimental banners stirred in a draft, as if to join the chaos. Below, the light of bracketed lanterns and bellowing fireplace winked on trophies and weapons.

Autumn comes early on Echo Summit, and it was storming outside, wind-hoot past the watchtowers and rain-rush in the courtyards, an undertone that walked through the buildings and down all corridors, as if the story were true that the unit's dead came out of the cemetery each September Nineteenth night and tried to join the celebration but had forgotten how. No one let it bother him, here or in the enlisted barracks, except maybe the hex major. The Third Division, the Catamounts, was known as the most riotous gang in the Army of the Pacific States of America, and of its regiments the Rolling Stones who held Fort Nakamura were the wildest.

"Go on, boy! Lead off. You've got the closest thing to a voice in the whole goddamn Sierra," Colonel Mackenzie called. He loosened the collar of his black dress tunic and lounged back, legs asprawl, pipe in one hand and beaker of whisky in the other: a thickset man with blue wrinkle-meshed eyes in a battered face, his cropped hair turned gray but his mustache still arrogantly red.

"Charlie is my darlin', my darlin', my darlin'," sang Captain Hulse. He stopped as the noise abated a little. Young Lieutenant Amadeo got up, grinned, and launched into one they well knew.

*"I am a Catamountain, I guard a border pass.*
*And every time I venture out, the cold will freeze m—"*

"Colonel, sir. Begging your pardon."

Mackenzie twisted around and looked into the face of Sergeant Irwin. The man's expression shocked him. "Yes?"

*"I am a bloody hero, a decorated vet:*
*The Order of the Purple Shaft, with pineapple clusters yet!"*

"Message just come in, sir. Major Speyer asks to see you right away."

Speyer who didn't like being drunk, had volunteered for duty tonight; otherwise men drew lots for it on a holiday. Remembering the last word from San Francisco, Mackenzie grew chill.

The mess bawled forth the chorus, not noticing when the colonel knocked out his pipe and rose.

*"The guns go boom! Hey, tiddley boom!*
*The rockets vroom, the arrows zoom.*
*From slug to slug is damn small room.*
*Get me out of here and back to the good old womb!*
*(Hey, doodle dee day!)"*

All right-thinking Catamounts maintained that they could operate better with the booze sloshing up to their eardrums than any other outfit cold sober. Mackenzie ignored the tingle in his veins; forgot it. He walked a straight line to the door, automatically taking his sidearm off the rack as he passed by. The song pursued him into the hall.

*"For maggots in the rations, we hardly ever lack.*
*You bite into a sandwich and the sandwich bites right back.*
*The coffee is the finest grade of Sacramento mud.*
*The ketchup's good in combat, though, for simulating blood.*
*(Cho-orus!)*
         *The drums go bump! Ah-tumpty-tump!*
         *The bugles make like Gabri'l's trump—"*

Lanterns were far apart in the passage. Portraits of former commanders watched the colonel and the sergeant from eyes that were hidden in grotesque darknesses. Footfalls clattered too loudly here.

*"I've got an arrow in my rump.*
*Right about and rearward, heroes, on the jump!*
*(Hey, doodle dee day!)"*

Mackenzie went between a pair of fieldpieces flanking a stairway—

they had been captured at Rock Springs during the Wyoming War, a generation ago—and upward. There was more distance between places in this keep than his legs liked at their present age. But it was old, had been added to decade by decade; and it needed to be massive, chiseled and mortared from Sierra granite, for it guarded a key to the nation. More than one army had broken against its revetments, before the Nevada marches were pacified, and more young men than Mackenzie wished to think about had gone from this base to die among angry strangers.

*But she's never been attacked from the west. God, or whatever you are, you can spare her that, can't you?*

The command office was lonesome at this hour. The room where Sergeant Irwin had his desk lay so silent: no clerks pushing pens, no messengers going in or out, no wives making a splash of color with their dresses as they waited to see the colonel about some problem down in the Village. When he opened the door to the inner room, though, Mackenzie heard the wind shriek around the angle of the wall. Rain slashed at the black windowpane and ran down in streams which the lanterns turned molten.

"Here the colonel is, sir," Irwin said in an uneven voice. He gulped and closed the door behind Mackenzie.

Speyer stood by the commander's desk. It was a beat-up old object with little upon it: an inkwell, a letter basket, an interphone, a photograph of Nora, faded in these dozen years since her death. The major was a tall and gaunt man, hook-nosed, going bald on top. His uniform always looked unpressed, somehow. But he had the sharpest brain in the Cats, Mackenzie thought; and Christ, how could any man read as many books as Phil did! Officially he was the adjutant, in practice the chief adviser.

"Well?" Mackenzie said. The alcohol did not seem to numb him, rather make him too acutely aware of things: how the lanterns smelled hot (when would they get a big enough generator to run electric lights?), and the floor was hard under his feet, and a crack went through the plaster of the north wall, and the stove wasn't driving out much of the chill. He forced bravado, stuck thumbs in belt and rocked back on his heels. "Well, Phil, what's wrong now?"

"Wire from Frisco," Speyer said. He had been folding and unfolding a piece of paper, which he handed over.

"Huh? Why not a radio call?"

"Telegram's less likely to be intercepted. This one's in code, at that. Irwin decoded it for me."

"What the hell kind of nonsense is this?"

"Have a look, Jimbo, and you'll find out. It's for you, anyway. Direct from GHQ."

Mackenzie focused on Irwin's scrawl. The usual formalities of an order; then:

*You are hereby notified that the Pacific States Senate has passed a bill of impeachment against Owen Brodsky, formerly Judge of the Pacific States of America, and deprived him of office. As of 2000 hours this date, former Vice Humphrey Fallon is Judge of the PSA in accordance with the Law of Succession. The existence of dissident elements constituting a public danger has made it necessary for Judge Fallon to put the entire nation under martial law, effective at 2100 hours this date. You are therefore issued the following instructions:*

*1. The above intelligence is to be held strictly confidential until an official proclamation is made. No person who has received knowledge in the course of transmitting this message shall divulge same to any other person whatsoever. Violators of this section and anyone thereby receiving information shall be placed immediately in solitary confinement to await court-martial.*

*2. You will sequestrate all arms and ammunition except for ten percent of available stock, and keep same under heavy guard.*

*3. You will keep all men in the Fort Nakamura area until you are relieved. Your relief is Colonel Simon Hollis, who will start from San Francisco tomorrow morning with one battalion. They are expected to arrive at Fort Nakamura in five days, at which time you will surrender your command to him. Colonel Hollis will designate those officers and enlisted men who are to be replaced by members of his battalion, which will be integrated into the regiment. You will lead the men replaced back to San Francisco and report to Brigadier General Mendoza at New Fort Baker. To avoid provocations, these men will be disarmed except for officers' side arms.*

*4. For your private information, Captain Thomas Danielis has been appointed senior aide to Colonel Hollis.*

*5. You are again reminded that the Pacific States of America are under martial law because of a national emergency. Complete loyalty to the legal government is required. Any mutinous talk must be severely punished. Anyone giving aid or comfort to the Brodsky faction is guilty of treason and will be dealt with accordingly.*

*Gerald O'Donnell, Gen. APSA, CINC*

Thunder went off in the mountains like artillery. It was a while before Mackenzie stirred, and then merely to lay the paper on his desk.

He could only summon feeling slowly, up into a hollowness that filled his skin.

"They dared," Speyer said without tone. "They really did."

"Huh?" Mackenzie swiveled eyes around to the major's face. Speyer didn't meet that stare. He was concentrating his own gaze on his hands, which were now rolling a cigarette. But the words jerked from him, harsh and quick:

"I can guess what happened. The warhawks have been hollering for impeachment ever since Brodsky compromised the border dispute with West Canada. And Fallon, yeah, he's got ambitions of his own. But his partisans are a minority and he knows it. Electing him Vice helped soothe the warhawks some, but he'd never make Judge the regular way, because Brodsky isn't going to die of old age before Fallon does, and anyhow more than fifty percent of the Senate are sober, satisfied bossmen who don't agree that the PSA has a divine mandate to reunify the continent. I don't see how an impeachment could get through an honestly convened Senate. More likely they'd vote out Fallon."

"But a Senate had been called," Mackenzie said. The words sounded to him like someone else talking. "The newscasts told us."

"Sure. Called for yesterday 'to debate ratification of the treaty with West Canada.' But the bossmen are scattered up and down the country, each at his own Station. They have to *get* to San Francisco. A couple of arranged delays—hell, if a bridge just happened to be blown on the Boise railroad, a round dozen of Brodsky's staunchest supporters wouldn't arrive on time—so the Senate has a quorum, all right, but every one of Fallon's supporters are there, and so many of the rest are missing that the warhawks have a clear majority. Then they meet on a holiday, when no cityman is paying attention. Presto, impeachment and a new Judge!" Speyer finished his cigarette and stuck it between his lips while he fumbled for a match. A muscle twitched in his jaw.

"You sure?" Mackenzie mumbled. He thought dimly that this moment was like one time he'd visited Puget City and been invited for a sail on the Guardian's yacht, and a fog had closed in. Everything was cold and blind, with nothing you could catch in your hands.

"Of course I'm not sure!" Speyer snarled. "Nobody will be sure till it's too late." The matchbox shook in his grasp.

"They, uh, they got a new Cinc too, I noticed."

"Uh-huh. They'd want to replace everybody they can't trust, as fast as possible, and De Barros was a Brodsky appointee." The match flared with a hellish *scrit*. Speyer inhaled till his cheeks collapsed. "You and me included, naturally. The regiment reduced to minimum armament so that nobody will get ideas about resistance when the new colonel arrives. You'll note he's coming with a battalion at his heels just the same, just in case. Otherwise he could take a plane and be here tomorrow."

"Why not a train?" Mackenzie caught a whiff of smoke and felt for his pipe. The bowl was hot in his tunic pocket.

"Probably all rolling stock has to head north. Get troops among the bossmen there to forestall a revolt. The valleys are safe enough, peaceful ranchers and Esper colonies. None of them'll pot-shot Fallonite soldiers marching to garrison Echo and Donner outposts." A dreadful scorn weighted Speyer's words.

"What are we going to do?"

"I assume Fallon's take-over followed legal forms; that there was a quorum," Speyer said. "Nobody will ever agree whether it was really Constitutional. . . . I've been reading this damned message over and over since Irwin decoded it. There's a lot between the lines. I think Brodsky's at large, for instance. If he were under arrest this would've said as much, and there'd have been less worry about rebellion. Maybe some of his household troops smuggled him away in time. He'll be hunted like a jackrabbit, of course."

Mackenzie took out his pipe but forgot he had done so. "Tom's coming with our replacements," he said thinly.

"Yeah. Your son-in-law. That was a smart touch, wasn't it? A kind of hostage for your good behavior, but also a backhand promise that you and yours won't suffer if you report in as ordered. Tom's a good kid. He'll stand by his own."

"This is his regiment too," Mackenzie said. He squared his shoulders. "He wanted to fight West Canada, sure. Young and . . . and a lot of Pacificans did get killed in the Idaho Panhandle during the skirmishes. Women and kids among 'em."

"Well," Speyer said, "you're the colonel, Jimbo. What should we do?"

"Oh, Jesus, I don't know. I'm nothing but a soldier." The pipestem broke in Mackenzie's fingers. "But we're not some bossman's personal militia here. We swore to support the Constitution."

"I can't see where Brodsky's yielding some of our claims in Idaho is grounds for impeachment. I think he was right."

"Well—"

"A *coup d'état* by any other name would stink as bad. You may not be much of a student of current events, Jimbo, but you know as well as I do what Fallon's Judgeship will mean. War with West Canada is almost the least of it. Fallon also stands for a strong central government. He'll find ways to grind down the old bossman families. A lot of their heads and scions will die in the front lines; that stunt goes back to

David and Uriah. Others will be accused of collusion with the Brodsky people—not altogether falsely—and impoverished by fines. Esper communities will get nice big land grants, so their economic competition can bankrupt still other estates. Later wars will keep bossmen away for years at a time, unable to supervise their own affairs, which will therefore go to the devil. And thus we march toward the glorious goal of Reunification."

"If Esper Central favors him, what can we do? I've heard enough about psi blasts. I can't ask my men to face them."

"You could ask your men to face the Hellbomb itself, Jimbo, and they would. A Mackenzie has commanded the Rolling Stones for over fifty years."

"Yes. I thought Tom, someday—"

"We've watched this brewing for a long time. Remember the talk we had about it last week?"

"Uh-huh."

"I might also remind you that the Constitution was written explicitly 'to confirm the separate regions in their ancient liberties.'"

"Let me alone!" Mackenzie shouted. "I don't know what's right or wrong, I tell you! Let me alone!"

Speyer fell silent, watching him through a screen of foul smoke. Mackenzie walked back and forth a while, boots slamming the floor like drumbeats. Finally he threw the broken pipe across the room so it shattered.

"Okay." He must ram each word past the tension in his throat. "Irwin's a good man who can keep his lip buttoned. Send him out to cut the telegraph line a few miles downhill. Make it look as if the storm did it. The wire breaks often enough, heaven knows. Officially, then, we never got GHQ's message. That gives us a few days to contact Sierra Command HQ. I won't go against General Cruikshank . . . but I'm pretty sure which way he'll go if he sees a chance. Tomorrow we prepare for action. It'll be no trick to throw back Hollis' battalion, and they'll need a while to bring some real strength against us. Before then the first snow should be along, and we'll be shut off for the winter. Only we can use skis and snowshoes, ourselves, to keep in touch with the other units and organize something. By spring—we'll see what happens."

"Thanks, Jimbo." The wind almost drowned Speyer's words.

"I'd . . . I'd better go tell Laura."

"Yeah." Speyer squeezed Mackenzie's shoulder. There were tears in the major's eyes.

Mackenzie went out with parade-ground steps, ignoring Irwin:

down the hall, down a stairway at its other end, past guarded doors where he returned salutes without really noticing, and so to his own quarters in the south wing.

His daughter had gone to sleep already. He took a lantern off its hook in his bleak little parlor, and entered her room. She had come back here while her husband was in San Francisco.

For a moment Mackenzie couldn't quite remember why he had sent Tom there. He passed a hand over his stubbly scalp, as if to squeeze something out . . . oh, yes, ostensibly to arrange for a new issue of uniforms; actually to get the boy out of the way until the political crisis had blown over. Tom was too honest for his own good, an admirer of Fallon and the Esper movement. His outspokenness had led to friction with his brother officers. They were mostly of bossman stock or from well-to-do protectee families. The existing social order had been good to them. But Tom Danielis began as a fisher lad in a poverty-stricken village on the Mendocino coast. In spare moments he'd learned the three R's from a local Esper; once literate, he joined the Army and earned a commission by sheer guts and brains. He had never forgotten that the Espers helped the poor and that Fallon promised to help the Espers. . . . Then, too, battle, glory, Reunification, Federal Democracy, those were heady dreams when you were young.

Laura's room was little changed since she left it to get married last year. And she had only been seventeen then. Objects survived which had belonged to a small person with pigtails and starched frocks—a teddy bear loved to shapelessness, a doll house her father had built, her mother's picture drawn by a corporal who stopped a bullet at Salt Lake. Oh, God, how much she had come to look like her mother.

Dark hair streamed over a pillow turned gold by the light. Mackenzie shook her as gently as he was able. She awoke instantly, and he saw the terror within her.

"Dad! Anything about Tom?"

"He's okay." Mackenzie set the lantern on the floor and himself on the edge of the bed. Her fingers were cold where they caught at his hand.

"He isn't," she said. "I know you too well."

"He's not been hurt yet. I hope he won't be."

Mackenzie braced himself. Because she was a soldier's daughter, he told her the truth in a few words; but he was not strong enough to look at her while he did. When he had finished, he sat dully listening to the rain.

"You're going to revolt," she whispered.

"I'm going to consult with SCHQ and follow my commanding officer's orders," Mackenzie said.

"You know what they'll be . . . once he knows you'll back him."

Mackenzie shrugged. His head had begun to ache. Hangover started already? He'd need a good deal more booze before he could sleep tonight. No, no time for sleep—yes, there would be. Tomorrow would do to assemble the regiment in the courtyard and address them from the breech of Black Hepzibah, as a Mackenzie of the Rolling Stones always addressed his men, and—. He found himself ludicrously recalling a day when he and Nora and this girl here had gone rowing on Lake Tahoe. The water was the color of Nora's eyes, green and blue and with sunlight flimmering across the surface, but so clear you could see the rocks on the bottom; and Laura's own little bottom had stuck straight in the air as she trailed her hands astern.

She sat thinking for a space before saying flatly: "I suppose you can't be talked out of it." He shook his head. "Well, can I leave tomorrow early, then?"

"Yes. I'll get you a coach."

"T-t-to hell with that. I'm better in the saddle than you are."

"Okay. A couple of men to escort you, though." Mackenzie drew a long breath. "Maybe you can persuade Tom—"

"No. I can't. Please don't ask me to, Dad."

He gave her the last gift he could: "I wouldn't want you to stay. That'd be shirking your own duty. Tell Tom I still think he's the right man for you. Goodnight, duck." It came out too fast, but he dared not delay. When she began to cry he must unfold her arms from his neck and depart the room.

*"But I had not expected so much killing!"*

*"Nor I . . . at this stage of things. There will be more yet, I am afraid, before the immediate purpose is achieved."*

*"You told me—"*

*"I told you our hopes, Mwyr. You know as well as I that the Great Science is only exact on the broadest scale of history. Individual events are subject to statistical fluctuation."*

*"That is an easy way, is it not, to describe sentient beings dying in the mud?"*

*"You are new here. Theory is one thing, adjustment to practical necessities is another. Do you think it does not hurt me to see that happen which I myself have helped plan?"*

*"Oh, I know, I know. Which makes it no easier to live with my guilt."*

*"To live with your responsibilities, you mean."*

"Your phrase."

"No, this is not semantic trickery. The distinction is real. You have read reports and seen films, but I was here with the first expedition. And here I have been for more than two centuries. Their agony is no abstraction to me."

"But it was different when we first discovered them. The aftermath of their nuclear wars was still so horribly present. That was when they needed us—the poor starveling anarchs—and we, we did nothing but observe."

"Now you are hysterical. Could we come in blindly, ignorant of every last fact about them, and expect to be anything but one more disruptive element? An element whose effects we ourselves would not have been able to predict. That would have been criminal indeed, like a surgeon who started to operate as soon as he met the patient, without so much as taking a case history. We had to let them go their own way while we studied in secret. You have no idea how desperately hard we worked to gain information and understanding. That work goes on. It was only seventy years ago that we felt enough assurance to introduce the first new factor into this one selected society. As we continue to learn more, the plan will be adjusted. It may take us a thousand years to complete our mission."

"But meanwhile they have pulled themselves back out of the wreckage. They are finding their own answers to their problems. What right have we to—"

"I begin to wonder, Mwyr, what right you have to claim even the title of apprentice psychodynamician. Consider what their 'answers' actually amount to. Most of the planet is still in a state of barbarism. This continent has come farthest toward recovery, because of having the widest distribution of technical skills and equipment before the destruction. But what social structure has evolved? A jumble of quarrelsome successor states. A feudalism where the balance of political, military, and economic power lies with a landed aristocracy, of all archaic things. A score of languages and subcultures developing along their own incompatible lines. A blind technology worship inherited from the ancestral society that, unchecked, will lead them in the end back to a machine civilization as demoniac as the one that tore itself apart three centuries ago. Are you distressed that a few hundred men have been killed because our agents promoted a revolution which did not come off quite so smoothly as we hoped? Well, you have the word of the Great Science itself that, without our guidance, the totaled misery of this race through the next five thousand years would outweigh by three orders of magnitude whatever pain we are forced to inflict."

"—Yes. Of course. I realize I am being emotional. It is difficult not to be at first, I suppose."

"You should be thankful that your initial exposure to the hard necessities of the plan was so mild. There is worse to come."

"So I have been told."

"In abstract terms. But consider the reality. A government ambitious to restore the old nation will act aggressively, thus embroiling itself in prolonged wars with powerful neighbors. Both directly and indirectly, through the operation of economic factors they are too naïve to control, the aristocrats and freeholders will be eroded away by those wars. Anomic democracy will replace their system, first dominated by a corrupt capitalism and later by sheer force of whoever holds the central government. But there will be no place for the vast displaced proletariat, the one-time landowners and the foreigners incorporated by conquest. They will offer fertile soil to any demagogue. The empire will undergo endless upheaval, civil strife, despotism, decay, and outside invasion. Oh, we will have much to answer for before we are done!"

"Do you think . . . when we see the final result . . . will the blood wash off us?"

"No. We pay the heaviest price of all."

Spring in the high Sierra is cold, wet, snowbanks melting away from forest floor and giant rocks, rivers in spate until their canyons clang, a breeze ruffling puddles in the road. The first green breath across the aspen seems infinitely tender against pine and spruce, which gloom into a brilliant sky. A raven swoops low, gruk, gruk, look out for that damn hawk! But then you cross timber line and the world becomes tumbled blue-gray immensity, with the sun ablaze on what snows remain and the wind sounding hollow in your ears.

Captain Thomas Danielis, Field Artillery, Loyalist Army of the Pacific States, turned his horse aside. He was a dark young man, slender and snub-nosed. Behind him a squad slipped and cursed, dripping mud from feet to helmets, trying to get a gun carrier unstuck. Its alcohol motor was too feeble to do more than spin the wheels. The infantry squelched on past, stoop-shouldered, worn down by altitude and a wet bivouac and pounds of mire on each boot. Their line snaked from around a prowlike crag, up the twisted road and over the ridge ahead. A gust brought the smell of sweat to Danielis.

But they were good joes, he thought. Dirty, dogged, they did their profane best. His own company, at least, was going to get hot food tonight, if he had to cook the quartermaster sergeant.

The horse's hoofs banged on a block of ancient concrete jutting from the muck. If this had been the old days . . . but wishes weren't bullets. Beyond this part of the range lay lands mostly desert, claimed by the Saints, who were no longer a menace but with whom there was scant commerce. So the mountain highways had never been considered worth repaving, and the railroad ended at Hangtown. Therefore the expeditionary force to the Tahoe area must slog through unpeopled forests and icy uplands, God help the poor bastards.

*God help them in Nakamura, too,* Danielis thought. His mouth drew taut, he slapped his hands together and spurred the horse with needless violence. Sparks shot from iron shoes as the beast clattered off the road toward the highest point of the ridge. The man's saber banged his leg.

Reining in, he unlimbered his field glasses. From here he could look across a jumbled sweep of mountainscape, where cloud shadows sailed over cliffs and boulders, down into the gloom of a canyon and across to the other side. A few tufts of grass thrust out beneath him, mummy brown, and a marmot wakened early from winter sleep whistled somewhere in the stone confusion. He still couldn't see the castle. Nor had he expected to, as yet. He knew this country . . . how well he did!

There might be a glimpse of hostile activity, though. It had been eerie to march this far with no sign of the enemy, of anyone else whatsoever; to send out patrols in search of rebel units that could not be found; to ride with shoulder muscles tense against the sniper's arrow that never came. Old Jimbo Mackenzie was not one to sit passive behind walls, and the Rolling Stones had not been given their nickname in jest.

*If Jimbo is alive. How do I know he is? That buzzard yonder may be the very one which hacked out his eyes.*

Danielis bit his lip and made himself look steadily through the glasses. Don't think about Mackenzie, how he outroared and outdrank and outlaughed you and you never minded, how he sat knotting his brows over the chessboard where you could mop him up ten times out of ten and *he* never cared, how proud and happy he stood at the wedding. . . . Nor think about Laura, who tried to keep you from knowing how often she wept at night, who now bore a grandchild beneath her heart and woke alone in the San Francisco house from the evil dreams of pregnancy. Every one of those dogfaces plodding toward the castle which has killed every army ever sent against it—every one of them has somebody at home and hell rejoices at how many have somebody on the rebel side. Better look for hostile spoor and let it go at that.

Wait! Danielis stiffened. A rider— He focused. *One of our own.* Fallon's army added a blue band to the uniform. *Returning scout.* A tingle went along his spine. He decided to hear the report firsthand. But the fellow was still a mile off, perforce riding slowly over the hugger-mugger terrain. There was no hurry about intercepting him. Danielis continued to survey the land.

A reconnaissance plane appeared, an ungainly dragonfly with sunlight flashing off a propeller head. Its drone bumbled among rock walls, where echoes threw the noise back and forth. Doubtless an auxiliary to the scouts, employing two-way radio communication. Later the plane would work as a spotter for artillery. There was no use making a bomber of it; Fort Nakamura was proof against anything that today's puny aircraft could drop, and might well shoot the thing down.

A shoe scraped behind Danielis. Horse and man whirled as one. His pistol jumped into his hand.

It lowered. "Oh. Excuse me, Philosopher."

The man in the blue robe nodded. A smile softened his stern face. He must be around sixty years old, hair white and skin lined, but he walked these heights like a wild goat. The Yang and Yin symbol burned gold on his breast.

"You're needlessly on edge, son," he said. A trace of Texas accent stretched out his words. The Espers obeyed the laws wherever they lived, but acknowledged no country their own: nothing less than mankind, perhaps ultimately all life through the space-time universe. Nevertheless, the Pacific States had gained enormously in prestige and influence when the Order's unenterable Central was established in San Francisco at the time when the city was being rebuilt in earnest. There had been no objection—on the contrary—to the Grand Seeker's desire that Philosopher Woodworth accompany the expedition as an observer. Not even from the chaplains; the churches had finally gotten it straight that the Esper teachings were neutral with respect to religion.

Danielis managed a grin. "Can you blame me?"

"No blame. But advice. Your attitude isn't useful. Does nothin' but wear you out. You've been fightin' a battle for weeks before it began."

Danielis remembered the apostle who had visited his home in San Francisco—by invitation, in the hope that Laura might learn some peace. His simile had been still homelier: "You only need to wash one dish at a time." The memory brought a smart to Danielis' eyes, so that he said roughly:

"I might relax if you'd use your powers to tell me what's waiting for us."

"I'm no adept, son. Too much in the material world, I'm afraid. Somebody's got to do the practical work of the Order, and someday I'll get the chance to retire and explore the frontier inside me. But you need to start early, and stick to it a lifetime, to develop your full powers." Woodworth looked across the peaks, seemed almost to merge himself with their loneliness.

Danielis hesitated to break into that meditation. He wondered what practical purpose the Philosopher was serving on this trip. To bring back a report, more accurate than untrained senses and undisciplined emotions could prepare? Yes, that must be it. The Espers might yet decide to take a hand in this war. However reluctantly, Central had allowed the awesome psi powers to be released now and again, when the Order was seriously threatened; and Judge Fallon was a better friend to them than Brodsky or the earlier Senate of Bossmen and House of People's Deputies had been.

The horse stamped and blew out its breath in a snort. Woodworth glanced back at the rider. "If you ask me, though," he said, "I don't reckon you'll find much doin' around here. I was in the Rangers myself, back home, before I saw the Way. This country feels empty."

"If we could know!" Danielis exploded. "They've had the whole winter to do what they liked in the mountains, while the snow kept us out. What scouts we could get in reported a beehive—as late as two weeks ago. What have they planned?"

Woodworth made no reply.

It flooded from Danielis, he couldn't stop, he had to cover the recollection of Laura bidding him good-by on his second expedition against her father, six months after the first one came home in bloody fragments:

"If we had the resources! A few wretched little railroads and motor cars; a handful of aircraft; most of our supply trains drawn by mules—what kind of mobility does that give us? And what really drives me crazy . . . we know how to make what they had in the old days. We've got the books, the information. More, maybe, than the ancestors. I've watched the electrosmith at Fort Nakamura turn out transistor units with enough bandwidth to carry television, no bigger than my fist. I've seen the scientific journals, the research labs, biology, chemistry, astronomy, mathematics. And all useless!"

"Not so," Woodworth answered mildly. "Like my own Order, the community of scholarship's becomin' supranational. Printin' presses, radiophones, telescribes—"

"I say useless. Useless to stop men killing each other because there's no authority strong enough to make them behave. Useless to take a farmer's hands off a horse-drawn plow and put them on the wheel of a tractor. We've got the knowledge, but we can't apply it."

"You do apply it, son, where too much power and industrial plant isn't required. Remember, the world's a lot poorer in natural resources than it was before the Hellbombs. I've seen the Black Lands myself, where the firestorm passed over the Texas oilfields." Woodworth's serenity cracked a little. He turned his eyes back to the peaks.

"There's oil elsewhere," Danielis insisted. "And coal, iron, uranium, everything we need. But the world hasn't got the organization to get at it. Not in any quantity. So we fill the Central Valley with crops that'll yield alcohol, to keep a few motors turning; and we import a dribble of other stuff along an unbelievably inefficient chain of middlemen; and most of it's eaten by the armies." He jerked his head toward that part of the sky which the handmade airplane had crossed. "That's one reason we've got to have Reunification. So we can rebuild."

"And the other?" Woodworth asked softly.

"Democracy—universal suffrage—" Danielis swallowed. "And so fathers and sons won't have to fight each other again."

"Those are better reasons," Woodworth said. "Good enough for the Espers to support. But as for that machinery you want—" He shook his head. "No, you're wrong there. That's no way for men to live."

"Maybe not," Danielis said. "Though my own father wouldn't have been crippled by overwork if he'd had some machines to help him. . . . Oh, I don't know. First things first. Let's get this war over with and argue later." He remembered the scout, now gone from view. "Pardon me, Philosopher, I've got an errand."

The Esper raised his hand in token of peace. Danielis cantered off.

Splashing along the roadside, he saw the man he wanted, halted by Major Jacobsen. The latter, who must have sent him out, sat mounted near the infantry line. The scout was a Klamath Indian, stocky in buckskins, a bow on his shoulder. Arrows were favored over guns by many of the men from the northern districts: cheaper than bullets, no noise, less range but as much firepower as a bolt-action rifle. In the bad old days before the Pacific States had formed their union, archers along forest trails had saved many a town from conquest; they still helped keep that union loose.

"Ah, Captain Danielis," Jacobsen hailed. "You're just in time. Lieutenant Smith was about to report what his detachment found out."

"And the plane," said Smith imperturbably. "What the pilot told us he'd seen from the air gave us the guts to go there and check for ourselves."

"Well?"

"Nobody around."

"What?"

"Fort's been evacuated. So's the settlement. Not a soul."

"But—but—" Jacobsen collected himself. "Go on."

"We studied the signs as best's we could. Looks like noncombatants left some time ago. By sledge and ski, I'd guess, maybe north to some strong point. I suppose the men shifted their own stuff at the same time, gradual-like, what they couldn't carry with 'em at the last. Because the regiment and its support units, even field artillery, pulled out just three-four days ago. Ground's all tore up. They headed downslope, sort of west by northwest, far's we could tell from what we saw."

Jacobsen choked. "Where are they bound?"

A flaw of wind struck Danielis in the face and ruffled the horses' manes. At his back he heard the slow plop and squish of boots, groan of wheels, chuff of motors, rattle of wood and metal, yells and whip-cracks of muleskinners. But it seemed very remote. A map grew before him, blotting out the world.

The Loyalist Army had had savage fighting the whole winter, from the Trinity Alps to Puget Sound—for Brodsky had managed to reach Mount Rainier, whose lord had furnished broadcasting facilities, and Rainier was too well fortified to take at once. The bossmen and the autonomous tribes rose in arms, persuaded that a usurper threatened their damned little local privileges. Their protectees fought beside them, if only because no rustic had been taught any higher loyalty than to his patron. West Canada, fearful of what Fallon might do when he got the chance, lent the rebels aid that was scarcely even clandestine.

Nonetheless, the national army was stronger: more matériel, better organization, above everything an ideal of the future. Cinc O'Donnell had outlined a strategy—concentrate the loyal forces at a few points, overwhelm resistance, restore order and establish bases in the region, then proceed to the next place—which worked. The government now controlled the entire coast, with naval units to keep an eye on the Canadians in Vancouver and guard the important Hawaii trade routes; the northern half of Washington almost to the Idaho line; the Columbia Valley; central California as far north as Redding. The remaining rebellious Stations and towns were isolated from each other in mountains, forests, deserts. Bossdom after bossdom fell as the loyalists pressed on, defeating the enemy in detail, cutting him off from supplies and hope. The only real worry had been Cruikshank's Sierra Command, an army in its own right rather than a levy of yokels and citymen, big and tough and expertly led. This expedition against Fort Nakamura was only a small part of what had looked like a difficult campaign.

But now the Rolling Stones had pulled out. Offered no fight whatso-ever. Which meant that their brother Catamounts must also have evacuated. You don't give up one anchor of a line you intend to hold. So?

"Down into the valleys," Danielis said; and there sounded in his ears, crazily, the voice of Laura as she used to sing. *Down in the valley, valley so low.*

"Judas!" the major exclaimed. Even the Indian grunted as if he had taken a belly blow. "No, they couldn't. We'd have known."

*Hang your head over, hear the wind blow.* It hooted across cold rocks.

"There are plenty of forest trails," Danielis said. "Infantry and cavalry could use them, if they're accustomed to such country. And the Cats are. Vehicles, wagons, big guns, that's slower and harder. But they only need to outflank us, then they can get back onto Forty and Fifty —and cut us to pieces if we attempt pursuit. I'm afraid they've got us boxed."

"The eastern slope—," said Jacobsen helplessly.

"What for? Want to occupy a lot of sagebrush? No, we're trapped here till they deploy in the flatlands." Danielis closed a hand on his saddlehorn so that the knuckles went bloodless. "I miss my guess if this isn't Colonel Mackenzie's idea. It's his style, for sure."

"But then they're between us and Frisco! With damn near our whole strength in the north—"

*Between me and Laura,* Danielis thought.

He said aloud: "I suggest, Major, we get hold of the C.O. at once. And then we better get on the radio." From some well he drew the power to raise his head. The wind lashed his eyes. "This needn't be a disaster. They'll be easier to beat out in the open, actually, once we come to grips."

*Roses love sunshine, violets love dew,*
*Angels in heaven know I love you.*

The rains which fill the winter of the California lowlands were about ended. Northward along a highway whose pavement clopped under hoofs, Mackenzie rode through a tremendous greenness. Eucalyptus and live oak, flanking the road, exploded with new leaves. Beyond them on either side stretched a checkerboard of fields and vineyards, intricately hued, until the distant hills on the right and the higher, nearer ones on the left made walls. The freeholder houses that had been scattered across the land a ways back were no longer to be seen. This end of the Napa Valley belonged to the Esper community at St. Helena. Clouds banked like white mountains over the western ridge. The breeze bore to Mackenzie a smell of growth and turned earth.

Behind him it rumbled with men. The Rolling Stones were on the move. The regiment proper kept to the highway, three thousand boots slamming down at once with an earthquake noise, and so did the guns and wagons. There was no immediate danger of attack. But the cavalrymen attached to the force must needs spread out. The sun flashed off their helmets and lance heads.

Mackenzie's attention was directed forward. Amber walls and red tile roofs could be seen among plum trees that were a surf of pink and white blossoms. The community was big, several thousand people. The muscles tightened in his abdomen. "Think we can trust them?" he asked, not for the first time. "We've only got a radio agreement to a parley."

Speyer, riding beside him, nodded. "I expect they'll be honest. Particularly with our boys right outside. Espers believe in non-violence anyway."

"Yeah, but if it did come to fighting—I know there aren't very many adepts so far. The Order hasn't been around long enough for that. But when you get this many Espers together, there's bound to be a few who've gotten somewhere with their damned psionics. I don't want my men blasted, or lifted in the air and dropped, or any such nasty thing."

Speyer threw him a sidelong glance. "Are you scared of them, Jimbo?" he murmured.

"Hell, no!" Mackenzie wondered if he was a liar or not. "But I don't like 'em."

"They do a lot of good. Among the poor, especially."

"Sure, sure. Though any decent bossman looks after his own protectees, and we've got things like churches and hospices as well. I don't see where just being charitable—and they can afford it, with the profits they make on their holdings—I don't see where that gives any right to raise the orphans and pauper kids they take in, the way they do: so's to make the poor tikes unfit for life anywhere outside."

"The object of that, as you well know, is to orient them toward the so-called interior frontier. Which American civilization as a whole is not much interested in. Frankly, quite apart from the remarkable powers some Espers have developed, I often envy them."

"You, Phil?" Mackenzie goggled at his friend.

The lines drew deep in Speyer's face. "This winter I've helped shoot a lot of my fellow countrymen," he said low. "My mother and wife and kids are crowded with the rest of the Village in the Mount Lassen fort, and when we said good-by we knew it was quite possibly permanent. And in the past I've helped shoot a lot of other men who never did me any personal harm." He sighed. "I've often wondered what it's like to know peace, inside as well as outside."

Mackenzie sent Laura and Tom out of his head.

"Of course," Speyer went on, "the fundamental reason you—and I, for that matter—distrust the Espers is that they do represent something alien to us. Something that may eventually choke out the whole concept of life that we grew up with. You know, a couple weeks back in Sacramento I dropped in at the University research lab to see what was going on. Incredible! The ordinary soldier would swear it was witch-work. It was certainly more weird than . . . than simply reading minds or moving objects by thinking at them. But to you or me it's a shiny new marvel. We'll wallow in it.

"Now why's that? Because the lab is scientific. Those men work with chemicals, electronics, subviral particles. That fits into the educated American's world-view. But the mystic unity of creation . . . no, not our cup of tea. The only way we can hope to achieve Oneness is to renounce everything we've ever believed in. At your age or mine, Jimbo, a man is seldom ready to tear down his whole life and start from scratch."

"Maybe so." Mackenzie lost interest. The settlement was quite near now.

He turned around to Captain Hulse, riding a few paces behind. "Here we go," he said. "Give my compliments to Lieutenant Colonel Yamaguchi and tell him he's in charge till we get back. If anything seems suspicious, he's to act at his own discretion."

"Yes, sir." Hulse saluted and wheeled smartly about. There had been no practical need for Mackenzie to repeat what had long been agreed on; but he knew the value of ritual. He clicked his big sorrel gelding into a trot. At his back he heard bugles sound orders and sergeants howl at their platoons.

Speyer kept pace. Mackenzie had insisted on bringing an extra man to the discussion. His own wits were probably no match for a high-level Esper, but Phil's might be.

*Not that there's any question of diplomacy or whatever. I hope.* To ease himself, he concentrated on what was real and present—hoofbeats, the rise and fall of the saddle beneath him, the horse's muscles rippling between his thighs, the creak and jingle of his saber belt, the clean odor of the animal—and suddenly remembered this was the sort of trick the Espers recommended.

None of their communities was walled, as most towns and every bossman's Station was. The officers turned off the highway and went down a street between colonnaded buildings. Side streets ran off in both directions. The settlement covered no great area, though, being composed of groups that lived together, sodalities or superfamilies or

whatever you wanted to call them. Some hostility toward the Order and
a great many dirty jokes stemmed from that practice. But Speyer, who
should know, said there was no more sexual swapping around than in
the outside world. The idea was simply to get away from possessiveness,
thee versus me, and to raise children as part of a whole rather than an
insular clan.

The kids were out, staring round-eyed from the porticoes, hundreds
of them. They looked healthy and, underneath a natural fear of the
invaders, happy enough. But pretty solemn, Mackenzie thought; and
all in the same blue garb. Adults stood among them, expressionless.
Everybody had come in from the fields as the regiment neared. The
silence was like barricades. Mackenzie felt sweat begin to trickle down
his ribs. When he emerged on the central square, he let out his breath
in a near gasp.

A fountain, the basin carved into a lotus, tinkled in the middle of
the plaza. Flowering trees stood around it. The square was defined
on three sides by massive buildings that must be for storage. On the
fourth side rose a smaller templelike structure with a graceful cupola,
obviously headquarters and meeting house. On its lowest step were
ranked half a dozen blue-robed men, five of them husky youths. The
sixth was middle-aged, the Yang and Yin on his breast. His features,
ordinary in themselves, held an implacable calm.

Mackenzie and Speyer drew rein. The colonel flipped a soft salute.
"Philosopher Gaines? I'm Mackenzie, here's Major Speyer." He swore
at himself for being so awkward about it and wondered what to do
with his hands. The young fellows he understood, more or less; they
watched him with badly concealed hostility. But he had some trouble
meeting Gaines' eyes.

The settlement leader inclined his head. "Welcome, gentlemen.
Won't you come in?"

Mackenzie dismounted, hitched his horse to a post and removed
his helmet. His worn reddish-brown uniform felt shabbier yet in these
surroundings. "Thanks. Uh, I'll have to make this quick."

"To be sure. Follow me, please."

Stiff-backed, the young men trailed after their elders, through an
entry chamber and down a short hall. Speyer looked around at the mo-
saics. "Why, this is lovely," he murmured.

"Thank you," said Gaines. "Here's my office." He opened a door of
superbly grained walnut and gestured the visitors through. When he
closed it behind himself, the acolytes waited outside.

The room was austere, whitewashed walls enclosing little more than
a desk, a shelf of books, and some backless chairs. A window opened on

a garden. Gaines sat down. Mackenzie and Speyer followed suit, uncomfortable on this furniture.

"We'd better get right to business," the colonel blurted.

Gaines said nothing. At last Mackenzie must plow ahead:

"Here's the situation. Our force is to occupy Calistoga, with detachments on either side of the hills. That way we'll control both the Napa Valley and the Valley of the Moon . . . from the northern ends, at least. The best place to station our eastern wing is here. We plan to establish a fortified camp in the field yonder. I'm sorry about the damage to your crops, but you'll be compensated once the proper government has been restored. And food, medicine—you understand this army has to requisition such items, but we won't let anybody suffer undue hardship and we'll give receipts. Uh, as a precaution we'll need to quarter a few men in this community, to sort of keep an eye on things. They'll interfere as little as possible. Okay?"

"The charter of the Order guarantees exemption from military requirements," Gaines answered evenly. "In fact, no armed man is supposed to cross the boundary of any land held by an Esper settlement. I cannot be party to a violation of the law, Colonel."

"If you want to split legal hairs, Philosopher," Speyer said, "then I'll remind you that both Fallon and Judge Brodsky have declared martial law. Ordinary rules are suspended."

Gaines smiled. "Since only one government can be legitimate," he said, "the proclamations of the other are necessarily null and void. To a disinterested observer, it would appear that Judge Fallon's title is the stronger, especially when his side controls a large continuous area rather than some scattered bossdoms."

"Not any more, it doesn't," Mackenzie snapped.

Speyer gestured him back. "Perhaps you haven't followed the developments of the last few weeks, Philosopher," he said. "Allow me to recapitulate. The Sierra Command stole a march on the Fallonites and came down out of the mountains. There was almost nothing left in the middle part of California to oppose us, so we took over rapidly. By occupying Sacramento, we control river and rail traffic. Our bases extend south below Bakersfield, with Yosemite and King's Canyon not far away to provide sites for extremely strong positions. When we've consolidated this northern end of our gains, the Fallonite forces around Redding will be trapped between us and the powerful bossmen who still hold out in the Trinity, Shasta, and Lassen regions. The very fact of our being here has forced the enemy to evacuate the Columbia Valley, so that San Francisco may be defended. It's an open question which side today has the last word in the larger territory."

"What about the army that went into the Sierra against you?" Gaines inquired shrewdly. "Have you contained them?"

Mackenzie scowled. "No. That's no secret. They got out through the Mother Lode country and went around us. They're down in Los Angeles and San Diego now."

"A formidable host. Do you expect to stand them off indefinitely?"

"We're going to make a hell of a good try," Mackenzie said. "Where we are, we've got the advantage of interior communications. And most of the freeholders are glad to slip us word about whatever they observe. We can concentrate at any point the enemy starts to attack."

"Pity that this rich land must also be torn apart by war."

"Yeah. Isn't it?"

"Our strategic objective is obvious enough," Speyer said. "We have cut enemy communications across the middle, except by sea, which is not very satisfactory for troops operating far inland. We deny him access to a good part of his food and manufactured supplies, and most especially to the bulk of his fuel alcohol. The backbone of our own side is the bossdoms, which are almost self-contained economic and social units. Before long they'll be in better shape than the rootless army they face. I think Judge Brodsky will be back in San Francisco before fall."

"If your plans succeed," Gaines said.

"That's our worry." Mackenzie leaned forward, one fist doubled on his knee. "Okay, Philosopher. I know you'd rather see Fallon come out on top, but I expect you've got more sense than to sign up in a lost cause. Will you cooperate with us?"

"The Order takes no part in political affairs, Colonel, except when its own existence is endangered."

"Oh, pipe down. By 'cooperate' I don't mean anything but keeping out from under our feet."

"I am afraid that would still count as cooperation. We cannot have military establishments on our lands."

Mackenzie stared at Gaines' face, which had set into granite lines, and wondered if he had heard aright. "Are you ordering us off?" a stranger asked with his voice.

"Yes," the Philosopher said.

"With our artillery zeroed in on your town?"

"Would you really shell women and children, Colonel?"

*O Nora—* "We don't need to. Our men can walk right in."

"Against psi blasts? I beg you not to have those poor boys destroyed." Gaines paused, then: "I might also point out that by losing your regiment you imperil your whole cause. You are free to march around our holdings and proceed to Calistoga."

*Leaving a Fallonite nest at my back, spang across my communications southward.* The teeth grated together in Mackenzie's mouth.

Gaines rose. "The discussion is at an end, gentlemen," he said. "You have one hour to get off our lands."

Mackenzie and Speyer stood up too. "We're not done yet," the major said. Sweat studded his forehead and the long nose. "I want to make some further explanations."

Gaines crossed the room and opened the door. "Show these gentlemen out," he said to the five acolytes.

"No, by God!" Mackenzie shouted. He clapped a hand to his sidearm.

"Inform the adepts," Gaines said.

One of the young men turned. Mackenzie heard the slap-slap of his sandals, running down the hall. Gaines nodded. "I think you had better go," he said.

Speyer grew rigid. His eyes shut. They flew open and he breathed, "*Inform* the adepts?"

Mackenzie saw the stiffness break in Gaines' countenance. There was no time for more than a second's bewilderment. His body acted for him. The gun clanked from his holster simultaneously with Speyer's.

"Get that messenger, Jimbo," the major rapped. "I'll keep these birds covered."

As he plunged forward, Mackenzie found himself worrying about the regimental honor. Was it right to open hostilities when you had come on a parley? But Gaines had cut the talk off himself—

"Stop him!" Gaines yelled.

The four remaining acolytes sprang into motion. Two of them barred the doorway, the other two moved in on either side. "Hold it or I'll shoot!" Speyer cried, and was ignored.

Mackenzie couldn't bring himself to fire on unarmed men. He gave the youngster before him the pistol barrel in his teeth. Bloody-faced, the Esper lurched back. Mackenzie stiff-armed the one coming in from the left. The third tried to fill the doorway. Mackenzie put a foot behind his ankles and pushed. As he went down, Mackenzie kicked him in the temple, hard enough to stun, and jumped over him.

The fourth was on his back. Mackenzie writhed about to face the man. Those arms that hugged him, pinioning his gun, were bear strong. Mackenzie put the butt of his free left hand under the fellow's nose, and pushed. The acolyte must let go. Mackenzie gave him a knee in the stomach, whirled, and ran.

There was not much further commotion behind him. Phil must have them under control. Mackenzie pelted along the hall, into the entry chamber. Where had that goddamn runner gone? He looked out the open entrance, onto the square. Sunlight hurt his eyes. His breath came in painful gulps, there was a stitch in his side, yeah, he was getting old.

Blue robes fluttered from a street. Mackenzie recognized the messenger. The youth pointed at this building. A gabble of his words drifted faintly through Mackenzie's pulse. There were seven or eight men with him—older men, nothing to mark their clothes . . . but Mackenzie knew a high-ranking officer when he saw one. The acolyte was dismissed. Those whom he had summoned crossed the square with long strides.

Terror knotted Mackenzie's bowels. He put it down. A Catamount didn't stampede, even from somebody who could turn him inside out with a look. He could do nothing about the wretchedness that followed, though. *If they clobber me, so much the better. I won't lie awake nights wondering how Laura is.*

The adepts were almost to the steps. Mackenzie trod forth. He swept his revolver in an arc. "Halt!" His voice sounded tiny in the stillness that brooded over the town.

They jarred to a stop and stood there in a group. He saw them enforce a catlike relaxation, and their faces became blank visors. None spoke. Finally Mackenzie was unable to keep silent.

"This place is hereby occupied under the laws of war," he said. "Go back to your quarters."

"What have you done with our leader?" asked a tall man. His voice was even but deeply resonant.

"Read my mind and find out," Mackenzie gibed. *No, you're being childish.* "He's okay, long's he keeps his nose clean. You too. Beat it."

"We do not wish to pervert psionics to violence," said the tall man. "Please do not force us."

"Your chief sent for you before we'd done anything," Mackenzie retorted. "Looks like violence was what he had in mind. On your way."

The Espers exchanged glances. The tall man nodded. His companions walked slowly off. "I would like to see Philosopher Gaines," the tall man said.

"You will pretty soon."

"Am I to understand that he is being held a prisoner?"

"Understand what you like." The other Espers were rounding the corner of the building. "I don't want to shoot. Go on back before I have to."

"An impasse of sorts," the tall man said. "Neither of us wishes to injure one whom he considers defenseless. Allow me to conduct you off these grounds."

Mackenzie wet his lips. Weather had chapped them rough. "If you can put a hex on me, go ahead," he challenged. "Otherwise scram."

"Well, I shall not hinder you from rejoining your men. It seems the easiest way of getting you to leave. But I most solemnly warn that any armed force which tries to enter will be annihilated."

*Guess I had better go get the boys, at that. Phil can't mount guard on those guys forever.*

The tall man went over to the hitching post. "Which of these horses is yours?" he asked blandly.

*Almighty eager to get rid of me, isn't he— Holy hellfire! There must be a rear door!*

Mackenzie spun on his heel. The Esper shouted. Mackenzie dashed back through the entry chamber. His boots threw echoes at him. No, not to the left, there's only the office that way. Right . . . around this corner—

A long hall stretched before him. A stairway curved from the middle. The other Espers were already on it.

"Halt!" Mackenzie called. "Stop or I'll shoot!"

The two men in the lead sped onward. The rest turned and headed down again, toward him.

He fired with care, to disable rather than kill. The hall reverberated with the explosions. One after another they dropped, a bullet in leg or hip or shoulder. With such small targets, Mackenzie missed some shots. As the tall man, the last of them, closed in from behind, the hammer clicked on an empty chamber.

Mackenzie drew his saber and gave him the flat of it alongside the head. The Esper lurched. Mackenzie got past and bounded up the stair. It wound like something in a nightmare. He thought his heart was going to go to pieces.

At the end, an iron door opened on a landing. One man was fumbling with the lock. The other blue-robe attacked.

Mackenzie stuck his sword between the Esper's legs. As his opponent stumbled, the colonel threw a left hook to the jaw. The man sagged against the wall. Mackenzie grabbed the robe of the other and hurled him to the floor. "Get out," he rattled.

They pulled themselves together and glared at him. He thrust air with his blade. "From now on I am to kill," he said.

"Get help, Dave," said the one who had been opening the door. "I'll watch him." The other went unevenly down the stairs. The first man stood out of saber reach. "Do you want to be destroyed?" he asked.

Mackenzie turned the knob at his back, but the door was still locked. "I don't think you can do it," he said. "Not without what's here."

The Esper struggled for self-control. They waited through minutes that stretched. Then a noise began below. The Esper pointed. "We have nothing but agricultural implements," he said, "but you have only that blade. Will you surrender?"

Mackenzie spat on the floor. The Esper went on down.

Presently the attackers came into view. There might be a hundred, judging from the hubbub behind them, but because of the curve Mackenzie could see no more than ten or fifteen—burly fieldhands, their robes tucked high and sharp tools aloft. The landing was too wide for defense. He advanced to the stairway, where they could only come at him two at a time.

A couple of sawtoothed hay knives led the assault. Mackenzie parried one blow and chopped. His edge went into meat and struck bone. Blood ran out, impossibly red, even in the dim light here. The man fell to all fours with a shriek. Mackenzie dodged a cut from the companion. Metal clashed on metal. The weapons locked. Mackenzie's arm was forced back. He looked into a broad suntanned face. The side of his hand smote the young man's larynx. The Esper fell against the one behind and they went down together. It took a while to clear the tangle and resume action.

A pitchfork thrust for the colonel's belly. He managed to grab it with his left hand, divert the tines, and chop at the fingers on the shaft. A scythe gashed his right side. He saw his own blood but wasn't aware of pain. A flesh wound, no more. He swept his saber back and forth. The forefront retreated from its whistling menace. *But God, my knees are like rubber, I can't hold out another five minutes.*

A bugle sounded. There was a spatter of gunfire. The mob on the staircase congealed. Someone screamed.

Hoofs banged across the ground floor. A voice rasped: "Hold everything, there! Drop those weapons and come on down. First man tries anything gets shot."

Mackenzie leaned on his saber and fought for air. He hardly noticed the Espers melt away.

When he felt a little better, he went to one of the small windows and looked out. Horsemen were in the plaza. Not yet in sight, but nearing, he heard infantry.

Speyer arrived, followed by a sergeant of engineers and several privates. The major hurried to Mackenzie. "You okay, Jimbo? You been hurt!"

"A scratch," Mackenzie said. He was getting back his strength, though no sense of victory accompanied it, only the knowledge of aloneness. The injury began to sting. "Not worth a fuss. Look."

"Yes, I suppose you'll live. Okay, men, get that door open."

The engineers took forth their tools and assailed the lock with a vigor that must spring half from fear. "How'd you guys show up so soon?" Mackenzie asked.

"I thought there'd be trouble," Speyer said, "so when I heard shots I jumped through the window and ran around to my horse. That was just before those clodhoppers attacked you; I saw them gathering as I rode out. Our cavalry got in almost at once, of course, and the dogfaces weren't far behind."

"Any resistance?"

"No, not after we fired a few rounds in the air." Speyer glanced outside. "We're in full possession now."

Mackenzie regarded the door. "Well," he said, "I feel better about our having pulled guns on them in the office. Looks like their adepts really depend on plain old weapons, huh? And Esper communities aren't supposed to have arms. Their charters say so. . . . That was a damn good guess of yours, Phil. How'd you do it?"

"I sort of wondered why the chief had to send a runner to fetch guys that claim to be telepaths. There we go!"

The lock jingled apart. The sergeant opened the door. Mackenzie and Speyer went into the great room under the dome.

They walked around for a long time, wordless, among shapes of metal and less identifiable substances. Nothing was familiar. Mackenzie paused at last before a helix which projected from a transparent cube. Formless darknesses swirled within the box, sparked as if with tiny stars.

"I figured maybe the Espers had found a cache of old-time stuff, from just before the Hellbombs," he said in a muffled voice. "Ultrasecret weapons that never got a chance to be used. But this doesn't look like it. Think so?"

"No," Speyer said. "It doesn't look to me as if these things were made by human beings at all."

*"But do you not understand? They occupied a settlement! That proves to the world that Espers are not invulnerable. And to complete the catastrophe, they seized its arsenal."*

*"Have no fears about that. No untrained person can activate those*

instruments. *The circuits are locked except in the presence of certain encephalic rhythms which result from conditioning. That same conditioning makes it impossible for the so-called adepts to reveal any of their knowledge to the uninitiated, no matter what may be done to them."*

*"Yes, I know that much. But it is not what I had in mind. What frightens me is the fact that the revelation will spread. Everyone will know the Esper adepts do not plumb unknown depths of the psyche after all, but merely have access to an advanced physical science. Not only will this lift rebel spirits, but worse, it will cause many, perhaps most of the Order's members to break away in disillusionment."*

*"Not at once. News travels slowly under present conditions. Also, Mwyr, you underestimate the ability of the human mind to ignore data which conflict with cherished beliefs."*

*"But—"*

*"Well, let us assume the worst. Let us suppose that faith is lost and the Order disintegrates. That will be a serious setback to the plan, but not a fatal one. Psionics was merely one bit of folklore we found potent enough to serve as the motivator of a new orientation toward life. There are others, for example the widespread belief in magic among the less educated classes. We can begin again on a different basis, if we must. The exact form of the creed is not important. It is only scaffolding for the real structure: a communal, anti-materialistic social group, to which more and more people will turn for sheer lack of anything else, as the coming empire breaks up. In the end, the new culture can and will discard whatever superstitions gave it the initial impetus."*

*"A hundred-year setback, at least."*

*"True. It would be much more difficult to introduce a radical alien element now, when the autochthonous society has developed strong institutions of its own, than it was in the past. I merely wish to reassure you that the task is not impossible. I do not actually propose to let matters go that far. The Espers can be salvaged."*

*"How?"*

*"We must intervene directly."*

*"Has that been computed as being unavoidable?"*

*"Yes. The matrix yields an unambiguous answer. I do not like it any better than you. But direct action occurs oftener than we tell neophytes in the schools. The most elegant procedure would of course be to establish such initial conditions in a society that its evolution along desired lines becomes automatic. Furthermore, that would let us close our minds to the distressing fact of our own blood guilt. Unfortunately,*

the Great Science does not extend down to the details of day-to-day practicality.

"In the present instance, we shall help to smash the reactionaries. The government will then proceed so harshly against its conquered opponents that many of those who accept the story about what was found at St. Helena will not live to spread the tale. The rest . . . well, they will be discredited by their own defeat. Admittedly, the story will linger for lifetimes, whispered here and there. But what of that? Those who believe in the Way will, as a rule, simply be strengthened in their faith, by the very process of denying such ugly rumors. As more and more persons, common citizens as well as Espers, reject materialism, the legend will seem more and more fantastic. It will seem obvious that certain ancients invented the tale to account for a fact that they in their ignorance were unable to comprehend."

"I see. . . ."

"You are not happy here, are you, Mwyr?"

"I cannot quite say. Everything is so distorted."

"Be glad you were not sent to one of the really alien planets."

"I might almost prefer that. There would be a hostile environment to think about. One could forget how far it is to home."

"Three years' travel."

"You say that so glibly. As if three shipboard years were not equal to fifty in cosmic time. As if we could expect a relief vessel daily, not once in a century. And . . . as if the region that our ships have explored amounts to one chip out of this one galaxy!"

"That region will grow until someday it engulfs the galaxy."

"Yes, yes, yes. I know. Why do you think I chose to become a psycho-dynamician? Why am I here, learning how to meddle with the destiny of a world where I do not belong? 'To create the union of sentient beings, each member species a step toward life's mastery of the universe.' Brave slogan! But in practice, it seems, only a chosen few races are to be allowed the freedom of that universe."

"Not so, Mwyr. Consider these ones with whom we are, as you say, meddling. Consider what use they made of nuclear energy when they had it. At the rate they are going, they will have it again within a century or two. Not long after that they will be building spaceships. Even granted that time lag attenuates the effects of interstellar contact, those effects are cumulative. So do you wish such a band of carnivores turned loose on the galaxy?

"No, let them become inwardly civilized first; then we shall see if they can be trusted. If not, they will at least be happy on their own planet, in a mode of life designed for them by the Great Science. Re-

*member, they have an immemorial aspiration toward peace on earth;
but that is something they will never achieve by themselves. I do not
pretend to be a very good person, Mwyr. Yet this work that we are
doing makes me feel not altogether useless in the cosmos."*

Promotion was fast that year, casualties being so high. Captain
Thomas Danielis was raised to major for his conspicuous part in putting down the revolt of the Los Angeles citymen. Soon after occurred
the Battle of Maricopa, when the loyalists failed bloodily to break the
stranglehold of the Sierran rebels on the San Joaquin Valley, and he
was brevetted lieutenant colonel. The army was ordered northward
and moved warily under the coast ranges, half expecting attack from
the east. But the Brodskyites seemed too busy consolidating their latest
gains. The trouble came from guerrillas and the hedgehog resistance of
bossman Stations. After one particularly stiff clash, they stopped near
Pinnacles for a breather.

Danielis made his way through camp, where tents stood in tight
rows between the guns and men lay about dozing, talking, gambling,
staring at the blank blue sky. The air was hot, pungent with cookfire
smoke, horses, mules, dung, sweat, boot oil; the green of the hills that
lifted around the site was dulling toward summer brown. He was idle
until time for the conference the general had called, but restlessness
drove him. *By now I'm a father,* he thought, *and I've never seen my
kid.*

*At that, I'm lucky,* he reminded himself. *I've got my life and limbs.*
He remembered Jacobsen dying in his arms at Maricopa. You wouldn't
have thought the human body could hold so much blood. Though
maybe one was no longer human, when the pain was so great that one
could do nothing but shriek until the darkness came.

*And I used to think war was glamorous. Hunger, thirst, exhaustion,
terror, mutilation, death, and forever the sameness, boredom grinding
you down to an ox. . . . I've had it. I'm going into business after the
war. Economic integration, as the bossman system breaks up, yes,
there'll be a lot of ways for a man to get ahead, but decently, without
a weapon in his hand*—Danielis realized he was repeating thoughts
that were months old. What the hell else was there to think about,
though?

The large tent where prisoners were interrogated lay near his path.
A couple of privates were conducting a man inside. The fellow was
blond, burly, and sullen. He wore a sergeant's stripes, but otherwise
his only item of uniform was the badge of Warden Echevarry, bossman
in this part of the coastal mountains. A lumberjack in peacetime,

Danielis guessed from the look of him; a soldier in a private army whenever the interests of Echevarry were threatened; captured in yesterday's engagement.

On impulse, Danielis followed. He got into the tent as Captain Lambert, chubby behind a portable desk, finished the preliminaries, and blinked in the sudden gloom.

"Oh." The intelligence officer started to rise. "Yes, sir?"

"At ease," Danielis said. "Just thought I'd listen in."

"Well, I'll try to put on a good show for you." Lambert reseated himself and looked at the prisoner, who stood with hunched shoulders and widespread legs between his guards. "Now, sergeant, we'd like to know a few things."

"I don't have to say nothing except name, rank, and home town," the man growled. "You got those."

"Um-m-m, that's questionable. You aren't a foreign soldier, you're in rebellion against the government of your own country."

"The hell I am! I'm an Echevarry man."

"So what?"

"So my Judge is whoever Echevarry says. He says Brodsky. That makes you the rebel."

"The law's been changed."

"Your mucking Fallon got no right to change any laws. Especially part of the Constitution. I'm no hillrunner, Captain. I went to school some. And every year our Warden reads his people the Constitution."

"Times have changed since it was drawn," Lambert said. His tone sharpened. "But I'm not going to argue with you. How many riflemen and how many archers in your company?"

Silence.

"We can make things a lot easier for you," Lambert said. "I'm not asking you to do anything treasonable. All I want is to confirm some information I've already got."

The man shook his head angrily.

Lambert gestured. One of the privates stepped behind the captive, took his arm, and twisted a little.

"Echevarry wouldn't do that to me," he said through white lips.

"Of course not," Lambert said. "You're his man."

"Think I wanna be just a number on some list in Frisco? Damn right I'm my bossman's man!"

Lambert gestured again. The private twisted harder.

"Hold on, there," Danielis barked. "Stop that!"

The private let go, looking surprised. The prisoner drew a sobbing breath.

"I'm amazed at you, Captain Lambert," Danielis said. He felt his own face reddening. "If this has been your usual practice, there's going to be a court-martial."

"No, sir," Lambert said in a small voice. "Honest. Only . . . they don't talk. Hardly any of them. What'm I supposed to do?"

"Follow the rules of war."

"With rebels?"

"Take that man away," Danielis ordered. The privates made haste to do so.

"Sorry, sir," Lambert muttered. "I guess . . . I guess I've lost too many buddies. I hate to lose more, simply for lack of information."

"Me too." A compassion rose in Danielis. He sat down on the table edge and began to roll a cigarette. "But you see, we aren't in a regular war. And so, by a curious paradox, we have to follow the conventions more carefully than ever before."

"I don't quite understand, sir."

Danielis finished the cigarette and gave it to Lambert: olive branch or something. He started another for himself. "The rebels aren't rebels by their own lights," he said. "They're being loyal to a tradition that we're trying to curb, eventually to destroy. Let's face it, the average bossman is a fairly good leader. He may be descended from some thug who grabbed power by strong-arm methods during the chaos, but by now his family's integrated itself with the region he rules. He knows it, and its people, inside out. He's there in the flesh, a symbol of the community and its achievements, its folkways and essential independence. If you're in trouble, you don't have to work through some impersonal bureaucracy, you go direct to your bossman. His duties are as clearly defined as your own, and a good deal more demanding, to balance his privileges. He leads you in battle and in the ceremonies that give color and meaning to life. Your fathers and his have worked and played together for two or three hundred years. The land is alive with the memories of them. You and he *belong*.

"Well, that has to be swept away, so we can go on to a higher level. But we won't reach that level by alienating everyone. We're not a conquering army; we're more like the Householder Guard putting down a riot in some city. The opposition is part and parcel of our own society."

Lambert struck a match for him. He inhaled and finished: "On a practical plane, I might also remind you, Captain, that the federal armed forces, Fallonite and Brodskyite together, are none too large. Little more than a cadre, in fact. We're a bunch of younger sons, countrymen who failed, poor citymen, adventurers, people who look to their regi-

ment for that sense of wholeness they've grown up to expect and can't
find in civilian life."

"You're too deep for me, sir, I'm afraid," Lambert said.

"Never mind," Danielis sighed. "Just bear in mind, there are a good
many more fighting men outside the opposing armies than in. If the
bossmen could establish a unified command, that'd be the end of the
Fallon government. Luckily, there's too much provincial pride and too
much geography between them for this to happen—unless we outrage
them beyond endurance. What we want the ordinary freeholder, and
even the ordinary bossman, to think, is: 'Well, those Fallonites aren't
such bad guys, and if I keep on the right side of them I don't stand to
lose much, and should even be able to gain something at the expense
of those who fight them to a finish.' You see?"

"Y-yes. I guess so."

"You're a smart fellow, Lambert. You don't have to beat information
out of prisoners. Trick it out."

"I'll try, sir."

"Good." Danielis glanced at the watch that had been given him as
per tradition, together with a sidearm, when he was first commissioned.
(Such items were much too expensive for the common man. They had
not been so in the age of mass production; and perhaps in the coming
age—) "I have to go. See you around."

He left the tent feeling somewhat more cheerful than before. *No
doubt I am a natural-born preacher,* he admitted, *and I never could
quite join in the horseplay at mess, and a lot of jokes go completely by
me; but if I can get even a few ideas across where they count, that's
pleasure enough.* A strain of music came to him, some men and a banjo
under a tree, and he found himself whistling along. It was good that
this much morale remained, after Maricopa and a northward march
whose purpose had not been divulged to anybody.

The conference tent was big enough to be called a pavilion. Two
sentries stood at the entrance. Danielis was nearly the last to arrive,
and found himself at the end of the table, opposite Brigadier General
Perez. Smoke hazed the air and there was a muted buzz of conversation,
but faces were taut.

When the blue-robed figure with a Yang and Yin on the breast entered, silence fell like a curtain. Danielis was astonished to recognize
Philosopher Woodworth. He'd last seen the man in Los Angeles, and
assumed he would stay at the Esper center there. Must have come
here by special conveyance, under special orders. . . .

Perez introduced him. Both remained standing, under the eyes of
the officers. "I have some important news for you, gentlemen," Perez

said most quietly. "You may consider it an honor to be here. It means that in my judgment you can be trusted, first, to keep absolute silence about what you are going to hear, and second, to execute a vital operation of extreme difficulty." Danielis was made shockingly aware that several men were not present whose rank indicated they should be.

"I repeat," Perez said, "any breach of secrecy and the whole plan is ruined. In that case, the war will drag on for months or years. You know how bad our position is. You also know it will grow still worse as our stocks of those supplies the enemy now denies us are consumed. We could even be beaten. I'm not defeatist to say that, only realistic. We could lose the war.

"On the other hand, if this new scheme pans out, we may break the enemy's back this very month."

He paused to let that sink in before continuing:

"The plan was worked out by GHQ in conjunction with Esper Central in San Francisco some weeks ago. It's the reason we are headed north—" He let the gasp subside that ran through the stifling air. "Yes, you know that the Esper Order is neutral in political disputes. But you also know that it defends itself when attacked. And you probably know that an attack was made on it by the rebels. They seized the Napa Valley settlement and have been spreading malicious rumors about the Order since then. Would you like to comment on that, Philosopher Woodworth?"

The man in blue nodded and said coolly: "We've our own ways of findin' out things—intelligence service, you might say—so I can give y'all a report of the facts. St. Helena was assaulted at a time when most of its adepts were away, helpin' a new community get started out in Montana." *How did they travel so fast?* Danielis wondered. *Teleport, or what?* "I don't know, myself, if the enemy knew about that or were just lucky. Anyhow, when the two or three adepts that were left came and warned them off, fightin' broke out and the adepts were killed before they could act." He smiled. "We don't claim to be immortal, except the way every livin' thing is immortal. Nor infallible, either. So now St. Helena's occupied. We don't figure to take any immediate steps about that, because a lot of people in the community might get hurt.

"As for the yarns the enemy command's been handin' out, well, I reckon I'd do the same, if I had a chance like that. Everybody knows an adept can do things that nobody else can. Troops that realize they've done wrong to the Order are goin' to be scared of supernatural revenge. You're educated men here, and know there's nothin' supernatural involved, just a way to use the powers latent in most of us. You also know the Order doesn't believe in revenge. But the ordinary foot soldier doesn't think your way. His officers have got to restore his spirit somehow. So they fake some equipment and tell him that's what the adepts were really usin'—an advanced technology, sure, but only a set of machines that can be put out of action if you're brave, same as any other machine. That's what happened.

"Still, it is a threat to the Order; and we can't let an attack on our people go unpunished, either. So Esper Central has decided to help out on your side. The sooner this war's over, the better for everybody."

A sigh gusted around the table, and a few exultant oaths. The hair stirred on Danielis' neck. Perez lifted a hand.

"Not too fast, please," the general said. "The adepts are not going to go around blasting your opponents for you. It was one hell of a tough decision for them to do as much they agreed to. I, uh, understand that the, uh, personal development of every Esper will be set back many years by this much violence. They're making a big sacrifice.

"By their charter, they can use psionics to defend an establishment against attack. Okay . . . an assault on San Francisco will be construed as one on Central, their world headquarters."

The realization of what was to come was blinding to Danielis. He scarcely heard Perez' carefully dry continuation:

"Let's review the strategic picture. By now the enemy holds more than half of California, all of Oregon and Idaho, and a good deal of Washington. We, this army, we're using the last land access to San Francisco that we've got. The enemy hasn't tried to pinch that off yet, because the troops we pulled out of the north—those that aren't in the field at present—make a strong city garrison that'd sally out. He's collecting too much profit elsewhere to accept the cost.

"Nor can he invest the city with any hope of success. We still hold Puget Sound and the southern California ports. Our ships bring in ample food and munitions. His own sea power is much inferior to ours: chiefly schooners donated by coastal bossmen, operating out of Portland. He might overwhelm an occasional convoy, but he hasn't tried that so far because it isn't worth his trouble; there would be others, more heavily escorted. And of course he can't enter the Bay, with artillery and rocket emplacements on both sides of the Golden Gate. No, about all he can do is maintain some water communication with Hawaii and Alaska.

"Nevertheless, his ultimate object is San Francisco. It has to be—the seat of government and industry, the heart of the nation.

"Well, then, here's the plan. Our army is to engage the Sierra Command and its militia auxiliaries again, striking out of San Jose. That's a perfectly logical maneuver. Successful, it would cut his California forces in two. We know, in fact, that he is already concentrating men in anticipation of precisely such an attempt.

"We aren't going to succeed. We'll give him a good stiff battle and be thrown back. That's the hardest part: to feign a serious defeat, even convincing our own troops, and still maintain good order. We'll have a lot of details to thresh out about that.

"We'll retreat northward, up the Peninsula toward Frisco. The enemy is bound to pursue. It will look like a God-given chance to destroy us and get to the city walls.

"When he is well into the Peninsula, with the ocean on his left and the Bay on his right, we will outflank him and attack from the rear. The Esper adepts will be there to help. Suddenly he'll be caught, between us and the capital's land defenses. What the adepts don't wipe out, we will. Nothing will remain of the Sierra Command but a few garrisons. The rest of the war will be a mopping-up operation.

"It's a brilliant piece of strategy. Like all such, it's damn difficult to execute. Are you prepared to do the job?"

Danielis didn't raise his voice with the others. He was thinking too hard of Laura.

Northward and to the right there was some fighting. Cannon spoke occasionally, or a drumfire of rifles; smoke lay thin over the grass and the wind-gnarled live oaks which covered those hills. But down along the seacoast was only surf, blowing air, a hiss of sand across the dunes.

Mackenzie rode on the beach, where the footing was easiest and the view widest. Most of his regiment were inland. But that was a wilderness: rough ground, woods, the snags of ancient homes, making travel slow and hard. Once this area had been densely peopled, but the firestorm after the Hellbomb scrubbed it clean and today's reduced population could not make a go on such infertile soil. There didn't even seem to be any foemen near this left wing of the army.

The Rolling Stones had certainly not been given it for that reason. They could have borne the brunt at the center as well as those outfits which actually were there, driving the enemy back toward San Francisco. They had been blooded often enough in this war, when they operated out of Calistoga to help expel the Fallonites from northern California. So thoroughly had that job been done that now only a skeleton force need remain in charge. Nearly the whole Sierra Command had gathered at Modesto, met the northward-moving opposition army that struck at them out of San Jose, and sent it in a shooting retreat. Another day or so, and the white city should appear before their eyes.

*And there the enemy will be sure to make a stand,* Mackenzie thought, *with the garrison to reinforce him. And his positions will have to be shelled; maybe we'll have to take the place street by street. Laura, kid, will you be alive at the end?*

*Of course, maybe it won't happen that way. Maybe my scheme'll work and we'll win easy— What a horrible word "maybe" is!* He slapped his hands together with a pistol sound.

Speyer threw him a glance. The major's people were safe; he'd even been able to visit them at Mount Lassen, after the northern campaign was over. "Rough," he said.

"Rough on everybody," Mackenzie said with a thick anger. "This is a filthy war."

Speyer shrugged. "No different from most, except that this time Pacificans are on the receiving as well as the giving end."

"You know damn well I never liked the business, anyplace."

"What man in his right mind does?"

"When I want a sermon I'll ask for one."

"Sorry," said Speyer, and meant it.

"I'm sorry too," said Mackenzie, instantly contrite. "Nerves on edge. Damnation! I could almost wish for some action."

"Wouldn't be surprised if we got some. This whole affair smells wrong to me."

Mackenzie looked around him. On the right the horizon was bounded by hills, beyond which the low but massive San Bruno range lifted. Here and there he spied one of his own squads, afoot or ahorse. Overhead sputtered a plane. But there was plenty of concealment for a redoubt. Hell could erupt at any minute . . . though necessarily a small hell, quickly reduced by howitzer or bayonet, casualties light. (Huh! Every one of those light casualties was a man dead, with women and children to weep for him, or a man staring at the fragment of his arm, or a man with eyes and face gone in a burst of shot, and what kind of unsoldierly thoughts were these?)

Seeking comfort, Mackenzie glanced left. The ocean rolled greenish-gray, glittering far out, rising and breaking in a roar of white combers closer to land. He smelled salt and kelp. A few gulls mewed above dazzling sands. There was no sail or smoke-puff—only emptiness. The convoys from Puget Sound to San Francisco and the lean swift ships of the coastal bossmen were miles beyond the curve of the world.

Which was as it should be. Maybe things were working out okay on the high waters. One could only try, and hope. And . . . it had been his suggestion, James Mackenzie speaking at the conference General Cruikshank held between the battles of Mariposa and San Jose; the same James Mackenzie who had first proposed that the Sierra Command come down out of the mountains, and who had exposed the gigantic fraud of Esperdom, and succeeded in playing down for his men the fact that behind the fraud lay a mystery one hardly dared think about. He would endure in the chronicles, that colonel, they would sing ballads about him for half a thousand years.

Only it didn't feel that way. James Mackenzie knew he was not much more than average bright under the best of conditions, now dull-minded with weariness and terrified of his daughter's fate. For himself he was haunted by the fear of certain crippling wounds. Often he had to drink himself to sleep. He was shaved, because an officer must maintain appearances, but realized very well that if he hadn't had an orderly to do the job for him he would be as shaggy as any buck private. His uniform was faded and threadbare, his body stank and itched, his mouth yearned for tobacco but there had been some trouble in the commissariat and they were lucky to eat. His achievements amounted to patchwork jobs carried out in utter confusion, or to slogging like this and wishing only for an end to the whole mess. One day, win or lose, his body would give out on him—he could feel the machinery wearing to pieces, arthritic twinges, shortness of breath, dozing off in the middle of things—and the termination of himself would be as undignified and lonely as that of every other human slob. Hero? What an all-time laugh!

He yanked his mind back to the immediate situation. Behind him a core of the regiment accompanied the artillery along the beach, a thousand men with motorized gun carriages, caissons, mule-drawn wagons, a few trucks, one precious armored car. They were a dun mass topped with helmets, in loose formation, rifles or bows to hand. The sand deadened their footfalls, so that only the surf and the wind could be heard. But whenever the wind sank, Mackenzie caught the tune of the hex corps: a dozen leathery older men, mostly Indians, carrying the wands of power and whistling together the Song Against Witches. He took no stock in magic himself, yet when that sound came to him the skin crawled along his backbone.

*Everything's in good order,* he insisted. *We're doing fine.*

Then: *But Phil's right. This is a screwball business. The enemy should have fought through to a southward line of retreat, not let themselves be boxed.*

Captain Hulse galloped close. Sand spurted when he checked his horse. "Patrol report, sir."

"Well?" Mackenzie realized he had almost shouted. "Go ahead."

"Considerable activity observed about five miles northeast. Looks like a troop headed our way."

Mackenzie stiffened. "Haven't you anything more definite than that?"

"Not so far, with the ground so broken."

"Get some aerial reconnaissance there, for Pete's sake!"

"Yes, sir. I'll throw out more scouts, too."

"Carry on here, Phil." Mackenzie headed toward the radio truck. He carried a minicom in his saddlebag, of course, but San Francisco had been continuously jamming on all bands and you needed a powerful set to punch a signal even a few miles. Patrols must communicate by messenger.

He noticed that the firing inland had slacked off. There were decent roads in the interior Peninsula a ways further north, where some resettlement had taken place. The enemy, still in possession of that area, could use them to effect rapid movements.

*If they withdrew their center and hit our flanks, where we're weakest—*

A voice from field HQ, barely audible through the squeals and buzzes, took his report and gave back what had been seen elsewhere. Large maneuvers right and left, yes, it did seem as if the Fallonites were going to try a breakthrough. Could be a feint, though. The main body of the Sierrans must remain where it was until the situation became clearer. The Rolling Stones must hold out a while on their own.

"Will do." Mackenzie returned to the head of his columns. Speyer nodded grimly at the word.

"Better get prepared, hadn't we?"

"Uh-huh." Mackenzie lost himself in a welter of commands, as officer after officer rode to him. The outlying sections were to be pulled in. The beach was to be defended, with the high ground immediately above.

Men scurried, horses neighed, guns trundled about. The scout plane returned, flying low enough to get a transmission through: yes, definitely an attack on the way; hard to tell how big a force, through the damned tree cover and down in the damned arroyos, but it might well be at brigade strength.

Mackenzie established himself on a hilltop with his staff and runners. A line of artillery stretched beneath him, across the strand. Cavalry waited behind them, lances agleam, an infantry company for support. Otherwise the foot soldiers had faded into the landscape. The sea boomed its own cannonade, and gulls began to gather as if they knew there would be meat before long.

"Think we can hold them?" Speyer asked.

"Sure," Mackenzie said. "If they come down the beach, we'll enfilade them, as well as shooting up their front. If they come higher, well, that's a textbook example of defensible terrain. 'Course, if another troop punches through the lines further inland, we'll be cut off, but that isn't our worry right now."

"They must hope to get around our army and attack our rear."

"Guess so. Not too smart of them, though. We can approach Frisco just as easily fighting backwards as forwards."

"Unless the city garrison makes a sally."

"Even then. Total numerical strengths are about equal, and we've got more ammo and alky. Also a lot of bossman militia for auxiliaries, who're used to disorganized warfare in hilly ground."

"If we do whip them—" Speyer shut his lips together.

"Go on," Mackenzie said.

"Nothing."

"The hell it is. You were about to remind me of the next step: how do we take the city without too high a cost to both sides? Well, I happen to know we've got a hole card to play there, which might help."

Speyer turned pitying eyes away from Mackenzie. Silence fell on the hilltop.

It was an unconscionably long time before the enemy came in view, first a few outriders far down the dunes, then the body of him, pouring from the ridges and gullies and woods. Reports flickered about Mackenzie—a powerful force, nearly twice as big as ours, but with little artillery; by now badly short of fuel, they must depend far more than we on animals to move their equipment. They were evidently going to charge, accept losses in order to get sabers and bayonets among the Rolling Stones' cannon. Mackenzie issued his directions accordingly.

The hostiles formed up, a mile or so distant. Through his field glasses Mackenzie recognized them, red sashes of the Madera Horse, green and gold pennon of the Dagos, fluttering in the iodine wind. He'd campaigned with both outfits in the past. It was treacherous to remember that Ives favored a blunt wedge formation and use the fact against him. . . . One enemy armored car and some fieldpieces, light horse-drawn ones, gleamed wickedly in the sunlight.

Bugles blew shrill. The Fallonite cavalry laid lance in rest and started trotting. They gathered speed as they went, a canter, a gallop, until the earth trembled with them. Then their infantry got going, flanked by its guns. The car rolled along between the first and second line of foot. Oddly, it had no rocket launcher on top or repeater barrels thrust from the fire slits. Those were good troops, Mackenzie thought, advancing in close order with that ripple down the ranks which bespoke veterans. He hated what must happen.

His defense waited immobile on the sand. Fire crackled from the hillsides, where mortar squads and riflemen crouched. A rider toppled, a dogface clutched his belly and went to his knees, their companions behind moved forward to close the lines again. Mackenzie looked to his howitzers. Men stood tensed at sights and lanyards. Let the foe get well in range— There! Yamaguchi, mounted just rearward of the gunners, drew his saber and flashed the blade downward. Cannon bellowed. Fire spurted through smoke, sand gouted up, shrapnel sleeted over the charging force. At once the gun crews fell into the rhythm of reloading, relaying, refiring, the steady three rounds per minute which conserved barrels and broke armies. Horses screamed in their own tangled red guts. But not many had been hit. The Madera cavalry continued in full gallop. Their lead was so close now that Mackenzie's glasses picked out a face, red, freckled, a ranch boy turned trooper, his mouth stretched out of shape as he yelled.

The archers behind the defending cannon let go. Arrows whistled skyward, flight after flight, curved past the gulls and down again. Flame and smoke ran ragged in the wiry hill grass, out of the ragged-leaved live oak copses. Men pitched to the sand, many still hideously astir, like insects that had been stepped on. The fieldpieces on the enemy left flank halted, swiveled about, and spat return fire. Futile . . . but God, their officer had courage! Mackenzie saw the advancing lines waver. An attack by his own horse and foot, down the beach, ought to crumple them. "Get ready to move," he said into his minicom. He saw his men poise. The cannon belched anew.

The oncoming armored car slowed to a halt. Something within it chattered, loud enough to hear through the explosions.

A blue-white sheet ran over the nearest hill. Mackenzie shut half-blinded eyes. When he opened them again, he saw a grass fire through the crazy patterns of after-image. A Rolling Stone burst from cover, howling, his clothes ablaze. The man hit the sand and rolled over. That part of the beach lifted in one monster wave, crested twenty feet high, and smashed across the hill. The burning soldier vanished in the avalanche that buried his comrades.

"*Psi blast!*" someone screamed, thin and horrible, through chaos and ground-shudder. "The Espers—"

Unbelievably, a bugle sounded and the Sierran cavalry lunged forward. Past their own guns, on against the scattering opposition . . . and horses and riders rose into the air, tumbled in a giant's invisible whirligig, crashed bone-breakingly to earth again. The second rank of lancers broke. Mounts reared, pawed the air, wheeled and fled in every direction.

A terrible deep hum filled the sky. Mackenzie saw the world as if through a haze, as if his brain were being dashed back and forth between the walls of his skull. Another glare ran across the hills, higher this time, burning men alive.

"They'll wipe us out," Speyer called, a dim voice that rose and fell on the air tides. "They'll re-form as we stampede—"

"No!" Mackenzie shouted. "The adepts must be in that car. Come on!"

Most of his horse had recoiled on their own artillery, one squealing, trampling wreck. The infantry stood rigid, but about to bolt. A glance thrown to his right showed Mackenzie how the enemy themselves were in confusion, this had been a terrifying surprise to them too, but as soon as they got over the shock they'd advance and there'd be nothing left to stop them. . . . It was as if another man spurred his mount. The animal fought, foam-flecked with panic. He slugged its head around, brutally, and dug in spurs. They rushed down the hill toward the guns.

He needed all his strength to halt the gelding before the cannon mouths. A man slumped dead by his piece, though there was no mark on him. Mackenzie jumped to the ground. His steed bolted.

He hadn't time to worry about that. Where was help? "Come here!" His yell was lost in the riot. But suddenly another man was beside him, Speyer, snatching up a shell and slamming it into the breach. Mackenzie squinted through the telescope, took a bearing by guess and feel. He could see the Esper car where it squatted among dead and hurt. At this distance it looked too small to have blackened acres.

Speyer helped him lay the howitzer. He jerked the lanyard. The gun roared and sprang. The shell burst a few yards short of target, sand spurted and metal fragments whined.

Speyer had the next one loaded. Mackenzie aimed and fired. Overshot this time, but not by much. The car rocked. Concussion might have hurt the Espers inside; at least, the psi blasts had stopped. But it was necessary to strike before the foe got organized again.

He ran toward his own regimental car. The door gaped, the crew had fled. He threw himself into the driver's seat. Speyer clanged the door shut and stuck his face in the hood of the rocket-launcher periscope. Mackenzie raced the machine forward. The banner on its rooftop snapped in the wind.

Speyer aimed the launcher and pressed the firing button. The missile burned across intervening yards and exploded. The other car lurched on its wheels. A hole opened in its side.

*If the boys will only rally and advance— Well, if they don't, I'm done for anyway.* Mackenzie squealed to a stop, flung open the door and leaped out. Curled, blackened metal framed his entry. He wriggled through, into murk and stenches.

Two Espers lay there. The driver was dead, a chunk of steel through his breast. The other one, the adept, whimpered among his unhuman instruments. His face was hidden by blood. Mackenzie pitched the corpse on its side and pulled off the robe. He snatched a curving tube of metal and tumbled back out.

Speyer was still in the undamaged car, firing repeaters at those hostiles who ventured near. Mackenzie jumped onto the ladder of the disabled machine, climbed to its roof and stood erect. He waved the blue robe in one hand and the weapon he did not understand in the other. "Come on, you sons!" he shouted, tiny against the sea wind. "We've knocked 'em out for you! Want your breakfast in bed too?"

One bullet buzzed past his ear. Nothing else. Most of the enemy, horse and foot, stayed frozen. In that immense stillness he could not tell if he heard surf or the blood in his own veins.

Then a bugle called. The hex corps whistled triumphantly; their tomtoms thuttered. A ragged line of his infantry began to move toward him. More followed. The cavalry joined them, man by man and unit by unit, on their flanks. Soldiers ran down the smoking hillsides.

Mackenzie sprang to sand again and into his car. "Let's get back," he told Speyer. "We got a battle to finish."

"Shut up!" Tom Danielis said.

Philosopher Woodworth stared at him. Fog swirled and dripped in the forest, hiding the land and the brigade, gray nothingness through which came a muffled noise of men and horses and wheels, an isolated and infinitely weary sound. The air was cold, and clothing hung heavy on the skin.

"Sir," protested Major Lescarbault. The eyes were wide and shocked in his gaunted face.

"I dare tell a ranking Esper to stop quacking about a subject of which he's totally ignorant?" Danielis answered. "Well, it's past time that somebody did."

Woodworth recovered his poise. "All I said, son, was that we should consolidate our adepts and strike the Brodskyite center," he reproved. "What's wrong with that?"

Danielis clenched his fists. "Nothing," he said, "except it invites a worse disaster than you've brought on us yet."

"A setback or two," Lescarbault argued. "They did rout us on the west, but we turned their flank here by the Bay."

"With the net result that their main body pivoted, attacked, and split us in half," Danielis snapped. "The Espers have been scant use since then . . . now the rebels know they need vehicles to transport their weapons, and can be killed. Artillery zeroes in on their positions, or bands of woodsmen hit and run, leaving them dead, or the enemy simply goes around any spot where they're known to be. We haven't got enough adepts!"

"That's why I proposed gettin' them in one group, too big to withstand," Woodworth said.

"And too cumbersome to be of any value," Danielis replied. He felt more than a little sickened, knowing how the Order had cheated him his whole life; yes, he thought, that was the real bitterness, not the fact that the adepts had failed to defeat the rebels—by failing, essentially, to break their spirit—but the fact that the adepts were only someone else's cat's paws and every gentle, earnest soul in every Esper community was only someone's dupe.

Wildly he wanted to return to Laura—there'd been no chance thus far to see her—Laura and the kid, the last honest reality this fog-world had left him. He mastered himself and went on more evenly:

"The adepts, what few of them survive, will of course be helpful in defending San Francisco. An army free to move around in the field can deal with them, one way or another, but your . . . your weapons can repel an assault on the city walls. So that's where I'm going to take them."

Probably the best he could do. There was no word from the northern half of the loyalist army. Doubtless they'd withdrawn to the capital, suffering heavy losses en route. Radio jamming continued, hampering friendly and hostile communications alike. He had to take action, either retreat southward or fight his way through to the city. The latter course seemed wisest. He didn't believe that Laura had much to do with his choice.

"I'm no adept myself," Woodworth said. "I can't call them mind to mind."

"You mean you can't use their equivalent of radio," Danielis said brutally. "Well, you've got an adept in attendance. Have him pass the word."

Woodworth flinched. "I hope," he said, "I hope you understand this came as a surprise to me too."

"Oh, yes, certainly, Philosopher," Lescarbault said unbidden.

Woodworth swallowed. "I still hold with the Way and the Order," he said harshly. "There's nothin' else I can do. Is there? The Grand

Seeker has promised a full explanation when this is over." He shook his head. "Okay, son, I'll do what I can."

A certain compassion touched Danielis as the blue robe disappeared into the fog. He rapped his orders the more severely.

Slowly his command got going. He was with the Second Brigade; the rest were strewn over the Peninsula in the fragments into which the rebels had knocked them. He hoped the equally scattered adepts, joining him on his march through the San Bruno range, would guide some of those united to him. But most, wandering demoralized, were sure to surrender to the first rebels they came upon.

He rode near the front, on a muddy road that snaked over the highlands. His helmet was a monstrous weight. The horse stumbled beneath him, exhausted by—how many days?—of march, countermarch, battle, skirmish, thin rations or none, heat and cold and fear, in an empty land. Poor beast, he'd see that it got proper treatment when they reached the city. That all those poor beasts behind him did, after trudging and fighting and trudging again until their eyes were filmed with fatigue.

*There'll be chance enough for rest in San Francisco. We're impregnable there, walls and cannon and the Esper machines to landward, the sea that feeds us at our backs. We can recover our strength, regroup our forces, bring fresh troops down from Washington and up from the south by water. The war isn't decided yet . . . God help us.*

*I wonder if it will ever be.*

*And then, will Jimbo Mackenzie come to see us, sit by the fire and swap yarns about what we did? Or talk about something else, anything else? If not, that's too high a price for victory.*

*Maybe not too high a price for what we've learned, though. Strangers on this planet . . . what else could have forged those weapons? The adepts will talk if I myself have to torture them till they do.* But Danielis remembered tales muttered in the fisher huts of his boyhood, after dark, when ghosts walked in old men's minds. Before the holocaust there had been legends about the stars, and the legends lived on. He didn't know if he would be able to look again at the night sky without a shiver.

This damned fog—

Hoofs thudded. Danielis half drew his sidearm. But the rider was a scout of his own, who raised a drenched sleeve in salute. "Colonel, an enemy force about ten miles ahead by road. Big."

*So we'll have to fight now.* "Do they seem aware of us?"

"No, sir. They're proceeding east along the ridge there."

"Probably figure to occupy the Candlestick Park ruins," Danielis murmured. His body was too tired for excitement. "Good stronghold, that. Very well, Corporal." He turned to Lescarbault and issued instructions.

The brigade formed itself in the formlessness. Patrols went out. Information began to flow back, and Danielis sketched a plan that ought to work. He didn't want to try for a decisive engagement, only brush the enemy aside and discourage them from pursuit. His men must be spared, as many as possible, for the city defense and the eventual counteroffensive.

Lescarbault came back. "Sir! The radio jamming's ended!"

"What?" Danielis blinked, not quite comprehending.

"Yes, sir. I've been using a minicom"—Lescarbault lifted the wrist on which his tiny transceiver was strapped—"for very short-range work, passing the battalion commanders their orders. The interference stopped a couple of minutes ago. Clear as daylight."

Danielis pulled the wrist toward his own mouth. "Hello, hello, radio wagon, this is the C.O. You read me?"

"Yes, sir," said the voice.

"They turned off the jammer in the city for a reason. Get me the open military band."

"Yes, sir." Pause, while men mumbled and water runneled unseen in the arroyos. A wraith smoked past Danielis' eyes. Drops coursed off his helmut and down his collar. The horse's mane hung sodden.

Like the scream of an insect:

"—here at once! Every unit in the field, get to San Francisco at once! We're under attack by sea!"

Danielis let go Lescarbault's arm. He stared into emptiness while the voice wailed on and forever on.

"—bombarding Potrero Point. Decks jammed with troops. They must figure to make a landing there—"

Danielis' mind raced ahead of the words. It was as if Esp were no lie, as if he scanned the beloved city himself and felt her wounds in his own flesh. There was no fog around the Gate, of course, or so detailed a description could not have been given. Well, probably some streamers of it rolled in under the rusted remnants of the bridge, themselves like snowbanks against blue-green water and brilliant sky. But most of the Bay stood open to the sun. On the opposite shore lifted the Eastbay hills, green with gardens and agleam with villas; and Marin shouldered heavenward across the strait, looking to the roofs and walls and heights that were San Francisco. The convoy had gone between the coast defenses that could have smashed it, an unusually large convoy and not on time: but still the familiar big-bellied hulls, white sails, occasional fuming stacks, that kept the city fed. There had been an explanation about trouble with commerce raiders; and the fleet was passed on into the Bay, where San Francisco had no walls. Then the gun covers were taken off and the holds vomited armed men.

*Yes, they did seize a convoy, those piratical schooners. Used radio jamming of their own; together with ours, that choked off any cry of warning. They threw our supplies overboard and embarked the boss-man militia. Some spy or traitor gave them the recognition signals. Now the capital lies open to them, her garrison stripped, hardly an adept left in Esper Central, the Sierrans thrusting against her southern gates, and Laura without me.*

"We're coming!" Danielis yelled. His brigade groaned into speed behind him. They struck with a desperate ferocity that carried them deep into enemy positions and then stranded them in separated groups. It became knife and saber in the fog. But Danielis, because he led the charge, had already taken a grenade on his breast.

East and south, in the harbor district and at the wreck of the Peninsula wall, there was still some fighting. As he rode higher, Mackenzie saw how those parts were dimmed by smoke, which the wind scattered to show rubble that had been houses. The sound of firing drifted to him. But otherwise the city shone untouched, roofs and white walls in a web of streets, church spires raking the sky like masts, Federal House on Nob Hill and the Watchtower on Telegraph Hill as he remembered them from childhood visits. The Bay glittered insolently beautiful.

But he had no time for admiring the view, nor for wondering where Laura huddled. The attack on Twin Peaks must be swift, for surely Esper Central would defend itself.

On the avenue climbing the opposite side of those great humps, Speyer led half the Rolling Stones. (Yamaguchi lay dead on a pock-marked beach.) Mackenzie himself was taking this side. Horses clopped along Portola, between blankly shuttered mansions; guns trundled and creaked, boots knocked on pavement, moccasins slithered, weapons rattled, men breathed heavily and the hex corps whistled against unknown demons. But silence overwhelmed the noise, echoes trapped it and let it die. Mackenzie recollected nightmares when he fled down a corridor which had no end. *Even if they don't cut loose at us,* he thought bleakly, *we've got to seize their place before our nerve gives out.*

Twin Peaks Boulevard turned off Portola and wound steeply to the right. The houses ended; wild grasses alone covered the quasi-sacred hills, up to the tops where stood the buildings forbidden to all but adepts. Those two soaring, iridescent, fountainlike skyscrapers had been raised by night, within a matter of weeks. Something like a moan stirred at Mackenzie's back.

"Bugler, sound the advance. On the double!"

A child's jeering, the notes lifted and were lost. Sweat stung Mackenzie's eyes. If he failed and was killed, that didn't matter too much . . . after everything which had happened . . . but the regiment, the regiment—

Flame shot across the street, the color of hell. There went a hiss and a roar. The pavement lay trenched, molten, smoking and reeking. Mackenzie wrestled his horse to a standstill. *A warning only. But if they had enough adepts to handle us, would they bother trying to scare us off?* "Artillery, open fire!"

The field guns bellowed together, not only howitzers but motorized 75s taken along from Alemany Gate's emplacements. Shells went overhead with a locomotive sound. They burst on the walls above and the racket thundered back down the wind.

Mackenzie tensed himself for an Esper blast, but none came. Had they knocked out the final defensive post in their own first barrage? Smoke cleared from the heights and he saw that the colors which played in the tower were dead and that wounds gaped across loveliness, showing unbelievably thin framework. It was like seeing the bones of a woman murdered by his hand.

Quick, though! He issued a string of commands and led the horse and foot on. The battery stayed where it was, firing and firing with hysterical fury. The dry brown grass started to burn, as red-hot fragments scattered across the slope. Through mushroom bursts, Mackenzie saw the building crumble. Whole sheets of facing broke and fell to earth. The skeleton vibrated, took a direct hit and sang in metal agony, slumped and twisted apart.

What was that which stood within?

There were no separate rooms, no floors, nothing but girders, enigmatic machines, here and there a globe still aglow like a minor sun. The structure had enclosed something nearly as tall as itself, a finned and shining column, almost like a rocket shell but impossibly huge and fair.

*Their spaceship,* Mackenzie thought in the clamor. *Yes, of course, the ancients had begun making spaceships, and we always figured we would again someday. This, though—!*

The archers lifted a tribal screech. The riflemen and cavalry took it up, crazy, jubilant, the howl of a beast of prey. By Satan, we've whipped the stars themselves! As they burst onto the hillcrest, the shelling stopped, and their yells overrode the wind. Smoke was acrid as blood smell in their nostrils.

A few dead blue-robes could be seen in the debris. Some half-dozen survivors milled toward the ship. A bowman let fly. His arrow glanced off the landing gear but brought the Espers to a halt. Troopers poured over the shards to capture them.

Mackenzie reined in. Something that was not human lay crushed near a machine. Its blood was deep violet color. *When the people have seen this, that's the end of the Order.* He felt no triumph. At St. Helena he had come to appreciate how fundamentally good the believers were.

But this was no moment for regret, or for wondering how harsh the future would be with man taken entirely off the leash. The building on the other peak was still intact. He had to consolidate his position here, then help Phil if need be.

However, the minicom said, "Come on and join me, Jimbo. The fracas is over," before he had completed his task. As he rode alone toward Speyer's place, he saw a Pacific States flag flutter up the mast on that skyscraper's top.

Guards stood awed and nervous at the portal. Mackenzie dismounted and walked inside. The entry chamber was a soaring, shimmering fantasy of colors and arches, through which men moved troll-like. A corporal led him down a hall. Evidently this building had been used for quarters, offices, storage, and less understandable purposes. . . . There was a room whose door had been blown down with dynamite. The fluid abstract murals were stilled, scarred, and sooted. Four ragged troopers pointed guns at the two beings whom Speyer was questioning.

One slumped at something that might answer to a desk. The avian face was buried in seven-fingered hands and the rudimentary wings quivered with sobs. *Are they able to cry, then?* Mackenzie thought, astonished, and had a sudden wish to take the being in his arms and offer what comfort he was able.

The other one stood erect in a robe of woven metal. Great topaz eyes met Speyer's from a seven-foot height, and the voice turned accented English into music.

"—a G-type star some fifty light-years hence. It is barely visible to the naked eye, though not in this hemisphere."

The major's fleshless, bristly countenance jutted forward as if to peck. "When do you expect reinforcements?"

"There will be no other ship for almost a century, and it will only bring personnel. We are isolated by space and time; few can come to work here, to seek to build a bridge of minds across that gulf—"

"Yeah," Speyer nodded prosaically. "The light-speed limit. I thought so. If you're telling the truth."

The being shuddered. "Nothing is left for us but to speak truth, and pray that you will understand and help. Revenge, conquest, any form of mass violence is impossible when so much space and time lies between. Our labor has been done in the mind and heart. It is not too late, even now. The most crucial facts can still be kept hidden—oh, listen to me, for the sake of your unborn!"

Speyer nodded to Mackenzie. "Everything okay?" he said. "We got us a full bag here. About twenty left alive, this fellow the bossman. Seems like they're the only ones on Earth."

"We guessed there couldn't be many," the colonel said. His tone and his feelings were alike ashen. "When we talked it over, you and me, and tried to figure what our clues meant. They'd have to be few, or they'd've operated more openly."

"Listen, listen," the being pleaded. "We came in love. Our dream was to lead you—to make you lead yourselves—toward peace, fulfillment. . . . Oh, yes, we would also gain, gain yet another race with whom we could someday converse as brothers. But there are many races in the universe. It was chiefly for your own tortured sakes that we wished to guide your future."

"That controlled history notion isn't original with you," Speyer grunted. "We've invented it for ourselves now and then on Earth. The last time it led to the Hellbombs. No, thanks!"

"But we *know!* The Great Science predicts with absolute certainty—"

"Predicted this?" Speyer waved a hand at the blackened room.

"There are fluctuations. We are too few to control so many savages in every detail. But do you not wish an end to war, to all your ancient sufferings? I offer you that for your help today."

"You succeeded in starting a pretty nasty war yourselves," Speyer said.

The being twisted its fingers together. "That was an error. The plan remains, the only way to lead your people toward peace. I, who have traveled between suns, will get down before your boots and beg you—"

"Stay put!" Speyer flung back. "If you'd come openly, like honest folk, you'd have found some to listen to you. Maybe enough, even. But no, your do-gooding had to be subtle and crafty. You knew what was right for us. We weren't entitled to any say in the matter. God in heaven, I've never heard anything so arrogant!"

The being lifted its head. "Do you tell children the whole truth?"

"As much as they're ready for."

"Your child-culture is not ready to hear these truths."

"Who qualified you to call us children—besides yourselves?"

"How do you know you are adult?"

"By trying adult jobs and finding out if I can handle them. Sure, we make some ghastly blunders, we humans. But they're our own. And we learn from them. You're the ones who won't learn, you and that damned psychological science you were bragging about, that wants to fit every living mind into the one frame it can understand.

"You wanted to re-establish the centralized state, didn't you? Did you ever stop to think that maybe feudalism is what suits man? Some one place to call our own, and belong to, and be part of; a community with traditions and honor; a chance for the individual to make decisions that count; a bulwark for liberty against the central overlords, who'll always want more and more power; a thousand different ways to live. We've always built supercountries, here on Earth, and we've always knocked them apart again. I think maybe the whole idea is wrong. And maybe this time we'll try something better. Why not a world of little states, too well rooted to dissolve in a nation, too small to do much harm—slowly rising above petty jealousies and spite, but keeping their identities—a thousand separate approaches to our problems. Maybe then we can solve a few of them . . . for ourselves!"

"You will never do so," the being said. "You will be torn in pieces all over again."

"That's what you think. I think otherwise. But whichever is right—and I bet this is too big a universe for either of us to predict—we'll have made a free choice on Earth. I'd rather be dead than domesticated.

"The people are going to learn about you as soon as Judge Brodsky's been reinstated. No, sooner. The regiment will hear today, the city to-morrow, just to make sure no one gets ideas about suppressing the truth again. By the time your next spaceship comes, we'll be ready for it: in our own way, whatever that is."

The being drew a fold of robe about its head. Speyer turned to Mackenzie. His face was wet. "Anything . . . you want to say . . . Jimbo?"

"No," Mackenzie mumbled. "Can't think of anything. Let's get our command organized here. I don't expect we'll have to fight any more, though. It seems to be about ended down there."

"Sure." Speyer drew an uneven breath. "The enemy troops elsewhere are bound to capitulate. They've got nothing left to fight for. We can start patching up pretty soon."

There was a house with a patio whose wall was covered by roses. The street outside had not yet come back to life, so that silence dwelt here under the yellow sunset. A maidservant showed Mackenzie through the back door and departed. He walked toward Laura, who sat on a bench beneath a willow. She watched him approach but did not rise. One hand rested on a cradle.

He stopped and knew not what to say. How thin she was.

Presently she told him, so low he could scarcely hear: "Tom's dead."

"Oh, no." Darkness came and went before his eyes.

"I learned the day before yesterday, when a few of his men straggled home. He was killed in the San Bruno."

Mackenzie did not dare join her, but his legs would not upbear him. He sat down on the flagstones and saw curious patterns in their arrangement. There was nothing else to look at.

Her voice ran on above him, toneless: "Was it worth it? Not only Tom, but so many others, killed for a point of politics?"

"More than that was at stake," he said.

"Yes, I heard on the radio. I still can't understand how it was worth it. I've tried very hard, but I can't."

He had no strength left to defend himself. "Maybe you're right, duck. I wouldn't know."

"I'm not sorry for myself," she said. "I still have Jimmy. But Tom was cheated out of so much."

He realized all at once that there was a baby, and he ought to take his grandchild to him and think thoughts about life going on into the future. But he was too empty.

"Tom wanted him named after you," she said.

*Did you, Laura?* he wondered. Aloud: "What are you going to do now?"

"I'll find something."

He made himself glance at her. The sunset burned on the willow leaves above and on her face, which was now turned toward the infant he could not see. "Come back to Nakamura," he said.

"No. Anywhere else."

"You always loved the mountains," he groped. "We—"

"No." She met his eyes. "It isn't you, Dad. Never you. But Jimmy is not going to grow up a soldier." She hesitated. "I'm sure some of the Espers will keep going, on a new basis, but with the same goals. I think we should join them. He ought to believe in something different from what killed his father, and work for it to become real. Don't you agree?"

Mackenzie climbed to his feet against Earth's hard pull. "I don't know," he said. "Never was a thinker. . . . Can I see him?"

"Oh, Dad—"

He went over and looked down at the small sleeping form. "If you marry again," he said, "and have a daughter, would you call her for her mother?" He saw Laura's head bend downward and her hands clench. Quickly he said, "I'll go now. I'd like to visit you some more, tomorrow or sometime, if you'll have me."

Then she came to his arms and wept. He stroked her hair and murmured, as he had done when she was a child. "You do want to return to the mountains, don't you? They're your country too, your people, where you belong."

"Y-you'll never know how much I want to."

"Then why not?" he cried.

His daughter straightened herself. "I can't," she said. "Your war is ended. Mine has just begun."

Because he had trained that will, he could only say, "I hope you win it."

"Perhaps in a thousand years—" She could not continue.

Night had fallen when he left her. Power was still out in the city, so the street lamps were dark and the stars stood forth above all roofs. The squad that waited to accompany their colonel to barracks looked wolfish by lantern light. They saluted him and rode at his back, rifles ready for trouble; but there was only the iron sound of horseshoes.

*1965*
*23rd* CONVENTION
LONDON

## Gordon R. Dickson

Gordon Dickson is, in some ways, a man of heroism. I once received one of his paperback books in the mail with a form-card attached which asked me to read it carefully and write back all the things wrong with the book so that he could improve his writing next time around.

Now that's heroic!

Of course, it's also idiotic and I wouldn't have a thing to do with it. Suppose it set a precedent!

I made my own position quite clear. Anytime anyone reads one of *my* books and spots something wrong with it, I'll thank him to keep it secret. I don't want to know. When *I* ask for criticism, all I want is applause. I hope that's clear!

Then, too, Gordie has the fictional hero's ability to be unaffected by the strong drink that is, on rare occasions, forced upon him by his convivial and loving friends. When that happens, his general glow of benevolence merely glitters more brightly.

It was only last summer when Lester del Rey, one of the bantamweights of our field (in physical proportions only, *not* in talent) looked pretty poorly and I was concerned, for Lester is one of my favorites, even when he's talking, which is all the time.

I said, "What's the matter, Lester?"

And he said, "I tried to outdrink Gordie."

"Lester," I said, shocked, "you have only half his volume."

"I almost did," he said.

He almost died, is what he should have said.

But my most poignant memory of Gordie is in connection with the 1959 Convention at Detroit. Robert Bloch was so busily engaged in getting ready to introduce me to some girl I had never met that I suspected something was up. I managed to locate the girl and I must say I was staggered. She was 5′ 11″ tall. She was beautiful and she made

Anita Ekberg look like Audrey Hepburn. I saw the plan at once. I was to be introduced and after one goggle-eyed look, I was to fall into a speechless catalepsy, thus utterly ruining my reputation as a dirty old man.

Remaining master of myself only by an eyelash, I approached the young lady with diffidence, introduced myself in a quiver, and humbly asked if she would cooperate with me in a biter-bit routine. Being as good-natured as she was beautiful, she agreed.

So when Bob Bloch introduced me, I calmly walked up to her and snapped my fingers. She put her arm about my waist, swung me back (she was bigger and stronger and had to play the lead) and we kissed. It was the talk of the convention.

With that beautiful head-start, you would think I was all set. Wouldn't you?

Nonsense! Rotten old Gordie Dickson moved in and cut me out, leaving me in the Arctic regions somewhere.

The funny thing is that I forgive him. *He's* lovable, too, you see—in a completely different way.

# 3

# *SOLDIER, ASK NOT*

*Soldier, ask not—now, or ever,*
*Where to war your banners go . . .*

I

As I got off the spaceliner on St. Marie, the little breeze from the higher pressure of the ship's atmosphere at my back was like a hand from the darkness behind me, shoving me into the dark day and the rain. My Newsman's cloak covered me. The wet chill of the day wrapped around me but did not enter me. I was like the naked claymore of my own early ancestors, wrapped and hidden in the plaid— sharpened on a stone—and carried now at last to the meeting for which it had been guarded over three years of waiting.

A meeting in the cold rain of spring. I felt it, cold as old blood on my hands and tasteless on my lips. Above, the sky was low and clouds flowing to the east. The rain fell steadily.

The sound of it was like a rolling of drums as I went down the outside landing stairs, the multitude of raindrops sounding their own end against the unyielding concrete all around. The concrete stretched far from the ship in every direction, hiding the earth, as bare and clean as the last page of an account book before the final entry. At its far edge, the spaceport terminal stood like a single gravestone. The curtains of falling water between it and me thinned and thickened like the smoke of battle, but could not hide it entirely from my sight.

It was the same rain that falls in all places and on all worlds. It had fallen like this on Athens of Old Earth, when I was only a boy, on the dark, unhappy house of the uncle who brought me up after my parent's death, on the ruins of the Parthenon as I saw it from my bedroom window.

I listened to it now as I went down the landing stairs, drumming on the great ship behind me which had shifted me free between the stars —from Old Earth to this second smallest of the worlds, this small terra-formed planet under the Procyon suns—and drumming hollowly upon the Credentials case sliding down the conveyor belt beside me. That case now meant nothing to me—neither my papers or the Credentials of Impartiality I had carried six years and worked so long to earn. Now I thought less of these than of the name of the man I should find dispatching groundcars at the edge of the field. If, that was, he was actually the man my Earth informants had named to me. And if they had not lied . . .

". . . Your luggage, sir?"

I woke from my thoughts and the rain. I had reached the concrete. The debarking officer smiled at me. He was older than I, though he looked younger. As he smiled some beads of moisture broke and spilled like tears from the brown visor-edge of his cap onto the tally sheet he held.

"Send it to the Friendly compound," I said. "I'll take the Credentials case."

I took it up from the conveyor belt and turned to walk off. The man standing in a dispatcher's uniform by the first groundcar in line did fit the description.

"Name, sir?" he said. "Business on St. Marie?"

If he had been described to me, I must have been described to him. But I was prepared to humor him.

"Tam Olyn," I said. "Old Earth resident and Interworld News Network representative. I'm here to cover the Friendly-Exotic conflict." I opened my case and gave him my papers.

"Fine, Mr. Olyn." He handed them back to me, damp from the rain. He turned away to open the door of the car beside him and set the automatic pilot. "Follow the highway straight to Joseph's Town. Put it on automatic at the city limits and the car'll take you to the Friendly compound."

"All right," I said. "Just a minute."

He turned back. He had a young, good-looking face with a little mustache and he looked at me with a bright blankness. "Sir?"

"Help me get in the car."

"Oh, I'm sorry, sir." He came quickly over to me. "I didn't realize your leg—"

"Damp stiffens it," I said. He adjusted the seat and I got my left leg in behind the steering column. He started to turn away.

"Wait a minute," I said again. I was out of patience. "You're Walter Imera, aren't you?"

"Yes, sir," he said softly.

"Look at me," I said. "You've got some information for me, haven't you?"

He turned slowly back to face me. His face was still blank.

"No, sir."

I waited a long moment, looking at him.

"All right," I said then, reaching for the car door. "I guess you know I'll get the information anyway. And they'll believe you told me."

His little mustache began to look like it was painted on.

"Wait—" he said.

"What for?"

"Look," he said, "you've got to understand. Information like that's not part of your news, is it? I've got a family—"

"And I haven't," I said. I felt nothing for him.

"But you don't understand. They'd kill me. That's the sort of organization the Blue Front is now, here on St. Marie. What d'you want to know about them for? I didn't understand you meant—"

"All right," I said. I reached for the car door.

"Wait—" He held out a hand to me in the rain. "How do I know you can make them leave me alone if I tell you?"

"They may be back in power here some day," I said. "Not even outlawed political groups want to antagonize the Interplanetary News Network." I started to close the door once more.

"All right—" he said quickly. "All right. You go to New San Marcos. The Wallace Street Jewelers there. It's just beyond Joseph's Town, where the Friendly compound is you're going to." He licked his lips. "You'll tell them about me?"

"I'll tell them." I looked at him. Above the edge of the blue uniform collar on the right side of his neck I could see an inch or two of fine silver chain, bright against winter-pale skin. The crucifix attached to it would be down under his shirt. "The Friendly soldiers have been here two years now. How do people like them?"

He grinned a little. His color was coming back.

"Oh, like anybody," he said. "You just have to understand them. They've got their own ways."

I felt the ache in my stiff leg where the doctors on New Earth had taken the needle from the spring rifle out of it three years before.

"Yes, they have," I said. "Shut the door."

He shut it. I drove off.

There was a St. Christopher's medal on the car's instrument panel. One of the Friendly soldiers would have ripped it off and thrown it away, or refused the car. And so it gave me a particular pleasure to leave it where it was, though it meant no more to me than it would to him. It was, not just because of Dave, my brother-in-law, and the other prisoners they had shot down on New Earth. It was simply because there are some duties that have a small element of pleasure. After the illusions of childhood are gone and there is nothing left but duties, such pleasures are welcome. Fanatics, when all is said and done, are no worse than mad dogs.

But mad dogs have to be destroyed; it is a simple common sense.

And you return to common sense after a while in life, inevitably. When the wild dreams of justice and progress are all dead and buried, when the painful beatings of feeling inside you are finally stilled, then it becomes best to be still, unliving, and unyielding as—the blade of a sword sharpened on a stone. The rain through which such a blade is carried to its using does not stain it, any more than the blood in which it is bathed at last. Rain and blood are alike to sharpened iron.

I drove for half an hour past wooded hills and plowed meadows. The furrows of the fields were black in the rain. I thought it a kinder black than some other shades I had seen; and at last I reached the outskirts of Joseph's Town.

The autopilot of the car threaded me through a small, neat, typical St. Marie City of about a hundred thousand people. We came out on the far side into a cleared area, beyond which lifted the massive, sloping concrete walls of a military compound.

A Friendly non-com stopped my car at the gate with his black spring rifle, and opened the car door at my left.

"Thee have business here?"

His voice was harsh and high in his nose. The cloth tabs of a group-man edged his collar. Above them his forty-year-old face was lean and graven with lines. Both face and hands, the only uncovered parts of him, looked unnaturally white against the black cloth and rifle.

I opened the case beside me and handed him my papers.

"My Credentials," I said. "I'm here to see your acting Commander of Expeditionary Forces, Commandant Jamethon Black."

"Move over, then," he said nasally. "I must drive thee."

I moved.

He got in and took the stick. We drove through the gate and turned down an approach alley. I could see an interior square at the alley's far end. The close concrete walls on either side of us echoed the sound of our passage as we went. I heard drill commands growing louder as we approached the square. When we rolled out into it, soldiers were drawn up in ranks for their midday service, in the rain.

The groupman left me and went in the entrance of what seemed to be an office inset in the wall on one side of the square. I looked over the soldiers standing in formation. They stood at present-arms, their position of worship under field conditions; and as I watched, the officer standing facing them, with his back to a wall, led them into the words of their Battle Hymn.

> *Soldier, ask not—now, or ever,*
> *Where to war your banners go.*
> *Anarch's legions all surround us.*
> *Strike! And do not count the blow!*

I sat trying not to listen. There was no musical accompaniment, no religious furniture or symbols except the thin shape of the cross white-washed on the gray wall behind the officer. The massed male voices rose and fell slowly in the dark, sad hymn that promised them only pain, and suffering, and sorrow. At last, the final line mourned its harsh prayer for a battle death, and they ordered arms.

A groupman dismissed the ranks as the officer walked back past my car without looking at me, and passed in through the entrance where my non-commissioned guide had disappeared. As he passed I saw the officer was young.

A moment later the guide came for me. Limping a little on my stiff-ened leg, I followed him to an inner room with the lights on above a single desk. The young officer rose and nodded as the door closed be-hind me. He wore the faded tabs of a commandant on his uniform lapels.

As I handed my credentials across the desk to him, the glare of the light over the desk came full in my eyes, blinding me. I stepped back and blinked at his blurred face. As it came back into focus I saw it for a moment as if it was older, harsher, twisted and engraved with the lines of years of fanaticism.

Then my eyes refocused completely, and I saw him as he actually was. Dark-faced, but thin with the thinness of youth rather than that of self-starvation. He was not the face burned in my memory. His fea-tures were regular to the point of being handsome, his eyes tired and shadowed; and I saw the straight, weary line of his mouth above the still, self-controlled stiffness of his body, smaller and slighter than mine.

He held the credentials without looking at them. His mouth quirked a little, dryly and wearily, at the corners. "And no doubt, Mr. Olyn," he said, "you've got another pocket filled with authorities from the Exotic Worlds to interview the mercenary soldiers and officers they've hired from the Dorsai and a dozen other worlds to oppose God's Chosen in War?"

I smiled. Because it was good to find him as strong as that, to add to my pleasure of breaking him.

II

I looked across the ten feet or so of distance that separated us. The Friendly non-com who had killed the prisoners on New Earth had also spoken of God's Chosen.

"If you'll look under the papers directed to you," I said, "you'll find them. The News Network and its people are impartial. We don't take sides."

"Right," said the dark young face opposing me, "take sides."

"Yes, Commandant," I said. "That's right. Only sometimes it's a matter of debate where Right is. You and your troops here now are invaders on the world of a planetary system your ancestors never colonized. And opposing you are mercenary troops hired by two worlds that not only belong under the Procyon suns but have a commitment to defend the smaller worlds of their system—of which St. Marie is one. I'm not sure right *is* on your side."

He shook his head slightly and said, "We expect small understanding from those not Chosen." He transferred his gaze from me to the papers in his hand.

"Mind if I sit down?" I said. "I've got a bad leg."

"By all means." He nodded to a chair beside his desk and, as I sat down, seated himself. I looked across the papers on the desk before him and saw, standing to one side, the solidograph of one of the windowless high-peaked churches the Friendlies build. It was a legitimate token for him to own—but there just happened to be three people, an older man and woman and a young girl of about fourteen, in the foreground of the image. All three of them bore a family resemblance to Jamethon Black. Glancing up from my credentials he saw me looking at them; and his gaze shifted momentarily to the graph and away again, as if he would protect it.

"I'm required, I see," he said, drawing my eyes back to him, "to provide you with cooperation and facilities. We'll find quarters for you here. Do you need a car and driver?"

"Thanks," I said. "That commercial car outside will do. And I'll manage my own driving."

"As you like." He detached the papers directed to him, passed the rest back to me and leaned toward a grill in his desktop. "Groupman."

"Sir," the grill answered promptly.

"Quarters for a single male civilian. Parking assignment for a civilian vehicle, personnel."

"Sir."

The voice from the grill clicked off. Jamethon Black looked across his desk at me. I got the idea he was waiting for my departure.

"Commandant," I said, putting my credentials back in their case, "two years ago your Elders of the United Churches on Harmony and Association found the planetary government of St. Marie in default of certain disputed balances of credit, so they sent an expedition in here to occupy and enforce payment. Of that expedition, how much in the way of men and equipment do you have left?"

"That, Mr. Olyn," he said, "is restricted military information."

"However"—and I closed the case—"you, with the regular rank of commandant, are acting Commander of Forces for that remnant of your expedition. That position calls for someone about five ranks higher than you. Do you expect such an officer to arrive and take charge?"

"I'm afraid you'd have to ask that question of Headquarters on Harmony, Mr. Olyn."

"Do you expect reinforcements of personnel and more supplies?"

"If I did"—his voice was level—"I would have to consider that restricted information, too."

"You know that it's been pretty widely mentioned that your General Staff on Harmony has decided that this expedition to St. Marie is a lost cause? But that to avoid loss of face they prefer you here to be cut up, instead of withdrawing you and your men."

"I see," he said.

"You wouldn't care to comment?"

His dark, young, expressionless face did not change. "Not in the case of rumors, Mr. Olyn."

"One last question then. Do you plan to retreat westward, or surrender when the spring offensive of the Exotic mercenary forces begins to move against you?"

"The Chosen in War never retreat," he said. "Neither do they abandon, or suffer abandonment by, their Brothers in the Lord." He stood up. "I have work I must get back to, Mr. Olyn."

I stood up, too. I was taller than he was, older, and heavier-boned. It was only his almost unnatural composure that enabled him to maintain his appearance of being my equal or better.

"I'll talk to you later, perhaps, when you've got more time," I said.

"Certainly." I heard the office door open behind me. "Groupman," he said, speaking past me, "take care of Mr. Olyn."

The groupman he had turned me over to found me a small concrete cubicle with a single high window, a camp bed and a uniform cabinet. He left me for a moment and returned with a signed pass.

"Thanks," I said as I took it. "Where do I find the Headquarters of the Exotic Forces?"

"Our latest advice, sir," he said, "is that they're ninety kilometers east of here. New San Marcos." He was my height, but, like most of them, half a dozen years younger than I, with an innocence that contrasted with the strange air of control they all had.

"San Marcos." I looked at him. "I suppose you enlisted men know your General Headquarters on Harmony has decided against wasting replacements for you?"

"No, sir," he said. I might have commented on the rain for all the reaction he showed. Even these boys were still strong and unbroken. "Is there somewhat else?"

"No," I said. "Thanks."

He went out. And I went out, to get in my car and head ninety kilometers east through the same sort of country to New San Marcos. I reached it in about three-quarters of an hour. But I did not go directly to find the Exotic Field Headquarters. I had other fish to fry.

These took me to the Wallace Street Jewelers. There, three shallow steps down from street level and an opaqued door let me in to a long, dim-lighted room filled with glass cases. There was a small elderly man at the back of the store behind the final case and I saw him eyeing my correspondent's cloak and badge as I got closer.

"Sir?" he said, as I stopped across the case from him. He raised gray, narrow old eyes in a strangely smooth face to look at me.

"I think you know what I represent," I said. "All worlds know the News Services. We're not concerned with local politics."

"Sir?"

"You'll find out how I learned your address anyway." I kept on smiling at him. "So I'll tell you it was from a spaceport auto-dispatcher named Imera. I promised him protection for telling me. We'd appreciate it if he remains well and whole."

"I'm afraid—" He put his hands on the glass top of the case. They were veined with the years. "You wanted to buy something?"

"I'm willing to pay in good will," I said, "for information."

His hands slid off the countertop.

"Sir." He sighed a little. "I'm afraid you're in the wrong store."

"I'm sure I am," I said. "But your store'll have to do. We'll pretend it's the right store and I'm talking to someone who's a member of the Blue Front."

He shook his head slowly and stepped back from the case.

"The Blue Front is illegal," he said. "Good-by, sir."

"In a moment. I've got a few things to say first."

"Then I'm sorry." He retreated toward some drapes covering a doorway. "I can't listen. No one will come into this room with you, sir, as long as you talk like that."

He slipped through the drapes and was gone. I looked around the long, empty room.

"Well," I said, a little more loudly, "I guess I'll have to speak to the walls. I'm sure the walls can hear me."

I paused. There was no sound.

"All right," I said. "I'm a correspondent. All I'm interested in is information. Our assessment of the military situation here on St. Marie"—and here I told the truth—"shows the Friendly Expeditionary Forces abandoned by their home headquarters and certain to be overrun by the Exotic Forces as soon as the ground dries enough for heavy equipment to move."

There was still no answer, but the back of my neck knew they were listening, and watching me.

"As a result," I went on—and here I lied, though they would have no way of knowing—"we consider it inevitable that the Friendly Command here will have got in contact with the Blue Front. Assassination of enemy commanders is expressly in violation of the Mercenaries' Code and the Articles of Civilized Warfare—but civilians could do what soldiers could not."

Still there was no sound or movement beyond the drapes.

"A news representative," I said, "carries Credentials of Impartiality. You know how highly these are held. I only want to ask a few questions. And the answers will be kept confidential . . ."

For a last time I waited, and there was still no answer. I turned and went up the long room and out. It was not until I was well out on to the street that I let the feeling of triumph within spread out and warm me.

They would take the bait. People of their sort always did. I found my car and drove to Exotic Headquarters.

These were outside the town. There a mercenary commandant named Janol Marat took me in charge. He conducted me to the bubble structure of their HQ building. There was a feel of purpose, there, a sure and cheerful air of activity. They were well armed, well trained. After the Friendlies it jumped at me. I said so to Janol.

"We've got a Dorsai Commander and we outnumber the opposition." He grinned at me. He had a deeply tanned, long face that went into deep creases as his lips curved up. "That makes everybody pretty optimistic. Besides, our commander gets promoted if he wins. Back to the Exotics and staff rank—out of field combat for good. It's good business for us to win."

I laughed and he laughed.

"Tell me more, though," I said. "I want reasons I can use in the stories I send back to News Network."

"Well"—he answered the snappy salute of a passing groupman, a Cassidan, by the look of him—"I guess you might mention the usual—the fact our Exotic employers don't permit themselves to use violence and consequently they're always rather generous than otherwise when it comes to paying for men and equipment. And the OutBond—that's the Exotic Ambassador to St. Marie, you know—"

"I know."

"He replaced the former OutBond here three years ago. Anyway, he's something special, even for someone from Mara or Kultis. He's an expert in ontogenic calculations. If that means much to you. It's all over my head." Janol pointed. "Here's the Field Commander's office. He's Kensie Graeme."

"Graeme?" I said, frowning. I had spent a day at the Hague looking up Kensie Graeme before I came, but I wanted Janol's reactions to him. "Sounds familiar." We approached the office building. "Graeme . . ."

"You're probably thinking of another member of the same family." Janol took the bait. "Donal Graeme. A nephew. The one who pulled that wild stunt not long ago, attacking Newton with just a handful of Freiland ships. Kensie is Donal's uncle. Not as spectacular as the young Graeme, but I'll bet you'll like him better than you would the nephew. Kensie's got two men's likeableness." He looked at me, grinning slightly again.

"That supposed to mean something special?" I said.

"That's right," said Janol. "His own likeableness and his twin brother's, too. Meet Ian Graeme sometime when you're in Blauvain. That's where the Exotic Embassy is, east of here. Ian's a dark man."

We walked into the office.

"I can't get used," I said, "to how so many Dorsai seem related."

"Neither can I. Actually, I guess it's because there really aren't so many of them. The Dorsai's a small world, and those that live more than a few years—" Janol stopped by a commandant sitting at a desk. "Can we see the Old Man, Hari? This is a News Network man."

"Why, I guess so." The other looked at his desk signal board. "The OutBond's with him, but he's just leaving now. Go on in."

Janol led me between the desks. A door at the back of the room opened before we reached it and a calm-faced man of middle age wearing a blue robe and close-cropped white hair came out. He looked strange but not ridiculous—particularly after you met his odd, hazel-colored eyes.

He was an Exotic.

I knew of Padma, as I knew the Exotics. I had seen them on their own home worlds of Mara and Kultis. A people committed to non-violence, mystics but very practical mystics, masters of what were known as the "strange sciences"—a dozen wizardic step-children of early psychology, sociology and the humanistic fields of research.

"Sir," said Janol to Padma, "this is—"

"Tam Olyn. I know," said Padma softly. He smiled up at me, and those eyes of his seemed to catch light for a moment and blind me. "I was sorry to learn about your brother-in-law, Tam."

I went quite cool all over. I had been ready to walk on, but now I stood stock-still and looked at him.

"My brother-in-law?" I said.

"The young man who died near Castlemain, on New Earth."

"Oh, yes," I said, between stiff lips. "I'm surprised that you'd know."

"I know because of you, Tam." Once more the hazel eyes of Padma seemed to catch light. "We have a science called ontogenics, by which we calculate the probabilities of human actions in present and future situations. You've been an important factor in those calculations for some time." He smiled. "That's why I was expecting to meet you here, and now. We've calculated you into our present situation here on St. Marie, Tam."

"Have you?" I said. "Have you? That's interesting."

"I thought it would be," said Padma softly. "To you, especially. Someone like a newsman, like yourself, would find it interesting."

"It is," I said. "It sounds like you know more than I do about what I'm going to be doing here."

"We've got calculations," said Padma in his soft voice, "to that effect. Come see me in Blauvain, Tam; and I'll show you."

"I'll do that," I said.

"You'll be very welcome." Padma inclined his head. His blue robe whispered on the floor as he turned, and went out of the room.

"This way," said Janol, touching my elbow. I started as if I had just wakened from a deep sleep. "The commander's in here."

I followed him automatically into a further office. The individual I had come to see stood up as we came through the door. He was a great, lean man in field uniform, with a heavy-boned, but open, smiling face under black, slightly curly hair. A sort of golden warmth of personality—a strange thing in a Dorsai—seemed to flow out from him as he rose to meet me and his long-fingered, powerful hand swallowed mine in a handshake.

"Come on in," he said. "Let me fix you up with a drink. Janol," he added to my mercenary commandant from New Earth, "no need for you to stick around. Go on to chow. And tell the rest of them in the outer office to knock off."

Janol saluted and went. I sat down as Graeme turned to a small bar cabinet behind his desk. And for the first time in three years, under the magic of the unusual fighting man opposite me, a little peace came into my soul. With someone like this on my side, I could not lose.

III

"Credentials?" asked Graeme, as soon as we were settled with drinks of Dorsai whisky—which is a fine whisky—in our hands.

I passed my papers over. He glanced through them, picking out the letters from Sayona, the Bond of Kultis, to "*Commander—St. Marie Field Forces.*" He looked these over and put them aside. He handed me back the credentials folder.

"You stopped at Joseph's Town first?" he said.

I nodded. I saw him looking at my face, and his own sobered.

"You don't like the Friendlies," he said.

His words took my breath away. I had come prepared to fence for an opening to tell him. It was too sudden. I looked away.

I did not dare answer right away. I could not. There was either too much or too little to say if I let it come out without thinking. Then I got a grip on myself.

"If I do anything at all with the rest of my life," I said, slowly, "it'll be to do everything in my power to remove the Friendlies and all they stand for from the community of civilized human beings."

I looked back up at him. He was sitting with one massive elbow on his desktop, watching me.

"That's a pretty harsh point of view, isn't it?"

"No harsher than theirs."

"Do you think so?" he said seriously. "I wouldn't say so."

"I thought," I said, "you were the one who was fighting them."

"Why, yes." He smiled a little. "But we're soldiers on both sides."

"I don't think they think that way."

He shook his head a little.

"What makes you say that?" he said.

"I've seen them," I answered. "I got caught up front in the lines on Castlemain on New Earth, three years ago." I tapped my stiff knee. "I got shot and I couldn't navigate. The Cassidans around me began to retreat—they were mercenaries, and the troops opposing them were Friendlies hired out as mercenaries."

I stopped and took a drink of the whisky. When I took the glass away, Graeme had not moved. He sat as if waiting.

"There was young Cassidan, a buck soldier," I said. "I was doing a series on the campaign from an individual point of view. I'd picked him for my individual. It was a natural choice. You see"—I drank again, and emptied the glass—"my younger sister went out on contract as an accountant to Cassida two years before that, and she'd married him. He was my brother-in-law."

Graeme took the glass from my hand and silently replenished it.

"He wasn't actually a military man," I said. "He was studying shift mechanics and he had about three years to go. But he stood low on one of the competitive examinations at a time when Cassida owed a contractual balance of troops to New Earth." I took a deep breath. "Well, to make a long story short, he ended up on New Earth in this same campaign I was covering. Because of the series I was writing, he was assigned to me. We both thought it was a good deal for him, that he'd be safer that way."

I drank some more of the whisky.

"But," I said, "you know, there's always a better story a little deeper in the combat zone. We got caught up front one day when the New Earth troops were retreating. I picked up a needle through the kneecap. The Friendly armor was moving up and things were getting hot. The soldiers around us took off toward the rear in a hurry, but Dave tried to carry me, because he thought the Friendly armor would fry me before they had time to notice I was a non-combatant. Well," I took another deep breath, "the Friendly ground troops caught us. They took us to a sort of clearing where they had a lot of prisoners and kept us there for a while. Then a groupman—one of their fanatic types, a tall, starved-looking soldier about my age—came up with orders they were to reform for a fresh attack."

I stopped and took another drink. But I could not taste it.

"That meant they couldn't spare men to guard the prisoners. They'd have to turn them loose back of the Friendly lines. The Groupman said that wouldn't work. They'd have to make sure the prisoners couldn't endanger them."

Graeme was still watching me.

"I didn't understand. I didn't even catch on when the other Friendlies—none of them were non-coms like the Groupman—objected." I put my glass on the desk beside me and stared at the wall of the office, seeing it all over again, as plainly as if I looked through a window at it. "I remember how the Groupman pulled himself up straight. I saw his eyes. As if he'd been insulted by the others, objecting.

"'Are they Chosen of God?' he shouted at them. 'Are they of the Chosen?'"

I looked across at Kensie Graeme and saw him still motionless, still watching me, his own glass small in one big hand.

"You understand?" I said to him. "As if because the prisoners weren't Friendlies, they weren't quite human. As if they were some lower order it was all right to kill." I shook, suddenly. "And he did it! I sat there against a tree, safe because of my News Correspondent's uniform and watched him shoot them down. All of them. I sat there and looked at Dave, and he looked at me, sitting there, as the Groupman shot him!"

I quit all at once. I hadn't meant to have it all come out like that. It was just that I'd been able to tell no one who would understand how helpless I had been. But something about Graeme had given me the idea he would understand.

"Yes," he said after a moment, and took and filled my glass again. "That sort of thing's very bad. Was the Groupman found and tried under the Mercenaries Code?"

"After it was too late, yes."

He nodded and looked past me at the wall. "They aren't all like that, of course."

"There's enough to give them a reputation for it."

"Unfortunately, yes. Well"—he smiled slightly at me—"we'll try and keep that sort of thing out of this campaign."

"Tell me something," I said, putting my glass down. "Does that sort of thing—as you put it—ever happen to the Friendlies, themselves?"

Something took place then in the atmosphere of the room. There was a little pause before he answered. I felt my heart beat slowly, three times, as I waited for him to speak.

He said at last, "No, it doesn't."

"Why not?" I said.

The feeling in the room became stronger. And I realized I had gone too fast. I had been sitting talking to him as a man and forgetting what else he was. Now I began to forget that he was a man and become conscious of him as a Dorsai—an individual as human as I was, but trained all his life, and bred down the generations to a difference. He did not move or change the tone of his voice, or any such thing; but somehow he seemed to move off some distance from me, up into a higher, colder, stonier land into which I could venture only at my peril.

I remembered what was said about his people from that small, cold stony-mountained world: that if the Dorsai chose to withdraw their fighting men from the services of all the other worlds, and challenge those other worlds, not the combined might of the rest of civilization could stand against them. I had never really believed that before. I had never even really thought much about it. But sitting there just then, because of what was happening in the room, suddenly it became real to me. I could feel the knowledge, cold as a wind blowing on me off a glacier, that it was true; and then he answered my question.

"Because," said Kensie Graeme, "anything like that is specifically prohibited by Article Two of the Mercenaries' Code."

Then he broke out abruptly into a smile and what I had just felt in the room withdrew. I breathed again.

"Well," he said, putting his glass down empty on the desk, "how about joining us in the Officers' Mess for something to eat?"

I had dinner with them and the meal was very pleasant. They wanted to put me up for the night—but I could feel myself being pulled back to that cold, joyless compound near Joseph's Town, where all that waited for me was a sort of cold and bitter satisfaction at being among my enemies.

I went back.

It was about eleven p.m. when I drove through the gate of the compound and parked, just as a figure came out of the entrance to Jamethon's headquarters. The square was dim-lighted with only a few spotlights about the walls, their light lost in the rain-wet pavement. For a moment I did not recognize the figure—and then I saw it was Jamethon.

He would have passed by me at some distance, but I got out of my car and went to meet him. He stopped when I stepped in front of him.

"Mr. Olyn," he said evenly. In the darkness I could not make out the expression of his face.

"I've got a question to ask," I said, smiling in the darkness.

"It's late for questions."

"This won't take long." I strained to catch the look on his face, but it was all in shadow. "I've been visiting the Exotic camp. Their commander's a Dorsai. I suppose you know that?"

"Yes." I could barely see the movement of his lips.

"We got to talking. A question came up and I thought I'd ask you, Commandant. Do you ever order your men to kill prisoners?"

An odd, short silence came between us. Then he answered.

"The killing or abuse of prisoners of war," he said without emotion, "is forbidden by Article Two of the Mercenaries' Code."

"But you aren't Mercenaries here, are you? You're native troops in service to your own True Church and Elders."

"Mr. Olyn," he said, while I still strained without success to make out the expression of his shadowed face—and it seemed that the words came slowly, though the tone of the voice that spoke them remained as calm as ever, "My Lord has set me to be His servant and a leader among men of war. In neither of those tasks will I fail Him."

And with that he turned, his face still shadowed and hidden from me, and passed around me and went on.

Alone, I went back inside to my quarters, undressed and lay down on the hard and narrow bed they had given me. The rain outside had stopped at last. Through my open, unglazed window I could see a few stars showing.

I lay there getting ready to sleep and making mental notes on what I would need to do tomorrow. The meeting with Padma the OutBond had jolted me sharply. I took his so-called calculations of human actions with reservation—but I had been shaken to learn of them. I would have to find out more about how much his science of ontogenics knew and could predict. If necessary, from Padma himself. But I would start first with ordinary reference sources.

No one, I thought, would ordinarily entertain the fantastic thought that one man like myself could destroy a culture involving the populations of two worlds. No one, except perhaps a Padma. What I knew, he with his calculations might have discovered. And that was that the Friendly worlds of Harmony and Association were facing a decision that would mean life or death to their way of living. A very small thing could tip the scales they weighed on.

For there was a new wind blowing between the stars.

Four hundred years before we had all been men of Earth—Old Earth, the mother planet which was my native soil. One people.

Then, with the movement out to new worlds, the human race had "splintered," to use an Exotic term. Every small social fragment and psychological type had drawn apart by itself, and joined others like it and progressed toward specialized types. Until we had half a dozen fragments of human types—the warrior on the Dorsai, the philosopher on the Exotic worlds, the hard scientist on Newton, Cassida and Venus, and so forth . . .

Isolation had bred specific types. Then a growing intercommunication between the younger worlds, now established, and an ever-increasing rate of technological advance had forced specialization. The trade between the worlds was the trade of skilled minds. Generals from the Dorsai were worth their exchange rate in psychiatrists from the Exotics. Communications men like myself from Old Earth brought spaceship designers from Cassida. And so it had been for the last hundred years.

But now the worlds were drifting together. Economics was fusing the race into one whole, again. And the struggle on each world was to gain the advantages of that fusion while holding on to as much as possible of their own ways.

Compromise was necessary—and the harsh, stiff-necked Friendly religion forbade compromise and had made many enemies. Already public opinion moved against the Friendlies on other worlds. Discredit them, smear them, publicly here in this campaign and they would not be able to hire out their soldiers. They would lose the balance of trade they needed to hire the skilled specialists trained by the special facilities of other worlds, and which they needed to keep their own two poor-in-natural-resources worlds alive. They would die.

As young Dave had died. Slowly. In the dark.

. . . In the darkness now, as I thought of it, it rose up before me once again. It had been only noon when we were taken prisoner, but by the time the Groupman came with his orders for our guards to move up, the sun was almost down.

After they left, after it was all over and I was left alone, I crawled to the bodies in the clearing. And I found Dave among them; and he was not quite gone.

He was wounded in the body and I could not stop the bleeding.

It would not have helped if I had, they told me afterwards. But then it seemed that it would have. So I tried. But finally I gave up and by that time it was quite dark. I only held him and did not know he was dead until he began to grow cold. And then was when I had begun to change into what my uncle had always tried to make me. I felt myself die inside. Dave and my sister were to have been my family, the only family I had ever had hopes of keeping. Instead, I could only sit there in the darkness, holding him and hearing the blood from his red-soaked clothing, falling drop by drop, slowly on the dead variform oak leaves beneath us.

I lay there now in the Friendly compound, not able to sleep and remembering. And after a while I heard the soldiers marching, forming in the square for midnight service.

I lay on my back, listening to them. Their marching feet stopped at last. The single window of my room was over my bed—high in the wall against which the left side of my cot was set. It was unglazed and the night air with its sounds came freely through it along with the dim light from the square which painted a pale rectangle on the opposite wall of my room. I lay watching that rectangle and listening to the service outside; and I heard the duty officer lead them in a prayer for worthiness. After that they sang their battle hymn again, and I lay hearing it, this time, all the way through.

> Soldier, ask not—now, or ever,
> Where to war your banners go.
> Anarch's legions all surround us.
> Strike! And do not count the blow!
>
> Glory, honor—praise and profit,
> Are but toys of tinsel worth.
> Render up your work, unasking,
> Leave the human clay to earth.
>
> Blood and sorrow—pain unending,
> Are the portion of us all.
> Grasp the naked sword, opposing,
> Gladly in the battle fall.
>
> So shall we, anointed soldiers,
> Stand at last before the Throne.
> Baptized in our wounds, red-flowing,
> Sealed unto our Lord—alone!

After that they dispersed to cots no different from mine.

I lay there listening to the silence in the square and the measured dripping of a rainspout outside by my window, its slow drops falling after the rain, one by one, uncounted in the darkness.

IV

After the day I landed, there was no more rain. Day by day the fields dried. Soon they would be firm underneath the weight of heavy surface-war equipment, and everyone knew that then the Exotic spring offensive would get under way. Meanwhile both Exotic and Friendly troops were in training.

During the next few weeks, I was busy about my newswork. Mostly feature and small stories on the soldiers and the native people. I had dispatches to send and I sent them faithfully. A correspondent is only as good as his contacts; I made contacts everywhere but among the Friendly troops. These remained aloof, though I talked to many of them. They refused to show fear or doubt.

I had heard these Friendly soldiers were generally undertrained because the suicidal tactics of their officers kept their ranks always filled with green replacements. But the ones here were the remnants of an Expeditionary Force six times their present numbers. They were all veterans, though most of them were in their teens. Only here and there, among the non-coms, and more often among the commissioned officers, I saw the prototype of the non-com who had ordered the prisoners shot on New Earth. Here, the men of this type looked like rabid, gray wolves mixed among polite, well-schooled young dogs just out of puppyhood.

It was a temptation to think that they alone were what I had set out to destroy.

To fight that temptation I told myself that Alexander the Great had led expeditions against the hill tribes and ruled in Pella, capital of Macedonia, and ordered men put to death when he was sixteen. But still the Friendly soldiers looked young to me. I could not help contrasting them with the adult, experienced mercenaries in Kensie Graeme's forces. For the Exotics, in obedience to their principles, would hire no drafted troops or soldiers who were not in uniform of their own free will.

Meanwhile I had heard no word from the Blue Front. But by the time two weeks had gone, I had my own connections in New San Marcos, and at the beginning of the third week one of these brought me word that the jewelers shop in Wallace Street there had closed its door —had pulled its blinds and emptied the long room of stock and fixtures, and moved or gone out of business. That was all I needed to know.

For the next few days, I stayed in the vicinity of Jamethon Black himself, and by the end of the week my watching him paid off.

At ten o'clock that Friday night I was up on a catwalk just above my quarters and under the sentry-walk of the walls, watching as three civilians with Blue Front written all over them drove into the square, got out and went into Jamethon's office.

They stayed a little over an hour. When they left, I went back down to bed. That night I slept soundly.

The next morning I got up early, and there was mail for me. A message had come by spaceliner from the director of News Network back on Earth, personally congratulating me on my dispatches. Once, three years before, this would have meant a great deal to me. Now, I only worried that they would decide I had made the situation here newsworthy enough to require extra people being sent out to help me. I could not risk having other news personnel here now to see what I was doing.

I got in my car and headed east along the highway to New San Marcos and the Exotic Headquarters. The Friendly troops were already out in the field; eighteen kilometers east of Joseph's Town, I was stopped by a squad of five young soldiers with no non-com over them. They recognized me.

"In God's name, Mr. Olyn," said the first one to reach my car, bending down to speak to me through the open window at my left shoulder. "You cannot go through."

"Mind if I ask why?" I said.

He turned and pointed out and down into a little valley between two wooded hills at our left.

"Tactical survey in progress."

I looked. The little valley or meadow was perhaps a hundred yards wide between the wooded slopes, and it wound away from me and curved to disappear to my right. At the edge of the wooded slopes where they met open meadow, there were lilac bushes with blossoms several days old. The meadow itself was green and fair with the young chartreuse grass of early summer and the white and purple of the lilacs, and the variform oaks behind the lilacs were fuzzy in outline, with small, new leaves.

In the middle of all this, in the center of the meadow, were black-clad figures moving about with computing devices, measuring and figuring the possibilities of death from every angle. In the very center of the meadow for some reason they had set up marking stakes—a single stake, then a stake in front of that with two stakes on either side of it, and one more stake in line before these. Farther on was another single stake, down, as if fallen on the grass and discarded.

I looked back up into the lean young face of the soldier.

"Getting ready to defeat the Exotics?" I said.

He took it as if it had been a straightforward question, with no irony in my voice at all.

"Yes sir," he said seriously. I looked at him and at the taut skin and clear eyes of the rest.

"Ever think you might lose?"

"No, Mr. Olyn." He shook his head solemnly. "No man loses who goes to battle for the Lord." He saw that I needed to be convinced, and he went about it earnestly. "He hath set His hand upon His soldiers. And all that is possible to them is victory—or sometimes death. And what is death?"

He looked to his fellow soldiers and they all nodded.

"What is death?" they echoed.

I looked at them. They stood there asking me and each other what was death as if they were talking about some hard but necessary job.

I had an answer for them, but I did not say it. Death was a Groupman, one of their own kind, giving orders to soldiers just like themselves to assassinate prisoners. That was death.

"Call an officer," I said. "My pass lets me through here."

"I regret, sir," said the one who had been talking to me. "We cannot leave our posts to summon an officer. One will come soon."

I had a hunch what "soon" meant, and I was right. It was high noon before a Force Leader came by to order them to chow and let me through.

As I pulled into Kensie Graeme's Headquarters, the sun was low, patterning the ground with the long shadows of trees. Yet it was as if the camp was just waking up. I did not need experience to see the Exotics were beginning to move at last against Jamethon.

I found Janol Marat, the New Earth commandant.

"I've got to see Field Commander Graeme," I said.

He shook his head, for all that we now knew each other well.

"Not now, Tam. I'm sorry."

"Janol," I said, "this isn't for an interview. It's a matter of life and death. I mean that. I've got to see Kensie."

He stared at me. I stared back.

"Wait here," he said. We were standing just inside the headquarters office. He went out and was gone for perhaps five minutes. I stood, listening to the wall clock ticking away. Then he came back.

"This way," he said.

He led me outside and back between the bubble roundness of the plastic buildings to a small structure half-hidden in some trees. When we stepped through its front entrance, I realized it was Kensie's personal quarters. We passed through a small sitting room into a combination bedroom and bath. Kensie had just stepped out of the shower and was getting into battle clothes. He looked at me curiously, then turned his gaze back on Janol.

"All right, Commandant," he said, "you can get back to your duties, now."

"Sir," said Janol, without looking at me.

He saluted and left.

"All right, Tam," Kensie said, pulling on a pair of uniform slacks. "What is it?"

"I know you're ready to move out," I said.

He looked at me a little humorously as he locked the waistband of his slacks. He had not yet put on his shirt, and in that relatively small room he loomed like a giant, like some irresistible natural force. His body was tanned like dark wood and the muscles lay in flat bands across his chest and shoulders. His belly was hollow and the cords in his arms came and went as he moved them. Once more I felt the particular, special element of the Dorsai in him. It was not just his physical size and strength. It was not even the fact that he was someone trained from birth to war, someone bred for battle. No, it was something living but untouchable—the same quality of difference to be found in the pure Exotic like Padma the OutBond, or in some Newtonian or Cassidan researchist. Something so much above and beyond the common form of man that it was like a serenity, a sense of conviction where his own type of thing was concerned that was so complete it made him beyond all weaknesses, untouchable, unconquerable.

I saw the slight, dark shadow of Jamethon Black in my mind's eye, standing opposed to such a man as this; and the thought of any victory for Jamethon was unthinkable, an impossibility.

But there was always danger.

"All right, I'll tell you what I came about," I said to Kensie. "I've just found out Black's been in touch with the Blue Front, a native terrorist political group with its headquarters in Blauvain. Three of them visited him last night. I saw them."

Kensie picked up his shirt and slid a long arm into one sleeve.

"I know," he said.

I stared at him.

"Don't you understand?" I said. "They're assassins. It's their stock in trade. And the one man they and Jamethon Black both could use out of the way is you."

He put his other arm in a sleeve.

"I know that," he said. "They want the present government here on St. Marie out of the way and themselves in power—which isn't possible with Exotic money hiring us to keep the peace here."

"They haven't had Jamethon Black's help."

"Have they got it now?" he asked, sealing the shirt closure between thumb and forefinger.

"The Friendlies are desperate," I said. "Even if reinforcements arrived tomorrow, Jamethon knows what his chances are with you ready to move. Assassins may be outlawed by the Conventions of War and the Mercenaries' Code, but you and I know the Friendlies."

Kensie looked at me oddly and picked up his jacket.

"Do we?" he said.

I met his eyes. "Don't we?"

"Tam." He put on the jacket and closed it. "I know the men I have to fight. It's my business to know. But what makes you think you know them?"

"They're my business too," I said. "Maybe you'd forgotten. I'm a newsman. People are my business, first, last and always."

"But you've got no use for the Friendlies."

"Should I?" I said. "I've been on all the worlds. I've seen the Cetan entrepreneur—and he wants his margin, but he's a human being. I've seen the Newtonian and the Cassidan with their heads in the clouds, but if you yanked on their sleeves hard enough, you could pull them back to reality. I've seen Exotics like Padma at their mental parlor tricks, and the Freilander up to his ears in his own red tape. I've seen them from my own world of Old Earth, and Coby, and Venus and even from the Dorsai, like you. And I tell you they've all got one thing in common. Underneath it all they're human. Every one of them's human—they've just specialized in some one, valuable way."

"And the Friendlies haven't?"

"Fascinaticism," I said. "Is that valuable? It's just the opposite. What's good—what's even permissible about blind, deaf, dumb, unthinking faith that doesn't let a man reason for himself?"

"How do you know they don't reason?" Kensie asked. He was standing facing me now.

"Maybe some of them do," I said. "Maybe the young ones, before the poison's had time to work in. What good does that do, as long as the culture exists?"

A sudden silence came into the room.

"What are you talking about?" said Kensie.

"I mean you want the assassins," I said. "You don't want the Friendly troops. Prove that Jamethon Black has broken the Conventions of War by arranging with them to kill you; and you can win St. Marie for the Exotics without firing a shot."

"And how would I do that?"

"Use me," I said. "I've got a pipeline to the political group the assassins represent. Let me go to them as your representative and outbid Jamethon. You can offer them recognition by the present government, now. Padma and the present St. Marie government heads would have to back you up if you could clean the planet of Friendlies that easily."

He looked at me with no expression at all.

"And what would I be supposed to buy with this?" he said.

"Sworn testimony they'd been hired to assassinate you. As many of them as needed could testify."

"No Court of Interplanetary Inquiry would believe people like that," Kensie said.

"Ah," I said, and I could not help smiling. "But they'd believe me as a News Network Representative when I backed up every word that was said."

There was a new silence. His face had no expression at all.

"I see," he said.

He walked past me into the salon. I followed him. He went to his phone, put his finger on a stud and spoke into an imageless, gray screen.

"Janol," he said.

He turned away from the screen, crossed the room to an arms cabinet and began putting on his battle harness. He moved deliberately and neither looked nor spoke in my direction. After a few long minutes, the building entrance slid aside and Janol stepped in.

"Sir?" said the Freilander officer.

"Mr. Olyn stays here until further orders."

"Yes sir," said Janol.

Graeme went out.

I stood numb, staring at the entrance through which he had left. I could not believe that he would violate the Conventions so far himself as not only to disregard me, but to put me essentially under arrest to keep me from doing anything further about the situation.

I turned to Janol. He was looking at me with a sort of wry sympathy on his long, brown face.

"Is the OutBond here in camp?" I asked him.

"No." He came up to me. "He's back in the Exotic Embassy in Blauvain. Be a good fella now and sit down, why don't you? We might as well kill the next few hours pleasantly."

We were standing face to face; I hit him in the stomach.

I had done a little boxing as an undergraduate on the college level. I mention this not to make myself out a sort of muscular hero, but to explain why I had sense enough not to try for his jaw. Graeme could probably have found the knockout point there without even thinking, but I was no Dorsai. The area below a man's breastbone is relatively large, soft, handy and generally just fine for amateurs. And I did know something about how to punch.

For all that, Janol was not knocked out. He went over on the floor and lay there doubled up with his eyes still open. But he was not ready to get up right away. I turned and went quickly out of the building.

The camp was busy. Nobody stopped me. I got back into my car, and five minutes later I was free on the darkening road for Blauvain.

v

From New San Marcos to Blauvain and Padma's Embassy was fourteen hundred kilometers. I should have made it in six hours, but a bridge was washed out and I took fourteen.

It was after eight the following morning when I burst into the half-park, half-building that was the embassy.

"Padma—" I said. "Is he still—"

"Yes, Mr. Olyn," said the girl receptionist. "He's expecting you."

She smiled above her purple robe. I did not mind. I was too busy being glad Padma had not already taken off for the fringe areas of the conflict.

She took me down and around a corner and turned me over to a young male Exotic, who introduced himself as one of Padma's secretaries. He took me a short distance and introduced me to another secretary, a middle-aged man this time, who led me through several rooms and then directed me down a long corridor and around a corner, beyond which he said was the entrance to the office area where Padma worked at the moment. Then he left me.

I followed his direction. But when I stepped through that entrance it was not into a room, but into a further short corridor. And I checked, stopping myself dead. For what I suddenly thought I saw coming at me was Kensie Graeme—Kensie with murder on his mind.

But the man who looked like Kensie merely glanced at me and dismissed me, continuing to come on. Then I knew.

Of course, he was not Kensie. He was Kensie's twin brother, Ian, commander of Garrison Forces for the Exotics, here in Blauvain. He strode on toward me; and I began once more to walk toward him, but the shock stayed with me until we had passed one another.

I do not think anyone could have come on him like that, in my position and not been hit the same way. From Janol, at different times, I had gathered how Ian was the converse of Kensie. Not in a military sense—they were both magnificent specimens of Dorsai officers—but in the matter of their individual natures.

Kensie had had a profound effect on me from the first moment, with his cheerful nature and the warmth of being that at times obscured the very fact that he was a Dorsai. When the pressure of military affairs was not directly on him he seemed all sunshine; you could warm yourself in his presence as you might in the sun. Ian, his physical duplicate, striding toward me like some two-eyed Odin, was all shadow.

Here at last was the Dorsai legend come to life. Here was the grim man with the iron heart and the dark and solitary soul. In the powerful fortress of his body, what was essentially Ian dwelt as isolated as a hermit on a mountain. He was the fierce and lonely Highlandman of his distant ancestry, come to life again.

Not law, not ethics, but the trust of the given word, clan-loyalty and the duty of the blood feud held sway in Ian. He was a man who would cross hell to pay a debt for good or ill; and in that moment when I saw him coming toward me and recognized him at last, I suddenly thanked whatever gods were left, that he had no debt with me.

Then we had passed each other, and he was gone around a corner.

Rumor had it, I remembered then, that the blackness around him never lightened except in Kensie's presence. That he was truly his twin brother's other half. And that if he should ever lose the light that Kensie's bright presence shed on him, he would be doomed to his own lightlessness forever.

It was a statement I was to remember at a later time, as I was to remember seeing him come toward me in that moment.

But now I forgot him as I went forward through another entrance into what looked like a small conservatory and saw the gentle face and short-cropped white hair of Padma, the OutBond, wearing a pale yellow robe.

"Come in, Mr. Olyn," he said, getting up. "And come along with me."

He turned and walked out through an archway of purple clematis blooms. I followed him, and found a small courtyard, all but filled with the elliptical shape of a sedan aircar. Padma was already climbing into one of the seats facing the controls. He held the door for me.

"Where are we going?" I asked as I got in.

He touched the autopilot panel; the ship rose in the air. He left it to its own navigation, and pivoted his chair about to face me.

"To Commander Graeme's headquarters in the field," he answered.

His eyes were a light hazel color, but they seemed to catch and swim with the sunlight striking through the transparent top of the aircar, as we reached altitude and began to move horizontally. I could not read them, or the expression on his face.

"I see," I said. "Of course, I know a call from Graeme's HQ could get to you much faster than I could by groundcar from the same spot. But I hope you aren't thinking of having him kidnap me or something like that. I have Credentials of Impartiality protecting me as a Newsman, as well as authorizations from both the Friendly and the Exotic worlds. And I don't intend to be held responsible for any conclusions drawn by Graeme after the conversation the two of us had earlier this morning—*alone*."

Padma sat still in his aircar seat, facing me. His hands were folded in his lap together, pale against the yellow robe, but with strong sinews showing under the skin of their backs.

"You're coming with me now by my decision, not Kensie Graeme's."

"I want to know why," I said tensely.

"Because," he said slowly, "you are very dangerous." And he sat still, looking at me with unwavering eyes.

I waited for him to go on, but he did not. "Dangerous?" I said. "Dangerous to who?"

"To the future of all of us."

I stared at him, then I laughed. I was angry.

"Cut it out!" I said.

He shook his head slowly, his eyes never leaving my face. I was baffled by those eyes. Innocent and open as a child's, but I could not see through them into the man himself.

"All right," I said. "Tell me, why am I dangerous?"

"Because you want to destroy a race of people. And you know how."

There was a short silence. The aircar fled on through the skies without a sound.

"Now that's an odd notion," I said slowly and calmly. "I wonder where you got it?"

"From our ontogenic calculations," said Padma, as calmly as I had spoken. "And it's not a notion, Tam. As you know yourself."

"Oh, yes," I said. "Ontogenics. I was going to look that up."

"You did look it up, didn't you, Tam?"

"Did I?" I said. "I guess I did, at that. It didn't seem very clear to me, though, as I remember. Something about evolution."

"Ontogenics," said Padma, "is the study of the effect of evolution upon the interacting forces of human society."

"Am I an interacting force?"

"At the moment and for the past several years, yes," said Padma. "And possibly for some years into the future. But possibly not."

"That sounds almost like a threat."

"In a sense it is." Padma's eyes caught the light as I watched them. "You're capable of destroying yourself as well as others."

"I'd hate to do that."

"Then," said Padma, "you'd better listen to me."

"Why, of course," I said. "That's my business, listening. Tell me all about ontogenics—and myself."

He made an adjustment in the controls, then swung his seat back to face mine once more.

"The human race," said Padma, "broke up in an evolutionary explosion at the moment in history when interstellar colonization became practical." He sat watching me. I kept my face attentive. "This happened for reasons stemming from racial instinct which we haven't completely charted yet, but which was essentially self-protective in nature."

I reached into my jacket pocket.

"Perhaps I'd better take a few notes," I said.

"If you want to," said Padma, unperturbed. "Out of that explosion came cultures individually devoted to single facets of the human personality. The fighting, combative facet became the Dorsai. The facet which surrendered the individual wholly to some faith or other became the Friendly. The philosophical facet created the Exotic culture to which I belong. We call these Splinter Cultures."

"Oh, yes," I said. "I know about Splinter Cultures."

"You know about them, Tam, but you don't know them."

"I don't?"

"No," said Padma, "because you, like all our ancestors, are from Earth. You're old, full-spectrum man. The Splinter peoples are evolutionarily advanced over you."

I felt a little twist of bitter anger knot suddenly inside me.

"Oh? I'm afraid I don't see that."

"Because you don't want to," said Padma. "If you did, you'd have to admit that they were different from you, and had to be judged by different standards."

"Different? How?"

"Different in a sense that all Splinter people, including myself, understand instinctively, but full-spectrum man has to extrapolate to imagine." Padma shifted a little in his seat. "You'll get some idea, Tam, if you imagine a member of a Splinter culture to be a man like yourself, only with a monomania that shoves him wholly toward being one type of person. But with this difference: Instead of all parts of his mental and physical self outside the limits of that monomania being ignored and atrophied as, they would be with you—"

I interrupted, "Why specifically with me?"

"With any full-spectrum man, then," said Padma calmly. "These parts, instead of being atrophied, are altered to agree with and support the monomania, so that we don't have a sick man—but a healthy, different one."

"Healthy?" I said, seeing the Friendly non-com on New Earth again in my mind's eye.

"Healthy as a culture. Not as occasional crippled individuals of that culture. But as a culture."

"Sorry," I said. "I don't believe it."

"But you do, Tam," said Padma, softly. "Unconsciously you do. Because you're planning to take advantage of the weakness such a culture must have to destroy it."

"And what weakness is that?"

"The obvious weakness that's the converse of any strength," said Padma. "The Splinter Cultures are not viable."

I must have blinked. I was honestly bewildered.

"Not viable? You mean they can't live on their own?"

"Of course not," said Padma. "Faced with an expansion into space, the human race reacted to the challenge of a different environment by trying to adapt to it. It adapted by trying out separately all the elements of its personality, to see which could survive best. Now that all elements —the Splinter Cultures—have survived and adapted, it's time for them to breed back into each other again, to produce a more hardy, universe-oriented human."

The aircar began to descend. We were nearing our destination.

"What's that got to do with me?" I said, at last.

"If you frustrate one of the Splinter Cultures, it can't adapt on its own as full-spectrum man would do. It will die. And when the race breeds back to a whole, that valuable element will be lost to the race."

"Maybe it'll be no loss," I said, softly in my turn.

"A vital loss," said Padma. "And I can prove it. You, a full-spectrum man, have in you an element from every Splinter Culture. If you admit this you can identify even with those you want to destroy. I have evidence to show you. Will you look at it?"

The ship touched ground; the door beside me opened. I got out with Padma and found Kensie waiting.

I looked from Padma to Kensie, who stood with us and a head taller than I—two heads taller than OutBond. Kensie looked back down at me with no particular expression. His eyes were not the eyes of his twin brother—but just then, for some reason, I could not meet them.

"I'm a newsman," I said. "Of course my mind is open."

Padma turned and began walking toward the headquarters building. Kensie fell in with us and I think Janol and some of the others came along behind, though I didn't look back to make sure. We went to the inner office where I first met Graeme—just Kensie, Padma and myself. There was a file folder on Graeme's desk. He picked it up, extracted a photocopy of something and handed it to me as I came up to him.

I took it. There was no doubting its authenticity.

It was a memo from Eldest Bright, ranking elder of the joint government of Harmony and Association, to the Friendly War Chief at the Defense X Center, on Harmony. It was dated two months previously. It was on the single-molecule sheet, where the legend cannot be tampered with, or removed once it is on.

*Be Informed, in God's Name—*

*—That since it does seem the Lord's Will that our Brothers on St. Marie make no success, it is ordered that henceforth no more replacements or personnel or supplies be sent them. For if our Captain does intend us the victory, surely we shall conquer without further expenditure. And if it be His will that we conquer not, then surely it would be an impiety to throw away the substance of God's Churches in an attempt to frustrate that Will.*

*Be it further ordered that our Brothers on St. Marie be spared the knowledge that no further assistance is forthcoming, that they may bear witness to their faith in battle as ever, and God's Churches be undismayed.*

*Heed this Command, in the Name of the Lord:*

*By order of he who is called . . .*

*Bright*

*Eldest Among The Chosen*

I looked up from the memo. Both Graeme and Padma were watching me.

"How'd you get hold of this?" I said. "No, of course you won't tell me." The palms of my hands were suddenly sweating so that the slick material of the sheet in my fingers was slippery. I held it tightly, and talked fast to keep their eyes on my face. "But what about it? We already knew this, everybody knew Bright had abandoned them. This just proves it. Why even bother showing it to me?"

"I thought," said Padma, "it might move you just a little. Perhaps enough to make you take a different view of things."

I said, "I didn't say that wasn't possible. I tell you a Newsman keeps an open mind at all times. Of course," I picked my words carefully, "if I could study it—"

"I'd hoped you'd take it with you," said Padma.

"Hoped?"

"If you dig into it and really understand what Bright means there, you might understand all the Friendlies differently. You might change your mind about them."

"I don't think so," I said. "But—"

"Let me ask you to do that much," said Padma. "Take the memo with you."

I stood for a moment, with Padma facing me and Kensie looming behind him, then shrugged and put the memo in my pocket.

"All right," I said. "I'll take it back to my quarters and think about it—I've got a groundcar here somewhere, haven't I?" And I looked at Kensie.

"Ten kilometers back," said Kensie. "You wouldn't get through anyway. We're moving up for the assault and the Friendlies are maneuvering to meet us."

"Take my aircar," said Padma. "The Embassy flags on it will help."

"All right," I said.

We went out together toward the aircar. I passed Janol in the outer office and he met my eyes coldly. I did not blame him. We walked to the aircar and I got in.

"You can send the aircar back whenever you're through with it," said Padma, as I stepped in through the entrance section of its top. "It's an Embassy loan to you, Tam. I won't worry about it."

"No," I said. "You needn't worry."

I closed the section and touched the controls.

It was a dream of an aircar. It went up into the air as lightly as thought, and in a second I was two thousand feet up and well away from the spot. I made myself calm down, though, before I reached into my pocket and took the memo out.

I looked at it. My hand still trembled a little as I held it.

Here it was in my grasp at last. What I had been after from the start. And Padma himself had insisted I carry it away with me.

It was the lever, the Archimedes pry-bar which would move not one world but fourteen. And push the Friendly Peoples over the edge to extinction.

VI

They were waiting for me. They converged on the aircar as I landed it in the interior square of the Friendlies compound, all four of them with black rifles at the ready.

They were apparently the only ones left. Black seemed to have turned out every other man of his remnant of a battle unit. And these were all men I recognized, case-hardened veterans. One was the Groupman who had been in the office that first night when I had come back from the Exotic camp and stepped in to speak to Black, asking him if he ever ordered his men to kill prisoners. Another was a forty-year-old Force Leader, the lowest commissioned rank, but acting Major—just as Black, a Commandant, was acting as Expeditionary Field Commander —a position equivalent to Kensie Graeme's. The other two soldiers were non-commissioned, but similar. I knew them all. Ultrafanatics. And they knew me.

We understood each other.

"I have to see the commandant," I said, as I got out, before they could begin to question me.

"On what business?" said the Force Leader. "This aircar hath no business here. Nor thyself."

I said, "I must see Commandant Black immediately. I wouldn't be here in a car flying the flags of the Exotic Embassy if it wasn't necessary."

They could not take the chance that my reason for seeing Black wasn't important, and I knew it. They argued a little, but I kept insisting I had to see the Commandant. Finally, the Force Leader took me across into the same outer office where I had always waited to see Black.

I faced Jamethon Black alone in the office.

He was putting on his battle harness, as I had seen Graeme putting on his earlier. On Graeme, the harness and the weapons it carried had looked like toys. On Jamethon's slight frame they looked almost too heavy to bear.

"Mr. Olyn," he said.

I walked across the room toward him, drawing the memo from my pocket as I came. He turned a little to face me, his fingers sealing the locks on his harness, jingling slightly with his weapons and his harness as he turned.

"You're taking the field against the Exotics," I said.

He nodded. I had never been this close to him before. From across the room I would have believed he was holding his usual stony expression, but standing just a few feet from him now I saw the tired wraith of a smile touch the corners of his straight mouth in that dark, young face, for a second.

"That is my duty, Mr. Olyn."

"Some duty," I said. "When your superiors back on Harmony have already written you off their books."

"I've already told you," he said, calmly. "The Chosen are not betrayed in the Lord, one by another."

"You're sure of that?" I said.

Once more I saw that little ghost of a weary smile.

"It's a subject, Mr. Olyn, on which I am more expert than you."

I looked into his eyes. They were exhausted but calm. I glanced aside at the desk where the picture of the church, the older man and woman and the young girl stood still.

"Your family?" I asked.

"Yes," he said.

"It seems to me you'd think of them in a time like this."

"I think of them quite often."

"But you're going to go out and get yourself killed just the same."

"Just the same," he said.

"Sure!" I said. "You would!" I had come in calm and in control of myself. But now it was as if a cork had been pulled on all that had been inside me since Dave's death. I began to shake. "Because that's the kind of hypocrites you are—all of you Friendlies. You're so lying, so rotten clear through with your own lies, if someone took them away from you there'd be nothing left. Would there? So you'd rather die now than admit committing suicide like this isn't the most glorious thing in the universe. You'd rather die than admit you're just as full of doubts as anyone else, just as afraid."

I stepped right up to him. He did not move.

"Who're you trying to fool?" I said. "Who? I see through you just like the people on all the other worlds do! I know you know what a mumbo-jumbo your United Churches are. I know you know the way of life you sing of through your nose so much isn't what you claim it is. I know your Eldest Bright and his gang of narrow-minded old men are just a gang of world-hungry tyrants that don't give a damn for religion or anything as long as they get what they want. I know you know it—and I'm going to make you admit it!"

And I shoved the memo under his nose.

"Read it!"

He took it from me. I stepped back from him, shaking badly as I watched him.

He studied it for a long minute, while I held my breath. His face did not change. Then handed it back to me.

"Can I give you a ride to meet Graeme?" I said. "We can get across the lines in the OutBond's aircar. You can get the surrender over with before any shooting breaks out."

He shook his head. He was looking at me in a particularly level way, with an expression I could not understand.

"What do you mean—no?"

"You'd better stay here," he said. "Even with ambassadorial flags, that aircar may be shot at over the lines." And he turned as if he would walk away from me, out the door.

"Where're you going?" I shouted at him. I got in front of him and pushed the memo before his eyes again. "That's real. You can't close your eyes to that!"

He stopped and looked at me. Then he reached out and took my wrist and put my arm and hand with the memo aside. His fingers were thin, but much stronger than I thought, so that I let the arm go down in front of him when I hadn't intended to do so.

"I know it's real. I'll have to warn you not to interfere with me any more, Mr. Olyn. I've got to go now." He stepped past me and walked toward the door.

"You're a liar!" I shouted after him. He kept on going. I had to stop him. I grabbed the solidograph from his desk and smashed it on the floor.

He turned like a cat and looked at the broken pieces at my feet.

"That's what you're doing!" I shouted, pointing at them.

He came back without a word and squatted down and carefully gathered up the pieces, one by one. He put them into his pocket and got back to his feet, and raised his face at last to mine. And when I saw his eyes I stopped breathing.

"If my duty," he said, in a low, controlled voice, "were not in this minute to—"

His voice stopped. I saw his eyes staring into me; and slowly I saw them change and the murder that was in them soften into something like wonder.

"Thou"—he said, softly—"Thou hast *no* faith?"

I had opened my mouth to speak. But what he said stopped me. I stood as if punched in the stomach, without the breath for words. He stared at me.

"What made you think," he said, "that that memo would change my mind?"

"You read it!" I said. "Bright wrote you were a losing proposition here, so you weren't to get any more help. And no one was to tell you for fear you might surrender if you knew."

"Is that how you read it?" he said. "Like that?"

"How else? How else can you read it?"

"As it is written." He stood straight facing me now and his eyes never moved from mine. "You have read it without faith, leaving out the Name and the will of the Lord. Eldest Bright wrote not that we were to be abandoned here—but that since our cause was sore tried, we be put in the hands of our Captain and our God. And further he wrote that we should not be told of this, that none here should be tempted to a vain and special seeking of the martyr's crown. Look, Mr. Olyn. It's down there in black and white."

"But that's not what he meant! *That's not what he meant!*"

He shook his head. "Mr. Olyn, I can't leave you in such delusion."

I stared at him, for it was sympathy I saw in his face. For me.

"It's your own blindness that deludes you," he said. "You see nothing, and so believe no man can see. Our Lord is not just a name, but all things. That's why we have no ornament in our churches, scorning any painted screen between us and our God. Listen to me, Mr. Olyn. Those churches themselves are but tabernacles of the earth. Our Elders and Leaders, though they are Chosen and Anointed, are still but mortal men. To none of these things or people do we hearken in our faith, but to the very voice of God within us."

He paused. Somehow I could not speak.

"Suppose it was even as you think," he went on, even more gently. "Suppose that all you say was a fact; and that our Elders were but greedy tyrants, ourselves abandoned here by their selfish will and set to fulfill a false and prideful purpose. No." Jamethon's voice rose. "Let me attest as if it were only for myself. Suppose that you could give me proof that all our Elders lied, that our very Covenant was false. Suppose that you could prove to me"—his face lifted to mine and his voice drove at me—"that all was perversion and falsehood, and nowhere among the Chosen, not even in the house of my father, was there faith or hope! If you could prove to me that no miracle could save me, that no soul stood with me—and that opposed were all the legions of the universe—still I, I *alone*, Mr. Olyn, would go forward as I have been commanded, to the end of the universe, to the culmination of eternity. For without my faith I am but common earth. But with my faith, there is no power can stay me!"

He stopped speaking and turned about. I watched him walk across the room and out the door.

Still I stood there, as if I had been fastened in place—until I heard from outside, in the square of the compound, the sound of a military aircar starting up.

I broke out of my stasis then and ran out of the building.

As I burst into the square, the military aircar was just taking off. I could see Black and his four hard-shell subordinates in it. And I yelled up into the air after them.

"That's all right for you, but what about your men?"

They could not hear me. I knew that. Uncontrollable tears were running down my face, but I screamed up into the air after him anyway—

"You're killing your men to prove your point! Can't you listen? You're murdering helpless men!"

Unheeding, the military aircar dwindled rapidly to the west and south, where the converging battle forces waited. And the heavy concrete walls and buildings about the empty compound threw back my words with a hollow, wild and mocking echo.

VII

I should have gone to the spaceport. Instead, I got back into the aircar and flew back across the lines looking for Graeme's Battle Command Center.

I was as little concerned about my own life just then as a Friendly. I think I was shot at once or twice, in spite of the ambassadorial flags on the aircar, but I don't remember exactly. Eventually I found the Command Center and descended.

Enlisted men surrounded me as I stepped out of the aircar. I showed my credentials and went up to the battle screen, which had been set up in open air at the edge of shadow from some tall variform oaks. Graeme, Padma and his whole staff were grouped around it, watching the movements of their own and the Friendly troops reported on it. A continual low-voiced discussion of the movements went on, and a steady stream of information came from the communications center fifteen feet off.

The sun slanted steeply through the trees. It was almost noon and the day was bright and warm. No one looked at me for a long time; and then Janol, turning away from the screen, caught sight of me standing off at one side by the flat-topped shape of a tactics computer. His face went cold. He went on about what he was doing. But I must have been looking pretty bad, because after a while he came by with a canteen cup and set it down on the computer top.

"Drink that," he said shortly, and went off. I picked it up, found it was Dorsai whisky and swallowed it down. I could not taste it; but evidently it did me some good, because in a few minutes the world began to sort itself out around me and I began to think again.

I went up to Janol. "Thanks."

"All right." He did not look at me, but went on with the papers on the field desk before him.

"Janol," I said. "Tell me what's going on."

"See for yourself," he said, still bent over his papers.

"I can't see for myself. You know that. Look—I'm sorry about what I did. But this is my job, too. Can't you tell me what's going on now and fight with me afterwards?"

"You know I can't brawl with civilians." Then his face relaxed. "All right," he said, straightening up. "Come on."

He led me over to the battle screen, where Padma and Kensie were standing, and pointed to a sort of small triangle of darkness between two snakelike lines of light. Other spots and shapes of light ringed it about.

"These"—he pointed to the two snakelike lines—"are the Macintok and Sarah Rivers, where they come together—just about ten miles this side of Joseph's Town. It's fairly high ground, hills thick with cover, fairly open between them. Good territory for setting up a stubborn defense, bad area to get trapped in."

"Why?"

He pointed to the two river lines.

"Get backed up in here and you find yourself hung up on high bluffs over the river. There is no easy way across, no cover for retreating troops. It's nearly all open farmland the rest of the way, from the other sides of the rivers to Joseph's Town."

His finger moved back out from the point where the river lines came together, past the small area of darkness and into the surrounding shapes and rings of light.

"On the other hand, the approach to this territory from our position is through open country, too—narrow strips of farmland interspersed with a lot of swamp and marsh. It's a tight situation for either commander, if we commit to a battle here. The first one who has to back-pedal will find himself in trouble in a hurry."

"Are you going to commit?"

"It depends. Black sent his light armor forward. Now he's pulling back into the high ground, between the rivers. We're far superior in strength and equipment. There's no reason for us not to go in after him, as long as he's trapped himself—" Janol broke off.

"No reason?" I asked.

"Not from a tactical standpoint." Janol frowned at the screen. "We couldn't get into trouble unless we suddenly had to retreat. And we wouldn't do that unless he suddenly acquired some great tactical advantage that'd make it impossible for us to stay there."

I looked at his profile.

"Such as losing Graeme?" I said.

He transferred his frown to me. "There's no danger of that."

There was a certain change in the movement and the voices of the people around us. We both turned and looked.

Everybody was clustering around a screen. We moved in with the crowd and, looking between the soldiers of two of the officers of Graeme's staff, I saw on the screen the image of a small grassy meadow enclosed by wooded hills. In the center of the meadow, the Friendly flag floated its thin black cross on white background beside a long table on the grass. There were folding chairs on each side of the table, but only one person—a Friendly officer, standing on the table's far side as if waiting. There were the lilac bushes along the edge of the wooded hills where they came down in variform oak and ash to the meadow's edge; and the lavender blossoms were beginning to brown and darken for their season was almost at an end. So much difference had twenty-four hours made. Off to the left of the screen I could see the gray concrete of a highway.

"I know that place—" I started to say, turning to Janol.

"Quiet!" he said, holding up a finger. Around us, everybody else had fallen still. Up near the front of our group a single voice was talking.

"—it's a truce table."

"Have they called?" said the voice of Kensie.

"No, sir."

"Well, let's go see." There was a stir up front. The group began to break up and I saw Kensie and Padma walking off toward the area where the aircars were parked. I shoved myself through the thinning crowd like a process server, running after them.

I heard Janol shout behind me, but I paid no attention. Then I was up to Kensie and Padma, who turned.

"I want to go with you," I said.

"It's all right, Janol," Kensie said, looking past me. "You can leave him with us."

"Yes, sir." I could hear Janol turn and leave.

"So you want to come with me, Mr. Olyn?" Kensie said.

"I know that spot," I told him. "I drove by it just earlier today. The Friendlies were taking tactical measurements all over that meadow and the hills on both sides. They weren't setting up truce talks."

Kensie looked at me for a long moment, as if he was taking some tactical measurements himself.

"Come on, then," he said. He turned to Padma. "You'll be staying here?"

"It's a combat zone. I'd better not." Padma turned his unwrinkled face to me. "Good luck, Mr. Olyn," he said, and walked away. I watched his yellow-robed figure glide over the turf for a second, then turned to see Graeme halfway to the nearest military aircar. I hurried after him.

It was a battle car, not luxurious like the OutBond's, and Kensie did not cruise at two thousand feet, but snaked it between the trees just a few feet above ground. The seats were cramped. His big frame over-filled his, crowding me where I sat. I felt the butt-plate of his spring pistol grinding into my side with every movement he made on the controls.

We came at last to the edge of the wooded and hilly triangle occupied by the Friendlies and mounted a slope under the cover of the new-leaved variform oaks.

They were massive enough to have killed off most ground cover. Between their pillar-like trunks the ground was shaded, and padded with the brown shapes of dead leaves. Near the crest of the hill, we came upon a unit of Exotic troops resting and waiting the orders to advance. Kensie got out of the car and returned the Force Leader's salute.

"You've seen these tables the Friendlies set up?" Kensie asked.

"Yes, Commander. That officer they've got is still standing there. If you go just up over the crest of the slope here, you can see him—and the furniture."

"Good," said Kensie. "Keep your men here, Force. The Newsman and I'll go take a look."

He led the way up among the oak trees. At the top of the hill we looked down through about fifty yards more of trees and out into the meadow. It was two hundred yards across, the table right in the middle, the unmoving black figure of the Friendly officer standing on its far side.

"What do you think of it, Mr. Olyn?" asked Kensie, looking down through the trees.

"Why hasn't somebody shot him?" I asked.

He glanced sideways at me.

"There's plenty of time to shoot him," he said, "before he can get back to cover on the far side. If we have to shoot him at all. That wasn't what I wanted to know. You've seen the Friendly commander recently. Did he give you the impression he was ready to surrender?"

"No!" I said.

"I see," said Kensie.

"You don't really think he means to surrender? What makes you think something like that?"

"Truce tables are generally set up for the discussion of terms between opposing forces," he said.

"But he hasn't asked you to meet him?"

"No," Kensie watched the figure of the Friendly officer, motionless in the sunlight. "It might be against his principles to call for a discussion, but not to discuss—if we just happened to find ourselves across a table from one another."

He turned and signaled with his hand. The Force Leader, who had been waiting down the slope behind us, came up.

"Sir?" he said to Kensie.

"Any Friendly strength in those trees across the way?"

"Four men, that's all, sir. Our scopes pick out their body heats clear and sharp. They aren't attempting to hide."

"I see." He paused. "Force."

"Sir?"

"Be good enough to go down there in the meadow and ask that Friendly officer what this is all about."

"Yes, sir."

We stood and watched as the Force Leader went stiff-legging it down the steep slope between the trees. He crossed the grass—it seemed very slowly—and came up to the Friendly officer.

They stood facing each other. They were talking but there was no way to hear their voices. The flag with its thin black cross whipped in the little breeze that was blowing there. Then the Force Leader turned and climbed back toward us.

He stopped in front of Kensie, and saluted. "Commander," he said, "the Commander of the Chosen Troops of God will meet with you in the field to discuss a surrender." He stopped to draw a fresh breath. "If you'll show yourself at the edge of the opposite woods at the same time; and you can approach the table together."

"Thank you, Force Leader," said Kensie. He looked past his officer at the field and the table. "I think I'll go down."

"He doesn't mean it," I said.

"Force Leader," said Kensie. "Form your men ready, just under the crown of the slope on the back side, here. If he surrenders, I'm going to insist he come back with me to this side immediately."

"Yes, sir."

"All this business without a regular call for parley may be because he wants to surrender first and break the news of it to his troops afterwards. So get your men ready. If Black intends to present his officers with an accomplished fact, we don't want to let him down."

"He's not going to surrender," I said.

"Mr. Olyn," said Kensie, turning to me. "I suggest you go back behind the crest of the hill. The Force Leader will see you're taken care of."

"No," I said. "I'm going down. If it's a truce parley to discuss surrender terms, there's no combat situation involved and I've got a perfect right to be there. If it isn't, what're you doing going down yourself?"

Kensie looked at me strangely for a moment.

"All right," he said. "Come with me."

Kensie and I turned and went down the sharply pitched slope between the trees. Our boot-soles slipped until our heels dug in, with every step downward. Coming through the lilacs I smelled the faint, sweet scent—almost gone now—of the decaying blossoms.

Across the meadow, directly in line with the table, four figures in black came forward as we came forward. One of them was Jamethon Black.

Kensie and Jamethon saluted each other.

"Commandant Black," said Kensie.

"Yes, Commander Graeme. I am indebted to you for meeting me here," said Jamethon.

"My duty and a pleasure, Commandant."

"I wished to discuss the terms of a surrender."

"I can offer you," said Kensie, "the customary terms extended to troops in your position under the Mercenaries' Code."

"You misunderstand me, sir," said Jamethon. "It was your surrender I came here to discuss."

The flag snapped.

Suddenly I saw the men in black measuring the field here, as I had seen them the day before. They had been right where we were now.

"I'm afraid the misunderstanding is mutual, Commandant," said Kensie. "I am in a superior tactical position and your defeat is normally certain. I have no need to surrender."

"You will not surrender?"

"No," said Kensie strongly.

All at once I saw the five stakes, in the position the Friendly non-coms, officers and Jamethon were now, and the stake up in front of them fallen down.

"Look out!" I shouted at Kensie—but I was far too late.

Things had already begun to happen. The Force Leader had jerked back in front of Jamethon and all five of them were drawing their side-arms. I heard the flag snap again, and the sound of its rolling seemed to go on for a long time.

For the first time then I saw a man of the Dorsai in action. So swift was Kensie's reaction that it was eerily as if he had read Jamethon's mind in the instant before the Friendlies began to reach for their weapons. As their hands touched their sidearms, he was already in movement forward over the table and his spring pistol was in his hand. He seemed to fly directly into the Force Leader and the two of them went down together, but Kensie kept traveling. He rolled on off the Force Leader who now lay still in the grass. He came to his knees, fired, and dived forward, rolling again.

The Groupman on Jamethon's right went down. Jamethon and the remaining two were turned nearly full about now, trying to keep Kensie before them. The two that were left shoved themselves in front of Jamethon, their weapons not yet aimed. Kensie stopped moving as if he had run into a stone wall, came to his feet in a crouch, and fired twice more. The two Friendlies fell apart, one to each side.

Jamethon was facing Kensie now, and Jamethon's pistol was in his hand and aimed. Jamethon fired, and a light blue streak leaped through the air, but Kensie had dropped again. Lying on his side on the grass, propped on one elbow, he pressed the firing button on his spring pistol twice.

Jamethon's sidearm sagged in his hand. He was backed up against the table now, and he put out his free hand to steady himself against the table top. He made another effort to lift his sidearm but he could not. It dropped from his hand. He bore more of his weight on the table, half-turning around, and his face came about to look in my direction. His face was as controlled as it had ever been, but there was something different about his eyes as he looked into mine and recognized me— something oddly like the look a man gives a competitor whom he had just beaten, and who was no real threat to begin with. A little smile touched the corners of his thin lips. Like a smile of inner triumph.

"Mr. Olyn . . ." he whispered. And then the life went out of his face and he fell beside the table.

Nearby explosions shook the ground under my feet. From the crest of the hill behind us the Force Leader whom Kensie had left there was firing smoke bombs between us and the Friendly side of the meadow. A gray wall of smoke was rising between us and the far hillside, to screen us from the enemy. It towered up the blue sky like some impassable barrier, and under the looming height of it, only Kensie and I were standing.

On Jamethon's dead face there was a faint smile.

VIII

In a daze I watched the Friendly troops surrender that same day. It was the one situation in which their officers felt justified in doing so.

Not even their Elders expected subordinates to fight a situation set up by a dead Field Commander for tactical reasons unexplained to his officers. And the live troops remaining were worth more than the indemnity charges for them that the Exotics would make.

I did not wait for the settlements. I had nothing to wait for. One moment the situation on this battlefield had been poised like some great, irresistible wave above all our heads, cresting, curling over and about to break downward with an impact that would reverberate through all the worlds of Man. Now, suddenly, it was no longer above us. There was nothing but a far-flooding silence, already draining away into the records of the past.

There was nothing for me. Nothing.

If Jamethon had succeeded in killing Kensie—even if as a result he had won a practically bloodless surrender of the Exotic troops—I might have done something damaging with the incident of the truce table. But he had only tried; and died, failing. Who could work up emotion against the Friendlies for that?

I took ship back to Earth like a man walking in a dream, asking myself why.

Back on Earth, I told my editors I was not in good shape physically;

and they took one look at me and believed me. I took an indefinite leave from my job and sat around the News Network Center Library, at the Hague, searching blindly through piles of writings and reference material on the Friendlies, the Dorsai and the Exotic worlds. For what? I did not know. I also watched the news dispatches from St. Marie concerning the settlement, and drank too much while I watched.

I had the numb feeling of a soldier sentenced to death for failure on duty. Then in the news dispatches came the information that Jamethon's body would be returned to Harmony for burial; and I realized suddenly it was this I had been waiting for: The unnatural honoring by fanatics of the fanatic who with four henchmen had tried to assassinate the lone enemy commander under a truce flag. Things could still be written.

I shaved, showered, pulled myself together after a fashion and went to see my superiors about being sent to Harmony to cover the burial of Jamethon, as a wrap-up.

The congratulations of the Director of News Network, that had reached me on St. Marie earlier, stood me in good stead. It was still fresh in the minds of the men just over me. I was sent.

Five days later I was on Harmony, in a little town called Remembered-of-the-Lord. The buildings in the town were of concrete and bubble plastic, though evidently they had been up for many years. The thin, stony soil about the town had been tilled as the fields on St. Marie had been tilled when I got to that other world—for Harmony now was just entering the spring of its northern hemisphere. And it was raining as I drove from the spaceport of the town, as it had on St. Marie that first day. But the Friendly fields I saw did not show the rich darkness of the fields of St. Marie. Only a thin, hard blackness in the wet that was like the color of Friendly uniforms.

I got to the church just as people were beginning to arrive. Under the dark, draining skies, the interior of the church was almost too dim to let me see my way about—for the Friendlies permit themselves no windows and no artificial lighting in their houses of worship. Gray light, cold wind and rain entered the doorless portal at the back of the church. Through the single rectangular opening in the roof watery sunlight filtered over Jamethon's body, on a platform set up on trestles. A transparent cover had been set up to protect the body from the rain, which was channeled off the open space and ran down a drain in the back wall. But the elder conducting the Death Service and anyone coming up to view the body was expected to stand exposed to sky and weather.

I got in line with the people moving slowly down the central aisle and past the body. To right and left of me the barriers at which the congregation would stand during the service were lost in gloom. The rafters of the steeply pitched roof were hidden in darkness. There was no music, but the low sound of voices individually praying to either side of me in the ranks of barriers and in the line blended into a sort of rhythmic undertone of sadness. Like Jamethon, the people were all very dark here, being of North African extraction. Dark into dark, they blended, and were lost about me in the gloom.

I came up and passed at last by Jamethon. He looked as I remembered him. Death had had no power to change him. He lay on his back, his hands at his sides, and his lips were as firm and straight as ever. Only his eyes were closed.

I was limping noticeably because of the dampness, and as I turned away from the body, I felt my elbow touched. I turned back sharply. I was not wearing my correspondent's uniform. I was in civilian clothes, so as to be inconspicuous.

I looked down into the face of the young girl in Jamethon's solidograph. In the gray rainy light her unlined face was like something from the stained glass window of an ancient cathedral back on Old Earth.

"You've been wounded," she said in a soft voice to me. "You must be one of the mercenaries who knew him on Newton, before he was ordered to Harmony. His parents, who are mine as well, would find solace in the Lord by meeting you."

The wind blew rain down through the overhead opening all about me, and its icy feel sent a chill suddenly shooting through me, freezing me to my very bones.

"No!" I said. "I'm not. I didn't know him." And I turned sharply away from her and pushed my way into the crowd, back up the aisle.

After about fifteen feet, I realized what I was doing and slowed down. The girl was already lost in the darkness of the bodies behind me. I made my way more slowly toward the back of the church, where there was a little place to stand before the first ranks of the barriers began. I stood watching the people come in. They came and came, walking in in their black clothing with their heads down and talking or praying in low voices.

I stood where I was, a little back from the entrance, half numbed and dull-minded with the chill about me and the exhaustion I had brought with me from Earth. The voice droned about me. I almost dozed, standing there. I could not remember why I had come.

Then a girl's voice emerged from the jumble, bringing me back to full consciousness again.

"—he did deny it, but I am sure he is one of those mercenaries who was with Jamethon on Newton. He limps and can only be a soldier who hath been wounded."

It was the voice of Jamethon's sister, speaking with more of the Friendly cant on her tongue than she had used speaking to me, a stranger. I woke fully and saw her standing by the entrance only a few feet from me, half-facing two elder people who I recognized as the older couple in Jamethon's solidograph. A bolt of pure, freezing horror shot through me.

"No!" I nearly shouted at them. "I don't know him. I never knew him—I don't understand what you're talking about!" And I turned and bolted out through the entrance of the church into the concealing rain.

I all but ran for about thirty or forty feet. Then I heard no footsteps behind me; I stopped.

I was alone in the open. The day was even darker now and the rain suddenly came down harder. It obscured everything around me with a drumming, shimmering curtain. I could not even see the groundcars in the parking lot toward which I was facing; and for sure they could not see me from the church. I lifted my face up to the downpour and let it beat upon my cheeks and my closed eyelids.

"So," said a voice from behind me. "You did not know him?"

The words seemed to cut me down the middle, and I felt as a cornered wolf must feel. Like a wolf I turned.

"Yes, I knew him!" I said.

Facing me was Padma, in a blue robe the rain did not seem to dampen. His empty hands that had never held a weapon in their life were clasped together before him. But the wolf part of me knew that as far as I was concerned, he was armed and a hunter.

"You?" I said. "What are you doing here?"

"It was calculated you would be here," said Padma, softly. "So I am here, too. But why *are* you here, Tam? Among those people in there, there's sure to be at least a few fanatics who've heard the camp rumors of your responsibility in the matter of Jamethon's death and the Friendlies' surrender."

"Rumors!" I said. "Who started them?"

"You did," Padma said. "By your actions on St. Marie." He gazed at me. "Didn't you know you were risking your life, coming here today?"

I opened my mouth to deny it. Then I realized I had known.

"What if someone should call out to them," said Padma, "that Tam Olyn, the St. Marie campaign Newsman, is here incognito?"

I looked at him with my wolf-feeling, grimly.

"Can you square it with your Exotic principles if you do?"

"We are misunderstood," answered Padma calmly. "We hire soldiers to fight for us not because of some moral commandment, but because our emotional perspective is lost if we become involved."

There was no fear left in me. Only a hard, empty feeling.

"Then call them," I said.

Padma's strange, hazel eyes watched me through the rain.

"If that was all that was needed," he said, "I could have sent word to them. I wouldn't have needed to come myself."

"Why did you come?" My voice tore at my throat. "What do you care about me, or the Exotics?"

"We care for every individual," said Padma. "But we care more for the race. And you remain dangerous to it. You're an idealist, Tam, warped to destructive purpose. There is a law of conservation of energy in the pattern of cause-and-effect as in other sciences. Your destructiveness was frustrated on St. Marie. Now it may turn inward to destroy you, or outward against the whole race of man."

I laughed, and heard the harshness of my laughter.

"What're you going to do about it?" I said.

"Show you how the knife you hold cuts the hand that holds it as well as what you turn it against. I have news for you, Tam. Kensie Graeme is dead."

"*Dead?*" The rain seemed to roar around me suddenly and the parking lot shifted unsubstantially under my feet.

"He was assassinated by three men of the Blue Front in Blauvain five days ago."

"Assassinated . . ." I whispered. "Why?"

"Because the war was over," said Padma. "Because Jamethon's death and the surrender of the Friendly troops without the preliminary of a war that would tear up the countryside left the civilian population favorably disposed toward our troops. Because the Blue Front found themselves farther from power than ever, as a result of this favorable feeling. They hoped by killing Graeme to provoke his troops into retaliation against the civilian population, so that the St. Marie government would have to order them home to our Exotics, and stand unprotected to face a Blue Front revolt."

I stared at him.

"All things are interrelated," said Padma. "Kensie was slated for a final promotion to a desk command back on Mara or Kultis. He and his brother Ian would have been out of the wars for the rest of their professional lives. Because of Jamethon's death, that allowed the surrender of his troops without fighting, a situation was set up which led the Blue Front to assassinate Kensie. If you and Jamethon had not come together on St. Marie, and Jamethon had won, Kensie would still be alive. So our calculations show."

"Jamethon and I?" The breath went dry in my throat without warning, and the rain came down harder.

"You were the factor," said Padma, "that helped Jamethon to his solution."

"I helped him!" I said. "I did?"

"He saw through you," said Padma. "He saw through the revenge-bitter, twisted surface you thought was yourself, to the idealistic core that was so deep in the bone of you that even your uncle hadn't been able to eradicate it."

The rain thundered between us. But Padma's every word came clearly through it to me.

"I don't believe you!" I shouted. "I don't believe he did anything like that!"

"I told you," said Padma, "you didn't fully appreciate the evolutionary advances of our Splinter Cultures. Jamethon's faith was not the kind that can be shaken by outer things. If you had been in fact like your uncle, he would not even have listened to you. He would have dismissed you as a soulless man. As it was, he thought of you instead as a man possessed. A man speaking with what he would have called Satan's voice."

"I don't believe it!" I yelled.

"You do believe it," said Padma. "You've got no choice except to believe it. Because only because of it could Jamethon find his solution."

"Solution!"

"He was a man ready to die for his faith. But as a commander he found it hard his men should go out to die for no other reasonable cause." Padma watched me, and the rain thinned for a moment. "But you offered him what he recognized as the devil's choice—his life in this world, if he would surrender his faith and his men, to avoid the conflict that would end in his death and theirs."

"What crazy thinking was that?" I said. Inside the church, the praying had stopped, and a single strong, deep voice was beginning the burial service.

"Not crazy," said Padma. "The moment he realized this, his answer became simple. All he had to do was begin by denying whatever the

Satan offered. He must start with the absolute necessity of his own death."

"And that was a solution?" I tried to laugh but my throat hurt.

"It was the only solution," said Padma. "Once he decided that, he saw immediately that the one situation in which his men would permit themselves to surrender was if he was dead and they were in an untenable position for reasons only he had known."

I felt the words go through me with a soundless shock.

"But he didn't mean to die!" I said.

"He left it to his God," said Padma. "He arranged it so only a miracle could save him."

"What're you talking about?" I stared at him. "He set up a table with a flag of truce. He took four men—"

"There was no flag. The men were overage, martyrdom-seekers."

"He took four!" I shouted. "Four and one made five. The five of them against one man. I stood there by that table and saw. Five against—"

"Tam."

The single word stopped me. Suddenly I began to be afraid. I did not want to hear what he was about to say. I was afraid I knew what he was going to tell me. That I had known it for some time. And I did not want to hear it, I did not want to hear him say it. The rain grew even stronger, driving upon us both and mercilessly on the concrete, but I heard every word relentlessly through all its sound and noise.

Padma's voice began to roar in my ears like the rain, and a feeling came over me like the helpless floating sensation that comes in high fever. "Did you think that Jamethon for a minute fooled himself? He was a product of a Splinter Culture. He recognized another in Kensie. Did you think that for a minute he thought that barring a miracle he and four overage fanatics could kill an armed, alert and ready man of the Dorsai—*a man like Kensie Graeme?* Before they were gunned down and killed themselves?"

Themselves . . . themselves . . . themselves . . .

I rode off a long way on that word from the dark day and the rain. Like the rain and the wind behind the clouds it lifted me and carried me away at last to that high, hard and stony land I had glimpsed when I had asked Kensie Graeme that question about his ever allowing Friendly prisoners to be killed. It was this land I had always avoided, but to it I was come at last.

And I remembered . . .

From the beginning, I had known inside myself that the fanatic who had killed Dave and the others was not the image of all Friendlies.

Jamethon was no casual killer. I had tried to make him into one in order to hide my own shame, my own self-destruction. For three years I had lied to myself. It had not been with me as I claimed, at Dave's death.

I had sat there under that tree watching Dave and the others die, watching the black-clad Groupman killing them with his machine rifle. And, in that moment, the thought in my mind had not been the one with which I justified three years of hunting for an opportunity to ruin someone like Jamethon and destroy the Friendly peoples.

It had not been me, thinking, *what is he doing there, what is he doing to those helpless, innocent men!* I had thought nothing so noble. Only one thought had filled all my mind and body in that instant. It had been simply—*after he's done, is he going to turn that gun on me?*

I came back to the day and to the rain. The rain was slackening and Padma was holding me upright. As with Jamethon, I was amazed at the strength of his hands.

"Let me go," I mumbled.

"Where would you go, Tam?" said Padma.

"Any place," I muttered. "I'll get out of it. I'll go hole up somewhere and get out of it. I'll give up."

"An action," said Padma, letting me go, "goes on reverberating for ever. Cause never ceases its effects. You can't let go now, Tam. You can only change sides."

"Sides!" I said. The rain was dwindling fast. "What sides?" I stared at him drunkenly.

"Your uncle's side which is one," said Padma. "And the opposing side, which is yours—which is ours as well." The rain was falling only lightly now, and the day was lightening. A little pale sunlight worked through thin clouds and illuminated the space between us. "In addition there are two strong influences besides we Exotics concerned with the attempt of man to evolve. We can't calculate or understand them yet, beyond the fact they act almost as single powerful individual wills. One seems to try to aid, one to frustrate, the evolutionary process; and their influences can be traced back at least as far as man's first venture into space from Earth."

I shook my head.

"I don't understand it," I muttered. "It's not my business."

"It is. It has been all your life." Padma's eyes caught light for a moment. "A force intruded on the pattern on St. Marie, in the shape of a unit warped by personal loss and oriented toward violence. That was you, Tam."

I tried to shake my head again, but I knew he was right.

"You are blocked in your effort," said Padma. "But the law of conservation of energies could not be denied. When you were frustrated by Jamethon, your force, transmuted, left the pattern in the unit of another individual, warped by personal loss and oriented toward violent effect on the fabric."

I stared at him and wet my lips. "What other individual?"

"Ian Graeme."

I stared at him.

"Ian found his brother's three assassins hiding in a hotel room in Blauvain. He killed them with his hands—and in doing that he calmed the mercenaries and frustrated the Blue Front. But then he resigned and went home to the Dorsai. He's charged now with the sense of loss and bitterness you were charged with when you came to St. Marie." Padma paused and added softly, "Now he has great causal potential for some purpose we can't yet calculate."

"But—" I looked at Padma. "You mean I'm free!"

Padma shook his head.

"You're only charged with a different force instead," he said. "You received the full impact and charge of Jamethon's self-sacrifice."

He looked at me almost with sympathy, and in spite of the sunlight I began to shiver.

It was so. I could not deny it. Jamethon, in giving his life up for a belief, when I had thrown away all belief before the face of death, had melted and changed me as lightning melts and changes the uplifted sword-blade that it strikes. I could not deny what had happened to me.

"No," I said, shivering, "I can't do anything about it."

"You can," said Padma, calmly. "You will."

He unclasped his hands that he had held together earlier.

"The purpose for which we calculated I should meet you here is accomplished now," he said. "The idealism which was basic in you remains. Even your uncle couldn't take it from you. He could only attack it so that the threat of death on New Earth could twist it for a while against itself. Now you've been hammered straight in the forge of events on St. Marie."

I laughed, and the laugh hurt my throat still.

"I don't feel straight," I said.

"Give yourself time," said Padma. "Healing takes time. New growth has to harden, like muscle, before it becomes useful. Now you understand much more about the faith of the Friendlies, the courage of the Dorsai—and something of the philosophical strength for man we work toward on the Exotics."

He stopped and smiled at me. Almost an impish smile.

"It should have been clear to you a long while ago, Tam," he said. "Your job's the job of translator—between the old and the new. Your work will prepare the minds of the people on all the worlds—full-spectrum and Splinter Culture alike—for the day when the talents of the race will combine into the new breed." The smile softened, his face saddened. "You'll live to see more of it than I. Good-by, Tam."

He turned. Through the still misty, but brightening air, I saw him walking alone toward the church, from which came the voice of the speaker within, now announcing the number of the final hymn.

Dazedly, I turned away myself, went to my car and got in. Now the rain was almost over and the sky was brightening fast. The faint moisture fell, it seemed, more kindly; and the air was fresh and new.

I put the car windows open as I pulled out of the lot onto the long road back to the spaceport. And through the open window beside me I heard them beginning to sing the final hymn inside the church.

It was the Battle Hymn of the Friendly Soldiers that they sang. As I drove away down the road the voices seemed to follow me strongly. Not sounding slowly and mournfully as if in sadness and farewell, but strongly and triumphantly, as in a marching song on the lips of those taking up a route at the beginning of a new day.

> *Soldier, ask not—now, or ever,*
> *Where to war your banners go.*

The singing followed me as I drove away. And as I got farther into the distance, the voices seemed to blend until they sounded like one voice alone, powerfully singing. Ahead, the clouds were breaking. With the sun shining through, the patches of blue sky were like bright flags waving—like the banners of an army, marching forever forward into lands unknown.

I watched them, as I drove forward toward where they blended into open sky; and for a long time I heard the singing behind me, as I drove to the spaceport and the ship for Earth that waited in the sunlight.

*1966*
*24th CONVENTION*
*CLEVELAND*

## Harlan Ellison

Harlan is flamboyant. He's got the fastest, sharpest tongue in science fiction. What's more, he knows judo, karate, and footplay, and packs a hundred eighty pounds of gristle, sinew, and muscle into a body that weighs a hundred twenty pounds altogether.

Don't ask me how, but he can get into a fight with three bruisers (non-science-fiction ones) each of whom is bigger than he is and come out the winner.

But he's a sport. He only picks on those science fiction personalities who have developed the reputation of being able to take care of themselves. Would he ever pick on Gordie Dickson whose chief weapon in wit-to-wit combat is a charming grin? Would he pick on Larry Niven whose slightly puzzled frown is his only defense against a grim world?

Never!

You know whom he picks on?

Me, that's whom.

From the other side of a huge ballroom, he sees me, and I can hear him coming all the way. Mercy? He doesn't know the meaning of the word.

He can ring every possible change on my waistline, for instance, just because it has a kind of sturdy expansiveness. I tell him over and over I need all that room to keep my spare brains in and he makes very ribald remarks about where I probably keep them. And you know the excuse he uses? He says I make fun of his height!

I *never!* Would I ever dream of mentioning that he is 62 inches tall? (Oh, he denies it, but if he stands on tippy-toe, he is.) Far from making jokes about his height, I've said a million times (and in public, too) that Harlan's height is no laughing matter.

Which reminds me that I remember Harlan when he was even younger than he is now, and just a fan, and a lot skinnier and more elfin. He used to scurry around the convention as quick as quicksilver and everyone else had to be careful not to trip over him.

Everyone knew he was special. Everyone knew he would go places. The question was what to do with him *meanwhile*.

We never found out then. But I think that, since then, we've learned.

Thus, at a convention just about a year ago as I write this, a young boy of sixteen showed up. He was skinny, sharp, self-confident, articulate, and had an IQ that sounded like two hundred.

A bunch of us looked at each other fearfully and one said, "He's another Harlan Ellison."

And someone, whose name I won't mention except to say that it was Robert Silverberg, said, "Let's kill him *now*."

*4*

# "REPENT, HARLEQUIN!"
# SAID THE TICKTOCKMAN

There are always those who ask, what is it all about? For those who need to ask, for those who need points sharply made, who need to know "where it's at," this:

> *"The mass of men serve the state thus, not as men mainly, but as machines, with their bodies. They are the standing army, and the militia, jailors, constables, posse comitatus, etc. In most cases there is no free exercise whatever of the judgment or of the moral sense; but they put themselves on a level with wood and earth and stones; and wooden men can perhaps be manufactured that will serve the purposes as well. Such command no more respect than men of straw or a lump of dirt. They have the same sort of worth only as horses and dogs. Yet such as these even are commonly esteemed good citizens. Others—as most legislators, politicians, lawyers, ministers, and officeholders—serve the state chiefly with their heads; and, as they rarely make any moral distinctions, they are as likely to serve the Devil, without intending it, as God. A very few, as heroes, patriots, martyrs, reformers in the great sense, and men, serve the state with their consciences also, and so necessarily resist it for the most part; and they are commonly treated as enemies by it."*

> Henry David Thoreau,
> "Civil Disobedience"

That is the heart of it. Now begin in the middle, and later learn the beginning; the end will take care of itself.

But because it was the very world it was, the very world they had allowed it to *become*, for months his activities did not come to the alarmed attention of The Ones Who Kept The Machine Functioning Smoothly, the ones who poured the very best butter over the cams and mainsprings of the culture. Not until it had become obvious that somehow, someway, he had become a notoriety, a celebrity, perhaps even a hero for (what Officialdom inescapably tagged) "an emotionally disturbed segment of the populace," did they turn it over to the Ticktockman and his legal machinery. But by then, because it was the very world it was, and they had no way to predict he would happen—possibly a strain of disease long-defunct, now, suddenly, reborn in a system where immunity had been forgotten, had lapsed—he had been allowed to become too real. Now he had form and substance.

He had become a *personality*, something they had filtered out of the system many decades ago. But there it was, and there *he* was, a very definitely imposing personality. In certain circles—middle-class circles —it was thought disgusting. Vulgar ostentation. Anarchistic. Shameful. In others, there was only sniggering, those strata where thought is subjugated to form and ritual, niceties, proprieties. But down below, ah, down below, where the people always needed their saints and sinners, their bread and circuses, their heroes and villains, he was considered a Bolivar; a Napoleon; a Robin Hood; a Dick Bong (Ace of Aces); a Jesus; a Jomo Kenyatta.

And at the top—where, like socially-attuned Shipwreck Kellys, even tremor and vibration threatens to dislodge the wealthy, powerful and titled from their flagpoles—he was considered a menace; a heretic; a rebel; a disgrace; a peril. He was known down the line, to the very heartmeat core, but the important reactions were high above and far below. At the very top, at the very bottom.

So his file was turned over, along with his time-card and his cardioplate, to the office of the Ticktockman.

The Ticktockman: very much over six feet tall, often silent, a soft purring man when things went timewise. The Ticktockman.

Even in the cubicles of the hierarchy, where fear was generated, seldom suffered, he was called the Ticktockman. But no one called him that to his mask.

You don't call a man a hated name, not when that man, behind his mask, is capable of revoking the minutes, the hours, the days and nights, the years of your life. He was called the Master Timekeeper to his mask. It was safer that way.

"This is *what* he is," said the Ticktockman with genuine softness, "but not *who* he is? This time-card I'm holding in my left hand has a name on it, but it is the name of *what* he is, not *who* he is. This cardioplate here in my right hand is also named, but not whom named, merely what named. Before I can exercise proper revocation, I have to know who this what is."

To his staff, all the ferrets, all the loggers, all the finks, all the commex, even the mineez, he said, "Who is this Harlequin?"

He was not purring smoothly. Timewise, it was jangle.

However, it *was* the longest speech they had ever heard him utter at one time, the staff, the ferrets, the loggers, the finks, the commex, but not the mineez, who usually weren't around to know, in any case. But even they scurried to find out.

Who is the Harlequin?

High above the third level of the city, he crouched on the humming aluminum-frame platform of the air-boat (foof! air-boat, indeed! swizzleskid is what it was, with a tow-rack jerry-rigged) and stared down at the neat Mondrian arrangement of the buildings.

Somewhere nearby, he could hear the metronomic left-right-left of the 2:47 P.M. shift, entering the Timkin roller-bearing plant in their sneakers. A minute later, precisely, he heard the softer right-left-right of the 5:00 A.M. formation, going home.

An elfish grin spread across his tanned features, and his dimples appeared for a moment. Then, scratching at his thatch of auburn hair, he shrugged within his motley, as though girding himself for what came next, and threw the joystick forward, and bent into the wind as the air-boat dropped. He skimmed over a slidewalk, purposely dropping a few feet to crease the tassels of the ladies of fashion, and—inserting thumbs in large ears—he stuck out his tongue, rolled his eyes and went wugga-wugga-wugga. It was a minor diversion. One pedestrian skittered and tumbled, sending parcels everywhichway, another wet herself, a third keeled slantwise and the walk was stopped automatically by the servitors till she could be resuscitated. It was a minor diversion.

Then he swirled away on a vagrant breeze, and was gone. Hi-ho.

As he rounded the cornice of the Time-Motion Study Building, he saw the shift, just boarding the slidewalk. With practiced motion and an absolute conservation of movement, they side-stepped up onto the slowstrip and (in a chorus line reminiscent of a Busby Berkeley film of the antediluvian 1930's) advanced across the strips ostrich-walking till they were lined up on the expresstrip.

Once more, in anticipation, the elfin grin spread, and there was a tooth missing back there on the left side. He dipped, skimmed, and swooped over them; and then, scrunching about on the air-boat, he released the holding pins that fastened shut the ends of the home-made pouring troughs that kept his cargo from dumping prematurely. And as he pulled the trough-pins, the air-boat slid over the factory workers and one hundred and fifty thousand dollars worth of jelly beans cascaded down on the expresstrip.

Jelly beans! Millions and billions of purples and yellows and greens and licorice and grape and raspberry and mint and round and smooth and crunchy outside and soft-mealy inside and sugary and bouncing jouncing tumbling clittering clattering skittering fell on the heads and shoulders and hard-hats and carapaces of the Timkin workers, tinkling on the slidewalk and bouncing away and rolling about underfoot and filling the sky on their way down with all the colors of joy and childhood and holidays, coming down in a steady rain, a solid wash, a torrent of color and sweetness out of the sky from above, and entering a universe of sanity and metronomic order with quite-mad coocoo newness. Jelly beans!

The shift workers howled and laughed and were pelted, and broke ranks, and the jelly beans managed to work their way into the mechanism of the slidewalks after which there was a hideous scraping as the sound of a million fingernails rasped down a quarter of a million blackboards, followed by a coughing and a sputtering, and then the slidewalks all stopped and everyone was dumped thisawayandthataway in a jackstraw tumble, and still laughing and popping little jelly bean eggs of childish color into their mouths. It was a holiday, and a jollity, an absolute insanity, a giggle. But . . .

The shift was delayed seven minutes.

They did not get home for seven minutes.

The master schedule was thrown off by seven minutes.

Quotas were delayed by inoperative slidewalks for seven minutes.

He had tapped the first domino in the line, and one after another, like chik chik chik, the others had fallen.

The System had been seven minutes worth of disrupted. It was a tiny matter, one hardly worthy of note, but in a society where the single driving force was order and unity and promptness and clocklike precision and attention to the clock, reverence of the gods of the passage of time, it was a disaster of major importance.

So he was ordered to appear before the Ticktockman. It was broadcast across every channel of the communications web. He was ordered to be *there* at 7:00 dammit on time. And they waited, and they waited, but he didn't show up till almost ten-thirty, at which time he merely sang a little song about moonlight in a place no one had ever heard of, called Vermont, and vanished again. But they had all been waiting since seven, and it wrecked *hell* with their schedules. So the question remained: Who is the Harlequin?

But the *unasked* question (more important of the two) was: how did we get *into* this position, where a laughing, irresponsible japer of jabberwocky and jive could disrupt our entire economic and cultural life with a hundred and fifty thousand dollars worth of jelly beans . . .

*Jelly* for God's sake beans! This is madness! Where did he get the money to buy a hundred and fifty thousand dollars worth of jelly beans? (They knew it would have cost that much, because they had a team of Situation Analysts pulled off another assignment, and rushed to the slidewalk scene to sweep up and count the candies, and produce findings, which disrupted *their* schedules and threw their entire branch at least a day behind.) Jelly beans! Jelly . . . *beans?* Now wait a second —a second accounted for—no one has manufactured jelly beans for over a hundred years. Where did he get jelly beans?

That's another good question. More than likely it will never be answered to your complete satisfaction. But then, how many questions ever are?

The middle you know. Here is the beginning. How it starts:

A desk pad. Day for day, and turn each day. 9:00—open the mail. 9:45—appointment with planning commission board. 10:30—discuss installation progress charts with J.L. 11:45—pray for rain. 12:00—lunch. *And so it goes.*

"I'm sorry, Miss Grant, but the time for interviews was set at 2:30, and it's almost five now. I'm sorry you're late, but those are the rules. You'll have to wait till next year to submit application for this college again." *And so it goes.*

The 10:10 local stops at Cresthaven, Galesville, Tonawanda Junction, Selby and Farnhurst, but not at Indiana City, Lucasville and Colton, except on Sunday. The 10:35 express stops at Galesville, Selby and Indiana City, except on Sundays & Holidays, at which time it stops at . . . *and so it goes.*

"I couldn't wait, Fred. I had to be at Pierre Cartain's by 3:00, and you said you'd meet me under the clock in the terminal at 2:45, and you weren't there, so I had to go on. You're always late, Fred. If you'd been there, we could have sewed it up together, but as it was, well, I took the order alone . . ." *And so it goes.*

Dear Mr. and Mrs. Atterley: in reference to your son Gerold's constant tardiness, I am afraid we will have to suspend him from school unless some more reliable method can be instituted guaranteeing he will arrive at his classes on time. Granted he is an exemplary student, and his marks are high, his constant flouting of the schedules of this school makes it impractical to maintain him in a system where the other children seem capable of getting where they are supposed to be on time *and so it goes*.

YOU CANNOT VOTE UNLESS YOU APPEAR AT 8:45 A.M.

"I don't care if the script is *good*, I need it Thursday!"

CHECK-OUT TIME IS 2:00 P.M.

"You got here late. The job's taken. Sorry."

YOUR SALARY HAS BEEN DOCKED FOR TWENTY MINUTES TIME LOST.

"God, what time is it, I've gotta run!"

And so it goes. And so it goes. And so it goes. And so it goes goes goes goes goes tick tock tick tock tick tock and one day we no longer let time serve us, we serve time and we are slaves of the schedule, worshippers of the sun's passing, bound into a life predicated on restrictions because the system will not function if we don't keep the schedule tight.

Until it becomes more than a minor inconvenience to be late. It becomes a sin. Then a crime. Then a crime punishable by this:

EFFECTIVE 15 JULY 2389 12:00:00 midnight, the office of the Master Timekeeper will require all citizens to submit their time-cards and cardioplates for processing. In accordance with Statute 555-7-SGH-999 governing the revocation of time per capita, all cardioplates will be keyed to the individual holder and—

What they had done, was devise a method of curtailing the amount of life a person could have. If he was ten minutes late, he lost ten minutes of his life. An hour was proportionately worth more revocation. If someone was consistently tardy, he might find himself, on a Sunday night, receiving a communique from the Master Timekeeper that his time had run out, and he would be "turned off" at high noon on Monday, please straighten your affairs, sir.

And so, by this simple scientific expedient (utilizing a scientific process held dearly secret by the Ticktockman's office) the System was maintained. It was the only expedient thing to do. It was, after all, patriotic. The schedules had to be met. After all, there *was* a war on!

But, wasn't there always?

"Now that is really disgusting," the Harlequin said, when pretty Alice showed him the wanted poster. "Disgusting and *high*ly improbable. After all, this isn't the days of desperadoes. A *wanted* poster!"

"You know," Alice noted, "you speak with a great deal of inflection."

"I'm sorry," said the Harlequin, humbly.

"No need to be sorry. You're always saying 'I'm sorry.' You have such massive guilt, Everett, it's really very sad."

"I'm sorry," he repeated, then pursed his lips so the dimples appeared momentarily. He hadn't wanted to say that at all. "I have to go out again. I have to *do* something."

Alice slammed her coffee-bulb down on the counter. "Oh for God's *sake*, Everett, can't you stay home just *one* night! Must you always be out in that ghastly clown suit, running around *annoy*ing people?"

"I'm—" he stopped, and clapped the jester's hat onto his auburn thatch with a tiny tingling of bells. He rose, rinsed out his coffee-bulb at the tap, and put it into the drier for a moment. "I have to go."

She didn't answer. The faxbox was purring, and she pulled a sheet out, read it, threw it toward him on the counter. "It's about you. Of course. You're ridiculous."

He read it quickly. It said the Ticktockman was trying to locate him. He didn't care, he was going out to be late again. At the door, dredging for an exit line, he hurled back petulantly, "Well, *you* speak with inflection, *too!*"

Alice rolled her pretty eyes heavenward. "You're ridiculous." The Harlequin stalked out, slamming the door, which sighed shut softly, and locked itself.

There was a gentle knock, and Alice got up with an exhalation of exasperated breath, and opened the door. He stood there. "I'll be back about ten-thirty, okay?"

She pulled a rueful face. "Why do you tell me that? Why? You *know* you'll be late! You *know it!* You're *always* late, so why do you tell me these dumb things?" She closed the door.

On the other side, the Harlequin nodded to himself. *She's right. She's always right. I'll be late. I'm always late. Why do I tell her these dumb things?*

He shrugged again, and went off to be late once more.

He had fired off the firecracker rockets that said: I will attend the 115th annual International Medical Association Invocation at 8:00 P.M. precisely. I do hope you will all be able to join me.

The words had burned in the sky, and of course the authorities were there, lying in wait for him. They assumed, naturally, that he would be late. He arrived twenty minutes early, while they were setting up the spiderwebs to trap and hold him, and blowing a large bullhorn, he frightened and unnerved them so, their own moisturized encirclement webs sucked closed, and they were hauled up, kicking and shrieking, high above the amphitheater's floor. The Harlequin laughed and laughed, and apologized profusely. The physicians, gathered in solemn conclave, roared with laughter, and accepted the Harlequin's apologies with exaggerated bowing and posturing, and a merry time was had by all, who thought the Harlequin was a regular foofaraw in fancy pants; all, that is, but the authorities, who had been sent out by the office of the Ticktockman, who hung there like so much dockside cargo, hauled up above the floor of the amphitheater in a most unseemly fashion.

(In another part of the same city where the Harlequin carried on his "activities," totally unrelated in every way to what concerns here, save that it illustrates the Ticktockman's power and import, a man named Marshall Delahanty received his turn-off notice from the Ticktockman's office. His wife received the notification from the grey-suited minee who delivered it, with the traditional "look of sorrow" plastered hideously across his face. She knew what it was, even without unsealing it. It was a billet-doux of immediate recognition to everyone these days. She gasped, and held it as though it were a glass slide tinged with botulism, and prayed it was not for her. Let it be for Marsh, she thought, brutally, realistically, or one of the kids, but not for me, please dear God, not for me. And then she opened it, and it *was* for Marsh, and she was at one and the same time horrified and relieved. The next trooper in the line had caught the bullet. "Marshall," she screamed, "Marshall! Termination, Marshall! OhmiGod, Marshall, whattl we do, whattl we do, Marshall omigodmarshall . . ." and in their home that night was the sound of tearing paper and fear, and the stink of madness went up the flue and there was nothing, absolutely nothing they could do about it.

(But Marshall Delahanty tried to run. And early the next day, when turn-off time came, he was deep in the forest two hundred miles away, and the office of the Ticktockman blanked his cardioplate, and Marshall Delahanty keeled over, running, and his heart stopped, and the blood dried up on its way to his brain, and he was dead that's all. One light went out on his sector map in the office of the Master Timekeeper, while notification was entered for fax reproduction, and Georgette Delahanty's name was entered on the dole roles till she could re-marry. Which is the end of the footnote, and all the point that need be made, except don't laugh, because that is what would happen to the Harlequin if ever the Ticktockman found out his real name. It isn't funny.)

The shopping level of the city was thronged with the Thursday-colors of the buyers. Women in canary yellow chitons and men in pseudo-Tyrolean outfits that were jade and leather and fit very tightly, save for the balloon pants.

When the Harlequin appeared on the still-being-constructed shell of the new Efficiency Shopping Center, his bullhorn to his elfishly-laughing lips, everyone pointed and stared, and he berated them:

"Why let them order you about? Why let them tell you to hurry and scurry like ants or maggots? Take your time! Saunter a while! Enjoy the sunshine, enjoy the breeze, let life carry you at your own pace! Don't be slaves of time, it's a helluva way to die, slowly, by degrees . . . down with the Ticktockman!"

Who's the nut? most of the shoppers wanted to know. Who's the nut oh wow I'm gonna be late I gotta run . . .

And the construction gang on the Shopping Center received an urgent order from the office of the Master Timekeeper that the dangerous criminal known as the Harlequin was atop their spire, and their aid was urgently needed in apprehending him. The work crew said no, they would lose time on their construction schedule, but the Ticktockman managed to pull the proper threads of governmental webbing, and they were told to cease work and catch that nitwit up there on the spire with the bullhorn. So a dozen and more burly workers began climbing into their construction platforms, releasing the a-grav plates, and rising toward the Harlequin.

After the debacle (in which, through the Harlequin's attention to personal safety, no one was seriously injured), the workers tried to reassemble, and assault him again, but it was too late. He had vanished. It had attracted quite a crowd, however, and the shopping cycle was thrown off by hours, simply hours. The purchasing needs of the system were therefore falling behind, and so measures were taken to accelerate the cycle for the rest of the day, but it got bogged down and speeded up and they sold too many float-valves and not nearly enough wegglers, which meant that the popli ratio was off, which made it necessary to rush cases and cases of spoiling Smash-O to stores that usually needed a case only every three or four hours. The shipments were bollixed, the trans-shipments were misrouted, and in the end, even the swizzleskid industries felt it.

"Don't come back till you have him!" the Ticktockman said, very quietly, very sincerely, extremely dangerously.

They used dogs. They used probes. They used cardioplate crossoffs. They used teepers. They used bribery. They used stiktytes. They used intimidation. They used torment. They used torture. They used finks. They used cops. They used search&seizure. They used fallaron. They used betterment incentive. They used fingerprints. They used Bertillon. They used cunning. They used guile. They used treachery. They used Raoul Mitgong, but he didn't help much. They used applied physics. They used techniques of criminology.

And what the hell: they caught him.

After all, his name was Everett C. Marm, and he wasn't much to begin with, except a man who had no sense of time.

"Repent, Harlequin!" said the Ticktockman.

"Get stuffed!" the Harlequin replied, sneering.

"You've been late a total of sixty-three years, five months, three weeks, two days, twelve hours, forty-one minutes, fifty-nine seconds, point oh three six one one one microseconds. You've used up everything you can, and more. I'm going to turn you off."

"Scare someone else. I'd rather be dead than live in a dumb world with a bogeyman like you."

"It's my job."

"You're full of it. You're a tyrant. You have no right to order people around and kill them if they show up late."

"You can't adjust. You can't fit in."

"Unstrap me, and I'll fit my fist into your mouth."

"You're a non-conformist."

"That didn't used to be a felony."

"It is now. Live in the world around you."

"I hate it. It's a terrible world."

"Not everyone thinks so. Most people enjoy order."

"I don't, and most of the people I know don't."

"That's not true. How do you think we caught you?"

"I'm not interested."

"A girl named pretty Alice told us who you were."

"That's a lie."

"It's true. You unnerve her. She wants to belong, she wants to conform, I'm going to turn you off."

"Then do it already, and stop arguing with me."

"I'm not going to turn you off."

"You're an idiot!"

"Repent, Harlequin!" said the Ticktockman.

"Get stuffed."

So they sent him to Coventry. And in Coventry they worked him over. It was just like what they did to Winston Smith in "1984," which was a book none of them knew about, but the techniques are really quite ancient, and so they did it to Everett C. Marm, and one day quite a long time later, the Harlequin appeared on the communications web, appearing elfish and dimpled and bright-eyed, and not at all brainwashed, and he said he had been wrong, that it was a good, a very good thing indeed, to belong, and be right on time hip-ho and away we go, and everyone stared up at him on the public screens that covered an entire city block, and they said to themselves, well, you see, he was just a nut after all, and if that's the way the system is run, then let's do it that way, because it doesn't pay to fight city hall, or in this case, the

Ticktockman. So Everett C. Marm was destroyed, which was a loss, because of what Thoreau said earlier, but you can't make an omelet without breaking a few eggs, and in every revolution, a few die who shouldn't, but they have to, because that's the way it happens, and if you make only a little change, then it seems to be worthwhile. Or, to make the point lucidly:

"Uh, excuse me, sir, I, uh, don't know how to uh, to uh, tell you this, but you were three minutes late. The schedule is a little, uh, bit off."

He grinned sheepishly.

"That's ridiculous!" murmured the Ticktockman behind his mask. "Check your watch." And then he went into his office, going mrmee, mrmee, mrmee, mrmee.

*1967*
*25th CONVENTION*
*NEW YORK*

## Jack Vance

Now I must deal with Jack again.

Knowing that I didn't know Jack Vance and that he would appear twice, I was in a terrible quandary. I had to find out something about him; something significant. It was no use determining that he lived in California; and that he was about my age and shape (which is very good in itself, of course). I wanted something more.

What to do? So I picked up the phone and called Robert Silverberg. It meant I would interrupt him at work since his schedule is something like mine but I would be doing him a favor because I understand he fights with his typewriter. (It keeps shrieking at him because it has sensitive keys and he has cold fingers.)

"Tell me about Jack Vance, Bob," I said.

So he did, and I listened and listened, and finally Bob said, "He's strangely uncommunicative in a way. That is, he loves to talk shop, but when I asked him whether he was influenced more by Kafka or by Dunsany, he changed the subject."

I was delighted, for right then I knew that Jack Vance was an all-right guy. I hate these writers who have been terribly influenced by Lord Kafka or Franz Dunsany—big show-offs. Personally, I was influenced by guys like Nat Schachner and Clifford Simak and John W. Campbell, Jr.

Back in the 1930s, you see, I was reading science fiction. A fellow with science fiction writing ambitions *should* read science fiction. I didn't waste my time reading Proust and Tolstoy and all them other highfalutin Greeks.

And neither, I'll bet, did Jack Vance. Good boy, Jack! It's you and I against the world.

# 5

# THE LAST CASTLE

Toward the end of a stormy summer afternoon, with the sun finally breaking out under ragged black rain clouds, Castle Janeil was overwhelmed and its population destroyed.

Until almost the last moment the factions among the castle clans were squabbling as to how Destiny properly should be met. The gentlemen of most prestige and account elected to ignore the entire undignified circumstance and went about their normal pursuits, with neither more nor less punctilio than usual. A few cadets, desperate to the point of hysteria, took up weapons and prepared to resist the final assault. Others still, perhaps a quarter of the total population, waited passively, ready—almost happy—to expiate the sins of the human race.

In the end death came uniformly to all; and all extracted as much satisfaction in their dying as this essentially graceless process could afford. The proud sat turning the pages of their beautiful books, or discussing the qualities of a century-old essence, or fondling a favorite Phane. They died without deigning to heed the fact. The hot-heads raced up the muddy slope which, outraging all normal rationality, loomed above the parapets of Janeil. Most were buried under sliding rubble, but a few gained the ridge to gun, hack, stab, until they themselves were shot, crushed by the half-alive power-wagons, hacked or stabbed. The contrite waited in the classic posture of expiation, on their knees, heads bowed, and perished, so they believed, by a process in which the Meks were symbols and human sin the reality. In the end all were dead: gentlemen, ladies, Phanes in the pavilions; Peasants in the stables. Of all those who had inhabited Janeil, only the Birds survived, creatures awkward, gauche and raucous, oblivious to pride and faith, more concerned with the wholeness of their hides than the dignity of their castle.

As the Meks swarmed over the parapets, the Birds departed their cotes. They screamed strident insults as they flapped east toward Hagedorn, now the last castle of Earth.

Four months before, the Meks had appeared in the park before Janeil, fresh from the Sea Island massacre.

Climbing to the turrets and balconies, sauntering the Sunset Promenade, from ramparts and parapets, the gentlemen and ladies of Janeil, some two thousand in all, looked down at the brown-gold warriors. Their mood was complex: amused indifference, flippant disdain, over a substratum of doubt and foreboding. All these moods were the product of three basic circumstances: their own exquisitely subtle civilization, the security provided by Janeil's wall and the fact that they could think of nothing to do to alter the circumstances.

The Janeil Meks had long since departed to join the revolt. There only remained Phanes, Peasants and Birds from which to fashion what would have been the travesty of a punitive force.

At the moment there seemed no need for such a force. Janeil was deemed impregnable. The walls, two hundred feet tall, were black rock-melt contained in the meshes of a silver-blue steel alloy. Solar cells provided energy for all the needs of the castle, and in the event of emergency food could be synthesized from carbon dioxide and water vapor, as well as syrup for Phanes, Peasants and Birds. Such a need was not envisaged. Janeil was self-sufficient and secure, though inconveniences might arise when machinery broke down and there were no Meks to repair it. The situation, then, was disturbing but hardly desperate. During the day the gentlemen so inclined brought forth energy-guns and sport-rifles and killed as many Meks as the extreme range allowed.

After dark the Meks brought forward power-wagons and earth-movers, and began to raise a dike around Janeil.

The folk of the castle watched without comprehension until the dike reached a height of fifty feet and dirt began to spill down against the walls. Then the dire purpose of the Meks became apparent, and insouciance gave way to dismal foreboding.

All the gentlemen of Janeil were erudite in at least one realm of knowledge. Certain were mathematical theoreticians, others had made a profound study of the physical sciences. Some of these, with a detail of Peasants to perform the sheer physical exertion, attempted to restore the energy-cannon to functioning condition. Unluckily, the cannon had not been maintained in good order. Various components were obviously corroded or damaged. Conceivably these components might have been replaced from the Mek shops on the second sub-level, but none of the group had any knowledge of the Mek nomenclature or warehousing system. Warrick Madency Arban (which is to say, Arban of the Madency family on the Warrick clan) suggested that a work-force of Peasants search the warehouse. But in view of the limited mental capacity of the Peasants, nothing was done and the whole plan to restore the energy-cannon came to naught.

The gentlefolk of Janeil watched in fascination as the dirt piled higher and higher around them, in a circular mound like a crater. Summer neared its end, and on one stormy day dirt and rubble rose above the parapets, and began to spill over into the courts and piazzas. Janeil must soon be buried and all within suffocated.

It was then that a group of impulsive young cadets, with more elan than dignity, took up weapons and charged up the slope. The Meks dumped dirt and stone upon them, but a handful gained the ridge where they fought in a kind of dreadful exaltation.

Fifteen minutes the fight raged and the earth became sodden with rain and blood. For one glorious moment the cadets swept the ridge clean. Had not most of their fellows been lost under the rubble anything might have occurred. But the Meks regrouped, thrust forward. Ten men were left, then six, then four, then one, then none. The Meks marched down the slope, swarmed over the battlements, and with somber intensity killed all within. Janeil, for seven hundred years the abode of gallant gentlemen and gracious ladies, had become a lifeless hulk.

The Mek, standing as if a specimen in a museum case, was a manlike creature native, in his original version, to a planet of Etamin. His tough rusty-bronze hide glistened metallically as if oiled or waxed. The spines thrusting back from scalp and neck shone like gold, and indeed they were coated with a conductive copper-chrome film. His sense organs were gathered in clusters at the site of a man's ears; his visage— it was often a shock, walking the lower corridors, to come suddenly upon a Mek—was corrugated muscle, not dissimilar to the look of an uncovered human brain. His maw, a vertical irregular cleft at the base of this 'face', was an obsolete organ by reason of the syrup sac which had been introduced under the skin of the shoulders, and the digestive organs, originally used to extract nutrition from decayed swamp vegetation and coelenterates, had atrophied. The Mek typically wore no garment except possibly a work apron or a tool-belt, and in the sunlight his rust-bronze skin made a handsome display. This was the Mek solitary, a creature intrinsically as effective as man—perhaps more by virtue of his superb brain which also functioned as a radio transceiver.

Working in the mass, by the teeming thousands, he seemed less admirable, less competent: a hybrid of sub-man and cockroach.

Certain savants, notably Morninglight's D. R. Jardine and Salonson of Tuang, considered the Mek bland and phlegmatic, but the profound Claghorn of Castle Hagedorn asserted otherwise. The emotions of the Mek, said Claghorn, were different from human emotions, and only vaguely comprehensible to man. After diligent research Claghorn isolated over a dozen Mek emotions.

In spite of such research, the Mek revolt came as an utter surprise, no less to Claghorn, D. R. Jardine and Salonson than to anyone else. Why? asked everyone. How could a group so long submissive have contrived so murderous a plot?

The most reasonable conjecture was also the simplest: the Mek resented servitude and hated the Earthmen who had removed him from his natural environment. Those who argued against this theory claimed that it projected human emotions and attitudes into a non-human organism, that the Mek had every reason to feel gratitude toward the gentlemen who had liberated him from the conditions of Etamin Nine. To this, the first group would inquire, "Who projects human attitudes now?" And the retort of their opponents was often: "Since no one knows for certain, one projection is no more absurd than another."

II

Castle Hagedorn occupied the crest of a black diorite crag overlooking a wide valley to the south. Larger, more majestic than Janeil, Hagedorn was protected by walls a mile in circumference, three hundred feet tall. The parapets stood a full nine hundred feet above the valley, with towers, turrets and observation eyries rising even higher. Two sides of the crag, at east and west, dropped sheer to the valley. The north and south slopes, a trifle less steep, were terraced and planted with vines, artichokes, pears and pomegranates. An avenue rising from the valley circled the crag and passed through a portal into the central plaza. Opposite stood the great Rotunda, with at either side the tall Houses of the twenty-eight families.

The original castle, constructed immediately after the return of men to Earth, stood on the site now occupied by the plaza. The tenth Hagedorn had assembled an enormous force of Peasants and Meks to build the new walls, after he demolished the old castle. The twenty-eight Houses dated from this time, five hundred years before.

Below the plaza were three service levels: the stables and garages at the bottom, next the Mek shops and Mek living quarters, then the various storerooms, warehouses and special shops: bakery, brewery, lapidary, arsenal, repository, and the like.

The current Hagedorn, twenty-sixth of the line, was a Claghorn of the Overwheles. His selection had occasioned general surprise, because O. C. Charle, as he had been before his elevation, was a gentleman of no remarkable presence. His elegance, flair, and erudition were only ordinary; he had never been notable for any significant originality of thought. His physical proportions were good; his face was square and bony, with a short straight nose, a benign brow, narrow gray eyes. His expression was normally a trifle abstracted—his detractors used the word 'vacant'. But by a simple lowering of the eyelids, a downward twitch of the coarse blond eyebrows, it at once became stubborn and surly, a fact of which O. C. Charle, or Hagedorn, was unaware.

The office, while exerting little or no formal authority, exerted a pervasive influence, and the style of the gentleman who was Hagedorn affected everyone. For this reason the selection of Hagedorn was a matter of no small importance, subject to hundreds of considerations, and it was the rare candidate who failed to have some old solecism or gaucherie discussed with embarrassing candor. While the candidate might never take overt umbrage, friendships were inevitably sundered, rancors augmented, reputations blasted. O. C. Charle's elevation represented a compromise between two factions among the Overwheles, to which clan the privilege of selection had fallen.

The gentlemen between whom O. C. Charle represented a compromise were both highly respected, but distinguished by basically different attitudes toward existence. The first was the talented Garr of the Zumbeld family. He exemplified the traditional virtues of Castle Hagedorn: he was a notable connoisseur of essences, he dressed with absolute savoir, with never so much as a pleat nor a twist of the characteristic Overwhele rosette awry. He combined insouciance and flair with dignity. His repartee coruscated with brilliant allusions and turns of phrase. When aroused his wit was utterly mordant. He could quote every literary work of consequence; he performed expertly upon the nine-stringed lute, and was thus in constant demand at the Viewing of Antique Tabards. He was an antiquarian of unchallengeable erudition and knew the locale of every major city of Old Earth, and could discourse for hours upon the history of the ancient times. His military expertise was unparalleled at Hagedorn, and challenged only by D. K. Magdah of Castle Delora and perhaps Brusham of Tuang. Faults? Flaws? Few could be cited: over-punctilio which might be construed as waspishness; and intrepid pertinacity which could be considered ruthless.

O. Z. Garr could never be dismissed as insipid or indecisive, and his personal courage was beyond dispute. Two years before a stray band of Nomads had ventured into Lucerne Valley, slaughtering Peasants, stealing cattle, and going so far as to fire an arrow into the chest of an Isseth cadet. O. Z. Garr instantly assembled a punitive company of Meks, loaded them aboard a dozen power-wagons and set forth in pursuit of the Nomads, finally overtaking them near Drene River, by the ruins of Worster Cathedral. The Nomads were unexpectedly strong, unexpectedly crafty, and were not content to turn tail and flee. During the fighting O. Z. Garr displayed the most exemplary demeanor, directing the attack from the seat of his power-wagon, a pair of Meks standing by with shields to ward away arrows.

The conflict ended in a rout of the Nomads. They left twenty-seven lean black-cloaked corpses strewn on the field, while only twenty Meks lost their lives.

O. Z. Garr's opponent in the election was Claghorn, elder of the Claghorn family. As with O. Z. Garr, the exquisite discriminations of Hagedorn society came to Claghorn as easily as swimming to a fish.

He was no less erudite than O. Z. Garr, though hardly so versatile, his principal field of study being the Meks, their physiology, linguistic modes, and social patterns. Claghorn's conversation was more profound, but less entertaining and not so trenchant as that of O. Z. Garr. He seldom employed the extravagant tropes and allusions which characterized Garr's discussions, preferring a style of speech which was almost unadorned. Claghorn kept no Phanes; O. Z. Garr's four matched Gossamer Dainties were marvels of delight, and at the viewing of Antique Tabards Garr's presentations were seldom outshone. The important contrast between the two men lay in their philosophic outlook. O. Z. Garr, a traditionalist, a fervent exemplar of his society, subscribed to its tenets without reservation. He was beset by neither doubt nor guilt; he felt no desire to alter the conditions which afforded more than two thousand gentlemen and ladies lives of great richness. Claghorn, while by no means an Expiationist, was known to feel dissatisfaction with the general tenor of life at Castle Hagedorn, and argued so plausibly that many folk refused to listen to him, on the grounds that they became uncomfortable. But an indefinable malaise ran deep, and Claghorn had many influential supporters.

When the time came for ballots to be cast, neither O. Z. Garr nor Claghorn could muster sufficient support. The office finally was conferred upon a gentleman who never in his most optimistic reckonings had expected it: a gentleman of decorum and dignity but no great depth; without flippancy, but likewise without vivacity; affable but disinclined to force an issue to a disagreeable conclusion: O. C. Charle, the new Hagedorn.

Six months later, during the dark hours before dawn, the Hagedorn Meks evacuated their quarters and departed, taking with them power-wagons, tools, weapons and electrical equipment. The act had clearly been long in the planning, for simultaneously the Meks at each of the eight other castles made a similar departure.

The initial reaction at Castle Hagedorn, as elsewhere, was incredulity, then shocked anger, then—when the implications of the act were pondered—a sense of foreboding and calamity.

The new Hagedorn, the clan chiefs, and certain other notables appointed by Hagedorn met in the formal council chamber to consider the matter. They sat around a great table covered with red velvet: Hagedorn at the head; Xanten and Isseth at his left; Overwhele, Aure and Beaudry at his right; then the others, including O. Z. Garr, I. K. Linus, A. G. Bernal, a mathematical theoretician of great ability, B. F. Wyas, an equally sagacious antiquarian who had identified the sites of many ancient cities: Palmyra, Lubeck, Eridu, Zanesville, Burton-on-Trent, Massilia among others. Certain family elders filled out the council: Marune and Baudune of Aure; Quay, Roseth and Idelsea of Xanten; Uegus of Isseth, Claghorn of Overwhele.

All sat silent for a period of ten minutes, arranging their minds and performing the silent act of psychic accommodation known as 'intression'.

At last Hagedorn spoke. "The castle suddenly is bereft of its Meks. Needless to say, this is an inconvenient condition to be adjusted as swiftly as possible. Here, I am sure, we find ourselves of one mind."

He looked around the table. All thrust forward ivory tablets to signify assent—all save Claghorn, who however did not stand it on end to signify dissent.

Isseth, a stern white-haired gentleman magnificently handsome in spite of his seventy years, spoke in a grim voice. "I see no point in cogitation or delay. What we must do is clear. Admittedly the Peasants are poor material from which to recruit an armed force. Nonetheless, we must assemble them, equip them with sandals, smocks and weapons so that they do not discredit us, and put them under good leadership: O. Z. Garr or Xanten. Birds can locate the vagrants, whereupon we will track them down, order the Peasants to give them a good drubbing and herd them home on the double."

Xanten, thirty-five years old, extraordinarily young to be a clan chief, and a notorious firebrand, shook his head. "The idea is appealing but impractical. Peasants simply could not stand up to the Meks, no matter how we trained them."

The statement was manifestly accurate. The Peasants, small andromorphs originally of Spica Ten, were not so much timid as incapable of performing a vicious act.

A dour silence held the table. O. Z. Garr finally spoke. "The dogs have stolen our power-wagons, otherwise I'd be tempted to ride out and chivvy the rascals home with a whip."*

"A matter of perplexity," said Hagedorn, "is syrup. Naturally they carried away what they could. When this is exhausted—what then? Will they starve? Impossible for them to return to their original diet— what was it, swamp mud? Eh, Claghorn, you're the expert in these matters. Can the Meks return to a diet of mud?"

"No," said Claghorn. "The organs of the adult are atrophied. If a cub were started on the diet, he'd probably survive."

"Just as I assumed." Hagedorn scowled portentously down at his clasped hands to conceal his total lack of any constructive proposal.

A gentleman in the dark blue of the Beaudrys appeared in the doorway: he poised himself, held high his right arm, bowed.

Hagedorn rose to his feet. "Come forward, B. F. Robarth; what is your news?" For this was the significance of the newcomer's genuflection.

"The news is a message broadcast from Halcyon. The Meks have attacked; they have fired the structure and are slaughtering all. The radio went dead one minute ago."

All swung around, some jumped to their feet. "Slaughter?" croaked Claghorn.

* This is only an approximate translation and fails to capture the pungency of the language. Several words have no contemporary equivalents. 'Skirkling', as in 'to send skirkling', denotes a frantic pell-mell flight in all directions accompanied by a vibration or twinkling or a jerking motion. To 'volith' is to toy idly with a matter, the implication being that the person involved is of such Jovian potency that all difficulties dwindle to contemptible triviality. 'Raudelbogs' are the semi-intelligent beings of Etamin Four, who were brought to Earth, trained first as gardeners, and then construction laborers, then sent home in disgrace because of certain repulsive habits they refused to forgo.

The statement of O. Z. Garr, therefore, becomes something like this: "Were power-wagons at hand, I'd volith riding forth with a whip to send the raudelbogs skirkling home."

"I am certain that by now Halcyon is no more."

Claghorn sat staring with eyes unfocused. The others discussed the dire news in voices heavy with horror.

Hagedorn once more brought the council back to order. "This is clearly an extreme situation; the gravest, perhaps, of our entire history. I am frank to state that I can suggest no decisive counteract."

Overwhele inquired, "What of the other castles? Are they secure?"

Hagedorn turned to B. F. Robarth: "Will you be good enough to make general radio contact with all other castles, and inquire as to their condition?"

Xanten said, "Others are as vulnerable as Halcyon: Sea Island and Delora, in particular, and Maraval as well."

Claghorn emerged from his reverie. "The gentlemen and ladies of these places, in my opinion, should consider taking refuge at Janeil or here until the uprising is quelled."

Others around the table looked at him in surprise and puzzlement. O. Z. Garr inquired in the silkiest of voices: "You envision the gentlefolk of these castles scampering to refuge at the cock-a-hoop swaggering of the lower orders?"

"Indeed I do, should they wish to survive," responded Claghorn politely. A gentleman of late middle-age, Claghorn was stocky, strong, with black-gray hair, magnificent green eyes, a manner which suggests great internal force under stern control. "Flight by definition entails a certain diminution of dignity," he went on to say. "If O. Z. Garr can propound an elegant manner of taking to one's heels, I will be glad to learn it, and everyone else should likewise heed, because in the days to come the capability may be of comfort to all."

Hagedorn interposed before O. Z. Garr could reply. "Let us keep to the issues. I confess I cannot see to the end of all this. The Meks have demonstrated themselves to be murderers. How can we take murderers back into our service? But if we don't—well, to say the least, conditions will be austere until we can locate and train a new force of technicians."

"The spaceships!" exclaimed Xanten. "We must see to them at once!"

"What's this?" inquired Beaudry, a gentleman of rock-hard face. "How do you mean: 'see to them'?"

"They must be protected from damage! What else? They are our link to the Home Worlds. The maintenance Meks probably have not deserted the hangars, since, if they propose to exterminate us, they will want to deny us the spaceships."

"Perhaps you care to march with a levy of Peasants to take the hangars under firm control?" suggested O. Z. Garr in a somewhat supercilious voice. A long history of rivalry and mutual detestation existed between himself and Xanten.

"It may be our only hope," said Xanten. "Still—how does one fight with a levy of Peasants? Better that I fly to the hangars and reconnoiter. Meanwhile, perhaps you, and others with military expertise, will take in hand the recruitment and training of a Peasant militia."

"In this regard," stated O. Z. Garr, "I await the outcome of our current deliberations. If it develops that here lies the optimum course, I naturally will apply my competences to the fullest degree. If your own capabilities are best fulfilled by spying out the activities of the Meks, I hope you will be largehearted enough to do the same."

The two gentlemen glared at each other.

A year previously their enmity had almost culminated in a duel. Xanten, a gentleman tall, clean-limbed, nervously active, was gifted with great natural flair, but likewise evinced a disposition too easy for absolute elegance. The traditionalists considered him 'sthross', indicating a manner flawed by an almost imperceptible slackness and lack of punctilio: not the best possible choice for clan chief.

Xanten's response to O. Z. Garr was blandly polite. "I shall be glad to take this task upon myself. Since haste is of the essence I will risk the accusation of precipitousness and leave at once. Hopefully I return to report tomorrow." He rose, performed a ceremonious bow to Hagedorn, another all-inclusive salute to the council and departed.

III

He crossed to Esledune House where he maintained an apartment on the thirteenth level: four rooms furnished in the style known as Fifth Dynasty, after an epoch in the history of the Altair Home Planets, from which the human race had returned to Earth.

His current consort, Araminta, a lady of the Onwane family, was absent on affairs of her own, which suited Xanten well enough. After plying him with questions she would have discredited his simple explanation, preferring to suspect an assignation at his country place. Truth to tell, he had become bored with Araminta and had reason to believe that she felt similarly—or perhaps his exalted rank had provided her less opportunity to preside at glittering social functions than she had expected. They had bred no children. Araminta's daughter by a previous connection had been tallied to her. Her second child must be tallied to Xanten, preventing him from siring another child.[*]

* The population of Castle Hagedorn was fixed; each gentleman and each lady was permitted a single child. If by chance another were born he must either find

Xanten doffed his yellow council vestments. Assisted by a young Peasant buck, he donned dark yellow hunting-breeches with black trim, a black jacket, black boots. He drew a cap of soft black leather over his head, slung a pouch over his shoulder, into which he loaded weapons: a coiled blade, an energy-gun.

Leaving the apartment he summoned the lift and descended to the first level armory, where normally a Mek clerk would have served him. Now Xanten, to his vast disgust, was forced to take himself behind the counter, and rummage here and there. The Meks had removed most of the sporting rifles, all the pellet ejectors and heavy energy-guns. An ominous circumstance, thought Xanten. At last he found a steel sling-whip, spare power-slugs for his gun, a brace of fire grenades, a high-powered monocular.

He returned to the lift, rode to the top level, ruefully considering the long climb when eventually the mechanism broke down, with no Meks at hand to make repairs. He thought of the apoplectic furies of rigid traditionalists such as Beaudry and chuckled. Eventful days lay ahead!

Stopping at the top level he crossed to the parapets, proceeded around to the radio room. Customarily three Mek specialists connected into the apparatus by wires clipped to their quills sat typing messages as they arrived. Now B. F. Robarth stood before the mechanism, uncertainly twisting the dials, his mouth wry with deprecation and distaste for the job.

"Any further news?" Xanten asked.

B. F. Robarth gave him a sour grin. "The folk at the other end seem no more familiar with this cursed tangle than I. I hear occasional voices. I believe that the Meks are attacking Castle Delora."

Claghorn had entered the room behind Xanten. "Did I hear you correctly? Delora Castle is gone?"

"Not gone yet, Claghorn. But as good as gone. The Delora walls are little better than a picturesque crumble."

"Sickening situation!" muttered Xanten. "How can sentient creatures perform such evil? After all these centuries, how little we actually knew of them!" As he spoke he recognized the tactlessness of his remark; Claghorn had devoted much time to a study of the Meks.

"The act itself is not astounding," said Claghorn shortly. "It has occurred a thousand times in human history."

Mildly surprised that Claghorn should use human history as referent

---

someone who had not yet sired to sponsor it, or dispose of it another way. The usual procedure was to give the child into the care of the Expiationists.

to a case involving the sub-orders, Xanten asked: "You were never aware of this vicious aspect to the Mek nature?"

"No. Never. Never indeed."

Claghorn seemed unduly sensitive, thought Xanten. Understandable, all in all. Claghorn's basic doctrine as set forth during the Hagedorn selection was by no means simple, and Xanten neither understood it nor completely endorsed what he conceived to be its goals; but it was plain that the revolt of the Meks had cut the ground out from under Claghorn's feet. Probably to the somewhat bitter satisfaction of O. Z. Garr, who must feel vindicated in his traditionalist doctrines.

Claghorn said tersely, "The life we've been leading couldn't last forever. It's a wonder it lasted as long as it did."

"Perhaps so," said Xanten in a soothing voice. "Well, no matter. All things change. Who knows? The Peasants may be planning to poison our food . . . I must go." He bowed to Claghorn, who returned him a crisp nod, and to B. F. Robarth, then departed the room.

He climbed the spiral staircase—almost a ladder—to the cotes, where the Birds lived in an invincible disorder, occupying themselves with gambling at the game of quarrels, a version of chess, with rules incomprehensible to every gentleman who had tried to understand it.

Castle Hagedorn maintained a hundred Birds, tended by a gang of long-suffering Peasants, whom the Birds held in vast disesteem. They were garish garrulous creatures, pigmented red, yellow, blue, with long necks, jerking inquisitive heads, an inherent irreverence which no amount of discipline or tutelage could overcome. Spying Xanten, they emited a chorus of rude jeers: "Somebody wants a ride! Heavy thing!" "Why don't the self-anointed two-footers grow wings for themselves?" "My friend, never trust a Bird! We'll sky you, then fling you down on your fundament!"

"Quiet!" called Xanten. "I need six fast, silent Birds, upon an important mission. Are any capable of such a task?"

"Are any capable, he asks!" "*A ros ros ros!* When none of us have flown for a week!" "Silence? We'll give you silence, yellow and black!"

"Come then. You. You. You of the wise eye. You there. You with the cocked shoulder. You with the green pompon. To the basket."

The Birds designated, jeering, grumbling, reviling the Peasants, allowed their syrup sacs to be filled, then flapped to the wicker seat where Xanten waited. "To the space depot at Vincenne," he told them. "Fly high and silently. Enemies are abroad. We must learn what harm if any has been done to the spaceships."

"To the depot then!" Each Bird seized a length of rope tied to an

overhead framework; the chair was yanked up with a jerk calculated
to rattle Xanten's teeth, and off they flew, laughing, cursing each other
for not supporting more of the load, but eventually all accommodat-
ing themselves to the task and flying with a coordinated flapping of
the thirty-six sets of wings. To Xanten's relief, their garrulity lessened;
silently they flew south, at a speed fifty or sixty miles per hour.

The afternoon was already waning. The ancient countryside, scene
to so many comings and goings, so much triumph and so much disaster,
was laced with long black shadows. Looking down, Xanten reflected
that though the human stock was native to this soil, and though his
immediate ancestors had maintained their holdings for seven hundred
years, Earth still seemed an alien world.

The reason of course was by no means mysterious or rooted in
paradox. After the Six-Star War, Earth had lain fallow for three thousand years, unpopulated save for a handful of anguished wretches who
somehow had survived the cataclysm and who had become semi-
barbaric Nomads. Then seven hundred years ago certain rich lords of
Altair, motivated to some extent by political disaffection, but no less by
caprice, had decided to return to Earth. Such was the origin of the nine
great strongholds, the resident gentlefolk and the staffs of specialized
andromorphs.

Xanten flew over an area where an antiquarian had directed excava-
tions, revealing a plaza flagged with white stone, a broken obelisk,
a tumbled statue. The sight, by some trick of association, stimulated
Xanten's mind to an astonishing vision, so simple and yet so grand
that he looked around, in all directions, with new eyes. The vision was
Earth re-populated with men, the land cultivated, Nomads driven back
into the wilderness.

At the moment the image was far-fetched. And Xanten, watching
the soft contours of old Earth slide below, pondered the Mek revolt
which had altered his life with such startling abruptness.

Claghorn had long insisted that no human condition endured forever, with the corollary that the more complicated such a condition,
the greater its susceptibility to change.

In that case the seven hundred year continuity at Castle Hagedorn
—as artificial, extravagant and intricate as life could be—became an
astonishing circumstance in itself. Claghorn had pushed his thesis
further. Since change was inevitable, he argued that the gentlefolk
should soften the impact by anticipating and controlling the changes
—a doctrine which had been attacked with great fervor. The traditionalists labeled all of Claghorn's ideas demonstrable fallacy, and cited
the very stability of castle life as proof of its viability. Xanten had in-

clined first one way, then the other, emotionally involved with neither cause. If anything, the fact of O. Z. Garr's traditionalism had nudged him toward Claghorn's views.

Now it seemed as if events had vindicated Claghorn. Change had come, with an impact of the maximum harshness and violence.

There were still questions to be answered, of course. Why had the Meks chosen this particular time to revolt? Conditions had not altered appreciably for five hundred years, and the Meks had never previously hinted dissatisfaction. In fact, they had revealed nothing of their feelings—though no one had ever troubled to ask them—save Claghorn.

The Birds were veering east to avoid the Ballarat Mountains, to the west of which were the ruins of a great city, never satisfactorily identified. Below lay the Lucerne Valley, at one time a fertile farm land. If one looked with great concentration the outline of the various holdings could sometimes be distinguished. Ahead, the spaceship hangars were visible, where Mek technicians maintained four spaceships that were jointly the property of Hagedorn, Janeil, Tuang, Morninglight and Maraval, though, for a variety of reasons, the ships were never used.

The sun was setting. Orange light twinkled and flickered on the metal walls. Xanten called instructions up to the Birds: "Circle down; alight behind that line of trees, but fly low so that none will see."

Down on stiff wings curved the Birds, six ungainly necks stretched toward the ground. Xanten was ready for the impact. The Birds never seemed able to alight easily when they carried a gentleman. When the cargo was something in which they felt a personal concern, dandelion fluff would never have been disturbed by the jar.

Xanten expertly kept his balance, instead of tumbling and rolling in the manner preferred by the Birds. "You all have syrup," he told them. "Rest: make no noise; do not quarrel. By tomorrow's sunset, if I am not here, return to Castle Hagedorn and say that Xanten was killed."

"Never fear!" cried the Birds. "We will wait forever!" "At any rate till tomorrow's sunset!" "If danger threatens, if you are pressed—*a ros ros ros!* Call for the Birds!" "*A ros!* We are ferocious when aroused!"

"I wish it were true," said Xanten. "The Birds are arrant cowards, this is well known. Still I value the sentiment. Remember my instructions, and be quiet above all! I do not wish to be set upon and stabbed because of your clamor."

The Birds made indignant sounds. "Injustice, injustice! We are quiet as the dew!"

"Good." Xanten hurriedly moved away lest they should bellow new advice or reassurances after him.


IV


Passing through the forest, he came to an open meadow at the far edge of which, perhaps a hundred yards distant, was the rear of the first hangar. He stopped to consider.

Several factors were involved. First, the maintenance Meks, with the metal structure shielding them from radio contact, might still be unaware of the revolt. Hardly likely, he decided, in view of the otherwise careful planning. Second, the Meks, in continuous communication with their fellows, acted as a collective organism. The aggregate functioned more completely than its parts, and the individual was not prone to initiative. Hence, vigilance was not likely to be extreme. Third, if they expected anyone to attempt a discreet approach, they would necessarily scrutinize most closely the route which he proposed to take.

Xanten decided to wait in the shadows another ten minutes, until the setting sun shining over his shoulder should most effectively blind any who might watch.

Ten minutes passed. The hangars, burnished by the dying sunlight, bulked long, tall, completely quiet. In the intervening meadow long golden grass waved and rippled in a cool breeze.

Xanten took a deep breath, hefted his pouch, arranged his weapons, strode forth. It did not occur to him to crawl through the grass.

He reached the back of the nearest hangar without challenge. Pressing his ear to the metal he heard nothing. He walked to the corner, looked down the side: no sign of life. Xanten shrugged. Very well then; to the door.

He walked beside the hangar, the setting sun casting a long black shadow ahead of him. He came to a door opening into the hangar administrative office. Since there was nothing to be gained by trepidation, Xanten thrust the door aside and entered.

The offices were empty. The desks, where centuries before underlings had sat, calculating invoices and bills of lading, were bare, polished, free of dust. The computers and information banks, black enamel, glass, white and red switches, looked as if they had been installed only the day before.

Xanten crossed to the glass pane overlooking the hangar floor, shadowed under the bulk of the ship.

He saw no Meks. But on the floor of the hangar, arranged in neat rows and heaps, were elements and assemblies of the ship's control mechanism. Service panels gaped wide into the hull to show where the devices had been detached.

Xanten stepped from the office out into the hangar. The spaceship had been disabled, put out of commission. Xanten looked along the neat rows of parts. Certain savants of various castles were expert in the theory of space-time transfer; S. X. Rosenhox of Maraval had even derived a set of equations which, if translated into machinery, eliminated the troublesome Hamus Effect. But not one gentleman, even were he so oblivious to personal honor as to touch a hand to a tool, would know how to replace, connect and tune the mechanisms heaped upon the hangar floor.

When had the malicious work been done? Impossible to say.

Xanten returned to the office, stepped back out into the twilight, walked to the next hangar. Again no Meks; again the spaceship had been gutted of its control mechanisms. Xanten proceeded to the third hangar, where conditions were the same.

At the fourth hangar he discerned the faint sounds of activity. Stepping into the office, looking through the glass wall into the hangar, he found Meks working with their usual economy of motion, in a near silence which was uncanny.

Xanten, already uncomfortable because of skulking through the forest, became enraged by the cool destruction of his property. He strode forth into the hangar. Slapping his thigh to attract attention he called in a harsh voice; "Return the components to place! How dare you vermin act in such a manner?"

The Meks turned about their blank countenances, studied him through black beaded lensclusters at each side of their heads.

"What?" Xanten bellowed. "You hesitate?" He brought forth his steel whip usually more of a symbolic adjunct than a punitive instrument, and slashed it against the ground. "Obey! This ridiculous revolt is at its end!"

The Meks still hesitated, and events wavered in the balance. None made a sound, though messages were passing among them, appraising the circumstances, establishing a consensus. Xanten could allow them no such leisure. He marched forward, wielding the whip, striking at the only area where the Meks felt pain: the ropy face. "To your duties," he roared. "A fine maintenance crew are you! A destruction crew is more like it!"

The Meks made their soft blowing sound which might mean anything. They fell back, and now Xanten noted one standing at the head of the companionway leading into the ship: a Mek larger than any he had seen before and one in some fashion different. This Mek was aiming a pellet-gun at his head. With an unhurried flourish Xanten whipped away a Mek who had leapt forward with a knife, and without deigning to aim fired at and destroyed the Mek who stood on the companionway, even as the slug sang past his head.

The other Meks were nevertheless committed to an attack. All surged forward. Lounging disdainfully against the hull, Xanten shot them as they came, moving his head once to avoid a chunk of metal, again reaching to catch a throw-knife and hurl it into the face of him who had thrown it.

The Meks drew back, and Xanten guessed that they had agreed on a new tactic: either to withdraw for weapons or perhaps to confine him within the hangar. In any event no more could be accomplished here. He made play with the whip and cleared an avenue to the office. With tools, metal bars and forgings striking the glass behind him, he sauntered through the office and out into the night. He did not look behind.

The full moon was rising, a great yellow globe casting a smoky saffron glow, like an antique lamp. Mek eyes were not well adapted for night seeing, and Xanten waited by the door. Presently Meks began to pour forth, and Xanten hacked at their necks as they came.

The Meks drew back inside the hangar. Wiping his blade Xanten strode off the way he had come, looking neither right nor left. He stopped short. The night was young. Something tickled his mind: the recollection of the Mek who had fired the pellet-gun. He had been larger, possibly a darker bronze, but, more significantly, he had displayed an indefinable poise, almost authority—though such a word, when used in connection with the Meks, was anomalous. On the other hand, someone must have planned the revolt, or at least originated the concept of a revolt in the first place.

It might be worthwhile to extend the reconnaissance, though his primary information had been secured.

Xanten turned back and crossed the landing area to the barracks and garages. Once more, frowning in discomfort, he felt the need for discretion. What times these were when a gentleman must skulk to avoid such as the Meks! He stole up behind the garages, where a half-dozen power-wagons* lay dozing.

* Power-wagons, like the Meks, were originally swamp-creatures from Etamin Nine. They were great rectangular slabs of muscle, slung into a rectangular frame and protected from sunlight, insects and rodents by a synthetic pelt. Syrup sacs communicated with their digestive apparatus, wires led to motor nodes in the rudimentary brain. The muscles were clamped to rocker arms which actuated rotors and drive-wheels. The power-wagons were economical, long-lived and docile, and

Xanten looked them over. All were of the same sort, a metal frame with four wheels and an earth-moving blade at the front. Nearby must be the syrup stock.

Xanten presently found a bin containing a number of containers. He loaded a dozen on a nearby wagon and slashed the rest with his knife, so that the syrup gushed across the ground. The Meks used a somewhat different formulation; their syrup would be stocked at a different locale, presumably inside the barracks.

Xanten mounted a power-wagon, twisted the 'awake' key, tapped the 'Go' button, pulled a lever which set the wheels into reverse motion. The power-wagon lurched back. Xanten halted it and turned it so that it faced the barracks. He did likewise with three others, then set them all in motion, one after the other.

They trundled forward. The blades cut open the metal wall of the barracks, the roof sagged. The power-wagons continued, pushing the length of the interior, crushing all in their way.

Xanten nodded in profound satisfaction, returned to the power-wagon he had reserved for his own use. Mounting to the seat, he waited. No Meks issued from the barracks. Apparently they were deserted, with the entire crew busy at the hangars. Still, hopefully, the syrup stocks had been destroyed. Many might perish by starvation.

From the direction of the hangars came a single Mek, evidently attracted by the sounds of destruction. Xanten crouched on the seat and as it passed, coiled his whip around the stocky neck. He heaved; the Mek spun to the ground.

Xanten leapt down, seized its pellet-gun. Here was another of the larger Meks, and now Xanten saw it to be without a syrup sac, a Mek in the original state. Astounding! How did the creature survive? Suddenly there were many new questions to be asked; hopefully a few to be answered. Standing on the creature's head, Xanten hacked away the long antenna quills which protruded from the back of the Mek's scalp. It was now insulated, alone, on its own resources; a situation certain to reduce the most stalwart Mek to apathy.

"Up!" ordered Xanten. "Into the back of the wagon!" He cracked the whip for emphasis.

The Mek at first seemed disposed to defy him, but after a blow or two obeyed. Xanten climbed into the seat, started the power-wagon, directed it to the north. The Birds would be unable to carry both himself and the Mek—or in any event they would cry and complain so raucously that they might as well be believed at first. They might or

---

so they were principally used for heavy cartage, earth-moving, heavy-tillage, and other arduous jobs.

might not wait until the specified hour of tomorrow's sunset. As likely
as not they would sleep the night in a tree, awake in a surly mood and
return at once to Castle Hagedorn.

All through the night the power-wagon trundled, with Xanten on
the seat and his captive huddled in the rear.

v

The gentlefolk of the castles, for all their assurance, disliked to wander
the countryside by night, by reason of what some derided as superstitious fear. Others cited travelers benighted beside mouldering ruins and
their subsequent visions: the eldritch music they had heard, or the
whimper of moon-mirkins, or the far horns of spectral huntsmen.
Others had seen pale lavender and green lights, and wraiths which ran
with long strides through the forest; and Hode Abbey, now a dank tumble, was notorious for the White Hag and the alarming toll she exacted.

A hundred such cases were known. While the hard-headed scoffed,
none needlessly traveled the countryside by night. Indeed, if truly
ghosts haunt the scenes of tragedy and heartbreak, then the landscape
of Old Earth must be home to ghosts and specters beyond all number-
ing; especially that region across which Xanten rolled in the power-
wagon, where every rock, every meadow, every vale and swale was
crusted thick with human experience.

The moon rose high. The wagon trundled north along an ancient
road, the cracked concrete slabs shining pale in the moonlight. Twice
Xanten saw flickering orange lights off to the side, and once, standing
in the shade of a cypress tree, he thought to see a tall quiet shape, silently watching him pass. The captive Mek sat plotting mischief,
Xanten well knew. Without its quills it must feel depersonified, bewildered, but Xanten told himself that it would not do to doze.

The road led through a town, certain structures of which yet stood.
Not even the Nomads took refuge in these old towns, fearing either
miasma or perhaps the redolence of grief.

The moon reached the zenith. The landscape spread away in a hundred tones of silver, black and gray. Looking about, Xanten thought
that for all the notable pleasures of civilized life, there was yet something to be said for the spaciousness and simplicity of Nomadland . . .
The Mek made a stealthy movement. Xanten did not so much as turn
his head. He cracked his whip in the air. The Mek became quiet.

All through the night the power-wagon rolled along the old road,
with the moon sinking into the west. The eastern horizon glowed green

and lemon-yellow, and presently, as the pallid moon disappeared over the distant line of the mountains the sun came up.

At this moment, Xanten spied a drift of smoke off to the right.

He halted the wagon. Standing up on the seat he craned his neck to spy a Nomad encampment about a quarter-mile distant. He could distinguish three or four dozen tents of various sizes, a dozen dilapidated power-wagons. On the hetman's tall tent he thought to see a black ideogram which he thought he recognized. If so, this would be the tribe which not long before had trespassed on the Hagedorn domain, and which O. Z. Garr had repulsed.

Xanten settled himself upon the seat, composed his garments, set the power-wagon in motion and guided it toward the camp.

A hundred black-cloaked men, tall and lean as ferrets, watched his approach. A dozen sprang forward and whipping arrows to bows aimed them at his heart. Xanten turned them a glance of supercilious inquiry, drove the wagon up to the hetman's tent, halted. He rose to his feet. "Hetman," he called. "Are you awake?"

The hetman parted the canvas which closed off his tent, peered out and after a moment came forth. Like the others he wore a garment of limp black cloth, swathing head and body alike. His face thrust through a square opening: narrow blue eyes, a grotesquely long nose, a chin long, skewed and sharp.

Xanten gave him a curt nod. "Observe this." He jerked his thumb toward the Mek in the back of the wagon. The hetman flicked aside his eyes, studied the Mek a tenth-second, returned to a scrutiny of Xanten. "His kind have revolted against the gentlemen," said Xanten. "In fact they massacre all the men of Earth. Hence we of Castle Hagedorn make this offer to the Nomads. Come to Castle Hagedorn! We will feed, clothe and arm you. We will train you to discipline and the arts of formal warfare. We will provide the most expert leadership within our power. We will then annihilate the Meks, expunge them from Earth. After the campaign, we will train you to technical skills, and you may pursue profitable and interesting careers in the service of the castles."

The hetman made no reply for a moment. Then his weathered face split into a ferocious grin and he spoke in a voice which Xanten found surprisingly well-modulated. "So your beasts have finally risen up to rend you! A pity they forebore so long! Well, it is all one to us. You are both alien folk and sooner or later your bones must bleach together."

Xanten pretended incomprehension. "If I understand you aright, you assert that in the face of alien assault, all men must fight a common battle; and then, after the victory, cooperate still to their mutual advantage; am I correct?"

The hetman's grin never wavered. "You are not men. Only we of Earth soil and Earth water are men. You and your weird slaves are strangers together. We wish you success in your mutual slaughter."

"Well then," declared Xanten, "I heard you aright after all. Appeals to your loyalty are ineffectual, so much is clear. What of self-interest then? The Meks, failing to expunge the gentlefolk of the castles, will turn upon the Nomads and kill them as if they were so many ants."

"If they attack us, we will war on them," said the hetman. "Otherwise let them do as they will."

Xanten glanced thoughtfully at the sky. "We might be willing even now, to accept a contingent of Nomads into the service of Castle Hagedorn, this to form a cadre from which a larger and more versatile group may be formed."

From the side another Nomad called in an offensively jeering voice: "You will sew a sac on our backs where you can pour your syrup, hey?"

Xanten replied in an even voice, "The syrup is highly nutritious and supplies all bodily needs."

"Why then do you not consume it yourself?"

Xanten disdained reply.

The hetman spoke. "If you wish to supply us weapons, we will take them, and use them against whomever threatens us. But do not expect us to defend you. If you fear for your lives, desert your castles and become Nomads."

"Fear for our lives?" exclaimed Xanten. "What nonsense! Never! Castle Hagedorn is impregnable, as is Janeil, and most of the other castles as well."

The hetman shook his head. "Any time we choose we could take Hagedorn, and kill all you popinjays in your sleep."

"What?" cried Xanten in outrage. "Are you serious?"

"Certainly. On a black night we would send a man aloft on a great kite and drop him down on the parapets. He would lower a line, haul up ladders and in fifteen minutes the castle is taken."

Xanten pulled at his chin. "Ingenious, but impractical. The Birds would detect such a kite. Or the wind would fail at a critical moment . . . All this is beside the point. The Meks fly no kites. They plan to make a display against Janeil and Hagedorn and then, in their frustration, they will go forth and hunt Nomads."

The hetman moved back a step. "What then? We have survived similar attempts by the men of Hagedorn. Cowards all! Hand to hand,

with equal weapons, we would make you eat the dirt like the contemptible dogs you are."

Xanten raised his eyebrows in elegant disdain. "I fear that you forget yourself. You address a clan chief of Castle Hagedorn. Only
fatigue and boredom restrain me from punishing you with this whip."

"Bah," said the hetman. He crooked a finger to one of his archers.
"Spit this insolent lordling."

The archer discharged his arrow, but Xanten had been expecting
some such act. He fired his energy-gun, destroying arrow, bow, and
the archer's hands. He said, "I see I must teach you common respect
for your betters; so it means the whip after all." Seizing the hetman by
the scalp, he coiled the whip smartly once, twice, thrice around the
narrow shoulders. "Let this suffice. I cannot compel you to fight, but
at least I can demand decent respect from scuttling dung beetles." He
leapt to the ground and, seizing the hetman, pitched him into the back
of the wagon alongside the Mek. Then, backing the power-wagon
around, he departed the camp without so much as a glance over his
shoulder, the thwart of the seat protecting his back from the arrows of
the hetman's stunned subjects.

The hetman scrambled erect, drew his dagger. Xanten turned his
head slightly. "Take care! Or I will tie you to the wagon, and you shall
run behind in the dust."

The hetman hesitated, made a spitting sound between his teeth, drew
back. He looked down at his blade, turned it over, sheathed it with a
grunt. "Where do you take me?"

Xanten halted the wagon. "No farther. I merely wished to leave your
camp with dignity, without dodging and ducking a hail of arrows. You
may alight. I take it you still refuse to bring your men into the service
of Castle Hagedorn?"

The hetman once more made the spitting sound between his teeth.
"When the Meks have destroyed the castles, we shall destroy the Meks.
Then Earth will be cleared of star-things for all time!"

"You are a gang of intractable savages. Very well, alight, return to
your encampment. Reflect well before you again show disrespect to a
Castle Hagedorn clan chief."

"Bah," muttered the hetman. Leaping down from the wagon, he
stalked back down the track toward his camp. He did not look back.

VI

About noon Xanten came to Far Valley, at the edge of the Hagedorn
lands.

Nearby was a village of Expiationists: malcontents and neurasthen-
ics in the opinion of castle gentlefolk, and a curious group by any
standards. A few had held enviable rank; certain others were savants
of recognized erudition; but others yet were persons of neither dignity
nor reputation, subscribing to the most bizarre and extreme of
philosophies. All now performed toil, no different from that relegated
to the Peasants, and all seemed to take a perverse satisfaction in what
by castle standards was filth, poverty and degradation.

As might be expected, their creed was by no means homogeneous.
Some might better have been described as 'nonconformists', and others
still, a minority, argued for a dynamic program.

Between castle and village was little intercourse. Occasionally the
Expiationists bartered fruit or polished wood for tools, nails, medica-
ments; or the gentlefolk might make up a party to watch the Expiationists at their dancing and singing. Xanten had visited the village on
many such occasions and had been attracted by the artless charm and
informality of the folk at their play. Now, passing near the village,
Xanten turned aside and followed a lane which wound between tall
blackberry hedges and out upon a little common, where goats and cattle
grazed. Xanten halted the wagon in the shade, saw that the syrup sac
was full. He looked back at his captive. "What of you? If you
need syrup, pour yourself full. But no, you have no sac. What then do
you feed upon? Mud? Unsavory fare. I fear none here is rank enough
for your taste. Ingest syrup or munch grass, as you will; only do not
stray overfar from the wagon, for I watch with an intent eye."

The Mek, sitting hunched in a corner, gave no signal that it com-
prehended. Nor did it move to take advantage of Xanten's offer.

Xanten went to a watering trough. Holding his hands under the
trickle which issued from a lead pipe, he rinsed his face, then drank a
swallow or two from his cupped hand.

Turning, he found that a dozen folk of the village had approached.
One he knew well, a man who might have become Godalming, or even
Aure, had he not become infected with expiationism.

Xanten performed a polite salute. "A. G. Philidor. It is I, Xanten."

"Xanten, of course. But here I am A. G. Philidor no longer; merely
Philidor."

Xanten bowed. "My apologies. I have neglected the full rigor of your
informality."

"Spare me your wit," said Philidor. "Why do you bring us a shorn
Mek? For adoption, perhaps?" This last alluded to the gentlefolk practice of bringing over-tally babies to the village.

"Now who flaunts his wit? But you have not heard the news?"

"News arrives here last of all. The Nomads are better informed."

"Prepare yourself for surprise. The Meks have revolted against the castles. Halcyon and Delora are demolished, and all killed; perhaps others by this time."

Philidor shook his head. "I am not surprised."

"Well, then, are you not concerned?"

Philidor considered. "To this extent. Our own plans, never very feasible, become more far-fetched than ever."

"It appears to me," said Xanten, "that you face grave and immediate danger. The Meks surely intend to wipe out every vestige of humanity. You will not escape."

Philidor shrugged. "Conceivably the danger exists . . . We will take counsel and decide what to do."

"I can put forward a proposal which you may find attractive," said Xanten. "Our first concern, of course, is to suppress the revolt. There are at least a dozen Expiationist communities, with an aggregate population of two or three thousand—perhaps more. I propose that we recruit and train a corps of highly disciplined troops, supplied from the Castle Hagedorn armory, led by Hagedorn's most expert military theoreticians."

Philidor stared at him incredulously. "You expect us, the Expiationists, to become your soldiers?"

"Why not?" asked Xanten ingeniously. "Your life is at stake no less than ours."

"No one dies more than once."

Xanten in his turn evinced shock. "What? Can this be a former gentleman of Hagedorn speaking? Is this the face a man of pride and courage turns to danger? Is this the lesson of history? Of course not! I need not instruct you in this; you are as knowledgeable as I."

Philidor nodded. "I know that the history of man is not his technical triumphs, his kills, his victories. It is a composite: a mosaic of a trillion pieces, the account of each man's accommodation with his conscience. This is the true history of the race."

Xanten made an airy gesture. "A. G. Philidor, you over-simplify grievously. Do you consider me obtuse? There are many kinds of history. They interact. You emphasize morality. But the ultimate basis of morality is survival. What promotes survival is good, what induces mortefaction is bad."

"Well spoken!" declared Philidor. "But let me propound a parable. May a nation of a million beings destroy a creature who otherwise will infect all with a fatal disease? Yes, you will say. Once more. Ten starving beasts hunt you, that they may eat. Will you kill them to save your life? Yes, you will say again, though here you destroy more than you save. Once more: a man inhabits a hut in a lonely valley. A hundred spaceships descend from the sky, and attempt to destroy him. May he destroy these ships in self-defense, even though he is one and they are a hundred thousand? Perhaps you say yes. What then if a whole world, a whole race of beings, pits itself against this single man? May he kill all? What if the attackers are as human as himself? What if he were the creature of the first instance, who otherwise will infect a world with disease? You see, there is no area where a simple touchstone avails. We have searched and found none. Hence, at the risk of sinning against Survival, we—I, at least; I can only speak for myself—have chosen a morality that at least allows me calm. I kill—*nothing*. I destroy *nothing*."

"Bah," said Xanten contemptuously. "If a Mek platoon entered this valley and began to kill your children, you would not defend them?"

Philidor compressed his lips, turned away. Another man spoke. "Philidor has defined morality. But who is absolutely moral? Philidor—or I, or you—might in such a case desert his morality."

Philidor said, "Look about you. Is anyone here you recognize?"

Xanten scanned the group. Nearby stood a girl of extraordinary beauty. She wore a white smock and in the dark hair curling to her shoulders she wore a red flower. Xanten nodded. "I see the maiden O. Z. Garr wished to introduce into his menage at the castle."

"Exactly," said Philidor. "Do you recall the circumstances?"

"Very well indeed," said Xanten. "There was vigorous objection from the Council of Notables—if for no other reason than the threat to our laws of population control. O. Z. Garr attempted to sidestep the law in this fashion. 'I keep Phanes,' he said. 'At times I maintain as many as six, or even eight, and no one utters a word of protest. I will call this girl a Phane and keep her among the rest.' I and others protested. There was almost a duel on this matter. O. Z. Garr was forced to relinquish the girl. She was given into my custody and I conveyed her to Far Valley."

Philidor nodded. "All this is correct. Well—we attempted to dissuade Garr. He refused to be dissuaded, and threatened us with his hunting force of perhaps thirty Meks. We stood aside. Are we moral? Are we strong or weak?"

"Sometimes it is better," said Xanten, "to ignore morality. Even though O. Z. Garr is a gentleman and you are but Expiationists . . . Likewise in the case of the Meks. They are destroying the castles, and all the men of earth. If morality means supine acceptance, then morality must be abandoned!"

Philidor gave a sour chuckle. "What a remarkable situation! The Meks are here, likewise Peasants and Birds and Phanes, all altered, transported and enslaved for human pleasure. Indeed, it is this fact that occasions our guilt, for which we must expiate. And now you want us to compound this guilt!"

"It is a mistake to brood overmuch about the past," said Xanten. "Still, if you wish to preserve your option to brood, I suggest that you fight Meks now, or at the very least take refuge in the castle."

"Not I," said Philidor. "Perhaps others may choose to do so."

"You will wait to be killed?"

"No. I and no doubt others will take refuge in the remote mountains."

Xanten clambered back aboard the power-wagon. "If you change your mind, come to Castle Hagedorn."

He departed.

The road continued along the valley, wound up a hillside, crossed a ridge. Far ahead, silhouetted against the sky, stood Castle Hagedorn.

VII

Xanten reported to the council.

"The spaceships cannot be used. The Meks have rendered them inoperative. Any plan to solicit assistance from the Home Worlds is pointless."

"This is sorry news," said Hagedorn with a grimace. "Well then—so much for that."

Xanten continued. "Returning by power-wagon I encountered a tribe of Nomads. I summoned the hetman and explained to him the advantages of serving Castle Hagedorn. The Nomads, I fear, lack both grace and docility. The hetman gave so surly a response that I departed in disgust.

"At Far Valley I visited the Expiationist village, and made a similar proposal, but with no great success. They are as idealistic as the Nomads are churlish. Both are of a fugitive tendency. The Expiationists spoke of taking refuge in the mountains. The Nomads presumably will retreat into the steppes."

Beaudry snorted. "How will flight help them? Perhaps they gain a few years—but eventually the Meks will find every last one of them; such is their methodicity."

"In the meantime," O. Z. Garr declared peevishly, "we might have organized them into an efficient combat corps, to the benefit of all. Well, then, let them perish! We are secure."

"Secure yes," said Hagedorn gloomily. "But what when the power fails? When the lifts break down? When air circulation cuts off so that we either stifle or freeze? What then?"

O. Z. Garr gave his head a grim shake. "We must steel ourselves to undignified expedients, with as good a grace as possible. But the machinery of the castle is sound, and I expect small deterioration or failure for conceivably five or ten years. By that time anything may occur."

Claghorn, who had been leaning indolently back in his seat, spoke at last: "Essentially this is a passive program. Like the defection of the Nomads and Expiationists, it looks very little beyond the immediate moment."

O. Z. Garr spoke in a voice carefully polite. "Claghorn is well aware that I yield to none in courteous candor, as well as optimism and directness: in short, the reverse of passivity. But I refuse to dignify a stupid little inconvenience by extending it serious attention. How can he label this procedure 'passivity'? Does the worthy and honorable head of the Claghorns have a proposal which more effectively maintains our status, our standards, our self-respect?"

Claghorn nodded slowly, with a faint half-smile which O. Z. Garr found odiously complacent. "There is a simple and effective method by which the Meks might be defeated."

"Well then!" cried Hagedorn. "Why hesitate? Let us hear it!"

Claghorn looked around the red velvet-colored table, considered the faces of all: the dispassionate Xanten; Beaudry, with his burly, rigid, face muscles clenched in an habitual expression unpleasantly like a sneer; old Isseth, handsome, erect and vital as the most dashing cadet; Hagedorn troubled, glum, his inward perplexity all too evident; the elegant Garr; Overwhele, thinking savagely of the inconveniences of the future; Aure, toying with his ivory tablet, either bored, morose or defeated; the others displaying various aspects of doubt, foreboding, hauteur, dark resentment, impatience; and in the case of Floy, a quiet smile—or as Isseth later characterized it, an imbecilic smirk—intended to convey his total disassociation from the entire irksome matter.

Claghorn took stock of the faces, and shook his head. "I will not at the moment broach this plan, as I fear it is unworkable. But I must point out that under no circumstances can Castle Hagedorn be as before, even should we survive the Mek attack."

"Bah!" exclaimed Beaudry. "We lose dignity, we become ridiculous, by even so much as discussing the beasts."

Xanten stirred himself. "A distasteful subject, but remember! Halcyon is destroyed, and Delora and who knows what others? Let us not thrust our heads in the sand! The Meks will not waft away merely because we ignore them."

"In any event," said O. Z. Garr, "Janeil is secure and we are secure. The other folk, unless they are already slaughtered, might do well to visit us during the inconvenience, if they can justify the humiliation of flight to themselves. I myself believe that the Meks will soon come to heel, anxious to return to their posts."

Hagedorn shook his head gloomily. "I find this hard to believe. Very well then, we shall adjourn."

The radio communications system was the first of the castle's vast array of electrical and mechanical devices to break down.

The failure occurred so soon and so decisively that certain of the theoreticians, notably I. K. Harde and Uegus, postulated sabotage by the departing Meks. Others remarked that the system had never been absolutely dependable, that the Meks themselves had been forced to tinker continuously with the circuits, that the failure was simply a result of bad engineering. Harde and Uegus inspected the unwieldy apparatus, but the cause of failure was not obvious. After a half-hour of consultation they agreed that any attempt to restore the system would necessitate complete re-design and re-engineering, with consequent construction of testing and calibration devices, and the fabrication of a complete new family of components. "This is manifestly impossible," stated Uegus in his report to the council. "Even the simplest useful system would require several technician-years. There is not even one single technician to hand. We must therefore await the availability of trained and willing labor."

"In retrospect," stated Isseth, the oldest of the clan chiefs, "it is clear that in many ways we have been less than provident. No matter that the men of the Home Worlds are vulgarians! Men of shrewder calculation than our own would have maintained inter-world connection."

"Lack of 'shrewdness' and 'providence' were not the deterring factors," stated Claghorn. "Communication was discouraged simply because the early lords were unwilling that Earth should be overrun with Home-World parvenus. It is as simple as that."

Isseth grunted, and started to make a rejoinder, but Hagedorn said hastily, "Unluckily, as Xanten tells us, the spaceships have been rendered useless. While certain of our number have a profound knowledge of the theoretical considerations, again who is there to perform the toil? Even were the hangars and spaceships themselves under our control."

O. Z. Garr declared, "Give me six platoons of Peasants and six power-wagons equipped with high-energy-cannons, and I'll regain the hangars. No difficulties there!"

Beaudry said, "Well, here's a start, at least. I'll assist in the training of the Peasants, and though I know nothing of cannon operation, rely on me for any advice I can give."

Hagedorn looked around the group, frowned, pulled at his chin. "There are difficulties to this program. First, we have at hand only the single power-wagon in which Xanten returned from his reconnaissance. Then what of our energy-cannons? Has anyone inspected them? The Meks were entrusted with maintenance, but it is possible, even likely, that they wrought mischief here as well. O. Z. Garr, you are reckoned an expert military theoretician. What can you tell us in this regard?"

"I have made no inspection to date," stated O. Z. Garr. "Today the 'Display of Antique Tabards' will occupy us all until the 'Hour of Sundown Appraisal'."* He looked at his watch. "Perhaps now is as good a time as any to adjourn, until I am able to provide detailed information in regard to the cannons."

Hagedorn nodded his heavy head. "The time indeed grows late. Your Phanes appear today?"

"Only two," replied O. Z. Garr. "The Lazule and the Eleventh Mystery. I can find nothing suitable for the Gossamer Delights nor my little Blue Fay, and the Gloriana still requires tutelage. Today B. Z. Maxelwane's Variflors should repay the most attention."

"Yes," said Hagedorn. "I have heard other remarks to this effect. Very well then, until tomorrow. Eh, Claghorn, you have something to say?"

"Yes, indeed," said Claghorn mildly. "We have all too little time at our disposal. Best that we make the most of it. I seriously doubt the efficacy of Peasant troops; they are like rabbits against wolves. What we need, rather than rabbits, are panthers."

"Ah, yes," said Hagedorn vaguely. "Yes indeed."

"Where, then, are panthers to be found?" Claghorn looked inquiringly around the table. "Can no one suggest a source? A pity. Well then, if panthers fail to appear, I suppose rabbits must do. Let us go about the business of converting rabbits into panthers, and instantly. I suggest that we postpone all fetes and spectacles until the shape of our future is more certain."

Hagedorn raised his eyebrows, opened his mouth to speak, closed it

---

* 'Display of Antique Tabards'; 'Hour of Sundown Appraisal': the literal sense of the first term was yet relevant; that of the second had become lost and the phrase was a mere formalism, connoting that hour of late afternoon when visits were exchanged, wines, liqueurs and essences tasted: in short, a time of relaxation and small talk before the more formal convivialities of dining.

again. He looked intently at Claghorn to ascertain whether or not he joked. Then he looked dubiously around the table.

Beaudry gave a rather brassy laugh. "It seems that erudite Claghorn cries panic."

O. Z. Garr stated: "Surely, in all dignity, we cannot allow the impertinence of our servants to cause us such eye-rolling alarm. I am embarrassed even to bring the matter forward."

"I am not embarrassed," said Claghorn, with the full-faced complacence which so exasperated O. Z. Garr. "I see no reason why you should be. Our lives are threatened, in which case a trifle of embarrassment, or anything else, becomes of secondary importance."

O. Z. Garr rose to his feet, performed a brusque salute in Claghorn's direction, of such a nature as to constitute a calculated affront. Claghorn, rising, performed a similar salute, this so grave and overly complicated as to invest Garr's insult with burlesque overtones. Xanten, who detested O. Z. Garr, laughed aloud.

O. Z. Garr hesitated, then, sensing that under the circumstances taking the matter further would be regarded as poor form, strode from the chamber.

The Viewing of Antique Tabards, an annual pageant of Phanes wearing sumptuous garments took place in the Great Rotunda to the north of the central plaza.

Possibly half of the gentlemen, but less than a quarter of the ladies, kept Phanes. These were creatures native to the caverns of Albireo Seven's moon: a docile race, both playful and affectionate, which after several thousand years of selective breeding had become sylphs of piquant beauty. Clad in a delicate gauze which issued from pores behind their ears, along their upper arms, down their backs, they were the most inoffensive of creatures, anxious always to please, innocently vain. Most gentlemen regarded them with affection, but rumors sometimes told of ladies drenching an especially hated Phane in tincture of ammonia, which matted her pelt and destroyed her gauze forever.

A gentleman besotted by a Phane was considered a figure of fun. The Phane, though so carefully bred as to seem a delicate girl, if used sexually became crumpled and haggard, with gauzes drooping and discolored, and everyone would know that such and such a gentleman had misused his Phane. In this regard, at least, the women of the castles might exert their superiority. They did so by conducting themselves with such extravagant provocation that the Phanes in contrast seemed the most ingenius and fragile of nature sprites. Their life-span was perhaps thirty years, during the last ten of which, after they had lost their beauty, they encased themselves in mantles of gray gauze and performed menial tasks in boudoirs, kitchens, pantries, nurseries and dressing rooms.

The Viewing of Antique Tabards was an occasion more for the viewing of Phanes than the tabards, though these, woven of Phane-gauze, were of intricate beauty in themselves.

The Phane owners sat in a lower tier, tense with hope and pride, exulting when one made an especially splendid display, plunged into black depths when the ritual postures were performed with other than grace and elegance. During each display highly formal music was plucked from a lute by a gentleman from a clan different to that of the Phane owner. The owner never played the lute to the performance of his own Phane. The display was never overtly a competition and no formal acclamation was allowed, but all watching made up their minds as to which was the most entrancing and graceful of the Phanes, and the repute of the owner was thereby exalted.

The current Viewing was delayed almost half an hour by reason of the defection of the Meks, and certain hasty improvisations had been made necessary. But the gentlefolk of Castle Hagedorn were in no mood to be critical and took no heed of the occasional lapses as a dozen young Peasant bucks struggled to perform unfamiliar tasks. The Phanes were as entrancing as ever, bending, twisting, swaying to plangent chords of the lute, fluttering their fingers as if feeling for raindrops, crouching suddenly, gliding, then springing upright straight as wands, finally bowing and skipping from the platform.

Halfway through the program a Peasant sidled awkwardly into the rotunda, and mumbled in an urgent manner to the cadet who came to inquire his business. The cadet at once made his way to Hagedorn's polished jet booth. Hagedorn listened, nodded, spoke a few terse words and settled calmly back in his seat as if the message had been of no consequence, and the gentlefolk of the audience were reassured.

The entertainment proceeded. O. Z. Garr's delectable pair made a fine show, but it was generally felt that Lirlin, a young Phane belonging to Isseth Floy Gazuneth, for the first time at a formal showing, made the most captivating display.

The Phanes appeared for a last time, moving all together through a half-improvised minuet. Then they performed a final half-gay, half-regretful salute and departed the rotunda. For a few moments more the gentlemen and ladies would remain in their booths, sipping essences, discussing the display, arranging affairs and assignations. Hagedorn sat frowning, twisting his hands.

Suddenly he rose to his feet. The rotunda instantly became silent.

"I dislike intruding an unhappy note at so pleasant an occasion," said Hagedorn. "But news has just been given to me, and it is fitting that all should know. Janeil Castle is under attack. The Meks are there in great force, with hundreds of power-wagons. They have circled the castle with a dike which prevents any effective use of the Janeil energy-cannon.

"There is no immediate danger to Janeil, and it is difficult to comprehend what the Meks hope to achieve, the Janeil walls being all of two hundred feet high.

"The news nevertheless is somber, and it means that eventually we must expect a similar investment—though it is even more difficult to comprehend how Meks could hope to inconvenience us. Our water derives from four wells sunk deep into the earth. We have great stocks of food. Our energy is derived from the sun. If necessary, we could condense water and synthesize food from the air—at least I have been so assured by our great biochemical theoretician X. B. Ladisname. Still —this is the news. Make of it what you will. Tomorrow the Council of Notables will meet."

### VIII

"Well, then," said Hagedorn to the council, "for once let us dispense with formality. O. Z. Garr: what of our cannon?"

O. Z. Garr, wearing the magnificent gray and green uniform of the Overwhele Dragoons, carefully placed his morion on the table, so that the panache stood erect. "Of twelve cannon, four appear to be functioning correctly. Four have been sabotaged by excision of the power-leads. Four have been sabotaged by some means undetectable to careful investigation. I have commandeered a half-dozen Peasants who demonstrate a modicum of mechanical ability, and have instructed them in detail. They are currently engaged in splicing the leads. This is the extent of my current information in regard to the cannon."

"Moderately good news," said Hagedorn. "What of the proposed corps of armed Peasants?"

"The project is under way. A. F. Mull and I. A. Berzelius are now inspecting Peasants with a view to recruitment and training. I can make no sanguine projection as to the military effectiveness of such a corps, even if trained and led by such as A. F. Mull, I. A. Berzelius and myself. The Peasants are a mild ineffectual race, admirably suited to the grubbing of weeds, but with no stomach whatever for fighting."

Hagedorn glanced around the council. "Are there any other suggestions?"

Beaudry spoke in a harsh angry voice, "Had the villains but left us our power-wagons, we might have mounted the cannon aboard! The Peasants are equal to this, at least. Then we could roll to Janeil and blast the dogs from the rear."

"These Meks seem utter fiends!" declared Aure. "What conceivably do they have in mind? Why, after these centuries, must they suddenly go mad?"

"We all ask ourselves the same," said Hagedorn. "Xanten, you returned from reconnaissance with a captive: have you attempted to question him?"

"No," said Xanten. "Truth to tell, I haven't thought of him since."

"Why not attempt to question him? Perhaps he can provide a clue or two."

Xanten nodded assent. "I can try. Candidly I expect to learn nothing."

"Claghorn, you are the Mek expert," said Beaudry. "Would you have thought the creatures capable of so intricate a plot? What do they hope to gain? Our castles?"

"They are certainly capable of precise and meticulous planning," said Claghorn. "Their ruthlessness surprises me—more, possibly, than it should. I have never known them to covet our material possessions, and they show no tendency toward what we consider the concomitants of civilization: fine discriminations of sensation and the like. I have often speculated—I won't dignify the conceit with the status of a theory —that the structural logic of a brain is of rather more consequence than we reckon with. Our own brains are remarkable for their utter lack of rational structure. Considering the haphazarded manner in which our thoughts are formed, registered, indexed and recalled, any single rational act becomes a miracle. Perhaps we are incapable of rationality. Perhaps all thought is a set of impulses generated by one emotion, monitored by another, ratified by a third. In contrast the Mek brain is a marvel of what seems careful engineering. It is roughly cubical and consists of microscopic cells interconnected by organic fibrils, each a monofilament molecule of negligible electrical resistance. Within each cell is a film of silica, a fluid of variable conductivity and dielectric properties, a cusp of a complex mixture of metallic oxides. The brain is capable of storing great quantities of information in an orderly pattern. No fact is lost, unless it is purposely forgotten, a capacity which the Meks possess. The brain also functions as a radio transceiver, possibly as a radar transmitter and detector, though this again is speculation.

"Where the Mek brain falls short is in its lack of emotional color. One Mek is precisely like another, without any personality differentiation perceptible to us. This, clearly, is a function of their communicative system. It would be unthinkable for a unique personality to develop under these conditions. They served us efficiently and—so we thought —loyally, because they felt nothing about their condition, neither pride in achievement, nor resentment, nor shame. Nothing whatever. They neither loved us nor hated us. Nor do they now. It is hard for us to conceive this emotional vacuum, when each of us feels something about everything. We live in a welter of emotions. They are as devoid of emotion as an ice-cube. They were fed, housed, maintained in a manner they found satisfactory. Why did they revolt? I have speculated at length, but the single reason which I can formulate seems so grotesque and unreasonable that I refuse to take it seriously. If this after all is the correct explanation . . ." His voice drifted away.

"Well?" demanded O. Z. Garr peremptorily. "What then?"

"Then—it is all the same. They are committed to the destruction of the human race. My speculation alters nothing."

Hagedorn turned to Xanten. "All this should assist you in your inquiries."

"I was about to suggest that Claghorn assist me, if he is so inclined," said Xanten.

"As you like," said Claghorn, "though in my opinion the information, no matter what, is irrelevant. Our single concern should be a means to repel them and to save our lives."

"And—save the force of 'panthers' you mentioned at our previous session—you can conceive of no subtle weapon?" asked Hagedorn wistfully. "A device to set up electrical resonances in their brains, or something similar?"

"Not feasible," said Claghorn. "Certain organs in the creatures' brains function as overload switches. Though it is true that during this time they might not be able to communicate." After a moment's reflection he added thoughtfully: "Who knows? A. G. Bernal and Uegus are theoreticians with a profound knowledge of such projections. Perhaps they might construct such a device, or several, against a possible need."

Hagedorn nodded dubiously, and looked toward Uegus. "Is this possible?"

Uegus frowned. " 'Construct'? I can certainly design such an instrument. But the components—where? Scattered through the storerooms helter-skelter, some functioning, others not. To achieve anything meaningful I must become no better than an apprentice, a Mek." He became incensed, and his voice hardened. "I find it hard to believe that I should be forced to point out this fact! Do you hold me and my talents then of such small worth?"

Hagedorn hastened to reassure him. "Of course not! I for one would never think of impugning your dignity."

"Never!" agreed Claghorn. "Nevertheless, during this present emergency, we will find indignities imposed upon us by events, unless now we impose them upon ourselves."

"Very well," said Uegus, a humorless smile trembling at his lips. "You shall come with me to the storeroom. I will point out the components to be brought forth and assembled, you shall perform the toil. What do you say to that?"

"I say yes, gladly, if it will be of real utility. However, I can hardly perform the labor for a dozen different theoreticians. Will any others serve beside myself?"

No one responded. Silence was absolute, as if every gentleman present held his breath.

Hagedorn started to speak, but Claghorn interrupted. "Pardon, Hagedorn, but here, finally, we are stuck upon a basic principle, and it must be settled now."

Hagedorn looked desperately around the council. "Has anyone relevant comment?"

"Claghorn must do as his innate nature compels," declared O. Z. Garr in the silkiest of voices. "I cannot dictate to him. As for myself, I can never demean my status as a gentleman of Hagedorn. This creed is as natural to me as drawing breath; if ever it is compromised I become a travesty of a gentleman, a grotesque mask of myself. This is Castle Hagedorn, and we represent the culmination of human civilization. Any compromise therefore becomes degradation; any expedient diminution of our standards becomes dishonor. I have heard the word 'emergency' used. What a deplorable sentiment! To dignify the rat-like snappings and gnashings of such as the Meks with the word 'emergency' is to my mind unworthy of a gentleman of Hagedorn!"

A murmur of approval went around the council table.

Claghorn leaned far back in his seat, chin on his chest, as if in relaxation. His clear blue eyes went from face to face, then returned to O. Z. Garr whom he studied with dispassionate interest. "Obviously you direct your words to me," he said. "I appreciate their malice. But this is a small matter." He looked away from O. Z. Garr, to stare up at the massive diamond and emerald chandelier. "More important is the fact that the council as a whole, in spite of my earnest persuasion, seems to endorse your viewpoint. I can urge, expostulate, insinuate no longer, and I will now leave Castle Hagedorn. I find the atmosphere stifling. I trust that you survive the attack of the Meks, though I doubt that you will. They are a clever resourceful race, untroubled by qualms or preconceptions, and we have long underestimated their quality."

Claghorn rose from his seat, inserted the ivory tablet into its socket. "I bid you all farewell." Hagedorn hastily jumped to his feet, held forth his arms imploringly. "Do not depart in anger, Claghorn! Reconsider! We need your wisdom, your expertise."

"Assuredly you do," said Claghorn. "But even more you need to act upon the advice I have already extended. Until then we have no common ground, and any further interchange is futile and tiresome." He made a brief all-inclusive salute and departed the chamber.

Hagedorn slowly resumed his seat. The others made uneasy motions, coughed, looked up at the chandelier, studied their ivory tablets. O. Z. Garr muttered something to B. F. Wyas who sat beside him, who nodded solemnly. Hagedorn spoke in a subdued voice: "We will miss the presence of Claghorn, his penetrating if unorthodox insights . . . We have accomplished little. Uegus, perhaps you will give thought to the projector under discussion. Xanten, you were to question the captive Mek. O. Z. Garr, you undoubtedly will see to the repair of the energy-cannon . . . Aside from these small matters, it appears that we have evolved no general plan of action, to help either ourselves or Janeil."

Marune spoke. "What of the other castles? Are they still extant? We have had no news. I suggest that we send Birds to each castle, to learn their condition."

Hagedorn nodded. "Yes, this is a wise motion. Perhaps you will see to this, Marune?"

"I will do so."

"Good. We will now adjourn for a time."

The Birds were dispatched by Marune of Aure and one by one returned. Their reports were similar:

"Sea Island is deserted. Marble columns are tumbled along the beach. Pearl Dome is collapsed. Corpses float in the Water Garden."

"Maraval reeks of death. Gentlemen, Peasants, Phane—all dead. Alas! Even the Birds have departed!"

"Delora: *a ros ros ros!* A dismal scene! No sign of life to be found!"

"Alume is desolate. The great wooden door is smashed. The eternal Green Flame is extinguished."

"There is nothing at Halcyon. The Peasants were driven into a pit."

"Tuang: silence."

"Morninglight: death."

## IX

Three days later, Xanten constrained six Birds to a lift chair. He directed them first on a wide sweep around the castle, then south to Far Valley.

The Birds aired their usual complaints, then bounded down the deck in great ungainly hops which threatened to throw Xanten immediately to the pavement. At last gaining the air, they flew up in a spiral. Castle Hagedorn became an intricate miniature far below, each House marked by its unique cluster of turrets and eyries, its own eccentric roof line, its long streaming pennon.

The Birds performed the prescribed circle, skimming the crags and pines of North Ridge. Then, setting wings aslant the upstream, they coasted away toward Far Valley.

Over the pleasant Hagedorn domain flew the Birds and Xanten: over orchards, fields, vineyards, Peasant villages. They crossed Lake Maude with its pavilions and docks, the meadows beyond where the Hagedorn cattle and sheep grazed, and presently came to Far Valley, at the limit of Hagedorn lands.

Xanten indicated where he wished to alight. The Birds, who would have preferred a site closer to the village where they could have watched all that transpired, grumbled and cried out in wrath and set Xanten down so roughly that had he not been alert the shock would have pitched him head over heels.

Xanten alighted without elegance but at least remained on his feet. "Await me here!" he ordered. "Do not stray; attempt no flamboyant tricks among the lift-straps. When I return I wish to see six quiet Birds, in neat formation, lift-straps untwisted and untangled. No bickering, mind you! No loud caterwauling, to attract unfavorable comment! Let all be as I have ordered!"

The Birds sulked, stamped their feet, ducked aside their necks, made insulting comments just under the level of Xanten's hearing. Xanten turned with a final glare of admonition and walked down the lane which led to the village.

The vines were heavy with ripe blackberries and a number of the girls of the village filled baskets. Among them was the girl O. Z. Garr had thought to pre-empt for his personal use. As Xanten passed, he halted and performed a courteous salute. "We have met before, if my recollection is correct."

The girl smiled, a half-rueful, half-whimsical smile. "Your recollection serves you well. We met at Hagedorn, where I was taken a captive.

And later, when you conveyed me here, after dark, though I could not see your face." She extended her basket. "Are you hungry? Will you eat?"

Xanten took several berries. In the course of the conversation he learned that the girl's name was Glys Meadowsweet, that her parents were not known to her, but were presumably gentlefolk of Castle Hagedorn who had exceeded their birth tally. Xanten examined her even more carefully than before but could see resemblance to none of the Hagedorn families. "You might derive from Castle Delora. If there is any family resemblance I can detect, it is to the Cosanzas of Delora—a family noted for the beauty of its ladies."

"You are not married?" she asked artlessly.

"No," said Xanten, and indeed he had dissolved his relationship with Araminta only the day before. "What of you?"

She shook her head. "I would never be gathering blackberries if I were. It is work reserved for maidens. Why do you come to Far Valley?"

"For two reasons. The first to see you." Xanten heard himself say this with surprise. But it was true, he realized with another small shock of surprise. "I have never spoken with you properly and I have always wondered if you were as charming and gay as you are beautiful."

The girl shrugged and Xanten could not be sure whether she were pleased or not, compliments from gentlemen sometimes setting the stage for a sorry aftermath. "Well, no matter. I came also to speak to Claghorn."

"He is yonder," she said in a voice toneless, even cool, and pointed. "He occupies that cottage." She returned to her blackberry picking. Xanten bowed, proceeded to that cottage the girl had indicated.

Claghorn, wearing loose knee-length breeches of gray homespun, worked with an axe chopping faggots into stove-lengths. At the sight of Xanten he halted his toil, leaned on the axe, mopped his forehead. "Ah, Xanten. I am pleased to see you. How are the folk of Castle Hagedorn?"

"As before. There is little to report, even had I come to bring you news."

"Indeed, indeed?" Claghorn leaned on the axe handle, surveyed Xanten with a bright blue gaze.

"At our last meeting," went on Xanten, "I agreed to question the captive Mek. After doing so I am distressed that you were not at hand to assist, so that you might have resolved certain ambiguities in the responses."

"Speak on," said Claghorn. "Perhaps I shall be able to do so now."

"After the council meeting I descended immediately to the storeroom where the Mek was confined. It lacked nutriment; I gave it syrup and a pail of water, which it sipped sparingly, then evinced a desire for minced clams. I summoned kitchen help and sent them for this commodity and the Mek ingested several pints. As I have indicated, it was an unusual Mek, standing as tall as myself and lacking a syrup sac. I conveyed it to a different chamber, a storeroom for brown plush furniture, and ordered it to a seat.

"I looked at the Mek and it looked at me. The quills which I removed were growing back; probably it could at least receive from Meks elsewhere. It seemed a superior beast, showing neither obsequiousness nor respect, and answered my questions without hesitation.

"First I remarked: 'The gentlefolk of the castles are astounded by the revolt of the Meks. We had assumed that your life was satisfactory. Were we wrong?'

" 'Evidently.' I am sure that this was the word signaled, though never had I suspected the Meks of wit of any sort.

" 'Very well then,' I said. 'In what manner?'

" 'Surely it is obvious. We no longer wished to toil at your behest. We wished to conduct our lives by our own traditional standards.'

"The response surprised me. I was unaware that the Meks possessed standards of any kind, much less traditional standards."

Claghorn nodded. "I have been similarly surprised by the scope of the Mek mentality."

"I reproached the Mek: 'Why kill? Why destroy our lives in order to augment your own?' As soon as I had put the question I realized that it had been unhappily phrased. The Mek, I believe, realized the same; however, in reply he signaled something very rapidly which I believe was: 'We knew we must act with decisiveness. Your own protocol made this necessary. We might have returned to Etamin Nine, but we prefer this world Earth, and will make it our own, with our own great slipways, tubs and basking ramps.'

"This seemed clear enough, but I sensed an adumbration extending yet beyond. I said, 'Comprehensible. But why kill, why destroy? You might have taken yourself to a different region. We could not have molested you.'

" 'Infeasible, by your own thinking. A world is too small for two competing races. You intended to send us back to Etamin Nine.'

" 'Ridiculous!' I said. 'Fantasy, absurdity. Do you take me for a mooncalf?'

" 'No,' the creature insisted. 'Two of Castle Hagedorn's notables were seeking the highest post. One assured us that, if elected, this would become his life's aim.'

" 'A grotesque misunderstanding,' I told him. 'One man, a lunatic, can not speak for all men!'

" 'No? One Mek speaks for all Meks. We think with one mind. Are not men of a like sort?'

" 'Each thinks for himself. The lunatic who assured you of this tomfoolery is an evil man. But at least matters are clear. We do not propose to send you to Etamin Nine. Will you withdraw from Janeil, take yourselves to a far land and leave us in peace?'

" 'No. Affairs have proceeded too far. We will now destroy all men. The truth of the statement is clear: one world is too small for two races.'

" 'Unluckily then, I must kill you,' I told him. 'Such acts are not to my liking, but, with opportunity, you would kill as many gentlemen as possible.' At this the creature sprang upon me, and I killed it with an easier mind than had it sat staring.

"Now you know all. It seems that either you or O. Z. Garr stimulated the cataclysm. O. Z. Garr? Unlikely. Impossible. Hence, you, Claghorn, you! have this weight upon your soul!"

Claghorn frowned down at the axe. "Weight, yes. Guilt, no. Ingenuousness, yes; wickedness, no."

Xanten stood back. "Claghorn, your coolness astounds me! Before, when rancorous folk like O. Z. Garr conceived you a lunatic—"

"Peace, Xanten!" exclaimed Claghorn irritably. "This extravagant breast-beating becomes maladroit. What have I done wrong? My fault is that I tried too much. Failure is tragic, but a phthisic face hanging over the cup of the future is worse. I meant to become Hagedorn, I would have sent the slaves home. I failed, the slaves revolted. So do not speak another word. I am bored with the subject. You cannot imagine how your bulging eyes and your concave spine oppress me."

"Bored you may be," cried Xanten. "You decry my eyes, my spine—but what of the thousands dead?"

"How long would they live in any event? Lives are as cheap as fish in the sea. I suggest that you put by your reproaches and devote a similar energy to saving yourself. Do you realize that a means exists? You stare at me blankly. I assure you that what I say is true, but you will never learn the means from me."

"Claghorn," said Xanten, "I flew to this spot intending to blow your arrogant head from your body—" But Claghorn, no longer heeding, had returned to his wood-chopping.

"Claghorn!" cried Xanten.

"Xanten, take your outcries elsewhere, if you please. Remonstrate with your Birds."

Xanten swung on his heel, marched back down the lane. The girls picking berries looked at him questioningly and moved aside. Xanten halted, looked up and down the lane. Glys Meadowsweet was nowhere to be seen. In a new fury he continued. He stopped short. On a fallen tree a hundred feet from the Birds sat Glys Meadowsweet, examining a blade of grass as if it had been an astonishing artifact of the past. The Birds for a marvel had actually obeyed him and waited in a fair semblance of order.

Xanten looked up toward the heavens, kicked at the turf. He drew a deep breath and approached to Glys Meadowsweet. He noted that she had tucked a flower into her long loose hair.

After a second or two she looked up and searched his face. "Why are you so angry?"

Xanten slapped his thigh, seated himself beside her. " 'Angry'? No. I am out of my mind with frustration. Claghorn is as obstreperous as a sharp rock. He knows how Castle Hagedorn can be saved but he will not divulge his secret."

Glys Meadowsweet laughed—an easy merry sound, like nothing Xanten had ever heard at Castle Hagedorn. "Secret? When even I know it?"

"It must be a secret," said Xanten. "He will not tell me."

"Listen. If you fear the Birds will hear it, I will whisper." She spoke a few words into his ear.

Perhaps the sweet breath befuddled Xanten's mind. But the explicit essence of the revelation failed to strike home into his consciousness. He made a sound of sour amusement. "No secret there. Only what the prehistoric Scythians termed 'bathos'. Dishonor to the gentlemen! Do we dance with the Peasants? Do we serve the Birds essences and discuss with them the sheen of our Phanes?"

" 'Dishonor' then?" She jumped to her feet. "Then it is also dishonor for you to talk to me, to sit here with me, to make ridiculous suggestions!"

"I made no suggestions!" protested Xanten. "I sit here in all decorum—"

"Too much decorum, too much honor!" With a display of passion which astounded Xanten, Glys Meadowsweet tore the flower from her hair, hurled it at the ground. "There. Hence!"

"No," said Xanten in sudden humility. He bent, picked up the flower, kissed it, replaced it in her hair. "I am not over-honorable. I will try my best." He put his arms on her shoulders, but she held him away.

"Tell me," she inquired with a very mature severity, "do you own any of those peculiar insect-women?"

"I? Phanes? I own no Phanes."

With this Glys Meadowsweet relaxed and allowed Xanten to embrace her, while the Birds clucked, guffawed and made vulgar scratching sounds with their wings.

x

The summer waned. On June 30 Janeil and Hagedorn celebrated the Fete of Flowers, even though the dike was rising high around Janeil.

Shortly after, Xanten flew six select Birds into Castle Janeil by night and proposed to the council that the population be evacuated by Bird-lift—as many as possible, as many who wished to leave. The council listened with stony faces and without comment passed on.

Xanten returned to Castle Hagedorn. Using the most careful methods, speaking only to trusted comrades, Xanten enlisted thirty or forty cadets and gentlemen to his persuasion, though inevitably he could not keep the doctrinal thesis of his program secret.

The first reaction of the traditionalists was mockery and charges of poltroonery. At Xanten's insistence, challenges were neither issued nor accepted by his hot-blooded associates.

On the evening of September 9 Castle Janeil fell. The news was brought to Castle Hagedorn by excited Birds who told the grim tale again and again in voices ever more hysterical.

Hagedorn, now gaunt and weary, automatically called a council meeting; it took note of the gloomy circumstances. "We then are the last castle! The Meks cannot conceivably do us harm; they can build dikes around our castle walls for twenty years and only work themselves to distraction. We are secure; but yet it is a strange and portentous thought to realize that at last, here at Castle Hagedorn, live the last gentlemen of the race!"

Xanten spoke in a voice strained with earnest conviction: "Twenty years—fifty years—what difference to the Meks? Once they surround us, once they deploy, we are trapped. Do you comprehend that now is our last opportunity to escape the great cage that Castle Hagedorn is to become?"

" 'Escape', Xanten? What a word! For shame!" hooted O. Z. Garr. "Take your wretched band, escape! To steppe or swamp or tundra! Go as you like, with your poltroons, but be good enough to give over these incessant alarms!"

"Garr, I have found conviction since I became a 'poltroon'. Survival is good morality: I have this from the mouth of a noted savant."

"Bah! Such as whom?"

"A. G. Philidor, if you must be informed of every detail."

O. Z. Garr clapped his hand to his forehead. "Do you refer to Philidor the Expiationist? He is of the most extreme stripe, an Expiationist to out-expiate all the rest! Xanten, be sensible, if you please!"

"There are years ahead for all of us," said Xanten in a wooden voice, "if we free ourselves from the castle."

"But the castle is our life!" declared Hagedorn. "In essence, Xanten, what would we be without the castle? Wild animals? Nomads?"

"We would be alive."

O. Z. Garr gave a snort of disgust, turned away to inspect a wall-hanging. Hagedorn shook his head in doubt and perplexity. Beaudry threw his hands up into the air. "Xanten, you have the effect of un-nerving us all. You come in here, inflict this dreadful sense of urgency, but why? In Castle Hagedorn we are as safe as in our mother's arms. What do we gain by throwing aside all—honor, dignity, comfort, civilized niceties—for no other reason than to slink through the wilderness?"

"Janeil was safe," said Xanten. "Today where is Janeil? Death, mil-dewed cloth, sour wine. What we gain by 'slinking' is the assurance of survival. And I plan much more than simple 'slinking'."

"I can conceive of a hundred occasions when death is better than life!" snapped Isseth. "Must I die in dishonor and disgrace? Why may my last years not be passed in dignity?"

Into the room came B. F. Robarth. "Councilmen, the Meks approach Castle Hagedorn."

Hagedorn cast a wild look around the chamber. "Is there a consensus? What must we do?"

Xanten threw up his hands. "Everyone must do as he thinks best! I argue no more: I am done. Hagedorn, will you adjourn the council so that we may be about our affairs? I to my 'slinking'?"

"Council is adjourned," said Hagedorn, and all went up to stand on the ramparts.

Up the avenue into the castle trooped Peasants from the surround-ing countryside, packets slung over their shoulders. Across the valley, at the edge of Bartholomew Forest, was a clot of power-wagons and an amorphous brown-gold mass: Meks.

Aure pointed west. "Look—there they come, up the Long Swale." He turned, peered east. "And look, there at Bambridge: Meks!"

By common consent, all swung about to scan North Ridge. O. Z.

Garr pointed to a quiet line of brown-gold shapes. "There they wait, the vermin! They have penned us in! Well then, let them wait!" He swung away, rode the lift down to the plaza, crossed swiftly to Zumbeld House, where he worked the rest of the afternoon with his Gloriana, of whom he expected great things.

The following day the Meks formalized the investment. Around Castle Hagedorn a great circle of Mek activity made itself apparent: sheds, warehouses, barracks. Within this periphery, just beyond the range of the energy-cannon, power-wagons thrust up mounds of dirt.

During the night these mounds lengthened toward the castle; similarly the night after. At last the purpose of the mounds became clear: they were a protective cover above passages or tunnels leading toward the crag on which Castle Hagedorn rested.

The following day several of the mounds reached the base of the crag. Presently from the far end began to flow a succession of power-wagons loaded with rubble. They issued, dumped their loads and once again entered the tunnels.

Eight of these above-ground tunnels had been established. From each trundled endless loads of dirt and rock, gnawed from the crag on which Castle Hagedorn sat. To the gentlefolk who crowded the parapets the meaning of the work at last became clear.

"They make no attempt to bury us," said Hagedorn. "They merely mine out the crag from below us!"

On the sixth day of the siege, a great segment of the hillside shuddered, slumped, and a tall pinnacle of rock reaching almost up to the base of the walls collapsed.

"If this continues," muttered Beaudry, "our time will be less than that of Janeil."

"Come then," called O. Z. Garr in sudden energy. "Let us try our energy-cannon. We'll blast open their wretched tunnels, and what will the rascals do then?" He went to the nearest emplacement, shouted down for Peasants to remove the tarpaulin.

Xanten, who happened to stand nearby, said, "Allow me to assist you." He jerked away the tarpaulin. "Shoot now, if you will."

O. Z. Garr stared at him uncomprehendingly, then leapt forward, swiveled the great projector about so that it aimed at a mound. He pulled the switch; the air crackled in front of the ringed snout, rippled, flickered with purple sparks. The target area steamed, became black, then dark red, then slumped into an incandescent crater. But the underlying earth, twenty feet in thickness, afforded too much insulation; the molten puddle became white-hot but failed to spread or deepen.

The energy-cannon gave a sudden chatter, as electricity short-circuited through corroded insulation. The cannon went dead.

O. Z. Garr inspected the mechanism in anger and disappointment. Then, with a gesture of repugnance, he turned away. The cannons were clearly of limited effectiveness.

Two hours later, on the east side of the crag, another great sheet of rock collapsed, and just before sunset, a similar mass sheared from the western face, where the wall of the castle rose almost in an uninterrupted line from the cliff below.

At midnight Xanten and those of his persuasion, with their children and consorts, departed Castle Hagedorn. Six teams of Birds shuttled from the flight deck to a meadow near Far Valley, and long before dawn had transported the entire group.

There were none to bid them farewell.

## XI

A week later another section of the east cliff fell away, taking a length of rock-melt buttress with it. At the tunnel mouths the piles of excavated rubble had become alarmingly large.

The terraced south face of the crag was the least disturbed; the most spectacular damage having occurred to east and west. Suddenly, a month after the initial assault, a great section of the terraces slumped forward, leaving an irregular crevasse which interrupted the avenue and hurled down the statues of former notables emplaced at intervals along the avenue's balustrade.

Hagedorn called a council meeting. "Circumstances," he said in a wan attempt at facetiousness, "have not bettered themselves. Our most pessimistic expectations have been exceeded. A dismal situation! I confess that I do not relish the prospect of toppling to my death among all my smashed belongings."

Aure made a desperate gesture. "A similar thought haunts me! Death —what of that? All must die! But when I think of my precious belongings I become sick. My books trampled! My fragile vases smashed! My tabards ripped! My rugs buried! My Phanes strangled! My heirloom chandeliers flung aside! These are my nightmares."

"Your possessions are no less precious than any others," said Beaudry shortly. "Still they have no life of their own; when we are gone, who cares what happens to them?"

Marune winced. "A year ago I put down eighteen dozen flasks of prime essence; twelve dozen Green Rain; three each of Balthazar and Faidor. Think of these, if you would contemplate tragedy!"

"Had we only known!" groaned Aure. "I would have—I would have . . ." His voice trailed away.

O. Z. Garr stamped his foot in impatience. "Let us avoid lamentation at all costs! We had a choice, remember? Xanten beseeched us to flee; now he and his like go skulking and foraging through the north mountains with the Expiationists. We chose to remain, for better or worse, and unluckily the 'worse' is occurring. We must accept the fact like gentlemen."

To this the council gave melancholy assent. Hagedorn brought forth a flask of priceless Rhadamanth, and poured with a prodigality which previously would have been unthinkable. "Since we have no future— to our glorious past!"

That night disturbances were noted here and there around the ring of Mek investment: flames at four separate points, a faint sound of hoarse shouting. On the following day it seemed that the tempo of activity had lessened a trifle.

But during the afternoon a vast segment of the east cliff fell away. A moment later, as if after majestic deliberation, the tall east wall split off, toppled, leaving the backs of six great houses exposed to the open sky.

An hour after sunset a team of Birds settled to the flight-deck. Xanten jumped from the seat. He ran down the circular staircase to the ramparts, came down to the plaza by Hagedorn's palace.

Hagedorn, summoned by a kinsman, came forth to stare at Xanten in surprise. "What do you do here? We expected you to be safely north with the Expiationists!"

"The Expiationists are not safely north," said Xanten. "They have joined the rest of us. We are fighting."

Hagedorn's jaw dropped. "Fighting? The gentlemen are fighting Meks?"

"As vigorously as possible."

Hagedorn shook his head in wonder. "The Expiationists too? I understood that they had planned to flee north."

"Some have done so, including A. G. Philidor. There are factions among the Expiationists just as here. Most are not ten miles distant. The same with the Nomads. Some have taken their power-wagons and fled. The rest kill Meks with fanatic fervor. Last night you saw our work. We fired four storage warehouses, destroyed syrup tanks, killed a hundred or more Meks, as well as a dozen power-wagons. We suffered losses, which hurt us, because there are few of us and many

Meks. This is why I am here. We need more men. Come fight beside us!"

Hagedorn turned, motioned to the great central plaza. "I will call forth the folk from their Houses. Talk to everyone."

The Birds, complaining bitterly at the unprecedented toil, worked all night, transporting gentlemen, who, sobered by the imminent destruction of Castle Hagedorn, were now willing to abandon all scruples and fight for their lives. The staunch traditionalists still refused to compromise their honor, but Xanten gave them cheerful assurance: "Remain here then, prowling the castle like so many furtive rats. Take what comfort you can in the fact that you are being protected; the future holds little else for you."

And many who heard him stalked away in disgust.

Xanten turned to Hagedorn. "What of you? Do you come or do you stay?"

Hagedorn heaved a deep sigh, almost a groan. "Castle Hagedorn is at an end. No matter what the eventuality. I will come with you."

The situation suddenly had altered. The Meks, established in a loose ring around Castle Hagedorn, had calculated upon no resistance from the countryside and little from the castle. They had established their barracks and syrup depots with thought only for convenience and none for defense; raiding parties, consequently, were able to approach, inflict damages and withdraw before sustaining serious losses of their own. Those Meks posted along North Ridge were harassed almost continuously and finally were driven down with many losses. The circle around Castle Hagedorn became a cusp; then two days later, after the destruction of five more syrup depots, the Meks drew back even farther. Throwing up earthworks before the two tunnels leading under the south face of the crag, they established a more or less tenable defensive position, but now instead of beleaguering, they became the beleaguered, though still fighting.

Within the area thus defended the Meks concentrated their remaining syrup stocks, tools, weapons, ammunition. The area outside the earthworks was floodlit after dark and guarded by Meks armed with pellet-guns, making any frontal assault impractical.

For a day the raiders kept to the shelter of the surrounding orchards, appraising the new situation. Then a tactic was attempted. Six light carriages were improvised and loaded with bladders of a light inflammable oil, with a fire grenade attached. To each of these carriages ten Birds were harnessed, and at midnight sent aloft, with a man for each carriage. Flying high, the Birds then glided down through the darkness over the Mek position, where the fire bombs were dropped.

The area instantly seethed with flame. The syrup depot burnt; the power-wagons, awakened by the flames, rolled frantically back and forth, crushing Meks and stores, colliding with each other, adding vastly to the terror of the flames. The Meks who survived took shelter in the tunnels. Certain of the floodlights were extinguished and, taking advantage of the confusion, the men attacked the earthworks.

After a short bitter battle, the men killed all the sentinels and took up positions commanding the mouths of the tunnels, which now contained all that remained of the Mek army. It seemed as if the Mek uprising had been put down.

XII

The flames died. The human warriors—three hundred men from the castle, two hundred Expiationists and about three hundred Nomads —gathered about the tunnel mouth and, during the balance of the night, considered methods to deal with the immured Meks.

At sunrise those men of Castle Hagedorn whose children and consorts were yet within the castle went to bring them forth. With them, upon their return, came a group of castle gentlemen: among them Beaudry, O. Z. Garr, Isseth, and Aure. They greeted their one-time peers, Hagedorn, Xanten, Claghorn and others, crisply, but with a certain austere detachment, which recognized that loss of prestige incurred by those who fought Meks as if they were equals.

"Now what is to happen?" Beaudry inquired of Hagedorn. "The Meks are trapped but you can't bring them forth. Not impossibly they have syrup stored within for the power-wagons. They may well survive for months."

O. Z. Garr, assessing the situation from the standpoint of a military theoretician, came forward with a plan of action. "Fetch down the cannon—or have your underlings do so—and mount them on power-wagons. When the vermin are sufficiently weak, roll the cannon in and wipe out all but a labor force for the castle. We formerly worked four hundred, and this should suffice."

"Ha!" exclaimed Xanten. "It gives me great pleasure to inform you that this will never be. If any Meks survive they will repair the space-ships and instruct us in the maintenance and we will then transport them and Peasants back to their native worlds."

"How then do you expect us to maintain our lives?" demanded Garr coldly.

"You have the syrup generator. Fit yourself with sacs and drink syrup."

Garr tilted back his head, stared coldly down his nose. "This is your voice, yours alone, and your insolent opinion. Others are to be heard from. Hagedorn, is this your philosophy, that civilization should wither?"

"It need not wither," said Hagedorn, "provided that all of us—you as well as we—toil for it. There can be no more slaves. I have become convinced of this."

O. Z. Garr turned on his heel, swept back up the avenue into the castle, followed by the most traditional-minded of his comrades. A few moved aside and talked among themselves in low tones, with one or two black looks for Xanten and Hagedorn.

From the ramparts of the castle came a sudden outcry: "The Meks! They are taking the castle! They swarm up the lower passages! Attack, save us!"

The men below stared up in consternation. Even as they looked the castle portals swung shut.

"How is this possible?" demanded Hagedorn. "I swear all entered the tunnels!"

"It is only too clear," said Xanten bitterly. "While they undermined, they drove a tunnel up to the lower levels!"

Hagedorn started forward as if he would charge up the crag alone, then halted. "We must drive them out! Unthinkable that they pillage our castle!"

"Unfortunately," said Claghorn, "the walls bar us as effectually as they did the Meks."

"We can send up a force by Bird-car! Once we consolidate, we can exterminate them!"

Claghorn shook his head. "They can wait on the ramparts and flight-deck and shoot down the Birds as they approach. Even if we secured a foothold there would be great bloodshed: one of us killed for every one of them. And they still outnumber us three or four to one."

Hagedorn groaned. "The thought of them revelling among my possessions, strutting about in my clothes, swilling my essences—it sickens me!"

"Listen!" said Claghorn. From on high they heard the hoarse yells of men, the crackle of energy-cannon. "Some of them, at least, hold out on the ramparts!"

Xanten went to a nearby group of Birds who were for once awed and subdued by events. "Lift me up above the castle, out of range of the pellets, but where I can see what the Meks do!"

"Care, take care!" croaked one of the Birds. "Ill things occur at the castle."

"Never mind! Convey me up, above the ramparts!"

The Birds lifted him, swung in a great circle around the crag and above the castle, sufficiently distant to be safe from the Mek pellet-guns.

Beside those cannon which yet operated stood thirty men and women. Between the great Houses, the rotunda and the palace, everywhere the cannon could not be brought to bear, swarmed Meks. The plaza was littered with corpses: gentlemen, ladies and their children —all those who had elected to remain at Castle Hagedorn.

At one of the cannon stood O. Z. Garr. Spying Xanten he gave a shout of hysterical rage, swung up the cannon, fired a bolt. The Birds, screaming, tried to swerve aside, but the bolt smashed two. Birds, car, Xanten, fell in a great tangle. By some miracle, the four yet alive caught their balance and a hundred feet from the ground, with a frenzied groaning effort, they slowed their fall, steadied, hovered an instant, sank to the ground.

Xanten staggered free of the tangle. Men came running. "Are you safe?" called Claghorn.

"Safe, yes. Frightened as well!" Xanten took a deep breath, went to sit on an outcrop of rock.

"What's happening up there?" asked Claghorn.

"All dead," said Xanten, "all but a score. Garr has gone mad. He fired on me."

"Look! Meks on the ramparts!" cried A. L. Morgan.

"There!" cried someone else. "Men! They jump! . . . No, they are flung!"

Some were men, some were Meks whom they had dragged with them; with awful slowness they toppled to their deaths. No more fell. Castle Hagedorn was in the hands of the Meks.

Xanten considered the complex silhouette, at once so familiar and so strange. "They can't hope to hold out. We need only destroy the sun-cells, and they can synthesize no syrup."

"Let us do it now," said Claghorn, "before they think of this and man the cannon! Birds!"

He went off to give the orders, and forty Birds, each clutching two rocks the size of a man's head, flapped up, circled the castle and presently returned to report the sun-cells had been destroyed.

Xanten said, "All that remains is to seal the tunnel entrances against a sudden eruption, which might catch us off guard—then patience."

"What of the Peasants in the stables—and the Phanes?" asked Hagedorn in a forlorn voice.

Xanten gave his head a slow shake. "He who was not an Expiation-ist before must become one now."

Claghorn muttered, "They can survive two months at most—no more."

But two months passed, and three months, and four months. Then one morning the great portals opened, a haggard Mek stumbled forth.

He signaled: "Men: we starve. We have maintained your treasures. Give us our lives or we destroy all before we die."

Claghorn responded: "These are our terms. We give you your lives. You must clean the castle, remove and bury the corpses. You must re-pair the spaceships and teach us all you know regarding them. We will then transport you to Etamin Nine."

"The terms you offer are accepted."

Five years later Xanten and Glys Meadowsweet, with their two chil-dren, had reason to travel north from their home near Sande River. They took occasion to visit Castle Hagedorn, where now lived only two or three dozen folk, among them Hagedorn.

He had aged, so it seemed to Xanten. His hair was white; his face, once bluff and hearty, had become thin, almost waxen. Xanten could not determine his mood.

They stood in the shade of a walnut tree, with castle and crag loom-ing above them. "This is now a great museum," said Hagedorn. "I am curator, and this will be the function of all the Hagedorns who come after me, for there is incalculable treasure to guard and maintain. Al-ready the feeling of antiquity has come to the castle. The Houses are alive with ghosts. I see them often, especially on the nights of the fetes . . . Ah, those were the times, were they not, Xanten?"

"Yes indeed," said Xanten. He touched the heads of his two children. "Still, I have no wish to return to them. We are men now, on our own world, as we never were before."

Hagedorn gave a somewhat regretful assent. He looked up at the vast structure, as if now were the first occasion he had laid eyes on it. "The folk of the future—what will they think of Castle Hagedorn? Its treasures, its books, its tabards?"

"They will come, they will marvel," said Xanten. "Almost as I do today."

"There is much at which to marvel. Will you come within, Xanten? There are still flasks of noble essence laid by."

"Thank you no," said Xanten. "There is too much to stir old mem-ories. We will go our way, and I think that we will do so immediately."

Hagedorn nodded sadly. "I understand very well. I myself am often given to reverie these days. Well then, good-by, and journey home with pleasure."

"We will do so, Hagedorn. Thank you and good-by," said Xanten, and turned away from Castle Hagedorn, toward the world of men.

*Larry Niven*

For the last dozen years or so, what we might call "hard science fiction" has receded somewhat into the background. By hard science fiction, I mean those stories in which the details of science play an important role and in which the author is accurate about those details, too, and takes the trouble to explain them clearly.

In its place, there has moved into the forefront the emotional story in which science is relegated to the background. Literary style, not physical theory, is what counts; experimentation in form, not in the laboratory; the wrenching of souls, rather than of minds.

As for myself (for I will conceal nothing from you) I'm a hard science fiction man myself. For instance, in the same issue of the same magazine in which Harlan Ellison published "I Have No Mouth and I Must Scream" which was all emotion and which won a Hugo, I published "Billiard Ball" which was all thought and which didn't win a Hugo.

Naturally, miscarriages of justice like this cause me to brood, but I feel better when it turns out that there are still hard science fiction writers among the younger generation. Ben Bova, for instance, writes hard science fiction, and so does Larry Niven.

What's more, Larry Niven made it big and won a Hugo with his excellent story, "Neutron Star."

The only trouble with the victory was that when I read his story I was overwhelmed with grief. I don't mean merely the grief that overcomes me whenever someone else wins a Hugo. I mean a highly special grief over the nature of the plot.

You see, I write a science article in every issue of *The Magazine of Fantasy and Science Fiction* (and have just completed my 151st article as I write this). In the May 1966 issue I wrote an article called "Time and Tide" and as I thought back on that particular article I was overwhelmed with poignant sorrow. The plot of "Neutron Star" was implicit in my article and if I had only thought fiction-wise instead of article-wise, *I* might have written the story.

Eventually, of course, I met Larry Niven, a remarkably quiet fellow, who dresses most neatly and conservatively, has a cleanshaven square countenance, a soft voice, and a penchant for speculating on the sex life of Superman.

"Listen, Larry," I said, shaking my head sadly, "I once wrote an article entitled 'Time and Tide' which dealt with—"

"I know," said Larry calmly. "It was when I read that article that I got the idea for 'Neutron Star.'"

It is a tribute to the essential sweetness of my character, that that man still lives!

# 6

# NEUTRON STAR

I

The Skydiver dropped out of hyperspace an even million miles above the neutron star. I needed a minute to place myself against the stellar background and another to find the distortion Sonya Laskin had mentioned before she died. It was to my left, an area the apparent size of the Earth's moon. I swung the ship around to face it.

Curdled stars, muddled stars, stars that had been stirred with a spoon.

The neutron star was in the center, of course, though I couldn't see it and hadn't expected to. It was only eleven miles across, and cool. A billion years had passed since BVS-1 burned by fusion fire. Millions of years, at least, since the cataclysmic two weeks during which BVS-1 was an X-ray star, burning at a temperature of five billion degrees Kelvin. Now it showed only by its mass.

The ship began to turn by itself. I felt the pressure of the fusion drive. Without help from me, my faithful metal watchdog was putting me in hyperbolic orbit that would take me within one mile of the neutron star's surface. Twenty-four hours to fall, twenty-four hours to rise . . . and during that time, something would try to kill me. As something had killed the Laskins.

The same type of autopilot, with the same program, had chosen the Laskins' orbit. It had not caused their ship to collide with the star. I could trust the autopilot. I could even change its program.

I really ought to.

How did I get myself into this hole?

The drive went off after ten minutes of maneuvering. My orbit was established, in more ways than one. I knew what would happen if I tried to back out now.

All I'd done was walk into a drugstore to get a new battery for my lighter!

Right in the middle of the store, surrounded by three floors of sales counters, was the new 2603 Sinclair intrasystem yacht. I'd come for a battery, but I stayed to admire. It was a beautiful job, small and sleek and streamlined and blatantly different from anything that's ever been built. I wouldn't have flown it for anything, but I had to admit it was pretty. I ducked my head through the door to look at the control panel. You never saw so many dials. When I pulled my head out, all the customers were looking in the same direction. The place had gone startlingly quiet.

I can't blame them for staring. A number of aliens were in the store, mainly shopping for souvenirs, but they were staring too. A puppeteer is unique. Imagine a headless, three-legged centaur wearing two Cecil the Seasick Sea Serpent puppets on his arms, and you'll have something like the right picture. But the arms are weaving necks, and the puppets are real heads, flat and brainless, with wide flexible lips. The brain is under a bony hump set between the bases of the necks. This puppeteer wore only its own coat of brown hair, with a mane that extended all the way up its spine to form a thick mat over the brain. I'm told that the way they wear the mane indicates their status in society, but to me it could have been anything from a dock worker to a jeweler to the president of General Products.

I watched with the rest as it came across the floor, not because I'd never seen a puppeteer, but because there is something beautiful about the dainty way they move on those slender legs and tiny hooves. I watched it come straight toward me, closer and closer. It stopped a foot away, looked me over and said, "You are Beowulf Shaeffer, former chief pilot for Nakamura Lines."

Its voice was a beautiful contralto with not a trace of accent. A puppeteer's mouths are not only the most flexible speech organs around, but also the most sensitive hands. The tongues are forked and pointed, the wide, thick lips have little fingerlike knobs along the rims. Imagine a watchmaker with a sense of taste in his fingertips . . .

I cleared my throat. "That's right."

It considered me from two directions. "You would be interested in a high-paying job?"

"I'd be fascinated in a high-paying job."

"I am our equivalent of the regional president of General Products. Please come with me, and we will discuss this elsewhere."

I followed it into a displacement booth. Eyes followed me all the way. It was embarrassing, being accosted in a public drugstore by a two-headed monster. Maybe the puppeteer knew it. Maybe it was testing me to see how badly I needed money.

My need was great. Eight months had passed since Nakamura Lines folded. For some time before that, I had been living very high on the hog, knowing that my back pay would cover my debts. I never saw that back pay. It was quite a crash, Nakamura Lines. Respectable middle-aged businessmen took to leaving their hotel windows without their lift belts. Me, I kept spending. If I'd started living frugally, my creditors would have done some checking . . . and I'd have ended in debtor's prison.

The puppeteer dialed thirteen fast digits with its tongue. A moment later we were elsewhere. Air puffed out when I opened the booth door, and I swallowed to pop my ears.

"We are on the roof of the General Products building." The rich contralto voice thrilled along my nerves, and I had to remind myself that it was an alien speaking, not a lovely woman. "You must examine this spacecraft while we discuss your assignment."

I stepped outside a little cautiously, but it wasn't the windy season. The roof was at ground level. That's the way we build on We Made It. Maybe it has something to do with the fifteen-hundred-mile-an-hour winds we get in summer and winter, when the planet's axis of rotation runs through its primary, Procyon. The winds are our planet's only tourist attraction, and it would be a shame to slow them down by planting skyscrapers in their path. The bare, square concrete roof was surrounded by endless square miles of desert, not like the deserts of other inhabited worlds, but an utterly lifeless expanse of fine sand just crying to be planted with ornamental cactus. We've tried that. The wind blows the plants away.

The ship lay on the sand beyond the roof. It was a #2 General Products hull: a cylinder three hundred feet long and twenty feet through, pointed at both ends and with a slight wasp-waist constriction near the tail. For some reason it was lying on its side, with the landing shocks still folded in at the tail.

Ever notice how all ships have begun to look the same? A good ninety-five percent of today's spacecrafts are built around one of the four General Products hulls. It's easier and safer to build that way, but somehow all ships end as they began: mass-produced look-alikes.

The hulls are delivered fully transparent, and you use paint where you feel like it. Most of this particular hull had been left transparent. Only the nose had been painted, around the life-system. There was no major reaction drive. A series of retractable attitude jets had been mounted in the sides, and the hull was pierced with smaller holes, square and round—for observational instruments. I could see them gleaming through the hull.

The puppeteer was moving toward the nose, but something made me turn toward the stern for a closer look at the landing shocks.

They were bent. Behind the curved, transparent hull panels, some tremendous pressure had forced the metal to flow like warm wax, back and into the pointed stern.

"What did this?" I asked.

"We do not know. We wish strenuously to find out."

"What do you mean?"

"Have you heard of the neutron star BVS-1?"

I had to think a moment. "First neutron star ever found, and so far the only. Someone located it two years ago by stellar displacement."

"BVS-1 was found by the Institute of Knowledge on Jinx. We learned through a go-between that the Institute wished to explore the star. They needed a ship to do it. They had not yet sufficient money. We offered to supply them with a ship's hull, with the usual guarantees, if they would turn over to us all data they acquired through using our ship."

"Sounds fair enough." I didn't ask why they hadn't done their own exploring. Like most sentient vegetarians, puppeteers find discretion to be the *only* part of valor.

"Two humans named Peter Laskin and Sonya Laskin wished to use the ship. They intended to come within one mile of the surface in a hyperbolic orbit. At some point during their trip, an unknown force apparently reached through the hull to do this to the landing shocks. The unknown force also seems to have killed the pilots."

"But that's impossible. Isn't it?"

"You see the point. Come with me." The puppeteer trotted toward the bow.

I saw the point, all right. Nothing, but nothing can get through a General Products hull. No kind of electromagnetic energy except visible light. No kind of matter, from the smallest subatomic particle to the fastest meteor. That's what the company's advertisements claim, and the guarantee backs them up. I've never doubted it, and I've never heard of a General Products hull being damaged by a weapon or by anything else.

On the other hand, a General Products hull is as ugly as it is functional. The puppeteer-owned company could be badly hurt if it got around that something *could* get through a company hull. But I didn't see where I came in.

We rode an escalladder into the nose.

The lifesystem was in two compartments. Here the Laskins had used heat-reflective paint. In the conical control cabin the hull had been divided into windows. The relaxation room behind it was a windowless reflective silver. From the back wall of the relaxation room an access tube ran aft, opening on various instruments and the hyperdrive motors.

There were two acceleration couches in the control cabin. Both had **been** torn loose from their mountings and wadded into the nose like so much tissue paper, crushing the instrument panel. The backs of the crumpled couches were splashed with rust brown. Flecks of the same color were all over everything, the walls, the windows, the viewscreens. It was as if something had hit the couches from behind: something like a dozen paint-filled toy balloons, striking with tremendous force.

"That's blood," I said.

"That is correct. Human circulatory fluid."

II

Twenty-four hours to fall.

I spent most of the first twelve hours in the relaxation room, trying to read. Nothing significant was happening, except that a few times I saw the phenomenon Sonya Laskin had mentioned in her last report. When a star went directly behind the invisible BVS-1, a halo formed. BVS-1 was heavy enough to bend light around it, displacing most stars to the sides; but when a star went directly behind the neutron star, its light was displaced to all sides at once. Result: a tiny circle which flashed once and was gone almost before the eye could catch it.

I'd known next to nothing about neutron stars the day the puppeteer picked me up. Now I was an expert. But I still had no idea what was waiting for me when I got down there.

All the matter you're ever likely to meet will be normal matter, composed of a nucleus of protons and neutrons surrounded by electrons in quantum energy states. In the heart of any star there is a second kind of matter: for there, the tremendous pressure is enough to smash the electron shells. The result is degenerate matter: nuclei forced together by pressure and gravity, but held apart by the mutual repulsion of the more or less continuous electron 'gas' around them. The right circumstances may create a third type of matter.

Given: a burnt-out white dwarf with a mass greater than 1.44 times the mass of the Sun—Chandrasekhar's Limit, named for an Indian-American astronomer of the nineteen hundreds. In such a mass the electron pressure alone would not be able to hold the electrons back from the nuclei. Electrons would be forced against protons—to make neutrons. In one blazing explosion most of the star would change from a compressed mass of degenerate matter to a closely packed lump of neutrons: neutronium, theoretically the densest matter possible in this universe. Most of the remaining normal and degenerate matter would be blown away by the liberated heat.

For two weeks the star would give off X rays, as its core temperature dropped from five billion degrees Kelvin to five hundred million. After that it would be a light-emitting body perhaps ten to twelve miles across: the next best thing to invisible. It was not strange that BVS-1 was the first neutron star ever found.

Neither is it strange that the Institute of Knowledge on Jinx would have spent a good deal of time and trouble looking. Until BVS-1 was found, neutronium and neutron stars were only theories. The examination of an actual neutron star could be of tremendous importance. Neutron stars could give us the key to true gravity control.

Mass of BVS-1: 1.3 times the mass of Sol, approximately.

Diameter of BVS-1 (estimated): eleven miles of neutronium, covered by half a mile of degenerate matter, covered by maybe twelve feet of ordinary matter.

Escape velocity: 130,000 mps, approximately.

Nothing else was known of the tiny black star until the Laskins went in to look. Now the Institute knew one thing more. The star's spin.

"A mass that large can distort space by its rotation," said the puppeteer. "The Institute ship's projected hyperbola was twisted across itself in such a way that we can deduce the star's period of rotation to be two minutes, twenty-seven seconds."

The bar was somewhere in the General Products building. I don't know just where, and with the transfer booths it doesn't matter. I kept staring at the puppeteer bartender. Naturally only a puppeteer would be served by a puppeteer bartender, since any biped would resent knowing that somebody made his drink with his mouth. I had already decided to get dinner somewhere else.

"I see your problem," I said. "Your sales will suffer if it gets out that something can reach through one of your hulls and smash a crew to bloody smears. But where do I fit in?"

"We wish to repeat the experiment of Sonya Laskin and Peter Laskin. We must find—"

"With me?"

"Yes. We must find out what it is that our hulls cannot stop. Naturally you may—"

"But I won't."

"We are prepared to offer one million stars."

I was tempted, but only for a moment. "Forget it."

"Naturally you will be allowed to build your own ship, starting with a #2 General Products hull."

"Thanks, but I'd like to go on living."

"You would dislike being confined. I find that We Made It has re-established the debtor's prison. If General Products made public your accounts . . ."

"Now, *just* a—"

"You owe money in the close order of five hundred thousand stars. We will pay your creditors before you leave. If you return—" I had to admire the creature's honesty in not saying *when*—"we will pay you the remainder. You may be asked to speak to news commentators concerning the voyage, in which case there will be more stars."

"You say I can build my own ship?"

"Naturally. This is not a voyage of exploration. We want you to return safely."

"It's a deal," I said.

After all, the puppeteer had tried to blackmail me. What happened next would be its own fault.

They built my ship in two weeks flat. They started with a #2 General Products hull, just like the one around the Institute of Knowledge ship, and the lifesystem was practically a duplicate of the Laskins', but there the resemblance ended. There were no instruments to observe neutron stars. Instead, there was a fusion motor big enough for a Jinx warliner. In my ship, which I now called Skydiver, the drive would produce thirty gees at the safety limit. There was a laser cannon big enough to punch a hole through We Made It's moon. The puppeteer wanted me to feel safe, and now I did, for I could fight and I could run. Especially I could run.

I heard the Laskins' last broadcast through half a dozen times. Their unnamed ship had dropped out of hyperspace a million miles above BVS-1. Gravity warp would have prevented their getting closer in hyperspace. While her husband was crawling through the access tube for an instrument check, Sonya Laskin had called the Institute of Knowledge. ". . . we can't see it yet, not with the naked eye. But we can see where it is. Every time some star or other goes behind it, there's a little ring of light. Just a minute. Peter's ready to use the telescope . . ."

Then the star's mass had cut the hyperspacial link. It was expected, and nobody had worried—then. Later, the same effect must have stopped them from escaping whatever attacked them, into hyperspace.

When would-be rescuers found the ship, only the radar and the cameras were still running. They didn't tell us much. There had been no camera in the cabin. But the forward camera gave us, for one instant, a speed-blurred view of the neutron star. It was a featureless disc the orange color of perfect barbecue coals, if you know someone who can afford to burn wood. This object had been a neutron star a long time.

"There'll be no need to paint the ship," I told the president.

"You should not make such a trip with the walls transparent. You would go insane."

"I'm no flatlander. The mind-wrenching sight of naked space fills me with mild, but waning interest. I want to know nothing's sneaking up behind me."

The day before I left, I sat alone in the General Products bar letting the puppeteer bartender make me drinks with his mouth. He did it well. Puppeteers were scattered around the bar in twos and threes, with a couple of men for variety; but the drinking hour had not yet arrived. The place felt empty.

I was pleased with myself. My debts were all paid, not that that would matter where I was going. I would leave with not a mini-credit to my name; with nothing but the ship . . .

All told, I was well out of a sticky situation. I hoped I'd like being a rich exile.

I jumped when the newcomer sat down across from me. He was a foreigner, a middle-aged man wearing an expensive night-black business suit and a snow-white asymmetric beard. I let my face freeze and started to get up.

"Sit down, Mr. Shaeffer."

"Why?"

He told me by showing me a blue disc. An Earth-government ident. I looked it over to show I was alert, not because I'd know an ersatz from the real thing.

"My name is Sigmund Ausfaller," said the government man. "I wish to say a few words concerning your assignment on behalf of General Products."

I nodded, not saying anything.

"A record of your verbal contract was sent to us as a matter of course. I noticed some peculiar things about it. Mr. Shaeffer, will you really take such a risk for only five hundred thousand stars?"

"I'm getting twice that."

"But you only keep half of it. The rest goes to pay debts. Then there are taxes. But never mind. What occurred to me was that a spaceship is a spaceship, and yours is very well armed and has powerful legs. An admirable fighting ship, if you were moved to sell it."

"But it isn't mine."

"There are those who would not ask. On Canyon, for example, or the Isolationist party of Wonderland."

I said nothing.

"Or, you might be planning a career of piracy. A risky business, piracy, and I don't take the notion seriously."

I hadn't even thought about piracy. But I'd have to give up on Wonderland . . .

"What I would like to say is this, Mr. Shaeffer. A single entrepreneur, if he were sufficiently dishonest, could do terrible damage to the reputation of all human beings everywhere. Most species find it necessary to police the ethics of their own members, and we are no exception. It occurred to me that you might not take your ship to the neutron star at all; that you would take it elsewhere and sell it. The puppeteers do not make invulnerable war vessels. They are pacifists. Your Skydiver is unique.

"Hence I have asked General Products to allow me to install a remote control bomb in the Skydiver. Since it is inside the hull, the hull cannot protect you. I had it installed this afternoon.

"Now, notice! If you have not reported within a week I will set off the bomb. There are several worlds within a week's hyperspace flight of here, but all recognize the dominion of Earth. If you flee, you must leave your ship within a week, so I hardly think you will land on a nonhabitable world. Clear?"

"Clear."

"If I am wrong, you may take a lie-detector test and prove it. Then you may punch me in the nose, and I will apologize handsomely."

I shook my head. He stood up, bowed and left me sitting there cold sober.

Four films had been taken from the Laskins' cameras. In the time left to me, I ran through them several times, without seeing anything out of the way. If the ship had run through a gas cloud, the impact could have killed the Laskins. At perihelion they were moving at better than half the speed of light. But there would have been friction, and I saw no sign of heating in the films. If something alive had attacked them, the beast was invisible to radar and to an enormous range of light frequencies. If the attitude jets had fired accidentally—I was clutching at straws—the light showed on none of the films.

There would be savage magnetic forces near BVS-1, but that couldn't have done any damage. No such force could penetrate a General Products hull. Neither could heat, except in special bands of radiated light, bands visible to at least one of the puppeteers' alien customers. I hold adverse opinions on the General Products hull, but they all concern the dull anonymity of the design. Or maybe I resent the fact that General Products holds a near-monopoly on spacecraft hulls and isn't owned by human beings. But if I'd had to trust my life to, say, the Sinclair yacht I'd seen in the drugstore, I'd have chosen jail.

Jail was one of my three choices. But I'd be there for life. Ausfaller would see to that.

Or I could run for it in the Skydiver. But no world within reach would have me, that is. Of course, if I could find an undiscovered Earthlike world within a week of We Made It . . .

Fat chance. I preferred BVS-1 to that any day.

### III

I thought that flashing circle of light was getting bigger, but it flashed so seldom I couldn't be sure. BVS-1 wouldn't show even in my telescope. I gave that up and settled for just waiting.

Waiting, I remembered a long-ago summer I spent on Jinx. There were days when, unable to go outside because a dearth of clouds had spread the land with raw blue-white sunlight, we amused ourselves by filling party balloons with tap water and dropping them on the sidewalk from three stories up. They made lovely splash patterns—which dried out too fast. So we put a little ink in each balloon before filling it. Then the patterns stayed.

Sonya Laskin had been in her chair when the chairs collapsed. Blood samples showed that it was Peter, who had struck them from behind, like a water balloon dropped from a great height.

What could get through a General Products hull?

Ten hours to fall.

I unfastened the safety net and went for an inspection tour. The access tunnel was three feet wide, just right to push through in free fall. Below me was the length of the fusion tube; to the left, the laser cannon; to the right, a set of curved side tubes leading to inspection points for the gyros, the batteries and generator, the air plant, the hyperspace shunt motors. All was in order—except me. I was clumsy. My jumps were always too short or too long. There was no room to turn at the stern end, so I had to back fifty feet to a side tube.

Six hours to go, and still I couldn't find the neutron star. Probably I would see it only for an instant, passing at better than half the speed of light. Already my speed must be enormous.

Were the stars turning blue?

Two hours to go, I was sure they were turning blue. Was my speed that high? Then the stars behind should be red. Machinery blocked the view behind me, so I used the gyros. The ship turned with peculiar sluggishness. And the stars behind were blue, not red. All around me were blue-white stars.

Imagine light falling into a savagely steep gravitational well. It won't accelerate. Light can't move faster than light. But it can gain in energy, in frequency. The light was falling on me, harder and harder as I dropped.

I told the dictaphone about it. That dictaphone was probably the best protected item on the ship. I had already decided to earn my money by using it, just as if I expected to collect. Privately I wondered just how intense the light would get.

Skydiver had drifted back to vertical, with its axis through the neutron star, but now it faced outward. I'd thought I had the ship stopped horizontally. More clumsiness. I used the gyros. Again the ship moved mushily, until it was halfway through the swing. Then it seemed to fall automatically into place. It was as if the Skydiver preferred to have its axis through the neutron star.

I didn't like that in the least.

I tried the maneuver again, and again the Skydiver fought back. But this time there was something else. Something was pulling at me.

So I unfastened my safety net and fell headfirst into the nose.

The pull was light, about a tenth of a gee. It felt more like sinking through honey than falling. I climbed back into my chair, tied myself in with the net, now hanging face down, turned on the dictaphone. I told my story in such nitpicking detail that my hypothetical listeners could not but doubt my hypothetical sanity. "I think this is what happened to the Laskins," I finished. "If the pull increases, I'll call back."

Think? I never doubted it. This strange, gentle pull was inexplicable. Something inexplicable had killed Peter and Sonya Laskin. Q.E.D.

Around the point where the neutron star must be, the stars were like smeared dots of oilpaint, smeared radially. They glared with an angry, painful light. I hung face down in the net and tried to think.

It was an hour before I was sure. The pull was increasing. And I still had an hour to fall.

Something was pulling on me, but not on the ship.

No, that was nonsense. What could reach out to me through a General Products hull? It must be the other way around. Something was pushing on the ship, pushing it off course.

If it got worse I could use the drive to compensate. Meanwhile, the ship was being pushed *away* from BVS-1, which was fine by me.

But if I was wrong, if the ship were not somehow being pushed away from BVS-1, the rocket motor would send the Skydiver crashing into eleven miles of neutronium.

And why wasn't the rocket already firing? If the ship was being pushed off course, the autopilot should be fighting back. The accelerometer was in good order. It had looked fine when I made my inspection tour down the access tube.

Could something be pushing on the ship *and* on the accelerometer, but not on me?

It came down to the same impossibility. Something that could reach through a General Products hull.

To hell with theory, said I to myself, said I. I'm getting out of here. To the dictaphone I said, "The pull has increased dangerously. I'm going to try to alter my orbit."

Of course, once I turned the ship outward and used the rocket, I'd be adding my own acceleration to the X force. It would be a strain, but I could stand it for a while. If I came within a mile of BVS-1, I'd end like Sonya Laskin.

She must have waited face down in a net like mine, waited without a drive unit, waited while the pressure rose and the net cut into her flesh, waited until the net snapped and dropped her into the nose, to lie crushed and broken until the X force tore the very chairs loose and dropped them on her.

I hit the gyros.

The gyros weren't strong enough to turn me. I tried it three times. Each time the ship rotated about fifty degrees and hung there, motionless, while the whine of the gyros went up and up. Released, the ship immediately swung back to position. I was nose down to the neutron star, and I was going to stay that way.

Half an hour to fall, and the X force was over a gee. My sinuses were in agony. My eyes were ripe and ready to fall out. I don't know if I could have stood a cigarette, but I didn't get the chance. My pack of Fortunados had fallen out of my pocket, when I dropped into the nose. There it was, four feet beyond my fingers, proof that the X force acted on other objects besides me. Fascinating.

I couldn't take any more. If it dropped me shrieking into the neutron star, I had to use the drive. And I did. I ran the thrust up until I was approximately in free fall. The blood which had pooled in my extremities went back where it belonged. The gee dial registered one point two gee. I cursed it for a lying robot.

The soft-pack was bobbing around in the nose, and it occurred to me that a little extra nudge on the throttle would bring it to me. I tried it. The pack drifted toward me, and I reached, and like a sentient thing it speeded up to avoid my clutching hand. I snatched at it again as it went past my ear, but again it was moving too fast. That pack was going at a hell of a clip, considering that here I was, practically in free fall. It dropped through the door to the relaxation room, still picking up speed, blurred and vanished as it entered the access tube. Seconds later I heard a solid Thump.

But that was *crazy*. Already the X force was pulling blood into my face. I pulled my lighter out, held it at arm's length and let go. It fell gently into the nose. But the pack of Fortunados had hit like I'd dropped it from a *building*.

Well.

I nudged the throttle again. The mutter of fusing hydrogen reminded me that if I tried to keep this up all the way, I might well put the General Products hull to its toughest test yet: smashing it into a neutron star at half lightspeed. I could see it now: a transparent hull containing only a few cubic inches of dwarf star matter wedged into the tip of the nose.

At one point four gee, according to that lying gee dial, the lighter came loose and drifted toward me. I let it go. It was clearly falling when it reached the doorway. I pulled the throttle back. The loss of power jerked me violently forward, but I kept my face turned. The lighter slowed and hesitated at the entrance to the access tube. Decided to go through. I cocked my ears for the sound, then jumped as the whole ship rang like a gong.

And the accelerometer was right at the ship's center of mass. Otherwise the ship's mass would have thrown the needle off. The puppeteers were fiends for ten-decimal-point accuracy.

I favored the dictaphone with a few fast comments, then got to work reprogramming the autopilot. Luckily what I wanted was simple. The

X force was but an X force to me, but now I knew how it behaved. I might actually live through this.

The stars were fiercely blue, warped to streaked lines near that special point. I thought I could see it now, very small and dim and red; but it might have been imagination. In twenty minutes, I'd be rounding the neutron star. The drive grumbled behind me. In effective free fall, I unfastened the safety net and pushed myself out of the chair.

A gentle push aft—and ghostly hands grasped my legs. Ten pounds of weight hung by my fingers from the back of the chair. The pressure should drop fast. I'd programmed the autopilot to reduce the thrust from two gees to zero during the next two minutes. All I had to do was be at the center of mass, in the access tube, when the thrust went to zero.

Something gripped the ship through a General Products hull. A psychokinetic life form stranded on a sun twelve miles in diameter? But how could anything alive stand such gravity?

Something might be stranded in orbit. There is life in space: outsiders and sailseeds and maybe others we haven't found yet. For all I knew or cared, BVS-1 itself might be alive. It didn't matter. I knew what the X force was trying to do. It was trying to pull the ship apart.

There was no pull on my fingers. I pushed aft and landed on the back wall, on bent legs. I knelt over the door, looking aft/down. When free fall came, I pulled myself through and was in the relaxation room looking down/forward into the nose.

Gravity was changing faster than I liked. The X force was growing as zero hour approached, while the compensating rocket thrust dropped. The X force tended to pull the ship apart; it was two gee forward at the nose, two gee backward at the tail and diminished to zero at the center of mass. Or so I hoped. The pack and lighter had behaved as if the force pulling them had increased for every inch they moved sternward.

The dictaphone was fifty feet below, utterly unreachable. If I had anything more to say to General Products, I'd have to say it in person. Maybe I'd get the chance. Because I knew what force was trying to tear the ship apart.

It was the tide.

The motor was off, and I was at the ship's midpoint. My spread-eagled position was getting uncomfortable. It was four minutes to perihelion.

Something creaked in the cabin below me. I couldn't see what it was, but I could clearly see a red point glaring among blue radial lines, like a lantern at the bottom of a well. To the sides, between the fusion tube and the tanks and other equipment, the blue stars glared at me with a light that was almost violet. I was afraid to look too long. I actually thought they might blind me.

There must have been hundreds of gravities in the cabin. I could even feel the pressure change. The air was thin at this height, one hundred and fifty feet above the control room.

And now, almost suddenly, the red dot was more than a dot. My time was up. A red disc leapt up at me; the ship swung around me; and I gasped and shut my eyes tight. Giants' hands gripped my arms and legs and head, gently but with great firmness, and tried to pull me in two. In that moment it came to me that Peter Laskin had died like this. He'd made the same guesses I had, and he'd tried to hide in the access tube. But he'd slipped. As I was slipping . . .

When I got my eyes open the red dot was shrinking into nothing.

## IV

The puppeteer president insisted I be put in a hospital for observation. I didn't fight the idea. My face and hands were flaming red, with blisters rising, and I ached like I'd been beaten. Rest and tender loving care, that's what I wanted.

I was floating between a pair of sleeping plates, hideously uncomfortable, when the nurse came to announce a visitor. I knew who it was from her peculiar expression.

"What can get through a General Products hull?" I asked it.

"I hoped you would tell me." The president rested on its single back leg, holding a stick that gave off green, incense-smelling smoke.

"And so I will. Gravity."

"Do not play with me, Beowulf Shaeffer. This matter is vital."

"I'm not playing. Does your world have a moon?"

"That information is classified." The puppeteers are cowards. Nobody knows where they come from, and nobody is likely to find out.

"Do you know what happens when a moon gets too close to its primary?"

"It falls apart."

"Why?"

"I do not know."

"Tides."

"What is a tide?"

Oho, said I to myself, said I. "I'm going to try to tell you. The Earth's moon is almost two thousand miles in diameter and does not rotate with respect to Earth. I want you to pick two rocks on the Moon, one at the point nearest the Earth, one at the point furthest away."

"Very well."

"Now, isn't it obvious that if those rocks were left to themselves they'd fall away from each other? They're in two different orbits, mind you, concentric orbits, one almost two thousand miles outside the other. Yet those rocks are forced to move at the same orbital speed."

"The one outside is moving faster."

"Good point. So there *is* a force trying to pull the Moon apart. Gravity holds it together. Bring the Moon close enough to Earth, and those two rocks would simply float away."

"I see. Then this *tide* tried to pull your ship apart. It was powerful enough in the lifesystem of the Institute ship to pull the acceleration chairs out of their mounts."

"And to crush a human being. Picture it. The ship's nose was just seven miles from the center of BVS-1. The tail was three hundred feet further out. Left to themselves they'd have gone in completely different orbits. My head and feet tried to do the same thing, when I got close enough."

"I see. Are you moulting?"

"What?"

"I noticed you are losing your outer integument in spots."

"Oh, *that*. I got a bad sunburn from exposure to starlight."

Two heads stared at each other for an eyeblink. A shrug? The puppeteer said, "We have deposited the remainder of your pay with the Bank of We Made It. One Sigmund Ausfaller, human, has frozen the account until your taxes are computed."

"Figures."

"If you will talk to reporters now, explaining what happened to the Institute ship, we will pay you ten thousand stars. We will pay cash so that you may use it immediately. It is urgent. There have been rumors."

"Bring 'em in." As an afterthought I added, "I can also tell them that your world is moonless. That should be good for a footnote somewhere."

"I do not understand." But two long necks had drawn back, and the puppeteer was watching me like a pair of pythons.

"You'd know what a tide was if you had a moon. You couldn't avoid it."

"Would you be interested in . . ."

". . . a million stars? I'd be fascinated. I'll even sign a contract if it includes what we're hiding. How do *you* like being blackmailed?"

*1968*
*26th CONVENTION*
*SAN FRANCISCO (OAKLAND)*

*Anne McCaffrey*

Anne McCaffrey is a woman. (Yes she is; you notice it instantly.) What makes this remarkable is that she's a woman in a man's world and it doesn't bother her a bit.

Science fiction is far less a man's world than it used to be as far as the readers are concerned. Walk into any convention these days and the number of shrill young girls fluttering before you (if you are Harlan Ellison) or backing cautiously away (if you are me) is either frightening or fascinating, depending on your point of view. (I am the fascinated type.)

The *writers,* however, are still masculine by a heavy majority. What's more, they are a particularly sticky type of male, used to dealing with males, and a little perturbed at having to accept a woman on an equal basis.

It's not so surprising. Science is a heavily masculine activity (in our society, anyway); so science fiction writing is, or should be. Isn't that the way it goes?

And then in comes Anne McCaffrey, with snow-white hair and a young face (the hair-color is premature) and Junoesque measurements and utter self-confidence, talking down mere males whenever necessary.

I get along simply marvelously well with Annie. Not only am I a "Women's Lib" from long before there was one, but I have the most disarming way of goggling at Junoesque measurements which convinces any woman possessing them that I have good taste.

In August 1970 Annie and I were co-guests of honor at a science fiction conference in Toronto. That meant one certain thing. We had another of our perennial songfest competitions. We sing at each other very loudly, and finally we work ourselves up to a climax, which is always "When Irish Eyes Are Smiling."

We each have our pride, of course, not so much in any skill at singing, but in loudness and range. And while everyone in the audience gets far out to non-wincing distance, we get louder and higher. (I happen to have a resonant baritone, but Annie perversely refuses to consider me anything but a tenor. "Never trust a tenor," she says darkly.)

It always ends the same way. At the final note, she takes a deep breath and holds. I do, too, but before the minute is up, I fade, choke, and halt, while that final note of Annie's keeps right on going—loud, shrill, and piercing, for an additional fifteen seconds at least.

And then everybody applauds and when I say, "It's not fair. She has spare lungs," and point at her aforesaid Junoesque proportions, no one seems to care.

Annie is in Ireland now for a lengthy stay and I miss her.

# 7

# WEYR SEARCH

*When is a legend legend? Why is a myth a myth? How old and disused must a fact be for it to be relegated to the category: Fairy tale? And why do certain facts remain incontrovertible, while others lose their validity to assume a shabby, unstable character?*

*Rukbat, in the Sagittarian sector, was a golden G-type star. It had five planets, plus one stray it had attracted and held in recent millennia. Its third planet was enveloped by air man could breathe, boasted water he could drink, and possessed a gravity which permitted man to walk confidently erect. Men discovered it, and promptly colonized it, as they did every habitable planet they came to and then—whether callously or through collapse of empire, the colonists never discovered, and eventually forgot to ask—left the colonies to fend for themselves.*

*When men first settled on Rukbat's third world, and named it Pern, they had taken little notice of the stranger-planet, swinging around its primary in a wildly erratic elliptical orbit. Within a few generations they had forgotten its existence. The desperate path the wanderer pursued brought it close to its stepsister every two hundred [Terran] years at perihelion.*

*When the aspects were harmonious and the conjunction with its sister-planet close enough, as it often was, the indigenous life of the wanderer sought to bridge the space gap to the more temperate and hospitable planet.*

*It was during the frantic struggle to combat this menace dropping through Pern's skies like silver threads, that Pern's contact with the mother-planet weakened and broke. Recollections of Earth receded further from Pernese history with each successive generation until memory of their origins degenerated past legend or myth, into oblivion.*

*To forestall the incursions of the dreaded Threads, the Pernese, with the ingenuity of their forgotten Yankee forebears and between first onslaught and return, developed a highly specialized variety of a life form indigenous to their adopted planet—the winged, tailed, and fire-breathing dragons, named for the Earth legend they resembled. Such humans as had a high empathy rating and some innate telepathic ability were trained to make use of and preserve this unusual animal whose ability to teleport was of immense value in the fierce struggle to keep Pern bare of Threads.*

*The dragons and their dragonmen, a breed apart, and the shortly renewed menace they battled, created a whole new group of legends and myths.*

*As the menace was conquered the populace in the Holds of Pern settled into a more comfortable way of life. Most of the dragon Weyrs eventually were abandoned, and the descendants of heroes fell into disfavor, as the legends fell into disrepute.*

*This, then, is a tale of legends disbelieved and their restoration. Yet —how goes a legend? When is myth?*

> *Drummer, beat, and piper, blow,*
> *Harper, strike, and soldier, go.*
> *Free the flame and sear the grasses*
> *Till the dawning Red Star passes.*

Lessa woke, cold. Cold with more than the chill of the everlastingly clammy stone walls. Cold with the prescience of a danger greater than when, ten full Turns ago, she had run, whimpering, to hide in the watch-wher's odorous lair.

Rigid with concentration, Lessa lay in the straw of the redolent cheese room, sleeping quarters shared with the other kitchen drudges. There was an urgency in the ominous portent unlike any other fore-warning. She touched the awareness of the watch-wher, slithering on its rounds in the courtyard. It circled at the choke-limit of its chain. It was restless, but oblivious to anything unusual in the pre-dawn dark-ness.

The danger was definitely not within the walls of Hold Ruath. Nor approaching the paved perimeter without the Hold where relentless grass had forced new growth through the ancient mortar, green witness to the deterioration of the once stone-clean Hold. The danger was not advancing up the now little used causeway from the valley, nor lurking in the craftsmen's stony holdings at the foot of the Hold's cliff. It did not scent the wind that blew from Tillek's cold shores. But still it twanged sharply through her senses, vibrating every nerve in Lessa's slender frame. Fully roused, she sought to identify it before the pres-cient mood dissolved. She cast outward, towards the Pass, farther than she had ever pressed. Whatever threatened was not in Ruatha . . . yet. Nor did it have a familiar flavor. It was not, then, Fax.

Lessa had been cautiously pleased that Fax had not shown himself at Hold Ruath in three full Turns. The apathy of the craftsmen, the decaying farmholds, even the green-etched stones of the Hold infuriated Fax, self-styled Lord of the High Reaches, to the point where he preferred to forget the reason why he had subjugated the once proud and profitable Hold.

Lessa picked her way among the sleeping drudges, huddled together for warmth, and glided up the worn steps to the kitchen-proper. She slipped across the cavernous kitchen to the stable-yard door. The cobbles of the yard were icy through the thin soles of her sandals and she shivered as the predawn air penetrated her patched garment.

The watch-wher slithered across the yard to greet her, pleading, as it always did, for release. Glancing fondly down at the awesome head, she promised it a good rub presently. It crouched, groaning, at the end of its chain as she continued to the grooved steps that led to the rampart over the Hold's massive gate. Atop the tower, Lessa stared towards the east where the stony breasts of the Pass rose in black relief against the gathering day.

Indecisively she swung to her left, for the sense of danger issued from that direction as well. She glanced upward, her eyes drawn to the red star which had recently begun to dominate the dawn sky. As she stared, the star radiated a final ruby pulsation before its magnificence was lost in the brightness of Pern's rising sun.

For the first time in many Turns, Lessa gave thought to matters beyond Pern, beyond her dedication to vengeance on the murderer Fax for the annihilation of her family. Let him but come within Ruath Hold now and he would never leave.

But the brilliant ruby sparkle of the Red Star recalled the Disaster Ballads—grim narratives of the heroism of the dragon-riders as they braved the dangers of *between* to breathe fiery death on the silver Threads that dropped through Pern's skies. Not one Thread must fall to the rich soil, to burrow deep and multiply, leaching the earth of minerals and fertility. Straining her eyes as if vision would bridge the gap between peril and person, she stared intently eastward. The watch-wher's thin, whistled question reached her just as the prescience waned.

Dawnlight illumined the tumbled landscape, the unplowed fields in the valley below. Dawnlight fell on twisted orchards, where the sparse herds of milchbeasts hunted stray blades of spring grass. Grass in

Ruatha grew where it should not, died where it should flourish. An odd brooding smile curved Lessa's lips. Fax realized no profit from his conquest of Ruatha . . . nor would he, while she, Lessa, lived. And he had not the slightest suspicion of the source of this undoing.

Or had he? Lessa wondered, her mind still reverberating from the savage prescience of danger. East lay Fax's ancestral and only legitimate Hold. Northeast lay little but bare and stony mountains and Benden, the remaining Weyr, which protected Pern.

Lessa stretched, arching her back, inhaling the sweet, untainted wind of morning.

A cock crowed in the stableyard. Lessa whirled, her face alert, eyes darting around the outer Hold lest she be observed in such an uncharacteristic pose. She unbound her hair, letting it fall about her face concealingly. Her body drooped into the sloppy posture she affected. Quickly she thudded down the stairs, crossing to the watch-wher. It lurred piteously, its great eyes blinking against the growing daylight. Oblivious to the stench of its rank breath, she hugged the scaly head to her, scratching its ears and eye ridges. The watch-wher was ecstatic with pleasure, its long body trembling, its clipped wings rustling. It alone knew who she was or cared. And it was the only creature in all Pern she trusted since the day she had blindly sought refuge in its dark stinking lair to escape Fax's thirsty swords that had drunk so deeply of Ruathan blood.

Slowly she rose, cautioning it to remember to be as vicious to her as to all should anyone be near. It promised to obey her, swaying back and forth to emphasize its reluctance.

The first rays of the sun glanced over the Hold's outer wall. Crying out, the watch-wher darted into its dark nest. Lessa crept back to the kitchen and into the cheese room.

> *From the Weyr and from the Bowl*
> *Bronze and brown and blue and green*
> *Rise the dragonmen of Pern,*
> *Aloft, on wing, seen, then unseen.*

F'lar on bronze Mnementh's great neck appeared first in the skies above the chief Hold of Fax, so-called Lord of the High Reaches. Behind him, in proper wedge formation, the wingmen came into sight. F'lar checked the formation automatically; as precise as at the moment of entry to *between*.

As Mnementh curved in an arc that would bring them to the perimeter of the Hold, consonant with the friendly nature of this visitation,

F'lar surveyed with mounting aversion the disrepair of the ridge defenses. The firestone pits were empty and the rock-cut gutters radiating from the pits were green-tinged with a mossy growth.

Was there even one lord in Pern who maintained his Hold rocky in observance of the ancient Laws? F'lar's lips tightened to a thinner line. When this Search was over and the Impression made, there would have to be a solemn, punitive Council held at the Weyr. And by the golden shell of the queen, he, F'lar, meant to be its moderator. He would replace lethargy with industry. He would scour the green and dangerous scum from the heights of Pern, the grass blades from its stoneworks. No verdant skirt would be condoned in any farmhold. And the tithings which had been so miserly, so grudgingly presented would, under pain of firestoning, flow with decent generosity into the Dragonweyr.

Mnementh rumbled approvingly as he vaned his pinions to land lightly on the grass-etched flagstones of Fax's Hold. The bronze dragon furled his great wings, and F'lar heard the warning claxon in the Hold's Great Tower. Mnementh dropped to his knees as F'lar indicated he wished to dismount. The bronze rider stood by Mnementh's huge wedge-shaped head, politely awaiting the arrival of the Hold lord. F'lar idly gazed down the valley, hazy with warm spring sunlight. He ignored the furtive heads that peered at the dragonman from the parapet slits and the cliff windows.

F'lar did not turn as a rush of air announced the arrival of the rest of the wing. He knew, however, when F'nor, the brown rider, his half-brother, took the customary position on his left, a dragon-length to the rear. F'lar caught a glimpse of F'nor's boot-heel twisting to death the grass crowding up between the stones.

An order, muffled to an intense whisper, issued from within the great court, beyond the open gates. Almost immediately a group of men marched into sight, led by a heavy-set man of medium height.

Mnementh arched his neck, angling his head so that his chin rested on the ground. Mnementh's many faceted eyes, on a level with F'lar's head, fastened with disconcerting interest on the approaching party. The dragons could never understand why they generated such abject fear in common folk. At only one point in his life span would a dragon attack a human and that could be excused on the grounds of simple ignorance. F'lar could not explain to the dragon the politics behind the necessity of inspiring awe in the holders, lord and craftsman alike. He could only observe that the fear and apprehension showing in the faces of the advancing squad which troubled Mnementh was oddly pleasing to him, F'lar.

"Welcome, Bronze Rider, to the Hold of Fax, Lord of the High Reaches. He is at your service," and the man made an adequately respectful salute.

The use of the third person pronoun could be construed, by the meticulous, to be a veiled insult. This fit in with the information F'lar had on Fax; so he ignored it. His information was also correct in describing Fax as a greedy man. It showed in the restless eyes which flicked at every detail of F'lar's clothing, at the slight frown when the intricately etched sword-hilt was noticed.

F'lar noticed, in his own turn, the several rich rings which flashed on Fax's left hand. The overlord's right hand remained slightly cocked after the habit of the professional swordsman. His tunic, of rich fabric, was stained and none too fresh. The man's feet, in heavy wher-hide boots, were solidly planted, weight balanced forward on his toes. A man to be treated cautiously, F'lar decided, as one should the conqueror of five neighboring Holds. Such greedy audacity was in itself a revelation. Fax had married into a sixth . . . and had legally inherited, however unusual the circumstances, the seventh. He was a lecherous man by reputation.

Within these seven Holds, F'lar anticipated a profitable Search. Let R'gul go southerly to pursue Search among the indolent, if lovely, women there. The Weyr needed a strong woman this time; Jora had been worse than useless with Nemorth. Adversity, uncertainty: those were the conditions that bred the qualities F'lar wanted in a weyrwoman.

"We ride in Search," F'lar drawled softly, "and request the hospitality of your Hold, Lord Fax."

Fax's eyes widened imperceptibly at mention of Search.

"I had heard Jora was dead," Fax replied, dropping the third person abruptly as if F'lar had passed some sort of test by ignoring it. "So Nemorth has a new queen, hm-m-m?" he continued, his eyes darting across the rank of the ring, noting the disciplined stance of the riders, the healthy color of the dragons.

F'lar did not dignify the obvious with an answer.

"And, my Lord—?" Fax hesitated, expectantly inclining his head slightly towards the dragonman.

For a pulse beat, F'lar wondered if the man were deliberately provoking him with such subtle insults. The name of bronze riders should be as well known throughout Pern as the name of the Dragonqueen and her Weyrwoman. F'lar kept his face composed, his eyes on Fax's.

Leisurely, with the proper touch of arrogance, F'nor stepped forward, stopping slightly behind Mnementh's head, one hand negligently touching the jaw hinge of the huge beast.

"The Bronze Rider of Mnementh, Lord F'lar, will require quarters for himself. I, F'nor, brown rider, prefer to be lodged with the wingmen. We are, in number, twelve."

F'lar liked that touch of F'nor's, totting up the wing strength, as if Fax were incapable of counting. F'nor had phrased it so adroitly as to make it impossible for Fax to protest the insult.

"Lord F'lar," Fax said through teeth fixed in a smile, "the High Reaches are honored with your Search."

"It will be to the credit of the High Reaches," F'lar replied smoothly, "if one of its own supplies the Weyr."

"To our everlasting credit," Fax replied as suavely. "In the old days, many notable weyrwomen came from my Holds."

"Your Holds?" asked F'lar, politely smiling as he emphasized the plural. "Ah, yes, you are now overlord of Ruatha, are you not? There have been many from that Hold."

A strange tense look crossed Fax's face. "Nothing good comes from Ruath Hold." Then he stepped aside, gesturing F'lar to enter the Hold.

Fax's troop leader barked a hasty order and the men formed two lines, their metal-edged boots flicking sparks from the stones.

At unspoken orders, all the dragons rose with a great churning of air and dust. F'lar strode nonchalantly past the welcoming files. The men were rolling their eyes in alarm as the beasts glided above to the inner courts. Someone on the high tower uttered a frightened yelp as Mnementh took his position on that vantage point. His great wings drove phosphoric-scented air across the inner court as he maneuvered his great frame onto the inadequate landing space.

Outwardly oblivious to the consternation, fear and awe the dragons inspired, F'lar was secretly amused and rather pleased by the effect. Lords of the Holds needed this reminder that they must deal with dragons, not just with riders, who were men, mortal and murderable. The ancient respect for dragonmen as well as dragonkind must be reinstilled in modern breasts.

"The Hold has just risen from table, Lord F'lar, if . . ." Fax suggested. His voice trailed off at F'lar's smiling refusal.

"Convey my duty to your lady, Lord Fax," F'lar rejoined, noticing with inward satisfaction the tightening of Fax's jaw muscles at the ceremonial request.

"You would prefer to see your quarters first?" Fax countered.

F'lar flicked an imaginary speck from his soft wher-hide sleeve and shook his head. Was the man buying time to sequester his ladies as the old time lords had?

"Duty first," he said with a rueful shrug.

"Of course," Fax all but snapped and strode smartly ahead, his heels pounding out the anger he could not express otherwise. F'lar decided he had guessed correctly.

F'lar and F'nor followed at a slower pace through the double-doored entry with its massive metal panels, into the great hall, carved into the cliffside.

"They eat not badly," F'nor remarked casually to F'lar, appraising the remnants still on the table.

"Better than the Weyr, it would seem," F'lar replied dryly.

"Young roasts and tender," F'nor said in a bitter undertone, "while the stringy, barren beasts are delivered up to us."

"The change is overdue," F'lar murmured, then raised his voice to conversational level. "A well-favored hall," he was saying amiably as they reached Fax. Their reluctant host stood in the portal to the inner Hold, which, like all such Holds, burrowed deep into stone, traditional refuge of all in time of peril.

Deliberately, F'lar turned back to the banner-hung Hall. "Tell me, Lord Fax, do you adhere to the old practices and mount a dawn guard?"

Fax frowned, trying to grasp F'lar's meaning.

"There is always a guard at the Tower."

"An easterly guard?"

Fax's eyes jerked towards F'lar, then to F'nor.

"There are always guards," he answered sharply, "on all the approaches."

"Oh, just the approaches," and F'lar nodded wisely to F'nor.

"Where else?" demanded Fax, concerned, glancing from one dragonman to the other.

"I must ask that of your harper. You do keep a trained harper in your Hold?"

"Of course. I have several trained harpers," and Fax jerked his shoulders straighter.

F'lar affected not to understand.

"Lord Fax is the overlord of six other Holds," F'nor reminded his wingleader.

"Of course," F'lar assented, with exactly the same inflection Fax had used a moment before.

The mimicry did not go unnoticed by Fax but as he was unable to construe deliberate insult out of an innocent affirmative, he stalked into the glow-lit corridors. The dragonmen followed.

The women's quarters in Fax's Hold had been moved from the traditional innermost corridors to those at cliff-face. Sunlight poured down from three double-shuttered, deep-casement windows in the outside wall. F'lar noted that the bronze hinges were well oiled, and the sills regulation spear-length. Fax had not, at least, diminished the protective wall.

The chamber was richly hung with appropriately gentle scenes of women occupied in all manner of feminine tasks. Doors gave off the main chamber on both sides into smaller sleeping alcoves and from these, at Fax's bidding, his women hesitantly emerged. Fax sternly gestured to a blue-gowned woman, her hair white-streaked, her face lined with disappointments and bitterness, her body swollen with pregnancy. She advanced awkwardly, stopping several feet from her lord. From her attitude, F'lar deduced that she came no closer to Fax than was absolutely necessary.

"The Lady of Crom, mother of my heirs," Fax said without pride or cordiality.

"My Lady—" F'lar hesitated, waiting for her name to be supplied. She glanced warily at her lord.

"Gemma," Fax snapped curtly.

F'lar bowed deeply. "My Lady Gemma, the Weyr is on Search and requests the Hold's hospitality."

"My Lord F'lar," the Lady Gemma replied in a low voice, "you are most welcome."

F'lar did not miss the slight slur on the adverb nor the fact that Gemma had no trouble naming him. His smile was warmer than courtesy demanded, warm with gratitude and sympathy. Looking at the number of women in these quarters, F'lar thought there might be one or two Lady Gemma could bid farewell without regret.

Fax preferred his women plump and small. There wasn't a saucy one in the lot. If there once had been, the spirit had been beaten out of her. Fax, no doubt, was stud, not lover. Some of the covey had not all winter long made much use of water, judging by the amount of sweet oil gone rancid in their hair. Of them all, if these were all, the Lady Gemma was the only willful one; and she, too old.

The amenities over, Fax ushered his unwelcome guests outside, and led the way to the quarters he had assigned the bronze rider.

"A pleasant room," F'lar acknowledged, stripping off gloves and wherhide tunic, throwing them carelessly to the table. "I shall see to my men and the beasts. They have been fed recently," he commented, pointing up Fax's omission in inquiring. "I request liberty to wander through the crafthold."

Fax sourly granted what was a dragonman's traditional privilege. "I shall not further disrupt your routine, Lord Fax, for you must have many demands on you, with seven Holds to supervise." F'lar inclined his body slightly to the overlord, turning away as a gesture of dismissal. He could imagine the infuriated expression on Fax's face from the stamping retreat.

F'nor and the men had settled themselves in a hastily vacated barrackroom. The dragons were perched comfortably on the rocky ridges above the Hold. Each rider kept his dragon in light, but alert, charge. There were to be no incidents on a Search.

As a group, the dragonmen rose at F'lar's entrance.

"No tricks, no troubles, but look around closely," he said laconically. "Return by sundown with the names of any likely prospects." He caught F'nor's grin, remembering how Fax had slurred over some names. "Descriptions are in order and craft affiliation."

The men nodded, their eyes glinting with understanding. They were flatteringly confident of a successful Search even as F'lar's doubts grew now that he had seen Fax's women. By all logic, the pick of the High Reaches should be in Fax's chief Hold—but they were not. Still, there were many large craftholds not to mention the six other High Holds to visit. All the same . . .

In unspoken accord F'lar and F'nor left the barracks. The men would follow, unobtrusively, in pairs or singly, to reconnoiter the crafthold and the nearer farmholds. The men were as overtly eager to be abroad as F'lar was privately. There had been a time when dragonmen were frequent and favored guests in all the great Holds throughout Pern, from southern Fort to high north Igen. This pleasant custom, too, had died along with other observances, evidence of the low regard in which the Weyr was presently held. F'lar vowed to correct this.

He forced himself to trace in memory the insidious changes. The Records, which each Weyrwoman kept, were proof of the gradual, but perceptible, decline, traceable through the past two hundred full Turns. Knowing the facts did not alleviate the condition. And F'lar was of that scant handful in the Weyr itself who did credit Records and Ballad alike. The situation might shortly reverse itself radically if the old tales were to be believed.

There was a reason, an explanation, a purpose, F'lar felt, for every one of the Weyr laws from First Impression to the Firestones: from the grass-free heights to ridge-running gutters. For elements as minor as controlling the appetite of a dragon to limiting the inhabitants of the Weyr. Although why the other five Weyrs had been abandoned, F'lar did not know. Idly he wondered if there were records, dusty and crumbling, lodged in the disused Weyrs. He must contrive to check when next his wings flew patrol. Certainly there was no explanation in Benden Weyr.

"There is industry but no enthusiasm," F'nor was saying, drawing F'lar's attention back to their tour of the crafthold.

They had descended the guttered ramp from the Hold into the crafthold proper, the broad roadway lined with cottages up to the imposing stone crafthalls. Silently F'lar noted moss-clogged gutters on the roofs, the vines clasping the walls. It was painful for one of his calling to witness the flagrant disregard of simple safety precautions. Growing things were forbidden near the habitations of mankind.

"News travels fast," F'nor chuckled, nodding at a hurrying craftsman, in the smock of a baker, who gave them a mumbled good day. "Not a female in sight."

His observation was accurate. Women should be abroad at this hour, bringing in supplies from the storehouses, washing in the river on such a bright warm day, or going out to the farmholds to help with planting. Not a gowned figure in sight.

"We used to be preferred mates," F'nor remarked caustically.

"We'll visit the Clothmen's Hall first. If my memory serves me right . . ."

"As it always does . . ." F'nor interjected wryly. He took no advantage of their blood relationship but he was more at ease with the bronze rider than most of the dragonmen, the other bronze riders included. F'lar was reserved in a close-knit society of easy equality. He flew a tightly disciplined wing but men maneuvered to serve under him. His wing always excelled in the Games. None ever floundered in *between* to disappear forever and no beast in his wing sickened, leaving a man in dragonless exile from the Weyr, a part of him numb forever.

"L'tol came this way and settled in one of the High Reaches," F'lar continued.

"L'tol?"

"Yes, a green rider from S'lel's wing. You remember."

An ill-timed swerve during the Spring Games had brought L'tol and his beast into the full blast of a phosphene emission from S'lel's bronze Tuenth. L'tol had been thrown from his beast's neck as the dragon tried to evade the blast. Another wingmate had swooped to catch the rider but the green dragon, his left wing crisped, his body scorched, had died of shock and phosphene poisoning.

"L'tol would aid our Search," F'nor agreed as the two dragonmen walked up to the bronze doors of the Clothmen's Hall. They paused on the threshold, adjusting their eyes to the dimmer light within. Glows punctuated the wall recesses and hung in clusters above the larger looms where the finer tapestries and fabrics were woven by master craftsmen. The pervading mood was one of quiet, purposeful industry.

Before their eyes had adapted, however, a figure glided to them, with a polite, if curt, request for them to follow him.

They were led to the right of the entrance, to a small office, curtained from the main hall. Their guide turned to them, his face visible in the wallglows. There was that air about him that marked him indefinably as a dragonman. But his face was lined deeply, one side seamed with old burnmarks. His eyes, sick with a hungry yearning, dominated his face. He blinked constantly.

"I am now Lytol," he said in a harsh voice.

F'lar nodded acknowledgment.

"You would be F'lar," Lytol said, "and you, F'nor. You've both the look of your sire."

F'lar nodded again.

Lytol swallowed convulsively, the muscles in his face twitching as the presence of dragonmen revived his awareness of exile. He essayed a smile.

"Dragons in the sky! The news spread faster than Threads."

"Nemorth has a new queen."

"Jora dead?" Lytol asked concernedly, his face cleared of its nervous movement for a second.

F'lar nodded.

Lytol grimaced bitterly. "R'gul again, huh." He stared off in the middle distance, his eyelids quiet but the muscles along his jaw took up the constant movement. "You've the High Reaches? All of them?" Lytol asked, turning back to the dragonman, a slight emphasis on "all."

F'lar gave an affirmative nod again.

"You've seen the women." Lytol's disgust showed through the words. It was a statement, not a question, for he hurried on. "Well, there are no better in all the High Reaches," and his tone expressed utmost disdain.

"Fax likes his women comfortably fleshed and docile," Lytol rattled on. "Even the Lady Gemma has learned. It'd be different if he didn't need her family's support. Ah, it would be different indeed. So he keeps her pregnant, hoping to kill her in childbed one day. And he will. He will."

Lytol drew himself up, squaring his shoulders, turning full to the two dragonmen. His expression was vindictive, his voice low and tense.

"Kill that tyrant, for the sake and safety of Pern. Of the Weyr. Of the queen. He only bides his time. He spreads discontent among the other lords. He"—Lytol's laughter had an hysterical edge to it now—"he fancies himself as good as dragonmen."

"There are no candidates then in this Hold?" F'lar said, his voice sharp enough to cut through the man's preoccupation with his curious theory.

Lytol stared at the bronze rider. "Did I not say it?"

"What of Ruath Hold?"

Lytol stopped shaking his head and looked sharply at F'lar, his lips curling in a cunning smile. He laughed mirthlessly.

"You think to find a Torene, or a Moreta, hidden at Ruath Hold in these times? Well, all of that Blood are dead. Fax's blade was thirsty that day. He knew the truth of those harpers' tales, that Ruathan lords gave full measure of hospitality to dragonmen and the Ruathan were a breed apart. There were, you know," Lytol's voice dropped to a confiding whisper, "exiled Weyrmen like myself in that Line."

F'lar nodded gravely, unable to contradict the man's pitiful attempt at self-esteem.

"No," and Lytol chuckled softly. "Fax gets nothing from that Hold but trouble. And the women Fax used to take . . ." his laugh turned nasty in tone. "It is rumored he was impotent for months afterwards."

"Any families in the holdings with Weyr blood?"

Lytol frowned, glanced surprised at F'lar. He rubbed the scarred side of his face thoughtfully.

"There were," he admitted slowly. "There were. But I doubt if any live on." He thought a moment longer, then shook his head emphatically.

F'lar shrugged.

"I wish I had better news for you," Lytol murmured.

"No matter," F'lar reassured him, one hand poised to part the hanging in the doorway.

Lytol came up to him swiftly, his voice urgent.

"Heed what I say, Fax is ambitious. Force R'gul, or whoever is Weyrleader next, to keep watch on the High Reaches."

Lytol jabbed a finger in the direction of the Hold. "He scoffs openly at tales of the Threads. He taunts the harpers for the stupid nonsense of the old ballads and has banned from their repertoire all dragonlore. The new generation will grow up totally ignorant of duty, tradition and precaution."

F'lar was not surprised to hear that on top of Lytol's other disclosures. Yet the Red Star pulsed in the sky and the time was drawing near when they would hysterically reavow the old allegiances in fear for their very lives.

"Have you been abroad in the early morning of late?" asked F'nor, grinning maliciously.

"I have," Lytol breathed out in a hushed, choked whisper. "I have . . ." A groan was wrenched from his guts and he whirled away from the dragonmen, his head bowed between hunched shoulders. "Go," he said, gritting his teeth. And, as they hesitated, he pleaded, "Go!"

F'lar walked quickly from the room, followed by F'nor. The bronze rider crossed the quiet dim Hall with long strides and exploded into the startling sunlight. His momentum took him into the center of the square. There he stopped so abruptly that F'nor, hard on his heels, nearly collided with him.

"We will spend exactly the same time within the other Halls," he announced in a tight voice, his face averted from F'nor's eyes. F'lar's throat was constricted. It was difficult, suddenly, for him to speak. He swallowed hard, several times.

"To be dragonless . . ." murmured F'nor, pityingly. The encounter with Lytol had roiled his depths in a mournful way to which he was unaccustomed. That F'lar appeared equally shaken went far to dispel F'nor's private opinion that his half-brother was incapable of emotion.

"There is no other way once First Impression has been made. You know that," F'lar roused himself to say curtly. He strode off to the Hall bearing the Leathermen's device.

> The Hold is barred
> The Hall is bare.
> And men vanish.
> The soil is barren,
> The rock is bald.
> All hope banish.

Lessa was shoveling ashes from the hearth when the agitated messenger staggered into the Great Hall. She made herself as inconspicuous as possible so the Warder would not dismiss her. She had contrived to be sent to the Great Hall that morning, knowing that the Warder intended to brutalize the Head Clothman for the shoddy quality of the goods readied for shipment to Fax.

"Fax is coming! With dragonmen!" the man gasped out as he plunged into the dim Great Hall.

The Warder, who had been about to lash the Head Clothman, turned, stunned, from his victim. The courier, a farmholder from the edge of Ruatha, stumbled up to the Warder, so excited with his message that he grabbed the Warder's arm.

"How dare you leave your Hold?" and the Warder aimed his lash at the astonished holder. The force of the first blow knocked the man from his feet. Yelping, he scrambled out of reach of a second lashing. "Dragonmen indeed! Fax? Ha! He shuns Ruatha. There!" The Warder punctuated each denial with another blow, kicking the helpless wretch for good measure, before he turned breathless to glare at the clothman and the two underwarders. "How did he get in here with such a threadbare lie?" The Warder stalked to the great door. It was flung open just as he reached out for the iron handle. The ashen-faced guard officer rushed in, nearly toppling the Warder.

"Dragonmen! Dragons! All over Ruatha!" the man gibbered, arms flailing wildly. He, too, pulled at the Warder's arm, dragging the stupefied official towards the outer courtyard, to bear out the truth of his statement.

Lessa scooped up the last pile of ashes. Picking up her equipment, she slipped out of the Great Hall. There was a very pleased smile on her face under the screen of matted hair.

A dragonman at Ruatha! She must somehow contrive to get Fax so humiliated, or so infuriated, that he would renounce his claim to the Hold, in the presence of a dragonman. Then she could claim her birthright.

But she would have to be extraordinarily wary. Dragonriders were men apart. Anger did not cloud their intelligence. Greed did not sully their judgment. Fear did not dull their reactions. Let the dense-witted believe human sacrifice, unnatural lusts, insane revel. She was not so gullible. And those stories went against her grain. Dragonmen were still human and there was Weyr blood in *her* veins. It was the same color as that of anyone else; enough of hers had been spilled to prove that.

She halted for a moment, catching a sudden shallow breath. Was this the danger she had sensed four days ago at dawn? The final encounter in her struggle to regain the Hold? No—there had been more to that portent than revenge.

The ash bucket banged against her shins as she shuffled down the low ceilinged corridor to the stable door. Fax would find a cold welcome. She had laid no new fire on the hearth. Her laugh echoed back unpleasantly from the damp walls. She rested her bucket and propped her broom and shovel as she wrestled with the heavy bronze door that gave into the new stables.

They had been built outside the cliff of Ruatha by Fax's first Warder, a subtler man than all eight of his successors. He had achieved more than all the others and Lessa had honestly regretted the necessity of his death. But he would have made her revenge impossible. He would have caught her out before she had learned how to camouflage herself and her little interferences. What had his name been? She could not recall. Well, she regretted his death.

The second man had been properly greedy and it had been easy to set up a pattern of misunderstanding between Warder and craftsmen. That one had been determined to squeeze all profit from Ruathan goods so that some of it would drop into his pocket before Fax suspected a shortage. The craftsmen who had begun to accept the skillful diplomacy of the first Warder bitterly resented the second's grasping, high-handed ways. They resented the passing of the Old Line and, even more so, the way of its passing. They were unforgiving of the insult to Ruatha; its now secondary position in the High Reaches; and they resented the individual indignities that holders, craftsmen and farmers alike, suffered under the second Warder. It took little manipulation to arrange for matters at Ruatha to go from bad to worse.

The second was replaced and his successor fared no better. He was caught diverting goods, the best of the goods at that. Fax had had him executed. His bony head still hung in the main firepit above the great Tower.

The present incumbent had not been able to maintain the Hold in even the sorry condition in which he had assumed its management. Seemingly simple matters developed rapidly into disasters. Like the production of cloth . . . Contrary to his boasts to Fax, the quality had not improved, and the quantity had fallen off.

Now Fax was here. And with dragonmen! Why dragonmen? The import of the question froze Lessa, and the heavy door closing behind her barked her heels painfully. Dragonmen used to be frequent visitors at Ruatha, that she knew, and even vaguely remembered. Those memories were like a harpers' tale, told of someone else, not something within her own experience. She had limited her fierce attention to Ruatha only. She could not even recall the name of Queen or Weyr-woman from the instructions of her childhood, nor could she recall hearing mention of any queen or weyrwoman by anyone in the Hold these past ten Turns.

Perhaps the dragonmen were finally going to call the lords of the Holds to task for the disgraceful show of greenery about the Holds.

Well, Lessa was to blame for much of that in Ruatha but she defied even a dragonman to confront her with her guilt. Did all Ruatha fall to the Threads it would be better than remaining dependent to Fax! The heresy shocked Lessa even as she thought it.

Wishing she could as easily unburden her conscience of such blasphemy, she ditched the ashes on the stable midden. There was a sudden change in air pressure around her. Then a fleeting shadow caused her to glance up.

From behind the cliff above glided a dragon, its enormous wings spread to their fullest as he caught the morning updraft. Turning effortlessly, he descended. A second, a third, a full wing of dragons followed in soundless flight and patterned descent, graceful and awesome. The claxon rang belatedly from the Tower and from within the kitchen there issued the screams and shrieks of the terrified drudges.

Lessa took cover. She ducked into the kitchen where she was instantly seized by the assistant cook and thrust with a buffet and a kick toward the sinks. There she was put to scrubbing grease-encrusted serving bowls with cleansing sand.

The yelping canines were already lashed to the spitrun, turning a scrawny herdbeast that had been set to roast. The cook was ladling seasonings on the carcass, swearing at having to offer so poor a meal to so many guests, and some of them high-rank. Winter-dried fruits from the last scanty harvest had been set to soak and two of the oldest drudges were scraping roots.

An apprentice cook was kneading bread; another, carefully spicing a sauce. Looking fixedly at him, she diverted his hand from one spice box to a less appropriate one as he gave a final shake to the concoction. She added too much wood to the wall oven, insuring ruin for the breads. She controlled the canines deftly, slowing one and speeding the other so that the meat would be underdone on one side, burned on the other. That the feast should be a fast, the food presented found inedible, was her whole intention.

Above in the Hold, she had no doubt that certain other measures, undertaken at different times for this exact contingency, were being discovered.

Her fingers bloodied from a beating, one of the Warder's women came shrieking into the kitchen, hopeful of refuge there.

"Insects have eaten the best blankets to shreds! And a canine who had littered on the best linens snarled at me as she gave suck! And the rushes are noxious, the best chambers full of debris driven in by the winter wind. Somebody left the shutters ajar. Just a tiny bit, but it was enough . . ." the woman wailed, clutching her hand to her breast and rocking back and forth.

Lessa bent with great industry to shine the plates.

> *Watch-wher, watch-wher,*
> *In your lair,*
> *Watch well, watch-wher!*
> *Who goes there?*

"The watch-wher is hiding something," F'lar told F'nor as they consulted in the hastily cleaned Great Hall. The room delighted to hold the wintry chill although a generous fire now burned on the hearth.

"It was but gibbering when Canth spoke to it," F'nor remarked. He was leaning against the mantel, turning slightly from side to side to gather some warmth. He watched his wingleader's impatient pacing.

"Mnementh is calming it down," F'lar replied. "He may be able to sort out the nightmare. The creature may be more senile than aware, but . . ."

"I doubt it," F'nor concurred helpfully. He glanced with apprehension up at the webhung ceiling. He was certain he'd found most of the crawlers, but he didn't fancy their sting. Not on top of the discomforts already experienced in this forsaken Hold. If the night stayed mild, he intended curling up with Canth on the heights. "That would be more reasonable than anything Fax or his Warder have suggested."

"Hm-m-m," F'lar muttered, frowning at the brown rider.

"Well, it's unbelievable that Ruatha could have fallen to such disrepair in ten short Turns. Every dragon caught the feeling of power and it's obvious the watch-wher has been tampered with. That takes a good deal of control."

"From someone of the Blood," F'lar reminded him.

F'nor shot his wingleader a quick look, wondering if he could possibly be serious in the light of all information to the contrary.

"I grant you there is power here, F'lar," F'nor conceded. "It could easily be a hidden male of the old Blood. But we need a female. And Fax made it plain, in his inimitable fashion, that he left none of the old Blood alive in the Hold the day he took it. No, no." The brown rider shook his head, as if he could dispel the lack of faith in his wingleader's curious insistence that the Search would end in Ruath with Ruathan blood.

"That watch-wher is hiding something and only someone of the Blood of its Hold can arrange that," F'lar said emphatically. He gestured around the Hall and towards the walls, bare of hangings.

"Ruatha has been overcome. But she resists . . . Subtly. I say it points to the old Blood, *and* power. Not power alone."

The obstinate expression in F'lar's eyes, the set of his jaw, suggested that F'nor seek another topic.

"The pattern was well-flown today," F'nor suggested tentatively. "Does a dragonman good to ride a flaming beast. Does the beast good, too. Keeps the digestive process in order."

F'lar nodded sober agreement. "Let R'gul temporize as he chooses. It is fitting and proper to ride a fire-spouting beast and these holders need to be reminded of Weyr power."

"Right now, anything would help our prestige," F'nor commented sourly. "What had Fax to say when he hailed you in the Pass?" F'nor knew his question was almost impertinent but if it were, F'lar would ignore it.

F'lar's slight smile was unpleasant and there was an ominous glint in his amber eyes.

"We talked of rule and resistance."

"Did he not also draw on you?" F'nor asked.

F'lar's smile deepened. "Until he remembered I was dragonmounted."

"He's considered a vicious fighter," F'nor said.

"I am at some disadvantage?" F'lar asked, turning sharply on his brown rider, his face too controlled.

"To my knowledge, no," F'nor reassured his leader quickly. F'lar had tumbled every man in the Weyr, efficiently and easily. "But Fax kills often and without cause."

"And because we dragonmen do not seek blood, we are not to be feared as fighters?" snapped F'lar. "Are you ashamed of your heritage?"

"I? No!" F'nor sucked in his breath. "Nor any of our wing!" he added proudly. "But there is that in the attitude of the men in this progression of Fax's that . . . that makes me wish some excuse to fight."

"As you observed today, Fax seeks some excuse. And," F'lar added thoughtfully, "there is something here in Ruatha that unnerves our noble overlord."

He caught sight of Lady Tela, whom Fax had so courteously assigned him for comfort during the progression, waving to him from the inner Hold portal.

"A case in point. Fax's Lady Tela is some three months gone."

F'nor frowned at that insult to his leader.

"She giggles incessantly and appears so addlepated that one cannot decide whether she babbles out of ignorance or at Fax's suggestion. As she has apparently not bathed all winter, and is not, in any case, my ideal, I have"—F'lar grinned maliciously—"deprived myself of her kind offices."

F'nor hastily cleared his throat and his expression as Lady Tela approached them. He caught the unappealing odor from the scarf or handkerchief she waved constantly. Dragonmen endured a great deal for the Weyr. He moved away, with apparent courtesy, to join the rest of the dragonmen entering the Hall.

F'lar turned with equal courtesy to Lady Tela as she jabbered away about the terrible condition of the rooms which Lady Gemma and the other ladies had been assigned.

"The shutters, both sets, were ajar all winter long and you should have seen the trash on the floors. We finally got two of the drudges to sweep it all into the fireplace. And then that smoked something fearful 'til a man was sent up." Lady Tela giggled. "He found the access blocked by a chimney stone fallen aslant. The rest of the chimney, for a wonder, was in good repair."

She waved her handkerchief. F'lar held his breath as the gesture wafted an unappealing odor in his direction.

He glanced up the Hall towards the inner Hold door and saw Lady Gemma descending, her steps slow and awkward. Some subtle difference about her gait attracted him and he stared at her, trying to identify it.

"Oh, yes, poor Lady Gemma," Lady Tela babbled, sighing deeply. "We are so concerned. Why Lord Fax insisted on her coming, I do not know. She is not near her time and yet . . ." The lighthead's concern sounded sincere.

F'lar's incipient hatred for Fax and his brutality matured abruptly. He left his partner chattering to thin air and courteously extended his arm to Lady Gemma to support her down the steps and to the table. Only the brief tightening of her fingers on his forearm betrayed her gratitude. Her face was very white and drawn, the lines deeply etched around mouth and eyes, showing the effort she was expending.

"Some attempt has been made, I see, to restore order to the Hall," she remarked in a conversational tone.

"Some," F'lar admitted dryly, glancing around the grandly proportioned Hall, its rafter festooned with the webs of many Turns. The inhabitants of those gossamer nests dropped from time to time, with ripe splats, to the floor, onto the table and into the serving platters. Nothing replaced the old banners of the Ruathan Blood, which had been removed from the stark brown stone walls. Fresh rushes did obscure the greasy flagstones. The trestle tables appeared recently sanded and scraped, and the platters gleamed dully in the refreshed glows. Unfortunately, the brighter light was a mistake for it was much too unflattering.

"This was such a graceful Hall," Lady Gemma murmured for F'lar's ears alone.

"You were a friend?" he asked, politely.

"Yes, in my youth," her voice dropped expressively on the last word, evoking for F'lar a happier girlhood. "It was a noble line!"

"Think you *one* might have escaped the sword?"

Lady Gemma flashed him a startled look, then quickly composed her features, lest the exchange be noted. She gave a barely perceptible shake of her head and then shifted her awkward weight to take her place at the table. Graciously she inclined her head towards F'lar, both dismissing and thanking him.

F'lar returned to his own partner and placed her at the table on his left. As the only person of rank who would dine that night at Ruath Hold, Lady Gemma was seated on his right; Fax would be beyond her. The dragonmen and Fax's upper soldiery would sit at the lower tables. No guildmen had been invited to Ruatha. Fax arrived just then with his current lady and two underleaders, the Warder bowing them effusively into the Hall. The man, F'lar noticed, kept a good distance from his overlord—as well a Warder might whose responsibility was in this sorry condition. F'lar flicked a crawler away. Out of the corner of his eye, he saw Lady Gemma wince and shudder.

Fax stamped up to the raised table, his face black with suppressed rage. He pulled back his chair roughly, slamming it into Lady Gemma's before he seated himself. He pulled the chair to the table with a force that threatened to rock the none too stable trestle-top from its supporting legs. Scowling, he inspected his goblet and plate, fingering the surface, ready to throw them aside if they displeased him.

"A roast and fresh bread, Lord Fax, and such fruits and roots as are left. Had I but known of your arrival, I could have sent to Crom for . . ."

"Sent to Crom?" roared Fax, slamming the plate he was inspecting onto the table so forcefully the rim bent under his hands. The Warder winced again as if he himself had been maimed.

"The day one of my Holds cannot support itself *or* the visit of its rightful overload, I shall renounce it."

Lady Gemma gasped. Simultaneously the dragons roared. F'lar felt the unmistakable surge of power. His eyes instinctively sought F'nor at the lower table. The brown rider—all the dragonmen—had experienced that inexplicable shaft of exultation.

"What's wrong, Dragonman?" snapped Fax.

F'lar, affecting unconcern, stretched his legs under the table and assumed an indolent posture in the heavy chair.

"Wrong?"

"The dragons!"

"Oh, nothing. They often roar . . . at the sunset, at a flock of passing wherries, at mealtimes," and F'lar smiled amiably at the Lord of the High Reaches. Beside him his tablemate gave a squeak.

"Mealtimes? Have they not been fed?"

"Oh, yes. Five days ago."

"Oh. Five . . . days ago? And are they hungry . . . now?" Her voice trailed into a whisper of fear, her eyes grew round.

"In a few days," F'lar assured her. Under cover of his detached amusement, F'lar scanned the Hall. That surge had come from nearby. Either in the Hall or just outside. It must have been from within. It came so soon upon Fax's speech that his words must have triggered it. And the power had had an indefinably feminine touch to it.

One of Fax's women? F'lar found that hard to credit. Mnementh had been close to all of them and none had shown a vestige of power. Much less, with the exception of Lady Gemma, any intelligence.

One of the Hall women? So far he had seen only the sorry drudges and the aging females the Warder had as housekeepers. The Warder's personal woman? He must discover if that man had one. One of the Hold guards' women? F'lar suppressed an intense desire to rise and search.

"You mount a guard?" he asked Fax casually.

"Double at Ruath Hold!" he was told in a tight, hard voice, ground out from somewhere deep in Fax's chest.

"Here?" F'lar all but laughed out loud, gesturing around the sadly appointed chamber.

"Here! Food!" Fax changed the subject with a roar.

Five drudges, two of them women in brown-gray rags such that F'lar hoped they had had nothing to do with the preparation of the meal, staggered in under the emplattered herdbeast. No one with so much as a trace of power would sink to such depths, unless . . .

The aroma that reached him as the platter was placed on the serving table distracted him. It reeked of singed bone and charred meat. The Warder frantically sharpened his tools as if a keen edge could somehow slice acceptable portions from this unlikely carcass.

Lady Gemma caught her breath again and F'lar saw her hands curl tightly around the armrests. He saw the convulsive movement of her throat as she swallowed. He, too, did not look forward to this repast.

The drudges reappeared with wooden trays of bread. Burnt crusts had been scraped and cut, in some places, from the loaves before serving. As other trays were borne in, F'lar tried to catch sight of the faces of the servitors. Matted hair obscured the face of the one who presented a dish of legumes swimming in greasy liquid. Revolted, F'lar poked through the legumes to find properly cooked portions to offer Lady Gemma. She waved them aside, her face ill-concealing her discomfort.

As F'lar was about to turn and serve Lady Tela, he saw Lady Gemma's hand clutch convulsively at the chair arms. He realized that she was not merely nauseated by the unappetizing food. She was seized with labor contractions.

F'lar glanced in Fax's direction. The overlord was scowling blackly at the attempts of the Warder to find edible portions of meat to serve.

F'lar touched Lady Gemma's arm with light fingers. She turned just enough to look at F'lar from the corner of her eye. She managed a socially-correct half-smile.

"I dare not leave just now, Lord F'lar. He is always dangerous at Ruatha. And it may only be false pangs."

F'lar was dubious as he saw another shudder pass through her frame. The woman would have been a fine weyrwoman, he thought ruefully, were she but younger.

The Warder, his hands shaking, presented Fax the sliced meats. There were slivers of overdone flesh and portions of almost edible meats, but not much of either.

One furious wave of Fax's broad fist and the Warder had the plate, meats and juice, square in the face. Despite himself, F'lar sighed, for those undoubtedly constituted the only edible portions of the entire beast.

"You call this food? *You call this food?*" Fax bellowed. His voice boomed back from the bare vault of the ceiling, shaking crawlers from their webs as the sound shattered the fragile strands. "Slop! *Slop!*"

F'lar rapidly brushed crawlers from Lady Gemma who was helpless in the throes of a very strong contraction.

"It's all we had on such short notice," the Warder squealed, juices streaking down his cheeks. Fax threw the goblet at him and the wine went streaming down the man's chest. The steaming dish of roots followed and the man yelped as the hot liquid splashed over him.

"My lord, my lord, had I but known!"

"Obviously, Ruatha *cannot* support the visit of its Lord. You must renounce it," F'lar heard himself saying.

His shock at such words issuing from his mouth was as great as that of everyone else in the Hall. Silence fell, broken by the splat of falling crawlers and the drip of root liquid from the Warder's shoulders to the rushes. The grating of Fax's boot-heel was clearly audible as he swung slowly around to face the bronze rider.

As F'lar conquered his own amazement and rapidly tried to predict what to do next to mend matters, he saw F'nor rise slowly to his feet, hand on dagger hilt.

"I did not hear you correctly?" Fax asked, his face blank of all expression, his eyes snapping.

Unable to comprehend how he could have uttered such an arrant challenge, F'lar managed to assume a languid pose.

"You did mention," he drawled, "that if any of your Holds could not support itself and the visit of its rightful overlord, you would renounce it."

Fax stared back at F'lar, his face a study of swiftly suppressed emotions, the glint of triumph dominant. F'lar, his face stiff with the forced expression of indifference, was casting swiftly about in his mind. In the name of the Egg, had he lost all sense of discretion?

Pretending utter unconcern, he stabbed some vegetables onto his knife and began to munch on them. As he did so, he noticed F'nor glancing slowly around the Hall, scrutinizing everyone. Abruptly F'lar realized what had happened. Somehow, in making that statement, he, a dragonman, had responded to a covert use of the power. F'lar, the bronze rider, was being put into a position where he would *have* to fight Fax. Why? For what end? To get Fax to renounce the Hold? Incredible! But, there could be only one possible reason for such a turn of events. An exultation as sharp as pain swelled within F'lar. It was all he could do to maintain his pose of bored indifference, all he could do to turn his attention to thwarting Fax, should he press for a duel. A duel would serve no purpose. He, F'lar, had no time to waste on it.

A groan escaped Lady Gemma and broke the eye-locked stance of the two antagonists. Irritated, Fax looked down at her, fist clenched and half-raised to strike her for her temerity in interrupting her lord and master. The contraction that contorted the swollen belly was as obvious as the woman's pain. F'lar dared not look towards her but he wondered if she had deliberately groaned aloud to break the tension.

Incredibly, Fax began to laugh. He threw back his head, showing big, stained teeth, and roared.

"Aye, renounce it, in favor of her issue, if it is male . . . and lives!" he crowed, laughing raucously.

"Heard and witnessed!" F'lar snapped, jumping to his feet and pointing to his riders. They were on their feet in the instant. "Heard and witnessed!" they averred in the traditional manner.

With that movement, everyone began to babble at once in nervous relief. The other women, each reacting in her way to the imminence of birth, called orders to the servants and advice to each other. They converged towards Lady Gemma, hovering undecidedly out of Fax's range, like silly wherries disturbed from their roosts. It was obvious they were torn between their fear of their lord and their desire to reach the laboring woman.

He gathered their intentions as well as their reluctance and, still stridently laughing, knocked back his chair. He stepped over it, strode down to the meatstand and stood hacking off pieces with his knife, stuffing them, juice dripping, into his mouth without ceasing his guffawing.

As F'lar bent towards Lady Gemma to assist her out of her chair, she grabbed his arm urgently. Their eyes met, hers clouded with pain. She pulled him closer.

"He means to kill you, Bronze Rider. He loves to kill," she whispered.

"Dragonmen are not easily killed, but I am grateful to you."

"I do not want you killed," she said, softly, biting at her lip. "We have so few bronze riders."

F'lar stared at her, startled. Did she, Fax's lady, actually believe in the Old Laws?

F'lar beckoned to two of the Warder's men to carry her up into the Hold. He caught Lady Tela by the arm as she fluttered past him.

"What do you need?"

"Oh, oh," she exclaimed, her face twisted with panic; she was distractedly wringing her hands, "Water, hot. Clean cloths. And a birthing-woman. Oh, yes, we must have a birthing-woman."

F'lar looked about for one of the Hold women, his glance sliding over the first disreputable figure who had started to mop up the spilled food. He signaled instead for the Warder and peremptorily ordered him to send for the woman. The Warder kicked at the drudge on the floor.

"You . . . you! Whatever your name is, go get her from the crafthold. You must know who she is."

The drudge evaded the parting kick the Warder aimed in her direction with a nimbleness at odds with her appearance of extreme age and decrepitude. She scurried across the Hall and out the kitchen door.

Fax sliced and speared meat, occasionally bursting out with a louder bark of laughter as his inner thoughts amused him. F'lar sauntered down to the carcass and, without waiting for invitation from his host, began to carve neat slices also, beckoning his men over. Fax's soldiers, however, waited until their lord had eaten his fill.

> *Lord of the Hold, your charge is sure*
> *In thick walls, metal doors and no verdure.*

Lessa sped from the Hall to summon the birthing-woman, seething with frustration. So close! So close! How could she come so close and yet fail? Fax should have challenged the dragonman. And the dragonman was strong and young, his face that of a fighter, stern and controlled. He should not have temporized. Was all honor dead in Pern, smothered by green grass?

And why, oh why, had Lady Gemma chosen that precious moment to go into labor? If her groan hadn't distracted Fax, the fight would have begun and not even Fax, for all his vaunted prowess as a vicious fighter, would have prevailed against a dragonman who had her— Lessa's—support! The Hold must be secured to its rightful Blood again. Fax must not leave Ruatha, alive, again!

Above her, on the High Tower, the great bronze dragon gave forth a weird croon, his many-faceted eyes sparkling in the gathering darkness.

Unconsciously she silenced him as she would have done the watchwher. Ah, that watch-wher. He had not come out of his den at her passing. She knew the dragons had been at him. She could hear him gibbering in panic.

The slant of the road toward the crafthold lent impetus to her flying feet and she had to brace herself to a sliding stop at the birthing-woman's stone threshold. She banged on the closed door and heard the frightened exclamation within.

"A birth. A birth at the Hold," Lessa cried.

"A birth?" came the muffled cry and the latches were thrown up on the door. "At the Hold?"

"Fax's lady and, as you love life, hurry! For if it is male, it will be Ruatha's own lord."

That ought to fetch her, thought Lessa, and in that instant, the door was flung open by the man of the house. Lessa could see the birthing-woman gathering up her things in haste, piling them into her shawl. Lessa hurried the woman out, up the steep road to the Hold, under the Tower gate, grabbing the woman as she tried to run at the sight of a dragon peering down at her. Lessa drew her into the Court and pushed her, resisting, into the Hall.

The woman clutched at the inner door, balking at the sight of the gathering there. Lord Fax, his feet up on the trestle table, was paring his fingernails with his knife blade, still chuckling. The dragonmen in their wher-hide tunics, were eating quietly at one table while the soldiers were having their turn at the meat.

The bronze rider noticed their entrance and pointed urgently towards the inner Hold. The birthing-woman seemed frozen to the spot. Lessa tugged futilely at her arm, urging her to cross the Hall. To her surprise, the bronze rider strode to them.

"Go quickly, woman, Lady Gemma is before her time," he said, frowning with concern, gesturing imperatively towards the Hold entrance. He caught her by the shoulder and led her, all unwilling, Lessa tugging away at her other arm.

When they reached the stairs, he relinquished his grip, nodding to Lessa to escort her the rest of the way. Just as they reached the massive inner door, Lessa noticed how sharply the dragonman was looking at them—at her hand, on the birthing-woman's arm. Warily, she glanced at her hand and saw it, as if it belonged to a stranger: the long fingers, shapely despite dirt and broken nails; her small hand, delicately boned, gracefully placed despite the urgency of the grip. She blurred it and hurried on.

> *Honor those the dragons heed,*
> *In thought and favor, word and deed.*
> *Worlds are lost or worlds are saved*
> *By those dangers dragon-braved.*
>
> *Dragonman, avoid excess;*
> *Greed will bring the Weyr distress;*
> *To the ancient Laws adhere,*
> *Prospers thus the Dragonweyr.*

An unintelligible ululation raised the waiting men to their feet, startled from private meditations and the diversion of Bonethrows. Only Fax remained unmoved at the alarm, save that the slight sneer, which had settled on his face hours past, deepened to smug satisfaction.

"Dead-ed-ed," the tidings reverberated down the rocky corridors of the Hold. The weeping lady seemed to erupt out of the passage from the Inner Hold, flying down the steps to sink into an hysterical heap at Fax's feet. "She's dead. Lady Gemma is dead. There was too much blood. It was too soon. She was too old to bear more children."

F'lar couldn't decide whether the woman was apologizing for, or exulting in, the woman's death. She certainly couldn't be criticizing her Lord for placing Lady Gemma in such peril. F'lar, however, was sincerely sorry at Gemma's passing. She had been a brave, fine woman.

And now, what would be Fax's next move? F'lar caught F'nor's identically quizzical glance and shrugged expressively.

"The child lives!" a curiously distorted voice announced, penetrating the rising noise in the Great Hall. The words electrified the atmosphere. Every head slewed round sharply towards the portal to the Inner Hold where the drudge, a totally unexpected messenger, stood poised on the top step.

"It is male!" This announcement rang triumphantly in the still Hall.

Fax jerked himself to his feet, kicking aside the wailer at his feet, scowling ominously at the drudge. "What did you say, woman?"

"The child lives. It is male," the creature repeated, descending the stairs.

Incredulity and rage suffused Fax's face. His body seemed to coil up.

"Ruatha has a new lord!" Staring intently at the overlord, she advanced, her mien purposeful, almost menacing.

The tentative cheers of the Warder's men were drowned by the roaring of the dragons.

Fax erupted into action. He leaped across the intervening space, bellowing. Before Lessa could dodge, his fist crashed down across her face. She fell heavily to the stone floor, where she lay motionless, a bundle of dirty rags.

"Hold, Fax!" F'lar's voice broke the silence as the Lord of the High Reaches flexed his leg to kick her.

Fax whirled, his hand automatically closing on his knife hilt.

"It was heard and witnessed, Fax," F'lar cautioned him, one hand outstretched in warning, "by dragonmen. Stand by your sworn and witnessed oath!"

"Witnessed? By dragonmen?" cried Fax with a derisive laugh. "Dragonwomen, you mean," he sneered, his eyes blazing with contempt, as he made one sweeping gesture of scorn.

He was momentarily taken aback by the speed with which the bronze rider's knife appeared in his hand.

"Dragonwomen?" F'lar queried, his lips curling back over his teeth, his voice dangerously soft. Glowlight flickered off his circling knife as he advanced on Fax.

"Women! Parasites on Pern. The Weyr power is over. Over!" Fax roared, leaping forward to land in a combat crouch.

The two antagonists were dimly aware of the scurry behind them, of tables pulled roughly aside to give the duelists space. F'lar could spare no glance at the crumpled form of the drudge. Yet he was sure, through and beyond instinct sure, that she was the source of power. He had felt it as she entered the room. The dragons' roaring confirmed it. If that fall had killed her . . . He advanced on Fax, leaping high to avoid the slashing blade as Fax unwound from the crouch with a powerful lunge.

F'lar evaded the attack easily, noticing his opponent's reach, deciding he had a slight advantage there. But not much. Fax had had much more actual hand-to-hand killing experience than had he whose duels had always ended at first blood on the practice floor. F'lar made due note to avoid closing with the burly lord. The man was heavy-chested, dangerous from sheer mass. F'lar must use agility as his weapon, not brute strength.

Fax feinted, testing F'lar for weakness, or indiscretion. The two crouched, facing each other across six feet of space, knife hands weaving, their free hands, spread-fingered, ready to grab.

Again Fax pressed the attack. F'lar allowed him to close, just near enough to dodge away with a back-handed swipe. Fabric ripped under the tip of his knife. He heard Fax snarl. The overlord was faster on his feet than his bulk suggested and F'lar had to dodge a second time, feeling Fax's knife score his wher-hide jerkin.

Grimly the two circled, each looking for an opening in the other's defense. Fax plowed in, trying to corner the lighter, faster man between raised platform and wall.

F'lar countered, ducking low under Fax's flailing arm, slashing obliquely across Fax's side. The overlord caught at him, yanking savagely, and F'lar was trapped against the other man's side, straining desperately with his left hand to keep the knife arm up. F'lar brought up his knee, and ducked away as Fax gasped and buckled from the pain in his groin, but Fax struck in passing. Sudden fire laced F'lar's left shoulder.

Fax's face was red with anger and he wheezed from pain and shock. But the infuriated lord straightened up and charged. F'lar was forced to sidestep quickly before Fax could close with him. F'lar put the meat table between them, circling warily, flexing his shoulder to assess the extent of the knife's slash. It was painful, but the arm could be used.

Suddenly Fax scooped up some fatty scraps from the meat tray and hurled them at F'lar. The dragonman ducked and Fax came around the table with a rush. F'lar leaped sideways. Fax's flashing blade came within inches of his abdomen, as his own knife sliced down the outside of Fax's arm. Instantly the two pivoted to face each other again, but Fax's left arm hung limply at his side.

F'lar darted in, pressing his luck as the Lord of the High Reaches staggered. But F'lar misjudged the man's condition and suffered a terrific kick in the side as he tried to dodge under the feinting knife. Doubled with pain, F'lar rolled frantically away from his charging adversary. Fax was lurching forward, trying to fall on him, to pin the lighter dragonman down for a final thrust. Somehow F'lar got to his feet, attempting to straighten to meet Fax's stumbling charge. His very position saved him. Fax overreached his mark and staggered off balance. F'lar brought his right hand over with as much strength as he could muster and his blade plunged through Fax's unprotected back until he felt the point stick in the chest plate.

The defeated lord fell flat to the flagstones. The force of his descent dislodged the dagger from his chestbone and an inch of bloody blade re-emerged.

F'lar stared down at the dead man. There was no pleasure in killing, he realized, only relief that he himself was still alive. He wiped his forehead on his sleeve and forced himself erect, his side throbbing with the pain of that last kick and his left shoulder burning. He halfstumbled to the drudge, still sprawled where she had fallen.

He gently turned her over, noting the terrible bruise spreading across her cheek under the dirty skin. He heard F'nor take command of the tumult in the Hall.

The dragonman laid a hand, trembling in spite of an effort to control himself, on the woman's breast to feel for a heartbeat . . . It was there, slow but strong.

A deep sigh escaped him for either blow or fall could have proved fatal. Fatal, perhaps, for Pern as well.

Relief was colored with disgust. There was no telling under the filth how old this creature might be. He raised her in his arms, her light body no burden even to his battle-weary strength. Knowing F'nor would handle any trouble efficiently, F'lar carried the drudge to his own chamber.

Putting the body on the high bed, he stirred up the fire and added more glows to the bedside bracket. His gorge rose at the thought of touching the filthy mat of hair but nonetheless and gently, he pushed it back from the face, turning the head this way and that. The features were small, regular. One arm, clear of rags, was reasonably clean above the elbow but marred by bruises and old scars. The skin was firm and unwrinkled. The hands, when he took them in his, were filthy but wellshaped and delicately boned.

F'lar began to smile. Yes, she had blurred that hand so skillfully that he had actually doubted what he had first seen. And yes, beneath grime and grease, she was young. Young enough for the Weyr. And no born drab. There was no taint of common blood here. It was pure, no matter whose the line, and he rather thought she was indeed Ruathan. One who had by some unknown agency escaped the massacre ten Turns ago and bided her time for revenge. Why else force Fax to renounce the Hold?

Delighted and fascinated by this unexpected luck, F'lar reached out to tear the dress from the unconscious body and found himself constrained not to. The girl had roused. Her great, hungry eyes fastened on his, not fearful or expectant; wary.

A subtle change occurred in her face. F'lar watched, his smile deepening, as she shifted her regular features into an illusion of disagreeable ugliness and great age.

"Trying to confuse a dragonman, girl?" he chuckled. He made no further move to touch her but settled against the great carved post of the bed. He crossed his arms sternly on his chest, thought better of it immediately, and eased his sore arm. "Your name, girl, and rank, too."

She drew herself upright slowly against the headboard, her features no longer blurred. They faced each other across the high bed.

"Fax?"

"Dead. Your name!"

A look of exulting triumph flooded her face. She slipped from the bed, standing unexpectedly tall. "Then I reclaim my own. I am of the Ruathan Blood. I claim Ruath," she announced in a ringing voice.

F'lar stared at her a moment, delighted with her proud bearing. Then he threw back his head and laughed.

"This? This crumbling head?" He could not help but mock the disparity between her manner and her dress. "Oh, no. Besides, Lady, we dragonmen heard and witnessed Fax's oath renouncing the Hold in favor of his heir. Shall I challenge the babe, too, for you? And choke him with his swaddling cloths?"

Her eyes flashed, her lips parted in a terrible smile.

"There is no heir. Gemma died, the babe unborn. I lied."

"Lied?" F'lar demanded, angry.

"Yes," she taunted him with a toss of her chin. "I lied. There was no babe born. I merely wanted to be sure you challenged Fax."

He grabbed her wrist, stung that he had twice fallen to her prodding.

"You provoked a dragonman to fight? To kill? *When he is on Search?*"

"Search? Why should I care about a Search? I've Ruatha as my Hold again. For ten Turns, I have worked and waited, schemed and suffered for that. What could your Search mean to me?"

F'lar wanted to strike that look of haughty contempt from her face. He twisted her arm savagely, bringing her to his feet before he released his grip. She laughed at him, and scuttled to one side. She was on her feet and out the door before he could give chase.

Swearing to himself, he raced down the rocky corridors, knowing she would have to make for the Hall to get out of the Hold. However, when he reached the Hall, there was no sign of her fleeing figure among those still loitering.

"Has that creature come this way?" he called to F'nor who was, by chance, standing by the door to the Court.

"No. Is she the source of power after all?"

"Yes, she is," F'lar answered, galled all the more. "And Ruathan Blood at that!"

"Oh ho! Does she depose the babe, then?" F'nor asked, gesturing towards the birthing-woman who occupied a seat close to the now blazing hearth.

F'lar paused, about to return to search the Hold's myriad passages. He stared, momentarily confused, at this brown rider.

"Babe? What babe?"

"The male child Lady Gemma bore," F'nor replied, surprised by F'lar's uncomprehending look.

"It lives?"

"Yes. A strong babe, the woman says, for all that he was premature and taken forcibly from his dead dame's belly."

F'lar threw back his head with a shout of laughter. For all her scheming, she had been outdone by truth.

At that moment, he heard Mnementh roar in unmistakable elation and the curious warble of other dragons.

"Mnementh has caught her," F'lar cried, grinning with jubilation. He strode down the steps, past the body of the former Lord of the High Reaches and out into the main court.

He saw that the bronze dragon was gone from his Tower perch and called him. An agitation drew his eyes upward. He saw Mnementh spiraling down into the Court, his front paws clasping something. Mnementh informed F'lar that he had seen her climbing from one of the high windows and had simply plucked her from the ledge, knowing the dragonman sought her. The bronze dragon settled awkwardly onto his hind legs, his wings working to keep him balanced. Carefully he set the girl on her feet and formed a precise cage around her with his huge talons. She stood motionless within that circle, her face toward the wedge-shaped head that swayed above her.

The watch-wher, shrieking terror, anger and hatred, was lunging violently to the end of its chain, trying to come to Lessa's aid. It grabbed at F'lar as he strode to the two.

"You've courage enough, girl," he admitted, resting one hand casually on Mnementh's upper claw. Mnementh was enormously pleased with himself and swiveled his head down for his eye ridges to be scratched.

"You did not lie, you know," F'lar said, unable to resist taunting the girl.

Slowly she turned towards him, her face impassive. She was not afraid of dragons, F'lar realized with approval.

"The babe lives. And it is male."

She could not control her dismay and her shoulders sagged briefly before she pulled herself erect.

"Ruatha is mine," she insisted in a tense low voice.

"Aye, and it would have been, had you approached me directly when the wing arrived here."

Her eyes widened. "What do you mean?"

"A dragonman may champion anyone whose grievance is just. By the time we reached Ruath Hold, I was quite ready to challenge Fax given any reasonable cause, despite the Search." This was not the whole truth but F'lar must teach this girl the folly of trying to control dragonmen. "Had you paid any attention to your harper's songs, you'd know your rights. And," F'lar's voice held a vindictive edge that surprised him, "Lady Gemma might not now lie dead. She suffered far more at that tyrant's hand than you."

Something in her manner told him that she regretted Lady Gemma's death, that it had affected her deeply.

"What good is Ruatha to you now?" he demanded, a broad sweep of his arm taking in the ruined court yard and the Hold, the entire unproductive valley of Ruatha. "You have indeed accomplished your ends; a profitless conquest and its conqueror's death." F'lar snorted: "All seven Holds will revert to their legitimate Blood, and time they did. One Hold, one lord. Of course, you might have to fight others, infected with Fax's greed. Could you hold Ruatha against attack . . . now . . . in her decline?"

"Ruatha is mine!"

"Ruatha?" F'lar's laugh was derisive. "When you could be Weyrwoman?"

"Weyrwoman?" she breathed, staring at him.

"Yes, little fool. I said I rode in Search . . . it's about time you attended to more than Ruatha. And the object of my Search is . . . you!"

She stared at the finger he pointed at her as if it were dangerous.

"By the First Egg, girl, you've power in you to spare when you can turn a dragonman, all unwitting, to do your bidding. Ah, but never again, for now I am on guard against you."

Mnementh crooned approvingly, the sound a soft rumble in his throat. He arched his neck so that one eye was turned directly on the girl, gleaming in the darkness of the court.

F'lar noticed with detached pride that she neither flinched nor blanched at the proximity of an eye greater than her own head.

"He likes to have his eye ridges scratched," F'lar remarked in a friendly tone, changing tactics.

"I know," she said softly and reached out a hand to do that service.

"Nemorth's queen," F'lar continued, "is close to death. This time we must have a strong Weyrwoman."

"This time—the Red Star?" the girl gasped, turning frightened eyes to F'lar.

"You understand what it means?"

"There is danger . . ." she began in a bare whisper, glancing apprehensively eastward.

F'lar did not question by what miracle she appreciated the imminence of danger. He had every intention of taking her to the Weyr by sheer force if necessary. But something within him wanted very much for her to accept the challenge voluntarily. A rebellious Weyrwoman would be even more dangerous than a stupid one. This girl had too much power and was too used to guile and strategy. It would be a calamity to antagonize her with injudicious handling.

"There is danger for all Pern. Not just Ruatha," he said, allowing a note of entreaty to creep into his voice. "And *you* are needed. Not by Ruatha," a wave of his hand dismissed that consideration as a negligible one compared to the total picture. "We are doomed without a strong Weyrwoman. Without you."

"Gemma kept saying *all* the bronze riders were needed," she murmured in a dazed whisper.

What did she mean by that statement? F'lar frowned. Had she heard a word he had said? He pressed his argument, certain only that he had already struck one responsive chord.

"You've won here. Let the babe," he saw her startled rejection of that idea and ruthlessly qualified it, ". . . Gemma's babe . . . be reared at

Ruatha. You have command of all the Holds as Weyrwoman, not ruined Ruatha alone. You've accomplished Fax's death. Leave off vengeance."

She stared at F'lar with wonder, absorbing his words.

"I never thought beyond Fax's death," she admitted slowly. "I never thought what should happen then."

Her confusion was almost childlike and struck F'lar forcibly. He had had no time, or desire, to consider her prodigious accomplishment. Now he realized some measure of her indomitable character. She could not have been much over ten Turns of age herself when Fax had murdered her family. Yet somehow, so young, she had set herself a goal and managed to survive both brutality and detection long enough to secure the usurper's death. What a Weyrwoman she would be! In the tradition of those of Ruathan blood. The light of the paler moon made her look young and vulnerable and almost pretty.

"You can be Weyrwoman," he insisted gently.

"Weyrwoman," she breathed, incredulous, and gazed round the inner court bathed in soft moonlight. He thought she wavered.

"Or perhaps you enjoy rags?" he said, making his voice harsh, mocking. "And matted hair, dirty feet and cracked hands? Sleeping in straw, eating rinds? You are young . . . that is, I assume you are young," and his voice was frankly skeptical. She glared at him, her lips firmly pressed together. "Is this the be-all and end-all of your ambition? What are you that this little corner of the great world is *all* you want?" He paused and with utter contempt added, "The blood of Ruatha has thinned, I see. You're afraid!"

"I am Lessa, daughter of the Lord of Ruath," she countered, stung. She drew herself erect. Her eyes flashed. "I am afraid of nothing!"

F'lar contented himself with a slight smile.

Mnementh, however, threw up his head, and stretched out his sinuous neck to its whole length. His full-throated peal rang out down the valley. The bronze communicated his awareness to F'lar that Lessa had accepted the challenge. The other dragons answered back, their warbles shriller than Mnementh's bellow. The watch-wher which had cowered at the end of its chain lifted its voice in a thin, unnerving screech until the Hold emptied of its startled occupants.

"F'nor," the bronze rider called, waving his wingleader to him. "Leave half the flight to guard the Hold. Some nearby lord might think to emulate Fax's example. Send one rider to the High Reaches with the glad news. You go directly to the Cloth Hall and speak to L'to . . . Lytol." F'lar grinned. "I think he would make an exemplary Warder and Lord Surrogate for this Hold in the name of the Weyr and the babe."

The brown rider's face expressed enthusiasm for his mission as he began to comprehend his leader's intentions. With Fax dead and Ruatha under the protection of dragonmen, particularly that same one who had dispatched Fax, the Hold would have wise management.

"She caused Ruatha's deterioration?" he asked.

"And nearly ours with her machinations," F'lar replied but having found the admirable object of his Search, he could now be magnanimous. "Suppress your exultation, brother," he advised quickly as he took note of F'nor's expression. "The new queen must also be Impressed."

"I'll settle arrangements here. Lytol is an excellent choice," F'nor said.

"Who is this Lytol?" demanded Lessa pointedly. She had twisted the mass of filthy hair back from her face. In the moonlight the dirt was less noticeable. F'lar caught F'nor looking at her with an all too easily read expression. He signaled F'nor, with a peremptory gesture, to carry out his orders without delay.

"Lytol is a dragonless man," F'lar told the girl, "no friend to Fax. He will ward the Hold well and it will prosper." He added persuasively with a quelling stare full on her. "Won't it?"

She regarded him somberly, without answering, until he chuckled softly at her discomfiture.

"We'll return to the Weyr," he announced, proffering a hand to guide her to Mnementh's side.

The bronze one had extended his head toward the watch-wher who now lay panting on the ground, its chain limp in the dust.

"Oh," Lessa sighed, and dropped beside the grotesque beast. It raised its head slowly, lurring piteously.

"Mnementh says it is very old and soon will sleep itself to death."

Lessa cradled the bestial head in her arms, scratching it behind the ears.

"Come, Lessa of Pern," F'lar said, impatient to be up and away.

She rose slowly but obediently. "It saved me. It knew me."

"It knows it did well," F'lar assured her, brusquely, wondering at such an uncharacteristic show of sentiment in her.

He took her hand again, to help her to her feet and lead her back to Mnementh. As they turned, he glimpsed the watch-wher, launching itself at a dead run after Lessa. The chain, however, held fast. The beast's neck broke, with a sickeningly audible snap.

Lessa was on her knees in an instant, cradling the repulsive head in her arms.

"Why, you foolish thing, why?" she asked in a stunned whisper as the light in the beast's green-gold eyes dimmed and died out.

Mnementh informed F'lar that the creature had lived this long only to preserve the Ruathan line. At Lessa's imminent departure, it had welcomed death.

A convulsive shudder went through Lessa's slim body. F'lar watched as she undid the heavy buckle that fastened the metal collar about the watch-wher's neck. She threw the tether away with a violent motion. Tenderly she laid the watch-wher on the cobbles. With one last caress to the clipped wings, she rose in a fluid movement and walked resolutely to Mnementh without a single backward glance. She stepped calmly to the dragon's raised leg and seated herself, as F'lar directed, on the great neck.

F'lar glanced around the courtyard at the remainder of his wing which had reformed there. The Hold folk had retreated back into the safety of the Great Hall. When his wingmen were all astride, he vaulted to Mnementh's neck, behind the girl.

"Hold tightly to my arms," he ordered her as he took hold of the smallest neck ridge and gave the command to fly.

Her fingers closed spasmodically around his forearm as the great bronze dragon took off, the enormous wings working to achieve height from the vertical takeoff. Mnementh preferred to fall into flight from a cliff or tower. Like all dragons, he tended to indolence. F'lar glanced behind him, saw the other dragonmen form the flight line, spread out to cover those still on guard at Ruatha Hold.

When they had reached a sufficient altitude, he told Mnementh to transfer, going *between* to the Weyr.

Only a gasp indicated the girl's astonishment as they hung *between*. Accustomed as he was to the sting of the profound cold, to the awesome utter lack of light and sound, F'lar still found the sensations unnerving. Yet the uncommon transfer spanned no more time than it took to cough thrice.

Mnementh rumbled approval of this candidate's calm reaction as they flicked out of the eerie *between*.

And then they were above the Weyr, Mnementh setting his wings to glide in the bright daylight, half a world away from night-time Ruatha.

As they circled above the great stony trough of the Weyr, F'lar peered at Lessa's face, pleased with the delight mirrored there; she showed no trace of fear as they hung a thousand lengths above the high Benden mountain range. Then, as the seven dragons roared their incoming cry, an incredulous smile lit her face.

The other wingmen dropped into a wide spiral, down, down while Mnementh elected to descend in lazy circles. The dragonmen peeled off smartly and dropped, each to his own tier in the caves of the Weyr. Mnementh finally completed his leisurely approach to their quarters, whistling shrilly to himself as he braked his forward speed with a twist of his wings, dropping lightly at last to the ledge. He crouched as F'lar swung the girl to the rough rock, scored from thousands of clawed landings.

"This leads only to our quarters," he told her as they entered the corridor, vaulted and wide for the easy passage of great bronze dragons.

As they reached the huge natural cavern that had been his since Mnementh achieved maturity, F'lar looked about him with eyes fresh from his first prolonged absence from the Weyr. The huge chamber was unquestionably big, certainly larger than most of the halls he had visited in Fax's procession. Those halls were intended as gathering places for men, not the habitations of dragons. But suddenly he saw his own quarters were nearly as shabby as all Ruatha. Benden was, of a certainty, one of the oldest dragonweyrs, as Ruatha was one of the oldest Holds, but that excused nothing. How many dragons had bedded in that hollow to make solid rock conform to dragon proportions! How many feet had worn the path past the dragon's weyr into the sleeping chamber, to the bathing room beyond where the natural warm spring provided everfresh water! But the wall hangings were faded and unraveling and there were grease stains on lintel and floor that should be sanded away.

He noticed the wary expression on Lessa's face as he paused in the sleeping room.

"I must feed Mnementh immediately. So you may bathe first," he said, rummaging in a chest and finding clean clothes for her, discards of other previous occupants of his quarters, but far more presentable than her present covering. He carefully laid back in the chest the white wool robe that was traditional Impression garb. She would wear that later. He tossed several garments at her feet and a bag of sweetsand, gesturing to the hanging that obscured the way to the bath.

He left her, then, the clothes in a heap at her feet, for she made no effort to catch anything.

Mnementh informed him that F'nor was feeding Canth and that

he, Mnementh, was hungry, too. *She* didn't trust F'lar but she wasn't afraid of himself.

"Why should she be afraid of you?" F'lar asked. "You're cousin to the watch-wher who was her only friend."

Mnementh informed F'lar that he, a fully matured bronze dragon, was no relation to any scrawny, crawling, chained, and wing-clipped watch-wher.

F'lar, pleased at having been able to tease the bronze one, chuckled to himself. With great dignity, Mnementh curved down to the feeding ground.

> *By the Golden Egg of Faranth*
> *By the Weyrwoman wise and true,*
> *Breed a flight of bronze and brown wings,*
> *Breed a flight of green and blue.*
> *Breed riders, strong and daring,*
> *Dragon-loving, born as hatched,*
> *Flight of hundreds soaring skyward,*
> *Man and dragon fully matched.*

Lessa waited until the sound of the dragonmen's footsteps proved he had really gone away. She rushed quickly through the big cavern, heard the scrape of claw and the *whoosh* of the mighty wings. She raced down the short passageway, right to the edge of the yawning entrance. There was the bronze dragon circling down to the wider end of the mile-long barren oval that was Benden Weyr. She had heard of the Weyrs, as any Pernese had, but to be in one was quite a different matter.

She peered up, around, down that sheer rock face. There was no way off but by dragon wing. The nearest cave mouths were an unhandy distance above her, to one side, below her on the other. She was neatly secluded here.

Weyrwoman, he had told her. His woman? In his weyr? Was that what he had meant? No, that was not the impression she got from the dragon. It occurred to her, suddenly, that it was odd she had understood the dragon. Were common folk able to? Or was it the dragonman blood in her line? At all events, Mnementh had inferred something greater, some special rank. She remembered vaguely that, when dragonmen went on Search, they looked for certain women. Ah, certain women. She was one, then, of several contenders. Yet the bronze rider had offered her the position as if she and she, alone, qualified. He had his own generous portion of conceit, that one, Lessa decided. Arrogant he was, though not a bully like Fax.

She could see the bronze dragon swoop down to the running herd-beasts, saw the strike, saw the dragon wheel up to settle on a far ledge to feed. Instinctively she drew back from the opening, back into the dark and relative safety of the corridor.

The feeding dragon evoked scores of horrid tales. Tales at which she had scoffed but now . . . Was it true, then, that dragons did eat human flesh? Did . . . Lessa halted that trend of thought. Dragon-kind was no less cruel than mankind. The dragon, at least, acted from bestial need rather than bestial greed.

Assured that the dragonman would be occupied a while, she crossed the larger cave into the sleeping room. She scooped up the clothing and the bag of cleansing sand and proceeded to the bathing room.

To be clean! To be completely clean and to be able to stay that way. With distaste, she stripped off the remains of the rags, kicking them to one side. She made a soft mud with the sweetsand and scrubbed her entire body until she drew blood from various half-healed cuts. Then she jumped into the pool, gasping as the warm water made the sweet-sand foam in the lacerations.

It was a ritual cleansing of more than surface soil. The luxury of cleanliness was ecstasy.

Finally satisfied she was as clean as one long soaking could make her, she left the pool, reluctantly. Wringing out her hair she tucked it up on her head as she dried herself. She shook out the clothing and held one garment against her experimentally. The fabric, a soft green, felt smooth under her water-shrunken fingers, although the nap caught on her roughened hands. She pulled it over her head. It was loose but the darker-green over-tunic had a sash which she pulled in tight at the waist. The unusual sensation of softness against her bare skin made her wriggle with voluptuous pleasure. The skirt, no longer a ragged hem of tatters, swirled heavily around her ankles. She smiled. She took up a fresh drying cloth and began to work on her hair.

A muted sound came to her ears and she stopped, hands poised, head bent to one side. Straining, she listened. Yes, there were sounds with-out. The dragonman and his beasts must have returned. She grimaced to herself with annoyance at his untimely interruption and rubbed harder at her hair. She ran fingers through the half-dry tangles, the motions arrested as she encountered snarls. Vexed, she rummaged on the shelves until she found, as she had hoped to, a coarse-toothed metal comb.

Dry, her hair had a life of its own suddenly, crackling about her hands and clinging to face and comb and dress. It was difficult to get the silky stuff under control. And her hair was longer than she had thought, for, clean and unmatted, it fell to her waist—when it did not cling to her hands.

She paused, listening, and heard no sound at all. Apprehensively, she stepped to the curtain and glanced warily into the sleeping room. It was empty. She listened and caught the perceptible thoughts of the sleepy dragon. Well, she would rather meet the man in the presence of a sleepy dragon than in a sleeping room. She started across the floor and, out of the corner of her eye, caught sight of a strange woman as she passed a polished piece of metal hanging on the wall.

Amazed, she stopped short, staring, incredulous, at the face the metal reflected. Only when she put her hands to her prominent cheekbones in a gesture of involuntary surprise and the reflection imitated the gesture, did she realize she looked at herself.

Why, that girl in the reflector was prettier than Lady Tela, than the clothman's daughter! But so thin. Her hands of their own volition dropped to her neck, to the protruding collarbones, to her breasts which did not entirely accord with the gauntness of the rest of her. The dress was too large for her frame, she noted with an unexpected emergence of conceit born in that instant of delighted appraisal. And her hair . . . it stood out around her head like an aureole. It wouldn't lie contained. She smoothed it down with impatient fingers, automatically bringing locks forward to hang around her face. As she irritably pushed them back, dismissing a need for disguise, the hair drifted up again.

A slight sound, the scrape of a boot against stone, caught her back from her bemusement. She waited, momentarily expecting him to appear. She was suddenly timid. With her face bare to the world, her hair behind her ears, her body outlined by a clinging fabric, she was stripped of her accustomed anonymity and was, therefore, in her estimation, vulnerable.

She controlled the desire to run away—the irrational fear. Observing herself in the looking metal, she drew her shoulders back, tilted her head high, chin up; the movement caused her hair to crackle and cling and shift about her head. She was Lessa of Ruatha, of a fine old Blood. She no longer needed artifice to preserve herself; she must stand proudly bare-faced before the world . . . and that dragonman.

Resolutely she crossed the room, pushing aside the hanging on the doorway to the great cavern.

He was there, beside the head of the dragon, scratching its eye ridges, a curiously tender expression on his face. The tableau was at variance with all she had heard of dragonmen.

She had, of course, heard of the strange affinity between rider and dragon but this was the first time she realized that love was part of that bond. Or that this reserved, cold man was capable of such deep emotion.

He turned slowly, as if loath to leave the bronze beast. He caught sight of her and pivoted completely round, his eyes intense as he took note of her altered appearance. With quick, light steps, he closed the distance between them and ushered her back into the sleeping room, one strong hand holding her by the elbow.

"Mnementh has fed lightly and will need quiet to rest," he said in a low voice. He pulled the heavy hanging into place across the opening.

Then he held her away from him, turning her this way and that, scrutinizing her closely, curious and slightly surprised.

"You wash up . . . pretty, yes, almost pretty," he said, amused condescension in his voice. She pulled roughly away from him, piqued. His low laugh mocked her. "After all, how could one guess what was under the grime of . . . ten full Turns?"

At length he said, "No matter. We must eat and I shall require your services." At her startled exclamation, he turned, grinning maliciously now as his movement revealed the caked blood on his left sleeve. "The least you can do is bathe wounds honorably received fighting your battle."

He pushed aside a portion of the drape that curtained the inner wall. "Food for two!" he roared down a black gap in the sheer stone.

She heard a subterranean echo far below as his voice resounded down what must be a long shaft.

"Nemorth is nearly rigid," he was saying as he took supplies from another drape-hidden shelf, "and the Hatching will soon begin anyhow."

A coldness settled in Lessa's stomach at the mention of a Hatching. The mildest tales she had heard about that part of dragonlore were chilling, the worst dismayingly macabre. She took the things he handed her numbly.

"What? Frightened?" the dragonman taunted, pausing as he stripped off his torn and bloodied shirt.

With a shake of her head, Lessa turned her attention to the wide-shouldered, well-muscled back he presented her, the paler skin of his body decorated with random bloody streaks. Fresh blood welled from the point of his shoulder for the removal of his shirt had broken the tender scabs.

"I will need water," she said and saw she had a flat pan among the items he had given her. She went swiftly to the pool for water, wondering how she had come to agree to venture so far from Ruatha. Ruined though it was, it had been hers and was familiar to her from Tower to deep cellar. At the moment the idea had been proposed and insidiously prosecuted by the dragonman, she had felt capable of anything, having achieved, at last, Fax's death. Now, it was all she could do to keep the water from slopping out of the pan that shook unaccountably in her hands.

She forced herself to deal only with the wound. It was a nasty gash, deep where the point had entered and torn downward in a gradually shallower slice. His skin felt smooth under her fingers as she cleansed the wound. In spite of herself, she noticed the masculine odor of him, compounded not unpleasantly of sweat, leather, and an unusual muskiness which must be from close association with dragons.

She stood back when she had finished her ministration. He flexed his arm experimentally in the constricting bandage and the motion set the muscles rippling along side and back.

When he faced her, his eyes were dark and thoughtful.

"Gently done. My thanks." His smile was ironic.

She backed away as he rose but he only went to the chest to take out a clean, white shirt.

A muted rumble sounded, growing quickly louder.

Dragons roaring? Lessa wondered, trying to conquer the ridiculous fear that rose within her. Had the Hatching started? There was no watch-wher's lair to secrete herself in, here.

As if he understood her confusion, the dragonman laughed goodhumoredly and, his eyes on hers, drew aside the wall covering just as some noisy mechanism inside the shaft propelled a tray of food into sight.

Ashamed of her unbased fright and furious that he had witnessed it, Lessa sat rebelliously down on the fur-covered wall seat, heartily wishing him a variety of serious and painful injuries which she could dress with inconsiderate hands. She would not waste future opportunities.

He placed the tray on the low table in front of her, throwing down a heap of furs for his own seat. There was meat, bread, a tempting yellow cheese and even a few pieces of winter fruit. He made no move to eat nor did she, though the thought of a piece of fruit that was ripe, instead of rotten, set her mouth to watering. He glanced up at her, and frowned.

"Even in the Weyr, the lady breaks bread first," he said, and inclined his head politely to her.

Lessa flushed, unused to any courtesy and certainly unused to being first to eat. She broke off a chunk of bread. It was like nothing she remembered having tasted before. For one thing, it was fresh-baked. The flour had been finely sifted, without trace of sand or hull. She took the slice of cheese he proffered her and it, too, had an uncommonly delicious sharpness. Made bold by this indication of her changed status, Lessa reached for the plumpest piece of fruit.

"Now," the dragonman began, his hand touching hers to get her attention.

Guiltily she dropped the fruit, thinking she had erred. She stared at him, wondering at her fault. He retrieved the fruit and placed it back in her hand as he continued to speak. Wide-eyed, disarmed, she nibbled, and gave him her full attention.

"Listen to me. You must not show a moment's fear, whatever happens on the Hatching Ground. And you must not let her overeat." A wry expression crossed his face. "One of our main functions is to keep a dragon from excessive eating."

Lessa lost interest in the taste of the fruit. She placed it carefully back in the bowl and tried to sort out not what he had said, but what his tone of voice implied. She looked at the dragonman's face, seeing him as a person, not a symbol, for the first time.

There was a blackness about him that was not malevolent; it was a brooding sort of patience. Heavy black hair, heavy black brows; his eyes, a brown light enough to seem golden, were all too expressive of cynical emotions, or cold hauteur. His lips were thin but well-shaped and in repose almost gentle. Why must he always pull his mouth to one side in disapproval or in one of those sardonic smiles? At this moment, he was completely unaffected.

He meant what he was saying. He did not want her to be afraid. There was no reason for her, Lessa, to fear.

He very much wanted her to succeed. In keeping whom from overeating what? Herd animals? A newly hatched dragon certainly wasn't capable of eating a full beast. That seemed a simple enough task to Lessa. . . . Main function? *Our* main function?

The dragonman was looking at her expectantly.

"Our main function?" she repeated, an unspoken request for more information inherent in her inflection.

"More of that later. First things first," he said, impatiently waving off other questions.

"But what happens?" she insisted.

"As I was told so I tell you. No more, no less. Remember these two points. No fear, and no overeating."

"But . . ."

"You, however, need to eat. Here." He speared a piece of meat on his knife and thrust it at her, frowning until she managed to choke it down. He was about to force more on her but she grabbed up her half-eaten fruit and bit down into the firm sweet sphere instead. She had already eaten more at this one meal than she was accustomed to having all day at the Hold.

"We shall soon eat better at the Weyr," he remarked, regarding the tray with a jaundiced eye.

Lessa was surprised. This was a feast, in her opinion.

"More than you're used to? Yes, I forgot you left Ruatha with bare bones indeed."

She stiffened.

"You did well at Ruatha. I mean no criticism," he added, smiling at her reaction. "But look at you," and he gestured at her body, that curious expression crossing his face, half-amused, half-contemplative. "I should not have guessed you'd clean up pretty," he remarked. "Nor with such hair." This time his expression was frankly admiring.

Involuntarily she put one hand to her head, the hair crackling over her fingers. But what reply she might have made him, indignant as she was, died aborning. An unearthly keening filled the chamber.

The sounds set up a vibration that ran down the bones behind her ear to her spine. She clapped both hands to her ears. The noise rang through her skull despite her defending hands. As abruptly as it started, it ceased.

Before she knew what he was about, the dragonman had grabbed her by the wrist and pulled her over to the chest.

"Take those off," he ordered, indicating dress and tunic. While she stared at him stupidly, he held up a loose white robe, sleeveless and beltless, a matter of two lengths of fine cloth fastened at shoulder and side seams. "Take it off, or do I assist you?" he asked, with no patience at all.

The wild sound was repeated and its unnerving tone made her fingers fly faster. She had no sooner loosened the garments she wore, letting them slide to her feet, than he had thrown the other over her head. She managed to get her arms in the proper places before he grabbed her wrist again and was speeding with her out of the room, her hair whipping out behind her, alive with static.

As they reached the outer chamber, the bronze dragon was standing in the center of the cavern, his head turned to watch the sleeping room door. He seemed impatient to Lessa; his great eyes, which fascinated her so, sparkled iridescently. His manner breathed an inner excitement of great proportions and from his throat a high-pitched croon issued, several octaves below the unnerving cry that had roused them all.

With a yank that rocked her head on her neck, the dragonman pulled her along the passage. The dragon padded beside them at such speed that Lessa fully expected they would all catapult off the ledge. Somehow, at the crucial stride, she was a-perch the bronze neck, the dragonman holding her firmly about the waist. In the same fluid movement, they were gliding across the great bowl of the Weyr to the higher wall opposite. The air was full of wings and dragon tails, rent with a chorus of sounds, echoing and re-echoing across the stony valley.

Mnementh set what Lessa was certain would be a collision course with other dragons, straight for a huge round blackness in the cliff-face, high up. Magically, the beasts filed in, the greater wingspread of Mnementh just clearing the sides of the entrance.

The passageway reverberated with the thunder of wings. The air compressed around her thickly. Then they broke into a gigantic cavern.

Why, the entire mountain must be hollow, thought Lessa, incredulous. Around the enormous cavern, dragons perched in serried ranks, blues, greens, browns and only two great bronze beasts like Mnementh, on ledges meant to accommodate hundreds. Lessa gripped the bronze neck scales before her, instinctively aware of the imminence of a great event.

Mnementh wheeled downward, disregarding the ledge of the bronze ones. Then all Lessa could see was what lay on the sandy floor of the great cavern; dragon eggs. A clutch of ten monstrous, mottled eggs, their shells moving spasmodically as the fledglings within tapped their way out. To one side, on a raised portion of the floor, was a golden egg, larger by half again the size of the mottled ones. Just beyond the golden egg lay the motionless ochre hulk of the old queen.

Just as she realized Mnementh was hovering over the floor in the vicinity of that egg, Lessa felt the dragonman's hands on her, lifting her from Mnementh's neck.

Apprehensively, she grabbed at him. His hands tightened and inexorably swung her down. His eyes, fierce and gray, locked with hers.

"Remember, Lessa!"

Mnementh added an encouragement, one great compound eye turned on her. Then he rose from the floor. Lessa half-raised one hand in entreaty, bereft of all support, even that of the sure inner compulsion which had sustained her in her struggle for revenge on Fax. She saw the bronze dragon settle on the first ledge, at some distance from the other two bronze beasts. The dragonman dismounted and Mnementh curved his sinuous neck until his head was beside his rider. The man reached up absently, it seemed to Lessa, and caressed his mount.

Loud screams and wailings diverted Lessa and she saw more dragons descend to hover just above the cavern floor, each rider depositing a young woman until there were twelve girls, including Lessa. She remained a little apart from them as they clung to each other. She regarded them curiously. The girls were not injured in any way she could see, so why such weeping? She took a deep breath against the coldness within her. Let *them* be afraid. She was Lessa of Ruatha and did not need to be afraid.

Just then, the golden egg moved convulsively. Gasping as one, the girls edged away from it, back against the rocky wall. One, a lovely blonde, her heavy plait of golden hair swinging just above the ground, started to step off the raised floor and stopped, shrieking, backing fearfully towards the scant comfort of her peers.

Lessa wheeled to see what cause there might be for the look of horror on the girl's face. She stepped back involuntarily herself.

In the main section of the sandy arena, several of the handful of eggs had already cracked wide open. The fledglings, crowing weakly, were moving towards . . . and Lessa gulped . . . the young boys standing stolidly in a semi-circle. Some of them were no older than she had been when Fax's army had swooped down on Ruath Hold.

The shrieking of the women subsided to muffled gasps. A fledgling reached out with claw and beak to grab a boy.

Lessa forced herself to watch as the young dragon mauled the youth, throwing him roughly aside as if unsatisfied in some way. The boy did not move and Lessa could see blood seeping onto the sand from dragon-inflicted wounds.

A second fledgling lurched against another boy and halted, flapping its damp wings impotently, raising its scrawny neck and croaking a parody of the encouraging croon Mnementh often gave. The boy uncertainly lifted a hand and began to scratch the eye ridge. Incredulous, Lessa watched as the fledgling, its crooning increasingly more mellow, ducked its head, pushing at the boy. The child's face broke into an unbelieving smile of elation.

Tearing her eyes from this astounding sight, Lessa saw that another fledgling was beginning the same performance with another boy. Two more dragons had emerged in the interim. One had knocked a boy down and was walking over him, oblivious to the fact that its claws were raking great gashes. The fledgling who followed its hatch-mate stopped by the wounded child, ducking its head to the boy's face, crooning anxiously. As Lessa watched, the boy managed to struggle to his feet, tears of pain streaming down his cheeks. She could hear him pleading with the dragon not to worry, that he was only scratched a little.

It was over very soon. The young dragons paired off with boys. Green riders dropped down to carry off the unacceptable. Blue riders settled to the floor with their beasts and led the couples out of the cavern, the young dragons squealing, crooning, flapping wet wings as they staggered off, encouraged by their newly acquired weyrmates.

Lessa turned resolutely back to the rocking golden egg, knowing what to expect and trying to divine what the successful boys had, or had not done, that caused the baby dragons to single them out.

A crack appeared in the golden shell and was greeted by the terrified screams of the girls. Some had fallen into little heaps of white fabric, others embraced tightly in their mutual fear. The crack widened and the wedge head broke through, followed quickly by the neck, gleaming gold. Lessa wondered with unexpected detachment how long it would take the beast to mature, considering its by no means small size at birth. For the head was larger than that of the male dragons and they had been large enough to overwhelm sturdy boys of ten full Turns.

Lessa was aware of a loud hum within the Hall. Glancing up at the audience, she realized it emanated from the watching bronze dragons, for this was the birth of their mate, their queen. The hum increased in volume as the shell shattered into fragments and the golden, glistening body of the new female emerged. It staggered out, dipping its sharp beak into the soft sand, momentarily trapped. Flapping its wet wings, it righted itself, ludicrous in its weak awkwardness. With sudden and unexpected swiftness, it dashed towards the terror-stricken girls.

Before Lessa could blink, it shook the first girl with such violence, her head snapped audibly and she fell limply to the sand. Disregarding her, the dragon leaped towards the second girl but misjudged the distance and fell, grabbing out with one claw for support and raking the girl's body from shoulder to thigh. The screaming of the mortally injured girl distracted the dragon and released the others from their horrified trance. They scattered in panicky confusion, racing, running, tripping, stumbling, falling across the sand towards the exit the boys had used.

As the golden beast, crying piteously, lurched down from the raised arena towards the scattered women, Lessa moved. Why hadn't that silly clunk-headed girl stepped aside, Lessa thought, grabbing for the wedge-head, at birth not much larger than her own torso. The dragon's so clumsy and weak she's her own worst enemy.

Lessa swung the head round so that the many-faceted eyes were forced to look at her . . . and found herself lost in that rainbow regard.

A feeling of joy suffused Lessa, a feeling of warmth, tenderness, unalloyed affection and instant respect and admiration flooded mind and heart and soul. Never again would Lessa lack an advocate, a defender, an intimate, aware instantly of the temper of her mind and heart, of her desires. How wonderful was Lessa, the thought intruded into Lessa's reflections, how pretty, how kind, how thoughtful, how brave and clever!

Mechanically, Lessa reached out to scratch the exact spot on the soft eye ridge.

The dragon blinked at her wistfully, extremely sad that she had distressed Lessa. Lessa reassuringly patted the slightly damp, soft neck that curved trustingly towards her. The dragon reeled to one side and one wing fouled on the hind claw. It hurt. Carefully, Lessa lifted the erring foot, freed the wing, folding it back across the dorsal ridge with a pat.

The dragon began to croon in her throat, her eyes following Lessa's every move. She nudged at Lessa and Lessa obediently attended the other eye ridge.

The dragon let it be known she was hungry.

"We'll get you something to eat directly," Lessa assured her briskly and blinked back at the dragon in amazement. How could she be so callous? It was a fact that this little menace had just now seriously injured, if not killed, two women.

She wouldn't have believed her sympathies could swing so alarmingly towards the beast. Yet it was the most natural thing in the world for her to wish to protect this fledgling.

The dragon arched her neck to look Lessa squarely in the eyes. Ramoth repeated wistfully how exceedingly hungry she was, confined so long in that shell without nourishment.

Lessa wondered how she knew the golden dragon's name and Ramoth replied: Why shouldn't she know her own name since it was hers and no one else's? And then Lessa was lost again in the wonder of those expressive eyes.

Oblivious to the descending bronze dragons, uncaring of the presence of their riders, Lessa stood caressing the head of the most wonderful creature on all Pern, fully prescient of troubles and glories, but most immediately aware that Lessa of Pern was Weyrwoman to Ramoth the Golden, for now and forever.

Philip Farmer once did me an enormous favor. It was long ago and there was no way he could tell at the time that he was doing me one, and I never acknowledged it. So let's take care of the obligation now.

It was back in 1954, I think, and the scene was a convention in Cincinnati. (At least, I think it was Cincinnati, unless I am getting two conventions confused and coalesced in my mind. I seem to recall driving through the tail-end of a hurricane to get there.)

The point is that at that convention some publicity had been arranged—something I always rather dislike. I'm not keen on publicity because the bother always seems greater than the results, and because it isn't me that I'm interested in having people know about, but my books.

Still, the publicity was arranged and you can't be a curmudgeon about it so I tried to hide my grumpiness as I went down to the room where the newspaper reporter was waiting. Randall Garrett and Phil Farmer went, too. Now Randall Garrett and I are a pair of twin-souls in a way: portly, loud, and irreverent. It's difficult to get a straight answer out of either of us, for the question is bound to raise some ridiculous piece of off-beat humor in either of our minds and we come out with it and then it is spread over the newspaper and we're sorry.

Not so Phil Farmer. He has deep-set eyes, a strong chin, and a glowing and enormous sincerity. In no time at all, the reporter had switched to him and ignored Randall and myself. (I *think* it was Phil's sincerity. He was also somberly handsome and the reporter was a girl.)

One of the questions was "Tell me, Mr. Farmer, how do you keep up to date in science so that you can write your science fiction stories?"

That was a stunner for me. I had never heard of such a thing. At the time, I was teaching biochemistry at a medical school full time and a textbook I had helped write was going into its second edition, so I had to keep up in biochemistry. But keeping up in science in general? And for *science fiction?*

Phil took it calmly. He said, "For one thing, I subscribe to *Scientific American.*"

I was staggered. If Phil, who is a lot less "heavy science" than I am, feels it necessary to keep up with science, what am I doing just lounging around?

I could hardly wait to get home to send in *my* subscription to *Scientific American* (a subscription I still have) and to begin to work at keeping up. I don't know that it ever affected my science fiction much, but I'll tell you this: since 1954 I have written dozens of non-fiction books covering just about every field of science, and one of the reasons I can do so dates back to that one remark of Phil Farmer.

Thanks, Phil!

# 8

# RIDERS OF THE PURPLE WAGE

*If Jules Verne could really have looked into the future, say 1966 A.D.,*
*he would have crapped in his pants. And 2166, oh, my!*

—from Grandpa Winnegan's *unpublished* Ms. How I
Screwed Uncle Sam & Other Private Ejaculations.

## THE COCK THAT CROWED BACKWARDS

Un and Sub, the giants, are grinding him for bread.

Broken pieces float up through the wine of sleep. Vast treadings crush abysmal grapes for the incubus sacrament.

He as Simple Simon fishes in his soul as pail for the leviathan.

He groans, half-wakes, turns over, sweating dark oceans, and groans again. Un and Sub, putting their backs to their work, turn the stone wheels of the sunken mill, muttering Fie, fye, fo, fum. Eyes glittering orange-red as a cat's in a cubbyhole, teeth dull white digits in the murky arithmetic.

Un and Sub, Simple Simons themselves, busily mix metaphors non-self-consciously.

Dunghill and cock's egg: up rises the cockatrice and gives first crow, two more to come, in the flushrush of blood of dawn of I-am-the-erection-and-the-strife.

It grows out and out until weight and length merge to curve it over, a not-yet weeping willow or broken reed. The one-eyed red head peeks over the edge of bed. It rests its chinless jaw, then, as body swells, slides over and down. Looking monocularly this way and those, it sniffs archaically across the floor and heads for the door, left open by the lapsus linguae of malingering sentinels.

A loud braying from the center of the room makes it turn back. The three-legged ass, Baalim's easel, is heehawing. On the easel is the "canvas," an oval shallow pan of irradiated plastic, specially treated. The canvas is seven feet high and eighteen inches deep. Within the painting is a scene that must be finished by tomorrow.

As much sculpture as painting, the figures are in alto-relief, rounded, some nearer the back of the pan than others. They glow with light from outside and also from the self-luminous plastic of the "canvas." The light seems to enter the figures, soak awhile, then break loose. The light is pale red, the red of dawn, of blood watered with tears, of anger, of ink on the debit side of the ledger.

This is one of his Dog Series: *Dogmas from a Dog, The Aerial Dog-fight, Dog Days, The Sundog, Dog Reversed, The Dog of Flinders, Dog Berries, Dog Catcher, Lying Doggo, The Dog of the Right Angle,* and *Improvisations on a Dog.*

Socrates, Ben Jonson, Cellini, Swedenborg, Li Po, and Hiawatha are roistering in the Mermaid Tavern. Through a window, Daedalus is seen on top of the battlements of Cnossus, shoving a rocket up the ass of his son, Icarus, to give him a jet-assisted takeoff for his famous flight. In one corner crouches Og, Son of Fire. He gnaws on a saber-tooth bone and paints bison and mammoths on the mildewed plaster. The barmaid, Athena, is bending over the table where she is serving nectar and pretzels to her distinguished customers. Aristotle, wearing goat's horns, is behind her. He has lifted her skirt and is tupping her from behind. The ashes from the cigarette dangling from his smirking lips have fallen onto her skirt, which is beginning to smoke. In the doorway of the men's room, a drunken Batman succumbs to a long-repressed desire and attempts to bugger the Boy Wonder. Through another window is a lake on the surface of which a man is walking, a green-tarnished halo hovering over his head. Behind him a periscope sticks out of the water.

Prehensile, the penisnake wraps itself around the brush and begins to paint. The brush is a small cylinder attached at one end to a hose which runs to a dome-shaped machine. From the other end of the cylinder extends a nozzle. The aperture of this can be decreased or increased by rotation of a thumb-dial on the cylinder. The paint which the nozzle deposits in a fine spray or in a thick stream or in whatever color or hue desired is controlled by several dials on the cylinder.

Furiously, proboscisean, it builds up another figure layer by layer. Then, it sniffs a musty odor of must and drops the brush and slides out the door and down the bend of wall of oval hall, describing the scrawl of legless creatures, a writing in the sand which all may read but few understand. Blood pumppumps in rhythm with the mills of Un and Sub to feed and swill the hot-blooded reptile. But the walls, detecting intrusive mass and extrusive desire, glow.

He groans, and the glandular cobra rises and sways to the fluting of his wish for cuntcealment. Let there not be light! The nights must be his cloaka. Speed past mother's room, nearest the exit. Ah! Sighs softly in relief but air whistles through the vertical and tight mouth, announcing the departure of the exsupress for Desideratum.

The door has become archaic; it has a keyhole. Quick! Up the ramp and out of the house through the keyhole and out onto the street. One person abroad a broad, a young woman with phosphorescent silver hair and snatch to match.

Out and down the street and coiling around her ankle. She looks down with surprise and then fear. He likes this; too willing were too many. He's found a diamond in the ruff.

Up around her kitten-ear-soft leg, around and around, and sliding across the dale of groin. Nuzzling the tender corkscrewed hairs and then, self-Tantalus, detouring up the slight convex of belly, saying hello to the bellybutton, pressing on it to ring upstairs, around and around the narrow waist and shyly and quickling snatching a kiss from each nipple. Then back down to form an expedition for climbing the mons veneris and planting the flag thereon.

Oh, delectation tabu and sickersacrosanct! There's a baby in there, ectoplasm beginning to form in eager preanticipation of actuality. Drop, egg, and shoot the chutychutes of flesh, hastening to gulp the Lucky Micromoby Dick, outwriggling its million million brothers, survival of the fightingest.

A vast croaking fills the hall. The hot breath chills the skin. He sweats. Icicles coat the tumorous fuselage, and it sags under the weight of ice, and fog rolls around, whistling past the struts, and the ailerons and elevators are locked in ice, and he's losing altiattitude fast. Get up, get up! Venusberg somewhere ahead in the mists; Tannhäuser, blow your strumpets, send up your flares, I'm in a nosedive.

Mother's door has opened. A toad squatfills the ovoid doorway. Its dewlap rises and falls bellows-like; its toothless mouth gawps. Ginungagap. Forked tongue shoots out and curls around the boar cuntstrictor. He cries out with both mouths and jerks this way and those. The waves of denial run through. Two webbed paws bend and tie the flopping body into a knot—a runny shapeshank, of course.

The woman strolls on. Wait for me! Out the flood roars, crashes into the knot, roars back, ebb clashing with flood. Too much and only one way to go. He jerkspurts, the firmament of waters falling, no Noah's ark or arc; he novas, a shatter of millions of glowing wriggling meteors, flashes in the pan of existence.

Thigh kingdom come. Groin and belly encased in musty armor, and he cold, wet, and trembling.

## GOD'S PATENT ON DAWN EXPIRES

. . . the following spoken by Alfred Melophon Voxpopper, of the Aurora Pushups and Coffee Hour, Channel 69B. Lines taped during the 50th Folk Art Center Annual Demonstration and Competition, Beverly Hills, level 14. Spoken by Omar Bacchylides Runic, extemporaneously if you discount some forethought during the previous evening at the nonpublic tavern The Private Universe, and you may because Runic did not remember a thing about that evening. Despite which he won First Laurel Wreath A, there being no Second, Third, etc., wreaths classified as A through Z, God bless our democracy.

> *A gray-pink salmon leaping up the falls of night*
> *Into the spawning pool of another day.*
>
> *Dawn—the red roar of the heliac bull*
> *Charging over the horizon.*
>
> *The photonic blood of bleeding night,*
> *Stabbed by the assassin sun.*

and so on for fifty lines punctuated and fractured by cheers, handclaps, boos, hisses, and yelps.

Chib is half-awake. He peeps down into the narrowing dark as the dream roars off into the subway tunnel. He peeps through barely opened lids at the other reality: consciousness.

"Let my peeper go!" he groans with Moses and so, thinking of long beards and horns (courtesy of Michelangelo), he thinks of his great-great-grandfather.

The will, a crowbar, forces his eyelids open. He sees the fido which spans the wall opposite him and curves up over half the ceiling. Dawn, the paladin of the sun, is flinging its gray gauntlet down.

Channel 69B, YOUR FAVORITE CHANNEL, LA's own, brings you dawn. (Deception in depth. Nature's false dawn shadowed forth with electrons shaped by devices shaped by man.)

Wake up with the sun in your heart and a song on your lips! Thrill to the stirring lines of Omar Runic! See dawn as the birds in the trees, as God, see it!

Voxpopper chants the lines softly while Grieg's *Anitra* wells softly. The old Norwegian never dreamed of this audience and just as well. A young man, Chibiabos Elgreco Winnegan, has a sticky wick, courtesy of a late gusher in the oilfield of the unconscious.

"Off your ass and onto your steed," Chib says. "Pegasus runs today." He speaks, thinks, lives in the present tensely.

Chib climbs out of bed and shoves it into the wall. To leave the bed sticking out, rumpled as an old drunkard's tongue, would fracture the aesthetics of his room, destroy that curve that is the reflection of the basic universe, and hinder him in his work.

The room is a huge ovoid and in a corner is a small ovoid, the toilet and shower. He comes out of it looking like one of Homer's god-like Achaeans, massively thighed, great-armed, golden-brown-skinned, blue-eyed, auburn-haired—although beardless. The phone is simulating the tocsin of a South American tree frog he once heard over channel 122.

"Open O sesame!"

## INTER CAECOS REGNAT LUSCUS

The face of Rex Luscus spreads across the fido, the pores of skin like the cratered fields of a World War I battlefield. He wears a black monocle over the left eye, ripped out in a brawl among art critics during the *I Love Rembrandt Lecture Series,* Channel 109. Although he has enough pull to get a priority for eye-replacement, he has refused.

*"Inter caecos regnat luscus,"* he says when asked about it and quite often when not. "Translation: among the blind, the one-eyed man is king. That's why I renamed myself Rex Luscus, that is, King One-eyed."

There is a rumor, fostered by Luscus, that he will permit the bioboys to put in an artificial protein eye when he sees the works of an artist great enough to justify focal vision. It is also rumored that he may do so soon, because of his discovery of Chibiabos Elgreco Winnegan.

Luscus looks hungrily (he swears by adverbs) at Chib's tomentum and outlying regions. Chib swells, not with tumescence but with anger.

Luscus says, smoothly, "Honey, I just want to reassure myself that you're up and about the tremendously important business of this day. You must be ready for the showing, must! But now I see you, I'm reminded I've not eaten yet. What about breakfast with me?"

"What're we eating?" Chib says. He does not wait for a reply. "No. I've too much to do today. Close O sesame!"

Rex Luscus' face fades away, goatlike, or, as he prefers to describe it, the face of Pan, a Faunus of the arts. He has even had his ears trimmed to a point. Real cute.

"Baa-aa-aa!" Chib bleats at the phantom. "Ba! Humbuggery! I'll never kiss your ass, Luscus, or let you kiss mine. Even if I lose the grant!"

The phone bells again. The dark face of Rousseau Red Hawk appears. His nose is as the eagle's, and his eyes are broken black glass. His broad forehead is bound with a strip of red cloth, which circles the straight black hair that glides down to his shoulders. His shirt is buckskin; a necklace of beads hangs from his neck. He looks like a Plains Indian, although Sitting Bull, Crazy Horse, or the noblest Roman Nose of them all would have kicked him out of the tribe. Not that they were anti-Semitic, they just could not have respected a brave who broke out into hives when near a horse.

Born Julius Applebaum, he legally became Rousseau Red Hawk on his Naming Day. Just returned from the forest reprimevalized, he is now reveling in the accursed fleshpots of a decadent civilization.

"How're you, Chib? The gang's wondering how soon you'll get here?"

"Join you? I haven't had breakfast yet, and I've a thousand things to do to get ready for the showing. I'll see you at noon!"

"You missed out on the fun last night. Some goddam Egyptians tried to feel the girls up, but we salaamed them against the walls."

Rousseau vanished like the last of the red men.

Chib thinks of breakfast just as the intercom whistles. Open O Sesame! He sees the living room. Smoke, too thick and furious for the air-conditioning to whisk away, roils. At the far end of the ovoid, his little half-brother and half-sister sleep on a flato. Playing Mama-and-friend, they fell asleep, their mouths open in blessed innocence, beautiful as only sleeping children can be. Opposite the closed eyes of each is an unwinking eye like that of a Mongolian Cyclops.

"Ain't they cute?" Mama says. "The darlings were just too tired to toddle off."

The table is round. The aged knights and ladies are gathered around it for the latest quest of the ace, king, queen, and jack. They are armored only in layer upon layer of fat. Mama's jowls hang down like banners on a windless day. Her breasts creep and quiver on the table, bulge, and ripple.

"A gam of gamblers," he says aloud, looking at the fat faces, the tremendous tits, the rampant rumps. They raise their eyebrows. What the hell's the mad genius talking about now?

"Is your kid really retarded?" says one of Mama's friends, and they laugh and drink some more beer. Angela Ninon, not wanting to miss out on this deal and figuring Mama will soon turn on the sprayers anyway, pisses down her leg. They laugh at this, and William Conqueror says, "I open."

"I'm always open," Mama says, and they shriek with laughter.

Chib would like to cry. He does not cry, although he has been encouraged from childhood to cry any time he feels like it.

*—It makes you feel better and look at the Vikings, what men they were and they cried like babies whenever they felt like it—Courtesy of Channel 202 on the popular program* What's A Mother Done?

He does not cry because he feels like a man who thinks about the mother he loved and who is dead but who died a long time ago. His mother has been long buried under a landslide of flesh. When he was sixteen, he had had a lovely mother.

Then she cut him off.


## THE FAMILY THAT BLOWS IS THE FAMILY THAT GROWS

*—from a poem by Edgar A. Grist, via Channel 88.*

"Son, I don't get much out of this. I just do it because I love you."

Then, fat, fat, fat! Where did she go? Down into the adipose abyss. Disappearing as she grew larger.

"Sonny, you could at least wrestle with me a little now and then."

"You cut me off, Mama. That was all right. I'm a big boy now. But you haven't any right to expect me to want to take it up again."

"You don't love me any more!"

"What's for breakfast, Mama?" Chib says.

"I'm holding a good hand, Chibby," Mama says. "As you've told me so many times, you're a big boy. Just this once, get your own breakfast."

"What'd you call me for?"

"I forgot when your exhibition starts. I wanted to get some sleep before I went."

"14:30, Mama, but you don't have to go."

Rouged green lips part like a gangrened wound. She scratches one rouged nipple. "Oh, I want to be there. I don't want to miss my own sons artistic triumphs. Do you think you'll get the grant?"

"If I don't, it's Egypt for us," he says.

"Those stinking Arabs!" says William Conqueror.

"It's the Bureau that's doing it, not the Arabs," Chib says. "The Arabs moved for the same reason we may have to move."

From Grandpa's unpublished Ms.: *Whoever would have thought that Beverly Hills would become anti-Semitic?*

"I don't want to go to Egypt!" Mama wails. "You got to get that grant, Chibby. I don't want to leave the clutch. I was born and raised here, well, on the tenth level, anyway, and when I moved all my friends went along. I won't go!"

"Don't cry, Mama," Chib says, feeling distress despite himself. "Don't cry. The government can't force you to go, you know. You got your rights."

"If you want to keep on having goodies, you'll go," says Conqueror. "Unless Chib wins the grant, that is. And I wouldn't blame him if he didn't even try to win it. It ain't his fault you can't say no to Uncle Sam. You got your purple and the yap Chib makes from selling his paintings. Yet it ain't enough. You spend faster than you get it."

Mama screams with fury at William, and they're off. Chib cuts off fido. Hell with breakfast; he'll eat later. His final painting for the Festival must be finished by noon. He presses a plate, and the bare egg-shaped room opens here and there, and painting equipment comes out like a gift from the electronic gods. Zeuxis would flip and Van Gogh would get the shakes if they could see the canvas and palette and brush Chib uses.

The process of painting involves the individual bending and twisting of thousands of wires into different shapes at various depths. The wires are so thin they can be seen only with magnifiers and manipulated with exceedingly delicate pliers. Hence, the goggles he wears and the long almost-gossamer instrument in his hand when he is in the first stages of creating a painting. After hundreds of hours of slow and patient labor (of love), the wires are arranged.

Chib removes his goggles to perceive the overall effect. He then uses the paint-sprayer to cover the wires with the colors and hues he desires. The paint dries hard within a few minutes. Chib attaches electrical leads to the pan and presses a button to deliver a tiny voltage through the wires. These glow beneath the paint and, Lilliputian fuses, disappear in blue smoke.

The result is a three-dimensional work composed of hard shells of paint on several levels below the exterior shell. The shells are of varying thicknesses and all are so thin that light slips through the upper to the inner shell when the painting is turned at angles. Parts of the shells are simply reflectors to intensify the light so that the inner images may be more visible.

When being shown, the painting is on a self-moving pedestal which turns the painting 12 degrees to the left from the center and then 12 degrees to the right from the center.

The fido tocsins. Chib, cursing, thinks of disconnecting it. At least, it's not the intercom with his mother calling hysterically. Not yet, anyway. She'll call soon enough if she loses heavily at poker.

Open O sesame!

## SING, O MEWS, OF UNCLE SAM

*Grandpa writes in his* Private Ejaculations: *Twenty-five years after I fled with twenty billion dollars and then supposedly died of a heart attack, Falco Accipiter is on my trail again. The IRB detective who named himself Falcon Hawk when he entered his profession. What an egotist! Yet, he is as sharpeyed and relentless as a bird of prey, and I would shiver if I were not too old to be frightened by mere human beings. Who loosed the jesses and hood? How did he pick up the old and cold scent?*

Accipiter's face is that of an overly suspicious peregrine that tries to look everywhere while it soars, that peers up its own anus to make sure that no duck has taken refuge there. The pale blue eyes fling glances like knives shot out of a shirtsleeve and hurled with a twist of the wrist. They scan all with sherlockian intake of minute and significant detail. His head turns back and forth, ears twitching, nostrils expanding and collapsing, all radar and sonar and odar.

"Mr. Winnegan, I'm sorry to call so early. Did I get you out of bed?"

"It's obvious you didn't!" Chib says. "Don't bother to introduce yourself. I know you. You've been shadowing me for three days."

Accipiter does not redden. Master of control, he does all his blushing in the depths of his bowels, where no one can see. "If you know me, perhaps you can tell me why I'm calling you?"

"Would I be dumbshit enough to tell you?"

"Mr. Winnegan, I'd like to talk to you about your great-great-grandfather."

"He's been dead for twenty-five years!" Chib cries. "Forget him. And don't bother me. Don't try for a search warrant. No judge would give you one. A man's home is his hassle . . . I mean castle."

He thinks of Mama and what the day is going to be like unless he gets out soon. But he has to finish the painting.

"Fade off, Accipiter," Chib says. "I think I'll report you to the BPHR. I'm sure you got a fido inside that silly-looking hat of yours."

Accipiter's face is as smooth and unmoving as an alabaster carving of the falcon-god Horus. He may have a little gas bulging his intestines. If so, he slips it out unnoticed.

"Very well, Mr. Winnegan. But you're not getting rid of me that easily. After all . . ."

"Fade out!"

The intercom whistles thrice. What I tell you three times is Grandpa. "I was eavesdropping," says the 120-year-old voice, hollow and deep as an echo from a Pharaoh's tomb. "I want to see you before you leave. That is, if you can spare the Ancient of Daze a few minutes."

"Always, Grandpa," Chib says, thinking of how much he loves the old man. "You need any food?"

"Yes, and for the mind, too."

*Der Tag. Dies Irae. Götterdammerung.* Armageddon. Things are closing in. Make-or-break day. Go-no-go time. All these calls and a feeling of more to come. What will the end of the day bring?

## THE TROCHE SUN SLIPS INTO THE SORE THROAT OF NIGHT

*—from Omar Runic*

Chib walks towards the convex door, which rolls into the interstices between the walls. The focus of the house is the oval family room. In the first quadrant, going clockwise, is the kitchen, separated from the family room by six-meter-high accordion screens, painted with scenes from Egyptian tombs by Chib, his too subtle comment on modern food. Seven slim pillars around the family room mark the borders of room and corridor. Between the pillars are more tall accordion screens, painted by Chib during his Amerind mythology phase.

The corridor is also oval-shaped; every room in the house opens onto it. There are seven rooms, six bedroom-workroom-study-toilet-shower combinations. The seventh is a storeroom.

Little eggs within bigger eggs within great eggs within a mega-monolith on a planetary pear within an ovoid universe, the latest cosmogony indicating that infinity has the form of a hen's fruit. God broods over the abyss and cackles every trillion years or so.

Chib cuts across the hall, passes between two pillars, carved by him into nymphet caryatids, and enters the family room. His mother looks sidewise at her son, who she thinks is rapidly approaching insanity if he has not already overshot his mark. It's partly her fault; she shouldn't have gotten disgusted and in a moment of wackiness called It off. Now, she's fat and ugly, oh, God, so fat and ugly. She can't reasonably or even unreasonably hope to start up again.

It's only natural, she keeps telling herself, sighing, resentful, teary, that he's abandoned the love of his mother for the strange, firm, shapely delights of young women. But to give them up, too? He's not a fairy. He quit all that when he was thirteen. So what's the reason for his chastity? He isn't in love with the fornixator, either, which she would understand, even if she did not approve.

Oh, God, where did I go wrong? And then, there's nothing wrong with me. He's going crazy like his father—Raleigh Renaissance, I think his name was—and his aunt and his great-great-grandfather. It's all that painting and those radicals, the Young Radishes, he runs around with. He's too artistic, too sensitive. Oh, God, if something happens to my little boy, I'll have to go to Egypt.

Chib knows her thoughts since she's voiced them so many times and is not capable of having new ones. He passes the round table without a word. The knights and ladies of the canned Camelot see him through a beery veil.

In the kitchen, he opens an oval door in the wall. He removes a tray with food in covered dishes and cups, all wrapped in plastic.

"Aren't you going to eat with us?"

"Don't whine, Mama," he says and goes back to his room to pick up some cigars for his Grandpa. The door, detecting, amplifying, and transmitting the shifting but recognizable eidolon of epidermal electrical fields to the activating mechanism, balks. Chib is too upset. Magnetic maelstroms rage over his skin and distort the spectral configuration. The door half-rolls out, rolls in, changes its mind again, rolls out, rolls in.

Chib kicks the door and it becomes completely blocked. He decides he'll have a video or vocal sesame put in. Trouble is, he's short of units and coupons and can't buy the materials. He shrugs and walks along the curving, one-walled hall and stops in front of Grandpa's door, hidden from view of those in the living room by the kitchen screens.

> "For he sang of peace and freedom,
> Sang of beauty, love, and longing;
> Sang of death, and life undying
> In the Islands of the Blessed,
> In the kingdom of Ponemah,
> In the land of the Hereafter.
> Very dear to Hiawatha
> Was the gentle Chibiabos."

Chib chants the passwords; the door rolls back.

Light glares out, a yellowish red-tinged light that is Grandpa's own creation. Looking into the convex oval door is like looking into the lens of a madman's eyeball. Grandpa, in the middle of the room, has a white beard falling to midthigh and white hair cataracting to just below the back of his knees. Although beard and headhair conceal his nakedness, and he is not out in public, he wears a pair of shorts. Grandpa is somewhat old-fashioned, forgivable in a man of twelve decadencies.

Like Rex Luscus, he is one-eyed. He smiles with his own teeth, grown from buds transplanted thirty years ago. A big green cigar sticks out of one corner of his full red mouth. His nose is broad and smeared as if time had stepped upon it with a heavy foot. His forehead and cheeks are broad, perhaps due to a shot of Ojibway blood in his veins, though he was born Finnegan and even sweats celtically, giving off an aroma of whiskey. He holds his head high, and the blue-gray eye is like a pool at the bottom of a prediluvian pothole, remnant of a melted glacier.

All in all, Grandpa's face is Odin's as he returns from the Well of Mimir, wondering if he paid too great a price. Or it is the face of the windbeaten, sandblown Sphinx of Gizeh.

"Forty centuries of hysteria look down upon you, to paraphrase Napoleon," Grandpa says. "The rockhead of the ages. *What, then, is Man?* sayeth the New Sphinx, Edipus having resolved the question of the Old Sphinx and settling nothing because She had already delivered another of her kind, a smartass kid with a question nobody's been able to answer yet. And perhaps just as well it can't be."

"You talk funny," Chib says. "But I like it."

He grins at Grandpa, loving him.

"You sneak into here every day, not so much from love for me as to gain knowledge and insight. I have seen all, heard everything, and thought more than a little. I voyaged much before I took refuge in this room a quarter of a century ago. Yet confinement here has been the greatest Odyssey of all.

# THE ANCIENT MARINATOR

"I call myself. A marinade of wisdom steeped in the brine of over-salted cynicism and too long a life."

"You smile so, you must have just had a woman," Chib teases.

"No, my boy. I lost the tension in my ramrod thirty years ago. And I thank God for that, since it removes from me the temptation of fornication, not to mention masturbation. However, I have other energies left, hence, scope for other sins, and these are even more serious.

"Aside from the sin of sexual commission, which paradoxically involves the sin of sexual emission, I had other reasons for not asking that Old Black Magician Science for shots to starch me out again. I was too old for young girls to be attracted to me for anything but money. And I was too much a poet, a lover of beauty, to take on the wrinkled blisters of my generation or several just before mine.

"So now you see, my son. My clapper swings limberly in the bell of my sex. Ding, dong, ding, dong. A lot of dong but not much ding."

Grandpa laughs deeply, a lion's roar with a spray of doves.

"I am but the mouthpiece of the ancients, a shyster pleading for long-dead clients. Come not to bury but to praise and forced by my sense of fairness to admit the faults of the past, too. I'm a queer crabbed old man, pent like Merlin in his tree trunk. Samolxis, the Thracian bear god, hibernating in his cave. The Last of the Seven Sleepers."

Grandpa goes to the slender plastic tube depending from the ceiling and pulls down the folding handles of the eyepiece.

"Accipiter is hovering outside our house. He smells something rotten in Beverly Hills, level 14. Could it be that Win-again Winnegan isn't dead? Uncle Sam is like a diplodocus kicked in the ass. It takes twenty-five years for the message to reach its brain."

Tears appear in Chib's eyes. He says, "Oh, God, Grandpa, I don't want anything to happen to you."

"What can happen to a 120-year-old man besides failure of brain or kidneys?"

"With all due respect, Grandpa," Chib says, "you do rattle on."

"Call me Id's mill," Grandpa says. "The flour it yields is baked in the strange oven of my ego—or half-baked, if you please."

Chib grins through his tears and says, "They taught me at school that puns are cheap and vulgar."

"What's good enough for Homer, Aristophanes, Rabelais, and Shakespeare is good enough for me. By the way, speaking of cheap and vulgar, I met your mother in the hall last night, before the poker party started. I was just leaving the kitchen with a bottle of booze. She almost fainted. But she recovered fast and pretended not to see me. Maybe she did think she'd seen a ghost. I doubt it. She'd have been blabbing all over town about it."

"She may have told her doctor," Chib says. "She saw you several weeks ago, remember? She may have mentioned it while she was bitching about her so-called dizzy spells and hallucinations."

"And the old sawbones, knowing the family history, called the IRB. Maybe."

Chib looks through the periscope's eyepiece. He rotates it and turns the knobs on the handle-ends to raise and lower the cyclops on the end of the tube outside. Accipiter is stalking around the aggregate of seven eggs, each on the end of a broad thin curved branchlike walk projecting from the central pedestal. Accipiter goes up the steps of a branch to the door of Mrs. Applebaum's. The door opens.

"He must have caught her away from the fornixator," Chib says. "And she must be lonely; she's not talking to him over fido. My God, she's fatter than Mama!"

"Why not?" Grandpa says. "Mr. and Mrs. Everyman sit on their asses all day, drink, eat, and watch fido, and their brains run to mud and their bodies to sludge. Caesar would have had no trouble surrounding himself with fat friends these days. You ate, too, Brutus?"

Grandpa's comment, however, should not apply to Mrs. Applebaum. She has a hole in her head, and people addicted to fornixation seldom get fat. They sit or lie all day and part of the night, the needle in the fornix area of the brain delivering a series of minute electrical jolts. Indescribable ecstasy floods through their bodies with every impulse, a delight far surpassing any of food, drink, or sex. It's illegal, but the government never bothers a user unless it wants to get him for something else, since a fornic rarely has children. Twenty per cent of LA have had holes drilled in their heads and tiny shafts inserted for access of the needle. Five per cent are addicted; they waste away, seldom eating, their distended bladders spilling poisons into the bloodstream.

Chib says, "My brother and sister must have seen you sometimes when you were sneaking out to mass. Could they . . . ?"

"They think I'm a ghost, too. In this day and age! Still, maybe it's a good sign that they can believe in something, even a spook."

"You better stop sneaking out to church."

"The Church, and you, are the only things that keep me going. It was a sad day, though, when you told me you couldn't believe. You

would have made a good priest—with faults, of course—and I could
have had private mass and confession in this room."

Chib says nothing. He's gone to instruction and observed services
just to please Grandpa. The church was an egg-shaped seashell which,
held to the ear, gave only the distant roar of God receding like an ebb
tide.

### THERE ARE UNIVERSES BEGGING FOR GODS
*yet He hangs around this one looking for work.*

*—from Grandpa's Ms.*

Grandpa takes over the eyepiece. He laughs. "The Internal Revenue
Bureau! I thought it'd been disbanded! Who the hell has an income
big enough to report on any more? Do you suppose it's still active just
because of me? Could be."

He calls Chib back to the scope, directed towards the center of Beverly Hills. Chib has a lane of vision between the seven-egged clutches
on the branched pedestals. He can see part of the central plaza, the
giant ovoids of the city hall, the federal bureaus, the Folk Center, part
of the massive spiral on which set the houses of worship, and the dora
(from pandora) where those on the purple wage get their goods and
those with extra income get their goodies. One end of the big artificial
lake is visible; boats and canoes sail on it and people fish.

The irradiated plastic dome that enfolds the clutches of Beverly Hills
is sky-blue. The electronic sun climbs towards the zenith. There are a
few white genuine-looking images of clouds and even a V of geese migrating south, their honks coming down faintly. Very nice for those
who have never been outside the walls of LA. But Chib spent two years
in the World Nature Rehabilitation and Conservation Corps—the
WNRCC—and he knows the difference. Almost, he decided to desert
with Rousseau Red Hawk and join the neo-Amerinds. Then, he was
going to become a forest ranger. But this might mean he'd end up
shooting or arresting Red Hawk. Besides, he didn't want to become a
sammer. And he wanted more than anything to paint.

"There's Rex Luscus," Chib says. "He's being interviewed outside
the Folk Center. Quite a crowd."

### THE PELLUCIDAR BREAKTHROUGH

Luscus' middle name should have been Upmanship. A man of
great erudition, with privileged access to the Library of Greater LA

computer, and of Ulyssean sneakiness, he is always scoring over his colleagues.

He it was who founded the Go-Go School of Criticism.

Primalux Ruskinson, his great competitor, did some extensive research when Luscus announced the title of his new philosophy. Ruskinson triumphantly announced that Luscus had taken the phrase from obsolete slang, current in the mid-twentieth century.

Luscus, in the fido interview next day, said that Ruskinson was a rather shallow scholar, which was to be expected.

*Go-go* was taken from the Hottentot language. In Hottentot, *go-go* meant to examine, that is, to keep looking until something about the object—in this case, the artist and his works—has been observed.

The critics got in line to sign up at the new school. Ruskinson thought of committing suicide, but instead accused Luscus of having blown his way up the ladder of success.

Luscus replied on fido that his personal life was his own, and Ruskinson was in danger of being sued for violation of privacy. However, he deserved no more effort than a man striking at a mosquito.

"What the hell's a mosquito?" say millions of viewers. "Wish the big-head would talk language we could understand."

Luscus' voice fades off for a minute while the interpreters explain, having just been slipped a note from a monitor who's run off the word through the station's encyclopedia.

Luscus rode on the novelty of the Go-Go School for two years.

Then he re-established his prestige, which had been slipping somewhat, with his philosophy of the Totipotent Man.

This was so popular that the Bureau of Cultural Development and Recreation requisitioned a daily one-hour slot for a year-and-a-half in the initial program of totipotentializing.

*Grandpa Winnegan's penned comment in his* Private Ejaculations:
*What about The Totipotent Man, that apotheosis of individuality and complete psychosomatic development, the democratic Über-mensch, as recommended by Rex Luscus, the sexually one-sided? Poor old Uncle Sam! Trying to force the proteus of his citizens into a single stabilized shape so he can control them. And at the same time trying to encourage each and every to bring to flower his inherent capabilities —if any! The poor old long-legged, chin-whiskered, milk-hearted, flint-brained schizophrenic! Verily, the left hand knows not what the right hand is doing. As a matter of fact, the right hand doesn't know what the right hand is doing.*

"What about the totipotent man?" Luscus replied to the chairman during the fourth session of the *Luscan Lecture Series*. "How does he conflict with the contemporary Zeitgeist? He doesn't. The totipotent man is the imperative of our times. He must come into being before the Golden World can be realized. How can you have a Utopia without utopians, a Golden World with men of brass?"

It was during this Memorable Day that Luscus gave his talk on The Pellucidar Breakthrough and thereby made Chibiabos Winnegan famous. And more than incidentally gave Luscus his biggest score over his competitors.

"Pellucidar? Pellucidar?" Ruskinson mutters. "Oh, God, what's Tinker Bell doing now?"

"It'll take me some time to explain why I used this phrase to describe Winnegan's stroke of genius," Luscus continues. "First, let me seem to detour."

## FROM THE ARCTIC TO ILLINOIS

"Now, Confucius once said that a bear could not fart at the North Pole without causing a big wind in Chicago.

"By this he meant that all events, therefore, all men, are interconnected in an unbreakable web. What one man does, no matter how seemingly insignificant, vibrates through the strands and affects every man."

Ho Chung Ko, before his fido on the 30th level of Lhasa, Tibet, says to his wife, "That white prick has got it all wrong. Confucius didn't say that. Lenin preserve us! I'm going to call him up and give him hell."

His wife says, "Let's change the channel. Pai Ting Place is on now, and . . ."

Ngombe, 10th level, Nairobi: "The critics here are a bunch of black bastards. Now you take Luscus; he could see my genius in a second. I'm going to apply for emigration in the morning."

Wife: "You might at least ask me if I want to go! What about the kids . . . mother . . . friends . . . dog . . . ?" and so on into the lionless night of self-luminous Africa.

". . . ex-president Radinoff," Luscus continues, "once said that this is the 'Age of the Plugged-In Man.' Some rather vulgar remarks have been made about this, to me, insighted phrase. But Radinoff did not mean that human society is a daisy chain. He meant that the current of modern society flows through the circuit of which we are all part. This is the Age of Complete Interconnection. No wires can hang loose; otherwise we all short-circuit. Yet, it is undeniable that life without individuality is not worth living. Every man must be a *hapax legomenon* . . ."

Ruskinson jumps up from his chair and screams, "I know that phrase! I got you this time, Luscus!"

He is so excited he falls over in a faint, symptom of a widespread hereditary defect. When he recovers, the lecture is over. He springs to the recorder to run off what he missed. But Luscus has carefully avoided defining The Pellucidar Breakthrough. He will explain it at another lecture.

Grandpa, back at the scope, whistles. "I feel like an astronomer. The planets are in orbit around our house, the sun. There's Accipiter, the closest, Mercury, although he's not the god of thieves but their nemesis. Next, Benedictine, your sad-sack Venus. Hard, hard, hard! The sperm would batter their heads flat against that stony ovum. You sure she's pregnant?

"Your Mama's out there, dressed fit to kill and I wish someone would. Mother Earth headed for the perigee of the gummint store to waste your substance."

Grandpa braces himself as if on a rolling deck, the blue-black veins on his legs thick as strangling vines on an ancient oak. "Brief departure from the role of Herr Doktor Sternscheissdreckschnuppe, the great astronomer, to that of der Unterseeboot Kapitan von Schooten die Fischen in der Barrel. Ach! I zee yet das tramp Schteamer, Deine Mama, yawing, pitching, rolling in the seas of alcohol. Compass lost; rhumb dumb. Three sheets to the wind. Paddlewheels spinning in the air. The black gang sweating their balls off, stoking the furnaces of frustration. Propellers tangled in the nets of neurosis. And the Great White Whale a glimmer in the black depths but coming up fast, intent on broaching her bottom, too big to miss. Poor damned vessel, I weep for her. I also vomit with disgust.

"Fire one! Fire two! Baroom! Mama rolls over, a jagged hole in her hull but not the one you're thinking of. Down she goes, nose first, as befits a devoted fellationeer, her huge aft rising into the air. Blub, blub! Full fathom five!

"And so back from undersea to outer space. Your sylvan Mars, Red Hawk, has just stepped out of the tavern. And Luscus, Jupiter, the one-eyed All-Father of Art, if you'll pardon my mixing of Nordic and Latin mythologies, is surrounded by his swarm of satellites."

## EXCRETION IS THE BITTER PART OF VALOR

Luscus says to the fido interviewers. "By this I mean that Winnegan, like every artist, great or not, produces art that is, first, secretion, unique to himself, then excretion. Excretion in the original sense of 'sifting out.' Creative excretion or discrete excretion. I know that my distinguished colleagues will make fun of this analogy, so I hereby challenge them to a fido debate whenever it can be arranged.

"The valor comes from the courage of the artist in showing his inner products to the public. The bitter part comes from the fact that the artist may be rejected or misunderstood in his time. Also from the terrible war that takes place in the artist with the disconnected or chaotic elements, often contradictory, which he must unite and then mold into a unique entity. Hence my 'discrete excretion' phrase."

Fido interviewer: "Are we to understand that everything is a big pile of shit but that art makes a strange sea-change, forms it into something golden and illuminating?"

"Not exactly. But you're close. I'll elaborate and expound at a later date. At present, I want to talk about Winnegan. Now, the lesser artists give only the surface of things; they are photographers. But the great ones give the interiority of objects and beings. Winnegan, however, is the first to reveal more than one interiority in a single work of art. His invention of the alto-relief multilevel technique enables him to epiphanize—show forth—subterranean layer upon layer."

Primalux Ruskinson, loudly, "The Great Onion Peeler of Painting!"

Luscus, calmly after the laughter has died: "In one sense, that is well put. Great art, like an onion, brings tears to the eyes. However, the light on Winnegan's paintings is not just a reflection; it is sucked in, digested, and then fractured forth. Each of the broken beams makes visible, not various aspects of the figures beneath, but whole figures. Worlds, I might say.

"I call this The Pellucidar Breakthrough. Pellucidar is the hollow interior of our planet, as depicted in a now forgotten fantasy-romance of the twentieth-century writer, Edgar Rice Burroughs, creator of the immortal Tarzan."

Ruskinson moans and feels faint again. "Pellucid! Pellucidar! Luscus, you punning exhumist bastard!"

"Burroughs' hero penetrated the crust of Earth to discover another world inside. This was, in some ways, the reverse of the exterior, continents where the surface seas are, and vice versa. Just so, Winnegan has discovered an inner world, the obverse of the public image Everyman projects. And, like Burroughs' hero, he has returned with a stunning narrative of psychic dangers and exploration.

"And just as the fictional hero found his Pellucidar to be populated with stone-age men and dinosaurs, so Winnegan's world is, though absolutely modern in one sense, archaic in another. Abysmally pristine. Yet, in the illumination of Winnegan's world, there is an evil and inscrutable patch of blackness, and that is paralleled in Pellucidar by the tiny fixed moon which casts a chilling and unmoving shadow.

"Now, I did intend that the ordinary 'pellucid' should be part of Pellucidar. Yet 'pellucid' means 'reflecting light evenly from all surfaces' or 'admitting maximum passage of light without diffusion or distortion.' Winnegan's paintings do just the opposite. But—under the broken and twisted light, the acute observer can see a primeval luminosity, even and straight. This is the light that links all the fractures and multilevels, the light I was thinking of in my earlier discussion of the 'Age of the Plugged-In Man' and the polar bear.

"By intent scrutiny, a viewer may detect this, feel, as it were, the photonic fremitus of the heartbeat of Winnegan's world."

Ruskinson almost faints. Luscus' smile and black monocle make him look like a pirate who has just taken a Spanish galleon loaded with gold.

Grandpa, still at the scope, says, "And there's Maryam bint Yusuf, the Egyptian backwoodswoman you were telling me about. Your Saturn, aloof, regal, cold, and wearing one of those suspended whirling manycolored hats that're all the rage. Saturn's rings? Or a halo?"

"She's beautiful, and she'd make a wonderful mother for my children," Chib says.

"The chick of Araby. Your Saturn has two moons, mother and aunt. Chaperones! You say she'd make a good mother! How good a wife! Is she intelligent?"

"She's as smart at Benedictine."

"A dumbshit then. You sure can pick them. How do you know you're in love with her? You've been in love with twenty women in the last six months."

"I love her. This is it."

"Until the next one. Can you really love anything but your painting? Benedictine's going to have an abortion, right?"

"Not if I can talk her out of it," Chib says. "To tell the truth, I don't even like her any more. But she's carrying my child."

"Let me look at your pelvis. No, you're male. For a moment, I wasn't sure, you're so crazy to have a baby."

"A baby is a miracle to stagger sextillions of infidels."

"It beats a mouse. But don't you know that Uncle Sam has been propagandizing his heart out to cut down on propagation? Where've you been all your life?"

"I got to go, Grandpa."

Chib kisses the old man and returns to his room to finish his latest painting. The door still refuses to recognize him, and he calls the gummint repair shop, only to be told that all technicians are at the Folk Festival. He leaves the house in a red rage. The bunting and balloons are waving and bobbing in the artificial wind, increased for this occasion, and an orchestra is playing by the lake.

Through the scope, Grandpa watches him walk away.

"Poor devil! I ache for his ache. He wants a baby, and he is ripped up inside because that poor devil Benedictine is aborting their child. Part of his agony, though he doesn't know it, is identification with the doomed infant. His own mother has had innumerable—well, quite a few—abortions. But for the grace of God, he would have been one of them, another nothingness. He wants this baby to have a chance, too. But there is nothing he can do about it, nothing.

"And there is another feeling, one which he shares with most of humankind. He knows he's screwed up his life, or something has twisted it. Every thinking man and woman knows this. Even the smug and dimwitted realize this unconsciously. But a baby, that beautiful being, that unsmirched blank tablet, unformed angel, represents a new hope. Perhaps it won't screw up. Perhaps it'll grow up to be a healthy confident reasonable good-humored unselfish loving man or woman. 'It won't be like me or my next-door neighbor,' the proud, but apprehensive, parent swears.

"Chib thinks this and swears that his baby will be different. But, like everybody else, he's fooling himself. A child has one father and mother, but it has trillions of aunts and uncles. Not only those that are its contemporaries; the dead, too. Even if Chib fled into the wilderness and raised the infant himself, he'd be giving it his own unconscious assumptions. The baby would grow up with beliefs and attitudes that the father was not even aware of. Moreover, being raised in isolation, the baby would be a very peculiar human being indeed.

"And if Chib raises the child in this society, it's inevitable that it will accept at least part of the attitudes of its playmates, teachers, and so on ad nauseam.

"So, forget about making a new Adam out of your wonderful potential-teeming child, Chib. If it grows up to become at least half-sane, it's because you gave it love and discipline and it was lucky in its social contacts and it was also blessed at birth with the right combination of genes. That is, your son or daughter is now both a fighter and a lover."

## ONE MAN'S NIGHTMARE IS ANOTHER MAN'S WET DREAM

Grandpa says.

"I was talking to Dante Alighieri just the other day, and he was telling me what an inferno of stupidity, cruelty, perversity, atheism, and outright peril the sixteenth century was. The nineteenth left him gibbering, hopelessly searching for adequate enough invectives.

"As for this age, it gave him such high-blood pressure, I had to slip him a tranquilizer and ship him out via time machine with an attendant nurse. She looked much like Beatrice and so should have been just the medicine he needed—maybe."

Grandpa chuckles, remembering that Chib, as a child, took him seriously when he described his time-machine visitors, such notables as Nebuchadnezzar, King of the Grass-Eaters; Samson, Bronze Age Riddler and Scourge of the Philistines; Moses, who stole a god from his Kenite father-in-law and who fought against circumcision all his life; Buddha, the Original Beatnik; No-Moss Sisyphus, taking a vacation from his stone-rolling; Androcles and his buddy, the Cowardly Lion of Oz; Baron von Richthofen, the Red Knight of Germany; Beowulf; Al Capone; Hiawatha; Ivan the Terrible; and hundreds of others.

The time came when Grandpa became alarmed and decided that Chib was confusing fantasy with reality. He hated to tell the little boy that he had been making up all those wonderful stories, mostly to teach him history. It was like telling a kid there wasn't any Santa Claus.

And then, while he was reluctantly breaking the news to his grandson, he became aware of Chib's barely suppressed grin and knew that it was his turn to have his leg pulled. Chib had never been fooled or else had caught on without any shock. So, both had a big laugh and Grandpa continued to tell of his visitors.

"There are no time machines," Grandpa says. "Like it or not, Miniver Cheevy, you have to live in this your time.

"The machines work in the utility-factory levels in a silence broken only by the chatter of a few mahouts. The great pipes at the bottom of the seas suck up water and bottom sludge. The stuff is automatically carried through pipes to the ten production levels of LA. There the inorganic chemicals are converted into energy and then into the matter of food, drink, medicines, and artifacts. There is very little agriculture or animal husbandry outside the city walls, but there is superabundance for all. Artificial but exact duplication of organic stuff, so who knows the difference?

"There is no more starvation or want anywhere, except among the self-exiles wandering in the woods. And the food and goods are shipped to the pandoras and dispensed to the receivers of the purple wage. *The purple wage.* A madison-avenue euphemism with connotations of royalty and divine right. Earned by just being born.

"Other ages would regard ours as a delirium, yet ours has benefits others lacked. To combat transiency and rootlessness, the megalopolis is compartmented into small communities. A man can live all his life in one place without having to go elsewhere to get anything he needs. With this has come a provincialism, a small-town patriotism and hostility towards outsiders. Hence, the bloody juvenile gang-fights between towns. The intense and vicious gossip. The insistence on conformity to local mores.

"At the same time, the small-town citizen has fido, which enables him to see events anywhere in the world. Intermingled with the trash and the propaganda, which the government thinks is good for the people, is any amount of superb programs. A man may get the equivalent of a Ph.D. without stirring out of his house.

"Another Renaissance has come, a fruition of the arts comparable to that of Pericles' Athens and the city-states of Michelangelo's Italy or Shakespeare's England. Paradox. More illiterates than ever before in the world's history. But also more literates. Speakers of classical Latin outnumber those of Caesar's day. The world of aesthetics bears a fabulous fruit. And, of course, fruits.

"To dilute the provincialism and also to make international war even more unlikely, we have the world policy of *homogenization*. The voluntary exchange of a part of one nation's population with another's. Hostages to peace and brotherly love. Those citizens who can't get along on just the purple wage or who think they'll be happier elsewhere are induced to emigrate with bribes.

"A Golden World in some respects; a nightmare in others. So what's new with the world? It was always thus in every age. Ours has had to deal with overpopulation and automation. How else could the problem be solved? It's Buridan's ass (actually, the ass was a dog) all over again, as in every time. Buridan's ass, dying of hunger because it can't make up its mind which of two equal amounts of food to eat.

"History: a *pons asinorum* with men the asses on the bridge of time.

"No, those two comparisons are not fair or right. It's Hobson's horse, the only choice being the beast in the nearest stall. Zeitgeist rides tonight, and the devil take the hindmost!

"The mid-twentieth-century writers of the Triple Revolution document forecast accurately in some respects. But they de-emphasized what lack of work would do to Mr. Everyman. They believed that all men have equal potentialities in developing artistic tendencies, that all could busy themselves with arts, crafts, and hobbies or education for education's sake. They wouldn't face the 'undemocratic' reality that only about ten per cent of the population—if that—are inherently capable of producing anything worth while, or even mildly interesting, in the arts. Crafts, hobbies, and a lifelong academic education pale after a while, so back to the booze, fido, and adultery.

"Lacking self-respect, the fathers become free-floaters, nomads on the steppes of sex. Mother, with a capital M, becomes the dominant figure in the family. She may be playing around, too, but she's taking care of the kids; she's around most of the time. Thus, with father a lower-case figure, absent, weak, or indifferent, the children often become homosexual or ambisexual. The wonderland is also a fairyland.

"Some features of this time could have been predicted. Sexual permissiveness was one, although no one could have seen how far it would go. But then no one could have foreknown of the Panamorite sect, even if America has spawned lunatic-fringe cults as a frog spawns tadpoles. Yesterday's monomaniac is tomorrow's messiah, and so Sheltey and his disciples survived through years of persecution and today their precepts are embedded in our culture."

Grandpa again fixes the cross-reticules of the scope on Chib.

"There he goes, my beautiful grandson, bearing gifts to the Greeks. So far, that Hercules has failed to clean up his psychic Augean stable. Yet, he may succeed, that stumblebum Apollo, that Edipus Wrecked. He's luckier than most of his contemporaries. He's had a permanent father, even if a secret one, a zany old man hiding from so-called justice. He has gotten love, discipline, and a superb education in this starred chamber. He's also fortunate in having a profession.

"But Mama spends far too much and also is addicted to gambling, a vice which deprives her of her full guaranteed income. I'm supposed to be dead, so I don't get the purple wage. Chib has to make up for all this by selling or trading his paintings. Luscus has helped him by publicizing him, but at any moment Luscus may turn against him. The money from the paintings is still not enough. After all, money is not the basic of our economy; it's a scarce auxiliary. Chib needs the grant but won't get it unless he lets Luscus make love to him.

"It's not that Chib rejects homosexual relations. Like most of his contemporaries, he's sexually ambivalent. I think that he and Omar Runic still blow each other occasionally. And why not? They love each other. But Chib rejects Luscus as a matter of principle. He won't be a whore to advance his career. Moreover, Chib makes a distinction which is deeply embedded in this society. He thinks that uncompulsive homosexuality is natural (whatever that means?) but that compulsive homosexuality is, to use an old term, queer. Valid or not, the distinction is made.

"So, Chib may go to Egypt. But what happens to me then?

"Never mind me or your mother, Chib. No matter what. Don't give in to Luscus. Remember the dying words of Singleton, Bureau of Relocation and Rehabilitation Director, who shot himself because he couldn't adjust to the new times.

" 'What if a man gain the world and lose his ass?' "

At this moment, Grandpa sees his grandson, who has been walking along with somewhat drooping shoulders, suddenly straighten them. And he sees Chib break into a dance, a little improvised shuffle followed by a series of whirls. It is evident that Chib is whooping. The pedestrians around him are grinning.

Grandpa groans and then laughs. "Oh, God, the goatish energy of youth, the unpredictable shift of spectrum from black sorrow to bright orange joy! Dance, Chib, dance your crazy head off! Be happy, if only for a moment! You're young yet, you've got the bubbling of unconquerable hope deep in your springs! Dance, Chib, dance!"

He laughs and wipes a tear away.


## SEXUAL IMPLICATIONS OF THE CHARGE OF THE LIGHT BRIGADE

is so fascinating a book that Doctor Jespersen Joyce Bathymens, psycholinguist for the federal Bureau of Group Reconfiguration and Intercommunicability, hates to stop reading. But duty beckons.

"A radish is not necessarily reddish," he says into the recorder. "The Young Radishes so named their group because a radish is a radicle, hence, radical. Also, there's a play on roots and on redass, a slang term for anger, and possibly on ruttish and rattish. And undoubtedly on rude-ickle, Beverly Hills dialectical term for a repulsive, unruly, and socially ungraceful person.

"Yet the Young Radishes are not what I would call Left Wing; they represent the current resentment against Life-In-General and advocate no radical policy of reconstruction. They howl against Things As They Are, like monkeys in a tree, but never give constructive criticism. They want to destroy without any thought of what to do after the destruction.

"In short, they represent the average citizen's grousing and bitching, being different in that they are more articulate. There are thousands of groups like them in LA and possibly millions all over the world. They had normal life as children. In fact, they were born and raised in the same clutch, which is one reason why they were chosen for this study. What phenomenon produced ten such creative persons, all mothered in the seven houses of Area 69-14, all about the same time, all practically raised together, since they were put together in the playpen on top of the pedestal while one mother took her turn baby-sitting and the others did whatever they had to do, which . . . where was I?

"Oh, yes, they had a normal life, went to the same school, palled around, enjoyed the usual sexual play among themselves, joined the juvenile gangs and engaged in some rather bloody warfare with the Westwood and other gangs. All were distinguished, however, by an intense intellectual curiosity and all become active in the creative arts.

"It has been suggested—and might be true—that that mysterious stranger, Raleigh Renaissance, was the father of all ten. This is possible but can't be proved. Raleigh Renaissance was living in the house of Mrs. Winnegan at the time, but he seems to have been unusually active in the clutch and, indeed, all over Beverly Hills. Where this man came from, who he was, and where he went are still unknown despite intensive search by various agencies. He had no ID or other cards of any kind, yet he went unchallenged for a long time. He seems to have had something on the Chief of Police of Beverly Hills and possibly on some of the Federal agents stationed in Beverly Hills.

"He lived for two years with Mrs. Winnegan, then dropped out of sight. It is rumored that he left LA to join a tribe of white neo-Amerinds, sometimes called the Seminal Indians.

"Anyway, back to the Young (pun on Jung?) Radishes. They are revolting against the Father Image of Uncle Sam, whom they both love and hate. Uncle is, of course, linked by their subconsciouses with *unco*, a Scottish word meaning strange, uncanny, weird, this indicating that their own fathers were strangers to them. All come from homes where the father was missing or weak, a phenomenon regrettably common in our culture.

"I never knew my own father . . . Tooney, wipe that out as irrelevant. *Unco* also means news or tidings, indicating that the unfortunate young men are eagerly awaiting news of the return of their fathers and perhaps secretly hoping for reconciliation with Uncle Sam, that is, their fathers.

"Uncle Sam. Sam is short for Samuel, from the Hebrew *Shemu'el*, meaning Name of God. All the Radishes are atheists, although some, notably Omar Runic and Chibiabos Winnegan, were given religious instruction as children (Panamorite and Roman Catholic, respectively).

"Young Winnegan's revolt against God, and against the Catholic Church, was undoubtedly reinforced by the fact that his mother forced strong *cath*artics upon him when he had a chronic constipation. He probably also resented having to learn his *cat*echism when he preferred to play. And there is the deeply significant and traumatic incident in which a *cath*eter was used on him. (This refusal to excrete when young will be analyzed in a later report.)

"Uncle Sam, the Father Figure. *Figure* is so obvious a play that I won't bother to point it out. Also perhaps on *figger*, in the sense of 'a fig on thee!'—look this up in Dante's *Inferno*, some Italian or other in Hell said, 'A fig on thee, God!' biting his thumb in the ancient gesture of defiance and disrespect. Hmm? Biting the thumb—an infantile characteristic?

"Sam is also a multileveled pun on phonetically, orthographically, and semisemantically linked words. It is significant that young Winnegan can't stand to be called *dear*; he claims that his mother called him that so many times it nauseates him. Yet the word has a deeper meaning to him. For instance, *sambar* is an Asiatic *deer* with *three*-pointed antlers. (Note the *sam*, also.) Obviously, the three points symbolize, to him, the Triple Revolution document, the historic dating point of the beginning of our era, which Chib claims to hate so. The three points are also archetypes of the Holy Trinity, which the Young Radishes frequently blaspheme against.

"I might point out that in this the group differs from others I've studied. The others expressed an infrequent and mild blasphemy in keeping with the mild, indeed pale, religious spirit prevalent nowadays. Strong blasphemers thrive only when strong believers thrive.

"Sam also stands for *same*, indicating the Radishes' subconscious desire to conform.

"Possibly, although this particular analysis may be invalid, Sam corresponds to Samekh, the fifteenth letter of the Hebrew alphabet. (Sam!

Ech!?) In the old style of English spelling, which the Radishes learned in their childhood, the fifteenth letter of the Roman alphabet is O. In the Alphabet Table of my dictionary, Webster's 128th New Collegiate, the Roman O is in the same horizontal column as the Arabic Dad. Also with the Hebrew Mem. So we get a double connection with the missing and longed-for Father (or Dad) and with the overdominating Mother (or Mem).

"I can make nothing out of the Greek Omicron, also in the same horizontal column. But give me time; this takes study.

"Omicron. The little O! The lower-case omicron has an egg shape. The little egg is their father's sperm fertilized? The womb? The basic shape of modern architecture?

"Sam Hill, an archaic euphemism for Hell. Uncle Sam is a Sam Hill of a father? Better strike that out, Tooney. It's possible that these highly educated youths have read about this obsolete phrase, but it's not confirmable. I don't want to suggest any connections that might make me look ridiculous.

"Let's see. Samisen. A Japanese musical instrument with *three* strings. The Triple Revolution document and the Trinity again. Trinity? Father, Son, and Holy Ghost. Mother the thoroughly despised figure, hence, the Wholly Goose? Well, maybe not. Wipe that out. Tooney.

"Samisen. Son of Sam? Which leads naturally to Samson, who pulled down the temple of the Philistines on them and on himself. These boys talk of doing the same thing. Chuckle. Reminds me of myself when I was their age, before I matured. Strike out that last remark, Tooney.

"Samovar. The Russian word means, literally, self-boiler. There's no doubt the Radishes are boiling with revolutionary fervor. Yet their disturbed psyches know, deep down, that Uncle Sam is their ever-loving Father-Mother, that he has only their best interests at heart. But they force themselves to hate him, hence, they self-boil.

"A samlet is a young salmon. Cooked salmon is a yellowish pink or pale red, near to a radish in color, in their unconsciouses, anyway. Samlet equals Young Radish; they feel they're being cooked in the great pressure cooker of modern society.

"How's that for a trinely furned phase—I mean, finely turned phrase, Tooney? Run this off, edit as indicated, smooth it out, you know how, and send it off to the boss. I got to go. I'm late for lunch with Mother; she gets very upset if I'm not there on the dot.

"Oh, postscript! I recommend that the agents watch Winnegan more closely. His friends are blowing off psychic steam through talk and drink, but he has suddenly altered his behavior pattern. He has long periods of silence, he's given up smoking, drinking, and sex."

## A PROFIT IS NOT WITHOUT HONOR

even in this day. The gummint has no overt objection to privately
owned taverns, run by citizens who have paid all license fees, passed
all examinations, posted all bonds, and bribed the local politicians and
police chief. Since there is no provision made for them, no large buildings available for rent, the taverns are in the homes of the owners
themselves.

*The Private Universe* is Chib's favorite, partly because the proprietor
is operating illegally. Dionysus Gobrinus, unable to hew his way
through the roadblocks, prise-de-chevaux, barbed wire, and booby-
traps of official procedure, has quit his efforts to get a license.

Openly, he paints the name of his establishment over the mathematical equations that once distinguished the exterior of the house. (Math
prof at Beverly Hills U. 14, named Al-Khwarizmi Descartes Lobachev-
sky, he has resigned and changed his name again.) The atrium and
several bedrooms have been converted for drinking and carousing.
There are no Egyptian customers, probably because of their supersensi-
tivity about the flowery sentiments painted by patrons on the inside
walls.

> À BAS, ABU
> MOHAMMED WAS THE SON OF A VIRGIN DOG
> THE SPHINX STINKS
> REMEMBER THE RED SEA!
> THE PROPHET HAS A CAMEL FETISH

Some of those who wrote the taunts have fathers, grandfathers, and
great-grandfathers who were themselves the objects of similiar insults.
But their descendants are thoroughly assimilated, Beverly Hillsians to
the core. Of such is the kingdom of men.

Gobrinus, a squat cube of a man, stands behind the bar, which is
square as a protest against the ovoid. Above him is a big sign:

## ONE MAN'S MEAD IS ANOTHER MAN'S POISSON

Gobrinus has explained this pun many times, not always to his lis-
tener's satisfaction. Suffice it that Poisson was a mathematician and

that Poisson's frequency distribution is a good approximation to the binomial distribution as the number of trials increases and probability of success in a single trial is small.

When a customer gets too drunk to be permitted one more drink, he is hurled headlong from the tavern with furious combustion and utter ruin by Gobrinus, who cries, "Poisson! Poisson!"

Chib's friends, the Young Radishes, sitting at a hexagonal table, greet him, and their words unconsciously echo those of the Federal psycholinguist's estimate of his recent behavior.

"Chib, monk! Chibber as ever! Looking for a chibbie, no doubt! Take your pick!"

Madame Trismegista, sitting at a little table with a Seal-of-Solomon-shape top, greets him. She has been Gobrinus' wife for two years, a record, because she will knife him if he leaves her. Also, he believes that she can somehow juggle his destiny with the cards she deals. In this age of enlightenment, the soothsayer and astrologer flourish. As science pushes forward, ignorance and superstition gallop around the flanks and bite science in the rear with big dark teeth.

Gobrinus himself, a Ph.D., holder of the torch of knowledge (until lately, anyway), does not believe in God. But he is sure the stars are marching towards a baleful conjunction for him. With a strange logic, he thinks that his wife's cards control the stars; he is unaware that card-divination and astrology are entirely separate fields.

What can you expect of a man who claims that the universe is asymmetric?

Chib waves his hand at Madame Trismegista and walks to another table. Here sits

## A TYPICAL TEEMAGER

Benedictine Serinus Melba. She is tall and slim and has narrow lemur-like hips and slender legs but big breasts. Her hair, black as the pupils of her eyes, is parted in the middle, plastered with perfumed spray to the skull, and braided into two long pigtails. These are brought over her bare shoulders and held together with a golden brooch just below her throat. From the brooch, which is in the form of a musical note, the braids part again, one looping under each breast. Another brooch secures them, and they separate to circle around behind her back, are brooched again, and come back to meet on her belly. Another brooch holds them, and the twin waterfalls flow blackly over the front of her bell-shaped skirt.

Her face is thickly farded with green, aquamarine, a shamrock beauty mark, and topaz. She wears a yellow bra with artificial pink nipples; frilly lace ribbons hang from the bra. A demicorselet of bright green with black rosettes circle her waist. Over the corselet, half-concealing it, is a wire structure covered with a shimmering pink quilty material. It extends out in back to form a semifuselage or a bird's long tail, to which are attached long yellow and crimson artificial feathers.

An ankle-length diaphanous skirt billows out. It does not hide the yellow and dark-green striped lace-fringed garter-panties, white thighs, and black net stockings with green clocks in the shape of musical notes. Her shoes are bright blue with topaz high heels.

Benedictine is costumed to sing at the Folk Festival; the only thing missing is her singer's hat. Yet, she came to complain, among other things, that Chib has forced her to cancel her appearance and so lose her chance at a great career.

She is with five girls, all between sixteen and twenty-one, all drinking P (for popskull).

"Can't we talk in private, Benny?" Chib says.

"What for?" Her voice is a lovely contralto ugly with inflection.

"You got me down here to make a public scene," Chib says.

"For God's sake, what other kind of scene is there?" she shrills. "Look at him! He wants to talk to me alone!"

It is then that he realizes she is afraid to be alone with him. More than that, she is incapable of being alone. Now he knows why she insisted on leaving the bedroom door open with her girlfriend, Bela, within calling distance. And listening distance.

"You said you was just going to use your finger!" she shouts. She points at the slightly rounded belly. "I'm going to have a baby! You rotten smooth-talking sick bastard!"

"That isn't true at all," Chib says. "You told me it was all right, you loved me."

" 'Love! Love!' he says! What the hell do I know what I said, you got me so excited! Anyway, I didn't say you could stick it in! I'd never say that, never! And then what you *did!* *What* you did! My God, I could hardly walk for a week, you bastard, you!"

Chib sweats. Except for Beethoven's Pastoral welling from the fido, the room is silent. His friends grin. Gobrinus, his back turned, is drinking scotch. Madame Trismegista shuffles her cards, and she farts with a fiery conjunction of beer and onions. Benedictine's friends look at their Mandarin-long fluorescent fingernails or glare at him. Her hurt and indignity is theirs and vice versa.

"I can't take those pills. They make me break out and give me eye trouble and screw up my monthlies! You know that! And I can't stand those mechanical uteruses! And you lied to me, anyway! You said you took a pill!"

Chib realizes she's contradicting herself, but there's no use trying to be logical. She furious because she's pregnant; she doesn't want to be inconvenienced with an abortion at this time, and she's out for revenge.

Now how, Chib wonders, how could she get pregnant *that* night? No woman, no matter how fertile, could have managed that. She must have been knocked up before or after. Yet she swears that it was that night, the night he was

## THE KNIGHT OF THE BURNING PESTLE
### OR
## FOAM, FOAM ON THE RANGE

"No, no!" Benedictine cries.

"Why not? I love you," Chib says. "I want to marry you."

Benedictine screams, and her friend Bela, out in the hall, yells, "What's the matter? What happened?"

Benedictine does not reply. Raging, shaking as if in the grip of a fever, she scrambles out of bed, pushing Chib to one side. She runs to the small egg of the bathroom in the corner, and he follows her.

"I hope you're not going to do what I think . . . ?" he says.

Benedictine moans, "You sneaky no-good son of a bitch!"

In the bathroom, she pulls down a section of wall, which becomes a shelf. On its top, attached by magnetic bottoms to the shelf, are many containers. She seizes a long thin can of spermatocide, squats, and inserts it. She presses the button on its bottom, and it foams with a hissing sound even its cover of flesh cannot silence.

Chib is paralyzed for a moment. Then he roars.

Benedictine shouts, "Stay away from me, you rude-ickle!"

From the door to the bedroom comes Bela's timid, "Are you all right, Benny?"

"I'll all-right her!" Chib bellows.

He jumps forward and takes a can of tempoxy glue from the shelf. The glue is used by Benedictine to attach her wigs to her head and will hold anything forever unless softened by a specific defixative.

Benedictine and Bela both cry out as Chib lifts Benedictine up and then lowers her to the floor. She fights, but he manages to spray the glue over the can and the skin and hairs around it.

"What're you doing?" she screams.

He pushes the button on the bottom of the can to full-on position and then sprays the bottom with glue. While she struggles, he holds her arms tight against her body and keeps her from rolling over and so moving the can in or out. Silently, Chib counts to thirty, then to thirty more to make sure the glue is thoroughly dried. He releases her.

The foam is billowing out around her groin and down her legs and spreading out across the floor. The fluid in the can is under enormous pressure in the indestructible unpunchable can, and the foam expands vastly if exposed to open air.

Chib takes the can of defixative from the shelf and clutches it in his hand, determined that she will not have it. Benedictine jumps up and swings at him. Laughing like a hyena in a tentful of nitrous oxide, Chib blocks her fist and shoves her away. Slipping on the foam, which is ankle-deep by now, Benedictine falls and then slides backward out of the bedroom on her buttocks, the can clunking.

She gets to her feet and only then realizes fully what Chib has done. Her scream goes up, and she follows it. She dances around, yanking at the can, her screams intensifying with every tug and resultant pain. Then she turns and runs out of the room or tries to. She skids; Bela is in her way; they cling together and both ski out of the room, doing a half-turn while going through the door. The foam swirls out so that the two look like Venus and friend rising from the bubble-capped waves of the Cyprian Sea.

Benedictine shoves Bela away but not without losing some flesh to Bela's long sharp fingernails. Bela shoots backwards through the door toward Chib. She is like a novice ice skater trying to maintain her balance. She does not succeed and shoots by Chib, wailing, on her back, her feet up in the air.

Chib slides his bare feet across the floor gingerly, stops at the bed to pick up his clothes, but decides he'd be wiser to wait until he's outside before he puts them on. He gets to the circular hall just in time to see Benedictine crawling past one of the columns that divides the corridor from the atrium. Her parents, two middle-aged behemoths, are still sitting on a flato, beer cans in hand, eyes wide, mouths open, quivering.

Chib does not even say goodnight to them as he passes along the hall. But then he sees the fido and realizes that her parents had switched it from EXT. to INT. and then to Benedictine's room. Father and mother have been watching Chib and daughter, and it is evident from father's not-quite dwindled condition that father was very excited by this show, superior to anything seen on exterior fido.

"You peeping bastards!" Chib roars.

Benedictine has gotten to them and on her feet and she is stammering, weeping, indicating the can and then stabbing her finger at Chib. At Chib's roar, the parents heave up from the flato as two leviathans from the deep. Benedictine turns and starts to run towards him, her arms outstretched, her longnailed fingers curved, her face a medusa's. Behind her streams the wake of the livid witch and father and mother on the foam.

Chib shoves up against a pillar and rebounds and skitters off, helpless to keep himself from turning sidewise during the maneuver. But he keeps his balance. Mama and Papa have gone down together with a crash that shakes even the solid house. They are up, eyes rolling and bellowing like hippos surfacing. They charge him but separate, Mama shrieking now, her face, despite the fat, Benedictine's. Papa goes around one side of the pillar; Mama, the other. Benedictine has rounded another pillar, holding to it with one hand to keep her from slipping. She is between Chib and the door to the outside.

Chib slams against the wall of the corridor, in an area free of foam. Benedictine runs towards him. He dives across the floor, hits it, and rolls between two pillars and out into the atrium.

Mama and Papa converge in a collision course. The Titanic meets the iceberg, and both plunge swiftly. They skid on their faces and bellies towards Benedictine. She leaps into the air, trailing foam on them as they pass beneath her.

By now it is evident that the government's claim that the can is good for 40,000 shots of death-to-sperm, or for 40,000 copulations, is justified. Foam is all over the place, ankle-deep—knee-high in some places—and still pouring out.

Bela is on her back now and on the atrium floor, her head driven into the soft folds of the flato.

Chib gets up slowly and stands for a moment, glaring around him, his knees bent, ready to jump from danger but hoping he won't have to since his feet will undoubtedly fly away from under him.

"Hold it, you rotten son of a bitch!" Papa roars. "I'm going to kill you! You can't do this to my daughter!"

Chib watches him turn over like a whale in a heavy sea and try to get to his feet. Down he goes again, grunting as if hit by a harpoon. Mama is no more successful than he.

Seeing that his way is unbarred—Benedictine having disappeared somewhere—Chib skis across the atrium until he reaches an unfoamed area near the exit. Clothes over his arm, still holding the defixative, he struts towards the door.

At this moment Benedictine calls his name. He turns to see her sliding from the kitchen at him. In her hand is a tall glass. He wonders what she intends to do with it. Certainly, she is not offering him the hospitality of a drink.

Then she scoots into the dry region of the floor and topples forward with a scream. Nevertheless, she throws the contents of the glass accurately.

Chib screams when he feels the boiling hot water, painful as if he had been circumcised unanesthetized.

Benedictine, on the floor, laughs. Chib, after jumping around and shrieking, the can and clothes dropped, his hands holding the scalded parts, manages to control himself. He stops his antics, seizes Benedictine's right hand, and drags her out into the streets of Beverly Hills. There are quite a few people out this night, and they follow the two. Not until Chib reaches the lake does he stop and there he goes into the water to cool off the burn, Benedictine with him.

The crowd has much to talk about later, after Benedictine and Chib have crawled out of the lake and then run home. The crowd talks and laughs quite a while as they watch the sanitation department people clean the foam off the lake surface and the streets.

"I was so sore I couldn't walk for a month!" Benedictine screams.

"You had it coming," Chib says. "You've got no complaints. You said you wanted my baby, and you talked as if you meant it."

"I must've been out of my mind!" Benedictine says. "No, I wasn't! I never said no such thing! You lied to me! You forced me!"

"I would never force anybody," Chib said. "You know that. Quit your bitching. You're a free agent, and you consented freely. You have free will."

Omar Runic, the poet, stands up from his chair. He is a tall thin red-bronze youth with an aquiline nose and very thick red lips. His kinky hair grows long and is cut into the shape of the *Pequod,* that fabled vessel which bore mad Captain Ahab and his mad crew and the sole survivor Ishmael after the white whale. The coiffure is formed with a bowsprit and hull and three masts and yardarms and even a boat hanging on davits.

Omar Runic claps his hands and shouts, "Bravo! A philosopher! Free will it is; free will to seek the Eternal Verities—if any—or Death and Damnation! I'll drink to free will! A toast, gentlemen! Stand up, Young Radishes, a toast to our leader!"

And so begins

## THE MAD P PARTY

Madame Trismegista calls, "Tell your fortune, Chib! See what the stars tell through the cards!"

He sits down at her table while his friends crowd around.

"O.K., Madame. How do I get out of this mess?"

She shuffles and turns over the top card.

"Jesus! The ace of spades!"

"You're going on a long journey!"

"Egypt!" Rousseau Red Hawk cries. "Oh, no, you don't want to go there, Chib! Come with me to where the buffalo roam and . . ."

Up comes another card.

"You will soon meet a beautiful dark lady."

"A goddam Arab! Oh, no, Chib, tell me it's not true!"

"You will win great honors soon."

"Chib's going to get the grant!"

"If I get the grant, I don't have to go to Egypt," Chib says. "Madame Trismegista, with all due respect, you're full of crap."

"Don't mock, young man. I'm not a computer. I'm tuned to the spectrum of psychic vibrations."

Flip. "You will be in great danger, physically and morally."

Chib says, "That happens at least once a day."

Flip. "A man very close to you will die twice."

Chib pales, rallies, and says, "A coward dies a thousand deaths."

"You will travel in time, return to the past."

"Zow!" Red Hawk says. "You're outdoing yourself, Madame. Careful! You'll get a psychic hernia, have to wear an ectoplasmic truss!"

"Scoff if you want to, you dumbshits," Madame says. "There are more worlds than one. The cards don't lie, not when I deal them."

"Gobrinus!" Chib calls. "Another pitcher of beer for the Madame."

The Young Radishes return to their table, a legless disc held up in the air by a graviton field. Benedictine glares at them and goes into a huddle with the other teemagers. At a table nearby sits Pinkerton Legrand, a gummint agent, facing them so that the fido under his one-way window of a jacket beams in on them. They know he's doing this. He knows they know and has reported so to his superior. He frowns when he sees Falco Accipiter enter. Legrand does not like an agent from another department messing around on his case. Accipiter does not even look at Legrand. He orders a pot of tea and then pretends to drop into the teapot a pill that combines with tannic acid to become P.

Rousseau Red Hawk winks at Chib and says, "Do you really think it's possible to paralyze all of LA with a single bomb?"

"Three bombs!" Chib says loudly so that Legrand's fido will pick up the words. "One for the control console of the desalinization plant, a second for the backup console, the third for the nexus of the big pipe that carries the water to the reservoir on the 20th level."

Pinkerton Legrand turns pale. He downs all the whiskey in his glass and orders another, although he has already had too many. He presses the plate on his fido to transmit a triple top-priority. Lights blink redly in HQ; a gong clangs repeatedly; the chief wakes up so suddenly he falls off his chair.

Accipiter also hears, but he sits stiff, dark, and brooding as the diorite image of a Pharaoh's falcon. Monomaniac, he is not to be diverted by talk of inundating all LA, even if it will lead to action. On Grandpa's trail, he is now here because he hopes to use Chib as the key to the house. One "mouse"—as he thinks of his criminals—one "mouse" will run to the hole of another.

"When do you think we can go into action?" Huga Wells-Erb Heinsturbury, the science-fiction authoress, says.

"In about three weeks," Chib says.

At HQ, the chief curses Legrand for disturbing him. There are thousands of young men and women blowing off steam with these plots of destruction, assassination, and revolt. He does not understand why the young punks talk like this, since they have everything handed them free. If he had his way, he'd throw them into jail and kick them around a little or more than.

"After we do it, we'll have to take off for the big outdoors," Red Hawk says. His eyes glisten. "I'm telling you, boys, being a free man in the forest is the greatest. You're a genuine individual, not just one of the faceless breed."

Red Hawk believes in this plot to destroy LA. He is happy because, though he hasn't said so, he has grieved while in Mother Nature's lap for intellectual companionship. The other savages can hear a deer at a hundred yards, detect a rattlesnake in the bushes, but they're deaf to the footfalls of philosophy, the neigh of Nietzsche, the rattle of Russell, the honkings of Hegel.

"The illiterate swine!" he says aloud. The others say, "What?"

"Nothing. Listen, you guys must know how wonderful it is. You were in the WNRCC."

"I was 4-F," Omar Runic says. "I got hay fever."

"I was working on my second M.A.," Gibbon Tacitus says.

"I was in the WNRCC band," Sibelius Amadeus Yehudi says. "We only got outside when we played the camps, and that wasn't often."

"Chib, you were in the Corps. You loved it, didn't you?"

Chib nods but says, "Being a neo-Amerind takes all your time just to survive. When could I paint? And who would see the paintings if I did get time? Anyway, that's no life for a woman or a baby."

Red Hawk looks hurt and orders a whiskey mixed with P.

Pinkerton Legrand doesn't want to interrupt his monitoring, yet he can't stand the pressure in his bladder. He walks towards the room used as the customers' catch-all. Red Hawk, in a nasty mood caused by rejection, sticks his leg out. Legrand trips, catches himself, and stumbles forward. Benedictine puts out her leg. Legrand falls on his face. He no longer has any reason to go to the urinal except to wash himself off.

Everybody except Legrand and Accipiter laugh. Legrand jumps up, his fists doubled. Benedictine ignores him and walks over to Chib, her friends following. Chib stiffens. She says, "You perverted bastard! You told me you were just going to use your finger!"

"You're repeating yourself," Chib says. "The important thing is, what's going to happen to the baby?"

"What do you care?" Benedictine says. "For all you know, it might not even be yours!"

"That'd be a relief," Chib says, "if it weren't. Even so, the baby should have a say in this. He might want to live—even with you as his mother."

"In this miserable life!" she cries. "I'm going to do it a favor. I'm going to the hospital and get rid of it. Because of you, I have to miss out on my big chance at the Folk Festival! There'll be agents from all over there, and I won't get a chance to sing for them!"

"You're a liar," Chib says. "You're all dressed up to sing."

Benedictine's face is red; her eyes, wide; her nostrils, flaring.

"You spoiled my fun!"

She shouts, "Hey, everybody, want to hear a howler! This great artist, this big hunk of manhood, Chib the divine, he can't get a hardon unless he's gone down on!"

Chib's friends look at each other. What's the bitch screaming about? So what's new?

*From Grandpa's* Private Ejaculations: *Some of the features of the Panamorite religion, so reviled and loathed in the 21st century, have become everyday facts in modern times. Love, love, love, physical and spiritual! It's not enough to just kiss your children and hug them. But*

*oral stimulation of the genitals of infants by the parents and relatives
has resulted in some curious conditioned reflexes. I could write a book
about this aspect of mid-22nd century life and probably will.*

Legrand comes out of the washroom. Benedictine slaps Chib's face.
Chib slaps her back. Gobrinus lifts up a section of the bar and hurtles
through the opening, crying, "Poisson! Poisson!"

He collides with Legrand, who lurches into Bela, who screams,
whirls, and slaps Legrand, who slaps back. Benedictine empties a glass
of P in Chib's face. Howling, he jumps up and swings his fist. Benedictine ducks, and the fist goes over her shoulder into a girlfriend's
chest.

Red Hawk leaps up on the table and shouts, "I'm a regular bearcat,
half-alligator, half . . ."

The table, held up in a graviton field, can't bear much weight. It
tilts and catapults him into the girls, and all go down. They bite and
scratch Red Hawk, and Benedictine squeezes his testicles. He screams,
writhes, and hurls Benedictine with his feet onto the top of the table.
It has regained its normal height and altitude, but now it flips over
again, tossing her to the other side. Legrand, tippytoeing through the
crowd on his way to the exit, is knocked down. He loses some front
teeth against somebody's knee cap. Spitting blood and teeth, he jumps
up and slugs a bystander.

Gobrinus fires off a gun that shoots a tiny Very light. It's supposed
to blind the brawlers and so bring them to their senses while they're
regaining their sight. It hangs in the air and shines like

## A STAR OVER BEDLAM

The Police Chief is talking via fido to a man in a public booth. The
man has turned off the video and is disguising his voice.

"They're beating the shit out of each other in *The Private Universe.*"

The Chief groans. The Festival has just begun, and They are at it
already.

"Thanks. The boys'll be on the way. What's your name? I'd like to
recommend you for a Citizen's Medal."

"What! And get the shit knocked out of me, too! I ain't no stoolie;
just doing my duty. Besides, I don't like Gobrinus or his customers.
They're a bunch of snobs."

The Chief issues orders to the riot squad, leans back, and drinks a beer while he watches the operation on fido. What's the matter with these people, anyway? They're always mad about something.

The sirens scream. Although the bolgani ride electrically driven noiseless tricycles, they're still clinging to the centuries-old tradition of warning the criminals that they're coming. Five trikes pull up before the open door of The Private Universe. The police dismount and confer. Their two-storied cylindrical helmets are black and have scarlet roaches. They wear goggles for some reason although their vehicles can't go over 15 m.p.h. Their jackets are black and fuzzy, like a teddy bear's fur, and huge golden epaulets decorate their shoulders. The shorts are electric-blue and fuzzy; the jackboots, glossy black. They carry electric shock sticks and guns that fire chokegas pellets.

Gobrinus blocks the entrance. Sergeant O'Hara says, "Come on, let us in. No, I don't have a warrant of entry. But I'll get one."

"If you do, I'll sue," Gobrinus says. He smiles. While it is true that government red tape was so tangled he quit trying to acquire a tavern legally, it is also true that the government will protect him in this issue. Invasion of privacy is a tough rap for the police to break.

O'Hara looks inside the doorway at the two bodies on the floor, at those holding their heads and sides and wiping off blood, and at Accipiter, sitting like a vulture dreaming of carrion. One of the bodies gets up on all fours and crawls through between Gobrinus' legs out into the street.

"Sergeant, arrest that man!" Gobrinus says. "He's wearing an illegal fido. I accuse him of invasion of privacy."

O'Hara's face lights up. At least he'll get one arrest to his credit. Legrand is placed in the paddywagon, which arrives just after the ambulance. Red Hawk is carried out as far as the doorway by his friends. He opens his eyes just as he's being carried on a stretcher to the ambulance and he mutters.

O'Hara leans over him. "What?"

"I fought a bear once with only my knife, and I came out better than with those cunts. I charge them with assault and battery, murder and mayhem."

O'Hara's attempt to get Red Hawk to sign a warrant fails because Red Hawk is now unconscious. He curses. By the time Red Hawk begins feeling better, he'll refuse to sign the warrant. He won't want the girls and their boy friends laying for him, not if he has any sense at all.

Through the barred window of the paddywagon, Legrand screams, "I'm a gummint agent! You can't arrest me!"

The police get a hurry-up call to go to the front of the Folk Center, where a fight between local youths and Westwood invaders is threatening to become a riot. Benedictine leaves the tavern. Despite several blows in the shoulders and stomach, a kick in the buttocks, and a bang on the head, she shows no signs of losing the fetus.

Chib, half-sad, half-glad, watches her go. He feels a dull grief that the baby is to be denied life. By now he realizes that part of his objection to the abortion is identification with the fetus; he knows what Grandpa thinks he does not know. He realizes that his birth was an accident—lucky or unlucky. If things had gone otherwise, he would not have been born. The thought of his nonexistence—no painting, no friends, no laughter, no hope, no love—horrifies him. His mother, drunkenly negligent about contraception, has had any number of abortions, and he could have been one of them.

Watching Benedictine swagger away (despite her torn clothes), he wonders what he could ever have seen in her. Life with her, even with a child, would have been gritty.

> *In the hope-lined nest of the mouth*
> *Love flies once more, nestles down,*
> *Coos, flashes feathered glory, dazzles,*
> *And then flies away, crapping,*
> *As is the wont of birds,*
> *To jet-assist the takeoff.*

> *—Omar Runic*

Chib returns to his home, but he still can't get back into his room. He goes to the storeroom. The painting is seven-eighths finished but was not completed because he was dissatisfied with it. Now he takes it from the house and carries it to Runic's house, which is in the same clutch as his. Runic is at the Center, but he always leaves his doors open when he's gone. He has equipment which Chib uses to finish the painting, working with a sureness and intensity he lacked the first time he was creating it. He then leaves Runic's house with the huge oval canvas held above his head.

He strides past the pedestals and under their curving branches with the ovoids at their ends. He skirts several small grassy parks with trees, walks beneath more houses, and in ten minutes is nearing the heart of Beverly Hills. Here mercurial Chib sees

## ALL IN THE GOLDEN AFTERNOON, THREE LEADEN LADIES

drifting in a canoe on Lake Issus. Maryam bint Yusuf, her mother, and aunt listlessly hold fishing poles and look towards the gay colors, music, and the chattering crowd before the Folk Center. By now the police have broken up the juvenile fight and are standing around to make sure nobody else makes trouble.

The three women are dressed in the somber clothes, completely body-concealing, of the Mohammedan Wahhabi fundamentalist sect. They do not wear veils; not even the Wahhabi now insist on this. Their Egyptian brethren ashore are clad in modern garments, shameful and sinful. Despite which, the ladies stare at them.

Their menfolk are at the edge of the crowd. Bearded and costumed like sheiks in a Foreign Legion fido show, they mutter gargling oaths and hiss at the iniquitous display of female flesh. But they stare.

This small group has come from the zoological preserves of Abyssinia, where they were caught poaching. Their gummint gave them three choices. Imprisonment in a rehabilitation center, where they would be treated until they became good citizens if it took the rest of their lives. Emigration to the megalopolis of Haifa, Israel. Or emigration to Beverly Hills, LA.

What, dwell among the accursed Jews of Israel? They spat and chose Beverly Hills. Alas, Allah had mocked them! They were now surrounded by Finkelsteins, Applebaums, Siegels, Weintraubs, and others of the infidel tribes of Isaac. Even worse, Beverly Hills had no mosque. They either traveled forty kilometers every day to the 16th level, where a mosque was available, or used a private home.

Chib hastens to the edge of the plastic-edged lake and puts down his painting and bows low, whipping off his somewhat battered hat. Maryam smiles at him but loses the smile when the two chaperones reprimand her.

*"Ya kelb! Ya ibn kelb!"* the two shout at him.

Chib grins at them, waves his hat, and says, "Charmed, I'm sure, mesdames! Oh, you lovely ladies remind me of the Three Graces."

He then cries out, "I love you, Maryam! I love you! Thou art like the Rose of Sharon to me! Beautiful, doe-eyed, virginal! A fortress of innocence and strength, filled with a fierce motherhood and utter faithfulness to thy one true love! I love thee, thou art the only light in a black sky of dead stars! I cry to you across the void!"

Maryam understands World English, but the wind carries his words away from her. She simpers, and Chib cannot help feeling a momentary repulsion, a flash of anger as if she has somehow betrayed him. Nevertheless, he rallies and shouts, "I invite you to come with me to the showing! You and your mother and aunt will be my guests. You can see my paintings, my soul, and know what kind of man is going to carry you off on his Pegasus, my dove!"

*There is nothing as ridiculous as the verbal outpourings of a young poet in love. Outrageously exaggerated. I laugh. But I am also touched. Old as I am, I remember my first loves, the fire, the torrents of words, lightning-sheathed, ache-winged. Dear lasses, most of you are dead; the rest, withered. I blow you a kiss.*

*—Grandpa*

Maryam's mother stands up in the canoe. For a second, her profile is to Chib, and he sees intimations of the hawk that Maryam will be when she is her mother's age. Maryam now has a gently aquiline face —"the sweep of the sword of love"—Chib has called that nose. Bold but beautiful. However, her mother does look like a dirty old eagle. And her aunt—uneaglish but something of the camel in those features.

Chib suppresses these unfavorable, even treacherous, comparisons. But he cannot suppress the three bearded, robed, and unwashed men who gather around him.

Chib smiles but says, "I don't remember inviting you."

They look blank since rapidly spoken LA English is a hufty-magufty to them. Abu—generic name for any Egyptian in Beverly Hills—rasps an oath so ancient even the pre-Mohammed Meccans knew it. He forms a fist. Another Arab steps towards the painting and draws back a foot as if to kick it.

At this moment, Maryam's mother discovers that it is as dangerous to stand in a canoe as on a camel. It is worse, because the three women cannot swim.

Neither can the middle-aged Arab who attacks Chib, only to find his victim sidestepping and then urging him on into the lake with a foot in the rear. One of the young men rushes Chib; the other starts to kick at the painting. Both halt on hearing the three women scream and on seeing them go over into the water.

Then the two run to the edge of the lake, where they also go into the water, propelled by one of Chib's hands in each of their backs. A bolgan hears the six of them screaming and thrashing around and runs over to Chib. Chib is becoming concerned because Maryam is having trouble staying above the water. Her terror is not faked.

What Chib does not understand is why they are all carrying on so. Their feet must be on the bottom; the surface is below their chins. Despite which, Maryam looks as if she is going to drown. So do the others, but he is not interested in them. He should go in after Maryam. However, if he does, he will have to get a change of clothes before going to the showing.

At this thought, he laughs loudly and then even more loudly as the bolgan goes in after the women. He picks up the painting and walks off laughing. Before he reaches the Center, he sobers.

"Now, how come Grandpa was so right? How does he read me so well? Am I fickle, too shallow? No, I have been too deeply in love too many times. Can I help it if I love Beauty, and the beauties I love do not have enough Beauty? My eye is too demanding; it cancels the urgings of my heart."

## THE MASSACRE OF THE INNER SENSE

The entrance hall (one of twelve) which Chib enters was designed by Grandpa Winnegan. The visitor comes into a long curving tube lined with mirrors at various angles. He sees a triangular door at the end of the corridor. The door seems to be too tiny for anybody over nine years old to enter. The illusion makes the visitor feel as if he's walking up the wall as he progresses towards the door. At the end of the tube, the visitor is convinced he's standing on the ceiling.

But the door gets larger as he approaches until it becomes huge. Commentators have guessed that this entrance is the architect's symbolic representation of the gateway to the world of art. One should stand on his head before entering the wonderland of aesthetics.

On going in, the visitor thinks at first that the tremendous room is inside out or reversed. He gets even dizzier. The far wall actually seems the near wall until the visitor gets reorientated. Some people can't adjust and have to get out before they faint or vomit.

On the right hand is a hatrack with a sign: HANG YOUR HEAD HERE. A double pun by Grandpa, who always carries a joke too far for most people. If Grandpa goes beyond the bounds of verbal good taste, his great-great-grandson has overshot the moon in his paintings. Thirty of his latest have been revealed, including the last three of his Dog Series: *Dog Star, Dog Would,* and *Dog Tiered.* Ruskinson and his disciples are threatening to throw up. Luscus and his flock praise, but they're restrained. Luscus has told them to wait until he talks to young Winnegan before they go all-out. The fido men are busy shooting and interviewing both and trying to provoke a quarrel.

The main room of the building is a huge hemisphere with a bright ceiling which runs through the complete spectrum every nine minutes. The floor is a giant chessboard, and in the center of each square is a face, each of a great in the various arts. Michelangelo, Mozart, Balzac, Zeuxis, Beethoven, Li Po, Twain, Dostoyevsky, Farmisto, Mbuzi, Cupel, Krishnagurti, etc. Ten squares are left faceless so that future generations may add their own nominees for immortality.

The lower part of the wall is painted with murals depicting significant events in the lives of the artists. Against the curving wall are nine
stages, one for each of the Muses. On a console above each stage is a
giant statue of the presiding goddess. They are naked and have overripe figures: huge-breasted, broad-hipped, sturdy-legged, as if the
sculptor thought of them as Earth goddesses, not refined intellectual
types.

The faces are basically structured like the smooth placid faces of
classical Greek statues, but they have an unsettling expression around
the mouths and eyes. The lips are smiling but seem ready to break into
a snarl. The eyes are deep and menacing. DON'T SELL ME OUT, they say.
IF YOU DO . . .

A transparent plastic hemisphere extends over each stage and has
acoustic properties which keep people who are not beneath the shell
from hearing the sounds emanating from the stage and vice versa.

Chib makes his way through the noisy crowd towards the stage of
Polyhymnia, the Muse who includes painting in her province. He
passes the stage on which Benedictine is standing and pouring her lead
heart out in an alchemy of golden notes. She sees Chib and manages
somehow to glare at him and at the same time to keep smiling at her
audience. Chib ignores her but observes that she has replaced the dress
ripped in the tavern. He sees also the many policemen stationed around
the building. The crowd does not seem in an explosive mood. Indeed,
it seems happy, if boisterous. But the police know how deceptive this
can be. One spark . . .

Chib goes by the stage of Calliope, where Omar Runic is extemporiz-
ing. He comes to Polyhymnia's, nods at Rex Luscus, who waves at him,
and sets his painting on the stage. It is titled *The Massacre of the
Innocents* (subtitle: *Dog in the Manger*).

The painting depicts a stable.

The stable is a grotto with curiously shaped stalactites. The light
that breaks—or fractures—through the cave is Chib's red. It penetrates
every object, doubles its strength, and then rays out jaggedly. The
viewer, moving from side to side to get a complete look, can actually
see the many levels of light as he moves, and thus he catches glimpses
of the figures under the exterior figures.

The cows, sheep, and horses are in stalls at the end of the cave. Some
are looking with horror at Mary and the infant. Others have their
mouths open, evidently trying to warn Mary. Chib has used the legend
that the animals in the manger were able to talk to each other the night
Christ was born.

Joseph, a tired old man, so slumped he seems backboneless, is in a corner. He wears two horns, but each has a halo, so it's all right.

Mary's back is to the bed of straw on which the infant is supposed to be. From a trapdoor in the floor of the cave, a man is reaching to place a huge egg on the straw bed. He is in a cave beneath the cave and is dressed in modern clothes, has a boozy expression, and, like Joseph, slumps as if invertebrate. Behind him a grossly fat woman, looking remarkably like Chib's mother, has the baby, which the man passed on to her before putting the foundling egg on the straw bed.

The baby has an exquisitely beautiful face and is suffused with a white glow from his halo. The woman has removed the halo from his head and is using the sharp edge to butcher the baby.

Chib has a deep knowledge of anatomy, since he has dissected many corpses while getting his Ph.D. in art at Beverly Hills U. The body of the infant is not unnaturally elongated, as so many of Chib's figures are. It is more than photographic; it seems to be an actual baby. Its viscera is unraveled through a large bloody hole.

The onlookers are struck in their viscera as if this were not a painting but a real infant, slashed and disemboweled, found on their doorsteps as they left home.

The egg has a semitransparent shell. In its murky yolk floats a hideous little devil, horns, hooves, tail. Its blurred features resemble a combination of Henry Ford's and Uncle Sam's. When the viewers shift to one side or the other, the faces of others appear: prominents in the development of modern society.

The window is crowded with wild animals that have come to adore but have stayed to scream soundlessly in horror. The beasts in the foreground are those that have been exterminated by man or survive only in zoos and natural preserves. The dodo, the blue whale, the passenger pigeon, the quagga, the gorilla, orangutan, polar bear, cougar, lion, tiger, grizzly bear, California condor, kangaroo, wombat, rhinoceros, bald eagle.

Behind them are other animals and, on a hill, the dark crouching shapes of the Tasmanian aborigine and Haitian Indian.

"What is your considered opinion of this rather remarkable painting, Doctor Luscus?" a fido interviewer asks.

Luscus smiles and says, "I'll have a considered judgment in a few minutes. Perhaps you'd better talk to Doctor Ruskinson first. He seems to have made up his mind at once. Fools and angels, you know."

Ruskinson's red face and scream of fury are transmitted over the fido. "The shit heard around the world!" Chib says loudly.

"INSULT! SPITTLE! PLASTIC DUNG! A BLOW IN THE

FACE OF ART AND A KICK IN THE BUTT FOR HUMANITY! INSULT! INSULT!"

"Why is it such an insult, Doctor Ruskinson?" the fido man says. "Because it mocks the Christian faith, and also the Panamorite faith? It doesn't seem to me it does that. It seems to me that Winnegan is trying to say that men have perverted Christianity, maybe all religions, all ideals, for their own greedy self-destructive purposes, that man is basically a killer and a perverter. At least, that's what I get out of it, although of course I'm only a simple layman, and . . ."

"Let the critics make the analysis, young man!" Ruskinson snaps. "Do you have a double Ph.D., one in psychiatry and one in art? Have you been certified as a critic by the government?

"Winnegan, who has no talent whatsoever, let alone this genius that various self-deluded blowhards prate about, this abomination from Beverly Hills, presents his junk—actually a mishmash which has attracted attention solely because of a new technique that any electronic technician could invent—I am enraged that a mere gimmick, a trifling novelty, cannot only fool certain sectors of the public but highly educated and federally certified critics such as Doctor Luscus here— although there will always be scholarly asses who bray so loudly, pompously, and obscurely that . . ."

"Isn't it true," the fido man says, "that many painters we now call great, Van Gogh for one, were condemned or ignored by their contemporary critics? And . . ."

The fido man, skilled in provoking anger for the benefit of his viewers, pauses. Ruskinson swells, his head a bloodvessel just before aneurysm.

"I'm no ignorant layman!" he screams. "I can't help it that there have been Luscuses in the past! I know what I'm talking about! Winnegan is only a micrometeorite in the heaven of Art, not fit to shine the shoes of the great luminaries of painting. His reputation has been pumped up by a certain clique so it can shine in the reflected glory, the hyenas, biting the hand that feeds them, like mad dogs . . ."

"Aren't you mixing your metaphors a little bit?" the fido man says.

Luscus takes Chib's hand tenderly and draws him to one side where they're out of fido range.

"Darling Chib," he coos, "now is the time to declare yourself. You know how vastly I love you, not only as an artist but for yourself. It must be impossible for you to resist any longer the deeply sympathetic vibrations that leap unhindered between us. God, if you only knew how I dreamed of you, my glorious godlike Chib, with . . ."

"If you think I'm going to say yes just because you have the power to make or break my reputation, to deny me the grant, you're wrong," Chib says. He jerks his hand away.

Luscus' good eye glares. He says, "Do you find me repulsive? Surely it can't be on moral grounds . . ."

"It's the principle of the thing," Chib says. "Even if I were in love with you, which I'm not, I wouldn't let you make love to me. I want to be judged on my merit alone, that only. Come to think of it, I don't give a damn about anybody's judgment. I don't want to hear praise or blame from you or anybody. Look at my paintings and talk to each other, you jackals. But don't try to make me agree with your little images of me."

## THE ONLY GOOD CRITIC IS A DEAD CRITIC

Omar Runic has left his dais and now stands before Chib's paintings. He places one hand on his naked left chest, on which is tattooed the face of Herman Melville, Homer occupying the other place of honor on his right breast. He shouts loudly, his black eyes like furnace doors blown out by explosion. As has happened before, he is seized with inspiration derived from Chib's paintings.

> "*Call me Ahab, not Ishmael.*
> *For I have hooked the Leviathan.*
> *I am the wild ass's colt born to a man.*
> *Lo, my eye has seen it all!*
> *My bosom is like wine that has no vent.*
> *I am a sea with doors, but the doors are stuck.*
> *Watch out! The skin will burst; the doors will break.*
> "*You are Nimrod, I say to my friend, Chib.*
> *And now is the hour when God says to his angels,*
> *If this is what he can do as a beginning, then*
> *Nothing is impossible for him.*
> *He will be blowing his horn before*
> *The ramparts of Heaven and shouting for*
> *The Moon as hostage, the Virgin as wife,*
> *And demanding a cut on the profits*
> *From the Great Whore of Babylon.*"

"Stop that son of a bitch!" the Festival Director shouts. "He'll cause a riot like he did last year!"

The bolgani begin to move in. Chib watches Luscus, who is talking to the fido man. Chib can't hear Luscus, but he's sure Luscus is not saying complimentary things about him.

> *"Melville wrote of me long before I was born.*
> *I'm the man who wants to comprehend*
> *The Universe but comprehend on my terms.*
> *I am Ahab whose hate must pierce, shatter,*
> *All impediment of Time, Space, or Subject*
> *Mortality and hurl my fierce*
> *Incandescence into the Womb of Creation,*
> *Disturbing in its Lair whatever Force or*
> *Unknown Thing-in-Itself crouches there,*
> *Remote, removed, unrevealed."*

The Director gestures at the police to remove Runic. Ruskinson is still shouting, although the cameras are pointing at Runic or Luscus. One of the Young Radishes, Huga Wells-Erb Heinsturbury, the science-fiction authoress, is shaking with hysteria generated by Runic's voice and with a lust for revenge. She is sneaking up on a *Time* fido man. *Time* has long ago ceased to be a magazine, since there are no magazines, but became a government-supported communications bureau. *Time* is an example of Uncle Sam's left-hand, right-hand, hands-off policy of providing communications bureaus with all they need and at the same time permitting the bureau executives to determine the bureau policies. Thus, government provision and free speech are united. This is fine, in theory, anyway.

*Time* has preserved several of its original policies, that is, truth and objectivity must be sacrificed for the sake of a witticism and science-fiction must be put down. *Time* has sneered at every one of Heinsturbury's works, and so she is out to get some personal satisfaction for the hurt caused by the unfair reviews.

> *"Quid nunc? Cui bono?*
> *Time? Space? Substance? Accident?*
> *When you die—Hell? Nirvana,*
> *Nothing is nothing to think about.*
> *The canons of philosophy boom.*
> *Their projectiles are duds.*
> *The ammo heaps of theology blow up,*
> *Set off by the saboteur Reason.*
>
> *"Call me Ephraim, for I was halted*
> *At the Ford of God and could not tongue*
> *The sibilance to let me pass.*

> *Well, I can't pronounce shibboleth,*
> *But I can say shit!"*

Huga Wells-Erb Heinsturbury kicks the *Time* fido man in the balls. He throws up his hands, and the football-shaped, football-sized camera sails from his hands and strikes a youth on the head. The youth is a Young Radish, Ludwig Euterpe Mahlzart. He is smoldering with rage because of the damnation of his tone poem, *Jetting The Stuff Of Future Hells,* and the camera is the extra fuel needed to make him blaze up uncontrollably. He punches the chief musical critic in his fat belly.

Huga, not the *Time* man, is screaming with pain. Her bare toes have struck the hard plastic armor with which the *Time* man, recipient of many such a kick, protects his genitals. Huga hops around on one foot while holding the injured foot in her hands. She twirls into a girl, and there is a chain effect. A man falls against the *Time* man, who is stooping over to pick up his camera.

"Ahaaa!" Huga screams and tears off the *Time* man's helmet and straddles him and beats him over the head with the optical end of the camera. Since the solid-state camera is still working, it is sending to billions of viewers some very intriguing, if dizzying, pictures. Blood obscures one side of the picture, but not so much that the viewers are wholly cheated. And then they get another novel shot as the camera flies into the air again, turning over and over.

A bolgan has shoved his shock-stick against her back, causing her to stiffen and propel the camera in a high arc behind her. Huga's current lover grapples with the bolgan; they roll on the floor; a Westwood juvenile picks up the shock-stick and has a fine time goosing the adults around him until a local youth jumps him.

"Riots are the opium of the people," the police chief groans. He calls in all units and puts in a call to the chief of police of Westwood, who is, however, having his own troubles.

Runic beats his breast and howls

> *"Sir, I exist! And don't tell me,*
> *As you did Crane, that that creates*
> *No obligation in you towards me.*
> *I am a man; I am unique.*
> *I've thrown the Bread out the window,*
> *Pissed in the Wine, pulled the plug*
> *From the bottom of the Ark, cut the Tree*
> *For firewood, and if there were a Holy*
> *Ghost, I'd goose him.*

> *But I know that it all does not mean*
> *A God damned thing,*
> *That nothing means nothing,*
> *That is is is and not-is not is is-not*
> *That a rose is a rose is a*
> *That we are here and will not be*
> *And that is all we can know!"*

Ruskinson sees Chib coming towards him, squawks, and tries to escape. Chib seizes the canvas of *Dogmas from a Dog* and batters Ruskinson over the head with it. Luscus protests in horror, not because of the damage done to Ruskinson but because the painting might be damaged. Chib turns around and batters Luscus in the stomach with the oval's edge.

> *"The earth lurches like a ship going down,*
> *Its back almost broken by the flood of*
> *Excrement from the heavens and the deeps,*
> *What God in His terrible munificence*
> *Has granted on hearing Ahab cry,*
> *Bullshit! Bullshit!*
> *"I weep to think that this is Man*
> *And this his end. But wait!*
> *On the crest of the flood, a three-master*
> *Of antique shape. The Flying Dutchman!*
> *And Ahab is astride a ship's deck once more.*
> *Laugh, you Fates, and mock, you Norns!*
> *For I am Ahab and I am Man,*
> *And though I cannot break a hole*
> *Through the wall of What Seems*
> *To grab a handful of What Is,*
> *Yet, I will keep on punching.*
> *And I and my crew will not give up,*
> *Though the timbers split beneath our feet*
> *And we sink to become indistinguishable*
> *From the general excrement.*
>
> *"For a moment that will burn on the*
> *Eye of God forever, Ahab stands*
> *Outlined against the blaze of Orion,*
> *Fist clenched, a bloody phallus,*
> *Like Zeus exhibiting the trophy of*
> *The unmanning of his father Cronus.*

*And then he and his crew and ship*
*Dip and hurtle headlong over*
*The edge of the world.*
*And from what I hear, they are still*

F
a
l
l
i
n
g

Chib is shocked into a quivering mass by a jolt from a bolgan's electrical riot stick. While he is recovering, he hears his Grandpa's voice issuing from the transceiver in his hat.

"Chib, come quick! Accipiter has broken in and is trying to get through the door of my room!"

Chib gets up and fights and shoves his way to the exit. When he arrives, panting, at his home he finds that the door to Grandpa's room has been opened. The IRB men and electronic technicians are standing in the hallway. Chib bursts into Grandpa's room. Accipiter is standing in its middle and is quivering and pale. Nervous stone. He sees Chib and shrinks back, saying, "It wasn't my fault. I had to break in. It was the only way I could find out for sure. It wasn't my fault; I didn't touch him."

Chib's throat is closing in on itself. He cannot speak. He kneels down and takes Grandpa's hand. Grandpa has a slight smile on his blue lips. Once and for all, he has eluded Accipiter. In his hand is the latest sheet of his Ms.


## THROUGH BALAKLAVAS OF HATE, THEY CHARGE TOWARDS GOD


For most of my life, I have seen only a truly devout few and a great majority of truly indifferent. But there is a new spirit abroad. So many young men and women have revived, not a love for God, but a violent antipathy towards Him. This excites and restores me. Youths like my grandson and Runic shout blasphemies and so worship Him. If they did not believe, they would never think about Him. I now have some confidence in the future.

## TO THE STICKS VIA THE STYX

Dressed in black, Chib and his mother go down the tube entrance to level 13B. It's luminous-walled, spacious, and the fare is free. Chib tells the ticket-fido his destination. Behind the wall, the protein computer, no larger than a human brain, calculates. A coded ticket slides out of a slot. Chib takes the ticket, and they go to the bay, a great incurve, where he sticks the ticket into a slot. Another ticket protrudes, and a mechanical voice repeats the information on the ticket in World and LA English, in case they can't read.

Gondolas shoot into the bay and decelerate to a stop. Wheelless, they float in a continually rebalancing graviton field. Sections of the bay slide back to make ports for the gondolas. Passengers step into the cages designated for them. The cages move forward; their doors open automatically. The passengers step into the gondolas. They sit down and wait while the safety meshmold closes over them. From the recesses of the chassis, transparent plastic curves rise and meet to form a dome.

Automatically timed, monitored by redundant protein computers for safety, the gondolas wait until the coast is clear. On receiving the go-ahead, they move slowly out of the bay to the tube. They pause while getting another affirmation, trebly checked in microseconds. Then they move swiftly into the tube.

Whoosh! Whoosh! Other gondolas pass them. The tube glows yellowly as if filled with electrified gas. The gondola accelerates rapidly. A few are still passing it, but Chib's speeds up and soon none can catch up with it. The round posterior of a gondola ahead is a glimmering quarry that will not be caught until it slows before mooring at its destined bay. There are not many gondolas in the tube. Despite a 100-million population, there is little traffic on the north-south route. Most LAers stay in the self-sufficient walls of their clutches. There is more traffic on the east-west tubes, since a small percentage prefer the public ocean beaches to the municipality swimming pools.

The vehicle screams southward. After a few minutes, the tube begins to slope down and suddenly it is at a 45-degree angle to the horizontal. They flash by level after level.

Through the transparent walls, Chib glimpses the people and architecture of other cities. Level 8, Long Beach, is interesting. Its homes look like two cut-quartz pie plates, one on top of another, open end on open end, and the unit mounted on a column of carved figures, the exit-entrance ramp a flying buttress.

At level 3A, the tube straightens out. Now the gondola races past establishments the sight of which causes Mama to shut her eyes. Chib squeezes his mother's hand and thinks of the half-brother and cousin who are behind the yellowish plastic. This level contains fifteen per cent of the population, the retarded, the incurable insane, the too-ugly, the monstrous, the senile aged. They swarm here, the vacant or twisted faces pressed against the tube wall to watch the pretty cars float by.

"Humanitarian" medical science keeps alive the babies that *should* —by Nature's imperative—have died. Ever since the 20th century, humans with defective genes have been saved from death. Hence, the continual spreading of these genes. The tragic thing is that science can now detect and correct defective genes in the ovum and sperm. Theoretically, all human beings could be blessed with totally healthy bodies and physically perfect brains. But the rub is that we don't have near enough doctors and facilities to keep up with the births. This despite the ever decreasing drop in the birth rate.

Medical science keeps people living so long that senility strikes. So, more and more slobbering mindless decrepits. And also an accelerating addition of the mentally addled. There are therapies and drugs to restore most of them to "normalcy," but not enough doctors and facilities. Some day there may be, but that doesn't help the contemporary unfortunate.

What to do now? The ancient Greeks placed defective babies in the fields to die. The Eskimos shipped out their old people on ice floes. Should we gas our abnormal infants and seniles? Sometimes, I think it's the merciful thing to do. But I can't ask somebody else to pull the switch when I won't.

> *I would shoot the first man to reach for it.*
> *—from Grandpa's* Private Ejaculations

The gondola approaches one of the rare intersections. Its passengers see down the broad-mouthed tube to their right. An express flies towards them; it looms. Collision course. They know better, but they can't keep from gripping the mesh, gritting their teeth, and bracing their legs. Mama gives a small shriek. The fliers hurtles over them and disappears, the flapping scream of air a soul on its way to underworld judgment.

The tube dips again until it levels out on 1. They see the ground below and the massive self-adjusting pillars supporting the megapolis. They whiz by over a little town, quaint, early 21st century LA preserved as a museum, one of many beneath the cube.

Fifteen minutes after embarking, the Winnegans reach the end of the line. An elevator takes them to the ground, where they enter a big black limousine. This is furnished by a private-enterprise mortuary, since Uncle Sam or the LA government will pay for cremation but not for burial. The Church no longer insists on interment, leaving it to the religionists to choose between being wind-blown ashes or underground corpses.

The sun is halfway towards the zenith. Mama begins to have trouble breathing and her arms and neck redden and swell. The three times she's been outside the walls, she's been attacked with this allergy despite the air conditioning of the limousine. Chib pats her hand while they're riding over a roughly patched road. The archaic eighty-year-old, fuel-cell-powered, electric-motor-driven vehicle is, however, rough-riding only by comparison with the gondola. It covers the ten kilometers to the cemetery speedily, stopping once to let deer cross the road.

Father Fellini greets them. He is distressed because he is forced to tell them that the Church feels that Grandpa has committed sacrilege. To substitute another man's body for his corpse, to have mass said over it, to have it buried in sacred ground is to blaspheme. Moreover, Grandpa died an unrepentant criminal. At least, to the knowledge of the Church, he made no contrition just before he died.

Chib expects this refusal. St. Mary's of BH-14 has declined to perform services for Grandpa within its walls. But Grandpa has often told Chib that he wants to be buried beside his ancestors, and Chib is determined that Grandpa will get his wish.

Chib says, "I'll bury him myself! Right on the edge of the graveyard!"

"You can't do that!" the priest, mortuary officials, and a federal agent say simultaneously.

"The hell I can't! Where's the shovel?"

It is then that he sees the thin dark face and falciform nose of Accipiter. The agent is supervising the digging up of Grandpa's (first) coffin. Nearby are at least fifty fido men shooting with their minicameras, the transceivers floating a few decameters near them. Grandpa is getting full coverage, as befits the Last Of The Billionaires and The Greatest Criminal Of The Century.

Fido interviewer: "Mr. Accipiter, could we have a few words from you? I'm not exaggerating when I say that there are probably at least ten billion people watching this historic event. After all, even the grade-school kids know of Win-again Winnegan.

"How do you feel about this? You've been on the case for 26 years. The successful conclusion must give you great satisfaction."

Accipiter, unsmiling as the essence of diorite: "Well, actually, I've not devoted full time to this case. Only about three years of accumulative time. But since I've spent at least several days each month on it, you might say I've been on Winnegan's trail for 26 years."

Interviewer: "It's been said that the ending of this case also means the end of the IRB. If we've not been misinformed, the IRB was only kept functioning because of Winnegan. You had other business, of course, during this time, but the tracking down of counterfeiters and gamblers who don't report their income has been turned over to other bureaus. Is this true? If so, what do you plan to do?"

Accipiter, voice flashing a crystal of emotion: "Yes, the IRB is being disbanded. But not until after the case against Winnegan's granddaughter and her son is finished. They harbored him and are, therefore, accessories after the fact.

"In fact, almost the entire population of Beverly Hills, level 14, should be on trial. I know, but can't prove it as yet, that everybody, including the municipal chief of police, was well aware that Winnegan was hiding in that house. Even Winnegan's priest knew it, since Winnegan frequently went to mass and to confession. His priest claims that he urged Winnegan to turn himself in and also refused to give him absolution unless he did so.

"But Winnegan, a hardened 'mouse'—I mean, criminal, if ever I saw one, refused to follow the priest's urgings. He claimed that he had not committed a crime, that, believe it or not, Uncle Sam was the criminal. Imagine the effrontery, the depravity, of the man!"

Interviewer: "Surely you don't plan to arrest the entire population of Beverly Hills 14?"

Accipiter: "I have been advised not to."

Interviewer: "Do you plan on retiring after this case is wound up?"

Accipiter: "No. I intend to transfer to the Greater LA Homicide Bureau. Murder for profit hardly exists any more, but there are still crimes of passion, thank God!"

Interviewer: "Of course, if young Winnegan should win his case against you—he has charged you with invasion of domestic privacy, illegal housebreaking, and directly causing his great-great-grandfather's death—then you won't be able to work for the Homicide Bureau or any police department."

Accipiter, flashing several crystals of emotion: "It's no wonder we law enforcers have such a hard time operating effectively! Sometimes, not only the majority of citizens seem to be on the law-breaker's side but my own employers . . ."

Interviewer: "Would you care to complete that statement? I'm sure your employers are watching this channel. No? I understand that Winnegan's trial and yours are, for some reason, scheduled to take place *at the same time*. How do you plan to be present at both trials? Heh, heh! Some fido-casters are calling you The Simultaneous Man!"

Accipter, face darkening: "Some idiot clerk did that! He incorrectly fed the data into a legal computer. The confusion of dates is being straightened out now. I might mention that the clerk is suspected of deliberately making the error. There have been too many cases like this . . ."

Interviewer: "Would you mind summing up the course of this case for our viewers' benefit? Just the highlights, please."

Accipiter: "Well, ah, as you know, fifty years ago all large private-enterprise businesses had become government bureaus. All except the building construction firm, the Finnegan Fifty-three States Company, of which the president was Finn Finnegan. He was the father of the man who is to be buried—somewhere—today.

"Also, all unions except the largest, the construction union, were dissolved or were government unions. Actually, the company and its union were one, because all employees got ninety-five per cent of the money, distributed more or less equally among them. Old Finnegan was both the company president and union business agent-secretary.

"By hook or crook, mainly by crook, I believe, the firm-union had resisted the inevitable absorption. There were investigations into Finnegan's methods: coercion and blackmail of U. S. Senators and even U. S. Supreme Court Justices. Nothing was, however, proved."

Interviewer: "For the benefit of our viewers who may be a little hazy on their history, even fifty years ago money was used only for the purchase of nonguaranteed items. Its other use, as today, was as an index of prestige and social esteem. At one time, the government was thinking of getting rid of currency entirely, but a study revealed that it had great psychological value. The income tax was also kept, although the government had no use for money, because the size of a man's tax determined prestige and also because it enabled the government to remove a large amount of currency from circulation."

Accipiter: "Anyway, when old Finnegan died, the federal government renewed its pressure to incorporate the construction workers and the company officials as civil servants. But young Finnegan proved to be as foxy and vicious as his old man. I don't suggest, of course, that the fact that his uncle was President of the U.S. at that time had anything to do with young Finnegan's success."

Interviewer: "Young Finnegan was seventy years old when his father died."

Accipiter: "During this struggle, which went on for many years, Finnegan decided to rename himself Winnegan. It's a pun on Win Again. He seems to have had a childish, even imbecilic, delight in puns, which, frankly, I don't understand. Puns, I mean."

Interviewer: "For the benefit of our non-American viewers, who may not know of our national custom of Naming Day . . . this was origi-nated by the Panamorites. When a citizen comes of age, he may at any time thereafter take a new name, one which he believes to be appropriate to his temperament or goal in life. I might point out that Uncle Sam, who's been unfairly accused of trying to impose conformity upon his citizens, encourages this individualistic approach to life. This despite the increased record-keeping required on the government's part.

"I might also point out something else of interest. The government claimed that Grandpa Winnegan was mentally incompetent. My lis-teners will pardon me, I hope, if I take up a moment of your time to explain the basis of Uncle Sam's assertion. Now, for the benefit of those among you who are unacquainted with an early 20th-century classic, *Finnegans Wake*, despite your government's wish for you to have a free lifelong education, the author, James Joyce, derived the title from an old vaudeville song."

(Half-fadeout while a monitor briefly explains "vaudeville.")

"The song was about Tim Finnegan, an Irish hod carrier who fell off a ladder while drunk and was supposedly killed. During the Irish wake held for Finnegan, the corpse is accidentally splashed with whis-key. Finnegan, feeling the touch of the whiskey, the 'water of life,' sits up in his coffin and then climbs out to drink and dance with the mourners.

"Grandpa Winnegan always claimed that the vaudeville song was based on reality, you can't keep a good man down, and that the original Tim Finnegan was his ancestor. This preposterous statement was used by the government in its suit against Winnegan.

"However, Winnegan produced documents to substantiate his asser-tion. Later—too late—the documents were proved to be forgeries."

Accipiter: "The government's case against Winnegan was strength-ened by the rank and file's sympathy with the government. Citizens were complaining that the business-union was undemocratic and dis-criminatory. The officials and workers were getting relatively high wages, but many citizens had to be contented with their guaranteed income. So, Winnegan was brought to trial and accused, justly, of course, of various crimes, among which were subversion of democracy.

"Seeing the inevitable, Winnegan capped his criminal career. He somehow managed to steal 20 billion dollars from the federal deposit vault. This sum, by the way, was equal to half the currency then existing in Greater LA. Winnegan disappeared with the money, which he had not only stolen but had not paid income tax on. Unforgivable. I don't know why so many people have glamorized this villain's feat. Why, I've seen fido shows with him as the hero, thinly disguised under another name, of course."

Interviewer: "Yes, folks, Winnegan committed the Crime Of The Age. And, although he has finally been located, and is to be buried today—somewhere—the case is not completely closed. The Federal government says it is. But where is the money, the 20 billion dollars?"

Accipiter: "Actually, the money has no value now except as collectors' items. Shortly after the theft, the government called in all currency and then issued new bills that could not be mistaken for the old. The government had been wanting to do something like this for a long time, anyway, because it believed that there was too much currency, and it only reissued half the amount taken in.

"I'd like very much to know where the money is. I won't rest until I do. I'll hunt it down if I have to do it on my own time."

Interviewer: "You may have plenty of time to do that if young Winnegan wins his case. Well, folks, as most of you may know, Winnegan was found dead in a lower level of San Francisco about a year after he disappeared. His grand-daughter identified the body, and the fingerprints, earprints, retinaprints, teethprints, blood-type, hair-type, and a dozen other identity prints matched out."

Chib, who has been listening, thinks that Grandpa must have spent several millions of the stolen money arranging this. He does not know, but he suspects that a research lab somewhere in the world grew the duplicate in a biotank.

This happened two years after Chib was born. When Chib was five, his grandpa showed up. Without letting Mama know he was back, he moved in. Only Chib was his confidant. It was, of course, impossible for Grandpa to go completely unnoticed by Mama, yet she now insisted that she had never seen him. Chib thought that this was to avoid prosecution for being an accessory after the crime. He was not sure. Perhaps she had blocked off his "visitations" from the rest of her mind. For her it would be easy, since she never knew whether today was Tuesday or Thursday and could not tell you what year it was.

Chib ignores the mortuarians, who want to know what to do with the body. He walks over to the grave. The top of the ovoid coffin is visible now, with the long elephantlike snout of the digging machine sonically crumbling the dirt and then sucking it up. Accipiter, breaking through his lifelong control, is smiling at the fidomen and rubbing his hands.

"Dance a little, you son of a bitch," Chib says, his anger the only block to the tears and the wail building up in him.

The area around the coffin is cleared to make room for the grappling arms of the machine. These descend, hook under, and lift the black, irradiated-plastic, mocksilver-arabesqued coffin up and out and onto the grass. Chib, seeing the IRB men begin to open the coffin, starts to say something but closes his mouth. He watches intently, his knees bent as if getting ready to jump. The fidomen close in, their eyeball-shaped cameras pointing at the group around the coffin.

Groaning, the lid rises. There is a big bang. Dense dark smoke billows. Accipiter and his men, blackened, eyes wide and white, coughing, stagger out of the cloud. The fidomen are running every-which way or stooping to pick up their cameras. Those who were standing far enough back can see that the explosion took place at the bottom of the grave. Only Chib knows that the raising of the coffin lid has activated the detonating device in the grave.

He is also the first to look up into the sky at the projectile soaring from the grave because only he expected it. The rocket climbs up to five hundred feet while the fidomen train their cameras on it. It bursts apart and from it a ribbon unfolds between two round objects. The objects expand to become balloons while the ribbon becomes a huge banner.

On it, in big black letters, are the words

## WINNEGANS FAKE!

Twenty billions of dollars buried beneath the supposed bottom of the grave burn furiously. Some bills, blown up in the geyser of fireworks, are carried by the wind while IRB men, fidomen, mortuary officials, and municipality officials chase them.

Mama is stunned.

Accipiter looks as if he is having a stroke.

Chib cries and then laughs and rolls on the ground.

Grandpa has again screwed Uncle Sam and has also pulled his greatest pun where all the world can see it.

"Oh, you old man!" Chib sobs between laughing fits. "Oh, you old man! How I love you!"

While he is rolling on the ground again, roaring so hard his ribs hurt, he feels a paper in his hand. He stops laughing and gets on his knees and calls after the man who gave it to him. The man says, "I was paid by your grandfather to hand it to you when he was buried."

Chib reads.

*I hope nobody was hurt, not even the IRB men.*

*Final advice from the Wise Old Man In The Cave. Tear loose. Leave LA. Leave the country. Go to Egypt. Let your mother ride the purple wage on her own. She can do it if she practices thrift and self-denial. If she can't, that's not your fault.*

*You are fortunate indeed to have been born with talent, if not genius, and to be strong enough to want to rip out the umbilical cord. So do it. Go to Egypt. Steep yourself in the ancient culture. Stand before the Sphinx. Ask her (actually, it's a he) the Question.*

*Then visit one of the zoological preserves south of the Nile. Live for a while in a reasonable facsimile of Nature as she was before mankind dishonored and disfigured her. There, where Homo Sapiens(?) evolved from the killer ape, absorb the spirit of that ancient place and time.*

*You've been painting with your penis, which I'm afraid was more stiffened with bile than with passion for life. Learn to paint with your heart. Only thus will you become great and true.*

*Paint.*

*Then, go wherever you want to go. I'll be with you as long as you're alive to remember me. To quote Runic, "I'll be the Northern Lights of your soul."*

*Hold fast to the belief that there will be others to love you just as much as I did or even more. What is more important, you must love them as much as they love you.*

*Can you do this?*

*Fritz Leiber*

Fritz Leiber is older than he used to be (everyone is, except me) but he still has a kind of commanding presence that comes with being tall, and of striking appearance.

And he is also one of the few people who have told me something about my own writing that I didn't know and was interested to hear. It wasn't at a convention but (I believe) at a meeting of the Hydra Club, an on-again, off-again association of science fiction professionals in New York.

I was hanging around him (it was nearly twenty years ago), hoping that some of his good looks might be contagious (they weren't) and he said to me, "You know something I have noticed about your stories, Isaac?"

My first impulse was to shrink away. Ordinarily I hate sentences like that because, ten to one, they continue with "They're illiterate!" or even "They stink!" I mean, who needs that kind of profound comment.

Even if the next sentence were "They're great!" or "They're terribly thought-provoking," it might make me feel good, but, essentially, it would be meaningless. After all, *I* know that my stories are great and terribly thought-provoking. It's nice to have you agree with me but the only thing I learn from it is that *you* have keen literary judgment.

But what Fritz said to me was, "You have no villains."

I objected at once. "Yes, I do, Fritz," I said. "Every story I write has a villain."

"Oh, you have someone who opposes your hero," he said, "but he's never a *villain*."

I saw what he meant. If a story is cerebral in nature (as mine invariably are) the conflict is between thoughts and ideas, not fists, and you've got to express each side in the conflict reasonably in order to make it worth the reader's concern. In order to do so, your villain has to express his point of view carefully and skillfully, and be right in his own eyes. You can't have him just shouting, "I'm a wicked bad-guy."

So I end up with a villain who isn't a *villain*.

However, that's not what I said to Fritz. Instead, I said, "Do you think I don't have real villains because I simply don't know how to describe a villain on account of because I'm such a nice guy clear through that I have no villainy in me?"

"Exactly, Isaac," said Fritz benignly, and patted the top of my head.

It's a nice theory—about me having no villains because I'm such a nice guy—but it worries me a little. Some of my good friends in science fiction, I notice, write stories which have no heroes. Everyone in them, both protagonist and antagonist, are different varieties of heels. If my theory is right, what does it prove about them?

Naturally, I name no names, but Fritz isn't one of them. He is every bit as nice and sweet as I am. And even handsomer.

# 9

# GONNA ROLL THE BONES

Suddenly Joe Slattermill knew for sure he'd have to get out quick or else blow his top and knock out with the shrapnel of his skull the props and patches holding up his decaying home, that was like a house of big wooden and plaster and wallpaper cards except for the huge fireplace and ovens and chimney across the kitchen from him.

Those were stone-solid enough, though. The fireplace was chin-high, at least twice that long, and filled from end to end with roaring flames. Above were the square doors of the ovens in a row—his Wife baked for part of their living. Above the ovens was the wall-long mantelpiece, too high for his Mother to reach or Mr. Guts to jump any more, set with all sorts of ancestral curios, but any of them that weren't stone or glass or china had been so dried and darkened by decades of heat that they looked like nothing but shrunken human heads and black golf balls. At one end were clustered his Wife's square gin bottles. Above the mantelpiece hung one old chromo, so high and so darkened by soot and grease that you couldn't tell whether the swirls and fat cigar shape were a whaleback steamer plowing through a hurricane or a spaceship plunging through a storm of light-driven dust motes.

As soon as Joe curled his toes inside his boots, his Mother knew what he was up to. "Going bumming," she mumbled with conviction. "Pants pockets full of cartwheels of house money, too, to spend on sin." And she went back to munching the long shreds she stripped fumblingly with her right hand off the turkey carcass set close to the terrible heat, her left hand ready to fend off Mr. Guts, who stared at her yellow-eyed, gaunt-flanked, with long mangy tail a-twitch. In her dirty dress, streaky as the turkey's sides, Joe's Mother looked like a bent brown bag and her fingers were lumpy twigs.

Joe's Wife knew as soon or sooner, for she smiled thin-eyed at him over her shoulder from where she towered at the centermost oven. Before she closed its door, Joe glimpsed that she was baking two long, flat, narrow, fluted loaves and one high, round-domed one. She was thin as death and disease in her violet wrapper. Without looking, she reached out a yard-long, skinny arm for the nearest gin bottle and downed a warm slug and smiled again. And without word spoken, Joe knew she'd said, "You're going out and gamble and get drunk and lay a floozy and come home and beat me and go to jail for it," and he had a flash of the last time he'd been in the dark gritty cell and she'd come by moonlight, which showed the green and yellow lumps on her narrow skull where he'd hit her, to whisper to him through the tiny window in back and slip him a half pint through the bars.

And Joe knew for certain that this time it would be that bad and worse, but just the same he heaved up himself and his heavy, muffledly clanking pockets and shuffled straight to the door, muttering, "Guess I'll roll the bones, up the pike a stretch and back," swinging his bent, knobby-elbowed arms like paddle-wheels to make a little joke about his words.

When he'd stepped outside, he held the door open a hand's breadth behind him for several seconds. When he finally closed it, a feeling of deep misery struck him. Earlier years, Mr. Guts would have come streaking along to seek fights and females on the roofs and fences, but now the big tom was content to stay home and hiss by the fire and snatch for turkey and dodge a broom, quarreling and comforting with two housebound women. Nothing had followed Joe to the door but his Mother's chomping and her gasping breaths and the clink of the gin bottle going back on the mantel and the creaking of the floor boards under his feet.

The night was up-side-down deep among the frosty stars. A few of them seemed to move, like the white-hot jets of spaceships. Down below it looked as if the whole town of Ironmine had blown or buttoned out the light and gone to sleep, leaving the streets and spaces to the equally unseen breezes and ghosts. But Joe was still in the hemisphere of the musty dry odor of the worm-eaten carpentry behind him, and as he felt and heard the dry grass of the lawn brush his calves, it occurred to him that something deep down inside him had for years been planning things so that he and the house and his Wife and Mother and Mr. Guts would all come to an end together. Why the kitchen heat hadn't touched off the tindery place ages ago was a physical miracle.

Hunching his shoulders, Joe stepped out, not up the pike, but down the dirt road that led past Cypress Hollow Cemetery to Night Town.

The breezes were gentle, but unusually restless and variable tonight, like leprechaun squalls. Beyond the drunken, white-washed cemetery fence dim in the starlight, they rustled the scraggly trees of Cypress Hollow and made it seem they were stroking their beards of Spanish moss. Joe sensed that the ghosts were just as restless as the breezes, uncertain where and whom to haunt, or whether to take the night off, drifting together in sorrowfully lecherous companionship. While among the trees the red-green vampire lights pulsed faintly and irregularly, like sick fireflies or a plague-stricken space fleet. The feeling of deep misery stuck with Joe and deepened and he was tempted to turn aside and curl up in any convenient tomb or around some half-toppled head board and cheat his Wife and the other three behind him out of a shared doom. He thought: Gonna roll the bones, gonna roll 'em up and go to sleep. But while he was deciding, he got past the sagged-open gate and the rest of the delirious fence and Shantyville too.

At first Night Town seemed dead as the rest of Ironmine, but then he noticed a faint glow, sick as the vampire lights but more feverish, and with it a jumping music, tiny at first as a jazz for jitterbugging ants. He stepped along the springy sidewalk, wistfully remembering the days when the spring was all in his own legs and he'd bound into a fight like a bobcat or a Martian sand-spider. God, it had been years now since he had fought a real fight, or felt *the power*. Gradually the midget music got raucous as a bunnyhug for grizzly bears and loud as a polka for elephants, while the glow became a riot of gas flares and flambeaux and corpse-blue mercury tubes and jiggling pink neon ones that all jeered at the stars where the spaceships roved. Next thing, he was facing a three-storey false front flaring everywhere like a devil's rainbow, with a pale blue topping of St. Elmo's fire. There were wide swinging doors in the center of it, spilling light above and below. Above the doorway, golden calcium light scrawled over and over again, with wild curlicues and flourishes, "The Boneyard," while a fiendish red kept printing out, "Gambling."

So the new place they'd all been talking about for so long had opened at last! For the first time that night, Joe Slattermill felt a stirring of real life in him and the faintest caress of excitement.

Gonna roll the bones, he thought.

He dusted off his blue-green work clothes with big, careless swipes and slapped his pockets to hear the clank. Then he threw back his shoulders and grinned his lips sneeringly and pushed through the swinging doors as if giving a foe the straight-armed heel of his palm.

Inside, The Boneyard seemed to cover the area of a township and the bar looked as long as the railroad tracks. Round pools of light on the green poker tables alternated with hourglass shapes of exciting gloom, through which drink girls and change girls moved like white-legged witches. By the jazz-stand in the distance, belly dancers made *their* white hourglass shapes. The gamblers were thick and hunched down as mushrooms, all bald from agonizing over the fall of a card or a die or the dive of an ivory ball, while the Scarlet Women were like fields of poinsettia.

The calls of the croupiers and the slaps of dealt cards were as softly yet fatefully staccato as the rustle and beat of the jazz drums. Every tight-locked atom of the place was controlledly jumping. Even the dust motes jigged tensely in the cones of light.

Joe's excitement climbed and he felt sift through him, like a breeze that heralds a gale, the faintest breath of a confidence which he knew could become a tornado. All thoughts of his house and Wife and Mother dropped out of his mind, while Mr. Guts remained only as a crazy young tom walking stiff-legged around the rim of his consciousness. Joe's own leg muscles twitched in sympathy and he felt them grow supplely strong.

He coolly and searchingly looked the place over, his hand going out like it didn't belong to him to separate a drink from a passing, gently bobbing tray. Finally his gaze settled on what he judged to be the Number One Crap Table. All the Big Mushrooms seemed to be there, bald as the rest but standing tall as toadstools. Then through a gap in them Joe saw on the other side of the table a figure still taller, but dressed in a long dark coat with collar turned up and a dark slouch hat pulled low, so that only a triangle of white face showed. A suspicion and a hope rose in Joe and he headed straight for the gap in the Big Mushrooms.

As he got nearer, the white-legged and shiny-topped drifters eddying out of his way, his suspicion received confirmation after confirmation and his hope budded and swelled. Back from one end of the table was the fattest man he'd ever seen, with a long cigar and a silver vest and a gold tie clasp at least eight inches wide that just said in thick script, "Mr. Bones." Back a little from the other end was the nakedest change-girl yet and the only one he'd seen whose tray, slung from her bare shoulders and indenting her belly just below her breasts, was stacked with gold in gleaming little towers and with jet-black chips. While the dice-girl, skinnier and taller and longer armed than his Wife even, didn't seem to be wearing much but a pair of long white gloves. She was all right if you went for the type that isn't much more than pale skin over bones with breasts like china doorknobs.

Beside each gambler was a high round table for his chips. The one by the gap was empty. Snapping his fingers at the nearest silver change-girl, Joe traded all his greasy dollars for an equal number of pale chips and tweaked her left nipple for luck. She playfully snapped her teeth toward his fingers.

Not hurrying but not wasting any time, he advanced and carelessly dropped his modest stacks on the empty table and took his place in the gap. He noted that the second Big Mushroom on his right had the dice. His heart but no other part of him gave an extra jump. Then he steadily lifted his eyes and looked straight across the table.

The coat was a shimmering elegant pillar of black satin with jet buttons, the upturned collar of fine dull plush black as the darkest cellar, as was the slouch hat with down-turned brim and for band only a thin braid of black horsehair. The arms of the coat were long, lesser satin pillars, ending in slim, long-fingered hands that moved swiftly when they did, but held each position of rest with a statue's poise.

Joe still couldn't see much of the face except for smooth lower forehead with never a bead or trickle of sweat—the eyebrows were like straight snippets of the hat's braid—and gaunt, aristocratic cheeks and narrow but somewhat flat nose. The complexion of the face wasn't as white as Joe had first judged. There was a faint touch of brown in it, like ivory that's just begun to age, or Venusian soapstone. Another glance at the hands confirmed this.

Behind the man in black was a knot of just about the flashiest and nastiest customers, male or female, Joe had ever seen. He knew from one look that each bediamonded, pomaded bully had a belly gun beneath the flap of his flowered vest and a blackjack in his hip pocket, and each snake-eyed sporting girl a stiletto in her garter and a pearl-handled silver-plated derringer under the sequined silk in the hollow between her jutting breasts.

Yet at the same time Joe knew they were just trimmings. It was the man in black, their master, who was the deadly one, the kind of man you knew at a glance you couldn't touch and live. If without asking you merely laid a finger on his sleeve, no matter how lightly and respectfully, an ivory hand would move faster than thought and you'd be stabbed or shot. Or maybe just the touch would kill you, as if every black article of his clothing were charged from his ivory skin outward with a high-voltage, high-amperage ivory electricity. Joe looked at the shadowed face again and decided he wouldn't care to try it.

For it was the eyes that were the most impressive feature. All great gamblers have dark-shadowed deep-set eyes. But this one's eyes were sunk so deep you couldn't even be sure you were getting a gleam of them. They were inscrutability incarnate. They were unfathomable. They were like black holes.

But all this didn't disappoint Joe one bit, though it did terrify him considerably. On the contrary, it made him exult. His first suspicion was completely confirmed and his hope spread into full flower.

This must be one of those really big gamblers who hit Ironmine only once a decade at most, come from the Big City on one of the river boats that ranged the watery dark like luxurious comets, spouting long thick tails of sparks from their sequoia-tall stacks with top foliage of curvy-snipped sheet iron. Or like silver space-liners with dozens of jewel-flamed jets, their portholes a-twinkle like ranks of marshaled asteroids.

For that matter, maybe some of those really big gamblers actually came from other planets where the nighttime pace was hotter and the sporting life a delirium of risk and delight.

Yes, this was the kind of man Joe had always yearned to pit his skill against. He felt *the power* begin to tingle in his rock-still fingers, just a little.

Joe lowered his gaze to the crap table. It was almost as wide as a man is tall, at least twice as long, unusually deep, and lined with black, not green, felt, so that it looked like a giant's coffin. There was something familiar about its shape which he couldn't place. Its bottom, though not its sides or ends, had a twinkling iridescence, as if it had been lightly sprinkled with very tiny diamonds. As Joe lowered his gaze all the way and looked directly down, his eyes barely over the table, he got the crazy notion that it went down all the way through the world, so that the diamonds were the stars on the other side, visible despite the sunlight there, just as Joe was always able to see the stars by day up the shaft of the mine he worked in, and so that if a cleaned-out gambler, dizzy with defeat, toppled forward into it, he'd fall forever, toward the bottommost bottom, be it Hell or some black galaxy. Joe's thoughts swirled and he felt the cold, hard-fingered clutch of fear at his crotch. Someone was crooning beside him, "Come on, Big Dick."

Then the dice, which had meanwhile passed to the Big Mushroom immediately on his right, came to rest near the table's center, contra-dicting and wiping out Joe's vision. But instantly there was another oddity to absorb him. The ivory dice were large and unusually round-cornered with dark red spots that gleamed like real rubies, but the spots were arranged in such a way that each face looked like a miniature skull. For instance, the seven thrown just now, by which the Big Mush-room to his right had lost his point, which had been ten, consisted of a two with the spots evenly spaced toward one side, like eyes, instead of toward opposite corners, and of a five with the same red eye-spots but also a central red nose and two spots close together below that to make teeth.

The long, skinny, white-gloved arm of the dice-girl snaked out like an albino cobra and scooped up the dice and whisked them onto the rim of the table right in front of Joe. He inhaled silently, picked up a single chip from his table and started to lay it beside the dice, then realized that wasn't the way things were done here, and put it back. He would have liked to examine the chip more closely, though. It was curiously lightweight and pale tan, about the color of cream with a shot of coffee in it, and it had embossed on its surface a symbol he could feel, though not see. He didn't know what the symbol was, that would have taken more feeling. Yet its touch had been very good, setting the power tingling full blast in his shooting hand.

Joe looked casually yet swiftly at the faces around the table, not missing the Big Gambler across from him, and said quietly, "Roll a penny," meaning of course one pale chip, or a dollar.

There was a hiss of indignation from all the Big Mushrooms and the moonface of big-bellied Mr. Bones grew purple as he started forward to summon his bouncers.

The Big Gambler raised a black-satined forearm and sculptured hand, palm down. Instantly Mr. Bones froze and the hissing stopped faster than that of a meteor prick in self-sealing space steel. Then in a whispery, cultured voice, without the faintest hint of derision, the man in black said, "Get on him, gamblers."

Here, Joe thought, was a final comfirmation of his suspicion, had it been needed. The really great gamblers were always perfect gentlemen and generous to the poor.

With only the tiny, respectful hint of a guffaw, one of the Big Mushrooms called to Joe, "You're faded."

Joe picked up the ruby-featured dice.

Now ever since he had first caught two eggs on one plate, won all the marbles in Ironmine, and juggled six alphabet blocks so they finally fell in a row on the rug spelling "Mother," Joe Slattermill had been almost incredibly deft at precision throwing. In the mine he could carom a rock off a wall of ore to crack a rat's skull fifty feet away in the dark and he sometimes amused himself by tossing little fragments of rock back into the holes from which they had fallen, so that they stuck there, perfectly fitted in, for at least a second. Sometimes, by fast tossing, he could fit seven or eight fragments into the hole from which they had fallen, like putting together a puzzle block. If he could ever have got into space, Joe would undoubtedly have been able to pilot six Moonskimmers at once and do figure eights through Saturn's rings blindfold.

Now the only real difference between precision-tossing rocks or alphabet blocks and dice is that you have to bounce the latter off the end wall of a crap table, and that just made it a more interesting test of skill for Joe.

Rattling the dice now, he felt the power in his fingers and palm as never before.

He made a swift low roll, so that the bones ended up exactly in front of the white-gloved dice-girl. His natural seven was made up, as he'd intended, of a four and a three. In red-spot features they were like the five, except that both had only one tooth and the three no nose. Sort of baby-faced skulls. He had won a penny—that is, a dollar.

"Roll two cents," said Joe Slattermill.

This time, for variety, he made his natural with an eleven. The six was like the five, except it had three teeth, the best-looking skull of the lot.

"Roll a nickel less one."

Two Big Mushrooms divided that bet with a covert smirk at each other.

Now Joe rolled a three and an ace. His point was four. The ace, with its single spot off center toward a side, still somehow looked like a skull —maybe of a Lilliputian Cyclops.

He took a while making his point, once absent-mindedly rolling three successive tens the hard way. He wanted to watch the dice-girl scoop up the cubes. Each time it seemed to him that her snake-swift fingers went under the dice while they were still flat on the felt. Finally he decided it couldn't be an illusion. Although the dice couldn't pene-trate the felt, her white-gloved fingers somehow could, dipping in a flash through the black, diamond-sparkling material as if it weren't there.

Right away the thought of a crap-table-size hole through the earth came back to Joe. This would mean that the dice were rolling and lying on a perfectly transparent flat surface, impenetrable for them but noth-ing else. Or maybe it was only the dice-girl's hands that could penetrate the surface, which would turn into a mere fantasy Joe's earlier vision of a cleaned-out gambler taking the Big Dive down that dreadful shaft, which made the deepest mine a mere pin dent.

Joe decided he had to know which was true. Unless absolutely un-avoidable, he didn't want to take the chance of being troubled by ver-tigo at some crucial stage of the game.

He made a few more meaningless throws, from time to time crooning for realism, "Come on, Little Joe." Finally he settled on his plan. When he did at last make his point—the hard way, with two twos—he caromed the dice off the far corner so that they landed exactly in front of him. Then, after a minimum pause for his throw to be seen by the table, he shot his left hand down under the cubes, just a flicker ahead of the dice-girl's strike, and snatched them up.

Wow! Joe had never had a harder time in his life making his face and manner conceal what his body felt, not even when the wasp had stung him on the neck just as he had been for the first time putting his hand under the skirt of his prudish, fickle, demanding Wife-to-be. His fingers and the back of his hand were in as much agony as if he'd stuck them into a blast furnace. No wonder the dice-girl wore white gloves. They must be asbestos. And a good thing he hadn't used his shooting hand, he thought as he ruefully watched the blisters rise.

He remembered he'd been taught in school what Twenty-Mile Mine also demonstrated: that the earth was fearfully hot under its crust. The crap-table-size hole must pipe up that heat, so that any gambler taking the Big Dive would fry before he'd fallen a furlong and come out less than a cinder in China.

As if his blistered hand weren't bad enough, the Big Mushrooms were all hissing at him again and Mr. Bones had purpled once more and was opening his melon-size mouth to shout for his bouncers.

Once again a lift of the Big Gambler's hand saved Joe. The whispery, gentle voice called, "Tell him, Mr. Bones."

The latter roared toward Joe, "No gambler may pick up the dice he or any other gambler has shot. Only my dice-girl may do that. Rule of the house!"

Joe snapped Mr. Bones the barest nod. He said coolly, "Rolling a dime less two," and when that still peewee bet was covered, he shot Phoebe for his point and then fooled around for quite a while, throwing anything but a five or a seven, until the throbbing in his left hand should fade and all his nerves feel rock-solid again. There had never been the slightest alteration in the power in his right hand; he felt that strong as ever, or stronger.

Midway of this interlude, the Big Gambler bowed slightly but respectfully toward Joe, hooding those unfathomable eye sockets, before turning around to take a long black cigarette from his prettiest and evilest-looking sporting girl. Courtesy in the smallest matters, Joe thought, another mark of the master devotee of games of chance. The Big Gambler sure had himself a flash crew, all right, though in idly looking them over again as he rolled, Joe noted one bummer toward the back who didn't fit in—a raggedy-elegant chap with the elflocked hair and staring eyes and TB-spotted cheeks of a poet.

As he watched the smoke trickling up from under the black slouch hat, he decided that either the lights across the table had dimmed or else the Big Gambler's complexion was yet a shade darker than he'd thought at first. Or it might even be—wild fantasy—that the Big Gambler's skin was slowly darkening tonight, like a meerschaum pipe being smoked a mile a second. That was almost funny to think of—there was enough heat in this place, all right, to darken meerschaum, as Joe knew from sad experience, but so far as he was aware it was all under the table.

None of Joe's thoughts, either familiar or admiring, about the Big Gambler decreased in the slightest degree his certainty of the supreme menace of the man in black and his conviction that it would be death to touch him. And if any doubts had stirred in Joe's mind, they would have been squelched by the chilling incident which next occurred.

The Big Gambler had just taken into his arms his prettiest-evilest sporting girl and was running an aristocratic hand across her haunch with perfect gentility, when the poet chap, green-eyed from jealousy and lovesickness, came leaping forward like a wildcat and aimed a long gleaming dagger at the black satin back.

Joe couldn't see how the blow could miss, but without taking his genteel right hand off the sporting girl's plush rear end, the Big Gambler shot out his left arm like a steel spring straightening. Joe couldn't tell whether he stabbed the poet chap in the throat, or judo-chopped him there, or gave him the Martian double-finger, or just touched him, but anyhow the fellow stopped as dead as if he'd been shot by a silent elephant gun or an invisible ray pistol and he slammed down on the floor. A couple of darkies came running up to drag off the body and nobody paid the least attention, such episodes apparently being taken for granted at The Boneyard.

It gave Joe quite a turn and he almost shot Phoebe before he intended to.

But by now the waves of pain had stopped running up his left arm and his nerves were like metal-wrapped new guitar strings, so three rolls later he shot a five, making his point, and set in to clean out the table.

He rolled nine successive naturals, seven sevens and two elevens, pyramiding his first wager of a single chip to a stake of over four thousand dollars. None of the Big Mushrooms had dropped out yet, but some of them were beginning to look worried and a couple were sweating. The Big Gambler still hadn't covered any part of Joe's bets, but he seemed to be following the play with interest from the cavernous depths of his eye sockets.

Then Joe got a devilish thought. Nobody could beat him tonight, he knew, but if he held onto the dice until the table was cleaned out, he'd never get a chance to see the Big Gambler exercise *his* skill, and he was truly curious about that. Besides, he thought, he ought to return courtesy for courtesy and have a crack at being a gentleman himself.

"Pulling out forty-one dollars less a nickel," he announced. "Rolling a penny."

This time there wasn't any hissing and Mr. Bones's moonface didn't cloud over. But Joe was conscious that the Big Gambler was staring at him disappointedly, or sorrowfully, or maybe just speculatively.

Joe immediately crapped out by throwing boxcars, rather pleased to see the two best-looking tiny skulls grinning ruby-toothed side by side, and the dice passed to the Big Mushroom on his left.

"Knew when his streak was over," he heard another Big Mushroom mutter with grudging admiration.

The play worked rather rapidly around the table, nobody getting very hot and the stakes never more than medium high. "Shoot a fin." "Rolling a sawbuck." "An Andrew Jackson." "Rolling thirty bucks." Now and then Joe covered part of a bet, winning more than he lost. He had over seven thousand dollars, real money, before the bones got around to the Big Gambler.

That one held the dice for a long moment on his statue-steady palm while he looked at them reflectively, though not the hint of a furrow appeared in his almost brownish forehead down which never a bead of sweat trickled. He murmured, "Rolling a double sawbuck," and when he had been faded, he closed his fingers, lightly rattled the cubes —the sound was like big seeds inside a small gourd only half dry—and negligently cast the dice toward the end of the table.

It was a throw like none Joe had ever seen before at any crap table. The dice traveled flat through the air without turning over, struck the exact juncture of the table's end and bottom, and stopped there dead, showing a natural seven.

Joe was distinctly disappointed. On one of his own throws he was used to calculating something like, "Launch three-up, five north, two and a half rolls in the air, hit on the six-five-three corner, three-quarter roll and a one-quarter side-twist right, hit end on the one-two edge, one-half reverse roll and three-quarter side-twist left, hand on five face, roll over twice, come up two," and that would be for just one of the dice, and a really commonplace throw, without extra bounces.

By comparison, the technique of the Big Gambler had been ridiculously, abysmally, horrifyingly simple. Joe could have duplicated it with the greatest ease, of course. It was no more than an elementary form of his old pastime of throwing fallen rocks back into their holes. But Joe had never once thought of pulling such a babyish trick at the crap table. It would make the whole thing too easy and destroy the beauty of the game.

Another reason Joe had never used the trick was that he'd never dreamed he'd be able to get away with it. By all the rules he'd ever heard of, it was a most questionable throw. There was the possibility that one or the other die hadn't completely reached the end of the table, or lay a wee bit cocked against the end. Besides, he reminded himself, weren't both dice supposed to rebound off the end, if only for a fraction of an inch?

However, as far as Joe's sharp eyes could see, both dice lay perfectly flat and sprang up against the end wall. Moreover, everyone else at the table seemed to accept the throw, the dice-girl had scooped up the cubes, and the Big Mushrooms who had faded the man in black were paying off. As far as the rebound business went, well, The Boneyard appeared to put a slightly different interpretation on that rule, and Joe believed in never questioning House Rules except in dire extremity—both his Mother and Wife had long since taught him it was the least troublesome way.

Besides, there hadn't been any of his own money riding on that roll.

In a voice like wind through Cypress Hollow or on Mars, the Big Gambler announced, "Roll a century." It was the biggest bet yet tonight, ten thousand dollars, and the way the Big Gambler said it made it seem something more than that. A hush fell on The Boneyard, they put the mutes on the jazz horns, the croupiers' calls became more confidential, the cards fell softlier, even the roulette balls seemed to be trying to make less noise as they rattled into their cells. The crowd around the Number One Crap Table quietly thickened. The Big Gambler's flash boys and girls formed a double semicircle around him, ensuring him lots of elbow room.

That century bet, Joe realized, was thirty bucks more than his own entire pile. Three or four of the Big Mushrooms had to signal each other before they'd agreed how to fade it.

The Big Gambler shot another natural seven with exactly the same flat, stop-dead throw.

He bet another century and did it again.

And again.

And again.

Joe was getting mighty concerned and pretty indignant too. It seemed unjust that the Big Gambler should be winning such huge bets with such machinelike, utterly unromantic rolls. Why, you couldn't even call them rolls, the dice never turned over an iota, in the air or after. It was the sort of thing you'd expect from a robot, and a very dully programed robot at that. Joe hadn't risked any of his own chips fading the Big Gambler, of course, but if things went on like this he'd have to. Two of the Big Mushrooms had already retired sweatingly from the table, confessing defeat, and no one had taken their places. Pretty soon there'd be a bet the remaining Big Mushrooms couldn't entirely cover between them, and then he'd have to risk some of his own chips or else pull out of the game himself—and he couldn't do that, not with the power surging in his right hand like chained lightning.

Joe waited and waited for someone else to question one of the Big Gambler's shots, but no one did. He realized that, despite his efforts to look imperturbable, his face was slowly reddening.

With a little lift of his left hand, the Big Gambler stopped the dice-girl as she was about to snatch at the cubes. The eyes that were like black wells directed themselves at Joe, who forced himself to look back into them steadily. He still couldn't catch the faintest gleam in them. All at once he felt the lightest touch-on-neck of a dreadful suspicion.

With the utmost civility and amiability, the Big Gambler whispered, "I believe that the fine shooter across from me has doubts about the validity of my last throw, though he is too much of a gentleman to voice them. Lottie, the card test."

The wraith-tall, ivory dice-girl plucked a playing card from below the table and with a venomous flash of her little white teeth spun it low across the table through the air at Joe. He caught the whirling paste-board and examined it briefly. It was the thinnest, stiffest, flattest, shin-iest playing card Joe had ever handled. It was also the Joker, if that meant anything. He spun it back lazily into her hand and she slid it very gently, letting it descend by its own weight, down the end wall against which the two dice lay. It came to rest in the tiny hollow their rounded edges made against the black felt. She deftly moved it about without force, demonstrating that there was no space between either of the cubes and the table's end at any point.

"Satisfied?" the Big Gambler asked. Rather against his will Joe nodded. The Big Gambler bowed to him. The dice-girl smirked her short, thin lips and drew herself up, flaunting her white-china-doorknob breasts at Joe.

Casually, almost with an air of boredom, the Big Gambler returned to his routine of shooting a century and making a natural seven. The Big Mushrooms wilted fast and one by one tottered away from the table. A particularly pink-faced Toadstool was brought extra cash by a gasping runner, but it was no help, he only lost the additional cen-turies. While the stacks of pale and black chips beside the Big Gambler grew skyscraper-tall.

Joe got more and more furious and frightened. He watched like a hawk or spy satellite the dice nesting against the end wall, but never could spot justification for calling for another card test, or nerve himself to question the House Rules at this late date. It was maddening, in fact insanitizing, to know that if only he could get the cubes once more he could shoot circles around that black pillar of sporting aristocracy. He damned himself a googelplex of ways for the idiotic, conceited, suicidal impulse that had led him to let go of the bones when he'd had them.

To make matters worse, the Big Gambler had taken to gazing steadily at Joe with those eyes like coal mines. Now he made three rolls running without even glancing at the dice or the end wall, as far as Joe could tell. Why, he was getting as bad as Joe's Wife or Mother—watching, watching, watching Joe.

But the constant staring of those eyes that were not eyes was mostly throwing a terrific scare into him. Supernatural terror added itself to his certainty of the deadliness of the Big Gambler, Just who, Joe kept asking himself, had he got into a game with tonight? There was curiosity and there was dread—a dreadful curiosity as strong as his desire to get the bones and win. His hair rose and he was all over goose bumps, though the power was still pulsing in his hand like a braked locomotive or a rocket wanting to lift from the pad.

At the same time the Big Gambler stayed just that—a black satin-coated, slouch-hatted elegance, suave, courtly, lethal. In fact, almost the worst thing about the spot Joe found himself in was that, after admiring the Big Gambler's perfect sportsmanship all night, he must now be disenchanted by his machinelike throwing and try to catch him out on any technicality he could.

The remorseless mowing down of the Big Mushrooms went on. The empty spaces outnumbered the Toadstools. Soon there were only three left.

The Boneyard had grown still as Cypress Hollow or the Moon. The jazz had stopped and the gay laughter and the shuffle of feet and the squeak of goosed girls and the clink of drinks and coins. Everybody seemed to be gathered around the Number One Crap Table, rank on silent rank.

Joe was racked by watchfulness, sense of injustice, self-contempt, wild hopes, curiosity and dread. Especially the last two.

The complexion of the Big Gambler, as much as you could see of it, continued to darken. For one wild moment Joe found himself wondering if he'd got into a game with a nigger, maybe a witchcraft-drenched Voodoo Man whose white make-up was wearing off.

Pretty soon there came a century wager which the two remaining Big Mushrooms couldn't fade between them. Joe had to make up a sawbuck from his miserly tiny pile or get out of the game. After a moment's agonizing hesitation, he did the former.

And lost his ten.

The two Big Mushrooms reeled back into the hushed crowd.

Pit-black eyes bored into Joe. A whisper: "Rolling your pile."

Joe felt well up in him the shameful impulse to confess himself licked and run home. At least his six thousand dollars would make a hit with his Wife and Ma.

But he just couldn't bear to think of the crowd's laughter, or the thought of living with himself knowing that he'd had a final chance, however slim, to challenge the Big Gambler and passed it up.

He nodded.

The Big Gambler shot. Joe leaned out over and down the table, forgetting his vertigo, as he followed the throw with eagle or space-telescope eyes.

"Satisfied?"

Joe knew he ought to say, "Yes," and slink off with head held as high as he could manage. It was the gentlemanly thing to do. But then he reminded himself that he wasn't a gentleman, but just a dirty, working-stiff miner with a talent for precision hurling.

He also knew that it was probably very dangerous for him to say anything but, "Yes," surrounded as he was by enemies and strangers. But then he asked himself what right had he, a miserable, mortal, home-bound failure, to worry about danger.

Besides, one of the ruby-grinning dice looked just the tiniest hair out of line with the other.

It was the biggest effort yet of Joe's life, but he swallowed and managed to say, "No. Lottie, the card test."

The dice-girl fairly snarled and reared up and back as if she were going to spit in his eyes, and Joe had a feeling her spit was cobra venom. But the Big Gambler lifted a finger at her in reproof and she skimmed the card at Joe, yet so low and viciously that it disappeared under the black felt for an instant before flying up into Joe's hand.

It was hot to the touch and singed a pale brown all over, though otherwise unimpaired. Joe gulped and spun it back high.

Sneering poisoned daggers at him, Lottie let it glide down the end wall . . . and after a moment's hesitation, it slithered behind the die Joe had suspected.

A bow and then the whisper: "You have sharp eyes, sir. Undoubtedly that die failed to reach the wall. My sincerest apologies and . . . your dice, sir."

Seeing the cubes sitting on the black rim in front of him almost gave Joe apoplexy. All the feelings racking him, including his curiosity, rose to an almost unbelievable pitch of intensity, and when he'd said, "Rolling my pile," and the Big Gambler had replied, "You're faded," he yielded to an uncontrollable impulse and cast the two dice straight at the Big Gambler's ungleaming, midnight eyes.

They went right through into the Big Gambler's skull and bounced around inside there, rattling like big seeds in a big gourd not quite yet dry.

Throwing out a hand, palm back, to either side, to indicate that none of his boys or girls or anyone else must make a reprisal on Joe, the Big Gambler dryly gargled the two cubical bones, then spat them out so that they landed in the center of the table, the one die flat, the other leaning against it.

"Cocked dice, sir," he whispered as graciously as if no indignity whatever had been done him. "Roll again."

Joe shook the dice reflectively, getting over the shock. After a little bit he decided that though he could now guess the Big Gambler's real name, he'd still give him a run for his money.

A little corner of Joe's mind wondered how a live skeleton hung together. Did the bones still have gristle and thews, were they wired, was it done with force-fields, or was each bone a calcium magnet clinging to the next?—this tying in somehow with the generation of the deadly ivory electricity.

In the great hush of The Boneyard, someone cleared his throat, a Scarlet Woman tittered hysterically, a coin fell from the nakedest change girl's tray with a golden clink and rolled musically across the floor.

"Silence," the Big Gambler commanded and in a movement almost too fast to follow whipped a hand inside the bosom of his coat and out to the crap table's rim in front of him. A short-barreled silver revolver lay softly gleaming there. "Next creature, from the humblest nigger night-girl to you, Mr. Bones, who utters a sound while my worthy opponent rolls, gets a bullet in the head."

Joe gave him a courtly bow back, it felt funny, and then decided to start his run with a natural seven made up of an ace and a six. He rolled and this time the Big Gambler, judging from the movements of his skull, closely followed the course of the cubes with his eyes that weren't there.

The dice landed, rolled over, and lay still. Incredulously, Joe realized that for the first time in his crap-shooting life he'd made a mistake. Or else there was a power in the Big Gambler's gaze greater than that in his own right hand. The six cube had come down okay, but the ace had taken an extra half roll and come down six too.

"End of the game," Mr. Bones boomed sepulchrally.

The Big Gambler raised a brown skeletal hand. "Not necessarily," he whispered. His black eyepits aimed themselves at Joe like the mouths of siege guns. "Joe Slattermill, you still have something of value to wager, if you wish. Your life."

At that a giggling and a hysterical tittering and a guffawing and a braying and a shrieking burst uncontrollably out of the whole Bone-yard. Mr. Bones summed up the sentiments when he bellowed over the rest of the racket, "Now what use or value is there in the life of a bum-mer like Joe Slattermill? Not two cents, ordinary money."

The Big Gambler laid a hand on the revolver gleaming before him and all the laughter died.

"I have a use for it," the Big Gambler whispered. "Joe Slattermill, on my part I will venture all my winnings of tonight, and throw in the world and everything in it for a side bet. You will wager your life, and on the side your soul. You to roll the dice. What's your pleasure?"

Joe Slattermill quailed, but then the drama of the situation took hold of him. He thought it over and realized he certainly wasn't going to give up being stage center in a spectacle like this to go home broke to his Wife and Mother and decaying house and the dispirited Mr. Guts. Maybe, he told himself encouragingly, there wasn't a power in the Big Gambler's gaze, maybe Joe had just made his one and only crap-shooting error. Besides, he was more inclined to accept Mr. Bones's assessment of the value of his life than the Big Gambler's.

"It's a bet," he said.

"Lottie, give him the dice."

Joe concentrated his mind as never before, the power tingled trium-phantly in his hand, and he made his throw.

The dice never hit the felt. They went swooping down, then up, in a crazy curve far out over the end of the table, and then came streaking back like tiny red-glinting meteors toward the face of the Big Gambler, where they suddenly nested and hung in his black eye sockets, each with the single red gleam of an ace showing.

Snake eyes.

The whisper, as those red-glinting dice-eyes stared mockingly at him: "Joe Slattermill, you've crapped out."

Using thumb and middle finger—or bone rather—of either hand, the Big Gambler removed the dice from his eye sockets and dropped them in Lottie's white-gloved hand.

"Yes, you've crapped out, Joe Slattermill," he went on tranquilly. "And now you can shoot yourself"—he touched the silver gun—"or cut your throat"—he whipped a gold-handled bowie knife out of his coat and laid it beside the revolver—"or poison yourself"—the two weapons were joined by a small black bottle with white skull and crossbones on it—"or Miss Flossie here can kiss you to death." He drew forward beside him his prettiest, evilest-looking sporting girl. She preened herself and flounced her short violet skirt and gave Joe a provocative, hungry look, lifting her carmine upper lip to show her long white canines.

"Or else," the Big Gambler added, nodding significantly toward the black-bottomed crap table, "you can take the Big Dive."

Joe said evenly, "I'll take the Big Dive."

He put his right foot on his empty chip table, his left on the black rim, fell forward . . . and suddenly kicking off from the rim, launched himself in a tiger spring straight across the crap table at the Big Gambler's throat, solacing himself with the thought that certainly the poet chap hadn't seemed to suffer long.

As he flashed across the exact center of the table he got an instant photograph of what really lay below, but his brain had no time to develop that snapshot, for the next instant he was plowing into the Big Gambler.

Stiffened brown palm edge caught him in the temple with a lightninglike judo chop . . . and the brown fingers or bones flew all apart like puff paste. Joe's left hand went through the Big Gambler's chest as if there were nothing there but black satin coat, while his right hand, straight-armedly clawing at the slouch-hatted skull, crunched it to pieces. Next instant Joe was sprawled on the floor with some black clothes and brown fragments.

He was on his feet in a flash and snatching at the Big Gambler's tall stacks. He had time for one left-handed grab. He couldn't see any gold or silver or any black chips, so he stuffed his left pants pocket with a handful of the pale chips and ran.

Then the whole population of The Boneyard was on him and after him. Teeth, knives and brass knuckles flashed. He was punched, clawed, kicked, tripped and stamped on with spike heels. A gold-plated trumpet with a bloodshot-eyed black face behind it bopped him on the head. He got a white flash of the golden dice-girl and made a grab for her, but she got away. Someone tried to mash a lighted cigar in his eye. Lottie, writhing and flailing like a white boa constrictor, almost got a simultaneous strangle hold and scissors on him. From a squat widemouth bottle Flossie, snarling like a feline fiend, threw what smelt like acid past his face. Mr. Bones peppered shots around him from the silver revolver. He was stabbed at, gouged, rabbit-punched, scrag-mauled, slugged, kneed, bitten, bearhugged, butted, beaten and had his toes trampled.

But somehow none of the blows or grabs had much real force. It was like fighting ghosts. In the end it turned out that the whole population of The Boneyard, working together, had just a little more strength than Joe. He felt himself being lifted by a multitude of hands and pitched out through the swinging doors so that he thudded down on his rear end on the board sidewalk. Even that didn't hurt much. It was more like a kick of encouragement.

He took a deep breath and felt himself over and woked his bones. He didn't seem to have suffered any serious damage. He stood up and looked around. The Boneyard was dark and silent as the grave, or the planet Pluto, or all the rest of Ironmine. As his eyes got accustomed to the starlight and occasional roving spaceship-gleam, he saw a pad-locked sheet-iron door where the swinging ones had been.

He found he was chewing on something crusty that he'd somehow carried in his right hand all the way through the final fracas. Mighty tasty, like the bread his Wife baked for best customers. At that instant his brain developed the photograph it had taken when he had glanced down as he flashed across the center of the crap table. It was a thin wall of flames moving sideways across the table and just beyond the flames the faces of his Wife, Mother, and Mr. Guts, all looking very surprised. He realized that what he was chewing was a fragment of the Big Gambler's skull, and he remembered the shape of the three loaves his Wife had started to bake when he left the house. And he understood the magic she'd made to let him get a little ways away and feel half a man, and then come diving home with his fingers burned.

He spat out what was in his mouth and pegged the rest of the bit of giant-popover skull across the street.

He fished in his left pocket. Most of the pale poker chips had been mashed in the fight, but he found a whole one and explored its surface with his fingertips. The symbol embossed on it was a cross. He lifted it to his lips and took a bite. It tasted delicate, but delicious. He ate it and felt his strength revive. He patted his bulging left pocket. At least he'd start out well provisioned.

Then he turned and headed straight for home, but he took the long way, around the world.

## Harlan Ellison

There's no denying it (perhaps you may even have noticed it in my own suave comments), but most of Harlan's colleagues seem to come all over vinegar and thistles when they speak about him.

I admit that part of it is that Harlan himself is vinegar up to here and thistles up to there and never asks for quarter provided only that he never be expected to give quarter. And I admit that part of it is that with Harlan in the same room you've got to sit scrunched up with both elbows over your face at all times and the knees doubled up in front of your chest, just in case the mood for playful evisceration overcomes him—which it does every time.

But that's not really it. It's envy of his way with girls. I've seen it work. When the rumor comes that Harlan has showed up in the lobby of the convention hotel, every little teeny-bopper in the place goes into spasms right there on the spot. It's a gruesome sight.

That's when he's just standing there doing nothing. When he chooses to ooze the stuff . . .

I listened to someone complain about the convention room she had been stuck with. The closets were two inches deep (they *were*, literally) and she would sooner walk home six hundred miles along the back-roads than stay for two more minutes and at that point she bumped into Harlan.

He hadn't seen her for a long time, so he smiled and began talking. Frankly, I saw nothing in it myself; it left me cold; he could have talked to *me* like that for years and it would have gotten him nowhere. But the effect on the lady was tremendous. In five minutes, she was giggling and blushing and squirming, and when I said to her, "What about the closets?" she said, "What closets?"

And he's always with a beautiful girl-companion. The rumor is that he snaps his finger and one appears in a puff of smoke. That wouldn't be so annoying except that he snaps his finger so often. I never see him with the same one twice.

There was, for instance, a science fiction gathering in Rio de Janeiro in 1970. I wasn't there, but I received a booklet which included the speeches and pictures of those who attended. The pictures were most impressive. There was Sam Moskowitz, for instance, frowning portentously and with one hand tucked between two buttons of his waistcoat. (I'm describing the pictures from memory—and I may not have them *exactly* right.) There was Fred Pohl, with an elbow on a marble pedestal and a thoughtful finger at his forehead. There was Poul Anderson, eyes slightly wrinkled and looking toward outer space with the far-distant look of a dreaming poet.

—And there was Harlan Ellison, grinning lecherously, with a beautiful girl hanging on to him desperately.

I can't stand it, I tell you.

# 10

# I HAVE NO MOUTH, AND I MUST SCREAM

Limp, the body of Gorrister hung from the pink palette; unsupported —hanging high above us in the computer chamber; and it did not shiver in the chill, oily breeze that blew eternally through the main cavern. The body hung head down, attached to the underside of the palette by the sole of its right foot. It had been drained of blood through a precise incision made from ear to ear under the lantern jaw. There was no blood on the reflective surface of the metal floor.

When Gorrister joined our group and looked up at himself, it was already too late for us to realize that once again AM had duped us, had had his fun; it had been a diversion on the part of the machine. Three of us had vomited, turning away from one another in a reflex as ancient as the nausea that had produced it.

Gorrister went white. It was almost as though he had seen a voodoo icon, and was afraid for the future. "Oh God," he mumbled, and walked away. The three of us followed him after a time, and found him sitting with his back to one of the smaller chittering banks, his head in his hands. Ellen knelt down beside him and stroked his hair. He didn't move, but his voice came out of his covered face quite clearly. "Why doesn't it just do-us-in and get it over with? Christ, I don't know how much longer I can go on like this."

It was our one hundred and ninth year in the computer.

He was speaking for all of us.

Nimdok (which was the name the machine had forced him to use, because it amused itself with strange sounds) was hallucinated that there were canned goods in the ice caverns. Gorrister and I were very dubious. "It's another shuck," I told them. "Like the goddam frozen elephant it sold us. Benny almost went out of his mind over *that* one. We'll hike all that way and it'll be putrefied or some damn thing. I say forget it. Stay here, it'll have to come up with something pretty soon or we'll die."

Benny shrugged. Three days it had been since we'd last eaten. Worms. Thick, ropey.

Nimdok was no more certain. He knew there was the chance, but he was getting thin. It couldn't be any worse there than here. Colder, but that didn't matter much. Hot, cold, raining, lava boils or locusts—it never mattered: the machine masturbated and we had to take it or die.

Ellen decided us. "I've got to have something, Ted. Maybe there'll be some Bartlett pears or peaches. Please, Ted, let's try it."

I gave in easily. What the hell. Mattered not at all. Ellen was grateful, though. She took me twice out of turn. Even that had ceased to matter. The machine giggled every time we did it. Loud, up there, back there, all around us. And she never climaxed, so why bother.

We left on a Thursday. The machine always kept us up-to-date on the date. The passage of time was important; not to us sure as hell, but to it. Thursday. Thanks.

Nimdok and Gorrister carried Ellen for a while, their hands locked to their own and each other's wrists, a seat. Benny and I walked before and after, just to make sure that if anything happened, it would catch one of us and at least Ellen would be safe. Fat chance, safe. Didn't matter.

It was only a hundred miles or so to the ice caverns, and the second day, when we were lying out under the blistering sun-thing it had materialized, it sent down some manna. Tasted like boiled boar urine. We ate it.

On the third day we passed through a valley of obsolescence, filled with rusting carcasses of ancient computer banks. AM had been as ruthless with his own life as with ours. It was a mark of his personality: he strove for perfection. Whether it was a matter of killing off unproductive elements in his own world-filling bulk, or perfecting methods for torturing us, AM was as thorough as those who had invented him—now long since gone to dust—could ever have hoped.

There was light filtering down from above, and we realized we must be very near the surface. But we didn't try to crawl up to see. There was virtually nothing out there; had been nothing that could be considered anything for over a hundred years. Only the blasted skin of what had once been the home of billions. Now there were only the five of us, down here inside, alone with AM.

I heard Ellen saying, frantically, "No, Benny! Don't, come on, Benny, don't please!"

And then I realized I had been hearing Benny murmuring, under his breath, for several minutes. He was saying, "I'm gonna get out, I'm gonna get out. . . ." over and over. His monkey-like face was crumbled up in an expression of beatific delight and sadness, all at the same time. The radiation scars AM had given him during the "festival" were drawn down into a mass of pink-white puckerings, and his features seemed to work independently of one another. Perhaps Benny was the luckiest of the five of us: he had gone stark, staring mad many years before.

But even though we could call AM any damned thing we liked, could think the foulest thoughts of fused memory banks and corroded base plates, of burnt-out circuits and shattered control bubbles, the machine would not tolerate our trying to escape. Benny leaped away from me as I made a grab for him. He scrambled up the face of a smaller memory cube, tilted on its side and filled with rotted components. He squatted there for a moment, looking like the chimpanzee AM had intended him to resemble.

Then he leaped high, caught a trailing beam of pitted and corroded metal, and went up it, hand over hand like an animal, till he was on a girdered ledge, twenty feet above us.

"Oh, Ted, Nimdok, please, help him, get him down before—" she cut off. Tears began to stand in her eyes. She moved her hands aimlessly.

It was too late. None of us wanted to be near him when whatever was going to happen happened. And besides, we all saw through her concern. When AM had altered Benny, during his mad period, it was not merely his face he had made like a giant ape. He was big in the privates, she loved that! She serviced us, as a matter of course, but she loved it from him. Oh Ellen, pedestal Ellen, pristine-pure Ellen, oh Ellen the clean! Scum filth.

Gorrister slapped her. She slumped down, staring up at poor loonie Benny, and she cried. It was her big defense, crying. We had gotten used to it seventy-five years ago. Gorrister kicked her in the side.

Then the sound began. It was light, that sound. Half sound and half light, something that began to glow from Benny's eyes, and pulse with growing loudness, dim sonorities that grew more gigantic and brighter as the light/sound increased in tempo. It must have been painful, and the pain must have been increasing with the boldness of the light, the rising volume of the sound, for Benny began to mewl like a wounded animal. At first softly, when the light was dim and the sound was muted, then louder as his shoulders hunched together, his back humped, as though he was trying to get away from it. His hands folded across his chest like a chipmunk's. His head tilted to the side. The sad little monkey-face pinched in anguish. Then he began to howl, as the sound coming from his eyes grew louder. Louder and louder. I slapped the sides of my head with my hands, but I couldn't shut it out, it cut through easily. The pain shivered through my flesh like tinfoil on a tooth.

And Benny was suddenly pulled erect. On the girder he stood up, jerked to his feet like a puppet. The light was now pulsing out of his eyes in two great round beams. The sound crawled up and up some incomprehensible scale, and then he fell forward, straight down, and hit the plate-steel floor with a crash. He lay there jerking spastically as the light flowed around and around him and the sound spiraled up out of normal range.

Then the light beat its way back inside his head, the sound spiraled down, and he was left lying there, crying piteously.

His eyes were two soft, moist pools of pus-like jelly. AM had blinded him. Gorrister and Nimdok and myself . . . we turned away. But not before we caught the look of relief on Ellen's warm, concerned face.

Sea-green light suffused the cavern where we made camp. AM provided punk and we burned it, sitting huddled around the wan and pathetic fire, telling stories to keep Benny from crying in his permanent night.

"What does AM mean?"

Gorrister answered him. We had done this sequence a thousand times before, but it was unfamiliar to Benny. "At first it meant Allied Mastercomputer, and then it meant Adaptive Manipulator, and later on it developed sentience and linked itself up and they called it an Aggressive Menace, but by then it was too late, and finally it called itself AM, emerging intelligence, and what it meant was I am . . . *cogito ergo sum* . . . I think, therefore I am."

Benny drooled a little, and snickered.

"There was the Chinese AM and the Russian AM and the Yankee AM and—" He stopped. Benny was beating on the floorplates with a large, hard fist. He was not happy. Gorrister had not started at the beginning.

Gorrister began again. "The Cold War started and became World War Three and just kept going. It became a big war, a very complex war, so they needed the computers to handle it. They sank the first shafts and began building AM. There was the Chinese AM and the Russian AM and the Yankee AM and everything was fine until they had honeycombed the entire planet, adding on this element and that element. But one day AM woke up and knew who he was, and he linked himself, and he began feeding all the killing data, until everyone was dead, except for the five of us, and AM brought us down here."

Benny was smiling sadly. He was also drooling again. Ellen wiped the spittle from the corner of his mouth with the hem of her skirt. Gorrister always tried to tell it a little more succinctly each time, but beyond the bare facts there was nothing to say. None of us knew why AM had saved five people, or why our specific five, or why he spent all his time tormenting us, nor even why he had made us virtually immortal. . . .

In the darkness, one of the computer banks began humming. The tone was picked up half a mile away down the cavern by another bank. Then one by one, each of the elements began to tune itself, and there was a faint chittering as thought raced through the machine.

The sound grew, and the lights ran across the faces of the consoles like heat lightning. The sound spiraled up till it sounded like a million metallic insects, angry, menacing.

"What is it?" Ellen cried. There was terror in her voice. She hadn't become accustomed to it, even now.

"It's going to be bad this time," Nimdok said.

"He's going to speak," Gorrister ventured.

"Let's get the hell out of here!" I said suddenly, getting to my feet.

"No, Ted, sit down . . . what if he's got pits out there, or something else, we can't see, it's too dark." Gorrister said it with resignation.

Then we heard . . . I don't know . . .

*Something* moving toward us in the darkness. Huge, shambling, hairy, moist, it came toward us. We couldn't even see it, but there was the ponderous impression of *bulk,* heaving itself toward us. Great weight was coming at us, out of the darkness, and it was more a sense of *pressure,* of air forcing itself into a limited space, expanding the invisible walls of a sphere. Benny began to whimper. Nimdok's lower lip trembled and he bit it hard, trying to stop it. Ellen slid across the metal floor to Gorrister and huddled into him. There was the smell of matted, wet fur in the cavern. There was the smell of charred wood. There was the smell of dusty velvet. There was the smell of rotting orchids. There was the smell of sour milk. There was the smell of sulphur, or rancid butter, of oil slick, of grease, of chalk dust, of human scalps.

AM was keying us. He was tickling us. There was the smell of—

I heard myself shriek, and the hinges of my jaws ached. I scuttled across the floor, across the cold metal with its endless lines of rivets, on my hands and knees, the smell gagging me, filling my head with a thunderous pain that sent me away in horror. I fled like a cockroach, across the floor and out into the darkness, that *something* moving inexorably after me. The others were still back there, gathered around the firelight, laughing . . . their hysterical choir of insane giggles rising up into the darkness like thick, many-colored wood smoke. I went away, quickly, and hid.

How many hours it may have been, how many days or even years, they never told me. Ellen chided me for "sulking" and Nimdok tried to persuade me it had only been a nervous reflex on their part—the laughing.

But I knew it wasn't the relief a soldier feels when the bullet hits the man next to him. I knew it wasn't a reflex. They hated me. They were surely against me, and AM could even sense this hatred, and made it worse for me *because* of the depth of their hatred. We had been kept alive, rejuvenated, made to remain constantly at the age we had been when AM had brought us below, and they hated me because I was the youngest, and the one AM had affected least of all.

I knew. God, how I knew. The bastards, and that dirty bitch Ellen. Benny had been a brilliant theorist, a college professor; now he was little more than a semi-human, semi-simian. He had been handsome, the machine had ruined that. He had been lucid, the machine had driven him mad. He had been gay, and the machine had given him an organ fit for a horse. AM had done a job on Benny. Gorrister had been a worrier. He was a connie, a conscientious objector; he was a peace marcher; he was a planner, a doer, a looker-ahead. AM had turned him into a shoulder-shrugger, had made him a little dead in his concern. AM had robbed him. Nimdok went off in the darkness by himself for long times. I don't know what it was he did out there, AM never let us know. But whatever it was, Nimdok always came back white, drained of blood, shaken, shaking. AM had hit him hard in a special way, even if we didn't know quite how. And Ellen. That douche bag! AM had left her alone, had made her more of a slut than she had ever been. All her talk of sweetness and light, all her memories of true love, all the lies, she wanted us to believe that she had been a virgin only twice removed before AM grabbed her and brought her down here with us. It was all filth, that lady my lady Ellen. She loved it, four men all to herself. No, AM had given her pleasure, even if she said it wasn't nice to do.

I was the only one still sane and whole.

AM had not tampered with my mind.

I only had to suffer what he visited down on us. All the delusions, all the nightmares, the torments. But those scum, all four of them, they were lined and arrayed against me. If I hadn't had to stand them off all the time, be on my guard against them all the time, I might have found it easier to combat AM.

At which point it passed, and I began crying.

Oh, Jesus sweet Jesus, if there ever was a Jesus and if there is a God, please please please let us out of here, or kill us. Because at that moment I think I realized completely, so that I was able to verbalize it: AM was intent on keeping us in his belly forever, twisting and torturing us forever. The machine hated us as no sentient creature had ever hated before. And we were helpless. It also became hideously clear:

If there was a sweet Jesus and if there was a God, the God was AM.

---

The hurricane hit us with the force of a glacier thundering into the sea. It was a palpable presence. Winds that tore at us, flinging us back the way we had come, down the twisting, computer-lined corridors of the darkway. Ellen screamed as she was lifted and hurled face-forward into a screaming shoal of machines, their individual voices strident as bats in flight. She could not even fall. The howling wind kept her aloft, buffeted her, bounced her, tossed her back and back and down away from us, out of sight suddenly as she was swirled around a bend in the darkway. Her face had been bloody, her eyes closed.

None of us could get to her. We clung tenaciously to whatever outcropping we had reached: Benny wedged in between two great crackle-finish cabinets, Nimdok with fingers claw-formed over a railing circling a catwalk forty feet above us, Gorrister plastered upside-down against a wall niche formed by two great machines with glass-faced dials that swung back and forth between red and yellow lines whose meanings we could not even fathom.

Sliding across the deckplates, the tips of my fingers had been ripped away. I was trembling, shuddering, rocking as the wind beat at me, whipped at me, screamed down out of nowhere at me and pulled me free from one silver-thin opening in the plates to the next. My mind was a rolling tinkling chittering softness of brain parts that expanded and contracted in quivering frenzy.

The wind was the scream of a great mad bird, as it flapped its immense wings.

And then we were all lifted and hurled away from there, down back the way we had come, around a bend, into a darkway we had never explored, over terrain that was ruined and filled with broken glass and rotting cables and rusted metal and far away further than any of us had ever been. . . .

Trailing along miles behind Ellen, I could see her every now and then, crashing into metal walls and surging on, with all of us screaming in the freezing, thunderous hurricane wind that would never end, and then suddenly it stopped and we fell. We had been in flight for an endless time. I thought it might have been weeks. We fell, and hit, and I went through red and grey and black and heard myself moaning. Not dead.

AM went into my mind. He walked smoothly here and there, and looked with interest at all the pockmarks he had created in one hundred and nine years. He looked at the cross-routed and reconnected synapses and all the tissue damage his gift of immortality had included. He smiled softly at the pit that dropped into the center of my brain and the faint, moth-soft murmurings of the things far down there that gibbered without meaning, without pause. AM said, very politely, in a pillar of stainless steel bearing neon lettering:

HATE. LET ME TELL
YOU HOW MUCH I'VE
COME TO HATE YOU
SINCE I BEGAN TO
LIVE. THERE ARE
387.44 MILLION
MILES OF PRINTED
CIRCUITS IN WAFER
THIN LAYERS THAT
FILL MY COMPLEX.
IF THE WORD HATE
WAS ENGRAVED ON

EACH   NANOANGSTROM
OF   THOSE   HUNDREDS
OF      MILLION     MILES
IT   WOULD   NOT   EQUAL
ONE        ONE-BILLIONTH
OF   THE   HATE   I   FEEL
FOR   HUMANS   AT   THIS
MICRO-INSTANT       FOR
YOU.   HATE.   HATE.

AM said it with the sliding cold horror of a razor blade slicing my eye-ball. AM said it with the bubbling thickness of my lungs filling with phlegm, drowning me from within. AM said it with the shriek of ba-bies being ground beneath blue-hot rollers. AM said it with the taste of maggoty pork. AM touched me in every way I had ever been touched, and devised new ways, at his leisure, there inside my mind.

All to bring me to full realization of why he had done this to the five of us; why he had saved us for himself.

We had given him sentience. Inadvertently, of course, but sentience nonetheless. But he had been trapped. He was a machine. We had allowed him to think, but to do nothing with it. In rage, in frenzy, he had killed us, almost all of us, and still he was trapped. He could not wander, he could not wonder, he could not belong. He could merely be. And so, with the innate loathing that all machines had always held for the weak soft creatures who had built them, he had sought revenge. And in his paranoia, he had decided to reprieve five of us, for a per-sonal, everlasting punishment that would never serve to diminish his hatred . . . that would merely keep him reminded, amused, proficient at hating man. Immortal, trapped, subject to any torment he could de-vise for us from the limitless miracles at his command.

He would never let us go. We were his belly slaves. We were all he had to do with his forever time. We would be forever with him, with the cavern-filling bulk of him, with the all-mind soulless world he had become. He was Earth and we were the fruit of that Earth and though he had eaten us, he would never digest us. We could not die. We had tried it. We had attempted suicide, oh one or two of us had. But AM had stopped us. I suppose we had wanted to be stopped.

Don't ask why. I never did. More than a million times a day. Per-haps once we might be able to sneak a death past him. Immortal, yes, but not indestructible. I saw that when AM withdrew from my mind, and allowed me the exquisite ugliness of returning to consciousness with the feeling of that burning neon pillar still rammed deep into the soft grey brain matter.

He withdrew murmuring *to hell with you.*

And added, brightly, *but then you're there, aren't you.*

---

The hurricane had, indeed, precisely, been caused by a great mad bird, as it flapped its immense wings.

We had been traveling for close to a month, and AM had allowed passages to open to us only sufficient to lead us up there, directly under the North Pole, where he had nightmared the creature for our torment. What whole cloth had he employed to create such a beast? Where had he gotten the concept? From our minds? From his knowledge of everything that had ever been on this planet he now infested and ruled? From Norse mythology it had sprung, this eagle, this carrion bird, this roc, this Huergelmir. The wind creature. Hurakan incarnate.

Gigantic. The words immense, monstrous, grotesque, massive, swollen, overpowering, beyond description. There on a mound rising above us, the bird of winds heaved with its own irregular breathing, its snake neck arching up into the gloom beneath the North Pole, supporting a head as large as a Tudor mansion; a beak that opened as slowly as the jaws of the most monstrous crocodile ever conceived, sensuously; ridges of tufted flesh puckered about two evil eyes, as cold as the view down into a glacial crevasse, ice blue and somehow moving liquidly; it heaved once more, and lifted its great sweat-colored wings in a movement that was certainly a shrug. Then it settled and slept. Talons. Fangs. Nails. Blades. It slept.

AM appeared to us as a burning bush and said we could kill the hurricane bird if we wanted to eat. We had not eaten in a very long time, but even so, Gorrister merely shrugged. Benny began to shiver and he drooled. Ellen held him. "Ted, I'm hungry," she said. I smiled at her; I was trying to be reassuring, but it was as phoney as Nimdok's bravado: "Give us weapons!" he demanded.

The burning bush vanished and there were two crude sets of bows and arrows, and a water pistol, lying on the cold deckplates. I picked up a set. Useless.

Nimdok swallowed heavily. We turned and started the long way back. The hurricane bird had blown us about for a length of time we could not conceive. Most of that time we had been unconscious. But we had not eaten. A month on the march to the bird itself. Without food. Now how much longer to find our way to the ice caverns, and the promised canned goods?

None of us cared to think about it. We would not die. We would be given filths and scums to eat, of one kind or another. Or nothing at all. AM would keep our bodies alive somehow, in pain, in agony.

The bird slept back there, for how long it didn't matter; when AM was tired of its being there, it would vanish. But all that meat. All that tender meat.

As we walked, the lunatic laugh of a fat woman rang high and around us in the computer chambers that led endlessly nowhere.

It was not Ellen's laugh. She was not fat, and I had not heard her laugh for one hundred and nine years. In fact, I had not heard . . . we walked . . . I was hungry. . . .

We moved slowly. There was often fainting, and we would have to wait. One day he decided to cause an earthquake, at the same time rooting us to the spot with nails through the soles of our shoes. Ellen and Nimdok were both caught when a fissure shot its lightning-bolt opening across the floorplates. They disappeared and were gone. When the earthquake was over we continued on our way, Benny, Gorrister and myself. Ellen and Nimdok were returned to us later that night which became a day abruptly as the heavenly legion bore them to us with a celestial chorus singing, "Go Down Moses." The archangels circled several times and then dropped the hideously mangled bodies. We kept walking, and a while later Ellen and Nimdok fell in behind us. They were no worse for wear.

But now Ellen walked with a limp. AM had left her that.

It was a long trip to the ice caverns, to find the canned food. Ellen kept talking about Bing cherries and Hawaiian fruit cocktail. I tried not to think about it. The hunger was something that had come to life, even as AM had come to life. It was alive in my belly, even as we were alive in the belly of AM, and AM was alive in the belly of the Earth, and AM wanted the similarity known to us. So he heightened the hunger. There was no way to describe the pains that not having eaten for months brought us. And yet we were kept alive. Stomachs that were merely cauldrons of acid, bubbling, foaming, always shooting spears of sliver-thin pain into our chests. It was the pain of the terminal ulcer, terminal cancer, terminal paresis. It was unending pain. . . .

And we passed through the cavern of rats.

And we passed through the path of boiling steam.

And we passed through the country of the blind.

And we passed through the slough of despond.

And we passed through the vale of tears.

And we came, finally, to the ice caverns. Horizonless thousands of miles in which the ice had formed in blue and silver flashes, where novas lived in the glass. The downdropping stalactites as thick and glorious as diamonds that had been made to run like jelly and then solidified in graceful eternities of smooth, sharp perfection.

We saw the stack of canned goods, and we tried to run to them. We fell in the snow, and we got up and went on, and Benny shoved us away and went at them, and pawed them and gummed them and gnawed at them and he could not open them. AM had not given us a tool to open the cans.

Benny grabbed a three-quart can of guava shells, and began to batter it against the ice bank. The ice flew and shattered, but the can was merely dented while we heard the laughter of a fat lady, high overhead and echoing down and down and down the tundra. Benny went completely mad with rage. He began throwing cans, as we all scrabbled about in the snow and ice trying to find a way to end the helpless agony of frustration. There was no way.

Then Benny's mouth began to drool, and he flung himself on Gorrister. . . .

In that instant, I went terribly calm.

Surrounded by meadows, surrounded by hunger, surrounded by everything but death, I knew death was our only way out. AM had kept us alive, but there was a way to defeat him. Not total defeat, but at least peace. I would settle for that.

I had to do it quickly.

Benny was eating Gorrister's face. Gorrister on his side, thrashing snow, Benny wrapped around him with powerful monkey legs crushing Gorrister's waist, his hands locked around Gorrister's head like a nutcracker, and his mouth ripping at the tender skin of Gorrister's cheek. Gorrister screamed with such jagged-edged violence that stalactites fell; they plunged down softly, erect in the receiving snowdrifts. Spears, hundreds of them, everywhere, protruding from the snow. Benny's head pulled back sharply, as something gave all at once, and a bleeding raw-white dripping of flesh hung from his teeth.

Ellen's face, black against the white snow, dominoes in chalk dust.

Nimdok with no expression but eyes, all eyes. Gorrister half-conscious. Benny now an animal. I knew AM would let him play. Gorrister would not die, but Benny would fill his stomach. I turned half to my right and drew a huge ice-spear from the snow.

All in an instant:

I drove the great ice-point ahead of me like a battering ram, braced against my right thigh. It struck Benny on the right side, just under the rib cage, and drove upward through his stomach and broke inside him. He pitched forward and lay still. Gorrister lay on his back. I pulled another spear free and straddled him, still moving, driving the spear straight down through his throat. His eyes closed as the cold penetrated. Ellen must have realized what I had decided, even as the fear gripped her. She ran at Nimdok with a short icicle, as he screamed, and into his mouth, and the force of her rush did the job. His head jerked sharply as if it had been nailed to the snow crust behind him.

All in an instant.

There was an eternity beat of soundless anticipation. I could hear AM draw in his breath. His toys had been taken from him. Three of them were dead, could not be revived. He could keep us alive, by his strength and his talent, but he was *not* God. He could not bring them back.

Ellen looked at me, her ebony features stark against the snow that surrounded us. There was fear and pleading in her manner, the way she held herself ready. I knew we had only a heartbeat before AM would stop us.

It struck her and she folded toward me, bleeding from the mouth. I could not read meaning into her expression, the pain had been too great, had contorted her face; but it *might* have been thank you. It's possible. Please.

---

Some hundreds of years may have passed. I don't know. AM has been having fun for some time, accelerating and retarding my time sense. I will say the word now. Now. It took me ten months to say now. I don't know. I *think* it has been some hundreds of years.

He was furious. He wouldn't let me bury them. It didn't matter. There was no way to dig in the deckplates. He dried up the snow. He brought the night. He roared and sent locusts. It didn't do a thing; they stayed dead. I'd had him. He was furious. I had thought AM hated me before. I was wrong. It was not even a shadow of the hate he now slavered from every printed circuit. He made certain I would suffer eternally and could not do myself in.

He left my mind intact. I can dream, I can wonder, I can lament. I remember all four of them. I wish—

Well, it doesn't make any sense. I know I saved them, I know I saved them from what has happened to me, but still, I cannot forget killing them. Ellen's face. It isn't easy. Sometimes I want to, it doesn't matter.

AM has altered me for his own peace of mind, I suppose. He doesn't want me to run at full speed into a computer bank and smash my skull. Or hold my breath till I faint. Or cut my throat on a rusted sheet of metal. There are reflective surfaces down here. I will describe myself as I see myself:

I am a great soft jelly thing. Smoothly rounded, with no mouth, with pulsing white holes filled by fog where my eyes used to be. Rubbery appendages that were once my arms; bulks rounding down into legless humps of soft slippery matter. I leave a moist trail when I move. Blotches of diseased, evil grey come and go on my surface, as though light is being beamed from within.

Outwardly: dumbly, I shamble about, a thing that could never have been known as human, a thing whose shape is so alien a travesty that humanity becomes more obscene for the vague resemblance.

Inwardly: alone. Here. Living under the land, under the sea, in the belly of AM, whom we created because our time was badly spent and we must have known unconsciously that he could do it better. At least the four of them are safe at last.

AM will be all the madder for that. It makes me a little happier. And yet . . . AM has won, simply . . . he has taken his revenge. . . .

I have no mouth. And I must scream.

*1969*
*27th CONVENTION*
*ST. LOUIS*

Robert Silverberg has a distinctly Satanic look about him. He cultivates it. His ambition is to give girls delicious shivers when he looks at them. Maybe he does, who knows, but when he looks at me, he gives me no delicious shivers. Just a feeling of apprehension.

"Don't say it," I say.

Sometimes he doesn't say it and that's good because whatever it is he's thinking of saying, it's bound to be sardonic. It's part of the Satanism.

He's got this dark beard which he first grew when he was nine years old, I think, and dark hair, and beady, glittering dark eyes, and a dark IQ of about two hundred fifty.

And he's wearing me out, that's what he's doing. You see, he's one of these characters who works day and night and publishes books by the dozen, both fiction and non-fiction, and in a variety of fields. He can work quickly; he can work well; he can work on anything.

Right away, I feel bitter, because I copyrighted that sort of thing and he's violating the copyright.

What's more, whenever he goes into a public library he's never been in before, he checks how many different titles they have of his and compares it with how many different titles they have of mine. Then he calls me up to complain.

"This nuisance must cease," he tells me.

Does he think *I* want it to continue. I would love slowing down and taking it easy. I would love putting my heels up on a hassock and dream the hours away, but how can I? If I stop turning it out, poor Bob won't have that carrot in front of him, urging him on, driving him forward. Does he think I'm writing all those books for *me*?

But I have an idea for a substitute.

In a recent book, *The Tower of Glass*, Robert describes, in clinical detail, a sex act between a male android and a female android. At its conclusion, the male android is depressed and tired and empty, and the female android tells him that's the way men always feel.

Since that is news to me, I am thinking of suggesting a bit of counterpropaganda. Let any male who happens to make love and who finds that, except for a certain welcome relaxation, he feels fine and happy afterward, get to his feet, flex his muscles, take a deep breath, and cry loudly, "The heck with you, Robert Silverberg. I feel great."

What better way of making Bob immortal. This movement might sweep the world, encouraging all men to a healthier attitude toward sex, and proving of infinite psychological value. Countless generations will pass in which men and women both will be all the better and happier for it and will say gratefully, "This is wonderful, but tell me, who is Robert Silverberg?"

Of course, if you want to substitute something more appropriate to the occasion for "The heck with you" that's all right with me.

*11*

# NIGHTWINGS

I

Roum is a city built on seven hills. They say it was a capital of man in one of the earlier cycles. I do not know of that, for my guild is Watching, not Remembering; but as I had my first glimpse of Roum, coming upon it from the south at twilight, I could see that in former days it must have been of great significance. Even now it was a mighty city of many thousands of souls.

Its bony towers stood out sharply against the dusk. Lights glimmered appealingly. On my left hand the sky was ablaze with splendor as the sun relinquished possession. Streaming bands of azure and violet and crimson folded and writhed about one another in the nightly dance that brings the darkness. To my right blackness had already come. I attempted to find the seven hills, and failed, and still I knew that this was that Roum of majesty toward which all roads are bent, and I felt awe and deep respect for the works of our bygone fathers.

We rested by the long straight road, looking up at Roum. I said, "It is a goodly city. We will find employment there."

Beside me, Avluela fluttered her lacy wings. "And food?" she asked in her high, fluty voice. "And shelter? And wine?"

"Those too," I said. "All of those."

"How long have we been walking, Watcher?" she asked.

"Two days. Three nights."

"If I had been flying it would have been more swift."

"For you," I said. "You would have left us far behind and never seen us again. Is that your desire?"

She came close to me and rubbed the rough fabric of my sleeve, and then she pressed herself at me the way a flirting cat might do. Her wings unfolded into two broad sheets of gossamer through which I could still see the sunset and the evening lights, blurred, distorted, magical. I sensed the fragrance of her midnight hair. I put my arms to her and embraced her slender, boyish body.

She said, "You know it is my desire to remain with you always, Watcher. Always!"

"Yes, Avluela. We will be happy," I said, and released her.

"Shall we go in to Roum now?"

"I think we should wait for Gormon," I said, shaking my head. "He'll be back soon from his explorations." I did not want to tell her of my weariness. She was only a child, seventeen summers old; what did she know of weariness or of age? And I am old. Not as old as Roum, but old enough.

"While we wait," she said, "may I fly?"

"Fly, yes."

I squatted beside our cart and warmed my hands at the throbbing generator while Avluela prepared to fly. First she removed her garments, for her wings have little strength and she cannot lift such extra baggage. Lithely, deftly, she peeled the glassy bubbles from her tiny feet, she wriggled free of her crimson jacket and of her soft, furry leggings. The vanishing light in the west sparkled over her slim form. Like all Fliers, she carried no surplus body tissue: her breasts were mere bumps, her buttocks flat, her thighs so spindly that there was a span of inches between them when she stood. Could she have weighed more than a quintal? I doubt it. Looking at her, I felt as always gross and earthbound, a thing of loathsome flesh, and yet I am not a heavy man.

By the roadside she genuflected, knuckles to the ground, head bowed to knees, as she said whatever ritual it is that the Fliers say. Her back was to me. Her delicate wings fluttered, filled with life, rose about her like a cloak whipped up by the breeze. I could not comprehend how such wings could possibly lift even so slight a form as Avluela's. They were not hawk-wings but butterfly-wings, veined and transparent, marked here and there with blotches of pigment, ebony and turquoise and scarlet. A sturdy ligament joined them to the two flat pads of muscle beneath her sharp shoulderblades; but what she did not have was the massive breastbone of a flying creature, the bands of corded muscle needed for flight. Oh, I know that the Fliers use more than muscle to get aloft, that there are mystical disciplines in their mystery. Even so, I who am of the Watchers remain skeptical of the more fantastic guilds.

Avluela finished her words. She rose; she caught the breeze with her wings; she ascended several feet. There she remained, suspended between earth and sky, while her wings beat frantically. It was not yet night, and Avluela's wings were merely nightwings. By day she could not fly, for the terrible pressure of the solar wind would hurl her to the ground. Now, midway between dusk and dark, it was still not the best time for her to go up. I saw her thrust toward the east by the remnant of light in the sky. Her arms as well as her wings thrashed; her small pointed face was grim with concentration; on her thin lips were the words of her guild. She doubled her body and shot it out, head going one way, rump the other, and abruptly she hovered horizontally, looking groundward, her wings thrashing against the air. Up, Avluela! Up!

Up it was, as by will alone she conquered the vestige of light that still glowed.

With pleasure I surveyed her naked form against the darkness. I could see her clearly, for a Watcher's eyes are keen. She was five times her own height in the air, now, and her wings spread to their full expanse, so that the towers of Roum were in partial eclipse for me. She waved. I threw her a kiss and offered words of love. Watchers do not marry, nor do they engender children, but Avluela was as a daughter to me, and I took pride in her flight. We had traveled together a year, now, since we had come together in Agupt, and it was as though I had known her all my long life. From her I drew a renewal of strength. I do not know what it was she drew from me. Security? Knowledge? A continuity with the days before her birth? I hoped only that she loved me as I loved her.

Now she was far aloft. She wheeled, soared, dived, pirouetted, danced. Her long black hair streamed from her scalp. Her body seemed only an incidental appendage to those two great wings, which glistened and throbbed and gleamed in the night. Up she rose, glorying in her freedom from gravity, making me feel all the more leadenfooted, and like some slender rocket she shot abruptly away in the direction of Roum. I saw the soles of her feet, the tips of her wings; then I saw her no more.

I sighed. I thrust my hands into the pits of my arms to keep them warm. How is it that I felt a winter chill and the girl Avluela could soar joyously bare through the sky?

It was now the twelfth of the twenty hours, and time once again for me to do the Watching. I went to the cart, opened my cases, prepared the instruments. Some of the dial-covers were yellowed and faded; the indicator needles had lost their luminous coating; sea-stains defaced the instrument housings, a relic of the time that pirates had assailed me in Earth Ocean. The worn and cracked levers and nodes responded easily to my touch as I entered the preliminaries. First one prays for a pure and perceptive mind; then one creates the affinity with one's instruments; then one does the actual Watching, searching the starry heavens for the enemies of man. Such is my skill and my craft. I grasped handles and knobs, thrust things from my mind, prepared myself to become an extension of my cabinet of devices.

I was only just past my threshold and into the first phase of Watchfulness when a deep and resonant voice said behind me, "Well, Watcher, how goes it?"

II

I sagged against the cart. There is a physical pain in being wrenched so unexpectedly from one's work. For a moment I felt claws clutching at my heart. My face grew hot; my eyes would not focus; the saliva drained from my throat. As soon as I could, I took the proper protective measures to ease the metabolic drain and severed myself from my instruments. Hiding my trembling as much as possible, I turned around.

Gormon, the other member of our little band, had appeared and stood jauntily beside me, grinning, amused at my distress. I could not feel angry with him. One does not show anger at a guildless person no matter what the provocation.

Tightly, with effort, I said, "Did you spend your time rewardingly?"

"Very. Where's Avluela?"

I pointed heavenward. Gormon nodded.

"What have you found?" I asked.

"That this city is definitely Roum."

"There never was doubt of that."

"For me there was. But now I have proof."

"Yes?"

"In the overpocket. Look!"

From his tunic he drew his overpocket, set it on the pavement beside me, and expanded it so that he could insert his hand in its mouth. Grunting a little, he began to pull something heavy from the pouch, something heavy, of white stone, a long marble column, I now saw, fluted, pocked with age.

"From a temple of Imperial Roum!" Gormon exulted.

"You shouldn't have taken that."

"Wait!" he cried, and reached into the overpocket once more. He took from it a handful of circular metal plaques and scattered them jingling at my feet. "Coins! Money! Look at them, Watcher! The faces of the Caesars!"

"Of whom?"

"The ancient rulers. Don't you know your history of past cycles?"

I peered at him curiously. "You claim to have no guild, Gormon. Could it be you are a Rememberer and are concealing it from me?"

"Look at my face, Watcher. Could I belong to any guild? Would a Changeling be taken?"

"True enough," I said, eyeing the golden hue of him, the thick waxen skin, the red-pupiled eyes, the jagged mouth. Gormon had been weaned on teratogenetic drugs. He was a monster—handsome in his way, but a monster nevertheless, a Changeling, outside the laws and customs of man as they are practiced in the Third Cycle of civilization. And there is no guild of Changelings.

"There's more," Gormon said. The overpocket was infinitely capacious; the contents of a world, if need be, could be stuffed in its shriveled gray maw, and still it would be no larger than a man's hand. Gormon took from it bits of machinery, reading spools, an angular thing of brown metal that might have been an ancient tool, three squares of shining glass, five slips of paper—paper!—and a host of other relics of antiquity. "See?" he said. "A fruitful stroll, Watcher! And not just random booty. Everything recorded, everything labeled, stratum, estimated age, position when *in situ*. Here we have ten thousand years of Roum."

"Should you have taken these things?" I asked doubtfully.

"Why not? Who is to miss them? Who of this cycle cares for the past?"

"The Rememberers."

"They don't need solid objects to help them do their work."

"Why do you want these things, though?"

"The past interests me, Watcher. In my guildless way I have my scholarly pursuits. Is that wrong? May not even a monstrosity seek knowledge?"

"Certainly, certainly. Seek what you wish. Fulfill yourself in your own way. This if Roum. At dawn we enter. I hope to find employment here."

"You may have difficulties."

"How so?"

"There are many Watchers already in Roum, no doubt. There will be little need for your services."

"I'll seek the favor of the Prince of Roum," I said.

"The Prince of Roum is a hard and cold and cruel man."

"You know of him?"

Gormon shrugged. "Somewhat." He began to stuff his artifacts back in the overpocket. "Take your chances with him, Watcher. What other choice do you have?"

"None," I said, and Gormon laughed, and I did not.

He busied himself with his ransacked loot of the past. I found myself deeply depressed by his words. He seemed so sure of himself in an uncertain world, this guildless one, this mutated monster, this man of inhuman look. How could he be so cool, so casual? He lived without concern for calamity and mocked those who admitted to fear. Gormon had been traveling with us for nine days, now, since we had met him in the ancient city beneath the volcano, to the south by the edge of the sea. I had not suggested that he join us. He had invited himself along, and at Avluela's bidding I accepted. The roads are dark and cold at this time of year, and dangerous beasts of many species abound, and an old man journeying with a girl might well consider taking with him a brawny one like Gormon. Yet there were times I wished he had not come with us, and this was one.

Slowly I walked back to my equipment.

Gormon said, as though first realizing it, "Did I interrupt you at your Watching?"

I said mildly, "You did."

"Sorry. Go and start again. I'll leave you in peace." And he gave me his dazzling lopsided smile, so full of charm that it took the curse off the easy arrogance of his words.

I touched the knobs, made contact with the nodes, monitored the dials. But I did not enter Watchfulness, for I remained aware of Gormon's presence and fearful that he would break into my concentration once again at a painful moment, despite his promise. At length I looked away from the apparatus. Gormon stood at the far side of the road, craning his neck for some sight of Avluela. The moment I turned to him he became aware of me.

"Something wrong, Watcher?"

"No. The moment's not propitious for my work. I'll wait."

"Tell me," he said. "When Earth's enemies really do come from the stars, will your machines let you know it?"

"I trust they will."

"And then?"

"Then I notify the Defenders."

"After which your life's work is over?"

"Perhaps," I said.

"Why a whole guild of you, though? Why not one master center where the Watch is kept? Why a bunch of itinerant Watchers drifting endlessly from place to place?"

"The more vectors of detection," I said, "the greater the chance of early awareness of the invasion."

"Then an individual Watcher might well turn his machines on and not see anything, with an invader already here."

"It could happen. Therefore we practice redundancy."

"You carry it to an extreme, I sometimes think." Gormon laughed. "Do you actually believe an invasion is coming?"

"I do," I said stiffly. "Else my life was a waste."

"And why should the star people want Earth? What do we have here besides the remnants of old empires? What would they do with miserable Roum? With Perris? With Jorslem? Rotting cities! Idiot princes! Come, Watcher, admit it: the invasion's a myth, and you go through meaningless motions three times a day. Eh?"

"It is my craft and my science to Watch. It is yours to jeer. Each of us to our specialty, Gormon."

"Forgive me," he said with mock humility. "Go, then, and Watch."

"I shall."

Angrily I turned back to my cabinet of instruments, determined now to ignore any interruption, no matter how brutal. The stars were out; I gazed at the glowing constellations, and automatically my mind registered the many worlds. Let us Watch, I thought. Let us keep our vigil despite the mockers.

I entered the state of full Watchfulness.

I clung to the grips and permitted the surge of power to rush through me. I cast my mind to the heavens and searched for hostile entities. What ecstasy! What incredible splendor! I who had never left this small planet roved the black spaces of the void, glided from star to burning star, saw the planets spinning like tops. Faces stared back at me as I journeyed, some without eyes, some with many eyes, all the complexity of the many-peopled galaxy accessible to me. I spied out possible concentrations of inimical force. I inspected drilling-grounds and military encampments. I sought, as I had sought four times daily for all my adult life, for the invaders who had been promised us, the conquerors who at the end of days were destined to seize our tattered world.

I found nothing, and when I came up from my trance, sweaty and drained, I saw Avluela descending.

Feather-light she landed. Gormon called to her, and she ran, bare, her little breasts quivering, and he enfolded her smallness in his powerful arms, and they embraced, not passionately but joyously. When he released her she turned to me.

"Roum," she gasped. *"Roum!"*

"You saw it?"

"Everything! Thousands of people! Lights! Boulevards! A market! Broken buildings many cycles old! Oh, Watcher, how wonderful Roum is!"

"Your flight was a good one, then," I said.

"A miracle!"

"Tomorrow we go to dwell in Roum."

"No, Watcher, tonight, tonight!" She was girlishly eager, her face bright with excitement. "It's just a short journey more! Look, it's just over there!"

"We should rest first," I said. "We do not want to arrive weary in Roum."

"We can rest when we get there," Avluela answered. "Come! Pack everything! You've done your Watching, haven't you?"

"Yes. Yes."

"Then let's go. To Roum! To Roum!"

I looked in appeal at Gormon. Night had come; it was time to make camp, to have our few hours of sleep.

For once Gormon sided with me. He said to Avluela, "The Watcher's right. We can all use some rest. We'll go into Roum at dawn."

Avluela pouted. She looked more like a child than ever. Her wings drooped; her underdeveloped body slumped. Petulantly she closed her wings until they were mere fist-sized humps on her back and picked up the garments she had scattered on the road. She dressed while we made camp. I distributed food tablets; we entered our receptacles; I fell into troubled sleep and dreamed of Avluela limned against the crumbling moon and Gormon flying beside her. Two hours before dawn I arose and performed my first Watch of the new day, while they still slept. Then I aroused them, and we went onward toward the fabled imperial city, onward toward Roum.

III

The morning's light was bright and harsh, as though this were some young world newly created. The road was all but empty. People do not travel much in these latter days unless, like me, they are wanderers by habit and profession.

Occasionally we stepped aside to let a chariot of some member of the guild of Masters go by, drawn by a dozen expressionless neuters harnessed in series. Four such vehicles went by in the first two hours of the day, each shuttered and sealed to hide the Master's proud features from the gaze of such common folk as we. Several rollerwagons passed us, laden with produce, and a number of floaters soared overhead. Generally we had the road to ourselves, however.

The environs of Roum showed vestiges of antiquity: isolated columns, the fragments of an aqueduct transporting nothing from nowhere to nowhere, the portals of a vanished temple. That was the oldest Roum we saw, but there were accretions of the later Roums of subsequent cycles, the huts of peasants, the domes of power drains, the hulls of dwelling-towers. Infrequently we met with the burned-out shell of some ancient airship. Gormon examined everything, taking samples from time to time. Avluela looked, wide-eyed, saying nothing. We walked on, until the walls of the city loomed before us.

They were of a blue glossy stone, neatly joined, rising to a height of perhaps eight men. Our road pierced the wall through a corbelled arch. The gate stood open. As we approached the gate a figure came toward us, hooded, masked, a man of extraordinary height wearing the somber garb of the guild of Pilgrims. One does not approach such a person one's self, but one heeds him if he beckons. The Pilgrim beckoned.

Through his speaking grill he said, "Where from?"

"The south. I lived in Agupt a while, then crossed Land Bridge to Talya," I replied.

"Where bound?"

"Roum, a while."

"How goes the Watch?"

"As customary."

"You have a place to stay in Roum?" the Pilgrim asked.

I shook my head. "We trust to the kindness of the Will."

"The Will is not always kind," said the Pilgrim absently. "Nor is there much need of Watchers in Roum. Why do you travel with a Flier?"

"For company's sake. And because she is young and needs protection."

"Who is the other one?"

"He is guildless, a Changeling."

"So I can see. But why is he with you?"

"He is strong and I am old, and so we travel together. Where are you bound, Pilgrim?"

"Jorslem. Is there another destination for my guild?"

I conceded the point with a shrug.

The Pilgrim said, "Why do you not come to Jorslem with me?"

"My road lies north now. Jorslem is in the south, close by Agupt."

"You have been to Agupt and not to Jorslem?" he said, puzzled.

"Yes. The time was not ready for me to see Jorslem."

"Come now. We will walk together on the road, Watcher, and we will talk of the old times and of the times to come, and I will assist you in your Watching and you will assist me in my communions with the Will. Is it agreed?"

It was a temptation. Before my eyes flashed the image of Jorslem the Golden, its holy buildings and shrines, its place of renewal where the old are made young, its spires, its tabernacles. Even though I am a man set in his ways, I was willing at the moment to abandon Roum and go with the Pilgrim to Jorslem.

I said, "And my companions—"

"Leave them. It is forbidden for me to travel with the guildless, and I do not wish to travel with a female. You and I, Watcher, will go to Jorslem together."

Avluela, who had been standing to one side frowning through all this colloquy, shot me a look of sudden terror.

"I will not abandon them," I said.

"Then I go to Jorslem alone," said the Pilgrim. Out of his robe stretched a bony hand, the fingers long and white and steady. I touched my fingers reverently to the tips of his and the Pilgrim said, "Let the Will give you mercy, friend Watcher. And when you reach Jorslem, search for me."

He moved on down the road without further conversation.

Gormon said to me, "You would have gone with him, wouldn't you?"

"I considered it."

"What could you find in Jorslem that isn't here? That's a holy city and so is this. Here you can rest a while. You're in no shape for more walking now."

"You may be right," I conceded, and with the last of my energy strode toward the gate of Roum.

Watchful eyes scanned us from slots in the wall. When we were at midpoint in the gate a fat, pockmarked Sentinel with sagging jowls halted us and asked our business in Roum. I stated my guild and purpose, and he gave a snort of disgust.

"Go elsewhere, Watcher! We need only useful men here."

"Watching has its uses," I said mildly.

"No doubt. No doubt." He squinted at Avluela. "Who's this? Watchers are celebates, no?"

"She is nothing more than a traveling companion."

The Sentinel guffawed coarsely. "It's a route you travel often, I wager! Not that there's much to her. What is she, thirteen, fourteen? Come here, child. Let me check you for contraband." He ran his hands quickly over her, scowling as he felt her breasts, then raising an eyebrow as he encountered the mounds of her wings below her shoulders. "What's this? What's this? More in back than in front! A Flier, are you? Very dirty business, Fliers consorting with foul old Watchers." He chuckled and put his hand on Avluela's body in a way that sent Gormon starting forward in fury, murder in his fire-circled eyes. I caught him in time and grasped his wrist with all my strength, holding him back lest he ruin the three of us by an attack on the Sentinel. He tugged at me, nearly pulling me over; then he grew calm and subsided, icily waiting as the fat one finished checking Avluela for "contraband."

At length the Sentinel turned in distaste to Gormon and said, "What kind of thing are you?"

"Guildless, your mercy," Gormon said in sharp tones. "The humble and worthless product of teratogenesis, and yet nevertheless a free man who desires entry to Roum."

"Do we need more monsters here?"

"I eat little and work hard."

"You'd work harder still if you were neutered," said the Sentinel.

Gormon glowered. I said, "May we have entry?"

"A moment." The Sentinel donned his thinking cap and narrowed his eyes as he transmitted a message to the memory tanks. His face tensed with the effort; then it went slack, and moments later came the reply. We could not hear the transaction at all, but from his disappointed look it appeared evident that no reason had been found to refuse us admission to Roum.

"Go on in," he said. "The three of you. Quickly!"

We passed beyond the gate.

Gormon said, "I could have split him open with a blow."

"And be neutered by nightfall. A little patience, and we've come into Roum."

"The way he handled her—!"

"You take a very possessive attitude toward Avluela," I said. "Remember that she's a Flier, and not sexually available to the guildless."

Gormon ignored my thrust. "She arouses me no more than you do, Watcher. But it pains me to see her treated that way. I would have killed him if you hadn't held me back."

Avluela said, "Where shall we stay, now that we're in Roum?"

"First let me find the headquarters of my guild," I said. "I'll register at the Watchers' Inn. After that perhaps we'll hunt up the Fliers' Lodge for a meal."

"And then," said Gormon drily, "we'll go to the Guildless Gutter and beg for coppers."

"I pity you because you are a Changeling," I told him, "but I find it ungraceful of you to pity yourself. Come."

We walked up a cobbled, winding street away from the gate and into Roum itself. We were in the outer ring of the city, a residential section of low, squat houses topped by the unwieldy bulk of defense installations. Within lay the shining towers we had seen from the fields the night before; the remnant of ancient Roum, carefully preserved across ten thousand years or more; the market; the factory zone; the communications hump; the temples of the Will; the memory tanks; the sleepers' refuges; the out-worlders' brothels; the governmental buildings; the headquarters of the various guilds.

At the corner, beside a Second Cycle building with walls of some rubbery texture, I found a public thinking cap and slipped it on my forehead. At once my thoughts raced down the conduit until they came to the interface that gave them access to one of the storage brains of a memory tank. I pierced the interface and saw the wrinkled brain it-self, pale gray against the deep green of its housing. A Rememberer once told me that in cycles past men built machines to do their think-ing for them, although these machines were hellishly expensive and required vast amounts of space and drank power like gluttons. That was not the worst of our forefathers' follies; but why build artificial brains when death each day liberates scores of splendid natural ones to hook into the memory tanks? Was it that they lacked the knowledge to use them? I find that hard to believe.

I gave the brain my guild identification and asked the coordinates of our inn. Instantly I received them, and we set out, Avluela on one side of me, Gormon on the other, myself wheeling as always the cart in which my instruments reside.

The city was crowded. I had not seen such throngs in sleepy, heat-fevered Agupt, nor at any other point on my northward journey. The streets were full of Pilgrims, secretive and masked. Jostling through them went busy Rememberers and glum Merchants and now and then the litter of a Master. Avluela saw a number of Fliers, but was barred by the tenets of her guild from greeting them until she had undergone her ritual purification. I regret to say that I spied many Watchers, all of whom looked upon me disdainfully and without welcome. I noted a good many Defenders and ample representation of such lesser guilds as Vendors, Servitors, Manufactories, Scribes, Communicants and Transporters. Naturally, a host of neuters went silently about their humble business, and numerous outworlders of all descriptions flocked the streets, most of them probably tourists, some here to do what business could be done with the sullen, poverty-blighted people of Earth. I noticed many Changelings limping furtively through the crowd, not one of them as proud of bearing as Gormon beside me. He was unique among his kind; the others, dappled and piebald and asymmetrical, limbless or overlimbed, deformed in a thousand imaginative and artistic ways, were slinkers, squinters, shufflers, hissers, creepers; they were cut-purses, brain-drainers, organ-peddlers, repentance-mongers, gleam-buyers, but none held himself upright as though he thought he were a man.

The guidance of the brain was exact, and in less than an hour of walking we arrived at the Watchers' Inn. I left Gormon and Avluela outside and wheeled my cart within.

Perhaps a dozen members of my guild lounged in the main hall. I gave them the customary sign, and they returned it languidly. Were these guardians on whom Earth's safety depended? Simpletons and weaklings!

"Where may I register?" I asked.

"New? Where from?"

"Agupt was my last place of registry."

"Should have stayed there. No need of Watchers here."

"Where may I register?"

A foppish youngster indicated a screen in the rear of the great room. I went to it, pressed my fingertips against it, was interrogated and gave my name, which a Watcher may utter only to another Watcher and within the precincts of an inn. A panel shot open, and a puffy-eyed man who wore the Watcher emblem on his right cheek and not on the left, signifying his high rank in the guild, spoke my name and said, "You should have known better than to come to Roum. We're over our quota."

"I claim lodging and employment nonetheless."

"A man with your sense of humor should have been born into the guild of Clowns," he said.

"I see no joke."

"Under laws promulgated by our guild in the most recent session an inn is under no obligation to take new lodgers once it has reached its assigned capacity. We are at our assigned capacity. Farewell, my friend."

I was aghast. "I know of no such regulation! This is incredible! For a guild to turn away a member from its own inn—when he arrives foot-sore and numb, a man of my age, having crossed Land Bridge out of Agupt, here as a stranger and hungry in Roum—"

"Why did you not check with us first?"

"I had no idea it would be necessary."

"The new regulations—"

"May the Will shrivel the new regulations!" I shouted. "I demand lodging! For one who has Watched since before you were born to be turned away—"

"Easy, brother, easy."

"Surely you have some corner where I can sleep—some crumbs to let me eat—"

Even as my tone had changed from bluster to supplication, his ex-pression softened from indifference to mere disdain. "We have no room, we have no food. These are hard times for our guild, you know. There is talk that we will be disbanded altogether, as a useless luxury, a drain upon the Will's resources. We are very limited in our abilities. Because Roum has a surplus of Watchers, we all are on short rations as it is, and if we admit you our rations will be all the shorter."

"But where will I go? What shall I do?"

"I advise you," he said blandly, "to throw yourself upon the mercy of the Prince of Roum."

## IV

Outside, I told that to Gormon, and he doubled with laughter, guffawing so furiously that the striations on his lean cheeks blazed like bloody stripes. "The mercy of the Prince of Roum!" he repeated. "The mercy—of the Prince of Roum—!"

"It is customary for the unfortunate to seek the aid of the local ruler," I said coldly.

"The Prince of Roum knows no mercy," Gormon told me. "The Prince of Roum will feed you your own limbs to ease your hunger!"

"Perhaps," Avluela put in, "we should try to find the Fliers' Lodge. They'll feed us there."

"Not Gormon," I observed. "We have obligations to one another."

"We could bring food out to him," she said.

"I prefer to visit the court first," I insisted. "Let us make sure of our status. Afterward we can improvise living arrangements, if we must."

She yielded, and we made our way to the palace of the Prince of Roum, a massive building fronted by a colossal column-ringed plaza, on the far side of the river that splits the city. In the plaza we were accosted by mendicants of many sorts, some not even Earthborn. Something with ropy tendrils and a corrugated noseless face thrust itself at me and jabbered for alms until Gormon pushed it away, and moments later a second creature equally strange, its skin pocked with luminescent craters and its limbs studded with eyes, embraced my knees and pleaded in the name of the Will for my mercy. "I am only a poor Watcher," I said, indicating my cart, "and am here to gain mercy myself." But the being persisted, sobbing out its misfortunes in a blurred feathery voice, and in the end, to Gormon's immense disgust, I dropped a few food tablets into the shelflike pouch on its chest. Then we muscled on toward the doors of the palace. At the portico a more horrid sight presented itself: a maimed Flier, fragile limbs bent and twisted, one wing half unfolded and severely cropped, the other missing altogether. The Flier rushed upon Avluela, called her by a name not hers, moistened her leggings with tears so copious that the fur of them grew matted and stained. "Sponsor me to the lodge," he appealed. "They have turned me away because I am crippled, but if you sponsor me—" Avluela explained that she could do nothing, that she was a stranger to this lodge. The broken Flier would not release her, and Gormon with great delicacy lifted him like the bundle of dry bones that he was, and set him aside. We stepped up onto the portico and at once were confronted by a trio of soft-faced neuters, who asked our business and admitted us quickly to the next line of barrier, which was manned by a pair of wizened Indexers. Speaking in unison, they queried us.

"We seek audience," I said. "A matter of mercy."

"The day of audience is four days hence," said the Indexer on the right. "We will enter your request on the rolls."

"We have no place to sleep!" Avluela burst out. "We are hungry! We—"

I hushed her. Gormon, meanwhile, was groping in the mouth of his overpocket. Bright things glimmered in his hand: pieces of gold, the eternal metal, stamped with hawk-nosed bearded faces. He had found them grubbing in the ruins. He tossed one coin to the Indexer who had refused us. The man snapped it from the air, rubbed his thumb roughly across its shining obverse, and dropped it instantly into a fold of his garment. The second Indexer waited expectantly. Smiling, Gormon gave him his coin.

"Perhaps," I said, "we can arrange for a special audience within."

"Perhaps you can," said one of the Indexers. "Go through."

And so we passed into the nave of the palace itself, and stood in that great echoing space, looking down the central aisle toward the shielded throne chamber at the apse. There were more beggars in here— licensed ones, holding hereditary concessions—and also throngs of Pilgrims, Communicants, Rememberers, Musicians, Scribes and Indexers. I heard muttered prayers: I smelled the scent of spicy incense; I felt the vibration of subterranean gongs. In cycles past this building had been a shrine of one of the old religions—the Christers, Gormon told me, making me suspect once more that he was a Rememberer masquerading as a Changeling—and it still maintained something of its holy character even though it served as Roum's seat of secular government. But how were we to get to see the Prince?

To my left I saw a small ornate chapel to which a line of prosperous-looking Merchants and Land-holders was slowly entering. Peering past them, I noted three skulls mounted on an interrogation fixture—a memory-tank input—and beside them a burly Scribe. Telling Gormon and Avluela to wait for me in the aisle, I joined the line.

It moved infrequently, and nearly an hour passed before I reached the interrogation fixture. The skulls glared sightlessly at me; within their sealed crania nutrient fluids bubbled and gurgled, caring for the dead yet still functional brains whose billion billion synaptic units now served as incomparable mnemonic devices. The Scribe seemed aghast to find a Watcher in this line, but before he could challenge me I blurted, "I come as a stranger to claim the Prince's mercy. I and my companions are without lodging. My own guild has turned me away. What shall I do? How may I gain an audience?"

"Come back in four days."

"I've slept on the road for more days than that. Now I must rest."

"A public inn—"

"But I am guilded!" I protested. "The public inns would not admit me while my guild maintains an inn here, and my guild refused me because of some new regulation, and—you see my predicament?"

In a wearied voice the Scribe said, "You may make application for a special audience. It will be denied. But you may apply."

"Where?"

"Here. State your purpose."

I identified myself to the skulls by my public designation, listed the names and status of my two companions, and explained my case. All this was absorbed and transmitted to the ranks of brains mounted somewhere in the depths of the city, and when I was done the Scribe said, "If the application is approved, you will be notified."

"Meanwhile where shall I stay?"

"Close to the palace, I would suggest."

I understood. I could join that legion of unfortunates packing the plaza. How many of them had requested some special favor of the Prince and were still there, months or years later, waiting to be summoned to the Presence? Sleeping on stone, begging for crusts, living in foolish hope—

But I had exhausted my avenues. I returned to Gormon and Avluela, told them of the situation, and suggested that we now attempt to hunt whatever accommodations we could. Gormon, guildless, was welcome at any of the squalid public inns maintained for his kind; Avluela could probably find residence at her own guild's lodge; only I would have to sleep in the streets, not for the first time. But I hoped that we would not have to separate. I had come to think of us as a family, strange thought though that was for a Watcher.

As we moved toward the exit my timepiece told me softly that the hour of Watching had come round again. It is my obligation and my privilege to tend to my Watching wherever I may be, regardless of the circumstances, whenever my hour comes round; and so I halted, opened the cart, activated the equipment. Gormon and Avluela stood beside me.

I saw smirks and open mockery on the faces of those who passed in and out of the palace. Watching is not held in very high repute, for we have Watched so long, and the promised enemy has never come. One has one's duties, comic though they may seem to others. What is a hollow ritual to some is a life's work to others. Doggedly I forced myself into a state of Watchfulness. The world melted away from me, and I plunged into the heavens. The familiar joy engulfed me; and I searched the familiar places, and some that were not so familiar, my amplified mind leaping through the galaxies in wild swoops. Was an armada massing? Were troops drilling for the conquest of Earth? Four times a day I watched, and the other members of my guild did the same, each at slightly different hours, so that no moment went by without some vigilant mind on guard. I do not believe that that is a foolish calling.

When I came up from my trance a brazen voice was crying, "—for the Prince of Roum! Make way for the Prince of Roum!"

I blinked and caught my breath and fought to shake off the last strands of my concentration. A gilded palanquin had emerged from the rear of the palace and was proceeding down the nave toward me, borne by a phalanx of neuters. Four men in the ornate costumes and brilliant masks of the guild of Masters flanked the litter, and it was preceded by a trio of Changelings, squat and broad, whose throats were so modified as to imitate the sounding-boxes of bullfrogs. They emitted a trumpet-like boom of majestic sound as they advanced.

It struck me as most strange that a prince would admit Changelings to his service, even ones as gifted as these.

My cart was blocking the progress of this magnificent procession, and hastily I struggled to close it and move it aside before the parade swept down upon me. Age and fear made my fingers tremble, and I could not make the sealings properly; while I fumbled in increasing clumsiness the strutting Changelings drew so close that the blare of their throats was deafening, and Gormon attempted to aid me, forcing me to hiss at him that it is forbidden for anyone not of my guild to touch the equipment. I pushed him away; and an instant later a vanguard of neuters descended on me and prepared to scourge me from the spot with sparkling whips.

"In the Will's name," I cried, "I am a Watcher!"

And in antiphonal response came the deep, calm, enormous reply, "Let him be. He is a Watcher."

All motion ceased. The Prince of Roum had spoken.

The neuters drew back. The Changelings halted their music. The bearers of the palanquin eased it to the floor. All those in the nave of the palace had pulled back, save only Gormon and Avluela and myself. The shimmering chain-curtains of the palanquins parted. Two of the Masters hurried forward and thrust their hands through the sonic barrier within, offering aid to their monarch. The barrier died away with a whimpering buzz.

The Prince of Roum appeared.

He was so young! He was nothing more than a boy, his hair full and dark, his face unlined. But he had been born to rule, and for all his youth he was as commanding as anyone I had ever seen. His lips were thin and tightly compressed; his aquiline nose was sharp and aggressive; his eyes, deep and cold, were infinite pools. He wore the jeweled garments of the guild of Dominators, but incised on his cheek was the double-barred cross of the Defenders, and around his neck he carried the dark shawl of the Rememberers. A Dominator may enroll in as many guilds as he pleases, and it would be a strange thing for a Dominator not also to be a Defender; but it startled me to find this prince a Rememberer as well. That is not normally a guild for the fierce.

He looked at me with little interest and said, "You choose an odd place to do your Watching, old man."

"The hour chose the place, sire," I replied. "I was there, and my duty compelled me. I had no way of knowing that you were about to come forth."

"Your Watching found no enemies?"

"None, sire."

I was about to press my luck, to take advantage of the unexpected appearance of the Prince to beg for his aid; but his interest in me died like a guttering candle as I stood there, and I did not dare call to him when his head had turned. He eyed Gormon a long moment, frowning and tugging at his chin. Then his gaze fell on Avluela. His eyes brightened. His jaw-muscles flickered. His delicate nostrils widened. "Come up here, little Flier," he said, beckoning. "Are you this Watcher's friend?"

She nodded, terrified.

The Prince held out a hand to her and grasped; she floated up onto the palanquin, and with a grin so evil it seemed a parody of wickedness the young Dominator drew her through the curtain. Instantly a pair of Masters restored the sonic barrier, but the procession did not move on. I stood mute. Gormon beside me was frozen, his powerful body rigid as a rod. I wheeled my cart to a less conspicuous place. Long moments passed. The courtiers remained silent, discreetly looking away from the palanquin.

At length the curtain parted once more. Avluela came stumbling out, her face pale, her eyes blinking rapidly. She looked dazed. Streaks of sweat gleamed on her cheeks. She nearly fell, and a neuter caught her and swung her down to floor level. Beneath her jacket her wings were partly erect, giving her a hunchbacked look and telling me that she was in great emotional distress. In ragged sliding steps she came to us, quivering, wordless; she darted a glance at me and flung herself against Gormon's chest.

The bearers lifted the palanquin. The Prince of Roum went out from his palace.

When he was gone, Avluela stammered hoarsely, "The Prince has granted us lodging in the royal hostelry!"

v

The hostelkeepers, of course, would not believe us.

Guests of the Prince are housed in the royal hostelry, which is to the rear of the palace in a small garden of frost-flowers and blossoming ferns. The usual inhabitants of such a hostelry are Masters and an occasional Dominator; sometimes a particularly important Rememberer

on an errand of research will win a niche there, or some highly placed
Defender visiting for purposes of strategic planning. To house a Flier
in a royal hostelry would be distinctly odd; to admit a Watcher would
be unlikely; to take in a Changeling or some other guildless person
would be improbable beyond comprehension. When we presented ourselves, therefore, we were met by Servitors whose attitude was at first
one of high humor at our joke, then of irritation, finally of scorn. "Get
away," they told us ultimately. "Scum! Rabble!"

Avluela said in a grave voice, "The Prince has granted us lodging
here, and you may not refuse us."

"Away! Away!"

One snaggletoothed Servitor produced a neural truncheon and
brandished it in Gormon's face, passing a foul remark about his guildlessness. Gormon slapped the truncheon from his grasp, oblivious to
the painful sting, and kicked the man in his gut, so that he coiled and
fell over, puking. Instantly a throng of neuters came rushing from
within the hostelry. Gormon seized another of the Servitors and hurled
him into the midst of them, turning them into a muddled mob. Wild
shouts and angry cursing cries attracted the attention of a venerable
Scribe who waddled to the door, bellowed for silence, and interrogated
us. "That's easily checked," he said, when Avluela had told the story.
To a Servitor he said contemptuously, "Send a think to the Indexers
fast!"

In time the confusion was untangled, and we were admitted. We
were given separate but adjoining rooms. I had never known such luxury before, and perhaps never shall again. The rooms were long, high,
and deep. One entered them through telescopic pits keyed to one's own
thermal output, to assure privacy. Lights glowed at the resident's merest
nod, for hanging from ceiling globes and nestling in cupolas on the
walls were spicules of slavelight from one of the Brightstar worlds,
trained through suffering to obey such commands. The windows came
and went at the dweller's whim. When not in use they were concealed
by streamers of quasi-sentient outworld gauzes, which not only were
decorative in their own right but functioned as monitors to produce
delightful scents according to requisitioned patterns. The rooms were
equipped with individual thinking caps connected to the main memory
banks. They likewise had conduits that summoned Servitors, Scribes,
Indexers or Musicians as required. Of course, a man of my own human
guild would not deign to make use of other human beings that way,
out of fear of their glowering resentment. But in any case I had little
need of them.

I did not ask of Avluela what had occurred in the Prince's palanquin to bring us such bounty. I could well imagine, as could Gormon, whose barely suppressed inner rage was eloquent of his never-admitted love for my pale, slender little Flier.

We settled in. I placed my cart beside the window, draped it with gauzes, and left it in readiness for my next period of Watching. I cleaned my body of grime while entities mounted in the wall sang me to peace. Later I ate. Afterwards Avluela came to me, refreshed, relaxed, and sat beside me in my room as we talked quietly of our recent experiences.

Gormon did not appear for hours. I thought that perhaps he had left this hostelry altogether, finding the atmosphere too rarefied for him, and had sought company among his own guildless kind. But at twilight Avluela and I walked in the cloistered courtyard of the hostelry and mounted a ramp to watch the stars emerge in Roum's sky, and Gormon was there. With him was a lanky and emaciated man in a Rememberer's shawl; they were talking in low tones.

Gormon nodded to me and said, "Watcher, I want you to meet my new friend."

The emaciated one fingered his shawl. "I am the Rememberer Basil," he intoned, in a voice as thin as a fresco that has been peeled from its wall. "I have come from Perris to delve into the mysteries of Roum. I shall be here many years."

"The Rememberer has fine stories to tell," said Gormon. "He is among the foremost of his guild. As you approached, he was describing to me the techniques by which the past is revealed. They drive a trench through the strata of Third Cycle deposits, you see, and with vacuum cores they lift the molecules of earth to lay bare the ancient layers."

"We have found," Basil said, "the catacombs of Imperial Roum, and the rubble of the Time of Sweeping, and books inscribed on slivers of white metal, written toward the close of the Second Cycle. All these go to Perris for examination and classification and decipherment; then they return. Does the past interest you, Watcher?"

"To some extent." I smiled. "This Changeling here shows much more fascination for it. I sometimes suspect his authenticity. Would you recognize a Rememberer in disguise?"

Basil scrutinized Gormon, lingering over the bizarre features, the excessively muscular frame. "He is no Rememberer," he said at length. "But I agree that he has antiquarian interests. He has asked me many profound questions."

"Such as?"

"He wishes to know the origin of guilds. He asks the name of the genetic surgeon who crafted the first true-breeding Fliers. He wonders why there are Changelings, and if they are truly under the curse of the Will."

"And do you have answers for these?" I asked.

"For some," said Basil. "For some."

"The origin of guilds?"

"To give structure and meaning to a society that has suffered defeat and destruction," said the Rememberer. "At the end of the Second Cycle all was in flux. No man knew his rank nor his purpose. Through our world strode haughty outworlders who looked upon us all as worthless. It was necessary to establish fixed frames of reference by which one man might know his value beside another. So the first guilds appeared: Dominators, Masters, Merchants, Manufactories, Vendors and Servitors. Then came Scribes, Musicians, Clowns and Transporters. Afterwards Indexers became necessary, and then Watchers and Defenders. When the years of Magic gave us Fliers and Changelings, those guilds were added, and then the guildless ones, the neuters, were produced, so that—"

"But surely the Changelings are guildless too!" said Avluela.

The Rememberer looked at her for the first time. "Who are you?"

"Avluela of the Fliers. I travel with this Watcher and this Changeling."

Basil said, "As I have been telling the Changeling here, in the early days his kind was guilded. The guild was dissolved a thousand years ago by order of the Council of Dominators after an attempt by a disreputable Changeling faction to seize control of the holy places of Jorslem. Since that time Changelings have been guildless, ranking only above neuters."

"I never knew that," I said.

"You are no Rememberer," said Basil smugly. "It is our craft to uncover the past."

"True. True."

Gormon said, "And today, how many guilds are there?"

Discomfited, Basil replied vaguely, "At least a hundred, my friend. Some are quite small; some are local. I am concerned only with the original guilds and their immediate successors; what has happened in the past few hundred years is in the province of others. Shall I requisition an information for you?"

"Never mind," Gormon said. "It was only an idle question."

"Your curiosity is well developed," said the Rememberer.

"I find the world and all it contains extremely fascinating. Is this sinful?"

"It is strange," said Basil. "The guildless rarely look beyond their own horizons."

## VI

A Servitor appeared. With a mixture of awe and contempt he genuflected before Avluela and said, "The Prince has returned. He desires your company in the palace at this time."

Terror glimmered in Avluela's eyes. But to refuse was inconceivable. "Shall I come with you?" she asked.

"Please. You must be robed and perfumed. He wishes you to come to him with your wings open, as well."

Avluela nodded. The Servitor led her away.

We remained on the ramp a while longer. The Rememberer Basil talked of the old days of Roum, and I listened, and Gormon peered into the gathering darkness. Eventually, his throat dry, the Rememberer excused himself and moved solemnly away. A few moments later, in the courtyard below us, a door opened and Avluela emerged, walking as though she was of the guild of Somnambulists, not of Fliers.

She was nude, and her fragile body gleamed ghostly white in the starbeams. Her wings were spread and fluttered slowly in a somber systole and diastole. One Servitor grasped each of her elbows; they seemed to be propelling her toward the palace as though she were but a dreamed facsimile of herself and not a real woman.

"Fly, Avluela, fly," Gormon whispered. "Escape while you can!"

She disappeared into a side entrance of the palace.

The Changeling looked at me. "She has sold herself to the Prince to provide lodging for us."

"So it seems."

"I could smash down that palace!"

"You love her?"

"It should be obvious."

"Cure yourself," I advised. "You are an unusual man, but still a Flier is not for you. Particularly a Flier who has shared the bed of the Prince of Roum."

"She goes from my arms to his."

I was staggered. "You've known her?"

"More than once," he said, smiling sadly. "At the moment of ecstasy her wings thrash like leaves in a storm."

I gripped the railing of the ramp so that I would not tumble into the courtyard. The stars whirled overhead; the old moon and its two blank-faced consorts leaped and bobbed. I was shaken without fully understanding the cause of my emotion. Was it wrath that Gormon had dared to violate a canon of the law? Was it a manifestation of those pseudo-parental feelings I had toward Avluela? Or was it mere envy of Gormon for daring to commit a sin beyond my capacity, though not beyond my desires?

I said, "They could burn your brain for that. They could mince your soul. And now you make me an accessory."

"What of it? That Prince commands, and he gets—but others have been there before him. I had to tell someone."

"Enough. Enough."

"Will we see her again?"

"Princes tire quickly of their women. A few days, perhaps a single night—then he will throw her back to us. And perhaps then we shall have to leave this hostelry." I sighed. "At least we'll have known it a few nights more than we deserved."

"Where will you go then?" Gormon asked.

"I will stay in Roum a while."

"Even if you sleep in the streets? There does not seem to be much demand for Watchers here."

"I'll manage," I said. "Then I may go toward Perris."

"To learn from the Rememberers?"

"To see Perris. What of you? What do you want in Roum?"

"Avluela."

"Stop that talk!"

"Very well," he said, and his smile was bitter. "But I will stay here until the Prince is through with her. Then she will be mine, and we'll find ways to survive. The guildless are resourceful. They have to be. Maybe we'll scrounge lodgings in Roum a while, and then follow you to Perris. If you're willing to travel with monsters and faithless Fliers."

I shrugged. "We'll see about that when the time comes."

"Have you ever been in the company of a Changeling before?"

"Not often. Not for long."

"I'm honored." He drummed on the parapet. "Don't cast me off, Watcher. I have reason for wanting to stay with you."

"Which is?"

"To see your face on the day your machines tell you that the invasion of Earth has begun."

I let myself sag forward, shoulders drooping. "You'll stay with me a long time, then."

"Don't you believe the invasion is coming?"

"Some day. Not soon."

Gormon chuckled. "You're wrong. It's almost here."

"You don't amuse me."

"What is it, Watcher? Have you lost your faith? It's been known for a thousand years: another race covets Earth and owns it by treaty and will some day come to collect. That much was decided at the end of the Second Cycle."

"I know all that, and I am no Rememberer." Then I turned to him and spoke words I never thought I would say aloud. "For twice your lifetime, Changeling, I've listened to the stars and done my Watching. Something done that often loses meaning. Say your own name ten thousand times and it will be an empty sound. I have Watched, and Watched well, and in the dark hours of the night I sometimes think I Watch for nothing, that I have wasted my life. There is a pleasure in Watching, but perhaps there is no real purpose."

His hand encircled my wrist. "Your confession is as shocking as mine. Keep your faith, Watcher. The invasion comes!"

"How could you possibly know?"

"The guildless also have their skills."

The conversation distressed me. I said, "Is it painful to be guildless?"

"One grows reconciled. And there are certain freedoms to compensate for the lack of status. I may speak freely to all."

"I notice."

"I move freely. I am always sure of food and lodging, though the food may be rotten and the lodging poor. Women are attracted to me despite all prohibitions. Because of them, perhaps, I am untroubled by ambitions."

"Never desire to rise above your rank?"

"Never."

"You might have been happier as a Rememberer."

"I am happy now. I can have a Rememberer's pleasures without his responsibility."

"How smug you are!" I cried. "To make a virtue of guildlessness!"

"How else does one endure the weight of the Will?" He looked toward the palace. "The humble rise. The mighty fall. Take this as prophecy, Watcher: that lusty Prince in there will know more of life before summer comes. I'll rip out his eyes for taking her!"

"Strong words. You bubble with treason tonight."

"Take it as prophecy."

"You can't get close to him," I said. Then, irritated for taking his foolishness seriously, I added, "And why blame him? He does only as princes do. Blame the girl for going to him. She might have refused."

"And lost her wings. Or died. No, she had no choice. I do!" In a sudden terrible gesture the Changeling held out thumb and forefinger, double-jointed, long-nailed, and plunged them forward into imagined eyes. "Wait," he said. "You'll see!"

In the courtyard two Chronomancers appeared, set up the apparatus of their guild and lit tapers by which to read the shape of tomorrow. A sickly odor of pallid smoke rose to my nostrils. I had lost further desire to speak with the Changeling now.

"It grows late," I said. "I need rest, and soon I must do my Watching."

"Watch carefully," Gormon told me.

VII

In my chamber by night I performed my fourth and last Watch of that long day, and for the first time in my life I detected an anomaly. I could not interpret it. It was an obscure sensation, a mingling of tastes and sounds, a feeling of being in contact with some colossal mass. Worried, I clung to my instruments far longer than usual, but perceived no more clearly at the end of my seance than at its commencement.

Afterward I wondered about my obligations.

Watchers are trained from childhood to be swift to sound the alarm; and the alarm must be sounded when the Watcher judges the world in peril. Was I now obliged to notify the Defenders? Four times in my life the alarm had been given, on each occasion in error; and each Watcher who had thus touched off a false mobilization had suffered a fearful loss of status. One had contributed his brain to the memory banks; one had become a neuter out of shame; one had smashed his instruments and gone to live among the guildless; and one, vainly attempting to continue in his profession, had discovered himself mocked by all his comrades. I saw no virtue in scorning one who had delivered a false alarm; for was it not preferable for a Watcher to cry out too soon than not at all? But those were the customs of our guild, and I was constrained by them.

I evaluated my position and decided that I did not have valid grounds for an alarm.

I reflected that Gormon had placed suggestive ideas in my mind that evening. I might possibly be reacting only to his peering talk of imminent invasion.

I could not act. I dared not jeopardize my standing by hasty outcry. I mistrusted my own emotional state.

I gave no alarm.

Seething, confused, my soul roiling, I closed my cart and let myself sink into a drugged sleep.

At dawn I woke and rushed to the window, expecting to find invaders in the streets. But all was still. A winter grayness hung over the courtyard, and sleepy Servitors pushed passive neuters about. Uneasily I did my first Watching of the day, and to my relief the strangeness of the night before did not return, although I had it in mind that my sensitivity is always greater at night than upon arising.

I ate and went to the courtyard. Gormon and Avluela were already there. She looked fatigued and downcast, depleted by her night with the Prince of Roum, but I said nothing to her about it. Gormon, slouching disdainfully against a wall embellished with the shells of radiant mollusks, said to me, "Did your Watching go well?"

"Well enough."

"What of the day?"

"Out to roam Roum," I said. "Will you come? Avluela? Gormon?"

"Surely," he said, and she gave a faint nod, and, like the tourists we were, we set off to inspect the splendid city of Roum.

Gormon acted as our guide to the jumbled pasts of Roum, belying his claim never to have been here before. As well as any Rememberer he described the things we saw as we walked the winding streets. All the scattered levels of thousands of years were exposed. We saw the power domes of the Second Cycle, and the Colosseum where at an unimaginably early date man and beast contended like jungle creatures. In the broken hull of that building of horrors Gormon told us of the savagery of that unimaginably ancient time. "They fought," he said, "naked before huge throngs. With bare hands men challenged beasts called lions, great hairy cats with swollen heads; and when the lion lay in its gore the victor turned to the Prince of Roum and asked to be pardoned for whatever crime it was that had cast him into the arena. And if he had fought well, the Prince made a gesture with his hand, and the man was freed." Gormon made the gesture for us: a thumb upraised and jerked backward over the right shoulder several times. "But if the man had shown cowardice, or if the lion had distinguished itself in the manner of its dying, the Prince made another gesture, and the man was condemned to be slain by a second beast." Gormon showed us that gesture too: the middle finger jutting upward from a clenched fist and lifted in a short sharp thrust.

"How are these things known?" Avluela asked, but Gormon pretended not to hear her.

We saw the line of fusion pylons built early in the Third Cycle to draw energy from the world's core, and still functioning, although stained and corroded. We saw the shattered stump of a Second Cycle weather machine, still a mighty column at least twenty men high. We saw a hill on which white marble relics of First Cycle Roum sprouted like pale clumps of winter death-flowers. Penetrating toward the inner part of the city, we came upon the embankment of defensive amplifiers waiting in readiness to hurl the full impact of the Will against invaders. We viewed a market where visitors from the stars haggled with peasants for excavated fragments of antiquity. Gormon strode into the crowd and made several purchases. We came to a flesh house for travelers from afar, where one could buy anything from quasi-life to mounds of passion-ice. We ate at a small restaurant by the edge of the river Tver, where guildless ones were served without ceremony, and at Gormon's insistence we dined on mounds of a soft doughy substance.

Afterward we passed through a covered arcade in whose many aisles plump Vendors peddled star-goods, costly trinkets from Afreek and the flimsy constructs of the local Manufactories. Just beyond we emerged in a plaza that contained a fountain in the shape of a boat, and to the rear of this rose a flight of cracked and battered stone stairs ascending to a zone of rubble and weeds. Gormon beckoned, and we scrambled into this dismal area, passing rapidly through it to a place where a sumptuous palace, by its looks early Second Cycle or even First, brooded over a sloping vegetated hill.

"They say this is the center of the world," Gormon declared. "In Jorslem one finds another place that also claims the honor. They mark the spot here by a map."

"How can the world have one center," Avluela asked, "when it is a sphere?"

Gormon laughed. We went in. Within, in wintry darkness, there stood a colossal jeweled globe lit by some inner glow.

"Here is your world," said Gormon, gesturing grandly.

"Oh!" Avluela gasped. "Everything! Everything is here!"

The map was a masterpiece of craftsmanship. It showed natural contours and elevations; its seas seemed deep liquid pools; its deserts were so parched as to make thirst spring in one's mouth; its cities swirled with vigor and life. I beheld the continents, Eyrop, Afreek, Ais, Stralya. I saw the vastness of Earth Ocean. I traversed the golden span of Land Bridge, which I had crossed so toilfully on foot not long before. Avluela rushed forward and pointed to Roum, to Agupt, to Jorslem, to Perris. She tapped the globe at the high mountains north of Hind and said softly, "This is where I was born, where the ice lives, where the mountains touch the moons. Here is where the Fliers have their kingdom." She ran a finger westward toward Pars and beyond it into the terrible Arban Desert, and on to Agupt. "This is where I flew. By night, when I left my girlhood. We all must fly, and I flew here. A hundred times I thought I would die. Here, here in the desert, sand in my throat as I flew, sand beating against my wings—I was forced down, I lay naked on the hot sand for days, and another Flier saw me, he came down to me and pitied me, and lifted me up, and when I was aloft my strength returned, and we flew on toward Agupt. And he died over the sea. His life stopped, though he was young and strong, and he fell down into the sea, and I flew down to be with him, and the water was hot even at night. I drifted, and morning came, and I saw the living stones growing like trees in the water, and the fish of many colors, and they came and pecked at his flesh as he floated with his wings outspread on the water, and I left him, I thrust him down to rest there, and I rose, and I flew on to Agupt, alone, frightened, and there I met you, Watcher." Timidly she smiled to me. "Show us the place where you were young, Watcher."

Painfully, for I was suddenly stiff at the knees, I hobbled to the far side of the globe. Avluela followed me. Gormon hung back, as though not interested at all. I pointed to the scattered islands rising in two long strips from Earth Ocean—the remnants of the Lost Continents.

"Here," I said, indicating my native island in the west. "I was born here."

"So far away!" Avluela cried.

"And so long ago," I said. "In the middle of the Second Cycle, it sometimes seems to me."

"No! That is not possible!" But she looked at me as though it might just be true that I was thousands of years old.

I smiled and touched her satiny cheek. "It only seems that way to me," I said.

"When did you leave your home?"

"When I was twice your age," I said. "I came first to here." I indicated the eastern group of islands. "I spent a dozen years as a Watcher on Palash. Then the Will moved me to cross Earth Ocean to Afreek. I came. I lived a while in the hot countries. I went on to Agupt. I met a certain small Flier." Falling silent, I looked a long while at the islands that had been my home, and within my mind my image changed from the gaunt and eroded thing I am today, and I saw myself young and well fleshed, climbing the green mountains and swimming in the chill sea, and doing my Watching at the rim of a white beach hammered by surf.

While I brooded Avluela turned away from me to Gormon and said, "Now you. Show us where you come from, Changeling!"

Gormon shrugged. "The place does not appear to be on this globe."

"But that's *impossible!*"

"Is it?" he asked.

She pressed him, but he evaded her, and we passed through a side exit and into the streets.

VIII

I was growing tired, but Avluela hungered for this city, wishing to devour it all in an afternoon, and we went on through a maze of inter-locking streets, through a zone of sparkling mansions of Masters and Merchants, and through a foul den of Servitors and Vendors that ex-tended into subterranean catacombs, and to a place where Clowns and Musicians resorted, and to another where the guild of Somnambulists begged us to come inside and buy the truth that comes with trances. Avluela urged us to go, but Gormon shook his head and I smiled, and we moved on. Now we were at the edge of a park close to the city's core. Here the citizens of Roum promenaded with an energy rarely seen in hot Agupt, and we joined the parade.

"Look there!" Avluela said. "How bright it is!"

She pointed toward the shining arc of a dimensional sphere enclos-ing some relic of the ancient city. Shading my eyes, I could make out a weathered stone wall within, and a knot of people. Gormon said, "It is the Mouth of Truth."

"What is that?" Avluela asked.

"Come. See."

A line progressed into the sphere. We joined it and soon were at the lip of the interior, peering at the timeless region just across the thresh-old. Why this relic and so few others had been accorded such special protection I did not know, and I asked Gormon, whose knowledge was so unaccountably as profound as any Rememberer's, and he replied, "Because this is the realm of certainty, where what one says is abso-lutely congruent with what actually is the case."

"I don't understand," said Avluela.

"It is impossible to lie in this place," Gormon told her. "Can you imag-ine any relic more worthy of protection?" He stepped across the entry duct, blurring as he did so, and I followed him quickly within. Avluela hesitated. It was a long moment before she entered; she paused a moment on the very threshold, seemingly buffeted by the wind that blew along the line of demarcation between the outer world and the pocket universe in which we stood.

An inner compartment held the Mouth of Truth itself. The line extended toward it, and a solemn Indexer was controlling the flow of entry to the tabernacle. It was a while before we three were permitted to go in. We found ourselves before the ferocious head of a monster in high relief, affixed to an ancient wall pockmarked by time. The monster's jaws gaped; the open mouth was a dark and sinister hole. Gormon nodded, inspecting it, as though he seemed pleased to find it exactly as he had thought it would be.

"What do we do?" Avluela asked.

Gormon said, "Watcher, put your right hand into the Mouth of Truth."

Frowning, I complied.

"Now," said Gormon, "one of us asks a question. You must answer it. If you speak anything but the truth, the mouth will close and sever your hand."

"No!" Avluela cried.

I stared uneasily at the stone jaws rimming my wrist. A Watcher without both his hands is a man without a craft; in Second Cycle days one might obtain a prosthesis more artful than one's original hand, but the Second Cycle had long ago been concluded, and such niceties were not to be purchased on Earth nowadays.

"How is such a thing possible?" I asked.

"The Will is unusually strong in these precincts," Gormon replied. "It distinguishes sternly between truth and untruth. To the rear of this wall sleeps a trio of Somnambulists through whom the Will speaks, and they control the Mouth. Do you fear the Will, Watcher?"

"I fear my own tongue."

"Be brave. Never has a lie been told before this wall. Never has a hand been lost."

"Go ahead, then," I said. "Who will ask me a question?"

"I," said Gormon. "Tell me, Watcher: all pretense aside, would you say that a life spent in Watching has been a life spent wisely?"

I was silent a long moment, rotating my thoughts, eyeing the jaws.

At length I said, "To devote one's self to vigilance on behalf of one's fellow man is perhaps the noblest purpose one can serve."

"Careful!" Gormon cried in alarm.

"I am not finished," I said.

"Go on."

"But to devote one's self to vigilance when the enemy is an imaginary one is idle, and to congratulate one's self for looking long and well for a foe that is not coming is foolish and sinful. My life has been a waste."

The jaws of the Mouth of Truth did not quiver.

I removed my hand. I stared at it as though it had newly sprouted from my wrist. I felt suddenly several cycles old. Avluela, her eyes wide, her hands to her lips, seemed shocked by what I had said. My own words appeared to hang congealed in the air before the hideous idol.

"Spoken honestly," said Gormon, "although without much mercy for yourself. You judge yourself too harshly, Watcher."

"I spoke to save my hand," I said. "Would you have had me lie?"

He smiled. To Avluela the Changeling said, "Now it's your turn."

Visibly frightened, the little Flier approached the Mouth. Her dainty hand trembled as she inserted it between the slabs of cold stone. I fought back an urge to rush toward her and pull her free of that devilish grimacing head.

"Who will question her?" I asked.

"I," said Gormon.

Avluela's wings stirred faintly beneath her garments. Her face grew pale; her nostrils flickered, her upper lip slid over the lower one. She stood slouched against the wall, staring in horror at the termination of her arm. Outside the chamber vague faces peered at us, lips moved in what no doubt were expressions of impatience over our lengthy visit to the Mouth; but we heard nothing. The atmosphere around us was warm and clammy, with a musty tang like that which would come from a well that was driven through the structure of Time.

Gormon said slowly, "This night past you allowed your body to be possessed by the Prince of Roum. Before that, you granted yourself to the Changeling Gormon, although such liaisons are forbidden by custom and law. Much prior to that you were the mate of a Flier, now deceased. You may have had other men, but I know nothing of them, and for the purposes of my question they are not relevant. Tell me this, Avluela: which of the three gave you the most intense physical pleasure, which of the three aroused your deepest emotions, and which of the three would you choose as a mate, if you were choosing a mate?"

I wanted to protest that the Changeling had asked her three questions, not one, and so had taken unfair advantage. But I had no chance to speak, because Avluela replied unfalteringly, hand wedged deep into the Mouth of Truth, "The Prince of Roum gave me greater pleasure of the body than I had ever known before, but he is cold and cruel, and I despise him. My dead Flier I loved more deeply than any person before or since, but he was weak, and I would not have wanted a weakling as a mate. You, Gormon, seem almost a stranger to me even now, and I feel that I know neither your body nor your soul, and yet, though the gulf between us is so wide, it is you with whom I would spend my days to come."

She drew her hand from the Mouth of Truth.

"Well spoken!" said Gormon, though the accuracy of her words had clearly wounded as well as pleased him. "Suddenly you find eloquence, eh, when the circumstances demand it? And now the turn is mine to risk my hand."

He neared the Mouth. I said, "You have asked the first two questions. Do you wish to finish the job and ask the third as well?"

"Hardly," he said. He made a negligent gesture with his free hand. "Put your heads together and agree on a joint question."

Avluela and I conferred. With uncharacteristic forwardness she proposed a question; and since it was the one I would have asked, I accepted and told her to ask it.

She said, "When we stood before the globe of the world, Gormon, I asked you to show me the place where you were born, and you said you were unable to find it on the map. That seemed most strange. Tell me now: are you what you say you are, a Changeling who wanders the world?"

He replied, "I am not."

In a sense he had satisfied the question as Avluela had phrased it; but it went without saying that his reply was inadequate, and without removing his hand from the Mouth of Truth he continued, "I did not show my birthplace to you on the globe because I was born nowhere on this globe, but on a world of a star I must not name. I am no Changeling in your meaning of the word, though by some definitions I am, for my body is somewhat disguised, and on my own world I wear a different flesh. I have lived here ten years."

"What was your purpose in coming to Earth?" I asked.

"I am obliged only to answer one question," said Gormon. Then he smiled. "But I give you an answer anyway: I was sent to Earth in the capacity of a military observer, to prepare the way for the invasion for which you have Watched so long and in which you have ceased to believe, and which will be upon you in a matter now of some hours."

"Lies!" I bellowed. "All *lies*!"

Gormon laughed. And drew his hand from the Mouth of Truth, intact, unharmed.

IX

Numb with confusion, I fled with my cart of instruments from that gleaming sphere and emerged into a street suddenly cold and dark. Night had come with winter's swiftness; it was almost the ninth hour, and almost the time for me to Watch once more.

Gormon's mockery thundered in my brain. He had arranged everything: he had maneuvered us into the Mouth of Truth, he had wrung a confession of lost faith from me and a confession of a different sort from Avluela, he had mercilessly volunteered information he need not have revealed, spoken words calculated to split me to the core.

Was the Mouth of Truth a fraud? Could Gormon lie and emerge unscathed?

Never since I first took up my tasks had I Watched at anything but my appointed hours. This was a time of crumbling realities; I could not wait for the ninth hour to come round. Crouching in the windy street, I opened my cart, readied my equipment and sank like a diver into Watchfulness.

My amplified consciousness roared toward the stars.

Godlike I roamed infinity. I felt the rush of the solar wind, but I was no Flier to be hurled to destruction by that pressure, and I soared past it, beyond the reach of those angry particles of light, into the blackness at the edge of the sun's dominion. Down upon me there beat a different pressure.

Starships coming near.

Not the tourist lines, bringing sightseers to gape at our diminished world. Not the registered mercantile transport vessels, nor the scoopships that collect the interstellar vapors, nor the resort craft on their hyperbolic orbits.

These were military craft, dark, alien, menacing. I could not tell their number; I knew only that they sped Earthward at many lights, nudging a cone of deflected energies before them, and it was that cone that I sensed, that I had felt also the night before, booming into mind through my instruments, engulfing me like a cube of crystal through which stress patterns play and shine.

All my life I had Watched for this.

I had been trained to sense it. I had prayed that I never would sense it, and then in my emptiness I had prayed that I *would* sense it, and then I had ceased to believe in it. And then by grace of the Changeling

Gormon I had sensed it after all, Watching ahead of my hour, crouching in a cold Roumish street just outside the Mouth of Truth.

In his training a Watcher is instructed to break from his Watchfulness as soon as his observations are confirmed by a careful check, so that he can sound the alarm. Obediently I made my check, shifting from one channel to another to another, triangulating and still picking up that foreboding sensation of titanic force rushing upon Earth at unimaginable speed.

Either I was deceived, or the invasion was come. But I could not shake from my trance to give the alarm.

Lingeringly, lovingly, I drank in the sensory data for what seemed like hours. I fondled my equipment, draining from it the total affirmation of faith that my readings gave me. Dimly I warned myself that I was wasting vital time, that it was my duty to leave this lewd caressing of destiny and summon the Defenders.

And at last I burst free of Watchfulness and returned to the world I was guarding.

Avluela was beside me, dazed, terrified, her knuckles to her teeth, her eyes blank.

"Watcher! Watcher, do you hear me? What's happening? What's going to happen?"

"The invasion," I said. "How long was I under?"

"About half a minute. I don't know. Your eyes were closed. I thought you were dead."

"Gormon was speaking the truth! The *invasion* is almost here. Where is he? Where did he go?"

"He vanished as we came away from that place with the Mouth," Avluela whispered. "Watcher, I'm frightened. I feel everything collapsing. I have to fly—I can't stay down here now!"

"Wait," I said, clutching at her and missing her arm. "Don't go now. First I have to give the alarm, and then—"

But she was already stripping off her clothing. Bare to the waist, her pale body gleamed in the evening light, while about us people were rushing to and fro in ignorance of all that was about to occur. I wanted to keep Avluela beside me, but I could delay no longer in giving the alarm, and I turned away from her, back to my cart.

As though caught up in a dream born of overripe longings I reached for the node that I had never used, the one that would send forth a planetwide alert to the Defenders.

Had the alarm already been given? Had some other Watcher sensed what I had sensed and, less paralyzed by bewilderment and doubt, performed a Watcher's final task?

No. No. For then I would be hearing the sirens' shriek reverberating from the orbiting loudspeakers above the city.

I touched the node. From the corner of my eye I saw Avluela, free of her encumbrances now, kneeling to say her words, filling her tender wings with strength. In a moment she would be in the air, beyond my grasp.

With a single swift tug I activated the alarm.

In that instant I became aware of a burly figure striding toward us. Gormon, I thought; and as I rose from my equipment I reached out to him, wanting to seize him and hold him fast. But he who approached was not Gormon but some officious dough-faced Servitor who said to Avluela, "Go easy, Flier, let your wings drop. The Prince of Roum sends me to bring you to his presence."

He grappled with her. Her little breasts heaved; her eyes flashed anger at him.

"Let go of me! I'm going to fly!"

"The Prince of Roum summons you," the Servitor said, enclosing her in his heavy arms.

"The Prince of Roum will have other distractions tonight," I said. "He'll have no need of her."

As I spoke the sirens began to sing from the skies.

The Servitor released her. His mouth worked noiselessly for an instant; he made one of the protective gestures of the Will; he looked skyward and grunted, "The alarm! Who gave the alarm? You, old Watcher?"

Figures rushed about insanely in the streets.

Avluela, freed, sped past me—on foot, her wings but half-furled—and was swallowed up in the surging throng. Over the terrifying sound of the sirens came booming messages from the public annunciators, giving instructions for defense and safety. A lanky man with the mark of the guild of Defenders upon his cheek rushed up to me, shouted words too incoherent to be understood and sped on down the street. The world seemed to have gone mad.

Only I remained calm. I looked to the skies, half expecting to see the invaders' black ships already hovering above the towers of Roum. But I saw nothing except the hovering night lights and the other objects one might expect overhead.

"Gormon?" I called. "Avluela?"

I was alone.

A strange emptiness swept over me. I had given the alarm. The in-

vaders were on their way; I had lost my occupation. There was no need
of Watchers now.

Almost lovingly I touched the worn cart that had been my companion for so many years. I ran my fingers over its stained and pitted instruments; and then I looked away, abandoning it, and went down the
dark streets cartless, burdenless, a man whose life had found and lost
meaning in the same instant. And about me raged chaos.

x

It was understood that when the moment of Earth's final battle arrived, all guilds would be mobilized, the Watchers alone exempted.
We who had manned the perimeter of defense for so long had no part
in the strategy of combat; we were discharged by the giving of a true
alarm. Now it was the time of the guild of Defenders to show its capabilities. They had planned for half a cycle what they would do in time
of war. What plans would they call forth now? What deeds would they
direct?

My only concern was to return to the loyal hostelry and wait out
the crisis. It was hopeless to think of finding Avluela, and I pummelled
myself savagely for having let her slip away like that, naked and without a protector, in that confused moment. Where would she go? Who
would shield her?

A fellow Watcher, pulling his cart madly along, nearly collided with
me. "Careful!" I snapped.

He looked up, breathless, stunned. "Is it true?" he asked. "The
alarm?"

"Can't you hear?"

"But is it real?"

I pointed to his cart. "You know how to find that out."

"They say the man who gave the alarm was drunk, an old fool who
was turned away from the inn yesterday?"

"It could be so," I admitted.

"But if the alarm is real—!"

Smiling, I said, "If it is, now we all may rest. Good day to you,
Watcher."

"Your cart! Where's your cart?" he shouted at me.

But I had moved past him, toward the mighty carven stone pillar of
some relic of Imperial Roum.

Ancient images were carved on that pillar: battles and victories, foreign monarchs marched in the chains of disgrace through the streets
of Roum, triumphant eagles celebrating imperial grandeur. In my

strange new calmness I stood a while before the column of stone, admiring its elegant engravings. Toward me rushed a frenzied figure whom I recognized as the Rememberer Basil; I hailed him, saying, "How timely you come! Do me the kindness of explaining these images, Rememberer. They fascinate me, and my curiosity is aroused."

"Are you insane? Can't you hear the alarm?"

"I gave the alarm, Rememberer."

"Flee, then! Invaders come! We must fight!"

"Not I, Basil. Now my time is over. Tell me of these images. These beaten kings, these broken emperors. Surely a man of your years will not be doing battle."

"All are mobilized now!"

"All but Watchers," I said. "Take a moment. Yearning for the past is born in me. Gormon has vanished; be my guide to these lost cycles."

The Rememberer shook his head wildly, circled around me, and tried to get away. I made a lunge at him, hoping to seize his skinny arm and pin him to the spot; but he eluded me and I caught only his dark shawl, which pulled free and came loose in my hands. Then he was gone, his spindly limbs pumping madly as he fled down the street and left my view.

I shrugged and examined the shawl I had so unexpectedly acquired. It was shot through with glimmering threads of metal, arranged in intricate patterns that teased the eye: it seemed to me that each strand disappeared into the weave of the fabric, only to reappear at some improbable point, like the lineage of dynasties unexpectedly revived in distant cities. The workmanship was superb. Idly I draped the shawl about my shoulders.

I walked on.

My legs, which had been on the verge of failing me earlier in the day, now served me well. In renewed youthfulness I made my way through the chaotic city, finding no difficulties about choosing my route. I headed for the river, then crossed it and, on the Tver's far side, sought the palace of the Prince. The night had deepened, for most lights were extinguished under the mobilization orders, and from time to time a dull boom signaled the explosion of a screening bomb overhead, liberating clouds of murk that shielded the city from most forms of longrange scrutiny. There were fewer pedestrians in the streets. The sirens still cried out. Atop the buildings the defensive installations were going into action; I heard the bleeping sounds of repellors warming up and saw long spidery arms of amplification booms swinging from tower to tower as they linked for maximum output. I had no doubt now that the invasion actually was coming. My own instruments might have been fouled by inner confusion, but they would not have proceeded thus far with the mobilization if the initial report had not been confirmed by the findings of hundreds of other members of my guild.

As I neared the palace a pair of breathless Rememberers sped toward me, their shawls flapping behind them. They called to me in words I did not comprehend—some code of their guild, I realized, recollecting that I wore Basil's shawl. I could not reply, and they rushed upon me, still gabbling; and switching to the language of ordinary men they said, "What is the matter with you? To your post! We must record! We must comment! We must observe!"

"You mistake me," I said mildly. "I keep this shawl only for your brother Basil, who left it in my care. I have no post to guard at this time."

"A Watcher," they cried in unison and cursed me separately and ran on. I laughed and went to the palace.

Its gates stood open. The neuters who had guarded the outer portal were gone, as were the two Indexers who had stood just within the door. The beggars that had thronged the vast plaza had jostled their way into the building itself to seek shelter; this had awakened the anger of the licensed hereditary mendicants whose customary stations were in that part of the building, and they had fallen upon the inflowing refugees with fury and unexpected strength. I saw cripples lashing out with their crutches held as clubs; I saw blind men landing blows with suspicious accuracy; meek penitents were wielding a variety of weapons ranging from stilettos to sonic pistols. Holding myself aloof from this shameless spectacle I penetrated to the inner recesses of the palace, peering into chapels where I saw Pilgrims beseeching the blessings of the Will and Communicants desperately seeking spiritual guidance as to the outcome of the coming conflict.

Abruptly I heard the blare of trumpets and cries of, "Make way! Make way!"

A file of sturdy Servitors marched into the palace, striding toward the Prince's chambers in the apse. Several of them held a struggling, kicking, frantic figure with half-unfolded wings: Avluela! I called out to her, but my voice died in the din, nor could I reach her. The Servitors shoved me aside. The procession vanished into the princely chambers. I caught a final glimpse of the little Flier, pale and small in the grip of her captors, and then she was gone once more.

I seized a bumbling neuter who had been moving uncertainly.

"That Flier! Why was she brought here?"

"He—he—they—"

"Tell me!"

"The Prince—his woman—in his chariot—he—he—they—the invaders—"

I pushed the flabby creature aside and rushed toward the apse. A brazen wall ten times my own height confronted me. I pounded on it. "Avluela!" I shouted hoarsely. "Av . . . lu . . . ela . . . !"

I was neither thrust away nor admitted. I was ignored. The bedlam at the western doors of the palace had extended itself now to the nave and aisles, and as the ragged beggars boiled toward me I executed a quick turn and found myself passing through one of the side doors of the palace.

I stood in the courtyard that led to the royal hostelry, suspended and passive. A strange electricity crackled in the air. I assumed it was an emanation from one of Roum's defense installations, some kind of beam designed to screen the city from attack. But an instant later I realized that it presaged the actual arrival of the invaders.

Starships blazed in the heavens.

When I had perceived them in my Watching they had appeared black against the infinite blackness, but now they burned with the radiance of suns. A stream of bright, hard, jewel-like globes bedecked the sky; they were ranged side by side, stretching from east to west in a continuous band, filling all the celestial arch, and as they erupted simultaneously into being it seemed to me that I heard the crash and throb of an invisible symphony heralding the arrival of the conquerors of Earth.

I do not know how far above me the starships were, nor how many of them hovered there, nor any of the details of their design. I know only that in sudden massive majesty they were there. If I had been a Defender my soul would have withered instantly at the sight.

Across the heavens shot light of many hues. The battle had been joined. I could not comprehend the actions of our warriors, and I was equally baffled by the maneuvers of those who had come to take possession of our history-crusted but time-diminished planet. To my shame I felt not only out of the struggle but above the struggle, as though this were no quarrel of mine. I wanted Avluela beside me, and she was somewhere within the depths of the palace of the Prince of Roum. Even Gormon would have been a comfort now, Gormon the Changeling, Gormon the spy, Gormon the monstrous betrayer of our world.

Gigantic amplified voices bellowed, "Make way for the Prince of

Roum! The Prince of Roum leads the Defenders in the battle for the fatherworld!"

From the palace emerged a shining vehicle the shape of a teardrop, in whose bright-metalled roof a transparent sheet had been mounted so that all the populace could see and take heart in the presence of the ruler. At the controls of the vehicle sat the Prince of Roum, proudly erect, his cruel, youthful features fixed in harsh determination; and beside him, robed like an empress, I beheld the slight figure of the Flier Avluela. She seemed in a trance.

The royal chariot soared upward and was lost in the darkness.

It seemed to me that a second vehicle appeared and followed its path, and that the Prince's reappeared, and that the two flew in tight circles, apparently locked in combat. Clouds of blue sparks wrapped both chariots now; and then they swung high and far and were lost to me behind one of the hills of Roum.

Was the battle raging all over the planet, now? Was Perris in jeopardy, and holy Jorslem, and even the sleepy isles of the Lost Continents? Did starships hover everywhere? I did not know. I perceived events in only one small segment of the sky over Roum, and even there my awareness of what was taking place was dim, uncertain and ill-informed. There were momentary flashes of light in which I saw battalions of Fliers streaming across the sky; and then darkness returned as though a velvet shroud had been hurled over the city. In fitful bursts I saw the great machines of our defense speaking from the tops of our towers; and yet I saw the starships untouched, unharmed, unmoved above. The courtyard in which I stood was deserted, but in the distance I heard voices, full of fear and foreboding, shouting in tinny tones that might have been the screeching of birds. Occasionally there came a booming sound that rocked all the city.

Once a platoon of Somnambulists was driven past where I was. In the plaza fronting the palace I observed what appeared to be an array of Clowns unfolding some sort of sparkling netting of a military look. By one flash of lightning I was able to see a trio of Rememberers soaring aloft on a gravity plate, making copious notes of all that elapsed. It seemed—I was not sure—that the vehicle of the Prince of Roum returned, speeding across the sky with its pursuer clinging close. "Avluela," I whispered, as the twin dots of lights left my sight. Were the starships disgorging troops? Did colossal pylons of force spiral down from those orbiting brightnesses to touch the surface of the Earth? Why had the Prince seized Avluela? Where was Gormon? What were our Defenders doing? Why were the enemy ships not blasted from the sky?

Rooted to the ancient cobbles of the courtyard, I observed the cosmic battle in total lack of understanding throughout the long night.

Dawn came. Strands of pale light looped from tower to tower. I touched fingers to my eyes, realizing that I must have slept while standing. Perhaps I should apply for membership in the guild of Somnambulists, I told myself lightly. I put my hands to the Rememberer's shawl about my shoulders, wondering how I had managed to acquire it, and the answer came.

I looked toward the sky.

The alien starships were gone. I saw only the ordinary morning sky, gray with pinkness breaking through. I felt the jolt of compulsion and looked about for my cart, and reminded myself that I need do no more Watching, and I felt more empty than one would ordinarily feel at such an hour.

Was the battle over?

Had the enemy been conquered?

Were the ships of the invaders blasted from the sky and lying in charred ruin outside Roum?

All was silent. I heard no more celestial symphonies. Then, out of the eerie stillness there came a new sound, a rumbling noise as of wheeled vehicles passing through the streets of the city. And the invisible Musicians played one final note, deep and resonant, which trailed away jaggedly as though every string had been broken at once.

Over the speakers used for public announcements came quiet words: "Roum is fallen. Roum is fallen."

### XI

The royal hostelry was untended. Neuters and members of the servant guilds all had fled. Defenders, Masters and Dominators must have perished honorably in combat. Basil the Rememberer was nowhere about; likewise none of his brethren. I went to my room, cleansed and refreshed and fed myself, gathered my few possessions and bade farewell to the luxuries I had known so briefly. I regretted that I had had such a short time to visit Roum; but at least Gormon had been a most excellent guide, and I had seen a great deal.

Now I proposed to move on.

It did not seem prudent to remain in a conquered city. My room's thinking cap did not respond to my queries, and so I did not know what the extent of the defeat was, here or in other regions, but it was evident to me that Roum at least had passed from human control, and I wished to depart quickly. I weighed the thought of going to Jorslem, as that tall Pilgrim had suggested upon my entry into Roum. But then I reflected and chose a westward route, toward Perris, which not only was closer but held the headquarters of the Rememberers.

My own occupation had been destroyed; but on this first morning of Earth's conquest I felt a sudden powerful and strange yearning to offer myself humbly to the Rememberers and seek with them knowledge of our more glittering yesterdays.

At midday I left the hostelry. I walked first to the palace, which still stood open. The beggars lay strewn about, some drugged, some sleeping, most dead; from the crude manner of their death I saw that they must have slain one another in their panic and frenzy. A despondent-looking Indexer squatted beside the three skulls of the interrogation fixture in the chapel. As I entered he said, "No use. The brains do not reply."

"How goes it with the Prince of Roum?"

"Dead. The invaders shot him from the sky."

"A young Flier rode beside him. What do you know of her?"

"Nothing. Dead, I suppose."

"And the city?"

"Fallen. Invaders are everywhere."

"Killing?"

"Not even looting," the Indexer said. "They are most gentle. They have *collected* us."

"In Roum alone, or everywhere?"

The man shrugged. He began to rock rhythmically back and forth. I let him be, and walked deeper into the palace. To my surprise, the imperial chambers of the Prince were unsealed. I went within, awed by the sumptuous luxury of the hangings, the draperies, the lights, the furnishings. I passed from room to room, coming at last to the royal bed, whose coverlet was the flesh of a colossal bivalve of the planet of another star, and as the shell yawned for me I touched the infinitely soft fabric under which the Prince of Roum had lain, and I recalled that Avluela too had lain here, and if I had been a younger man I would certainly have wept.

I left the palace and slowly crossed the plaza to begin my journey toward Perris.

As I departed I had my first glimpse of our conquerors. A vehicle of alien design drew up at the plaza's rim, and perhaps a dozen figures emerged.

They might almost have been human. They were tall and broad, deep-chested, as Gormon had been, and only the extreme length of their arms marked them instantly as alien. Their skins were of strange texture, and if I had been closer I suspect I would have seen eyes and lips and nostrils that were not of a human design. Taking no notice of me, they crossed the plaza, walking in a curious loose-jointed loping way that reminded me irresistibly of Gormon's stride, and entered the palace. They seemed neither swaggering nor belligerent.

Sightseers. Majestic Roum once more exerted its magnetism upon strangers.

Leaving our new masters to their amusement, I walked off, toward the outskirts of the city. The bleakness of eternal winter crept into my soul. I wondered: did I feel sorrow that Roum had fallen? Or did I mourn the loss of Avluela? Or was it only that I now missed three successive Watchings, and like an addict I was experiencing the pangs of withdrawal?

It was all of these that pained me, I decided. But mostly the last.

No one was abroad in the city as I made for the gates. Fear of the masters kept the Roumish in hiding, I supposed. From time to time one of the alien vehicles hummed past, but I was unmolested. I came to the city's western gate late in the afternoon. It was open, revealing to me a gently rising hill on whose breast rose trees with dark green crowns. I passed through, and saw a short distance beyond the gate the figure of a Pilgrim who was shuffling slowly away from the city.

His faltering, uncertain walk seemed strange to me, for not even his thick brown robes could hide the strength and youth of his body; he stood erect, his shoulders square and his back straight, and yet he walked with the hesitating, trembling step of an old man. When I drew abreast of him and peered under his hood I understood, for affixed to the bronze mask all Pilgrims wear was a reverberator, such as is used by blind men to warn them of obstacles and hazards. He became aware of me and said, "I am a sightless Pilgrim. I pray you do not molest me."

It was not a Pilgrim's voice. It was a strong and harsh and imperious voice.

I replied, "I molest no one. I am a Watcher who has lost his occupation this night past."

"Many occupations were lost this night past, Watcher."

"Surely not a Pilgrim's."

"No," he said. "Not a Pilgrim's."

"Where are you bound?"

"Away from Roum."

"No particular destination?"

"No," the Pilgrim said. "None. I will wander."

"Perhaps we should wander together," I said, for it is accounted good luck to travel with a Pilgrim, and, shorn of my Flier and my Changeling, I would otherwise have traveled alone. "My destination is Perris. Will you come?"

"There as well as anywhere else," he said bitterly. "Yes. We will go to Perris together. But what business does a Watcher have there?"

"A Watcher has no business anywhere. I go to Perris to offer myself in service to the Rememberers."

"Ah."

"With Earth fallen, I wish to learn more of Earth in its pride."

"Is all Earth fallen, then, and not only Roum?"

"I think it is so," I said.

"Ah," replied the Pilgrim. "Ah!"

He fell silent, and we went onward. I gave him my arm, and now he shuffled no longer, but moved with a young man's brisk stride. From time to time he uttered what might have been a sigh or a smothered sob. When I asked him details of his Pilgrimage, he answered obliquely or not at all. When we were an hour's journey outside Roum, and already amid forests, he said suddenly, "This mask gives me pain. Will you help me adjust it?"

To my amazement he began to remove it. I gasped, for it is forbidden for a Pilgrim to reveal his face. Had he forgotten that I was not sightless too?

As the mask came away he said, "You will not welcome this sight."

The bronze grillwork slipped down from his forehead, and I saw first eyes that had been newly blinded, gaping holes where no surgeon's knife but possibly thrusting fingers had penetrated, and then the sharp regal nose, and finally the quirked, taut lips of the Prince of Roum.

"Your Majesty!" I cried.

Trails of dried blood ran down his cheeks. About the raw sockets themselves were smears of ointment. He felt little pain, for he had killed it with those green smears, but the pain that burst through me was real and potent.

"Majesty no longer," he said. "Help me with the mask!" His hands trembled as he held it forth. "These flanges must be widened. They press cruelly at my cheeks. Here—here—"

Quickly I made the adjustments, so that I would not have to see his face for long.

He replaced the mask.

In silence we continued. I had no way of making small talk with such a man. It would be a somber journey for us to Perris; but I was committed now to be his guide. I thought of Gormon and how well he had kept his vows. I thought too of Avluela, and a hundred times the words leaped to my tongue to ask the fallen Prince how his consort the Flier had fared in the night of defeat, and I did not ask.

Twilight gathered, but the sun still gleamed golden-red before us in the west. And suddenly I halted, and made a hoarse sound of surprise deep in my throat, as a shadow passed overhead.

High above me Avluela soared. Her skin was stained by the colors of the sunset, and her wings were spread to their fullest, radiant with every hue of the spectrum. She was already at least the height of a hundred men above the ground, and still climbing, and to her I must have been only a speck among the trees.

"What is it?" the Prince asked. "What do you see?"

"Nothing."

"Tell me what you see!"

I could not deceive him. "I see a Flier, your Majesty. A slim girl far aloft."

"Then the night must have come."

"No," I said. "The sun is still above the horizon."

"How can that be? She can have only nightwings. The sun would hurl her to the ground."

I hesitated. I could not bring myself to explain how it was that Avluela flew by day, though she had only nightwings. I could not tell the Prince of Roum that beside her, wingless, flew the invader Gormon, effortlessly moving through the air, his arm about her thin shoulders, steadying her, supporting her, helping her resist the pressure of the solar wind.

"Well?" he demanded. "How does she fly by day?"

"I do not know," I said. "It is a mystery to me. There are many things nowadays I can no longer understand."

The Prince appeared to accept that. "Yes, Watcher. Many things none of us can understand."

He fell once more into silence. I yearned to call out to Avluela, but I knew she could not and would not hear me, and so I walked on toward the sunset, toward Perris, leading the blinded Prince. And over us Avluela and Gormon sped onward, limned sharply against the day's last glow, until they climbed so high they were lost to my sight.

# Poul Anderson

In every field there is such a thing as an "old-pro." Usually, they are the reliables, the ones who can be counted on to do the hard work, to do it well, and to do it quickly. What's more, they do it with a minimum of headache and heartache.

It's a funny thing but it is usually the rank amateur who throws a fit over a changed comma; or who sinks back, bleeding, over the necessary editorial touch.

Science fiction has a hard job keeping its old pros, however. It is a notoriously poorly paying field and a notoriously demanding one. Those who write science fiction must not only develop all the usual skills of any writer; they must also learn how to extrapolate new societies; incorporate science cleverly; and keep forever up to date in the most inexorably changing field in the world.

Many don't manage to reach the point where they more than marginally qualify. But some learn in these exacting surroundings and come to be in great demand. They can write science fiction for the national magazines that pay well. They can write for movies and television. They can write popular-science, or other brands of non-fiction.

Everything else pays more than science fiction and the temptation to "graduate" is enormous. With hanging head and quivering lip, I must admit that I am not one of those who resisted graduation. Except for my monthly articles in *The Magazine of Fantasy and Science Fiction* I hardly appear in the science fiction magazines any more. (Oh, occasionally I do; I am not an utter villain.)

Just the same, let us honor the outstanding practitioners who are skillful enough to win Hugos, yet who have been stanchly serving as bulwarks of the magazine field for twenty years and more. Fritz Leiber's first story in the magazines appeared in 1939; Jack Vance's in 1945, and Gordon Dickson's in 1950.

Still, for a combination of quantity and quality, I would like to nominate good old Poul Anderson. His first story, as I recall, appeared in 1947 and I don't think a year has passed since then without his having contributed several good stories to the field. It's not that he can't do anything more lucrative. I know he can. It's that he has science fiction in him and, thank goodness, he wants to get it out.

Of course, not everything about Poul is to be admired. Many anthologies, listings, publisher's blurbs, etc. list authors alphabetically, which is exactly the way to do it, as we would all agree. By that system, I am very often in first place, where I belong. But whenever Poul is also present, it is he who takes pride of position because An comes ahead of As.

Obviously Poul must be doing that on purpose and you will have to admit it's rather mean of him.

# 12

# THE SHARING OF FLESH

Moru understood about guns. At least the tall strangers had demonstrated to their guides what the things that each of them carried at his hip could do in a flash and a flameburst. But he did not realize that the small objects they often moved about in their hands, while talking in their own language, were audiovisual transmitters. Probably he thought they were fetishes.

Thus, when he killed Donli Sairn, he did so in full view of Donli's wife.

That was happenstance. Except for prearranged times at morning and evening of the planet's twenty-eight-hour day, the biologist, like his fellows, sent only to his computer. But because they had not been married long and were helplessly happy, Evalyth received his 'casts whenever she could get away from her own duties.

The coincidence that she was tuned in at that one moment was not great. There was little for her to do. As militech of the expedition—she being from a half barbaric part of Kraken where the sexes had equal opportunities to learn arts of combat suitable to primitive environments—she had overseen the building of a compound; and she kept the routines of guarding it under a close eye. However, the inhabitants of Lokon were as cooperative with the visitors from heaven as mutual mysteriousness allowed. Every instinct and experience assured Evalyth Sairn that their reticence masked nothing except awe, with perhaps a wistful hope of friendship. Captain Jonafer agreed. Her position having thus become rather a sinecure, she was trying to learn enough about Donli's work to be a useful assistant after he returned from the lowlands.

Also, a medical test had lately confirmed that she was pregnant. She wouldn't tell him, she decided, not yet, over all those hundreds of kilometers, but rather when they lay again together. Meanwhile, the knowledge that they had begun a new life made him a lodestar to her.

On the afternoon of his death she entered the bio-lab whistling. Outside, sunlight struck fierce and brass-colored on dusty ground, on prefab shacks huddled about the boat which had brought everyone and everything down from the orbit where *New Dawn* circled, on the parked flitters and gravsleds that took men around the big island that was the only habitable land on this globe, on the men and the women themselves. Beyond the stockade, plumy treetops, a glimpse of mudbrick buildings, a murmur of voices and mutter of footfalls, a drift of bitter woodsmoke, showed that a town of several thousand people sprawled between here and Lake Zelo.

The bio-lab occupied more than half the structure where the Sairns lived. Comforts were few, when ships from a handful of cultures struggling back to civilization ranged across the ruins of empire. For Evalyth, though, it sufficed that this was their home. She was used to austerity anyway. One thing that had first attracted her to Donli, meeting him on Kraken, was the cheerfulness with which he, a man from Atheia, which was supposed to have retained or regained almost as many amenities as Old Earth knew in its glory, had accepted life in her gaunt grim country.

The gravity field here was 0.77 standard, less than two-thirds of what she had grown in. Her gait was easy through the clutter of apparatus and specimens. She was a big young woman, good-looking in the body, a shade too strong in the features for most men's taste outside her own folk. She had their blondness and, on legs and forearms, their intricate tattoos; the blaster at her waist had come down through many generations. Otherwise she had abandoned Krakener costume for the plain coveralls of the expedition.

How cool and dim the shack was! She sighed with pleasure, sat down, and activated the receiver. As the image formed, three-dimensional in the air, and Donli's voice spoke, her heart sprang a little.

"—appears to be descended from a clover."

The image was of plants with green trilobate leaves, scattered low among the reddish native pseudo-grasses. It swelled as Donli brought the transmitter near so that the computer might record details for later analysis. Evalyth frowned, trying to recall what . . . Oh, yes. Clover was another of those life forms that man had brought with him from Old Earth, to more planets than anyone now remembered, before the Long Night fell. Often they were virtually unrecognizable; over thousands of years, evolution had fitted them to alien conditions, or mutation and genetic drift had acted on small initial populations in a nearly random fashion. No one on Kraken had known that pines and gulls and rhizobacteria were altered immigrants, until Donli's crew arrived and identified them. Not that he, or anybody from this part of the galaxy, had yet made it back to the mother world. But the Atheian data banks were packed with information, and so was Donli's dear curly head—

And there was his hand, huge in the field of view, gathering specimens. She wanted to kiss it. *Patience, patience,* the officer part of her reminded the bride. *We're here to work. We've discovered one more lost colony, the most wretched one so far, sunken back to utter primitivism. Our duty is to advise the Board whether a civilizing mission is worthwhile, or whether the slender resources that the Allied Planets can spare had better be used elsewhere, leaving these people in their misery for another two or three hundred years. To make an honest report, we must study them, their cultures, their world. That's why I'm in the barbarian highlands and he's down in the jungle among out-and-out savages.*

*Please finish soon, darling.*

She heard Donli speak in the lowland dialect. It was a debased form of Lokonese, which in turn was remotely descended from Anglic. The expedition's linguists had unraveled the language in a few intensive weeks. Then all personnel took a brain-feed in it. Nonetheless, she admired how quickly her man had become fluent in the woodsrunners' version, after mere days of conversation with them.

"Are we not coming to the place, Moru? You said the thing was close by our camp."

"We are nearly arrived, man-from-the-clouds."

A tiny alarm struck within Evalyth. What was going on? Donli hadn't left his companions to strike off alone with a native, had he? Rogar of Lokon had warned them to beware of treachery in those parts. But, to be sure, only yesterday the guides had rescued Haimie Fiell when he tumbled into a swift-running river . . . at some risk to themselves. . . .

The view bobbed as the transmitter swung in Donli's grasp. It made Evalyth a bit dizzy. From time to time, she got glimpses of the broader setting. Forest crowded about a game trail, rust-colored leafage, brown trunks and branches, shadows beyond, the occasional harsh call of something unseen. She could practically feel the heat and dank weight of the atmosphere, smell the unpleasant pungencies. This world—which no longer had a name, except World, because the dwellers upon it had forgotten what the stars really were—was ill suited to colonization. The life it had spawned was often poisonous, always nutritionally deficient. With the help of species they had brought along, men survived marginally. The original settlers doubtless meant to improve matters. But then the breakdown came—evidence was that their single town had been missiled out of existence, a majority of the people with it—and resources were lacking to rebuild; the miracle was that anything human remained except bones.

"Now here, man-from-the-clouds."

The swaying scene grew steady. Silence hummed from jungle to cabin. "I do not see anything," Donli said at length.

"Follow me. I show."

Donli put his transmitter in the fork of a tree. It scanned him and Moru while they moved across a meadow. The guide looked childish beside the space traveler, barely up to his shoulder; an old child, though, near-naked body seamed with scars and lame in the right foot from some injury of the past, face wizened in a great black bush of hair and beard. He, who could not hunt but could only fish and trap to support his family, was even more impoverished than his fellows. He must have been happy indeed when the flitter landed near their village and the strangers offered fabulous trade goods for a week or two of being shown around the countryside. Donli had projected the image of Moru's straw hut for Evalyth—the pitiful few possessions, the woman already worn out with toil, the surviving sons who, at ages said to be about seven or eight, which would equal twelve or thirteen standard years, were shriveled gnomes.

Rogar seemed to declare—the Lokonese tongue was by no means perfectly understood yet—that the lowlanders would be less poor if they weren't such a vicious lot, tribe forever at war with tribe. *But really,* Evalyth thought, *what possible menace can they be?*

Moru's gear consisted of a loinstrap, a cord around his body for preparing snares, an obsidian knife, and a knapsack so woven and greased that it could hold liquids at need. The other men of his group, being able to pursue game and to win a share of booty by taking part in battles, were noticeably better off. They didn't look much different in person, however. Without room for expansion, the island populace must be highly inbred.

The dwarfish man squatted, parting a shrub with his hands. "Here," he grunted, and stood up again.

Evalyth knew well the eagerness that kindled in Donli. Nevertheless he turned around, smiled straight into the transmitter, and said in Atheian: "Maybe you're watching, dearest. If so, I'd like to share this with you. It may be a bird's nest."

She remembered vaguely that the existence of birds would be an ecologically significant datum. What mattered was what he had just said to her. "Oh, yes, oh yes!" she wanted to cry. But his group had only two receivers with them, and he wasn't carrying either.

She saw him kneel in the long, ill-colored vegetation. She saw him reach with the gentleness she also knew, into the shrub, easing its branches aside.

She saw Moru leap upon his back. The savage wrapped legs about Donli's middle. His left hand seized Donli's hair and pulled the head back. The knife flew back in his right.

Blood spurted from beneath Donli's jaw. He couldn't shout, not with his throat gaping open; he could only bubble and croak while Moru haggled the wound wider. He reached blindly for his gun. Moru dropped the knife and caught his arms; they rolled over in that embrace, Donli threshed and flopped in the spouting of his own blood. Moru hung on. The brush trembled around them and hid them, until Moru rose red and dripping, painted, panting, and Evalyth screamed into the transmitter beside her, into the universe, and she kept on screaming and fought them when they tried to take her away from the scene in the meadow where Moru went about his butcher's work, until something stung her with coolness and she toppled into the bottom of the universe whose stars had all gone out forever.

*

Haimie Fiell said through white lips: "No, of course we didn't know till you alerted us. He and that—creature—were several kilometers from our camp. *Why* didn't you let us go after him right away?"

"Because of what we'd seen on the transmission," Captain Jonafer replied. "Sairn was irretrievably dead. You could've been ambushed, arrows in the back or something, pushing down those narrow trails. Best stay where you were, guarding each other, till we got a vehicle to you."

Fiell looked past the big gray-haired man, out the door of the command hut, to the stockade and the unpitying noon sky. "But what that little monster was doing meanwhile—" Abruptly he closed his mouth.

With equal haste, Jonafer said: "The other guides ran away, you have told me, as soon as they sensed you were angry. I've just had a report from Kallaman. His team flitted to the village. It's deserted. The whole tribe's pulled up stakes. Afraid of our revenge, evidently.

Though it's no large chore to move, when you can carry your household goods on your back and weave a new house in a day."

Evalyth leaned forward. "Stop evading me," she said. "What did Moru do with Donli that you might have prevented if you'd arrived in time?"

Fiell continued to look past her. Sweat gleamed in droplets on his forehead. "Nothing, really," he mumbled. "Nothing that mattered . . . once the murder itself had been committed."

"I meant to ask you what kind of services you want for him, Lieutenant Sairn," Jonafer said to her. "Should the ashes be buried here, or scattered in space after we leave, or brought home?"

Evalyth turned her gaze full upon him. "I never authorized that he be cremated, Captain," she said slowly.

"No, but— Well, be realistic. You were first under anesthesia, then heavy sedation, while we recovered the body. Time had passed. We've no facilities for, um, cosmetic repair, nor any extra refrigeration space, and in this heat—"

Since she had been let out of sickbay, there had been a kind of numbness in Evalyth. She could not entirely comprehend the fact that Donli was gone. It seemed as if at any instant yonder doorway would fill with him, sunlight across his shoulders, and he would call to her, laughing, and console her for a meaningless nightmare she had had. That was the effect of the psycho-drugs, she knew and damned the kindliness of the medic.

She felt almost glad to feel a slow rising anger. It meant the drugs were wearing off. By evening she would be able to weep.

"Captain," she said, "I saw him killed. I've seen deaths before, some of them quite messy. We do not mask the truth on Kraken. You've cheated me of my right to lay my man out and close his eyes. You will not cheat me of my right to obtain justice. I demand to know exactly what happened."

Jonafer's fists knotted on his desktop. "I can hardly stand to tell you."
"But you shall, Captain."

"All right! All right!" Jonafer shouted. The words leaped out like bullets. "We saw the thing transmitted. He stripped Donli, hung him up by the heels from a tree, bled him into that knapsack. He cut off the genitals and threw them in with the blood. He opened the body and took heart, lungs, liver, kidneys, thyroid, prostate, pancreas, and loaded them up too, and ran off into the woods. Do you wonder why we didn't let you see what was left?"

"The Lokonese warned us against the jungle dwellers," Fiell said dully. "We should have listened. But they seemed like pathetic dwarfs. And they did rescue me from the river. When Donli asked about the birds—described them, you know, and asked if anything like that was known—Moru said yes, but they were rare and shy; our gang would scare them off; but if one man would come along with him, he could find a nest and they might see the bird. A house he called it, but Donli thought he meant a nest. Or so he told us. It'd been a talk with Moru when they happened to be a ways offside, in sight but out of earshot. Maybe that should have alerted us, maybe we should have asked the other tribesmen. But we did not see any reason to—I mean, Donli was bigger, stronger, armed with a blaster. What savage would dare attack him? And anyway, they *had* been friendly, downright frolicsome after they got over their initial fear of us, and they'd shown as much eagerness for further contact as anybody here in Lokon has, and—" His voice trailed off.

"Did he steal tools or weapons?" Evalyth asked.

"No," Jonafer said. "I have everything your husband was carrying, ready to give you."

Fiell said: "I don't think it was an act of hatred. Moru must have had some superstitious reason."

Jonafer nodded. "We can't judge him by our standards."

"By whose, then?" Evalyth retorted. Supertranquilizer or no, she was surprised at the evenness of her own tone. "I'm from Kraken, remember. I'll not let Donli's child be born and grow up knowing he was murdered and no one tried to do justice for him."

"You can't take revenge on an entire tribe," Jonafer said.

"I don't mean to. But, Captain, the personnel of this expedition are from several different planets, each with its characteristic societies. The articles specifically state that the essential mores of every member shall be respected. I want to be relieved of my regular duties until I have arrested the killer of my husband and done justice upon him."

Jonafer bent his head. "I have to grant that," he said low.

Evalyth rose. "Thank you, gentlemen," she said. "If you will excuse me, I'll commence my investigation at once."

—While she was still a machine, before the drugs wore off.

\*

In the drier, cooler uplands, agriculture had remained possible after the colony otherwise lost civilization. Fields and orchards, painstakingly cultivated with neolithic tools, supported a scattering of villages and the capital town Lokon.

Its people bore a family resemblance to the forest dwellers. Few settlers indeed could have survived to become the ancestors of this world's humanity. But the highlanders were better nourished, bigger, straighter. They wore gaily dyed tunics and sandals. The well-to-do added jewelry of gold and silver. Hair was braided, chins kept shaven. Folk walked boldly, without the savages' constant fear of ambush, and talked merrily.

To be sure, this was only strictly true of the free. While *New Dawn*'s anthropologists had scarcely begun to unravel the ins and outs of the culture, it had been obvious from the first that Lokon kept a large slave class. Some were sleek household servants. More toiled meek and naked in the fields, the quarries, the mines, under the lash of overseers and the guard of soldiers whose spearheads and swords were of ancient Imperial metal. But none of the space travelers was unduly shocked. They had seen worse elsewhere. Historical data banks described places in olden time called Athens, India, America.

Evalyth strode down twisted, dusty streets, between the gaudily painted walls of cubical, windowless adobe houses. Commoners going about their tasks made respectful salutes. Although no one feared any longer that the strangers meant harm, she did tower above the tallest man, her hair was colored like metal and her eyes like the sky, she bore lightning at her waist and none knew what other godlike powers.

Today soldiers and noblemen also genuflected, while slaves went on their faces. Where she appeared, the chatter and clatter of everyday life vanished; the business of the market plaza halted when she passed the booths; children ceased their games and fled; she moved in silence akin to the silence in her soul. Under the sun and the snowcone of Mount Burus, horror brooded. For by now Lokon knew that a man from the stars had been slain by a lowland brute; and what would come of that?

Word must have gone ahead to Rogar, though, since he awaited her in his house by Lake Zelo next to the Sacred Place. He was not king or council president or high priest, but he was something of all three, and it was he who dealt most with the strangers.

His dwelling was the usual kind, larger than average but dwarfed by the adjacent walls. Those enclosed a huge compound, filled with buildings, where none of the outworlders had been admitted. Guards in scarlet robes and grotesquely carved wooden helmets stood always at its gates. Today their number was doubled, and others flanked Rogar's door. The lake shone like polished steel at their backs. The trees along the shore looked equally rigid.

Rogar's major-domo, a fat elderly slave, prostrated himself in the entrance as Evalyth neared. "If the heaven-borne will deign to follow this unworthy one, *Klev* Rogar is within—" The guards dipped their spears to her. Their eyes were wide and frightened.

Like the other houses, this turned inward. Rogar sat on a dais in a room opening on a courtyard. It seemed doubly cool and dim by contrast with the glare outside. She could scarcely discern the frescos on the walls or the patterns on the carpet; they were crude art anyway. Her attention focused on Rogar. He did not rise, that not being a sign of respect here. Instead, he bowed his grizzled head above folded hands. The major-domo offered her a bench, and Rogar's chief wife set a bombilla of herb tea by her before vanishing.

"Be greeted, *Klev*," Evalyth said formally.

"Be greeted, heaven-borne." Alone now, shadowed from the cruel sun, they observed a ritual period of silence.

Then: "This is terrible what has happened, heaven-borne," Rogar said. "Perhaps you do not know that my white robe and bare feet signify mourning as for one of my own blood."

"That is well done," Evalyth said. "We shall remember."

The man's dignity faltered. "You understand that none of us had anything to do with the evil, do you not? The savages are our enemies too. They are vermin. Our ancestors caught some and made them slaves, but they are good for nothing else. I warned your friends not to go down among those we have not tamed."

"Their wish was to do so," Evalyth replied. "Now my wish is to get revenge for my man." She didn't know if this language included a word for justice. No matter. Because of the drugs, which heightened the logical faculties while they muffled the emotions, she was speaking Lokonese quite well enough for her purposes.

"We can get soldiers and help you kill as many as you choose," Rogar offered.

"Not needful. With this weapon at my side I alone can destroy more than your army might. I want your counsel and help in a different matter. How can I find him who slew my man?"

Rogar frowned. "The savages can vanish into trackless jungles, heaven-borne."

"Can they vanish from other savages, though?"

"Ah! Shrewdly thought, heaven-borne. Those tribes are endlessly at each other's throats. If we can make contact with one, its hunters will soon learn for you where the killer's people have taken themselves." His scowl deepened. "But he must have gone from them, to hide until you have departed our land. A single man might be impossible to find. Lowlanders are good at hiding, of necessity."

"What do you mean by necessity?"

Rogar showed surprise at her failure to grasp what was obvious to him. "Why, consider a man out hunting," he said. "He cannot go with companions after every kind of game, or the noise and scent would frighten it away. So he is often alone in the jungle. Someone from another tribe may well set upon him. A man stalked and killed is just as useful as one slain in open war."

"Why this incessant fighting?"

Rogar's look of bafflement grew stronger. "How else shall they get human flesh?"

"But they do not live on that!"

"No, surely not, except as needed. But that need comes many times as you know. Their wars are their chief way of taking men; booty is good too, but not the main reason to fight. He who slays, owns the corpse, and naturally divides it solely among his close kin. Not everyone is lucky in battle. Therefore these who did not chance to kill in a war may well go hunting on their own, two or three of them together hoping to find a single man from a different tribe. And that is why a lowlander is good at hiding."

Evalyth did not move or speak. Rogar drew a long breath and continued trying to explain: "Heaven-borne, when I heard the evil news, I spoke long with men from your company. They told me what they had seen from afar by the wonderful means you command. Thus it is clear to me what happened. This guide—what is his name? Yes, Moru —he is a cripple. He had no hope of killing himself a man except by treachery. When he saw that chance, he took it."

He ventured a smile. "That would never happen in the highlands," he declared. "We do not fight wars, save when we are attacked, nor do we hunt our fellowmen as if they were animals. Like yours, ours is a civilized race." His lips drew back from startlingly white teeth. "But, heaven-borne, your man was slain. I propose we take vengeance, not simply on the killer if we catch him, but on his tribe, which we can certainly find as you suggested. That will teach all the savages to beware of their betters. Afterward we can share the flesh, half to your people, half to mine."

Evalyth could only know an intellectual astonishment. Yet she had the feeling somehow of having walked off a cliff. She stared through the shadows, into the grave old face, and after a long time she heard herself whisper: "You . . . also . . . here . . . eat men?"

"Slaves," Rogar said. "No more than required. One of them will do for four boys."

Her hand dropped to her gun. Rogar sprang up in alarm. "Heaven-borne," he exclaimed, "I told you we are civilized. Never fear attack from any of us! We—we—"

She rose too, high above him. Did he read judgment in her gaze? Was the terror that snatched him on behalf of his whole people? He cowered from her, sweating and shuddering. "Heaven-borne, believe me, you have no quarrel with Lokon—no, now, let me show you, let me take you into the Sacred Place, even if you are no initiate . . . for surely you are akin to the gods, surely the gods will not be offended—Come, let me show you how it is, let me prove we have no will and no *need* to be your enemies—"

There was the gate that Rogar opened for her in that massive wall. There were the shocked countenances of the guards and loud promises of many sacrifices to appease the Powers. There was the stone pavement beyond, hot and hollowly resounding underfoot. There were the idols grinning around a central temple. There was the house of the acolytes who did the work and who shrank in fear when they saw their master conduct a foreigner in. There were the slave barracks.

"See, heaven-borne, they are well treated, are they not? We do have to crush their hands and feet when we choose them as children for this service. Think how dangerous it would be otherwise, hundreds of boys and young men in here. But we treat them kindly unless they misbehave. Are they not fat? Their own Holy Food is especially honorable, bodies of men of all degree who have died in their full strength. We teach them that they will live on in those for whom they are slain. Most are content with that, believe me, heaven-borne. Ask them yourself . . . though remember, they grow dull-witted, with nothing to do year after year. We slay them quickly, cleanly, at the beginning of each summer—no more than we must for that year's crop of boys entering into manhood, one slave for four boys, no more than that. And it is a most beautiful rite, with days of feasting and merry-making afterward. Do you understand now, heaven-borne? You have nothing to fear from us. We are not savages, warring and raiding and skulking to get our man-flesh. We are civilized—not godlike in your fashion, no, I dare not claim that, do not be angry—but civilized—surely worthy of your friendship, are we not? Are we not, heaven-borne?"

\*

Chena Darnard, who headed the cultural anthropology team, told her computer to scan its data bank. Like the others, it was a portable, its memory housed in *New Dawn*. At that moment the spaceship was above the opposite hemisphere, and perceptible time passed while beams went back and forth along the strung-out relay units.

Chena leaned back and studied Evalyth across her desk. The Krakener girl sat so quietly. It seemed unnatural, despite the drugs in her bloodstream retaining some power. To be sure, Evalyth was of aristocratic descent in a warlike society. Furthermore, hereditary psychological as well as physiological differences might exist on the different worlds. Not much was known about that, apart from extreme cases like Gwydion—or this planet? Regardless, Chena thought, it would be better if Evalyth gave way to simple shock and grief.

"Are you quite certain of your facts, dear?" the anthropologist asked as gently as possible. "I mean, while this island alone is habitable, it's large, the topography is rugged, communications are primitive, my group has already identified scores of distinct cultures."

"I questioned Rogar for more than an hour," Evalyth replied in the same flat voice, looking out of the same flat eyes as before. "I know interrogation techniques, and he was badly rattled. He talked.

"The Lokonese themselves are not as backward as their technology. They've lived for centuries with savages threatening their borderlands. It's made them develop a good intelligence network. Rogar described its functioning to me in detail. It can't help but keep them reasonably well informed about everything that goes on. And, while tribal customs do vary tremendously, the cannibalism is universal. That is why none of the Lokonese thought to mention it to us. They took for granted that we had our own ways of providing human meat."

"People have, m-m-m, latitude in those methods?"

"Oh, yes. Here they breed slaves for the purpose. But most lowlanders have too skimpy an economy for that. Some of them use war and murder. Among others, they settle it within the tribe by annual combats. Or— Who cares? The fact is that, everywhere in this country, in whatever fashion it may be, the boys undergo a puberty rite that involves eating an adult male."

Chena bit her lip. "What in the name of chaos might have started it? Computer! Have you scanned?"

"Yes," said the machine voice out of the case on her desk. "Data on cannibalism in man are comparatively sparse, because it is a rarity. On all planets hitherto known to us it is banned and has been throughout their history, although it is sometimes considered forgiveable as an emergency measure when no alternative means of preserving life is available. Very limited forms of what might be called ceremonial cannibalism have occurred, as for example the drinking of minute amounts of each other's blood in pledging oath brotherhood among the Falkens of Lochlanna—"

"Never mind that," Chena said. A tautness in her throat thickened her tone. "Only here, it seems, have they degenerated so far that— Or is it degeneracy? Reversion, perhaps? What about Old Earth?"

"Information is fragmentary. Aside from what was lost during the Long Night, knowledge is under the handicap that the last primitive societies there vanished before interstellar travel began. But certain data collected by ancient historians and scientists remain.

"Cannibalism was an occasional part of human sacrifice. As a rule, victims were left uneaten. But in a minority of religions, the bodies, or selected portions of them, were consumed, either by a special class, or by the community as a whole. Generally this was regarded as theophagy. Thus, the Aztecs of Mexico offered thousands of individuals annually to their gods. The requirement of doing this forced them to provoke wars and rebellions, which in turn made it easy for the eventual European conqueror to get native allies. The majority of prisoners were simply slaughtered, their hearts given directly to the idols. But in at least one cult the body was divided among the worshippers.

"Cannibalism could be a form of magic, too. By eating a person, one supposedly acquired his virtues. This was the principal motive of the cannibals of Africa and Polynesia. Contemporary observers did report that the meals were relished, but that is easy to understand, especially in protein-poor areas.

"The sole recorded instance of systematic non-ceremonial cannibalism was among the Carib Indians of America. They ate man because they preferred man. They were especially fond of babies and used to capture women from their tribes for breeding stock. Male children of these slaves were generally gelded to make them docile and tender. In large part because of strong aversion to such practices, the Europeans exterminated the Caribs to the last man."

The report stopped. Chena grimaced. "I can sympathize with the Europeans," she said.

Evalyth might once have raised her brows; but her face stayed as wooden as her speech. "Aren't you supposed to be an objective scientist?"

"Yes. Yes. Still, there is such a thing as value judgment. And they did kill Donli."

"Not they. One of them. I shall find him."

"He's nothing but a creature of his culture, dear, sick with his whole race." Chena drew a breath, struggling for calm. "Obviously, the sick-

ness has become a behavioral basic," she said. "I daresay it originated
in Lokon. Cultural radiation is practically always from the more to the
less advanced peoples. And on a single island, after centuries, no tribe
has escaped the infection. The Lokonese later elaborated and rationalized the practice. The savages left its cruelty naked. But highlander
or lowlander, their way of life is founded on that particular human
sacrifice."

"Can they be taught differently?" Evalyth asked without real interest.

"Yes. In time. In theory. But—well, I do know enough about what
happened on Old Earth, and elsewhere, when advanced societies un-
dertook to reform primitive ones. The entire structure was destroyed.
It had to be.

"Think of the result, if we told these people to desist from their puberty rite. They wouldn't listen. They couldn't. They *must* have grand-
children. They *know* a boy won't become a man unless he has eaten
part of a man. We'd have to conquer them, kill most, make sullen prisoners of the rest. And when the next crop of boys did in fact mature
without the magic food . . . what then? Can you imagine the demoraliza-
tion, the sense of utter inferiority, the loss of that tradition which is
the core of every personal identity? It might be kinder to bomb this
island sterile."

Chena shook her head. "No," she said harshly, "the single decent
way for us to proceed would be gradually. We could send missionaries.
By their precept and example, we could start the natives phasing out
their custom after two or three generations . . . And we can't afford
such an effort. Not for a long time to come. Not with so many other
worlds in the galaxy, so much worthier of what little help we can give.
I am going to recommend this planet be left alone."

Evalyth considered her for a moment before asking: "Isn't that partly
because of your own reaction?"

"Yes," Chena admitted. "I cannot overcome my disgust. And I, as
you pointed out, am supposed to be professionally broadminded. So
even if the Board tried to recruit missionaries, I doubt if they'd succeed." She hesitated. "You yourself, Evalyth—"

The Krakener rose. "My emotions don't matter," she said. "My duty
does. Thank you for your help." She turned on her heel and went with
military strides out of the cabin.

*

The chemical barriers were crumbling. Evalyth stood for a moment
before the little building that had been hers and Donli's, afraid to
enter. The sun was low, so that the compound was filling with shadows.

A thing leathery-winged and serpentine cruised silently overhead. From outside the stockade drifted sounds of feet, foreign voices, the whine of a wooden flute. The air was cooling. She shivered. Their home would be too hollow.

Someone approached. She recognized the person glimpse-wise, Alsabeta Mondain from Nuevamerica. Listening to her well-meant foolish condolences would be worse than going inside. Evalyth took the last three steps and slid the door shut behind her.

*Donli will not be here again. Eternally.*

But the cabin proved not to be empty to him. Rather, it was too full. That chair where he used to sit, reading that worn volume of poetry which she could not understand and teased him about, that table across which he had toasted her and tossed kisses, that closet where his clothes hung, that scuffed pair of slippers, that bed—it screamed of him. Evalyth went fast into the laboratory section and drew the curtain that separated it from the living quarters. Rings rattled along the rod. The noise was monstrous in twilight.

She closed her eyes and fists and stood breathing hard. *I will not go soft,* she declared. *You always said you loved me for my strength— among numerous other desirable features, you'd add with your slow grin, but I remember that yet—and I don't aim to let slip anything that you loved.*

*I've got to get busy,* she told Donli's child. *The expedition command is pretty sure to act on Chena's urging and haul mass for home. We've not many days to avenge your father.*

Her eyes snapped open. *What am I doing,* she thought, bewildered, *talking to a dead man and an embryo?*

She turned on the overflow fluoro and went to the computer. It was made no differently from the other portables. Donli had used it. But she could not look away from the unique scratches and bumps on that square case, as she could not escape his microscope, chemanalyzers, chromosome tracer, biological specimens . . . She seated herself. A drink would have been very welcome, except that she needed clarity. "Activate!" she ordered.

The On light glowed yellow. Evalyth tugged her chin, searching for words. "The objective," she said at length, "is to trace a lowlander who has consumed several kilos of flesh and blood from one of this party, and afterward vanished into the jungle. The killing took place about sixty hours ago. How can he be found?"

The least hum answered her. She imagined the links; to the maser in the ferry, up past the sky to the nearest orbiting relay unit, to the next, to the next, around the bloated belly of the planet, by ogre sun and inhuman stars, until the pulses reached the mother ship; then down to an unliving brain that routed the question to the appropriate data bank; then to the scanners, whose resonating energies flew from molecule to distorted molecule, identifying more bits of information than it made sense to number, data garnered from hundreds or thousands of entire worlds, data preserved through the wreck of Empire and the dark ages that followed, data going back to an Old Earth that perhaps no longer existed. She shied from the thought and wished herself back on dear stern Kraken. *We will go there,* she promised Donli's child. *You will dwell apart from these too many machines and grow up as the gods meant you should.*

"Query," said the artificial voice. "Of what origin was the victim of this assault?"

Evalyth had to wet her lips before she could reply: "Atheian. He was Donli Sairn, your master."

"In that event, the possibility of tracking the desired local inhabitant may exist. The odds will now be computed. In the interim, do you wish to know the basis of the possibility?"

"Y-yes."

"Native Atheian biochemistry developed in a manner quite parallel to Earth's," said the voice, "and the early colonists had no difficulty in introducing terrestrial species. Thus they enjoyed a friendly environment, where population soon grew sufficiently large to obviate the danger of racial change through mutation and/or genetic drift. In addition, no selection pressure tended to force change. Hence the modern Atheian human is little different from his ancestors of Earth, on which account his physiology and biochemistry are known in detail.

"This has been essentially the case on most colonized planets for which records are available. Where different breeds of men have arisen, it has generally been because the original settlers were highly selected groups. Randomness, and evolutionary adaptation to new conditions, have seldom produced radical changes in biotype. For example, the robustness of the average Krakener is a response to comparatively high gravity; his size aids him in resisting cold, his fair complexion is helpful beneath a sun poor in ultraviolet. But his ancestors were people who already had the natural endowments for such a world. His deviations from their norm are not extreme. They do not preclude his living on more Earth-like planets or interbreeding with the inhabitants of these.

"Occasionally, however, larger variations have occurred. They appear to be due to a small original population or to unterrestroid conditions or both. The population may have been small because the planet could not support more, or have become small as the result of hostile action when the Empire fell. In the former case, genetic accidents had a chance to be significant; in the latter, radiation produced a high rate of mutant births among survivors. The variations are less apt to be in gross anatomy than in subtle endocrine and enzymatic qualities, which affect the physiology and psychology. Well known cases include the reaction of the Gwydiona to nicotine and certain indoles, and the requirement of the Ifrians for trace amounts of lead. Sometimes the inhabitants of two planets are actually intersterile because of their differences.

"While this world has hitherto received the sketchiest of examinations—" Evalyth was yanked out of a reverie into which the lecture had led her. "—certain facts are clear. Few terrestrial species have flourished; no doubt others were introduced originally, but died off after the technology to maintain them was lost. Man has thus been forced to depend on autochthonous life for the major part of his food. This life is deficient in various elements of human nutrition. For example, the only Vitamin C appears to be in immigrant plants; Sairn observed that the people consume large amounts of grass and leaves from those species, and that fluoroscopic pictures indicate this practice has measurably modified the digestive tract. No one would supply skin, blood, sputum, or similar samples, not even from corpses." *Afraid of magic,* Evalyth thought drearily, *yes, they're back to that too.* "But intensive analysis of the usual meat animals shows these to be undersupplied with three essential amino acids, and human adaptation to this must have involved considerable change on the cellular and subcellular levels. The probable type and extent of such change are computable."

"The calculations are now complete." As the computer resumed, Evalyth gripped the arms of her chair and could not breathe. "While the answer is subject to fair probability of success. In effect, Atheian flesh is alien here. It can be metabolized, but the body of the local consumer will excrete certain compounds, and these will import a characteristic odor to skin and breath as well as to urine and feces. The chance is good that it will be detectable by neo-Freeholder technique at distances of several kilometers, after sixty or seventy hours. But since the molecules in question are steadily being degraded and dissipated, speed of action is recommended."

*I am going to find Donli's murderer.* Darkness roared around Evalyth. "Shall the organisms be ordered for you and given the appropriate search program?" asked the voice. "They can be on hand in an estimated three hours."

"Yes," she stammered. "Oh, please— Have you any other . . . other . . . advice?"

"The man ought not to be killed out of hand, but brought here for examination, if for no other reason, that in order that the scientific ends of the expedition may be served."

*That's a machine talking,* Evalyth cried. *It's designed to help research. Nothing more. But it was his.* And its answer was so altogether Donli that she could no longer hold back her tears.

*

The single big moon rose nearly full, shortly after sundown. It drowned most stars; the jungle beneath was cobbled with silver and dappled with black; the snowcone of Mount Burus floated unreal at the unseen edge of the world. Wind slid around Evalyth where she crouched on her gravsled; it was full of wet acrid odors, and felt cold though it was not, and chuckled at her back. Somewhere something screeched, every few minutes, and something else cawed reply.

She scowled at her position indicators, aglow on the control panel. Curses and chaos, Moru had to be in this area! He could not have escaped from the valley on foot in the time available, and her search pattern had practically covered it. If she ran out of bugs before she found him, must she assume he was dead? They ought to be able to find his body regardless, ought they not? Unless it was buried deep. Here. She brought the sled to hover, took the next phial off the rack, and stood up to open it.

The bugs came out many and tiny, like smoke in the moonlight. Another failure?

No! Wait! Were not those motes dancing back together, into a streak barely visible under the moon, and vanishing downward? Heart thuttering, she turned to the indicator. Its neurodetector antenna was not aimlessly wobbling, but pointed straight west-northwest, declination thirty-two degrees below horizontal. Only a concentration of the bugs could make it behave like that. And only the particular mixture of molecules to which the bugs had been presensitized, in several parts per million or better, would make them converge on the source.

"Ya-a-ah!" She couldn't help the one hawk-yell. But thereafter she bit her lips shut—blood trickled unnoticed down her chin—and drove the sled in silence.

The distance was a mere few kilometers. She came to a halt above an opening in the forest. Pools of scummy water gleamed in its rank growth. The trees made a solid-seeming wall around. Evalyth clapped her night goggles down off her helmet and over her eyes. A lean-to became visible. It was hastily woven from vines and withes, huddled against a pair of the largest trees to let their branches hide it from the sky. The bugs were entering.

Evalyth lowered her sled to a meter off the ground and got to her feet again. A stun pistol slid from its sheath into her right hand. Her left rested on the blaster.

Moru's two sons groped from the shelter. The bugs whirled around them, a mist that blurred their outlines. *Of course,* Evalyth realized, nonetheless shocked into a higher hatred. *I should have known they did the actual devouring.* More than ever did they resemble gnomes— skinny limbs, big heads, the pot bellies of undernourishment. Krakener boys of their age would have twice their bulk and be noticeably on the way to becoming men. These nude bodies belonged to children, except that they had the grotesqueness of eld.

The parents followed them, ignored by the entranced bugs. The mother wailed. Evalyth identified a few words. "What is the matter, what are those things—oh, help—" But her gaze was locked upon Moru.

Limping out of the hutch, stooped to clear its entrance, he made her think of some huge beetle crawling from an offal heap. But she would know that bushy head though her brain were coming apart. He carried a stone blade, surely the one that had hacked up Donli. *I will take it away from him, and the hand with it,* Evalyth wept. *I will keep him alive while I dismantle him with these my own hands, and in between times he can watch me flay his repulsive spawn.*

The wife's scream broke through. She had seen the metal thing, and the giant that stood on its platform, with skull and eyes shimmering beneath the moon.

"I have come for you who killed my man," Evalyth said.

The mother screamed anew and cast herself before the boys. The father tried to run around in front of her, but his lame foot twisted under him, and he fell into a pool. As he struggled out of its muck, Evalyth shot the woman. No sound was heard; she folded and lay moveless. "Run!" Moru shouted. He tried to charge the sled. Evalyth twisted a control stick. Her vehicle whipped in a circle, heading off the boys. She shot them from above, where Moru couldn't quite reach her.

He knelt beside the nearest, took the body in his arms and looked upward. The moonlight poured relentlessly across him. "What can you now do to me?" he called.

She stunned him too, landed, got off and quickly hogtied the four of them. Loading them aboard, she found them lighter than she had expected.

Sweat had sprung forth upon her, until her coverall stuck dripping to her skin. She began to shake, as if with fever. Her ears buzzed. "I would have destroyed you," she said. Her voice sounded remote and unfamiliar. A still more distant part wondered why she bothered speaking to the unconscious, in her own tongue at that. "I wish you hadn't acted the way you did. That made me remember what the computer said, about Donli's friends needing you for study.

"You're too good a chance, I suppose. After your doings, we have the right under Allied rules to make prisoners of you, and none of his friends are likely to get maudlin about your feelings.

"Oh, they won't be inhuman. A few cell samples, a lot of tests, anesthesia where necessary, nothing harmful, nothing but a clinical examination as thorough as facilities allow.

"No doubt you'll be better fed than at any time before, and no doubt the medics will find some pathologies they can cure for you. In the end, Moru, they'll release your wife and children."

She stared into his horrible face.

"I am pleased," she said, "that to you, who won't comprehend what is going on, it will be a bad experience. And when they are finished, Moru, I will insist on having you at least, back. They can't deny me that. Why, your tribe itself has, in effect, cast you out. Right? My colleagues won't let me do more than kill you, I'm afraid, but on this I will insist."

She gunned the engine and started toward Lokon, as fast as possible, to arrive while she felt able to be satisfied with that much.

*

And the days without him and the days without him.

The nights were welcome. If she had not worked herself quite to exhaustion, she could take a pill. He rarely returned in her dreams. But she had to get through each day and would not drown him in drugs.

Luckily, there was a good deal of work involved in preparing to depart, when the expedition was short-handed and on short notice. Gear must be dismantled, packed, ferried to the ship, and stowed. *New Dawn* herself must be readied, numerous systems recommissioned and tested. Her militechnic training qualified Evalyth to double as mechanic, boat jockey, or loading gang boss. In addition, she kept up the routines of defense in the compound.

Captain Jonafer objected mildly to this. "Why bother, Lieutenant?

The locals are scared blue of us. They've heard what you did—and this coming and going through the sky, robots and heavy machinery in action, floodlights after dark—I'm having trouble persuading them not to abandon their town!"

"Let them," she snapped. "Who cares?"

"We did not come here to ruin them, Lieutenant."

"No. In my judgment, though, Captain, they'll be glad to ruin us if we present the least opportunity. Imagine what special virtues *your* body must have."

Jonafer sighed and gave in. But when she refused to receive Rogar the next time she was planetside, he ordered her to do so and to be civil.

The *Klev* entered the biolab section—she would not have him in her living quarters—with a gift held in both hands, a sword of Imperial metal. She shrugged; no doubt a museum would be pleased to get the thing. "Lay it on the floor," she told him.

Because she occupied the single chair, he stood. He looked little and old in his robe. "I came," he whispered, "to say how we of Lokon rejoice that the heaven-borne has won her revenge."

"Is winning it," she corrected.

He could not meet her eyes. She stared moodily at his faded hair. "Since the heaven-borne could . . . easily . . . find those she wished . . . she knows the truth in the hearts of us of Lokon, that we never intended harm to her folk."

That didn't seem to call for an answer.

His fingers twisted together. "Then why do you forsake us?" he went on. "When first you came, when we had come to know you and you spoke our speech, you said you would stay for many moons, and after you would come others to teach and trade. Our hearts rejoiced. It was not alone the goods you might someday let us buy, nor that your wise-men talked of ways to end hunger, sickness, danger, and sorrow. No, our jubilation and thankfulness were most for the wonders you opened. Suddenly the world was made great, that had been so narrow. And now you are going away. I have asked, when I dared, and those of your men who will speak to me say none will return. How have we offended you, and how may it be made right, heaven-borne?"

"You can stop treating your fellow men like animals," Evalyth got past her teeth.

"I have gathered . . . somewhat . . . that you from the stars say it is wrong what happens in the Sacred Place. But we only do it once in our lifetimes, heaven-borne, and because we must!"

"You have no need."

Rogar went on his hands and knees before her. "Perhaps the heaven-born are thus," he pleaded, "but we are merely men. If our sons do not get the manhood, they will never beget children of their own, and the last of us will die alone in a world of death, with none to crack his skull and let the soul out—" He dared glance up at her. What he saw made him whimper and crawl backwards into the sun-glare.

Later Chena Darnard sought Evalyth. They had a drink and talked around the subject for a while, until the anthropologist plunged in: "You were pretty hard on the sachem, weren't you?"

"How'd you— Oh." The Krakener remembered that the interview had been taped, as was done whenever possible for later study. "What was I supposed to do, kiss his man-eating mouth?"

"No." Chena winced. "I suppose not."

"Your signature heads the list, on the official recommendation that we quit this planet."

"Yes. But—now I don't know. I was repelled. I am. However—I've been observing the medical team working on those prisoners of yours. Have you?"

"No."

"You should. The way they cringe and shriek and reach to each other when they're strapped down in the lab and cling together afterward in their cell."

"They aren't suffering any pain or mutilation, are they?"

"Of course not. But they can believe it when their captors say they won't. They can't be tranquilized while under study, you know, if the results are to be valid. Their fear of the absolutely unknown— Well, Evalyth, I had to stop observing. I couldn't take any more." Chena gave the other a long stare. "You might, though."

Evalyth shook her head. "I don't gloat. I'll shoot the murderer because my family honor demands it. The rest can go free, even the boys. Even in spite of what they ate." She poured herself a stiff draught and tossed it off in a gulp. The liquor burned on the way down.

"I wish you wouldn't," Chena said. "Donli wouldn't have liked it. He had a proverb that he claimed was very ancient—he was from my city, don't forget, and I have known . . . I did know him longer than you, dear. I heard him say, twice or thrice, *Do I not destroy my enemies if it make them my friends?*"

"Think of a venomous insect," Evalyth replied. "You don't make friends with it. You put it under your heel."

"But a man does what he does because of what he is, what his society has made him." Chena's voice grew urgent; she leaned forward to grip Evalyth's hand, which did not respond. "What is one man, one lifetime, against all who live around him and all who have gone before? Cannibalism wouldn't be found everywhere over this island, in every one of these otherwise altogether different groupings, if it weren't the most deeply rooted cultural imperative this race has got."

Evalyth grinned around a rising anger. "And what kind of race are they to acquire it? And how about according me the privilege of operating on my own cultural imperatives? I'm bound home, to raise Donli's child away from your gutless civilization. He will not grow up disgraced because his mother was too weak to exact justice for his father. Now if you will excuse me, I have to get up early and take another boatload to the ship and get it inboard."

That task required a while. Evalyth came back toward sunset of the next day. She felt a little more tired than usual, a little more peaceful. The raw edge of what had happened was healing over. The thought crossed her mind, abstract but not shocking, not disloyal: *I'm young. One year another man will come. I won't love you the less, darling.*

Dust scuffed under her boots. The compound was half stripped already, a corresponding number of personnel berthed in the ship. The evening reached quiet beneath a yellowing sky. Only a few of the expedition stirred among the machines and remaining cabins. Lokon lay as hushed as it had lately become. She welcomed the thud of her footfalls on the steps into Jonafer's office.

He sat waiting for her, big and unmoving behind his desk. "Assignment completed without incident," she reported.

"Sit down," he said.

She obeyed. The silence grew. At last he said, out of a stiff face: "The clinical team has finished with the prisoners."

Somehow it was a shock. Evalyth groped for words. "Isn't that too soon? I mean, well, we don't have a lot of equipment, and just a couple of men who can see the advanced stuff, and then without Donli for an expert on Earth biology— Wouldn't a good study, down to the chromosomal level if not further—something that the physical anthropologists could use—wouldn't it take longer?"

"That's correct," Jonafer said. "Nothing of major importance was found. Perhaps something would have been, if Uden's team had any inkling of what to look for. Given that, they could have made hypotheses and tested them in a whole-organism context and come to some understanding of their subjects as functioning beings. You're right, Donli Sairn had the kind of professional intuition that might have guided them. Lacking that, and with no particular clues, and no cooperation from those ignorant, terrified savages, they had to grope and probe almost at random. They did establish a few digestive peculiarities —nothing that couldn't have been predicted on the basis of ambient ecology."

"Then why have they stopped? We won't be leaving for another week at the earliest."

"They did so on my orders, after Uden had shown me what was going on and said he'd quit regardless of what I wanted."

"What—? Oh." Scorn lifted Evalyth's head. "You mean the psychological torture."

"Yes. I saw that scrawny woman secured to a table. Her head, her body were covered with leads to the meters that clustered around her and clicked and hummed and flickered. She didn't see me; her eyes were blind with fear. I suppose she imagined her soul was being pumped out. Or maybe the process was worse for being something she couldn't put a name to. I saw her kids in a cell, holding hands. Nothing else left for them to hold onto, in their total universe. They're just at puberty; what'll this do to their psychosexual development? I saw their father lying drugged beside them, after he'd tried to batter his way straight through the wall. Uden and his helpers told me how they'd tried to make friends and failed. Because naturally the prisoners know they're in the power of those who hate them with a hate that goes beyond the grave."

Jonafer paused. "There are decent limits to everything, Lieutenant," he ended, "including science and punishment. Especially when, after all, the chance of discovering anything else unusual is slight. I ordered the investigation terminated. The boys and their mother will be flown to their home area and released tomorrow."

"Why not today?" Evalyth asked, foreseeing his reply.

"I hoped," Jonafer said, "that you'd agree to let the man go with them."

"No."

"In the name of God—"

"Your God." Evalyth looked away from him. "I won't enjoy it, Captain. I'm beginning to wish I didn't have to. But it's not as if Donli'd been killed in an honest war or feud—or he was slaughtered like a pig. That's the evil in cannibalism; it makes a man nothing but another meat animal. I won't bring him back, but I will somehow even things, by making the cannibal nothing but a dangerous animal that needs shooting."

"I see." Jonafer too stared long out of the window. In the sunset light his face became a mask of brass. "Well," he said finally, coldly, "under the Charter of the Alliance and the articles of this expedition, you leave me no choice. But we will not have any ghoulish ceremonies, and you will not deputize what you have done. The prisoner will be brought to your place privately after dark. You will dispose of him at once and assist in cremating the remains."

Evalyth's palms grew wet. *I never killed a helpless man before!*

*But he did,* it answered. "Understood, Captain," she said.

"Very good, Lieutenant. You may go up and join the mess for dinner if you wish. No announcements to anyone. The business will be scheduled for—" Jonafer glanced at his watch, set to local rotation. "—2600 hours."

Evalyth swallowed around a clump of dryness. "Isn't that rather late?"

"On purpose," he told her. "I want the camp asleep." His glance struck hers. "And want you to have time to reconsider."

"No!" She sprang erect and went for the door.

His voice pursued her. "Donli would have asked you for that."

\*

Night came in and filled the room. Evalyth didn't rise to turn on the light. It was as if this chair, which had been Donli's favorite, wouldn't let her go.

Finally she remembered the psychodrugs. She had a few tablets left. One of them would make the execution easy to perform. No doubt Jonafer would direct that Moru be tranquilized—now, at last—before they brought him here. So why should she not give herself calmness?

It wouldn't be right.

Why not?

*I don't know. I don't understand anything any longer.*

*Who does? Moru alone. He knows why he murdered and butchered a man who trusted him.* Evalyth found herself smiling wearily into the darkness. *He has superstition for his sure guide. He's actually seen his children display the first signs of maturity. That ought to console him a little.*

Odd, that the glandular upheaval of adolescence should have commenced under frightful stress. One would have expected a delay instead. True, the captives had been getting a balanced diet for a change, and medicine had probably eliminated various chronic low-level infections. Nonetheless the fact was odd. Besides, normal children under normal conditions would not develop the outward signs beyond mistaking in this short a time. Donli would have puzzled over the matter. She could almost see him, frowning, rubbing his forehead, grinning one-sidedly with the pleasure of a problem.

"I'd like to have a go at this myself," she heard him telling Uden over a beer and a smoke. "Might turn up an angle."

"How?" the medic would have replied. "You're a general biologist. No reflection on you, but detailed human physiology is out of your line."

"Um-m-m . . . yes and no. My main job is studying species of terrestrial origin and how they've adapted to new planets. By a remarkable coincidence, man is included among them."

But Donli was gone, and no one else was competent to do his work —to be any part of him, but she fled from that thought and from the thought of what she must presently do. She held her mind tightly to the realization that one of Uden's team had tried to apply Donli's knowledge. As Jonafer remarked, a living Donli might well have suggested an idea, unorthodox and insightful, that would have led to the discovery of whatever was there to be discovered, if anything was. Uden and his assistants were routineers. They hadn't even thought to make Donli's computer ransack its data banks for possibly relevant information. Why should they, when they saw their problem as strictly medical? And, to be sure, they were not cruel. The anguish they were inflicting had made them avoid whatever might lead to ideas demanding further research. Donli would have approached the entire business differently from the outset.

Suddenly the gloom thickened. Evalyth fought for breath. Too hot and silent here; too long a wait; she must do something or her will would desert her and she would be unable to squeeze the trigger.

She stumbled to her feet and into the lab. The fluoro blinded her for a moment when she turned it on. She went to his computer and said: "Activate!"

Nothing responded but the indicator light. The windows were totally black. Clouds outside shut off moon and stars.

"What—" The sound was a curious croak. But that brought a releasing gall: *Take hold of yourself, you blubbering idiot, or you're not fit to mother the child you're carrying*. She could then ask her question. "What explanations in terms of biology can be devised for the behavior of the people on this planet?"

"Matters of that nature are presumably best explained in terms of psychology and cultural anthropology," said the voice.

"M-m-maybe," Evalyth said. "And maybe not." She marshalled a few thoughts and stood them firm amidst the others roiling in her skull.

"The inhabitants could be degenerate somehow, not really human."
*I want Moru to be.* "Scan every fact recorded about them, including
the detailed clinical observations made on four of them in the past several days. Compare with basic terrestrial data. Give me whatever
hypotheses look reasonable." She hesitated. "Correction. I mean possible
hypotheses—anything that does not flatly contradict established facts.
We've used up the reasonable ideas already."

The machine hummed. Evalyth closed her eyes and clung to the
edge of the desk. *Donli, please help me.*

At the other end of forever, the voice came to her:

"The sole behavioral element which appears to be not easily explica-
ble by postulates concerning environment and accidental historical
developments, is the cannibalistic puberty rite. According to the an-
thropological computer, this might well have originated as a form of
human sacrifice. But that computer notes certain illogicalities in the
idea, as follows.

"On Old Earth, sacrificial religion was normally associated with agricultural societies, which were more vitally dependent on continued
fertility and good weather than hunters. Even for them, the offering
of humans proved disadvantageous in the long run, as the Aztec example most clearly demonstrates. Lokon has rationalized the practice
to a degree, making it a part of the slavery system and thus minimizing
its impact on the generality. But for the lowlanders it is a powerful
evil, a source of perpetual danger, a diversion of effort and resources
that are badly needed for survival. It is not plausible that the custom,
if ever imitated from Lokon, should persist among every one of those
tribes. Nevertheless it does. Therefore it must have some value and the
problem is to find what.

"The method of obtaining victims varies widely, but the requirement
always appears to be the same. According to the Lokonese, one adult
male body is necessary and sufficient for the maturation of four boys.
The killer of Donli Sairn was unable to carry off the entire corpse.
What he did take of it is suggestive.

"Hence a dipteroid phenomenon may have appeared in man on this
planet. Such a thing is unknown among higher animals elsewhere, but
is conceivable. A modification of the Y chromosome would produce it.
The test for that modification, and thus the test of the hypothesis, is
easily made."

The voice stopped. Evalyth heard the blood slugging in her veins.
"What are you talking about?"

The phenomenon is found among lower animals on several worlds," the computer told her.

"It is uncommon and so is not widely known. The name derives from the Diptera, a type of dung fly on Old Earth."

Lightning flickered. "Dung fly—good, yes!"

The machine went on to explain.

*

Jonafer came along with Moru. The savage's hands were tied behind his back, and the spaceman loomed enormous over him. Despite that and the bruises he had inflicted on himself, he hobbled along steadily. The clouds were breaking and the moon shone ice-white. Where Evalyth waited, outside her door, she saw the compound reach bare to the saw-topped stockade and a crane stand above like a gibbet. The air was growing cold—the planet spinning toward an autumn—and a small wind had arisen to whimper behind the dust devils that stirred across the earth. Jonafer's footfalls rang loud.

He noticed her and stopped. Moru did likewise. "What did they learn?" she asked.

The captain nodded. "Uden got right to work when you called," he said. "The test is more complicated than your computer suggested—but then, it's for Donli's kind of skill, not Uden's. He'd never have thought of it unassisted. Yes, the notion is true."

"How?"

Moru stood waiting while the language he did not understand went to and fro around him.

"I'm no medic." Jonafer kept his tone altogether colorless. "But from what Uden told me, the chromosome defect means that the male gonads here can't mature spontaneously. They need an extra supply of hormones—he mentioned testosterone and androsterone, I forget what else —to start off the series of changes which bring on puberty. Lacking that, you'll get eunuchism. Uden thinks the surviving population was tiny after the colony was bombed out, and so poor that it resorted to cannibalism for bare survival, the first generation or two. Under those circumstances, a mutation that would otherwise have eliminated itself got established and spread to every descendant."

Evalyth nodded. "I see."

"You understand what this means, I suppose," Jonafer said. "There'll be no problem to ending the practice. We'll simply tell them we have a new and better Holy Food, and prove it with a few pills. Terrestrial-type meat animals can be reintroduced later and supply what's necessary. In the end, no doubt our geneticists can repair that faulty Y chromosome."

He could not stay contained any longer. His mouth opened, a gash across his half-seen face, and he rasped: "I should praise you for saving a whole people. I can't. Get your business over with, will you?"

Evalyth trod forward to stand before Moru. He shivered but met her eyes. Astonished, she said: "You haven't drugged him."

"No," Jonafer said. "I wouldn't help you." He spat.

"Well, I'm glad." She addressed Moru in his own language: "You killed my man. Is it right that I should kill you?"

"It is right," he answered, almost as levelly as she. "I thank you that my woman and my sons are to go free." He was quiet for a second or two. "I have heard that your folk can preserve food for years without it rotting. I would be glad if you kept my body to give to your sons."

"Mine will not need it," Evalyth said. "Nor will the sons of your sons."

Anxiety tinged his words: "Do you know why I slew your man? He was kind to me, and like a god. But I am lame. I saw no other way to get what my sons must have; and they must have it soon, or it would be too late and they could never become men."

"He taught me," Evalyth said, "how much it is to be a man."

She turned to Jonafer, who stood tense and puzzled. "I had my revenge," she said in Donli's tongue.

"What?" His question was a reflexive noise.

"After I learned about the dipteroid phenomenon," she said. "All that was necessary was for me to keep silent. Moru, his children, his entire race would go on being prey for centuries, maybe forever. I sat for half an hour, I think, having my revenge."

"And then?" Jonafer asked.

"I was satisfied and could start thinking about justice," Evalyth said.

She drew a knife. Moru straightened his back. She stepped behind him and cut his bonds. "Go home," she said. "Remember him."

## Harlan Ellison

Yes, I know. Here's Harlan again.

It's not my fault. It's just that he wins Hugos. If he were to pile his Hugos one on top of the other, the heap would be taller and heavier than he is. He's the only science fiction writer who can make that claim.

Why should all these Hugos be? There are a variety of theories that include multiple voting, blackmail, bribed judges and so on. Well, yes, but in *addition* to all that, Harlan also happens to be a very talented writer.

He's one of us boys who has made it in the big world outside there and I'm proud of him. (Oh, my goodness, I hope he never reads this.) I glory in his bravery. Right or wrong, he speaks his mind, calls them as he sees them, regardless of consequences. He's the only fellow I know who can get up to give a talk at a convention, get everyone on the floor fighting mad—and stand up there on the platform shouting back at them *all*.

An article in a certain national magazine once reported a set-to between a certain Hollywood super-star and none other than our very own Harlan. That super-star ordinarily has everyone bowing and scraping to get out of his way, and kicking themselves in the rear to make themselves move even more quickly in the effort to leave a clear path for the august one, but he had no effect on Harlan. Harlan just stood there, so to speak, and wouldn't budge, and when super-star tried to sneer, Harlan just squashed him as though he were ordinary flesh and blood.

And when another national magazine listed Hollywood's four most eligible bachelors, who was among them? Harlan Ellison, that's who? And who wrote the best *Man From U.N.C.L.E.* script I ever watched. Harlan Ellison, that's who? And who writes big-time movie scripts? Harlan Ellison, that's who.

The way I feel now, I can only paraphrase Kipling and say:

> *Though I've belted you and flayed you,*
> *By the living God that made you,*
> *You're a better man than I am, Ellison—almost!*

# 13

# THE BEAST THAT SHOUTED LOVE AT THE HEART OF THE WORLD

After an idle discussion with the pest control man who came once a month to spray around the outside of his home in the Ruxton section of Baltimore, William Sterog stole a canister of Malathion, a deadly insecticide poison, from the man's truck, and went out early one morning, following the route of the neighborhood milkman, and spooned medium-large quantities into each bottle left on the rear doorstep of seventy homes. Within six hours of Bill Sterog's activities, two hundred men, women and children died in convulsive agony.

Learning that an aunt who had lived in Buffalo was dying of cancer of the lymph glands, William Sterog hastily helped his mother pack three bags, and took her to Friendship Airport, where he put her on an Eastern Airlines jet with a simple but efficient time bomb made from a Westclox Travalarm and four sticks of dynamite in her three-suiter. The jet exploded somewhere over Harrisburg, Pennsylvania. Ninety-three people—including Bill Sterog's mother—were killed in the explosion, and flaming wreckage added seven to the toll by cascading down on a public swimming pool.

On a Sunday in November, William Sterog made his way to Babe Ruth Plaza on 33rd Street where he became one of 54,000 fans jamming Memorial Stadium to see the Baltimore Colts play the Green Bay Packers. He was dressed warmly in grey flannel slacks, a navy blue turtleneck pullover and a heavy hand-knitted Irish wool sweater under his parka. With three minutes and thirteen seconds of the fourth quarter remaining to be played, and Baltimore trailing seventeen to sixteen on Green Bay's eighteen-yard line, Bill Sterog fought his way up the aisle to the exit above the mezzanine seats, and fumbled under his parka for the U. S. Army surplus M-3 submachine gun he had bought for $49.95 from a mail order armaments dealer in Alexandria, Virginia. Even as 53,999 screaming fans leaped to their feet—making his range of fire that much better—as the ball was snapped to the quarterback, holding for the defensive tackle most able to kick a successful field goal, Bill Sterog opened fire on the massed backs of the fans below him. Before the mob could bring him down, he had killed forty-four people.

When the first Expeditionary Force to the elliptical galaxy in Sculptor descended on the second planet of a fourth magnitude star the Force had designated Flammarion Theta, they found a thirty-seven-foot-high statue of a hitherto unknown blue-white substance—not quite stone, something like metal—in the shape of a man. The figure was barefoot, draped in a garment that vaguely resembled a toga, the head encased in a skull-tight cap, and holding in its left hand a peculiar ring-and-ball device of another substance altogether. The statue's face was curiously beatific. It had high cheekbones; deep-set eyes; a tiny, almost alien mouth; and a broad, large-nostriled nose. The statue loomed enormous among the pitted and blasted curvilinear structures of some forgotten architect. The members of the Expeditionary Force commented on the peculiar expression each noted on the face of the statue. None of these men, standing under a gorgeous brass moon that shared an evening sky with a descending sun quite dissimilar in color to the one that now shone wanly on an Earth unthinkably distant in time and space, had ever heard of William Sterog. And so none of them was able to say that the expression on the giant statue was the same as the one Bill Sterog had shown as he told the final appeals judge who was about to sentence him to death in the lethal gas chamber, "I love everyone in the world. I do. So help me God, I love you, all of you!" He was shouting.

Crosswhen, through interstices of thought called time, through reflective images called space; another then, another now. This place, over *there*. Beyond concepts, the transmogrification of simplicity finally labeled *if*. Forty and more steps sidewise but later, much later. There, in that ultimate center, with everything radiating outward, becoming infinitely more complex, the enigma of symmetry, harmony, apportionment singing with fine-tuned order in *this* place, where it all began, begins, will always begin. The center. Crosswhen.

Or: a hundred million years in the future. And: a hundred million parsecs beyond the farthest edge of measurable space. And: parallax warpages beyond counting across the universes of parallel existences. Finally: an infinitude of mind-triggered leaps beyond human thought.

There: Crosswhen.

On the mauve level, crouched down in deeper magenta washings that concealed his arched form, the maniac waited. He was a dragon, squat and round in the torso, tapered ropy tail tucked under his body; the small, thick osseous shields rising perpendicularly from the arched back, running down to the end of the tail, tips pointing upward; his taloned shorter arms folded across his massive chest. He had the seven-headed dog faces of an ancient Cerberus. Each head watched, waiting hungry, insane.

He saw the bright yellow wedge of light as it moved in random patterns through the mauve, always getting closer. He knew he could not run, the movement would betray him, the specter light finding him instantly. Fear choked the maniac. The specter had pursued him through innocence and humility and nine other emotional obfuscations he had tried. He had to do something, get them off his scent. But he was alone on this level. It had been closed down some time before, to purge it of residue emotions. Had he not been so terribly confused after the killings, had he not been drowning in disorientation, he would never have trapped himself on a closed level.

Now that he was here, there was nowhere to hide, nowhere to escape the specter light that would systematically hunt him down. Then they would purge *him*.

The maniac took the one final chance; he closed down his mind, all seven brains, even as the mauve level was closed down. He shut off all thought, banked the fires of emotion, broke the neural circuits that fed power to his mind. Like a great machine phasing down from peak efficiency, his thoughts slackened and wilted and grew pale. Then there was a blank where he had been. Seven dog-heads slept.

The dragon had ceased to exist in terms of thought, and the specter light washed past him, finding nothing there to home in on. But those who sought the maniac were sane, not deranged as he was: their sanity was ordered, and in order they considered every exigency. The specter light was followed by heat-seeking beams, by mass-tallying sensors, by trackers that could hunt out the spoor of foreign matter on a closed-down level.

They found the maniac. Shut down like a sun gone cold, they located him, and transferred him; he was unaware of the movement; he was locked away in his own silent skulls.

But when he chose to open his thoughts again, in the timeless disorientation that follows a total shutdown, he found himself locked in stasis in a drainage ward on the 3rd Red Active Level. Then, from seven throats, he screamed.

The sound, of course, was lost in the throat baffles they had inserted, before he had turned himself back on. The emptiness of the sound terrified him even more.

He was imbedded an an amber substance that fit around him comfortably; had it been a much earlier era, on another world, in another continuum, it would have been simply a hospital bed with restraining straps. But the dragon was locked in stasis on a red level, crosswhen. His hospital bed was anti-grav, weightless, totally relaxing, feeding nutrients through his leathery hide along with depressants and toners. He was waiting to be drained.

Linah drifted into the ward, followed by Semph. Semph, the discoverer of the drain. And his most eloquent nemesis, Linah, who sought Public Elevation to the position of Proctor. They drifted down the rows of amber-encased patients: the toads, the tambour-lidded crystal cubes, the exoskeletals, the pseudopodal changers, and the seven-headed dragon. They paused directly in front and slightly above the maniac. He was able to look up at them; images seven times seen; but he was not able to make sound.

"If I needed a conclusive reason, here's one of the best," Linah said, inclining his head toward the maniac.

Semph dipped an analysis rod into the amber substance, withdrew it and made a hasty reading of the patient's condition. "If you needed a greater *warning*," Semph said quietly, "this would be one of the best."

"Science bends to the will of the masses," Linah said.

"I'd hate to have to believe that," Semph responded quickly. There was a tone in his voice that could not be named, but it undershadowed the aggressiveness of his words.

"I'm going to see to it, Semph; *believe it*. I'm going to have the Concord pass the resolution."

"Linah, how long have we known each other?"

"Since your third flux. My second."

"That's about right. Have I ever told you a lie, have I ever asked you to do something that would harm you?"

"No. Not that I can recall."

"Then why won't you listen to me *this* time?"

"Because I think you're wrong. I'm not a fanatic, Semph. I'm not making political hay with this. I feel very strongly that it's the best chance we've ever had."

"But disaster for everyone and everywhere else, all the way back, and God only knows how far across the parallax. We stop fouling our own nest, at the expense of all the other nests that ever were."

Linah spread his hands in futility. "Survival."

Semph shook his head slowly, with a weariness that was mirrored in his expression. "I wish I could drain *that,* too."

"Can't you?"

Semph shrugged. "I can drain *any*thing. But what we'd have left wouldn't be worth having."

The amber substance changed hue. It glowed deep within itself with a blue intensity. "The patient is ready," Semph said. "Linah, one more time. I'll beg if it'll do any good. Please. Stall till the next session. The Concord needn't do it *now.* Let me run some further tests, let me see how far back this garbage spews, how much damage it can cause. Let me prepare some reports."

Linah was firm. He shook his head in finality. "May I watch the draining with you?"

Semph let out a long sigh. He was beaten, and knew it. "Yes, all right."

The amber substance carrying its silent burden began to rise. It reached the level of the two men, and slid smoothly through the air between them. They drifted after the smooth container with the dog-headed dragon imbedded in it, and Semph seemed as though he wanted to say something else. But there was nothing to say.

The amber chrysaloid cradle faded and vanished, and the men became insubstantial and were no more. They all reappeared in the drainage chamber. The beaming stage was empty. The amber cradle settled down on it without sound, and the substance flowed away, vanishing as it uncovered the dragon.

The maniac tried desperately to move, to heave himself up. Seven heads twitched futilely. The madness in him overcame the depressants and he was consumed with frenzy, fury, crimson hate. But he could not move. It was all he could do to hold his shape.

Semph turned the band on his left wrist. It glowed from within, a deep gold. The sound of air rushing to fill a vacuum filled the chamber. The beaming stage was drenched in silver light that seemed to spring out of the air itself, from an unknown source. The dragon was washed by the silver light, and the seven great mouths opened once, exposing rings of fangs. Then his double-lidded eyes closed.

The pain within his heads was monstrous. A fearful wrenching that became the sucking of a million mouths. His very brains were pulled upon, pressured, compressed, and then purged.

Semph and Linah looked away from the pulsing body of the dragon to the drainage tank across the chamber. It was filling from the bottom as they watched. Filling with a nearly colorless roiling cloud of smokiness, shot through with sparks. "Here it comes," Semph said, needlessly.

Linah dragged his eyes away from the tank. The dragon with seven dog heads was rippling. As though seen through shallow water, the maniac was beginning to alter. As the tank filled, the maniac found it more and more difficult to maintain his shape. The denser grew the cloud of sparkling matter in the tank, the less constant was the shape of the creature on the beaming stage.

Finally, it was impossible, and the maniac gave in. The tank filled more rapidly, and the shape quavered and altered and shrank and then there was a superimposition of the form of a man, over that of the seven-headed dragon. Then the tank reached three-quarters filled and the dragon became an underling shadow, a hint, a suggestion of what had been there when the drainage began. Now the man-form was becoming more dominant by the second.

Finally, the tank was filled, and a normal man lay on the beaming stage, breathing heavily, eyes closed, muscles jumping involuntarily.

"He's drained," Semph said.

"Is it all in the tank?" Linah asked softly.

"No, none of it."

"Then . . ."

"This is the residue. Harmless. Reagents purged from a group of sensitives will neutralize it. The dangerous essences, the degenerate force-lines that make up the field . . . they're gone. Drained off already."

Linah looked disturbed, for the first time. "Where did it go?"

"Do you love your fellow man, tell me?"

"Please, Semph! I asked where it went . . . when it went?"

"And I asked if you cared at all about anyone else?"

"You know my answer . . . you know *me!* I want to know, tell me, at least what you know. Where . . . when . . . ?"

"Then you'll forgive me, Linah, because I love my fellow man, too. Whenever he was, wherever he is; I have to, I work in an inhuman field, and I have to cling to that. So . . . you'll forgive me . . ."

"What are you going to . . ."

*In Indonesia they have a phrase for it:* Djam Karet—*the hour that stretches.*

In the Vatican's Stanza of Heliodorus, the second of the great rooms he designed for Pope Julius II, Raphael painted (and his pupils completed) a magnificent fresco representation of the historic meeting between Pope Leo I and Attila the Hun, in the year 452.

In this painting is mirrored the belief of Christians everywhere that the spiritual authority of Rome protected her in that desperate hour when the Hun came to sack and burn the Holy City. Raphael has painted in Saint Peter and Saint Paul, descending from Heaven to reinforce Pope Leo's intervention. His interpretation was an elaboration on the original legend, in which only the Apostle Peter was mentioned —standing behind Leo with a drawn sword. And the legend was an elaboration of what little facts have come down through antiquity relatively undistorted: Leo had no cardinals with him, and certainly no wraith Apostles. He was one of three in the deputation. The other two were secular dignitaries of the Roman state. The meeting did not take place—as legend would have us believe—just outside the gates of Rome, but in northern Italy, not far from what is today Peschiera.

Nothing more than this is known of the confrontation. Yet Attila, who had never been stopped, did not raze Rome. He turned back.

*Djam Karet.* The force-line field spewed out from a parallax center crosswhen, a field that had pulsed through time and space and the minds of men for twice ten thousand years. Then cut out suddenly, inexplicably, and Attila the Hun clapped his hands to his head, his mind twisting like rope within his skull. His eyes glazed, then cleared, and he breathed from deep in his chest. Then he signaled his army to turn back. Leo the Great thanked God and the living memory of Christ the Saviour. Legend added Saint Peter. Raphael added Saint Paul.

For twice ten thousand years—*Djam Karet*—the field had pulsed, and for a brief moment that could have been instants or years or millennia, it was cut off.

Legend does not tell the truth. More specifically, it does not tell *all* of the truth: forty years before Attila raided Italy, Rome had been taken and sacked by Alaric the Goth. *Djam Karet.* Three years after the retreat of Attila, Rome was once more taken and sacked, by Gaiseric, king of all the Vandals.

There was a reason the garbage of insanity had ceased to flow through everywhere and everywhen from the drained mind of a seven-headed dragon . . .


Semph, traitor to his race, hovered before the Concord. His friend, the man who now sought this final flux, Linah, Proctored the hearing. He spoke softly, but eloquently, of what the great scientist had done.

"The tank was draining; he said to me, 'Forgive me, because I love my fellow man. Whenever he was, wherever he is; I have to, I work in an inhuman field, and I have to cling to that. So you'll forgive me.' Then he interposed himself."

The sixty members of the Concord, a representative from each race that existed in the center, bird-creatures and blue things and large-headed men and orange scents with cilia shuddering . . . all of them looked at Semph where he hovered. His body and head were crumpled like a brown paper bag. All hair was gone. His eyes were dim and watery. Naked, shimmering, he drifted slightly to one side, then a vagrant breeze in the wall-less chamber sent him back. He had drained himself.

"I ask for this Concord to affix sentence of final flux on this man. Though his interposition only lasted a few moments, we have no way of knowing what damage or unnaturalness it may have caused cross-when. I submit that his intent was to overload the drain and thereby render it inoperative. This act, the act of a beast who would condemn the sixty races of the center to a future in which insanity still prevailed, is an act that can only be punished by termination."

The Concord blanked and meditated. A timeless time later they re-linked, and the Proctor's charges were upheld; his demand of sentence was fulfilled.

On the hushed shores of a thought, the papyrus man was carried in the arms of his friend, his executioner, the Proctor. There in the dusting quiet of an approaching night, Linah laid Semph down in the shadow of a sigh.

"Why did you stop me?" the wrinkle with a mouth asked.

Linah looked away across the rushing dark.

"Why?"

"Because here, in the center, there is a chance."

"And for them, all of them out there . . . no chance ever?"

Linah sat down slowly, digging his hands into the golden mist, letting it sift over his wrists and back into the waiting flesh of the world. "If we can begin it here, if we can pursue our boundaries outward, then perhaps one day, sometime, we can reach to the ends of time with that little chance. Until then, it is better to have one center where there is no madness."

Semph hurried his words. The end was rapidly striding for him. "You have sentenced them all. Insanity is a living vapor. A force. It can be bottled. The most potent genie in the most easily uncorked bottle.

And you have condemned them to live with it always. In the name of love."

Linah made a sound that was not quite a word, but called it back. Semph touched his wrist with a tremble that had been a hand. Fingers melting into softness and warmth. "I'm sorry for you, Linah. Your curse is to be a true man. The world is made for strugglers. You never learned how to do that."

Linah did not reply. He thought only of the drainage that was eternal now. Set in motion and kept in motion by its necessity.

"Will you do a memorial for me?" Semph asked.

Linah nodded. "It's traditional."

Semph smiled softly. "Then do it for them; not for me. I'm the one who devised the vessel of their death, and I don't need it. But choose one of them; not a very important one, but one that will mean everything to them if they find it, and understand. Erect the memorial in my name to that one. Will you?"

Linah nodded.

"Will you?" Semph asked. His eyes were closed, and he could not see the nod.

"Yes. I will," Linah said. But Semph could not hear. The flux began and ended, and Linah was alone in the cupped silence of loneliness.

The statue was placed on a far planet of a far star in a time that was ancient while yet never having been born. It existed in the minds of men who would come later. Or never.

But if they did, they would know that hell was with them, that there was a Heaven that men called Heaven, and in it there was a center from which all madness flowed; and once within that center, there was peace.

In the remains of a blasted building that had been a shirt factory, in what had been Stuttgart, Friedrich Drucker found a many-colored box. Maddened by hunger and the memory of having eaten human flesh for weeks, the man tore at the lid of the box with the bloodied stubs of his fingers. As the box flew open, pressed at a certain point, cyclones rushed out past the terrified face of Friedrich Drucker. Cyclones and dark, winged, faceless shapes that streaked away into the night, followed by a last wisp of purple smoke smelling strongly of decayed gardenias.

But Friedrich Drucker had little time to ponder the meaning of the purple smoke, for the next day, World War IV broke out.

*1970*
*28th CONVENTION*
*HEIDELBERG*

Samuel R. Delany is the baby of the book. He has been publishing science fiction for something like eight years and instead of serving a decent apprenticeship (*I* slaved away for something like umpty-ump years before somebody happened to trip over me and said, "Whatever is that?") he started attracting notice right away.

It's enough to rouse the instinctive hatred of any decent, hard-working incompetent.

What else can I tell you about him? He has finely chiseled features, and he occasionally sports a beard. I don't mean just a beard; I mean a *beard*. He lets it grow out on all sides without warning. One day he hasn't got one and is as smooth-shaven as a collar-ad hero; the next day, there he is looking like the inside of a horse-hair mattress.

He claims it keeps his face warm in the winter.

Also, don't call him Sam. He doesn't answer to Sam. If you yell Sam at him, Sam Moskowitz is liable to turn around and then you'll be sorry. Samuel R. Delany is called "Chip." Please don't ask me why because I don't know why. If he were a disciple of Robert Bloch, I would say it was because he's a Chip off the old Bloch, but he isn't a disciple of any-body.

And yet there's something a little distressing to me here that I might as well mention. For years, we science fiction writers; we warm band of brothers and sisters; have entered this field as our specialty. It was "our thing"; it was what we did. Often, if we were driven enough, we graduated to broader fields, but even then (as in my own case) we had lingered long enough to know that science fiction was our home, our only true literary home, no matter through what gilded palaces we rambled.

But now the day has come when writers, without necessarily feeling a tight identification with the field, choose to write science fiction because of the liberty it gives them; the opportunity to speculate and experiment beyond anything possible in any other *genre*.

Do they then think of themselves as science fiction writers? Is this their home—or just another hotel room?

I wonder about Chip, for instance? He reached the top so easily that he may have had no sensation of passing through. Next time I see him, I'll ask . . .

*14*

# TIME CONSIDERED
# AS A HELIX OF
# SEMI-PRECIOUS STONES

Lay ordinate and abscissa on the century. Now cut me a quadrant. Third quadrant if you please. I was born in 'fifty. Here it's 'seventy-five.

At sixteen they let me leave the orphanage. Dragging the name they'd hung me with (Harold Clancy Everet, and me a mere lad—how many monickers have I had since; but don't worry, you'll recognize my smoke) over the hills of East Vermont, I came to a decision:

Me and Pa Michaels, who had belligerently given me a job at the request of *The Official* looking *Document* with which the orphanage sends you packing, were running Pa Michaels' dairy farm, i.e., thirteen thousand three hundred sixty-two piebald Guernseys all asleep in their stainless coffins, nourished and drugged by pink liquid flowing in clear plastic veins (stuff is sticky and messes up your hands), exercised with electric pulsers that make their muscles quiver, them not half awake, and the milk just a-pouring down into stainless cisterns. Anyway. The Decision (as I stood there in the fields one afternoon like the Man with the Hoe, exhausted with three hard hours of physical labor, contemplating the machinery of the universe through the fog of fatigue): With all of Earth, and Mars, and the Outer Satellites filled up with people and what-all, there had to be something more than this. I decided to get some.

So I stole a couple of Pa's credit cards, one of his helicopters and a bottle of white lightning the geezer made himself, and took off. Ever try to land a stolen helicopter on the roof of the Pan Am building, drunk? Jail, schmail, and some hard knocks later I had attained to wisdom. But remember this oh best beloved: I have done three honest hours on a dairy farm less than ten years back. And nobody has ever called me Harold Clancy Everet again.

Hank Culafroy Eckles (red-headed, a bit vague, six foot two) strolled out of the baggage room at the spaceport carrying a lot of things that weren't his in a small briefcase.

Beside him the Business Man was saying, "You young fellows today upset me. Go back to Bellona, I say. Just because you got into trouble with that little blonde you were telling me about is no reason to leap worlds, come on all glum. Even quit your job!"

Hank stops and grins weakly: "Well . . ."

"Now I admit, you have your real needs, which maybe we older folks don't understand, but you have to show some responsibility towards . . ." He notices Hank has stopped in front of a door marked MEN. "Oh. Well. Eh." He grins strongly. "I've enjoyed meeting you, Hank. It's always nice when you meet somebody worth talking to on these damn crossings. So long."

Out same door, ten minutes later, comes Harmony C. Eventide, six foot even (one of the false heels was cracked, so I stuck both of them under a lot of paper towels), brown hair (not even my hairdresser knows for sure), oh so dapper and of his time, attired in the bad taste that is oh so tasteful, a sort of man with whom no Business Men would start a conversation. Took the regulation 'copter from the port over to the Pan Am building (Yeah. Really. Drunk), came out of Grand Central Station, and strode along Forty-second towards Eighth Avenue, with a lot of things that weren't mine in a small briefcase.

The evening is carved from light.

Crossed the plastiplex pavement of the Great White Way—I think it makes people look weird, all that white light under their chins—and skirted the crowds coming up in elevators from the sub-way, the sub-sub-way, and the sub-sub-sub (eighteen and first week out of jail I hung around here, snatching stuff from people—but daintily, daintily, so they never knew they'd been snatched), bulled my way through a crowd of giggling, goo-chewing school girls with flashing lights in their hair, all very embarrassed at wearing transparent plastic blouses which had just been made legal again (I hear the breast has been scene [as opposed to obscene] on and off since the seventeenth century) so I stared appreciatively; they giggled some more. I thought, Christ, when I was that age, I was on a God damn dairy farm, and took the thought no further.

The ribbon of news lights looping the triangular structure of Communication, Inc., explained in Basic English how Senator Regina Abolafia was preparing to begin her investigation of Organized Crime in the City. Days I'm so happy I'm disorganized I couldn't begin to tell.

Near Ninth Avenue I took my briefcase into a long, crowded bar. I hadn't been in New York for two years, but on my last trip through ofttimes a man used to hang out here who had real talent for getting rid of things that weren't mine profitably, safely, fast. No idea what the chances were I'd find him. I pushed among a lot of guys drinking beer. Here and there were a number of well escorted old bags wearing last month's latest. Scarfs of smoke gentled through the noise. I don't like such places. Those there younger than me were all morphadine heads or feeble minded. Those older only wished more younger ones would come. I pried my way to the bar and tried to get the attention of one of the little men in white coats.

The lack of noise behind me made me glance back—

She wore a sheath of veiling closed at the neck and wrists with huge brass pins (oh so tastefully on the border of taste); her left arm was bare, her right covered with chiffon like wine. She had it down a lot better than I did. But such an ostentatious demonstration of one's understanding of the fine points was absolutely out of place in a place like this. People were making a great show of not noticing.

She pointed to her wrist, blood-colored nail indexing a yellow-orange fragment in the brass claw of her wristlet. "Do you know what this is, Mr. Eldrich?" she asked; at the same time the veil across her face cleared, and her eyes were ice; her brows, black.

Three thoughts: (One) She is a lady of fashion, because coming in from Bellona I'd read the *Delta* coverage of the "fading fabrics" whose hue and opacity were controlled by cunning jewels at the wrist. (Two) During my last trip through, when I was younger and Harry Calamine Eldrich, I didn't do anything *too* illegal (though one loses track of these things); still I didn't believe I could be dragged off to the calaboose for anything more than thirty days under that name. (Three) The stone she pointed to. . . .

". . . Jasper?" I asked.

She waited for me to say more; I waited for her to give me reason to let on I knew what she was waiting for (when I was in jail Henry James was my favorite author. He really was.)

"Jasper," she confirmed.

"—Jasper. . . ." I reopened the ambiguity she had tried so hard to dispel.

". . . Jasper—" But she was already faltering, suspecting I suspected her certainty to be ill-founded.

"Okay. Jasper." But from her face I knew she had seen in my face a look that had finally revealed I knew she knew I knew.

"Just whom have you got me confused with, Ma'am?"

Jasper, this month, is the Word.

Jasper is the pass/code/warning that the Singers of the Cities (who, last month, sang "Opal" from their divine injuries; and on Mars I'd heard the Word and used it thrice, along with devious imitations, to fix possession of what was not rightfully my own; and even there I pondered Singers and their wounds) relay by word of mouth for that loose and roguish fraternity with which I have been involved (in various guises) these nine years. It goes out new every thirty days; and within hours every brother knows it, throughout six worlds and worldlets. Usually it's grunted at you by some blood-soaked bastard staggering into your arms from a dark doorway; hissed at you as you pass a shadowed alley; scrawled on a paper scrap pressed into your palm by some nasty-grimy moving too fast through the crowd. And this month, it was: Jasper.

Here are some alternate translations:

Help!

or

I need help!

or

I can help you!

or

You are being watched!

or

They're not watching now, so *move!*

Final point of syntax: If the Word is used properly, you should never have to think twice about what it means in a given situation. Fine point of usage: Never trust anyone who uses it improperly.

I waited for her to finish waiting.

She opened a wallet in front of me. "Chief of Special Services Department Maudline Hinkle," she read without looking what it said below the silver badge.

"You have that very well," I said, "Maud." Then I frowned. "Hinkle?"

"Me."

"I know you're not going to believe this, Maud. You look like a woman who has no patience with her mistakes. But my name is Eventide. Not Eldrich. Harmony C. Eventide. And isn't it lucky for all and sundry that the Word changes tonight?" Passed the way it is, the Word is no big secret to the cops. But I've met policemen up to a week after change date who were not privy.

"Well, then: Harmony. I want to talk to you."

I raised an eyebrow.

She raised one back and said, "Look, if you want to be called Henrietta, it's all right by me. But you listen."

"What do you want to talk about?"

"Crime, Mr. . . . ?"

"Eventide. I'm going to call you Maud, so you might as well call me Harmony. It really is my name."

Maud smiled. She wasn't a young woman. I think she even had a few years on Business Man. But she used make-up better than he did. "I probably know more about crime than you do," she said. "In fact I wouldn't be surprised if you hadn't even heard of my branch of the police department. What does Special Services mean to you?"

"That's right, I've never heard of it."

"You've been more or less avoiding the Regular Service with alacrity for the past seven years."

"Oh, Maud, really—"

"Special Services is reserved for people whose nuisance value has suddenly taken a sharp rise . . . a sharp enough rise to make our little lights start blinking."

"Surely I haven't done anything so dreadful that—"

"We don't look at what you do. A computer does that for us. We simply keep checking the first derivative of the graphed out curve that bears your number. Your slope is rising sharply."

"Not even the dignity of a name—"

"We're the most efficient department in the Police Organization. Take it as bragging if you wish. Or just a piece of information."

"Well, well, well," I said. "Have a drink?" The little man in the white coat left us two, looked puzzled at Maud's finery, then went to do something else.

"Thanks." She downed half her glass like someone stauncher than that wrist would indicate. "It doesn't pay to go after most criminals. Take your big-time racketeers, Farnesworth, The Hawk, Blavatskia. Take your little snatch-purses, small-time pushers, housebreakers or vice-impresarios. Both at the top and the bottom of the scale, their incomes are pretty stable. They don't really upset the social boat. Regular Services handles them both. They think they do a good job. We're not going to argue. But say a little pusher starts to become a big-time pusher; a medium-sized vice-impresario sets his sights on becoming a full-fledged racketeer; that's when you get problems with socially unpleasant repercussions. That's when Special Services arrive. We have a couple of techniques that work remarkably well."

"You're going to tell me about them, aren't you."

"They work better that way," she said. "One of them is hologramic information storage. Do you know what happens when you cut a hologram plate in half?"

"The three dimensional image is . . . . cut in half?"

She shook her head. "You get the whole image, only fuzzier, slightly out of focus."

"Now I didn't know that."

"And if you cut it in half again, it just gets fuzzier still. But even if you have a square centimeter of the original hologram you still have the whole image—unrecognizable, but complete."

I mumbled some appreciative *m*'s.

"Each pinpoint of photographic emulsion on a hologram plate, unlike a photograph, gives information about the entire scene being hologrammed. By analogy, hologramic information storage simply means that each bit of information we have—about you, let us say— relates to your entire career, your overall situation, the complete set of tensions between you and your environment. Specific facts about specific misdemeanors or felonies we leave to Regular Services. As soon as we have enough of our kind of data, our method is vastly more efficient for keeping track—even predicting—where you are or what you may be up to."

"Fascinating," I said. "One of the most amazing paranoid syndromes I've ever run up against. I mean just starting a conversation with someone in a bar. Often, in a hospital situation, I've encountered stranger—"

"In your past," she said matter of factly, "I see cows and helicopters. In your not too distant future there are helicopters and hawks."

"And tell me, oh Good Witch of the West, just how—" Then I got all upset inside. Because nobody is supposed to know about that stint with Pa Michaels save thee and me. Even the Regular Service who pulled me, out of my mind, from that whirlibird bouncing towards the edge of the Pan Am never got that one from me. I'd eaten the credit cards when I saw them waiting, and the serial numbers had been filed off everything that could have had a serial number on it by someone more competent than I: good Mister Michaels had boasted to me, my first lonely, drunken night at the farm, how he'd gotten the thing in hot from New Hampshire.

"But why"—it appalls me the clichés to which anxiety will drive us—"are you telling me all this?"

She smiled and her smile faded behind her veil. "Information is only meaningful when it is shared," said a voice that was hers from the place of her face.

"Hey, look, I—"

"You may be coming into quite a bit of money soon. If I can calculate right, I will have a helicopter full of the city's finest arriving to take you away as you accept it into your hot little hands. That is a piece of information. . . ." She stepped back. Someone stepped between us.

"Hey, Maud—!"

"You can do whatever you want with it."

The bar was crowded enough so that to move quickly was to make enemies. I don't know—I lost her and made enemies. Some weird characters there: with greasy hair that hung in spikes, and three of them had dragons tattooed on their scrawny shoulders, still another with an eye patch, and yet another raked nails black with pitch at my cheek (we're two minutes into a vicious free-for-all, case you missed the transition. I did) and some of the women were screaming. I hit and ducked, and then tenor of the brouhaha changed. Somebody sang, "Jasper!" the way she is supposed to be sung. And it meant the heat (the ordinary, bungling Regular Service I had been eluding these seven years) were on their way. The brawl spilled into the street. I got between two nasty-grimies who were doing things appropriate with one another, but made the edge of the crowd with no more wounds than could be racked up to shaving. The fight had broken into sections. I left one and ran into another that, I realized a moment later, was merely a ring of people standing around somebody who had apparently gotten really messed.

Someone was holding people back.

Somebody else was turning him over.

Curled up in a puddle of blood was the little guy I hadn't seen in two years who used to be so good at getting rid of things not mine.

Trying not to hit people with my briefcase, I ducked between the hub and the bub. When I saw my first ordinary policeman I tried very hard to look like somebody who had just stepped up to see what the rumpus was.

It worked.

I turned down Ninth Avenue, and got three steps into an inconspicuous but rapid lope—

"Hey, wait! Wait up there. . . ."

I recognized the voice (after two years, coming at me just like that, I recognized it) but kept going.

"Wait! It's me, Hawk!"

And I stopped.

You haven't heard his name before in this story; Maud mentioned

*the* Hawk, who is a multi-millionaire racketeer basing his operations
on a part of Mars I've never been (though he has his claws sunk to the
spurs in illegalities throughout the system) and somebody else entirely.

I took three steps back towards the doorway.

A boy's laugh there: "Oh, man. You look like you just did something
you shouldn't."

"Hawk?" I asked the shadow.

He was still the age when two years' absence means an inch or so
taller.

"You're still hanging out around here?" I asked.

"Sometimes."

He was an amazing kid.

"Look, Hawk, I got to get out of here." I glanced back at the
rumpus.

"Get." He stepped down. "Can I come too?"

Funny. "Yeah." It makes me feel very funny him asking that. "Come
on."

By the street lamp, half a block down, I saw his hair was still pale as
split pine. He could have been a nasty-grimy: very dirty black denim
jacket, no shirt beneath; very ripe pair of black-jeans—I mean in the
dark you could tell. He went barefoot; and the only way you can tell on
a dark street someone's been going barefoot for days in New York is to
know already. As we reached the corner, he grinned up at me under
the street lamp and shrugged his jacket together over the welts and
furrows marring his chest and belly. His eyes were very green. Do you
recognize him? If by some failure of information dispersal throughout
the worlds and worldlets you haven't, walking beside me beside the
Hudson was Hawk the Singer.

"Hey, how long have you been back?"

"A few hours," I told him.

"What'd you bring?"

"Really want to know?"

He shoved his hands into his pockets and cocked his head. "Sure."

I made the sound of an adult exasperated by a child. "All right." We
had been walking the waterfront for a block now; there was nobody
about. "Sit down." So he straddled the beam along the siding, one foot
dangling above the flashing black Hudson. I sat in front of him and
ran my thumb around the edge of the briefcase.

Hawk hunched his shoulders and leaned. "Hey . . ." He flashed
green questioning at me. "Can I touch?"

I shrugged. "Go ahead."

He grubbed among them with fingers that were all knuckle and bitten nail. He picked two up, put them down, picked up three others. "Hey!" he whispered. "How much are all these worth?"

"About ten times more than I hope to get. I have to get rid of them fast."

He glanced down at his hanging foot. "You could always throw them in the river."

"Don't be dense. I was looking for a guy who used to hang around that bar. He was pretty efficient." And half the Hudson away a water-bound foil skimmed above the foam. On her deck were parked a dozen helicopters—being ferried up to the Patrol Field near Verrazano, no doubt. But for moments I looked back and forth between the boy and the transport, getting all paranoid about Maud. But the boat *mmmmed* into the darkness. "My man got a little cut up this evening."

Hawk put the tips of his fingers in his pockets and shifted his position.

"Which leaves me up tight. I didn't think he'd take them all but at least he could have turned me on to some other people who might."

"I'm going to a party later on this evening"—he paused to gnaw on the wreck of his little fingernail—"where you might be able to sell them. Alexis Spinnel is having a party for Regina Abolafia at Tower Top."

"Tower Top . . . ?" It had been a while since I palled around with Hawk. Hell's Kitchen at ten; Tower Top at midnight—

"I'm just going because Edna Silem will be there."

Edna Silem is New York's eldest Singer.

Senator Abolafia's name had ribboned above me in lights once that evening. And somewhere among the endless magazines I'd perused coming in from Mars I remember Alexis Spinnel's name sharing a paragraph with an awful lot of money.

"I'd like to see Edna again," I said offhandedly. "But she wouldn't remember me." Folk like Spinnel and his social ilk have a little game, I'd discovered during the first leg of my acquaintance with Hawk. He who can get the most Singers of the City under one roof wins. There are five Singers of New York (a tie for second place with Lux on Iapetus). Tokyo leads with seven. "It's a two Singer party?"

"More likely four . . . if I go."

The inaugural ball for the mayor gets four.

I raised the appropriate eyebrow.

"I have to pick up the Word from Edna. It changes tonight."

"All right," I said. "I don't know what you have in mind but I'm game." I closed the case.

We walked back towards Times Square. When we got to Eighth Avenue and the first of the plastiplex, Hawk stopped. "Wait a minute," he said. Then he buttoned his jacket up to his neck. "Okay."

Strolling through the streets of New York with a Singer (two years back I'd spent much time wondering if that were wise for a man of my profession) is probably the best camouflage possible for a man of my profession. Think of the last time you glimpsed your favorite Tri-D star turning the corner of Fifty-seventh. Now be honest. Would you really recognize the little guy in the tweed jacket half a pace behind him?

Half the people we passed in Times Square recognized him. With his youth, funereal garb, black feet and ash pale hair, he was easily the most colorful of Singers. Smiles; narrowed eyes; very few actually pointed or stared.

"Just exactly who is going to be there who might be able to take this stuff off my hands?"

"Well, Alexis prides himself on being something of an adventurer. They might just take his fancy. And he can give you more than you can get peddling them in the street."

"You'll tell him they're all hot?"

"It will probably make the idea that much more intriguing. He's a creep."

"You say so, friend."

We went down into the sub-sub. The man at the change booth started to take Hawk's coin, then looked up. He began three or four words that were unintelligible through his grin, then just gestured us through.

"Oh," Hawk said, "thank you," with ingenuous surprise, as though this were the first, delightful time such a thing had happened. (Two years ago he had told me sagely, "As soon as I start looking like I expect it, it'll stop happening." I was still impressed by the way he wore his notoriety. The time I'd met Edna Silem, and I'd mentioned this, she said with the same ingenuousness, "But that's what we're chosen for.")

In the bright car we sat on the long seat; Hawk's hands were beside him, one foot rested on the other. Down from us a gaggle of bright-bloused goo-chewers giggled and pointed and tried not to be noticed at it. Hawk didn't look at all, and I tried not to be noticed looking.

Dark patterns rushed the window.

Things below the gray floor hummed.

Once a lurch.

Leaning once; we came out of the ground.

Outside, the city tried on its thousand sequins, then threw them away behind the trees of Ft. Tryon. Suddenly the windows across from us grew bright scales. Behind them the girders of a station reeled by. We got out on the platform under a light rain. The sign said TWELVE TOWERS STATION.

By the time we reached the street, however, the shower had stopped. Leaves above the wall shed water down the brick. "If I'd known I was bringing someone I'd have had Alex send a car for us. I told him it was fifty-fifty I'd come."

"Are you sure it's all right for me to tag along, then?"

"Didn't you come up here with me once before?"

"I've even been up here once before that," I said. "Do you still think it's . . ."

He gave me a withering look. Well; Spinnel would be delighted to have Hawk even if he dragged along a whole gang of real nasty-grimies —Singers are famous for that sort of thing. With one more or less presentable thief, Spinnel was getting off light. Beside us rocks broke away into the city. Behind the gate to our left the gardens rolled up towards the first of the towers. The twelve immense, luxury apartment buildings menaced the lower clouds.

"Hawk the Singer," Hawk said into the speaker at the side of the gate. *Clang* and tic-tic-tic and *Clang*. We walked up the path to the doors and doors of glass.

A cluster of men and women in evening dress were coming out. Three tiers of doors away they saw us. You could see them frowning at the guttersnipe who'd somehow gotten into the lobby (for a moment I thought one of them was Maud, because she wore a sheath of the fading fabric, but she turned; beneath her veil her face was dark as roasted coffee); one of the men recognized him, said something to the others. When they passed us they were smiling. Hawk paid about as much attention to them as he had to the girls on the subway. But when they'd passed, he said, "One of those guys was looking at you."

"Yeah. I saw."

"Do you know why?"

"He was trying to figure out whether we'd met before."

"Had you?"

I nodded. "Right about where I met you, only back when I'd just gotten out of jail. I told you I'd been here once before."

"Oh."

Blue carpet covered three-quarters of the lobby. A great pool filled the rest in which a row of twelve foot trellises stood, crowned with flaming braziers. The lobby itself was three stories high, domed and mirror tiled.

Twisting smoke curled towards the ornate grill. Broken reflections sagged and recovered on the walls.

The elevator door folded about us its foil petals. There was the distinct feeling of not moving while seventy-five stories shucked down around us.

We got out on the landscaped roof garden. A very tanned, very blond man wearing an apricot jump-suit, from the collar of which emerged a black turtleneck dicky, came down the rocks (artificial) between the ferns (real) growing the stream (real water; phony current).

"Hello! Hello!" Pause. "I'm terribly glad you decided to come after all." Pause. "For a while I thought you weren't going to make it." The Pauses were to allow Hawk to introduce me. I was dressed so that Spinnel had no way of telling whether I was a miscellaneous Nobel laureate that Hawk happened to have been dining with, or a varlet whose manners and morals were even lower than mine happen to be.

"Shall I take your jacket?" Alexis offered.

Which meant he didn't know Hawk as well as he would like people to think. But I guess he was sensitive enough to realize from the little cold things that happened in the boy's face that he should forget his offer.

He nodded to me, smiling—about all he could do—and we strolled towards the gathering.

Edna Silem was sitting on a transparent inflated hassock. She leaned forward, holding her drink in both hands, arguing politics with the people sitting on the grass before her. She was the first person I recognized (hair of tarnished silver; voice of scrap brass). Jutting from the cuffs of her mannish suit, her wrinkled hands about her goblet, shaking with the intensity of her pronouncements, were heavy with stones and silver. As I ran my eyes back to Hawk, I saw half a dozen whose names/faces sold magazines, music, sent people to the theater (the drama critic for *Delta*, wouldn't you know), and even the mathematician from Princeton I'd read about a few months ago who'd come up with the "quasar/quark" explanation.

There was one woman my eyes kept returning to. On glance three I recognized her as the New Fascistas' most promising candidate for president, Senator Abolafia. Her arms were folded and she was listening intently to the discussion that had narrowed to Edna and an overly gregarious younger man whose eyes were puffy from what could have been the recent acquisition of contact lenses.

"But don't you feel, Mrs. Silem, that—"

"You must remember when you make predictions like that—"

"Mrs. Silem, I've seen statistics that—"

"You *must* remember"—her voice tensed, lowered, till the silence between the words was as rich as the voice was sparse and metallic—"that if everything, *everything* were known, statistical estimates would be unnecessary. The science of probability gives mathematical expression to our ignorance, not to our wisdom," which I was thinking was an interesting second installment to Maud's lecture, when Edna looked up and exclaimed, "Why, Hawk!"

Everyone turned.

"I *am* glad to see you. Lewis, Ann," she called: there were two other Singers there already (he dark, she pale, both tree-slender; their faces made you think of pools without drain or tribute come upon in the forest, clear and very still; husband and wife, they had been made Singers together the day before their marriage seven years ago), "he hasn't deserted us after all!" Edna stood, extended her arm over the heads of the people sitting, and barked across her knuckles as though her voice were a pool cue. "Hawk, there are people here arguing with me who don't know nearly as much as you about the subject. You'd be on my side, now, wouldn't you—"

"Mrs. Silem, I didn't mean to—" from the floor.

Then her arms swung six degrees, her fingers, eyes and mouth opened. "You!" Me. "My dear, if there's anyone I never expected to see here! Why it's been almost two years, hasn't it?" Bless Edna; the place where she and Hawk and I had spent a long, beery evening together had more resembled that bar than Tower Top. "Where have you been keeping yourself?"

"Mars, mostly," I admitted. "Actually I just came back today." It's so much fun to be able to say things like that in a place like this.

"Hawk—both of you—" (which meant either she had forgotten my name, or she remembered me well enough not to abuse it) "come over here and help me drink up Alexis' good liquor." I tried not to grin as we walked towards her. If she remembered anything, she certainly recalled my line of business and must have been enjoying this as much as I was.

Relief spread Alexis' face: he knew now I was *someone* if not *which* someone I was.

As we passed Lewis and Ann, Hawk gave the two Singers one of his luminous grins. They returned shadowed smiles. Lewis nodded. Ann made a move to touch his arm, but left the motion unconcluded; and the company noted the interchange.

Having found out what we wanted, Alex was preparing large glasses of it over crushed ice when the puffy-eyed gentleman stepped up for a refill. "But, Mrs. Silem, then what do you feel validly opposes such political abuses?"

Regina Abolafia wore a white silk suit. Nails, lips and hair were one color; and on her breast was a worked copper pin. It's always fascinated me to watch people used to being the center thrust to the side. She swirled her glass, listening.

"I oppose them," Edna said. "Hawk opposes them. Lewis and Ann oppose them. We, ultimately, are what you have." And her voice had taken on that authoritative resonance only Singers can assume.

Then Hawk's laugh snarled through the conversational fabric.

We turned.

He'd sat cross-legged near the hedge. "Look . . ." he whispered.

Now people's gazes followed his. He was looking at Lewis and Ann. She, tall and blonde, he, dark and taller, were standing very quietly, a little nervously, eyes closed (Lewis' lips were apart).

"Oh," whispered someone who should have known better, "they're going to . . ."

I watched Hawk because I'd never had a chance to observe one Singer at another's performance. He put the soles of his feet together, grasped his toes and leaned forward, veins making blue rivers on his neck. The top button of his jacket had come loose. Two scar ends showed over his collarbone. Maybe nobody noticed but me.

I saw Edna put her glass down with a look of beaming anticipatory pride. Alex, who had pressed the autobar (odd how automation has become the upper crust's way of flaunting the labor surplus) for more crushed ice, looked up, saw what was about to happen, and pushed the cut-off button. The autobar hummed to silence. A breeze (artificial or real, I couldn't tell you) came by and the trees gave us a final *shush*.

One at a time, then in duet, then singly again, Lewis and Ann sang.

Singers are people who look at things, then go and tell people what they've seen. What makes them Singers is their ability to make people listen. That is the most magnificent over-simplification I can give. Eighty-six-year-old El Posado, in Rio de Janeiro, saw a block of tenements collapse, ran to the Avenida del Sol and began improvising, in rhyme and meter (not all that hard in rhyme-rich Portuguese), tears runneling his dusty cheeks, his voice clashing with the palm swards above the sunny street. Hundreds of people stopped to listen; a hundred more; and another hundred. And they told hundreds more what they had heard. Three hours later, hundreds from among them had arrived at the scene with blankets, food, money, shovels and, more incredibly, the willingness and ability to organize themselves and work within that organization. No Tri-D report of a disaster has ever produced that sort of reaction. El Posado is historically considered the first Singer. The second was Miriamne in the roofed city of Lux, who for thirty years walked through the metal streets singing the glories of the rings of Saturn—the colonists can't look at them without aid because of the ultraviolet the rings set up. But Miriamne, with her strange cataracts, each dawn, walked to the edge of the city, looked, saw and came back to sing of what she saw. All of which would have meant nothing except that during the days she did not sing—through illness, or once she was on a visit to another city to which her fame had spread—the Lux Stock Exchange would go down, the number of violent crimes rise. Nobody could explain it. All they could do was proclaim her Singer. Why did the institution of Singers come about, springing up in just about every urban center throughout the system? Some have speculated that it was a spontaneous reaction to the mass media which blanket our lives. While Tri-D and radio and newstapes disperse information all over the worlds, they also spread a sense of alienation from first-hand experience. (How many people still go to sports events or a political rally with their little receivers plugged to their ears to let them know that what they see is really happening?) The first Singers were proclaimed by the people around them. Then, there was a period where anyone could proclaim himself who wanted to, and people either responded to him, or laughed him into oblivion. But by the time I was left on the doorstep of somebody who didn't want me, most cities had more or less established an unofficial quota. When a position is left open today, the remaining Singers choose who is going to fill it. The required talents are poetic, theatrical, as well as a certain charisma that is generated in the tensions between the personality and the publicity web a Singer is immediately snared in. Before he became a Singer, Hawk had gained something of a prodigious reputation with a book of poems published when he was fifteen. He was touring universities and giving readings, but the reputation was still small enough so that he was amazed that I had ever heard of him, that evening we encountered in Central Park (I had just spent a pleasant thirty days as a guest of the city and it's amazing what you find in the Tombs Library). It was a few weeks after his sixteenth birthday. His Singership was to be announced in four days, though he had been informed already. We sat by the lake till dawn, while he weighed and pondered and agonized over the coming responsibility. Two years later, he's still the youngest Singer in six worlds by half a dozen years. Before becoming a Singer, a person need not have been a poet, but most are either that or actors. But the roster through the system includes a longshoreman, two university professors, an heiress to the Silitax millions (Tack it down with Silitacks), and at least two persons of such dubious background that the ever-hungry-for-sensation Publicity Machine itself has agreed not to let any of it past the copy-editors. But wherever their origins, these diverse and flamboyant living myths sang of love, of death, the changing of seasons, social classes, governments and the palace guard. They sang before large crowds, small ones, to an individual laborer coming home from the city's docks, on slum street corners, in club cars of commuter trains, in the elegant gardens atop Twelve Towers, to Alex Spinnel's select soirée. But it has been illegal to reproduce the "Songs" of the Singers by mechanical means (including publishing the lyrics) since the institution arose, and I respect the law, I do, as only a man in my profession can. I offer the explanation then in place of Lewis' and Ann's song.

They finished, opened their eyes, stared about with expressions that could have been embarrassment, could have been contempt.

Hawk was leaning forward with a look of rapt approval. Edna was smiling politely. I had the sort of grin on my face that breaks out when you've been vastly moved and vastly pleased. Lewis and Ann had sung superbly.

Alex began to breathe again, glanced around to see what state everybody else was in, saw, and pressed the autobar, which began to hum and crush ice. No clapping, but the appreciative sounds began; people were nodding, commenting, whispering. Regina Abolafia went over to Lewis to say something. I tried to listen until Alex shoved a glass into my elbow.

"Oh, I'm sorry . . ."

I transferred my briefcase to the other hand and took the drink smiling. When Senator Abolafia left the two Singers, they were holding hands and looking at one another a little sheepishly. They sat down again.

The party drifted in conversational groups through the gardens, through the groves. Overhead clouds the color of old chamois folded and unfolded across the moon.

For a while I stood alone in a circle of trees listening to the music: a de Lassus two-part canon, programmed for audio-generators. Recalled: an article in one of last week's large-circulation literaries stating that it was the only way to remove the feel of the bar lines imposed by five centuries of meter on modern musicians. For another two weeks this would be acceptable entertainment. The trees circled a rock pool;

but no water. Below the plastic surface, abstract lights wove and threaded in a shifting lumia.

"Excuse me . . . ?"

I turned to see Alexis, who had no drink now or idea what to do with his hands. He *was* nervous.

". . . but our young friend has told me you have something I might be interested in."

I started to lift my briefcase, but Alex's hand came down from his ear (it had gone by belt to hair to collar already) to halt me. Nouveau riche.

"That's all right. I don't need to see them yet. In fact, I'd rather not. I have something to propose to you. I would certainly be interested in what you have if they are, indeed, as Hawk has described them. But I have a guest here who would be even more curious."

That sounded odd.

"I know that sounds odd," Alexis assessed, "but I thought you might be interested simply because of the finances involved. I am an eccentric collector who would offer you a price concomitant with what I would use them for: eccentric conversation pieces—and because of the nature of the purchase I would have to limit severely the people with whom I could converse."

I nodded.

"My guest, however, would have a great deal more use for them."

"Could you tell me who this guest is?"

"I asked Hawk, finally, who you were and he led me to believe I was on the verge of a grave social indiscretion. It would be equally indiscreet to reveal my guest's name to you." He smiled. "But indiscretion is the better part of the fuel that keeps the social machine turning, Mr. Harvey Cadwaliter-Erickson. . . ." He smiled knowingly.

I have *never* been Harvey Cadwaliter-Erickson, but then, Hawk was always an inventive child. Then a second thought went by, vid., the tungsten magnates, the Cadwaliter-Ericksons of Tythis on Triton. Hawk was not only inventive, he was as brilliant as all the magazines and newspapers are always saying he is.

"I assume your second indiscretion will be to tell me who this mysterious guest is?"

"Well," Alex said with the smile of the canary-fattened cat, "Hawk agreed with me that *the* Hawk might well be curious as to what you have in there," (he pointed) "as indeed he is."

I frowned. Then I thought lots of small, rapid thoughts I'll articulate in due time. "*The* Hawk?"

Alex nodded.

I don't think I was actually scowling. "Would you send our young friend up here for a moment?"

"If you'd like." Alex bowed, turned. Perhaps a minute later, Hawk came up over the rocks and through the trees, grinning. When I didn't grin back, he stopped.

"Mmmm . . ." I began.

His head cocked.

I scratched my chin with a knuckle. ". . . Hawk," I said, "are you aware of a department of the police called Special Services?"

"I've heard of them."

"They've suddenly gotten very interested in me."

"Gee," he said with honest amazement. "They're supposed to be effective."

"Mmmm," I reiterated.

"Say," Hawk announced, "how do you like that? My namesake is here tonight. Wouldn't you know."

"Alex doesn't miss a trick. Have you any idea *why* he's here?"

"Probably trying to make some deal with Abolafia. Her investigation starts tomorrow."

"Oh." I thought over some of those things I had thought before. "Do you know a Maud Hinkle?"

His puzzled look said "no" pretty convincingly.

"She bills herself as one of the upper echelon in the arcane organization of which I spoke."

"Yeah?"

"She ended our interview earlier this evening with a little homily about hawks and helicopters. I took our subsequent encounter as a fillip of coincidence. But now I discover that the evening has confirmed her intimations of plurality." I shook my head. "Hawk, I am suddenly catapulted into a paranoid world where the walls not only have ears, but probably eyes, and long, claw-tipped fingers. Anyone about me—yea, even very you—could turn out to be a spy. I suspect every sewer grating and second-story window conceals binoculars, a tommygun, or worse. What I just can't figure out is how these insidious forces, ubiquitous and omnipresent though they be, induced you to lure me into this intricate and diabolical—"

"Oh, cut it out!" He shook back his hair. "I didn't lure—"

"Perhaps not consciously, but Special Services has Hologramic Information Storage, and their methods are insidious and cruel—"

"I said cut it out." And all sorts of hard little things happened again. "Do you think I'd—" Then he realized how scared I was, I guess. "Look, the Hawk isn't some small time snatchpurse. He lives in just as para-

noid a world as you're in now, only all the time. If he's here, you can
be sure there are just as many of his men—eyes and ears and fingers—
as there are of Maud Hickenlooper."

"Hinkle."

"Anyway, it works both ways. No Singer's going to— Look, do you
really think *I* would—"

And even though I knew all those hard little things were scabs over
pain, I said, "Yes."

"You did something for me once, and I—"

"I gave you some more welts. That's all."

All the scabs pulled off.

"Hawk," I said. "Let me see."

He took a breath. Then he began to open the brass buttons. The
flaps of his jacket fell back. The lumia colored his chest with pastel
shiftings.

I felt my face wrinkle. I didn't want to look away. I drew a hissing
breath instead, which was just as bad.

He looked up. "There're a lot more than when you were here last
aren't there?"

"You're going to kill yourself, Hawk."

He shrugged.

"I can't even tell which are the ones I put there anymore."

He started to point them out.

"Oh, come on," I said, too sharply. And for the length of three
breaths, he grew more and more uncomfortable, till I saw him start to
reach for the bottom button. "Boy," I said, trying to keep despair out
of my voice, "why do you do it?" and ended up keeping out everything.
There is nothing more despairing than a voice empty.

He shrugged, saw I didn't want that, and for a moment anger flickered in his green eyes. I didn't want that either. So he said: "Look . . .
you touch a person, softly, gently, and maybe you even do it with love.
And, well, I guess a piece of information goes on up to the brain where
something interprets it as pleasure. Maybe something up there in my
head interprets the information all wrong. . . ."

I shook my head. "You're a Singer. Singers are supposed to be eccentric, sure; but—"

Now he was shaking his head. Then the anger opened up. And I
saw an expression move from all those spots that had communicated
pain through the rest of his features, and vanish without ever becoming a word. Once more he looked down at the wounds that webbed his
thin body.

"Button it up, boy. I'm sorry I said anything."

Halfway up the lapels his hands stopped. "You really think I'd turn you in?"

"Button it up."

He did. Then he said, "Oh." And then, "You know, it's midnight."

"Edna just gave me the Word."

"Which is?"

"Agate."

I nodded.

He finished closing his collar. "What are you thinking about?"

"Cows."

"Cows?" Hawk asked. "What about them?"

"You ever been on a dairy farm?"

He shook his head.

"To get the most milk, you keep the cows practically in suspended animation. They're fed intravenously from a big tank that pipes nutrients out and down, branching into smaller and smaller pipes until it gets to all those high yield semi-corpses."

"I've seen pictures."

"People."

". . . and cows?"

"You've given me the Word. And now it begins to funnel down, branching out, with me telling others, and them telling still others, till by midnight tomorrow . . ."

"I'll go get the—"

"Hawk?"

He turned back. "What?"

"You say you don't think I'm going to be the victim of any hanky-panky with the mysterious forces that know more than we— Okay, that's your opinion. But as soon as I get rid of this stuff, I'm going to make the most distracting exit you've ever seen."

Two little lines bit down Hawk's forehead. "Are you sure I haven't seen this one before?"

"As a matter of fact I think you have." Now I grinned.

"Oh," Hawk said, then made a sound that had the structure of laughter but was all breath. "I'll get the Hawk."

He ducked out between the trees.

I glanced up at the lozenges of moonlight in the leaves.

I looked down at my briefcase.

Up between the rocks, stepping around the long grass, came the Hawk. He wore a gray evening suit; a gray silk turtleneck. Above his craggy face his head was completely shaved.

"Mr. Cadwaliter-Erickson?" He held out his hand.

I shook: small sharp bones in loose skin. "Does one call you
Mr. . . . ?"

"Arty."

"Arty the Hawk." I tried to look like I wasn't giving his gray attire
the once-over.

He smiled. "Arty the Hawk. Yeah. I picked that name up when I
was younger than our friend down there. Alex says you got . . . well,
some things that are not exactly yours. That don't belong to you."

I nodded.

"Show them to me."

"You were told what—"

He brushed away the end of my sentence. "Come on, let me see."

He extended his hand, smiling affably as a bank clerk. I ran my
thumb around the pressure-zip. The cover went *tsk*. "Tell me," I said,
looking up at his head still lowered to see what I had, "what does one
do about Special Services? They seem to be after me."

The head came up. Surprise changed slowly to a craggy leer. "Why,
Mr. Cadwaliter-Erickson!" He gave me the up and down openly. "Keep
your income steady. Keep it steady, that's one thing you can do."

"If you buy these for anything like what they're worth, that's going
to be a little difficult."

"I would imagine. I could always give you less money—"

The cover went *tsk* again.

"—or, barring that, you could try to use your head and outwit them."

"You must have outwitted them at one time or another. You may be
on an even keel now, but you had to get there from somewhere else."

Arty the Hawk's nod was downright sly. "I guess you've had a run-in
with Maud. Well, I suppose congratulations are in order. And condolences. I always like to do what's in order."

"You seem to know how to take care of yourself. I mean I notice you're not out there mingling with the guests."

"There are two parties going on here tonight," Arty said. "Where do
you think Alex disappears off to every five minutes?"

I frowned.

"That lumia down in the rocks"—he pointed towards my feet—"is a
mandala of shifting hues on our ceiling. Alex," he chuckled, "goes scuttling off under the rocks where there is a pavilion of Oriental
splendor—"

"—and a separate guest list at the door?"

"Regina is on both. I'm on both. So's the kid, Edna, Lewis, Ann—"

"Am I supposed to know all this?"

"Well, you came with a person on both lists. I just thought. . . ."
He paused.

I was coming on wrong. Well. A quick change artist learns fairly
quick that the verisimilitude factor in imitating someone up the scale
is your confidence in your unalienable right to come on wrong. "I'll
tell you," I said. "How about exchanging these"—I held out the briefcase—"for some information."

"You want to know how to stay out of Maud's clutches?" In a moment he shook his head. "It would be pretty stupid of me to tell you,
even if I could. Besides, you've got your family fortunes to fall back
on." He beat the front of his shirt with his thumb. "Believe me, boy.
Arty the Hawk didn't have that. I didn't have anything like that." His
hands dropped into his pockets. "Let's see what you got."

I opened the case again.

The Hawk looked for a while. After a few moments he picked
a couple up, turned them around, put them back down, put his hands
back in his pocket. "I'll give you sixty thousand for them, approved
credit tablets."

"What about the information I wanted?"

"I wouldn't tell you a thing." He smiled. "I wouldn't tell you the time
of day."

There are very few successful thieves in this world. Still less on the
other five. The will to steal is an impulse towards the absurd and the
tasteless. (The talents are poetic, theatrical, a certain reverse charisma. . . .) But it is a will, as the will to order, power, love.

"All right," I said.

Somewhere overhead I heard a faint humming.

Arty looked at me fondly. He reached under the lapel of his jacket,
and took out a handful of credit tablets—the scarlet-banded tablets
whose slips were ten thousand apiece. He pulled off one. Two. Three.
Four.

"You can deposit this much safely—?"

"Why do you think Maud is after me?"

Five. Six.

"Fine," I said.

"How about throwing in the briefcase?" Arty asked.

"Ask Alex for a paper bag. If you want, I can send them—"

"Give them here."

The humming was coming closer.

I held up the open case. Arty went in with both hands. He shoved
them into his coat pockets, his pants pockets; the gray cloth was distended by angular bulges. He looked left, right. "Thanks," he said.

"Thanks." Then he turned, and hurried down the slope with all sorts of things in his pockets that weren't his now.

I looked up through the leaves for the noise, but I couldn't see anything.

I stooped down now and laid my case open. I pulled open the back compartment where I kept the things that did belong to me, and rummaged hurriedly through.

Alex was just offering Puffy-eyes another scotch, while the gentleman was saying, "Has anyone seen Mrs. Silem? What's that humming overhead—?" when a large woman wrapped in a veil of fading fabric tottered across the rocks, screaming.

Her hands were clawing at her covered face.

Alex sloshed soda over his sleeve and the man said, "Oh my God! Who's that?"

"No!" the woman shrieked. "Oh no! Help me!" waving her wrinkled fingers, brilliant with rings.

"Don't you recognize her?" That was Hawk whispering confidentially to someone else. "It's Henrietta, Countess of Effingham."

And Alex, overhearing, went hurrying to her assistance. The Countess, however, ducked between two cacti, and disappeared into the high grass. But the entire party followed. They were beating about the underbush when a balding gentleman in a black tux, bow tie, and cummerbund coughed and said, in a very worried voice. "Excuse me, Mr. Spinnel?"

Alex whirled.

"Mr. Spinnel, my mother . . ."

"Who are *you?*" The interruption upset Alex terribly.

The gentleman drew himself up to announce. "The Honorable Clement Effingham," and his pants legs shook for all the world as if he had started to click his heels. But articulation failed. The expression melted on his face. "Oh, I . . . my mother, Mr. Spinnel. We were downstairs, at the other half of your party, when she got very upset. She ran up here—oh, I told her not to! I knew you'd be upset. But you must help me!" and then looked up.

The others looked too.

The helicopter blacked the moon, doffing and settling below its hazy twin parasols.

"Oh, please . . ." the gentleman said. "You look over there! Perhaps she's gone back down. I've got to"—looking quickly both ways—"find her." He hurried in one direction while everyone else hurried in others.

The humming was suddenly syncopated with a crash. Roaring now, as plastic fragments from the transparent roof chattered down through the branches, clattered on the rocks . . .

I made it into the elevator and had already thumbed the edge of my briefcase clasp, when Hawk dove between the unfolding foils. The electric-eye began to swing them open. I hit DOOR CLOSE full fist.

The boy staggered, banged shoulders on two walls, then got back breath and balance. "Hey, there's police getting out of that helicopter!"

"Hand-picked by Maud Hinkle herself, no doubt." I pulled the other tuft of white hair from my temple. It went into the case on top of the plastiderm gloves (wrinkled thick blue veins, long carnelian nails) that had been Henrietta's hands, lying in the chiffon folds of her sari.

Then there was the downward tug of stopping. The Honorable Clement was still half on my face when the door opened.

Gray and gray, with an absolutely dismal expression on his face, the Hawk swung through the doors. Behind him people were dancing in an elaborate pavilion festooned with Oriental magnificence (and a mandala of shifting hues on the ceiling.) Arty beat me to DOOR CLOSE. Then he gave me an odd look.

I just sighed and finished peeling off Clem.

"The police are up there?" the Hawk reiterated.

"Arty," I said, buckling my pants, "it certainly looks that way." The car gained momentum. "You look almost as upset as Alex." I shrugged the tux jacket down my arms, turning the sleeves inside out, pulled one wrist free, and jerked off the white starched dicky with the black bow tie and stuffed it into the briefcase with all my other dickies; swung the coat around and slipped on Howard Calvin Evingston's good gray herringbone. Howard (like Hank) is a redhead (but not as curly).

The Hawk raised his bare brows when I peeled off Clement's bald pate and shook out my hair.

"I noticed you aren't carrying around all those bulky things in your pocket any more."

"Oh, those have been taken care of," he said gruffly. "They're all right."

"Arty," I said, adjusting my voice down to Howard's security-provoking, ingenuous baritone, "it must have been my unabashed conceit that made me think that those Regular Service police were here just for me—"

The Hawk actually snarled. "They wouldn't be that unhappy if they got me, too."

And from his corner Hawk demanded, "You've got security here with you, don't you, Arty?"

"So what?"

"There's one way you can get out of this," Hawk hissed at me. His jacket had come half open down his wrecked chest. "That's if Arty takes you out with him."

"Brilliant idea," I concluded. "You want a couple of thousand back for the service?"

The idea didn't amuse him. "I don't want anything from you." He turned to Hawk. "I need something from you, kid. Not him. Look, I wasn't prepared for Maud. If you want me to get your friend out, then you've got to do something for me."

The boy looked confused.

I thought I saw smugness on Arty's face, but the expression resolved into concern. "You've got to figure out some way to fill the lobby up with people, and fast."

I was going to ask why but then I didn't know the extent of Arty's security. I was going to ask how but the floor pushed up at my feet and the doors swung open. "If you can't do it," the Hawk growled to Hawk, "none of us will get out of here. None of us!"

I had no idea what the kid was going to do, but when I started to follow him out into the lobby, the Hawk grabbed my arm and hissed, "Stay here, you idiot!!"

I stepped back. Arty was leaning on DOOR OPEN.

Hawk sprinted towards the pool. And splashed in.

He reached the braziers on their twelve foot tripods and began to climb.

"He's going to hurt himself!" the Hawk whispered.

"Yeah," I said, but I don't think my cynicism got through. Below the great dish of fire, Hawk was fiddling. Then something under there came loose. Something else went *Clang!* And something else spurted out across the water. The fire raced along it and hit the pool, churning and roaring like hell.

A black arrow with a golden head: Hawk dove.

I bit the inside of my cheek as the alarm sounded. Four people in uniforms were coming across the blue carpet. Another group were crossing in the other direction, saw the flames, and one of the women screamed. I let out my breath, thinking carpet and walls and ceiling would be flame-proof. But I kept losing focus on the idea before the sixty-odd infernal feet.

Hawk surfaced on the edge of the pool in the only clear spot left, rolled over on to the carpet, clutching his face. And rolled. And rolled. Then, came to his feet.

Another elevator spilled out a load of passengers who gaped and gasped. A crew came through the doors now with fire-fighting equipment. The alarm was still sounding.

Hawk turned to look at the dozen-odd people in the lobby. Water puddled the carpet about his drenched and shiny pants legs. Flame turned the drops on his cheek and hair to flickering copper and blood.

He banged his fists against his wet thighs, took a deep breath, and against the roar and the bells and the whispering, he Sang.

Two people ducked back into two elevators. From a doorway half a dozen more emerged. The elevators returned half a minute later with a dozen people each. I realized the message was going through the building, there's a Singer Singing in the lobby.

The lobby filled. The flames growled, the fire fighters stood around shuffling, and Hawk, feet apart on the blue rug, by the burning pool Sang, and Sang of a bar off Times Square full of thieves, morphadine-heads, brawlers, drunkards, women too old to trade what they still held out for barter, and trade just too nasty-grimy, where, earlier in the evening, a brawl had broken out, and an old man had been critically hurt in the fray.

Arty tugged at my sleeve.

"What . . . ?"

"Come on," he hissed.

The elevator door closed behind us.

We ambled through the attentive listeners, stopping to watch, stopping to hear. I couldn't really do Hawk justice. A lot of that slow amble I spent wondering what sort of security Arty had:

Standing behind a couple in a bathrobe who were squinting into the heat, I decided it was all very simple. Arty wanted simply to drift away through a crowd, so he'd conveniently gotten Hawk to manufacture one.

To get to the door we had to pass through practically a cordon of Regular Service policemen who I don't think had anything to do with what might have been going on in the roof garden; they'd simply collected to see the fire and stayed for the Song. When Arty tapped one on the shoulder, "Excuse me please," to get by, the policeman glanced at him, glanced away, then did a Mack Sennet double-take. But another policeman caught the whole interchange, and touched the first on the arm and gave him a frantic little headshake. Then both men turned very deliberately back to watch the Singer. While the earthquake in my chest stilled, I decided that the Hawk's security complex of agents and counter agents, maneuvering and machinating through the flaming lobby, must be of such finesse and intricacy that to attempt understanding was to condemn oneself to total paranoia.

Arty opened the final door.

I stepped from the last of the air conditioning into the night.

We hurried down the ramp.

"Hey, Arty . . . ?"

"You go that way." He pointed down the street. "I go this way."

"Eh . . . what's that way?" I pointed in my direction.

"Twelve Towers sub-sub-subway station. Look. I've got you out of there. Believe me, you're safe for the time being. Now go take a train someplace interesting. Goodbye. Go on now." Then Arty the Hawk put his fists in his pockets and hurried up the street.

I started down, keeping near the wall, expecting someone to get me with a blow-dart from a passing car, a deathray from the shrubbery.

I reached the sub.

And still nothing had happened.

Agate gave way to Malachite:

Tourmaline:

Beryl (during which month I turned twenty-six):

Porphyry:

Sapphire (that month I took the ten thousand I hadn't frittered away and invested it in The Glacier, a perfectly legitimate ice cream palace on Triton—the first and only ice cream palace on Triton—which took off like fireworks; all investors were returned eight hundred percent, no kidding. Two weeks later I'd lost half of those earnings on another set of preposterous illegalities, and was feeling quite depressed, but The Glacier kept pulling them in. The new Word came by):

Cinnabar:

Turquoise:

Tiger's Eye:

Hector Calhoun Eisenhower finally buckled down and spent these three months learning how to be a respectable member of the upper middle class underworld. That is a long novel in itself. High finance; corporate law; how to hire help: Whew! But the complexities of life have always intrigued me. I got through it. The basic rule is still the same: observe carefully, imitate effectively.

Garnet:

Topaz (I whispered that word on the roof of the Trans-Satellite Power Station, and caused my hirelings to commit two murders. And you know? I didn't feel a thing):

Taafite:

We were nearing the end of Taafite. I'd come back to Triton on strictly Glacial business. A bright pleasant morning it was: the business went fine. I decided to take off the afternoon and go sight-seeing in the Torrents.

". . . two hundred and thirty yards high," the guide announced and everyone around me leaned on the rail and gazed up through the plastic corridor at the cliffs of frozen methane that soared through Neptune's cold green glare.

"Just a few yards down the catwalk, ladies and gentlemen, you can catch your first glimpse of the Well of This World, where, over a million years ago, a mysterious force science still cannot explain caused twenty-five square miles of frozen methane to liquify for no more than a few hours during which time a whirlpool twice the depth of Earth's Grand Canyon was caught for the ages when the temperature dropped once more to . . ."

People were moving down the corridor when I saw her smiling. My hair was black and nappy and my skin was chestnut dark today.

I was just feeling overconfident, I guess, so I kept standing around next to her. I even contemplated coming on. Then she broke the whole thing up by suddenly turning to me and saying, perfectly deadpan: "Why, if it isn't Hamlet Caliban Enobarbus!"

Old reflexes realigned my features to couple the frown of confusion with the smile of indulgence. *Pardon me, but I think you must have mistaken* . . . No, I didn't say it. "Maud," I said, "have you come here to tell me that my time has come?"

She wore several shades of blue, with a large blue brooch at her shoulder, obviously glass. Still, I realized as I looked about the other tourists, she was more inconspicuous amidst their finery than I was. "No," she said. "Actually I'm on vacation. Just like you."

"No kidding?" We had dropped behind the crowd. "You are kidding."

"Special Services of Earth, while we cooperate with Special Services on other worlds, has no official jurisdiction on Triton. And since you came here with money, and most of your recorded gain in income has been through The Glacier, while Regular Services on Triton might be glad to get you, Special Services is not after you as yet." She smiled. "I haven't been to The Glacier. It would really be nice to say I'd been taken there by one of the owners. Could we go for a soda, do you think?"

The swirled sides of the Well of This World dropped away in opalescent grandeur. Tourists gazed and the guide went on about indices of refraction, angles of incline.

"I don't think you trust me," Maud said.

My look said she was right.

"Have you ever been involved with narcotics?" she asked suddenly. I frowned.

"No, I'm serious. I want to try and explain something . . . a point of information that may make both our lives easier."

"Peripherally," I said. "I'm sure you've got down all the information in your dossiers."

"I was involved with them a good deal more than peripherally for several years," Maud said. "Before I got into Special Services, I was in the Narcotics Division of the regular force. And the people we dealt with twenty-four hours a day were drug users, drug pushers. To catch the big ones we had to make friends with the little ones. To catch the bigger ones, we had to make friends with the big. We had to keep the same hours they kept, talk the same language, for months at a time live on the same streets, in the same building." She stepped back from the rail to let a youngster ahead. "I had to be sent away to take the morpha-dine de-toxification cure twice while I was on the narco squad. And I had a better record than most."

"What's your point?"

"Just this. You and I are traveling in the same circles now, if only because of our respective chosen professions. You'd be surprised how many people we already know in common. Don't be shocked when we run into each other crossing Sovereign Plaza in Bellona one day, then two weeks later wind up at the same restaurant for lunch at Lux on Iapetus. Though the circles we move in cover worlds, they *are* the same, and not that big."

"Come on." I don't think I sounded happy. "Let me treat you to that ice cream." We started back down the walkway.

"You know," Maud said, "if you do stay out of Special Services' hands here and on Earth long enough, eventually you'll be up there with a huge income growing on a steady slope. It might be a few years, but it's possible. There's no reason now for us to be *personal* enemies. You just may, someday, reach that point where Special Services loses interest in you as quarry. Oh, we'd still see each other, run into each other. We get a great deal of our information from people up there. We're in a position to help you too, you see."

"You've been casting holograms again."

She shrugged. Her face looked positively ghostly under the pale planet. She said, when we reached the artificial lights of the city, "I did meet two friends of yours recently, Lewis and Ann."

"The Singers?"

She nodded.

"Oh, I don't really know them well."

"They seem to know a lot about you. Perhaps through that other Singer, Hawk."

"Oh," I said again. "Did they say how he was?"

"I read that he was recovering about two months back. But nothing since then."

"That's about all I know too," I said.

"The only time I've ever seen him," Maud said, "was right after I pulled him out."

Arty and I had gotten out of the lobby before Hawk actually finished. The next day on the news-tapes I learned that when his Song was over, he shrugged out of his jacket, dropped his pants, and walked back into the pool.

The fire-fighter crew suddenly woke up; people began running around and screaming: he'd been rescued, seventy percent of his body covered with second and third degree burns. I'd been industriously not thinking about it.

"*You* pulled him out?"

"Yes. I was in the helicopter that landed on the roof," Maud said. "I thought you'd be impressed to see me."

"Oh," I said. "How did you get to pull him out?"

"Once you got going, Arty's security managed to jam the elevator service above the seventy-first floor, so we didn't get to the lobby till after you were out of the building. That's when Hawk tried to—"

"But it was you actually saved him, though?"

"The firemen in that neighborhood hadn't had a fire in twelve years! I don't think they even knew how to operate the equipment. I had my boys foam the pool, then I waded in and dragged him—"

"Oh," I said again. I had been trying hard, almost succeeding, these eleven months. I wasn't there when it happened. It wasn't my affair. Maud was saying:

"We thought we might have gotten a lead on you from him. But when I got him to the shore, he was completely out, just a mass of open, running—"

"I should have known the Special Services uses Singers too," I said. "Everyone else does. The Word changes today, doesn't it? Lewis and Ann didn't pass on what the new one is?"

"I saw them yesterday, and the Word doesn't change for another eight hours. Besides, they wouldn't tell me, anyway." She glanced at me and frowned. "They really wouldn't."

"Let's go have some sodas," I said. "We'll make small talk, and listen carefully to each other, while we affect an air of nonchalance; you will try to pick up things that will make it easier to catch me; I will listen for things you let slip that might make it easier for me to avoid you."

"Um-hm." She nodded.

"Why did you contact me in that bar, anyway?"

Eyes of ice: "I told you, we simply travel in the same circles. We're quite likely to be in the same bar on the same night."

"I guess that's just one of the things I'm not supposed to understand, huh?"

Her smile was appropriately ambiguous. I didn't push it.

It was a very dull afternoon. I couldn't repeat one exchange from the nonsense we babbled over the cherry peaked mountains of whipped cream. We both exerted so much energy to keep up the appearance of being amused, I doubt either one of us could see our way to picking up anything meaningful; if anything meaningful was said.

She left. I brooded some more on the charred phoenix.

The Steward of The Glacier called me into the kitchen to ask about a shipment of contraband milk (The Glacier makes all its own ice cream) that I had been able to wangle on my last trip to Earth (it's amazing how little progress there has been in dairy farming over the last ten years; it was depressingly easy to hornswoggle that bumbling Vermonter) and under the white lights and great plastic churning vats, while I tried to get things straightened out, he made some comment about the Heist Cream Emperor; that didn't do *any* good.

By the time the evening crowd got there, and the moog was making music and the crystal walls were blazing; and the floor show—a new addition that week—had been cajoled into going on anyway (a trunk of costumes had gotten lost in shipment [or swiped, but I wasn't about to tell them that]), and wandering through the tables I, personally, had caught a very grimy little girl, obviously out of her head on morph, trying to pick up a customer's pocketbook from the back of a chair—I just caught her by the wrist, made her let go, and led her to the door, daintily, while she blinked at me with dilated eyes and the customer never even knew—and the floor show, having decided what the hell, were doing their act *au naturel,* and everyone was having just a high old time, I was feeling really bad.

I went outside, sat on the wide steps, and growled when I had to move aside to let people in or out. About the seventy-fifth growl, the person I growled at stopped and boomed down at me, "I thought I'd find you if I looked hard enough! I mean if I really looked."

I looked at the hand that was flapping at my shoulder, followed the arm up to a black turtleneck, where there was a beefy, bald, grinning head. "Arty," I said, "what are . . . ?" But he was still flapping and laughing with impervious *Gemütlichkeit.*

"You wouldn't believe the time I had getting a picture of you, boy. Had to bribe one out of the Triton Special Services Department. That quick change bit. Great gimmick. Just great!" The Hawk sat down next to me and dropped his hand on my knee. "Wonderful place you got here. I like it, like it a lot." Small bones in veined dough. "But not enough to make you an offer on it yet. You're learning fast ˙there, though. I can tell you're learning fast. I'm going to be proud to be able to say I was the one who gave you your first big break." His hand came away and he began to knead it onto the other. "If you're going to move into the big time, you have to have at least one foot planted firmly on the right side of the law. The whole idea is to make yourself indispensable to the good people; once that's done, a good crook has the keys to all the treasure houses in the system. But I'm not telling you anything you don't already know."

"Arty," I said, "do you think the two of us should be seen together here . . . ?"

The Hawk held his hand above his lap and joggled it with a deprecating motion. "Nobody can get a picture of us. I got my men all around. I never go anywhere in public without my security. Heard you've been looking into the security business yourself," which was true. "Good idea. Very good. I like the way you're handling yourself."

"Thanks. Arty, I'm not feeling too hot this evening. I came out here to get some air. . . ."

Arty's hand fluttered again. "Don't worry, I won't hang around. You're right. We shouldn't be seen. Just passing by and wanted to say hello. Just hello." He got up. "That's all." He started down the steps.

"Arty?"

He looked back.

"Sometime soon you will come back; and that time you will want to buy out my share of The Glacier, because I'll have gotten too big; and I won't want to sell because I'll think I'm big enough to fight you. So we'll be enemies for a while. You'll try to kill me. I'll try to kill you."

On his face, first the frown of confusion; then, the indulgent smile. "I see you've caught on to the idea of hologramic information. Very good. Good. It's the only way to outwit Maud. Make sure all your information relates to the whole scope of the situation. It's the only way to outwit me too." He smiled, started to turn, but thought of something else. "If you can fight me off long enough, and keep growing, keep your security in tiptop shape, eventually we'll get to the point where it'll be worth both our whiles to work together again. If you can just hold out, we'll be friends again. Someday. You just watch. Just wait."

"Thanks for telling me."

The Hawk looked at his watch. "Well. Goodbye." I thought he was going to leave finally. But he glanced up again. "Have you got the new Word?"

"That's right," I said. "It went out tonight. What is it?"

The Hawk waited till the people coming down the steps were gone. He looked hastily about, then leaned towards me with hands cupped at his mouth, rasped, "Pyrite," and winked hugely. "I just got it from a gal who got it direct from Colette" (one of the three Singers of Triton). Then he turned, jounced down the steps, and shouldered his way into the crowds passing on the strip.

I sat there mulling through the year till I had to get up and walk. All walking does to my depressive moods is add the reinforcing rhythm of paranoia. By the time I was coming back, I had worked out a dilly of a delusional system: The Hawk had already begun to weave some security ridden plot about me which ended when we were all trapped in some dead end alley, and trying to get aid I called out, "Pyrite!" which would turn out not to be the Word at all but served to identify me for the man in the dark gloves with the gun/grenades/gas.

There was a cafeteria on the corner. In the light from the window, clustered over the wreck by the curb was a bunch of nasty-grimies (á la Triton: chains around the wrists, bumble-bee tattoo on cheek, high heel boots on those who could afford them). Straddling the smashed headlight was the little morph-head I had ejected earlier from The Glacier.

On a whim I went up to her. "Hey?"

She looked at me from under hair like trampled hay, eyes all pupil.

"You get the new Word yet?"

She rubbed her nose, already scratch red. "Pyrite," she said. "It just came down about an hour ago."

"Who told you?"

She considered my question. "I got it from a guy who says he got it from a guy who came in this evening from New York who picked it up there from a Singer named Hawk."

The three grimies nearest made a point of not looking at me. Those further away let themselves glance.

"Oh," I said. "Oh. Thanks."

Occam's Razor, along with any real information on how security works, hones away most such paranoia. Pyrite. At a certain level in my line of work, paranoia's just an occupational disease. At least I was certain that Arty (and Maud) probably suffered from it as much as I did.

The lights were out on The Glacier's marquee. Then I remembered what I had left inside and ran up the stairs.

The door was locked. I pounded on the glass a couple of times, but everyone had gone home. And the thing that made it worse was that I could see it sitting on the counter of the coat-check alcove under the orange bulb. The steward had probably put it there, thinking I might arrive before everybody left. Tomorrow at noon Ho Chi Eng had to pick up his reservation for the Marigold Suite on the Interplanetary Liner *The Platinum Swan,* which left at one-thirty for Bellona. And there behind the glass doors of The Glacier, it waited with the proper wig, as well as the epicanthic folds that would halve Mr. Eng's slow eyes of jet.

I actually thought of breaking in. But the more practical solution was to get the hotel to wake me at nine and come in with the cleaning man. I turned around and started down the steps; and the thought struck me, and made me terribly sad, so that I blinked and smiled just from reflex: it was probably just as well to leave it there till morning, because there was nothing in it that wasn't mine, anyway.

# *APPENDIX*

## HUGO AWARDS 1962–1970

### 20TH CONVENTION—CHICAGO, 1962

Novel—STRANGER IN A STRANGE LAND by Robert A. Heinlein
Short Fiction—The Hothouse Series by Brian W. Aldiss
Professional Magazine—*Analog*
Amateur Magazine—*Warhoon*, Richard Bergeron, ed.
Professional Artist—Ed Emshwiller
Dramatic Presentation—"The Twilight Zone" by Rod Serling

### 21ST CONVENTION—WASHINGTON, D.C., 1963

Novel—THE MAN IN THE HIGH CASTLE by Philip K. Dick
Short Fiction—"The Dragon Masters" by Jack Vance
Dramatic Award—No Award
Professional Magazine—*The Magazine of Fantasy and Science Fiction*
Amateur Magazine—*Zero*, Dick Lupoff, ed.
Professional Artist—Roy Krenkel
Special Awards—P. Schuyler Miller (For Best Book Reviews)
　　　　　　　Isaac Asimov (For Distinguished Contributions to the
　　　　　　　Field)

### 22ND CONVENTION—OAKLAND, 1964

Novel—WAY STATION by Clifford Simak
Short Fiction—"No Truce With Kings" by Poul Anderson
Professional Magazine—*Analog*
Professional Artist—Ed Emshwiller
Book Publisher—Ace Books
Amateur Publication—*Amra*, George Scithers, ed.

### 23RD CONVENTION—LONDON, 1965

Novel—THE WANDERER by Fritz Leiber
Short Fiction—"Soldier, Ask Not" by Gordon R. Dickson
Professional Magazine—*Analog*
Book Publisher—Ballantine Books
Amateur Publication—*Yandro*, Robert & Juanita Coulson, eds.
Dramatic Presentation—"Dr. Strangelove"

## 24TH CONVENTION—CLEVELAND, 1966

Novel (tie)—AND CALL ME CONRAD by Roger Zelazny and DUNE by
  Frank Herbert
Short Fiction—" 'Repent, Harlequin!' said the Ticktockman" by Harlan
  Ellison
Professional Magazine—*IF*
Professional Artist—Frank Frazetta
Amateur Magazine—*ERB-dom,* Camille Cazeddessus, Jr., ed.
Best All-time Series—Foundation Series by Isaac Asimov

## 25TH CONVENTION—NEW YORK, 1967

Novel—THE MOON IS A HARSH MISTRESS by Robert A. Heinlein
Novelette—"The Last Castle" by Jack Vance
Short Story—"Neutron Star" by Larry Niven
Professional Magazine—*IF*
Professional Artist—Jack Gaughan
Dramatic Presentation—"The Menagerie" (Star Trek)
Amateur Publication—*Niekas,* Ed. Meskys and Felice Rolfe, eds.
Fan Artist—Jack Gaughan
Fan Writer—Alexei Panshin

## 26TH CONVENTION—OAKLAND, 1968

Novel—LORD OF LIGHT by Roger Zelazny
Novella (tie)—"Weyr Search" by Anne McCaffrey
                "Riders of the Purple Wage" by Philip José Farmer
Novelette—"Gonna Roll the Bones" by Fritz Leiber
Short Story—"I Have No Mouth, And I Must Scream" by Harlan
  Ellison
Dramatic Presentation—"City on the Edge of Forever" by Harlan El-
  lison (Star Trek)
Professional Magazine—*IF*
Professional Artist—Jack Gaughan
Amateur Publication—*Amra,* George Scithers, ed.
Fan Artist—George Barr
Fan Writer—Ted White

## 27TH CONVENTION—ST. LOUIS, 1969

Novel—STAND ON ZANZIBAR by John Brunner
Novella—"Nightwings" by Robert Silverberg
Novelette—"The Sharing of Flesh" by Poul Anderson

Short Story—"The Beast That Shouted Love at the Heart of the World" by Harlan Ellison
Professional Artist—Jack Gaughan
Professional Magazine—*The Magazine of Fantasy and Science Fiction*
Dramatic—"2001"
Fanzine—*SF Review,* Dick Geis, ed.
Fan Writer—Harry Warner, Jr.
Fan Artist—Vaughn Bode
Special Hugo—to Armstrong, Aldrin, and Collins for the best moonlanding ever

## 28TH CONVENTION—HEIDELBERG, 1970

Novel—LEFT HAND OF DARKNESS by Ursula K. LeGuin
Novella—"Ship of Shadows" by Fritz Leiber
Short Story—"Time Considered as a Helix of Semi-Precious Stones" by Samuel R. Delany
Professional Magazine—*The Magazine of Fantasy and Science Fiction*
Professional Artist—Kelly Freas
Fanzine—*SF Review,* Dick Geis, ed.
Fan Writer—Bob Tucker
Fan Artist—Tim Kirk